Zoran Chronicles Volume 2
Dragons, Power, Courts, and War

Vic Broquard

Zoran Chronicles Volume 2 Dragons, Power, Courts, and War

©2008, 2009, 2012, 2014 by Vic Broquard
Third Printing
ISBN: 978-1-941415-16-0

http://www.Broquard-ebooks.com
Broquard eBooks
103 Timberlane
East Peoria, IL 61611
author@Broquard-eBooks.com

Artwork by Crooked Willow Studios.

For Morgan and L. Ron Hubbard

Table of Contents

Chapter 1 The Solution to Yesterday's Problem Becomes Today's Problem

The slum town of Ningho lay on the outskirts of Nanchan, one of the three capital cities of the swamp planet of Jing. Baron Chen Meerong had retired, ceding his throne and Circle of Ascension to his eldest son, Baron Gang, who was now twenty-five. For his younger sons, Baron Jie, twenty-three, and Baron Li, twenty-one, he had had two more Circles of Ascension built at the other two larger cities of Chaohu and Zhouhan, but these cities lay some five hundred miles distant from Ningho and in opposite directions, more or less. Why? Solid ground was hard to find on this swamp planet, especially ground which would support larger cities and the needed stone fortresses to both support and defend these great Circles of Ascension that gave the barons and baronesses their powers.

Although Ningho was only some twenty miles from the castle of Baron Gang in Nanchan, ten of these were merely foggy swampland. The poorest of folks eked out marginal lives in and around Ningho. Yet here too was the home base of the Swamp Raiders, five like-minded folks who had banded together to tackle the ever-growing problem of the greens, that is the Green Dragons.

Chan Meerong, twenty-four, was their leader, while her younger sister, Wen, twenty-two, was her second in command. Three men in their late twenties had joined up with them, Kang Zu, Tao Wu, and Peng Long. The three men were skilled fighters, who once had been in Baron Chen's army. Baronesses Chan and Wen now lived in exile from the royal courts. Both had defied their father's arranged marriages to off-world men, each of whom had sought to solidify their political alliances against the "Zoran Crowd" — a derogatory term for Baron Zoran and his allied planets. Worse, both young ex-baronesses thought that their father's secret deals to bring hundreds of Green Dragons to Jing, giving them sanctuary here in return for their protection and allegiance, had been an awful, terrible blunder. Baron Chen had made that decision some nineteen years ago and now Jing was infested with these infernal beasts, as the two women called them, only when they were being polite about the dragons.

The five sat around a beat up table in Wu's Bar. The hour was late. Urine, stale swamp fog, and tobacco smoke fought for dominance in the dimly lit room. Kang knocked down another shot of low grade swamp whiskey, "God-damn greens! May they rot in the bayous!" They'd just heard another report of locals being attacked by the Green Dragons. A family of three were found dead, their flesh eaten away, leaving behind bleached bones. Green Dragon slime was exceedingly toxic to human flesh. This was the sole topic of many who had frequented Wu's this evening.

"Aye. Wish they were not so damnably hard to kill," Tao interjected angrily.

"Top of the food chain — isn't that what old Zoran used to say a score of years back?" Wen asked, searching her childhood memory. She was barely four when dragons suddenly came into existence, arriving on Jing.

"Damn dad to hell," Chan answered hostilely, banging her mug on the marred tabletop. "He should have known better than to bring those foul, wicked demons to Jing. It's all his god-damn fault. Now he's retired, sitting comfy in his fortress home, and what do our idiot brothers do? Nothing! Not a god-damn thing! Damn right, Wen, dragons *are* at the top of the food chain and our people *are* their food!"

"Actually, Chan, our people are not food for the greens. They don't eat us — just kill us. Greens hate humans and kill us for sport," Peng politely corrected his leader.

"Okay, okay, so they don't eat us," Chan amended herself, hiccupped, and countered. "No, they just dissolve our bodies and kill us. That's bad enough. Well, that's not entirely true, Peng. We now know that the greens only attack out here in the slums of Jing. They never attack the wealthier cities. I swear that they have a bargain of some kind with the barons. But, yes, it was a whole family this time. We're just going to have to go after that green and kill it before it has a chance to do that to another family!"

"Agreed. Tomorrow we go dragon hunting again," Kang added. "Say, how many have we killed so far? My mind is a little fuzzy tonight." He hiccupped.

Tao laughed, "Too much cheap whiskey, Kang. Muddled your brains. Good thing a green isn't here now; you'd be slimed in no time!" All laughed, but Kang knew that what Tao said was true. They'd returned three days ago from their last mission, successfully slaying another green that was on their "most wanted" list.

"Eighteen," Chan answered. "We've been at this five years now, gang, and we have a paltry eighteen to show for our hard work." She sounded disgusted.

"Yes, but that's eighteen more than any other hunters on Jing," Peng countered.

"But there aren't any other hunters on Jing," Wen protested. "We're it! We are the only ones fighting the accursed dragons."

"Hey, that we know of — we haven't been all over Jing, just in this area. Yes, the barons are turning a blind eye to the dragons as long as they don't attack them and their precious cities. Out here in the sticks, we folks are left on our own," Chan added. "They've only got us to protect them. Eighteen, damn, that's hardly a tree in the swamp around here. Pathetic gang, pathetic."

"Yes, but they are so damnably hard to kill, Chan. Keep that in mind, will ya?" Tao justified. "Seventy feet of pure fighting machine, scales so thick a sword can't cut through them, claws like razors."

"Don't forget they can pick up a dozen of us and fly off with us," Kang added, greatly exaggerating how much a dragon could carry and still fly.

"That's ignoring their slime spittle breath, to say nothing of their magic spells," Chan growled. Magic spells and slime breath — if the truth be told, those were what made these powerful creatures so hard to slay. Worse, from Green Dragon to Green Dragon, there was no predicting what spells any given beast would have. The last one they'd killed very nearly did them in when it shot a Ball of Flames at them as they charged it. All five had miraculously avoided the searing flames by diving into the swamp waters. The women's Duska senses had again saved the five from certain death. Indeed, Chan and Wen were convinced that only a Duska had any chance at all of killing a dragon and that was only a slim chance at best. She didn't ask her group how many dragons had successfully eluded them. It was far more than eighteen. The dragons could also Shadow Walk, though theirs was somehow different that the Duska's Shadow Walk — at least that's what many had said that old Zoran had said so many years ago. "Damn Zoran for bring the dragons into the federation!" she cursed her off-world, enemy baron.

When Chan and Wen turned fourteen and come of age, each had been given their birthright Ceremony of Ascension. Chan recalled her ceremony, during which her special gland at the base of her body's brain activated. Through the guidance of the Priestess, she'd been initiated into the Shadow Walk, which allowed her to walk through space to any of the sixteen planets within the Federation. Her first trip was nauseating, but by the last walk, she had mastered her fears and was now a true Duska, a Shadow Walker, which was her given birthright. All those who ruled throughout the Federation were Duska, both barons and baronesses.

Duska were special, multi-talented, different human beings, gifted by birth with an oversized gland, which, upon puberty, set them apart with special powers and abilities. Perhaps the greatest of these was their ability to Shadow Walk, in which they could transport themselves and others, if they chose, from one planet to another within the Federation of Planets. Also, their reaction times were phenomenal, and males usually made use of this by becoming master swordsmen, though often women were so trained as well. Certainly, all male Duskas were given standard fighter training from about the age of six onwards.

Magic was also prevalent throughout the Federation, though it took many shapes and forms. Although no one ever made an accurate assessment, popular opinion held that one in ten of every inhabitant had some latent magical skill, though often this amounted to little more than having a spoon stir a cooking pot or starting a fire in the fireplace — little, useful sort of things. From among those with magical skills, a relatively few had gotten some magical training and were able to cast limited formal, useful spells, these were called the Adepts. Often, they made their living by trading their spells for room and board or gold coins. Clean, Mend, and Polish were some of their main spells.

Even fewer still had the funds or backers to make a full time study of magic. These were called Mages. Armed with an array of spells, often power spells such as Ball of Fire, Lightning Bolt, and Killing Vapors, these men and women frequently found lucrative employment within the ruling baron's army of enforcers or even their armies proper. Those who did not, were often employed by the many warlords who controlled lands currently beyond the dominion of the barons and baronesses.

Exceedingly rare were those in the third category, that of the Archmage. These individuals had gone far beyond the mundane use of magical powers and spells, extending their knowledge of arcana to unknown limits. Wherever possible, every baron had one Archmage in their employ, who, among other duties, taught magic to those gifted few. Baron Gang Meerong, the women's older brother, still had the use and support of their father's Archmage Liang Don, who was now sixty-five. True, all three barons had several mages in their employ, but only the one, aging Archmage, a distinct disadvantage. Many other planets had several Archmages backing the barons there, none more so than on Adapazan and Baron Archmage Zoran Vladislov.

For over twenty years now, this had become a very sore point among the other many barons. Baron Archmage Zoran's wife, Baroness Archmage Zdenka, continued to turn out new Archmages at an unheard of and alarming rate. Hardly a year passed without her announcing that yet another of her mage students had achieved this exalted status. True, some fifteen years ago, many of the barons had challenged her products, claiming these supposed new Archmages were not in fact true Archmages. The High Council backed the challengers and conducted an extensive series of tests of these new Archmages and their spell casting abilities. To the dismay of the many challengers and barons, all of her new Archmages fully passed their rigorous tests. They were in fact Archmages, capable of casting the most powerful of all spells.

After that, many of these new Archmages sought employment on the Zoran-aligned planets. A few ended up working for the Neutral barons, but none for the Have-Not's, such as Jing. Long ago, Chan realized why her father had made the awful decision to bring the detested Green Dragons to Jing. Self-preservation. With their enemy barons loaded with Archmages and Golden Dragons, the very independence and survival of Jing was in question! The presence of the greens was supposed to act as a deterrent to their enemies. Perhaps it had, Chan sighed. Jing had not yet been attacked or invaded by armies, dragons, or magic users.

Assassinations, well that was an entirely different story! These came with the position of baron or baroness. Indeed, their mother had fallen victim to an assassin's poisoned blade, though their father, then Baron Chen, somehow escaped. It was not long after that that he had passed on his throne to his eldest son, Gang, and gone into retirement. In fact, Chan had not seen her father for many years, not since he had exiled Chan and Wen. She smiled, recalling the last bounty poster that Baron Gang had posted around Ningho. Each year, the bounty had risen. Today her head was worth fifty thousand gold and Wen's, forty thousand.

Here in Ningho, they need not worry. Eighteen kills had endeared them to the locals, who looked to them for their protection, not the baron who never came here or sent any aid, just the loathsome tax collectors. Most all of their kills had been viewed as revenge by many in Ningho, since the dead dragons had killed one or more of those who lived in and around this area of the swamps. No, they were relatively safe here in Ningho. Still, sooner or later Chan knew that Baron Gang would tire of the game and send out assassins to cut them down or sick Archmage Liang on them. The aged Archmage had trained them and he knew their strengths and weaknesses as well as their personalities. He would be a most worthy opponent, one that they might barely have a chance of eliminating, but only because they were Duskas. On that, the two rested all of their hopes.

Early on, they discovered that the greens loved gold and gems. Each green that they had slain had a den somewhere in the vast swamps. However, they had been successful in locating only ten of the eighteen, recovering quite a stash of gold and gems. Most of the gold they donated to the seneschal of Ningho, who doled it out to the residents, covering their yearly taxes for the most part. Again, this helped ensure that none in Ningho would betray them to the barons.

Wen spoke up, "Well, if we are going to go after number nineteen tomorrow, we had all best get some sleep." Chan agreed and had the others hold hands with hers, while she teleported them all to their secret base of operations in an isolated area of swampland.

They did not see a dark cloaked man rise, grin, and leave the inn after they left. He had been watching them all evening and once outside the inn, he too teleported away. He arrived within the walls of the Royal Palace in Nanchan.

Neither saw another dark cloaked man rise, grin, and leave the inn after both had left. Once outside and after a careful glance around him, the man simply vanished. No spell was cast.

None of these three saw yet another dark cloaked man rise, grin, and leave the inn after the others had left. He climbed into his boat and began poling his way through the shallow swamp waters, heading towards the city of Nanchan.

Finally, as the inn closed for the night, the barmaid Yan cast one of her few spells. A Message was sent.

"Ah back at last, Mage Hui," the twenty-five year old Baron Gang acknowledged the arrival of one of his mages. "Come share some wine with me." He poured out the red liquid into crystal goblets imported from one of the desert planets. The men were in his private study deep within the fortress and Circle, far from prying eyes.

"Anti-scrying?" asked the thirty-five year old Mage Hui Shihuan.

Baron Gang quickly cast a few protection spells and handed the expensive goblet to his mage, who had quickly vanished his grubby clothes, replacing them with his fine suit — a few quick spells cast.

He took the offering and sat down in the overstuffed, leather chair opposite the young baron. "It is as you suspected. The Swamp Raiders — your sisters — showed up at Wu's Bar, talking about their recent slaughters of the Green Dragons. Eighteen they claim that they have murdered, sir."

"Incredible! So many? I had no idea that they were killing so many. I guess that I should have upped the bounty on their heads long ago. This is getting way out of hand, Mage Hui. I simply cannot overlook their rebel behavior any longer."

"They did take the offered bait, Baron. I heard that they are planning to go after the green tomorrow sometime," Mage Hui continued, satisfied that it was safe for him to relay this bit of news. "Perhaps this will be the end of this annoying problem for you."

Baron Gang grinned, "Aye, perhaps it may well be so. Still, they are Duska trained. Eighteen? Incredible. Well, let's hope that their murdering spree comes to an end soon, Mage Hui." For the tiniest moment, Gang felt a twinge of regret for what was about to befall his two sisters. That feeling didn't last long, though. Ever since his father had banished the two, they had been nothing but constant trouble, both for his father and now for himself. "Lord knows that it is hard enough making ends meet for Jing without those two constantly messing everything up. With luck, tomorrow may bring us a new day, eh Hui?" He grinned at his mage.

"Aye, sir, that it may. On the off-chance that it fails, do you want me to get the Archmage involved in the search for their hideout?" Mage Hui asked. For weeks, the two had worked on an alternative scheme, one that depended upon knowing where the Swamp Raiders made their home. Once that was known, it would be a simple matter to send in shock troops and mages to capture them and put them out of business. The flaw in that plan, as Baron Gang often pointed out, was that the women were Duskas and would likely be able to escape by Shadow Walking.

"Let's see how this one works out first. I hate to get the Archmage involved if we don't have to — he's under orders to make as many mages as he can turn out." The two chatted a bit longer, and it was clear to Mage Hui that it was time for him to leave. He bowed and cast a Mystical Door to his own quarters, where his disguise clothes were now heaped on the floor, deposited there by his previous spell. He kicked them into a corner and plopped down on his bed. He had much to ponder. Tomorrow promised to be eventful.

Alone at last, Baron Gang made his Mink Link to his brothers. *Li, Jie! They took the bait. Tomorrow they will be going after the green. Are you prepared?*

Jie replied, *We certainly are. Our sisters are such an embarrassment to us all. They have to be stopped. Count on us, big brother. We will be totally focused on Shadow Walks tomorrow. You know that we can sense when anyone Shadow Walks now. It is a marvelous side-effect of our new Circles. Rather amazing.* Gang grimaced. He hated the fact that his two younger brothers now actually had more physical powers than he, who his father had chosen to be his heir! Still, he knew that he could do nothing about that, only continue to keep them aligned with himself.

Li added, *Gang, if our sisters attempt any Shadow Walking tomorrow, we will know about it and attempt to follow them or at least know where they went, if it is off-planet. One way or another, this constant interference of our sisters must be ended. Most likely, they will head back to their safe house, wherever that is. If they do, rest assured big brother, we will know their precise location. If so, are we still planning to raid them and capture them?*

Gang replied, *Yes, it would be ideal to make them pay for their crimes against Jing. Such would do wonders for our authority. They've been flaunting dad's and our rule around here for far too many years. It has to stop now.*

I still think that we ought to give them a choice between execution and marrying one of Baron Clav's men on Rehor, Jie added. *Getting them off-world permanently is better than execution. They are still Duska after all.*

Gang laughed, envisioning his sisters bedding one of the ugly Clav men on Rehor. *Well, first we have to capture them. Then we'll see. Time for bed. Tomorrow promises to be most interesting, brothers.*

Once that connection ended, Baron Gang made one more Mind Link. *Ah, Noble Ashford, Baron Gang here. The Swamp Raiders have taken the bait. They will be looking for the green tomorrow. I wish you the very best of luck with your trap. Keep me informed of the outcome, please.*

The Green Dragon smiled; his own spy had already reported in on the Swamp Raider's conversations around their table at Wu's Inn. He certainly didn't need this puny human's message. Still, the human was most useful for the time being. *Of course, Baron Gang. I will notify you of the outcome at soon as I hear it.* However, he didn't add that he would do so only when it suited him.

"Come Leeds, let's prepare this trap. I aim to personally devour these infernal death stalkers myself! Eighteen! Damn them to hell. No one kills eighteen of us without paying the ultimate penalty!" Ashford growled. He was the oldest of the greens here on Jing and their leader. Leeds was his second, though he longed to take Ashford's place. He thought that Ashford was being way, way too kind to these infernal humans on Jing. One sweep and the combined greens could put an end to this human infestation on their new beautiful homeland. Ashford continually refused to do any such thing. Quite why, Leeds had no idea. Ashford seldom relayed such information to the other Green Dragons, only his orders which they had to follow.

Of course, with Green Dragons, following orders was antipathetic to their very natures. Each thought of himself or herself as all important and capable of making their own orders. However, due to the near starvation of their species back on Voss, those that had come here via Ashford owed him a great debt. With a Green Dragon, a debt was taken almost as seriously as gems and magic. Hence, most all of the greens on Jing pretended at least to follow Ashford's orders, at least until the gems stopped coming from the barons.

Morning came to a remote portion of the swamp, some twenty miles from Ningho. Here on a small clump of ground above the water was the Swamp Raider's base camp. Long ago, they had discovered an abandoned bear cave here. With a bit of enlarging into the bedrock via magic spells, Chan had turned it into a small home. Actually, most of their cave was below the water level, but the solid bedrock kept the swamp waters out. The main chamber served as their all-purpose living room. Two small side chambers had been fixed up as bedrooms — one for the women, one for the three men. Outside, two small boats were hidden in the brush.

This area of the swamp was heavily infested with both gators and vipers, which acted as a natural protection force while they were away. When they were here, the women erected a Force Screen to prevent unwanted creatures from entering, though they added more spells to completely block and hide the entrance whenever they left their safe house.

Wen went about the task of fixing them breakfast, while Chan sharpened their many blades, along with the three men. "Well, Yan sent me a message last night after we all left Wu's. She said that three different suspicious men left after we did. She doesn't think that any of the three were aware of each other, but only us."

"Sounds like someone is on to us," Peng pointed out.

"Could be a trap that we are heading into today," Kang said, highly suspicious of this interesting tidbit of news. "Three of them? Do you suppose each of the Barons sent out spies looking for us?"

"That's what has been bothering me all night, guys. Gang has always run rough-shod over Li and Jie, who have always done pretty much whatever Gang says. I can't imagine all three of them sending out spies and not having their spies aware of each other and working together. It is not Gang's way. No, Gang is devious. I wouldn't put it past him to send out a spy to spy on the spy, but not three of them. His big thing is redundancy. If one thing doesn't work, always have a secondary backup plan. I would bet that one of the spies was spying on one of his spies, but the third? Honestly, that has me baffled. Who else wants our hides?"

Wen called out as the tea water boiled over, "The greens!"

"She's got a point, Chan," Peng put in. "Dragons can take human forms. Perhaps one of the spies was a dragon looking for us. If so, maybe this whole thing is a setup — a trap to ensnare us all."

"I agree with Peng," Tao added, nursing a slight hangover. "Maybe we should let this one slide."

"Ordinarily, I'd agree," Chan said, diving into the breakfast that Wen dished out, "but that was a family of three, helpless, defenseless, innocent people who were murdered by the green. We saw their bodies. We know it was a green's doing. I just cannot let that go, fellows. That family needs justice served."

"If we know or suspect that it is a trap, we can be extra cautious and not take any chances," Wen suggested.

"Fellows, this one might be way too dangerous for you to come on, so if you want to stay here and guard the fort, we will understand. We cannot keep on asking you to risk your lives fighting these vile greens," Chan explained, giving them a way to back out honorably.

"Nah, what else is there to do now on Jing except go after the vermin?" Peng replied. "I'm with you. If I have to die, let it be for something of value." The other two agreed with him.

Kang added, "Look, Chan, if we don't survive this one, at least we five can say that we alone took eighteen of them down with us! No one else on Jing has even gotten one of them, so I say we are heroes. Let's die like heroes. At least the folks in Ningho know that we are heroes." They all grinned at that.

After arming themselves with all of their weapons, the five left their safe house. Chan sealed it up and was the last to climb aboard their poled boat. The three men were in one, while the two women took the other boat. With Wen poling and Chan far forward as lookout, they led the way through the fog-filled swamp morning. Chan too held a pole which she used to encourage vipers hanging from branches to move out of their way. A dozen gators slipped into the waters from the nearby patches of semisolid ground. Great trees grew overhead; their roots often looked like giant tendrils dropping down into the water, as if even the trees hated to be in these semi-stagnant waters and were trying to pull themselves upwards.

The going was slow in the fog, but they all knew that it would soon burn off. Then, they could double their pace. Bird calls echoed through the trees, while flies and mosquitoes abounded. Occasionally, a deer darted off following the patches of semi-solid ground. Wildlife teamed in these swamps, just not humans. Oh, there were hardy pioneers who lived out here in the swamps, catching wildlife and trading furs and skins for other necessities of life in Ningho or other towns and cities, but they were in the minority. They were also the ones that the Green Dragons were preying upon the most — isolated swamp families. Well, eighteen of them would not be doing that any longer, Chan mused, as she deftly encouraged another viper to slither out of their way from an overhanging branch.

Around ten, the fog lifted and their pace doubled, though it was still slow by poled boat. In these bayous, about the only real means of transportation was by poled boat. These were very shallow bottomed boats, capable of floating in mere inches of water, which often occurred as one traveled around the swamps of Jing. Occasionally, beams of sunlight slanted down through gaps in the dense foliage above their heads.

They drifted along at lunchtime, snacking on the scraps that Wen had packed. Finished, they resumed their poling. One o'clock found the two boats near the deceased family's home. "Here's where we start out search," Chan announced. "Start looking for dragon signs."

The one thing that these dragon hunters had going for them is that Green Dragons seldom flew. They preferred to slither along the water like the snakes that they were. Oh, they were fast swimmers! The gators were one of their favorite delicacies here on Jing, though they also often ate the deer as well. Before long, Chan picked up the trail left by the vile creature who a few days before had slaughtered the family of three. No mistaking the path: crushed plants and grasses, even small saplings bore witness to the seventy foot long passage of these enormous beasts. The question was: was this the trail the green left leaving the murdered family or was it the path that it took when it came here? Chan could not be sure which it was just yet.

"Okay, circle around the area. Let's see if we can find a second trail," she ordered. The two boats split up and began making a huge sweep around the small hillock on which the wooden cabin stood. Before long, Peng called out that they found another path and Wen poled their boat over to the men's location.

After a bit of study, Chan announced, "Ah, this is the exit trail. See how the grasses are pushed that way, away from the cabin and hillock? Follow me. Stay sharp, this well could be a trap!" On they poled for another hour.

At last, Chan hastily flashed hand signals to the men behind her. Both her and Wen's inner Duska senses began warning them of danger. The swamp was deadly quiet as their two boats drifted along among the trees. They made little noise with their passage. Still to their ears, it sounded as though they were shouting their way along the waters. The five felt confident, primarily because Chan had already cast her most powerful protection spell upon them all, Skin of Stone. This had frequently saved their lives when attacked, as no weapon could pierce their skin until the spell wore off. Perhaps that was their downfall, depending too heavily upon this single protection spell. Chan later believed that this was so.

In the lead boat, Chan drew her weapons making as little noise as possible. Wen already had hers out and laying at her feet where she could grab them when she dropped her pole. Slowly, ever so slowly, the two boats slipped along the shallow waters. Still no birds, no gators, no deer could be seen or heard. Utter quiet, deathly quiet. Chan knew that they must be close now. Somewhere just ahead of them must lay the vile Green Dragon who wantonly murdered the helpless pioneer family. She was determined to get revenge for them. Wen gave their boat another silent push and they continued their gentle, forward glide. Chan's eyes were pealed, looking for any sign of the green. It would be hard to miss, likely being seventy feet long and ten feet in diameter along its mid-section. But where the devil was it?

Curled around tree, Ashford watched the wary humans in their two puny boats slowly drifting towards him. Just a bit closer, he thought to himself. Five other greens were wrapped around neighboring trees, all Invisible. He'd cast that spell on the other five, who did not know the spell. If they followed his orders, the lives of these infernal Swamp Raiders would be over in just another minute. Get a bit closer, he thought.

The problem with Green Dragons is simple: they hate to have to work together. One of the five began his spell cast chanting before Ashford gave the signal. Ashford saw this and hastened his signal to the others, who began their chanting as well. That was all that Chan and Wen needed. Their Duska senses triggered, warning them of an imminent attack!

"Trap! We're being attacked!" Chan screamed her warning to the others. Spells detonated. Wen and Chan both felt their Skin of Stone spells being nullified and knew that some of their attackers had cast Dispel Magic spells on them. Further, the six Green Dragons became visible at the very moment their spells fired. Chan saw them curled around the thick trees just ahead of them. She realized that it would have been far worse had the dragons waited a bit longer until they had moved further along. Then they would have been entirely surrounded! A volley of Magical Missiles struck Peng. A Lightning Bolt arced towards Wen, but with her lightning fast reaction times, it missed her entirely, striking the pole that she had been holding. Five seconds had thus far elapsed; the Swamp Raiders had yet to counterattack.

Ashford saw his spell missing Wen and chose to resort to his tried and true methods of dealing with these humans. Forgetting even his own orders to his companions, he belched forth a flood of slime from his mouth, aiming it towards the first boat. These pesky humans would now have no chance at all, he thought.

In a nearby tree, Leeds, who, following Ashford's orders, had shot a Dispel Magic, now regretted having done so, for he could see no reason to have used that spell at all. Thus, he also belched forth his flood of slime onto the second boat. Enough of this playing around with these humans, he thought. Besides he had no intention of eating their bodies. They tasted awful. After all, they had killed eighteen fellow dragons and harmed another ten. In his mind, they should pay with their fragile lives. He ignored Ashford's orders not to dissolve their bodies, though he knew that the puny Baron Gang had wanted visible proof that these Swamp Raiders were dead and that Chan and Wen were among them. Well, he could give them their bones at least.

Still in the middle of her flying dive out of the way of the lightning bolt, Wen saw Ashford's mouth opening and knew he was about to unleash his awful slime breath weapon on her boat. She saw the vile looking, greenish slime exploding out of his mouth in an expanding cone of devastation coming her way. Her hands reached the side of the boat and she used her falling motion to flip her body over the side into the foul-smelling swamp waters beneath the boat, hoping that the waters were deep enough to cover her body and protecting her from the highly corrosive slime. Wen felt the warm waters flowing over her face and she headed downwards, striking hard into the soft, muddy bottom some three feet below the surface. Instinctively, she knew that it was just enough to cover her from the slime. However, she had a brief glimpse of the others as she was falling into the waters. Her sister was facing the wrong direction! Had she even seen it coming? Worse, the three men had not reacted as fast as she. Damn, they were not Duska. By the time that she hit the waters, Wen knew that the three men would take a direct hit from the slime.

As she sank below the waters, she heard the pitiful, horror-pain filled screams from the three men and knew that she'd lost them forever. Damn! Chan and she should never have allowed these men to join them, she thought as she landed face down in the mucky bottom, three feet from the surface. Wen's thoughts now went to her sister, had she gotten out of the way?

Chan was facing sideways and from her left she saw Ashford's mouth opening and knew slime was sure to follow. Worse, from her right, she saw another green's mouth opening and knew that the three men were in a direct line of sight of this one. She delayed her own reaction long enough to scream to the three, "Dive! Dive! Dive!" Almost in slow motion, she saw how futile her warning was. The three men barely had time to look up at the dragon before the cone of foul, caustic, green slime shot out of its mouth directly towards them in an ever expanding cone! She was utterly helpless to prevent them from taking a direct hit and a horrible, painful, but quick death! Her delay in reacting to the slime coming her way in this last ditch attempt to save her three companions almost cost Chan her life. At the very last instant, she dove into the water, having seen that Wen was a spit second ahead of her.

Pain! Sharp, excruciating pain shot along her lower left arm and hand. Such pain she had never felt before and she knew that she'd been hit with slime herself. Sliding under the water, Chan felt the intense pain of having led her three companions to their death with her insane desires to get revenge for the slain family. Now she knew that she was dying as well. You bastard, she though. *If I am going to die, then so are you!* With her right hand, she drew her magical dagger and focused her will power, attempting to drown out the searing pain in her left lower arm and hand. She did a short Shadow Walk and landed precisely on Ashford's enormous head! With her legs wrapped around his long neck, she stabbed her dagger into his right eye!

Chan felt the dragon's body wildly lurching, waves of involuntary muscle reactions surging through its seventy foot long, snake-like body, but she willed her legs to hold on, gripping hard as if they were around a horse. She pulled the dagger out and fought to hang on as Ashford's body writhed in agony and began falling from the trunk of the tree. Again she stabbed her dagger down, this time into its left eye, thrusting it in with all of the force she could muster. Ashford's body jerked hard to the right and her dagger snapped with a loud cracking sound. She was falling. So was the dragon. Cold water hit her followed by a massive weight landing on her body. Chan knew that this was the end. The force of the dragon's weight shot the remaining air out of her lungs like a bursting balloon. Death would come quickly now.

Wen used her Duska skills to Mind Link to Chan and was momentarily overwhelmed with the searing pain coming from Chan's body. She was able to see the dagger snapping like a twig and the two falling down into the waters not far from her own body. She felt the massive exhale of air from Chan's body, just as Chan did. Wen acted. She Shadow Walked a few feet, grabbed a hold of her sister's right hand, and Shadow Walked them both back inside their safe haven cavern. She cast her Light spell and looked at herself and sister. They were drenched in swamp muck. Foul smelling waters dripped off of them onto the stone floor. Leeches wigged over her exposed flesh and she knew more were probably beneath their clothes. However, what commanded her instant attention was Chan's left lower arm and hand. The flesh was slowly dissolving right before her eyes! An awful rotting, foul-smelling vapor rose from the decaying flesh! She gagged. What could she do to stop it?

Chan's body lurched and her lungs and chest gave a huge gasp for air, startling Wen for a moment. Then, she saw her unconscious sister's body breathing again and she began wracking her mind for what she could do for the rotting arm.

Barons Jie and Li were with Baron Gang and his two Mages Hui and Ji, along with the assassin Li Shan. Both younger barons were using their special abilities that their new Circles of Ascension had given them. True, their eyes had also changed color to match the uniquely colored threads of their Circles, a swampy green and a pinkish green, respectively, much to their eternal annoyance. Yes, they'd cursed

Brother Jiri for not having told them that their eyes would take on the color of their Circle's threads, but it was too late for that. Still, their new Circles gave them an ability that their older brother Gang didn't have. While Gang had inherited their father's original Circle here on Jing, he did not inherit the many special abilities that an original owner of a new Circle had. Among these was one that the priestesses had: the ability to follow and monitor Shadow Walks.

"Hey, I got them!" Baron Jie called out.

"Right, me too. Now we got you, pesky sisters!" Baron Li added, not wanting to be left out in the eyes of his older brother, Gang.

"Brilliant, brothers. Let's go capture them. Looks like Ashford failed in his ambush attempt. Well, never trust a dragon, I always say. Come on, Jie. Take us to them. Chan and Wen, your rebel days are finally over!" Baron Gang exclaimed excitedly, punching his fist high into the air. He was about to do something that even his father had been unable to do for nearly a dozen years now: capture his renegade daughters, ending their constant meddling in planet affairs. He felt certain of victory now. Always make contingency, backup plans was his motto. Today, it worked to perfection. He wagered that Ashford would botch his carefully laid trap for the Swamp Raiders, but his backup plan was working to perfection!

The six men double checked their many weapons and then they held hands with Barons Jie and Li. Jie then stepped them all into the Shadows, a swirling mass of blackness, but with their own planet still visible beneath their feet. A moment later, Baron Jie stepped them out onto the foul smelling swamp land just in front of the mouth of the cavern and safe haven of the Swamp Raiders. Baron Gang attempted to move into the entrance, but ran smack into their Force Screen. "Damn, Force Wall."

Baron Li cast his Dispel Magic but it failed to bring the two walls down. Baron Jie attempted it a second time and also failed. "Let a man do it," Baron Gang teased his brothers, knowing that had nothing to do with it. This particular spell just merely had a chance to bring it down. However, his was successful, and he gave a smirking look to his younger brothers. "Li Shan, guard the entrance. Mages prepare defensive spells. Let we Duska enter. Remember, we want them alive if possible," Gang ordered. Then, he yelled loudly, "Okay, Chan, Wen, the game is up. Surrender peacefully and we won't harm you." He was a bit hesitant about just walking into this unknown cavern. After all, they had killed eighteen dragons.

Inside, Wen had begun to examine the rapidly dissolving lower arm of Chan, frantically trying to think of anything that she could do to arrest the corrosive action of the green slime that still covered the arm from just below the elbow on down. She tried to use a Create Water spell to wash it off, but that had no effect; the slime was somehow sticky. Just then, her Duska senses kicked in, warning her of an imminent attack! She cursed, "Damn! How did they find this place?" Suddenly, she realized that this whole thing had been a cleverly designed trap! Only another Duska could have possibly followed her Shadow Walk back here. That meant her brothers were coming after them and were likely right outside. Their protective Force Walls would delay them, but only briefly. She could not fight her brothers; they were far too strong for her. Besides, all of her weapons were back on the boat. She'd abandoned them while diving overboard.

Wen thought fast. If she Shadow Walked from here bringing the still unconscious Chan with her, her brothers would surely be able to follow her no matter where she went on Jing. Worse, she really didn't know where she could possibly go on Jing where she and Chan would be safe! She had to do something to save her sister and herself. They had to get away from her brothers, but Chan desperately needed medical attention. She fought down the idea that perhaps it was already too late for Chan. The sneering voice of Gang entered her ears, ordering her to surrender. In desperation, she did the only thing that she could think of doing to get them to safety. She took her sister's good arm in hers and again dragged Chan into another Shadow Walk. This time it was a long walk!

"Hey, they are Shadow Walking again!" Baron Jie yelled to Gang, as the older brother stepped cautiously into the dark cavern.

"Damn! Can you follow them or see where they are going this time?" Baron Gang yelled back, quickly rushing back outside to the others.

"Shit, they are going off-planet, deep into the Shadows!" Baron Li pronounced, growing more excited by the minute.

"Crap! We almost had them," Baron Gang admitted. "Well, see if you can follow them. Where the devil are they going now?"

Both brothers didn't answer; they were both off into the Shadows themselves, at least partially so, monitoring the route taken by their sisters. They followed a good deal behind the two fleeing sisters and before long saw that they were heading for Adapazan! *Damn,* Jie thought, *they are fleeing to our archenemies!* Both watched a little longer until their sisters finally left the Shadows, and then they returned to Jing.

"Well, they are on Adapazan now," Baron Jie proclaimed as he and his younger brother stepped back onto the swamp land.

"Well, good riddance. While it would have been best to have tried them for their crimes here, I guess this result is almost as good. At least they won't be meddling in Jing affairs any longer. You two, keep a sharp eye on any possible return to Jing that they might make in the future. I expect to be informed the moment that they return here. Come on; let's get out of this smelly swampland!" The six men quickly reappeared back in Gang's private study.

Chapter 2 Surprise Visitors

Baron Zoran Vladislov, now thirty-nine, stared at his huge maps of Adapazan and the Planets of the Federation. As the senior baron for Adapazan and all Free Peoples, as he often described himself to others, he shouldered an enormous responsibility. With most all of the previous generation of ruling barons now either deceased or retired, their children had taken over the reins of running the sixteen Planets of the Federation. Many of these, Zoran knew well and considered good friends, especially those of his allied planets. On Valtr, the hilly planet, and Gladno, a forested planet, his older sisters were the baronesses, and their husbands, Baron Stefan Pavel and Baron Leo Matous, he considered extremely good friends.

Both an Archmage and a Duska, Baron Zoran was still unique among all the barons. While most had Mage status, he alone was also an Archmage. With it, he assumed more responsibility than other barons. He had to, he often told himself, for he had merged the world of magic with that of the Duska. Still, he was not totally alone. Oh no. His incredible wife, Archmage Zdenka had continued to produce more Archmages than any other Archmage in history. She had a knack of pulling out the very best in her students. Conservative by nature, she never forced others, but merely guided them along with unseen hands.

They had three children. Baron Tomas, twenty, had just been installed in the third Fortress and Circle here on Adapazan. Over the years, Zoran had rebuilt Mikolas' fortress in the deserted Sholov Province, and just last year Brother Jiri Zar had built him a new Circle of Ascension there, installing Tomas as the new Baron.

Zoran's dear friends and constant companions, Jarka and Bernard Dragan, also had three children. Their eldest, Verushka, twenty, had married Tomas and was now Baroness Verushka. She was also one of the newest Archmages. Zdenka lavished all manner of training on all of their close friends' children. She and Zoran owed Jarka and Bernard much for their assistance over the years. Hence, Zdenka always gave their many children her all, and Verushka blossomed just as Zdenka had done so some twenty years ago herself.

However, Zoran took things one step beyond the ordinary or even the known territory. Until this point in time, only a Duska-born child between ten and twenty-one were given the Ceremony of Ascension, in which their special glands grew and became operational, giving them the vast abilities of a Duska and the ability to Shadow Walk. That is, only the children of a baron and baroness were given this ceremony. However, from the ancient writings of the first baron of Adapazan, he had learned that anyone could be given this Ceremony of Ascension, turning them into Duskas as well! Except for Zoran, no one in the Federation of the Sixteen Planets knew this detail. Originally, Zoran had wanted to give this precious gift to Zdenka, but he didn't because she was a little over twenty-one and he did not want to risk her life.

Not so with their three children, Tomas, Nadia, and Jarmila. Each was given the Ceremony of Ascension on their tenth birthday. Compounding matters was the simple fact that Zoran had rescued many other of his half-brothers and sisters and even two Duska born women from Asami, Chika and Akira. With all of these living here either in his Brn Fortress and Circle or Archmage Zdenka's tower, their many children were also given the Ceremony of Ascension, becoming Duskas themselves. Only Jarka and Bernard's three children were not "legally" of Duska birth.

Zoran owed these two much, Jarka and Bernard — to say nothing of Brother Jiri Zar and his priestess wife Anezka, who also now had two children. Hence, in secret, he insisted that Anezka perform the Ceremony of Ascension on five who would never have received this incredibly special gift. Thus, Baroness Archmage Verushka was also a Duska now, as were Jarka and Bernard's other two children, Dusan, nineteen, and Evsen, eighteen. Likewise, the two Zar children, Miroslav, eighteen, and Danika, sixteen, were Duska. Thus, Baroness Archmage Verushka alone joined Zoran, merging Duska with Archmage skills. She was an exceedingly powerful woman.

Compounding all else, many of their children had married their friends' children! Indeed, the Vladislov dinner table was packed each evening, though Baron Tomas and Baroness Archmage Verushka were now usually off in the Sholov Fortress Circle. Zoran's daughter Archmage Nadia had married Jarka's son Dusan. His daughter, Jarmila, had been far more interested in the priestess aspect of the Circles of Ascension, and, though she had a good deal of training from her mother, Zdenka, and was considered a mage, Jarmila had married the Zar's son, Miroslav. Just this past year, the Zars retired from making more Circles, passing the torch, as it were, to Miroslav and Jarmila. The Zar's daughter, Danika, was also a priestess and a Duska.

Archmage Karel Ambrose, the falconer, had married one of the Duska born mermaids that Zoran had rescued from Asami, Chika. She was now officially the Business Trader for all of Adapazan, a super-trader, as Zoran always called her. Their oldest daughter, Katerina, eighteen, had married Jarka's youngest son, Evsen. What of Akira, the other sister mermaid?

Zdenka's Door Warden, Marek, had become an Archmage, thanks to the added push from Zdenka, when she took over for Archmage Oldrich. Archmage Marek married Akira and they had three children. Their oldest was Dana and he was now nineteen. Their daughter, Kate, was seventeen and now dating seriously Karel and Chicka's son, Milan, who was also seventeen. Their youngest daughter, Milena, was sixteen.

All of these dined each evening at Zoran and Zdenka's giant table. Everyone present was at least of mage status and all of the children were also Duska trained. Zdenka's father, Janos Lavos was seventy-one, but he had long ago retired from being Zoran's Security Chief. He, too, was always present. Though he was getting rather old, his advice was still highly sought.

At this time, Zoran had three fortresses and Circles evenly spaced across the major land mass of Adapazan. His here in Brn Province was near the western edge, while his half-brother Baron Jan Vavrin controlled the original Circle of Adapazan in Dorum. He'd installed the then ten year old bastard son of the despised Baron Kazimir as the new Baron when Kazimir was slain some twenty years ago. Now Jan was of age and had married a cousin from Gladno, Baroness Reina Matous. Already they had two children of their own, Lilia, ten, and Vilemn eight.

While he was growing up, their half-brother, General Damek Kamil ran the castle as his regent. He'd married Marika and had two children: Jarmila, ten, and Boris, eight. Zoran promised that in two days, Priestess Jarmila Zar would perform the Ceremony of Ascension for Jarmila. When Boris was ten, Zoran promised his brother that he would also get the ceremony, making both children Duskas.

Jan's twin sister, Zusa, was thirty herself. She married Zdenk Pavel, one of the cousins of Viktor Pavel. He had become Baron Zdenk Pavel a few years back and now Zusa was his Baroness.

Kamila Lota, who had looked after Jan's Circle of Ascension for eight years until he became of age, had also found love off-world, marrying another of the Pavel clan, Baron Dragan Pavel, becoming Baroness Kamila. Thanks to the education of Zdenka, she was prepared for this lofty position and was a mage in her own right. Slowly, Zoran's political tendrils began expanding to other worlds.

As he studied the map, he acknowledged the second reason that he had gone ahead and had Priestess Anezka perform the five "illegal" Ceremony of Ascension: the dragons. While he really had no choice in bringing the Golden Dragons to Adapazan, his worst fears had materialized. Other barons had subsequently been bringing other species of dragons into the federation planets as well. Each of the sixteen worlds now had dragons on them. While the starvation of the dragon's home world of Voss was probably a thing of the past, now dragons seemed to be everywhere. Worse, some Red Dragons and Black Dragons had been making raids on villages here on Adapazan. This had been his second reason for attempting to perform the five "illegal" Ceremony of Ascensions, to ensure all five were also Duskas and capable of lightning fast reactions and warnings of impending attacks, to say nothing of being able to Shadow Walk themselves. Here at Fortress Brn, he had more Duskas, mages, and Archmages present than at any other Circle or fortress on any of the sixteen planets.

Of course, the Archmages needed their own towers. Zdenka had inherited her old teacher's tower, Archmage Oldrich. It rose five stores and was at the front western edge of his fortress. Archmage Nadia's tower was under construction, due to be finished by the following spring. Lying at the front eastern corner, its lower four floors were already inhabitable and in use. Archmage Marek's tower was located in the right rear corner of the fortress. Like Nadia's, his was under construction, but only the bottom floor was serviceable at this time. At Fortress Miklos in Sholov Province, Archmage Verushka's adjoining tower was finished only weeks ago. She was now getting everything there organized for her few students. She was just starting out teaching others magic.

It was late afternoon when Zoran's intricate ties to his sky blue threaded Circle of Ascension suddenly alerted him. Someone was attempting to arrive at his Circle! For twenty years now, he always was alerted when anyone tried to Shadow Walk to within about a quarter mile of his Circle, located in the depths of his frugal fortress here in Brn. He did not recognize the person or persons who were attempting to come, and he instantly stepped down to his Circle and reached out with his Mind Link. *Help! Help us, please. Zoran, help us!*

Come on in, he sent, quickly lowering his Circle's defenses which prevented unauthorized materializing at or around his Circle. At once, two young women materialized in the center of his circle. One was unconscious, and her arm looked awful; the other was terrified and in shock. "Help us please! Chan has been slimed by a Green Dragon! Her arm is dissolving! Can you help us, please," the younger woman begged. Both women were soaked in some kind of foul smelling water. Mud and muck covered their leather clothing and hair; their weapon sheaths were empty, he noted.

He quickly chanted off a Message to Zdenka and Jarka, asking them to meet him here at the Circle. "Don't touch her arm. If you get it on your fingers, sir, it will eat through your flesh too," the frightened woman cautioned him.

"Oh hell, that looks really bad!" Jarka interrupted her, arriving just ahead of Zdenka. Both had used their Mystical Door spells to get here as rapidly as possible. "Green Dragon slime is it?" she asked.

"Yes, please, help her. She's my sister. Please," Wen begged.

"Oh dear!" the mellow alto voice of Zdenka announced her arrival a second after Jarka's.

"Don't touch her. Back in a flash," Mage Jarka ordered. She cast another Mystical Door and stepped through it, vanishing from sight. Seconds later, the door reopened and she reappeared, the door then vanishing.

"Zoran, careful of her arm, but lift her head up. I'll try to get this down her throat," Jarka ordered. He did as she asked, lifting the soaking, filthy woman up so that Jarka could make her attempt. She did manage to get the small vial of liquid down the woman's throat. Involuntary muscle reactions allowed Chan to swallow it.

"Damn, it's not going to work, Zoran," Jarka stated flatly. "Damn! Look, there is nothing left of her fingers but bones! Worse, it's almost down to her arm bones! If we're going to save her, we are going to have to remove her arm there at her elbow, Zoran. Do it immediately! If that slime gets into her system, she could die!"

"Okay, I'll tie on a tourniquet; you get it off," Zoran answered. Wen slumped to the floor and began bawling. Jarka used her dagger and carefully cut through the bit of remaining muscle and flesh at the woman's elbow. She had to go slow to avoid touching the slime which was barely an inch below this spot. At last, she severed the limb.

"There! Okay, Zoran, you Vanish the arm and hand. Make sure you get all of that corrosive slime too. I'm going to pump her full of healing potions now. Zdenka, hold her head up please." She poured two more healing potions into the unconscious woman.

"Will — will she live?" Wen asked above her sobbing.

"Let you know in a minute, ma'am," Jarka replied, watching the severed elbow closely. She smiled and began unloosening the tourniquet. "Ah ha. It is holding. Good. Yes, we caught it in the nick of time. The wound is healing rapidly now. No need for a doctor's stitches — not when you have good old Jarka around. You certainly came to the right place and in the nick of time. A few more minutes and she probably would not have made it. God, you both stink! Muddy too."

Zoran cast one of his power spells. All traces of the slime and the nearly dissolved hand vanished from sight, appearing momentarily just above the surface of the sun, where it vaporized. He could not help but remember how, before he learned to cast that spell, his teacher Archmage Oldrich had done the very same thing, greatly humbling him.

"Okay, it has healed sufficiently. Zdenka, we need to get these women cleaned up pronto. God, what a smell!" Jarka announced and proclaimed. Zdenka didn't hesitate. She took both women's hands, teleporting them to their bathroom. Jarka followed along after her, leaving Zoran to clean up the small amount of mud and water that the women had left on his precious Circle of Ascension.

Later, the two brought the new arrivals into the packed Great Hall at dinnertime. Word had already spread throughout the fortress, and everyone was anxiously awaiting the two women, eager to hear their story. Life had been pretty much mundane for many years now and this was big news! Indeed, for Zoran and Zdenka, the past twenty years had been heavenly and peaceful.

Zdenka and Jarka escorted the two women into the Great Hall. The healing potions had done wonders for Chan, physically at least. Her stump was pinkish now and healing rapidly on its own. They wore borrowed simple white cotton dresses, similar to what all the women wore around this fortress and tower. While other off-planet barons and baronesses insisted on wearing only the latest in fashions, here in Brn, the women opted to follow Zdenka's lead and wore simple dresses like all of the other women of Brn. Only at the twice a year High Councils did the women dress up in the latest fashions. Well, they also sometimes did so for dances and other outings.

"Everyone, these are the daughters of retired Baron Chen Meerong. Baronesses Chan and Wen Meerong. They have been killing Green Dragons on Jing and were caught in a trap today. Their friends died and Chan lost her left arm to the dragon slime. Now then, let's eat," Zdenka announced for everyone's benefit. "They can tell you more after we eat."

Chan struggled to eat, but Zoran sensed immense grief in her, far beyond the losing of her hand. Something else was eating away at her, though he waited to hear their story. When the meal was finished and everyone began sipping their tea, Wen decided to speak for her sister. After all, these people had save them from disaster.

"When we were little, dad — Baron Chen — brought the Green Dragons to Jing. My sister and I argued with him, insisting this was a very bad idea, but he did it anyway. At first, it seemed to work out. I mean, the dragons stayed away from us humans for the most part. Then they started attacking harmless families who live far out in the swamps. Dad wouldn't do anything about it, so finally Chan and I took matters into our own hands."

Wen continued, "We became rebels and slowly built up the Swamp Raiders and went after those Green Dragons who murdered our people. Some we got, some escaped. Dad put a bounty on our heads, but we kept out of sight. Dad retired and now our oldest brother Gang is the Barron, along with our other two brothers who run the new Circles, Baron Jie and Baron Li. Both of them mostly take orders from Gang. Anyway, we continued to get revenge for the murdered families, and Gang continued to raise the bounty for our heads."

"A few days ago, a green murdered a whole family of three, and we swore to get revenge for them. Only now we think it must have been a trap set by Gang and the greens to murder us. Chan thought it might be a trap, but she wanted to get that green anyway."

Chan spoke up, "It's all my fault. They are all dead! I led them into the trap, I killed them!"

"No you didn't, Chan. The greens killed them with their slime," Wen countered. She then outlined what had happened, adding, "I am sure that Jie and Li followed us here, Baron Zoran! Now they'll probably come attacking you to get to us, but I didn't know where else we could go."

Zoran spoke up, "Wen, Chan, I grant you sanctuary here in Brn for as long as you desire. I will not let your brothers or anyone else from Jing get to you. You are safe here with us."

"Thank you, Baron. We've brought funds with us, so we can pay for our keep," Wen replied. Always the two women kept their accumulated treasures shrunk into small bags and on their person. Living out in the swamps, they had no place to keep their valuables except on their persons. This turned out to be very fortuitous for them. "We've at least killed nineteen of the wicked dragons, but now I don't know how we can kill more."

Chan spoke up, "We can't, Wen. We've lost our weapons, and my magical dagger broke when I killed that green that did this to me. We never should have allowed those three men to join up with us. All we did was get them horribly killed. It is all my fault, Wen. I knew it must be a trap, but I went ahead with it anyway."

Zdenka Messaged *Zoran, Do something! Say something. Can't you tell she's blaming herself?*

"Chen, the three men who lost their lives today — didn't they want to help free Jing from the evil Green Dragons?"

"Well, yes," she admitted.

"Men and women all want to help when evil threatens their land, their families, themselves. Some of us are more powerful and more able than others, such as yourselves. Yet, Chan, would you deny someone who is not a Duska to offer their help in ridding your land of its evil? Would you deny them their own self-respect and honor simply because they are not as able as you and Wen are?"

"Well, no," she responded meekly.

"Did these men volunteer of their own free will? Didn't they want to do their part, knowing well the awful danger that they would be facing? Terrible odds against them?"

"Sure, they knew that. Honestly, they saved us a couple of times but," she answered.

"Then, Chan, honor their memory. They did not die in vain; they died brave and free. They alone of the millions of your people had the pride and self-respect to stand up for what was right and to do the right thing. You should honor their incredibly brave sacrifices. Don't let the battle against the Green Dragons of Jing die with them."

"Baron, you are right. I must not let them down. So few have the guts to stand up to the dragons. Hardly anything will kill them. Peng, Kang, and Tao did their best and delivered a killing blow several times. You are right; they were proud of what they were doing for Jing, in spite of the bounty placed on our heads by our barons, our idiot bothers. Wen, somehow, we have to continue to fight the dragons, but right now, I don't know how," Chan decided.

Zoran added, "As far as your mistake about the trap, we are all human. We can make mistakes in judgment. The sign of a good leader is one who learns from his or her mistakes and continues the great battle. For that matter, the entire dragon problem is really my own doing, Chan. I was the one who first brought dragons into our federation."

"Well, you had no choice, if our version of your history is right," Wen interjected.

Zoran sighed, "Yes, I had very little choice. Had I not brought the Golden Dragons to Adapazan, none of us would likely be here today. Yet, what have I unleashed upon all our worlds?" He sighed again and then added, "Please consider joining us, Chan, Wen. Somehow, someway, I must undo what I've done with these dragons."

Wen replied, "Well, count me in, but I am more interested in getting rid of all the greens on Jing."

"Of course, Wen. Thank you," Zoran agreed.

"Me too," Chan sighed deeply, before adding, "but I am going to have to find us some more magical weapons. These dragons are almost impossible to kill without using magical weapons."

Zdenka grinned, "Well ladies, with all of the Archmages around here, that should not be too hard to do."

"Not at all, ma'am," Archmage Karel broke in. "I've been putting my talents to good use enchanting high quality blades. Come on up to our quarters tomorrow and see what I have. My charming wife, Chika here, keeps finding me nothing but the very best forged weapons in the entire federation!"

Chika grinned, "Well, I do have a knack for finding them for Karel. But honestly, how were you and your hero friends able to actually kill those dragons? I mean they are *so* powerful and strong and huge. I don't see how anyone could harm them. Our Gold Dragon Archmages are so strong and powerful. They are really quite good friends with us all and have helped us a whole lot. Your dragons must be really evil ones."

"The last one I stabbed in its eyes with my magical dagger. Must have hit its brain twice," Chan answered. "The Green Dragons on Jing are evil and wicked, murdering helpless women and children. We've never seen a Gold Dragon."

"Do they eat humans? The Golden Dragons here only eat antelope, not people," Mage Jarka asked. She added, "Emil once told me that we taste really bad. He's our Archmage Gold Dragon. You have to meet him and his sister, Archmage Renata sometime. I think that you'll like them."

Wen answered her. "No, they murder us and slime the bodies, leaving nothing but bleached bones behind to bury. They eat gators and sometimes deer, we think. From what we've seen of them, I think that they must despise humans. Yet, dad allowed them to come to Jing from Voss, where they claimed that they were starving to death, having overpopulated Voss. Perhaps that was just a made up story they fed to dad."

"No, that much was true, I'm as certain of that as I can be without having seen Voss firsthand," Zoran answered her. "I trust Emil and Renata and their parents completely. That is the story they stand by — overpopulation of Voss and starvation. Old Archmage Oldrich wrote a treatise on dragon-kind. She claims that there are a number of different species of dragons, and each one had a different viewpoint of humans. Red Dragons and Black Dragons supposedly have a great dislike of us, though they value our gems and magic."

Chan volunteered, "Well, greens sure dislike us, but they do want gems and gold. Show them Wen."

Wen produced a bag that she carried around her neck, stuffed safely within her bosom. She put it on the table and canceled her Shrink spell. "After we killed a green, we spent days looking for its lair. Often we never did find it, but when we did, this is what we found." She dumped the bag's contents onto the table. Exclamations came from all sides, as the large gathering stared at hundreds of gems, rubies, emeralds, and diamonds mostly, and all were quite large in size. She added, "This is only about a third of what we found. Some we gave to the families of their victims and to our friends who perished today."

Chan added, "There was also quite a lot of gold, but that we gave to the folks who live in Ningho, our safe haven village, to help them pay our brother's high taxes."

"Incredible, Wen. I wonder where these greens got so many huge gems? This collection here must be a fortune. If you like, when Emil or Renata or their father is around, I can have him appraise them for you," Baroness Archmage Zdenka asked and offered.

"Thanks, I suppose that we ought to do that, since we are now exiled here and can never go home. Like I said, we will pay for our keep, Archmage, Baron," Chan replied. As Wen began picking them up and returning them to her pouch, Chan grimaced. She could no longer hold the bag and pick them up. The reality of her missing hand began to raise its ugly head, and Chan fought back tears, bottling it within herself for the moment.

Wen sensed this and changed the topic slightly. "Some of these probably come from our secret mines." That got everyone's attention.

"I thought that Jing produced mostly skins, furs and rice," Chika commented, she was most curious about this aspect, feeling that she was about to gain some key inside information on Jing and its economy.

"Well, yes, our average folk hunt and trap, while in the east some are able to grow rice crops. However, the baron has always had secret mines that yield gold and gemstones," Wen explained. She looked at her sister for approval and then added, "Jing is mostly swamp lands. Over the centuries, our mages and Archmages have devised clever ways of mining deep underground. They built stone retaining walls to keep the swamp waters out of the mine entrances. Workers get lowered into the mines down these long shafts. It's all very hush-hush. The barons use the gems to purchase what the planet needs, but from what we've seen, they spend a whole lot of it on senseless things and don't really use all that much of it to really benefit the average person. Most eke out a marginal living by trapping and hunting, aided a bit by a little fishing. We have no idea where these mines are, though."

Chan decided to add her take to Wen's explanation. "Now that our brothers are controlling Jing and not dad, the problem seems to be getting worse. I'll wager our whole stash here that our brothers are paying off the Green Dragons with many of the gems that they mine."

"Well, that would make sense," Mage Jarka commented coyly. "Everyone knows that dragons of all kinds love big gems. Here on Adapazan, we pay our Gold Dragons in gems for their protection services."

Archmage Nadia explained, "True, because of them, dad and the rest of us have not ever had to keep and maintain any large armies. I think of all the planets, Adapazan has the tiniest army, right dad?"

"True. We mostly have security forces to help maintain law and order. After all the wars unleashed on Adapazan by my evil father, I just can't stomach building up an army," Baron Zoran admitted. "I've taken an awful lot of flak from our allied barons over this. They continue to harp on me to build up at least a huge defensive army, but I keep declining. I guess that I am too dependent upon our Golden Dragon friends to do that. Besides, the manpower is much more useful elsewhere."

"He's right," Archmage Nadia backed him up. "Already the Wild Lands are rapidly becoming quite civilized as a result. Putting men to work on useful construction projects that benefit everyone in a province is actually working to civilize what was once considered the uncivilized lands of Adapazan. The changes they've made — the strides forward during the last twenty years are miraculous. But still, dad, I see your point. Perhaps we have been too dependent upon the golds."

Zdenka ended the lengthy conversation. "Gang, I think that we've talked long enough with our new guests. They have been through a traumatic ordeal today. Why don't we let them retire for tonight? Let them get some rest." She didn't add that poor Chan was going to be going through a rough period learning to adjust to living life with one hand. This evening, everyone was pretty much ignoring what had happened to her. She sensed just how hard Chan was fighting to keep that awful reality from becoming visible to one and all.

"Of course, dear, you are right. Forgive us, Wen, Chan," Zoran said sympathetically. "You must be utterly exhausted. Dear, will you show them to their quarters? If you need anything, ladies, just let one of us know." His eyes met Chan's and he knew what she was thinking, but he did not have the power to grant that. She needed her arm and hand back.

Chapter 3 Adjustments

"Hi, I am Mage Dana Aceda. Dad says I am to get you two fully equipped and trained. Oh, dad is Archmage Marek, the door warden and one of the two blade enchanters. Archmage Karel Ambrose, my uncle, is the falconer and other blade enchanter," the lad said shyly. Breakfast was done and the two new guests had returned to their new room.

"So why are you staring at us?" Wen asked, figuring it was because her sister was now a cripple. Already Chan was experiencing many difficulties with their normal routines. Wen had to tie Chan's boots for her, to say nothing of helping her get dressed in their new leather outfits, compliments of Jarka.

"I — I've never met anyone from Jing before. You don't look too different from us," he replied, his face flushing.

"What did you expect us to look like?" Chan retorted.

"Well, I don't know, but it is such a different world, Jing — I mean. I sort of expected you to look different from us, somehow. Well, your skin has sort of a yellowish hue to it."

"Most everyone around here looks like white ghosts to us," Wen teased him, "excepting you and a few others. How come your skin is tanner?"

"Oh, I get that from my mother. She and my aunt are originally from Asami. Mom and my aunt are Duskas and so are we. I mean myself and my sisters as well as Uncle Karel and Aunt Chika's two teens. Anyway, Uncle Karel and dad want me to get you all equipped. Have you two really killed nineteen Green Dragons?" he asked curiously.

"What? You don't think two women can do that?" Chan asked slightly antagonistically, as she looked at her stump which had now fully healed, thanks to Jarka's healing potions.

Dana flushed, "Er, no. Well, yes. Well sort of. You are Duskas, but usually it is the male Duskas who get all the keen fighter training. Of course, the women Duskas get some; they have to be able to protect themselves and all that."

"I see. Well, it was our male Duskas that brought the vile greens to Jing and are permitting them to murder our people with impunity. So it has fallen to we women Duskas to put a stop to that," Chan replied snidely.

"Chan, I mean you no offense. I am just envious. I admit that I've never killed any dragons before, but I am a good fighter. I found the blades far more interesting than learning to do magic. I know, with two Archmages I ought to have worked more at it, but as Archmage Zdenka — she's the best magic teacher ever — as she says, we each learn as much as we are able. I go more for the combat arts, though we haven't seen much real fighting for two decades now. Anyway, retired General Janos Lavos says that I am one of the best that he's ever seen. That's why dad asked me to work with both of you, and particularly you, Chan."

"Why particularly me, eh? Cause of this?" Chan waved her left stump up and down.

Dana flushed, "Yes, of course. I don't mean to put you down or anything."

"But now you think I can't fight? Is that it? Now I am a helpless cripple?" Chan retorted, venting her pent up anger and loss. Dana's face crimsoned. He knew that he'd put his foot in his mouth big time. He was at a loss on how to extricate himself without upsetting her further.

Wen stepped in, "Chan, you know that they have a point. You can't pretend that you are unharmed from yesterday. I had to tie your shoes and help you into your clothes this morning. They have a right to doubt your skills now. Honestly, sis, he's just being totally honest with you.

Tears welled up in Chan's blue eyes. Her body slumped. At last, she could withhold her tragic loss any further. Crying like a baby, Chan mumbled, "I'd rather be dead than a helpless cripple. Why didn't you just let me die, Wen? How can I live like this? I'm only fooling myself with all this talk of being a dragon slayer. I'm not good for anything anymore."

"Incredible! This is exactly what both dad and Zoran said would happen! Wow! How did they know? Now that you've said it, I suppose I can see why, Chan," Dana exclaimed, totally taken aback by her sudden outburst and tears.

Sympathy for her, consoling words, a sorrowful demeanor, maybe even pity — Chan rather expected to hear such from this gangly teen, but not this. Baron Zoran expected this from her? The Archmage too? Chan stopped crying and looked up at Dana. "Well, I *am* a helpless cripple now," she insisted.

Dana signed, perhaps they were right, he thought. Rather annoyed, he replied, "Only if you want to be one, Chan. That's why they sent me. I'm the best fighter around here. So are you going to come with me and let me get you two fully equipped and trained or not?" Dana asked slightly annoyed. "Frankly, Chan, I didn't have you pegged as a loser."

"What? What do you mean?" Chan sniffled, wiping her eyes with her remaining hand and stump. "Loser? I helped slay nineteen dragons."

"Right, I didn't figure you for a quitter, Chan. Even if you are quitting, Chan, I am still supposed to rearm you both. Baron's orders."

"I'm not a loser or a quitter!" Chan said hostilely. "Okay, show us the weapons."

"Cool. Follow me," Dana said. He led them down the long corridor and into a large practice room. "Lots of mats. Come on, this way." He paused before a locked door. Dana waved his hand in air and magic triggered. The women heard a clunking noise and the door opened of its own accord. "Magical door. They keep their new magical weapons in here. Locked up and all that."

"Incredible!" Chan exclaimed.

"Wholly molley, wow!" Wen added. Both women stared at countless weapons, all nearly arranged by type. Shelves of weapons covered all three walls of the twenty-foot square room. Magical lights in the ceiling provided a daytime level of illumination.

"Okay, daggers first, my ladies," Dana explained moving to his right and the giant case of some twenty daggers. "Examine them all and take the one that feels the best in your hand."

"This is unbelievable! Are all these weapons magically enchanted?" asked Chan, rubbing her eyes with her right hand. Never had she seen so many magical blades in one place before. Here was a fortune if they were sold.

Wen and Chan began picking up the daggers, trying them out for balance and grip. Their hands were a bit smaller than Dana's and both realized that the makers had taken different hand sizes into account, creating a perfectly balanced dagger for a specific hand. Finally, each chose one that best suited them.

"Great. Now I doubt that you are into bows and arrows, right?" Dana asked. Wen said that they never used them. So naturally their eyes moved over to the lines upon lines of swords. Some were two-handed monsters which only the very strong could possibly wield them. Bastard swords predominated, but there was a goodly supply of broadswords, scimitars, and short swords. The two women headed for the short swords, for these were what they usually wielded.

As they began experimenting with the choice of nearly twenty, Dana suggested, "Might I offer a suggestion on your choices?"

"How so, Dana?" asked Wen.

"Here, put your fighting hand in mine and push against my hand please."

She did so and he slowly increased his force back against hers, forcing Wen to push all the harder against him. "Keep going until you have to back up, Wen. There. Okay," he suddenly released his hand. She looked at him like he was out of his mind.

"Okay, try this one, Wen," he said, looking the pile over and settling on one particular short sword. She picked that one up and gave a couple of swings, cutting the air. "I think that one will give you the best edge in a fight," Dana suggested. "I have a good feel for these things. Now you, Chan."

Chan was a bit reluctant at first, but seeing Wen's satisfied look, she hesitantly put her right hand against Dana's. He began to push back against hers, forcing her to resist and push back harder. "Come on, as hard as you can Chan," Dana pushed her. Annoyed, she pushed as hard as she could, holding back nothing, hoping to push this young lad off his feet. He met and balanced her force and then nodded, releasing his hand, causing her to move forward slightly. Involuntarily, her left hand came up to push against his body, but only her stump moved into position, further embarrassing her.

"Pay that no mind," Dana said almost completely ignoring her awkward move. Instead, his eyes were already surveying the rows of short swords. "Ah ha. This one should be perfect for you, Chan. Give it a try." He handed her the sword. While she was hesitantly swinging it, he added, "I know each of these swords. They give them to me to try out once they finish enchanting them. I never forget a sword. Sometimes, they try to fool me, but I get the last laugh."

Seeing the questioning looks, he explained further. "Last week, Uncle Karel brought me a supposedly just enchanted new bastard sword. I took one heft with it and said, 'Hey, you gave this very sword to me two weeks ago. What gives, Uncle?' He roared with laughter. He said that he was just testing me."

"That's pretty amazing," Wen complimented him. "How can you do that? Tell the difference between them?"

"Each weapon is unique. I have a good memory for such details, I guess. Okay, do you like these short swords?" he asked. Both enthusiastically said that they did. "Okay, then accept them as a present from Baron Zoran Vladislov as a token of his friendship. I hope I said that right. I am not so big on court formalities and politics

25

yet."

"Thank you, please relay our thanks to Baron Zoran for us," Wen replied.

"Will do. You can thank him yourselves at lunch. Now, I am supposed to be training you, if you want, Chan. Your call," he said, looking her over.

"Well, okay. I am already quite skilled, but we can see, I guess," Chan replied somewhat reluctantly.

"Good, I like that spirit. Come on. Into the arena. I took the liberty of fixing up a lot of mats last night. I figured that you would not be backing down, Chan. Okay, you've lost an arm. No matter what else you think, you simply are going to have to learn to work around that disadvantage. You've never tried to fight like this yet, so let's take it easy on you, and let you see just how it is going to impact your fighting ability. Once you've gotten that discovered, then you and I can find ways around it and perhaps find ways to even exploit it."

"Whatever are you talking about?" Chan asked.

"At first, you will be relying on your left hand as you have always done, only it isn't there now. That is going to seem terribly humiliating and awkward. Forget about that, Chan. If you are going to continue to be a dragon slayer, you are going to have to learn your new limits. From there, we can move onwards," he tried to explain. Dana knew that she would be in for a rough time of it, but if she had the steel determination that he guessed she must have, she ought to make it.

Thus began the most embarrassing round of practice combat that Chan had ever endured. She quickly began to realize that Dana was right. She had all of these routine motions and actions which utilized her left lower arm and hand in some manner. All of these failed her miserably, of course. Instead of teasing her or making fun of her pathetic fumbles, Dana cheerily said, "Okay, we found another one of your training patterns that we need to alter. Good going; let's find the rest!" She did not expect such replies, and soon she was throwing herself into the practice session.

An hour later, they stopped, Chan was dripping with sweat. So was Dana for that matter. "Okay, Wen, your turn. Let's see your stuff. I'll be looking for ways to improve your skills too." Wen then got a thorough workout as well.

"Okay ladies, that's enough for one day. Take the rest of the day off and visit with everyone. I need time to review what we've done today and work up what we need to do next. Tomorrow, at nine, we will resume in earnest." He bowed to the two and led them back to the long corridor.

"To the bath barrels," Wen whispered to Chan. Once in their own chambers, Wen helped Chan undress, and the two hopped into the warm waters of their bath barrels, soaking their rather fatigued muscles.

"Dana seems to really know how we fight, doesn't he, Chan? I mean he kept finding all the ways that you are handicapped now."

"Tell me about it! Embarrassing, Wen. I felt like a novice with the blade. Maybe I am fooling myself, Wen. Like this, I may never be more than a liability to you if we ever go dragon hunting again."

"I hope not, sis. Dana did say that he was going to help you work out ways around your missing arm. Maybe he can. He sure is cute, isn't he?" Wen said with a wry grin.

"Cute and bossy, but we'll see. I will say this: I got more out of that workout than we ever did in the days with dad's sword master."

"Probably because he thought of us as only needing to protect ourselves, Chan," Wen stated the rather obvious. "Say, you know you could maybe get a hook for your left arm. We've seen a few soldiers who lost an arm get them. I suppose that it helps them, sis."

Chan grimaced. She was humiliated enough with her stump and had no intention going around advertising it further with some metal hook where her hand should be. Later, while getting dressed, Chan finally began to use some of her useful magical spells to help herself get dressed. Wen smiled and thought that was a good sign.

A maid knocked and told them that lunch was in a half hour. The two finished dressing in their new cotton dresses and headed off to dine with their hosts. The first chance they got, both thanked Baron Zoran for his wonderful gifts of the magical weapons.

"Use them wisely, my ladies. Come, I want you to meet Archmages Emil and Renata Vogler. They are our dear Gold Dragon friends. Emil, Renata, these are the two Duskas that I told you about, Chan and Wen Meerong of Jing, the Green Dragon slayers." The two women looked at the golden hued man and woman and shook their hands hesitantly.

"Pleased to meet you. Archmages? Wow. I didn't know that dragons could be Archmages," Chan said.

Renata grinned, "Neither did we. We owe that to Archmage Oldrich. She was our teacher, but she's long since dead. Humans have such short lifetimes, you see. Archmage Zdenka, who was part of our team, has taken over here. Honestly, she is even better at it than Archmage Oldrich was."

Emil added, "Right now, we are working on the enchanting of some large gems. We've acquired some fist-sized emeralds and are experimenting to see just how much magical energies those vessels can hold. So far, our research is fascinating." He saw that the women were not so interested in gems and changed the topic. "Well, Green Dragon slayers are you?" Both nodded.

"Impressive. Well, even though they are dragons, I say good riddance. Greens are the scum of dragons. Can't be trusted with anything; they are only out for themselves."

"Well, our idiot dad made some kind of deal with them to bring them to Jing," Chan explained.

"Foolish human. Whatever deal he made with them, you can expect that the greens will not honor it any long than it suits them to do so. Untrustworthy, to say the very least. I wouldn't give a hoot for whatever deal he made with them. Greens don't like humans as a rule, excepting for any gems you might have — that and gold," Emil pointed out.

"We know, they've been murdering lots of our people," Chan replied. "Well, nineteen of them won't be doing that anymore." Emil smiled.

Baron Zoran added, "Chan, Wen, after lunch, I've asked Emil and Renata to attend a special briefing on dragon-kind. I would like you both to attend. Many of us here would like your input and observations to add to those of the golden Archmages." Both women nodded and smiled. Chan observed that Baron Zoran was not treating them like enemies, but rather as equals. Well, in a way, they could be, since they were in line for the thrones that their brothers now held or so Chan thought.

As they walked down more halls in this fortress-tower complex, Chan and Wen continued to see the same style constructions. Unlike their father's and more recently those of their two brother's fortresses, this one was exceptionally plain, but highly functional. A small valley stream fed a pond inside the walled grounds, providing water for myriad purposes including times of siege. The construction was either the red-brown granite or the blacker hornblende and basalt combinations, hewn from the mountains that lay behind the rear of the fortress. There was nothing fancy or elegant anywhere that these two had been or been shown since their arrival. Even the long corridors that led from the Circle of Ascension in the bowels of the fortress were just as simple and plain as everywhere else.

"The folks around here are not wealthy, so we kept the fortress simple," had been Baron Zoran's comment when Chan had asked about it earlier.

"This place is so different from ours, Wen," Chan commented while they were alone and awaiting the afternoon meeting.

"I don't get it, sis. Adapazan is like Jing. We are both not-have planets. Yet dad and mom have got a fabulously elegant main fortress and castle to house their original Circle. Even our younger brother's new fortress-castles are far, far fancier than Baron Zoran's here. Could these people be even poorer than we are on Jing?" Wen asked baffled by this incredible austerity.

"How can that be? They have all of this land, stone abounds. Where there are stone and mountains, there has to be mines and minerals galore. How could there not be gold, silver, iron, copper, and even gem mines?" Chan replied and asked.

"Defies imagination," Wen answered. "Surely they have them in quantity. So why build such an austere fortress? It is purely functional from what we have seen. I asked Archmage Nadia about it, and she said that they have no need for fancy court finery here. Well, she said that the original Castle Dorumova where the original Circle of Ascension is located is very huge and fancy. Baron Zoran's half-brother resides there, Baron Jan Vavrin. Apparently that one is the only fancy one on Adapazan."

"Well, I think this is rather fitting, Wen," Chan admitted. "After all, why take so much wealth away from the inhabitants just so you can have a fancy place to live at their expense?"

"We don't," the soft voice of Archmage Nadia broke in on their conversation. "We try not to tax our people for more than the basic necessities. After all, we'd not like to have to pay heavy taxes either. Around here, you will find that we do all that we can to not impose on those who depend upon us for their security and leadership. If you will come with me, the meeting is about to start. You know, we've never had such an all-encompassing meeting about the dragon situation before, but times are changing."

She opened a Mystical Door and the three stepped through it, arriving in another huge meeting room, where her husband Dusan took her aside to chat. The room was fifty feet square with a high ceiling. Twenty small windows located ten feet above the ground allowed light to filter in from above. Several tapestries covered one wall, while on the opposite wall, Zoran had mounted his precious maps. One showed details of the known world of Adapazan; the other showed what was known of the other fifteen worlds of the Federation. Additionally, he had accumulated more detailed maps of these other worlds and had them arranged on a third wall. Chan and Wen guessed this was likely Zoran's War Room.

In the center of the room three, plain but huge oak tables were arranged in a giant U-shape and dozens of practical chairs sat around them. Nowhere did the two see a fancy chair suitable for a baron. In fact, all of the chairs were identical. Apparently, Baron Zoran thought of all here as equals, Chan concluded as they entered, just as Archmage Zdenka finished conjuring pitchers of water and glasses, which appeared at strategic locations around the tables.

Chan observed this baroness and Archmage. She was forty but still looked youthful, wearing a simple sky blue cotton dress which matched her husband's eyes, Chan noted. Strange, Baroness Archmage Zdenka certainly did not look like the many other baronesses whom she had seen — a total absence of fancy court finery and pretense. Her mellow alto voice spoke volumes of her infinite patience with her many magic students.

Baron Zoran entered and quickly chatted with their daughter, Archmage Nadia and her husband, Dusan. The nineteen year old woman had her mother's facial features and blond hair. She also wore a light blue, simple dress. "I agree, dad, a fine mess we have," she was responding to something he'd said out of earshot of Chan.

Dusan grinned. He had long black hair like his father, Mage Bernard. Both he and Baron Zoran wore dark cotton pants and a loose fitting white cotton shirt. Each carried a short sword in a belt sheath, so unlike the other barons who carried huge swords. Dusan was a few inches taller than Zoran and thinner. Baron Zoran, Chan thought, looked like the middle aged man that he was. Again, nothing in his demeanor and clothing would suggest that Baron Archmage Zoran was the most powerful man on Adapazan and perhaps on many other worlds. Dusan's arm was around Nadia's. Chan grinned, young love, she thought.

Mages Jarka and Bernard, both forty-two, followed them into the room, along with a small dog, which Bernard was training. Jarka's piercing dark eyes missed nothing; Chan saw that Jarka noticed her noticing her and gave a barely perceptible nod towards Chan. Jarka was the shortest woman here, but extremely deadly. Chan had heard all manner of wild tales about this fiery woman who was both an accomplished thief and a powerful mage. Rumors suggested that she had killed some twenty assassins through the years, and yet she had made the healing potions which had saved Chan's life. Still, she felt Jarka's eyes on her from time to time during the meeting. Bernard looked positively bored, contenting himself to giving his puppy sit commands and ensuring the dog obeyed.

Archmage Karel and Mage Chika came into the room walking at a good clip; both were slightly out of breath. Chan felt his cold stare on her as the tall, black haired man entered. He wore a leather fighter's suit and had several weapons on his person. His wife, Chika, also wore a man's leather suit and carried a pouch of papers. She too carried several weapons around her waist. Both looked a bit harried. "Sorry for being late, Zoran. We just brought the grain wagons through from Gladno," she explained, adding, "I got a good deal this time."

Zoran chuckled, "When, my dear Chika, have you ever *not* gotten us the best of deals?" She flushed and smiled broadly. "You're not late. Everyone's gathering still. Thanks for handling the grain for Tratky."

"Well, it is still too darn dangerous for you to be making these commerce runs," Karel pointed out, a hint of hostility in his voice. Chan was momentarily distracted as Mage Dana entered, looked about, spotted her and Wen, and came over to sit beside them.

"Hi, not too pooped from our practice sessions, I see," Dana teased the two women. Before either could reply, Dana called out, "The other barons and the dragons have just arrived, Zoran. They'll be here directly."

Indeed, magic flashed and a Mystical Door opened. His son, Baron Tomas, and his half-brother, Baron Jan Vavrin, stepped into the room. Tomas looked much like his father, though he was thinner and perhaps an inch taller, well-muscled. "Hey pop, you didn't save me a seat," he teased Zoran youthfully.

"You can sit by Mage Jarka so she can keep an eye on you," Zoran teased his son back.

Jarka laughed, "Aye, Tomas, now you have to *behave* yourself." Several laughed, as Tomas took a seat beside Jarka. Baron Jan was thirty and of all these men looked the most ill at ease. Chan guessed that Jan held his position by birthright, not by competence or skill as the others here did. Jan quickly poured himself a glass of water.

Another Mystical Door opened and the two golden skinned twins stepped into the room. Emil and Renata strode solemnly over to Zoran and took the chairs he'd reserved for the two dragons. While they both wore leather clothing, Chan could not help noticing that each had a fist-sized emerald around their necks. She fought hard to keep from casting her Detect Magic spell; she felt certain that both gems were highly enchanted. Well, both of these were Archmages and golden dragons, she thought. Their eyes were strange, large black orbs. Chan had never seen such compelling eyes, vastly different than the Green Dragons that she'd slain. She sensed great power in the room and caught Zdenka's faint chanting and the flashing of magical energies.

"Dear, the anti-scrying spells are in-force," Archmage Zdenka said, her mellow voice hushing the assembled group.

During this time, Zoran had quietly been studying his two guests intently. He had a knack of observing one without their realizing that they were being studied, a skill he'd honed well. Such had served him well for the past twenty years at the bi-annual High Council meetings with the other barons and baronesses. Both of these Jing women had a yellowish hue to their skin. Their faces were oval and their blue eyes quite slanted. Well, their eyes were not actually slanted, he noted, it was the skin and eye lids which gave that appearance. Both wore their hair short as befitting the fighters they had been. Renegades, both women had defied their father and their ruling brothers for nearly ten years. How had they not been caught until now, he wondered. Both he and Zdenka had already cast numerous spells on the two and found no traces of any detection spells or devices, which he had suspected they would have been carrying had they been spies from Jing.

Ten years of surviving in the harsh wilderness had hardened both women. Both were strong and fit. Gone were all traces of court finery that he'd seen in them years ago when the High Council had been held on Jing. Dana had kept him fully appraised on Chan's progress, in particular. His observations now backed up Dana's — Chan had indeed made remarkable progress in the rehabilitation of her fighting skills. Somehow, she's going to need them, Zoran thought, thinking back to his own youthful flight to Brn from the assassination attempts on his life.

"This special meeting on the recent dragon attacks is now in session," Zoran spoke solemnly. "Archmages Emil and Renata, these are Duskas from the swamp planet of Jing, Chan and Wen Meerong. Their father retired and left their three brothers as the Jing barons. Apparently, their father invited the Green Dragons to Jing and that has not gone well. These two women are exiles, having slain nineteen Green Dragons who had murdered defenseless families. Their brothers have put a price on their heads. I've invited them to join us and add to our discussion as they can."

Emil's black eyes focused on Chan, "Dragon slayers? Well, greens are certainly at the bottom of the dragon heap. Never knew anything good about a green. Still, they are dragons, our kind." His tone was slightly hostile, as Zoran expected it would be in such a formal setting.

"I can understand your position, Emil," Zoran intervened on Chan's behalf. "If some powerful creatures were slaying our peasants, we would be angry too. I believe that Chan and Wen only killed those greens which murdered their people who had not harmed the greens in any way. Similarly, I would not be opposed to your kind slaying humans who killed innocent dragons which had not harmed humans in any way." Emil nodded, protocols apparently satisfied, Chan thought.

Renata spoke up, "Well, years ago, we told you these things would be likely to occur, Zoran, but you humans could not leave well enough alone."

Zoran smiled, "Well, I did start it, didn't I? I brought the Golden Dragons to Adapazan and to Terra, Cosma, Gladno, and Valtr."

Archmage Karel added hostilely, "That's one thing, Zoran, but the other barons brought their own dooms down upon themselves by inviting the other races of dragons to their worlds! Now we got reds, whites, greens, browns, blacks, blues, and grey dragons scattered across all the other worlds of the Federation."

"Well, Voss is devoid of food and they had little choice but to flee our home world," Renata justified. "They were all starving to death. Wouldn't you leap at a chance to avoid starvation?"

"Of course, Renata. It's just that some of races of dragons do not get along well with humans," Zdenka added, conservatively.

"And vice versa," Zoran added. "That's why I have asked both of you to come today. First, let me summarize what our situation is here on Adapazan today. Only Golden Dragons are legally allowed to be on our world. However, as you know, over the years, we have had a few visitors, particularly reds, and blacks, who have raided us, killing and stealing from our people before leaving Adapazan."

"Of course, that is to be expected, Zoran," Emil pointed out. "As we said long ago, once dragon-kind knows of a world, it is likely to be visited by just about any dragon. We've also seen whites and browns dropping by as well, though we know of no deadly encounters they had with humans."

"Yes, and we thank you and your friends for your timely interventions on our behalf," Zoran added diplomatically. He knew that the Golden Dragons had sent over fifty visiting dragons home already, most during the last ten years.

"Yes, but it is not random anymore, Emil," Jarka interjected. "Look," she conjured her massive diagram. A huge chart some twenty feet tall and forty wide suddenly appeared hanging in space in such a way that it was clearly visible to all present. Across the bottom was a time line, each tick indicating a day and covering the last six months of time. Black dots representing a dragon attack appeared above the ticks. Only a few were present six months ago. It was plainly obvious from the more frequent clustering of dots that the number of attacks had gone from three a month to now over a dozen so far this month. A vertical line ran from the dot upwards to a balloon caption which held the details of the encounter. The lettering was so large that everyone could easily read it.

"You see, the frequency of the raids is escalating *big* time. It's gone beyond mere reds and blacks and *now* is including browns and blues and whites," Jarka pointed out rather snidely. "I call your attention to just what the raids attacked. Within the last two months, hardly anything but *gem* shipments have been attacked. Now don't you think that *is* more than a bit unusual? I certainly do."

She didn't wait for anyone to respond before adding, "Of course, you *know* what this means, don't you?" Bernard gave a fake groan; Zoran figured he'd already heard a lot about this from his wife. "Spies. We've *got* spies on Adapazan who are telling the dragons where and when to strike!" She had that smug look on her face that said, "See, I know that I am absolutely right on this one."

Chika spoke up, "We've been making up their losses, Jarka. All told, we've covered about two hundred fifty thousand in gemstone losses by the other warlords and miners."

"That much? Wow. I didn't know. I should have added up the losses," Jarka commented.

"We haven't made it public knowledge, Jarka," Zoran added. "I've kept it low key, making up the financial losses that others are suffering."

"But you can't make up for the *lost* lives," she retorted.

"We must put a *stop* to these incursions!" Karel declared vehemently.

"Aye, we must. That's why we are here today," Zoran took charge of his meeting once more. "I think the first thing we must do is to work out where each species of dragon now dwells. Let's take the reds first."

"They love hills, mountains, forests, and plains, to say nothing of hating you humans," Emil pointed out. Zdenka began taking notes — well, actually her spell did all the writing as she paid close attention to Emil. "We believe that they have settled on Rehor, Gerde, Maeve, and Alta. Zdenka, since you are documenting this, for the record, the adult red bodies are often fifty feet long and they breathe out fire. At least the reds listen to reason and follow their leader's orders, unlike the greens, who will do so only if hard-pressed."

"The greens are more like a snake, similar to the blues. Greens hate humans as much as the reds and blacks and breath out a rotting slime. They favor swamps and forests where there is easy access to lots of water. Green adults have been known to reach seventy feet in length. As far as we know, greens are only on Jing and Maeve."

"We can attest to that fact," Chan muttered. Zoran had her and Wen describe their last battle for the twins, who both nodded. "I see what you mean about the greens not following orders," Chan added. "They took us by surprise. If they had worked as a team of six, neither Wen nor I would be here today."

Emil continued, "Okay, the blacks are the other species who hate you humans. They are about the same size as the reds, some say that they are cousins, but I doubt that. They breathe out a cone of acid that can dissolve a sword in nothing flat. Like the reds, they like mountains, hills, and forests, but not plains and open spaces. Blacks have settled on Rehor, Gerde, Maeve, and Alta — the same as the reds."

Renata took up the outline, "The other four colors are neutral towards you humans. The whites are the smallest species, growing only to forty feet. Mind you, Emil and I are giving you merely the length from head to their rears, not to the end of their tails or wingspan. These whites breathe out a cone of fierce cold, and they prefer to live in mountains and hills, especially areas where there is a large amount of cold and snow. Here in Brn, they would not settle; it is too warm for them most of the year. We know that some have settled on Rehor, Gerde, Alta, and on Dietmar. Dad believes that the largest numbers are on Dietmar at this time."

She went on, "The browns reach sixty feet long and shoot out an electrical bolt, similar to our lightning bolt spells. They prefer hills, plains, and especially deserts. Isi, Alta, Anwyn, and Chana are where they have made their new homes, particularly those last two which are desert worlds. Now the blues likewise reach seventy feet in length, and they prefer watery worlds and swamps. They breathe out a neuro-toxin which paralyzes its prey, nasty to you humans, I'm told. They too look to you as snake-like. We know that they have settled on Asami primarily, but some are on Jing as well. Of all the species, the blues are the least likely to have anything to do with humans. Finally, the greys reach fifty feet in length and breathe out a suffocating cloud of smoke. They prefer plains exclusively. The greys are on Isi almost exclusively, though dad says that they are working out a deal to also settle on Gonda. Greys are known to have dealings with humans, mostly of a neutral nature."

Emil then continued, "Now the reds and blacks are our worst enemies. We golds can't stand them, or they, us. The greys also dislike us intensely, though nowhere near as violently as the reds and blacks. On Voss, the starvation crisis forced us all to set aside our racial hatreds and work together somewhat. Now that most all dragons have abandoned Voss, that truce is long gone. That's one reason that we golds are helping repulse the red and black attacks here on Adapazan."

Nadia asked, "Emil, I know that you and your golds love magic and large gems. Does this hold true for all of the other colors?" She was quite curious, hearing more key facts about dragons than she'd been able to read in the late Archmage Oldrich's treatise, the very one that Zoran and his friends had read so long ago.

"Yes, to varying degrees. You will find that all dragons love magic, but some more than others. All of us like magical items, though only a very few of us are able to actually make them," he smiled and nodded to his sister. Both were Archmages and had been doing just that — making magical items, especially enchanting their large gemstones. "While all dragons love gemstones, some of the others also treasure gold and a few, silver. Thanks to Baroness Archmage Zdenka, there are more of we golden dragons who have made it to Archmage. I think that has terribly upset the reds and blacks, who have only a very few who have mastered power spells."

"Say, can I ask how these dragons can be easily slain?" Chan spoke up at last, asking what she thought was the most important question. "No offense, Emil, Renata. I mean, is there any easy way of killing those who have killed innocent humans and those who are robbing the baron's people?"

She saw that she had struck a nerve with Emil, who flinched slightly. Renata answered instead. "I've heard it said that dragons are at the top of the food chain. Yes, dragons are notoriously hard to slay. Your normal weapons are not strong enough to pierce our hides. Only magically enchanted blades can harm us. Besides, your magic spells are often not effective on we dragons."

"I've noticed that, Renata. Why is that?" Chan asked most curious about her response. She'd often seen her spells detonate on a green and yet have no effect on it at all. Other times, the very same spell did harm a green. She wondered why it was hit and miss with her spells.

Emil answered this one, "We dragons are highly magical creatures. Look, we can move through space from known planet to planet, much like you Duskas can. As a result, we all have some innate resistance to magical spells cast against us. None more so than we golds. The greens have the least such innate resistance to magic spells, and they have also the weakest spells of all dragon-kind. Seldom does a green ever achieve even mage level. The whites, browns, blues, and greys are about twice as resistant as the greens, while the blacks and reds are almost triple as resistant as the greens. We, of course, are more than five times as resistant as the lowly greens." He was rather proud of that fact.

Zdenka asked quietly, "Emil, what about the level of the magic spell caster? Do we Archmages have a better chance of impacting a dragon with our spells?"

Emil grinned, "Touché. Yes. If the spell is cast by an Archmages, then in all likelihood, our power would nullify the magical resistance of the dragon. So yes, only an Archmage has any real chance of impacting a dragon with a spell for certain, but a mere mage, not at all likely, though there is always some chance that it might."

Chan looked at Emil and then at Zoran, who sensed that she wanted to say something about all this. Zoran nodded slightly towards her and she made up her mind. "Say, that's pretty much what we Dragon Slayers have found. Normal blades do virtually nothing, so we had to always use enchanted ones, which we stole from our brothers, the barons. We did use a few spells, mostly to confuse the dragon. I think Emil is quite right, sometimes a spell actually does harm the dragon, but not often. Still, it confused the greens enough. We had our men attacking it from behind and its sides, while Wen and I executed a frontal assault. We depended on our Duska skills to keep us out of the way of its slime path. Obviously, I goofed up that last time. Normally, it takes five of us hacking away at a green's body to finally kill it."

Emil nodded, adding solemnly, "And greens are the easiest to kill. Reds and blacks will be far more formidable opponents. I will say this, do not try to use fire-based spells against a red or acid-based spells against a black or electrical-based spells against a brown."

Chan grasped what he was implying at once. "Right, whatever their breath weapon is, they must be immune to similar things. Whites are likely immune to cold-based spells, right?"

Emil grinned, "Quick study. You are right. We golds are immune to fire and electrical based effects as well."

Chan grinned back, "Don't worry, Emil. We have no intentions of ever harming a Golden Dragon — just the slimy, evil greens who have infested our Jing."

"This is all well and good," Jarka interrupted, "but what *are* we going to do about all the spies among us? That's what *I'd* like to know."

"Okay, okay, I can take a hint," Zoran teased her. "Can I leave that up to you, Mage Jarka?" Chan could not believe that Baron Zoran was leaving something of this importance up to a mere mage who was not even Duska!

"You may," she replied dryly. "However, Zoran, do we want to *safeguard* the valuable shipments or do we want to lay a *trap* and capture some of these raiding dragons? Obviously, that *I* need to know," Jarka replied.

"I say trap the dragons!" Karel burst out angrily.

Zoran rubbed his face. This, he obviously had to decide. His son spoke up, "Dad, I don't like the idea that there are spies among us."

"Hey, I agree with Tomas. That's scary. What if the spies are within our fortress and castle?" asked Baron Jan, rather worriedly. Chan was now convinced that Jan was not a major player, but more of a figurehead for Adapazan.

"Difficult choices, gang," Zoran mused aloud. "On the one hand, I'd like nothing better than to root out all of the off-world spies."

"Hey, they might not be off-world spies," Jarka interrupted him, mid-thought, something Chan would never dare to do.

"True, they could well be our own people," Zoran amended himself. "I'd like to capture some of these dragons and see if we can find out where they came from and perhaps why they were here."

"Dad, it is probably Politics at works again," Nadia suggested. "I would not put it past those barons on Rehor or Gerde to be behind all this. Is there any way that we really could find out such information if we could capture a red or black dragon? If not, then we ought to protect our gem shipments and root out the spies."

"But — but how could we possibly capture a fifty foot beast, whose breath could kill all of us?" asked a nervous Baron Jan.

"Aye, we could chain its mouth shut!" Karel said hostilely. "Damn, then it couldn't answer our questions. Cancel that thought." He'd realized his mistake at once, but it was too late to take it back.

Emil spoke up. "If you promise not to kill them, we golds can capture the reds and get that information from them."

"Thank you, Emil. I was rather hoping that you would make such an offer. I give you my word that we will not kill them, if they are captured," Zoran stated with a huge sigh of relief. "Jarka, you and Chika work out one special transfer of gems that we will use for bait. Handle all of the other transfers on a top secret, need to know basis. It's high time that we mages earn our keep around here. We'll teleport the gems from place to place from now on — that is, after we capture some dragons."

"You got it! Come on, Chika, we have *plans* to make," Jarka grinned. Her days of boredom were now over at last.

Seeing the meeting breaking up, Chan volunteered, "Baron Zoran, we'd like to help you capturing the dragons. We're quite experienced, after all."

Jarka flashed Zoran a cutting glance. He squared to her and answered, "Chan, Wen, I will gladly accept your help with the dragon problem, but only after Dana pronounces you both are ready for such a fight. As an experienced field leader, you know what the liabilities of having fighters with you who are not yet ready for such an undertaking. I would feel horrible if anything happened to you before we had done our best to get the both of you as fully trained as we possibly can. I give you my word that just as soon as Dana gives me his okay, I'll let you both in on the action. I have a nagging hunch this is not over, but only the barest scratch of a beginning."

Chan's face fell at first, but Zoran's words were true. As she was now, one armed, she would be a liability to have on such a dangerous mission, Duska senses or no Duska senses. Fortunately for her, Wen replied. "Thanks, Baron. We appreciate all that you are doing for us. You can count on us when Dana thinks we are ready." Zoran nodded and followed the others out of the room, leaving Chan, Wen, and Dana alone in the huge hall.

"Well, that went well, don't you think?" Dana asked the two.

"What do you mean?" Wen asked not grasping his intent.

"Zoran is quite the guy. He got Emil to handle the interrogation of any captured dragons and to help in their capture. Clever, eh?" Dana replied.

"Well, yes, I rather had the feeling that dragons would stick up for each other," Chan commented seriously.

"They do, so this is why Zoran is the best. Anyway, ladies, we have time for one practice session before the dance."

"What dance?" asked Chan. Thus far, she'd seen nothing here that remotely resembled courtly life at her parent's fortress in the past or those of her brothers in the present.

"Sorry. My ladies, will you give me the honor of coming to our dance this evening right after supper? Unfortunately, I will be playing part of the time, but I can get away with a dance or two with you both," Dana answered her.

"But we have no fancy dresses to wear," Wen stated the obvious, recalling how her mother had dressed for their dances and all of the pretty ball gowns that she and Chan had worn when they were growing up.

"You wear what you have on now. Everyone else does. Around here, dances are for fun and relaxation. I'm told that they are nothing like the formal dances that our leaders attend at the off-world High Council meetings. Please, you must come," Dana insisted. Both agreed, finding more and more adjustments had to be made and not just by themselves. Zoran was also adjusting to the changing situations as well.

Chapter 4 Meetings

Dana picked up the two Jing women around seven, leading them into the huge ballroom, where already nearly everyone had begun to gather. "Who are all these people?" asked Chan. She and Wen saw well over a hundred men, women, and children already in the huge hall with more still arriving.

"Yes, who are they? There must be a hundred here already. How big is this dance?" asked Wen. Both were surprised. Back home when they were in their early teens, their parents often held dances for the nobles, but always these were a formal affair, and the two had to wear fancy gowns.

"Oh, these are all of the workers and their families who help maintain the fortress here and Zdenka's tower. Rumor has it that Zoran and Zdenka loved all the dances they attended off-world when he first became a baron, and they wanted to do that here. We don't abide by many formalities around here. This gives everyone who works for Zoran and Zdenka a chance to relax and enjoy themselves and their families. Come on. I'll introduce you to a few friends of mine, but then I got to go play the harpsichord for a while. When I finish my set, then I can dance with you both for the next set," Dana explained.

"You play music too? Amazing," Wen acknowledged him, very surprised to discover that their master swordsman was also a musician.

"Sure, don't you two play something?" he asked rather surprised with their reaction. Both shook their heads and he shrugged his shoulders.

Zoran gave the musicians a wave, starting the dance. Nothing formal at all, Chan saw. The music was quaint to their ears, dance tunes of Adapazan played on a variety of instruments, crumhorns, shawms, drums, and harpsichord. Later, a set of viols replaced Dana and several others, who now had their opportunity to dance as well.

When the two finally entered their bedroom that night, both were very impressed with life here on this planet. It was so different from Jing. "It is so homey, so laid back and relaxed here, Wen."

"Yes, incredible. I am beginning to really like it here, sis."

Chika and Jarka sat in Baron Tomas' private room waiting for the others to arrive. Baron Tomas and Baroness Archmage Verushka finally entered; she was a bit flushed and both women guessed what the two had been doing this early morning. Chika had Shadow Walked Jarka and herself here to the new Fortress-Circle of Mikolas, Sholov Province. Zoran had rebuilt the fortress which his father had destroyed and already many of those who had fled the province had returned to rebuild their lives. Zoran had his three Circles evenly spaced across the continent. He had named the fortress after the warlord who had discovered Bandar Zar's hidden room and the priceless documents that allowed Brother Jiri to build new Circles of Ascension. Mikolas had died trying to preserve those documents and had donated all of his funds to help finance the construction of the first new Circle in centuries, Zoran's Circle in Brn Province. It was only fitting, Zoran often explained his reasoning.

"Sorry we are a bit late," Tomas admitted sheepishly.

The two older women grinned. They were double these two's age and knew well why. Jarka could not resist a tease, though. "We were once your age too. I hope you didn't hurry her." Verushka flushed and lowered her eyes.

Chika took control. "Okay, we've worked out a way to lure the dragons to a gem shipment. We're going to use your province as the location, Tomas. We want you to announce that you are expecting a big shipment of gem stones from your northern mine. They will be leaving on the 25th of June and are expected to arrive here at Fortress Mikolas on the 27th. You will need to see that the miners there see a large amount of gems being loaded onto the wagon. But do a clever switch. We want most of the sacks to hold merely quartz crystals instead. Keep the real gems safe."

"So I am to be the bait. Okay, what else do I need to do?" Tomas asked.

Jarka took up the plan from here. "Have two men on the wagon as usual, driver and guard. Send along eight more guards for the shipment. Once they get about two miles from the mine, the road is no longer in sight from anyone at the mine. That's where you'll be waiting. You and Verushka are to teleport the ten men safely into your fortress and hide them where they cannot be seen by others. It's just for those few days. After you teleport them away, Emil, Renata, and eight other golds will take their places and continue on down the road. They will take it from there."

"So they will try to capture the raiding dragons themselves? Well, that ought to be safer than us getting involved," Verushka commented, greatly relieved.

"Yes, Emil wants to make sure that we humans don't get involved in killing dragons. I can see his point," Chika replied.

"*Honestly*, I don't see how *we* could *possibly* kill dragons!" Jarka added.

"If we don't get some answers soon, mom," Baroness Archmage Verushka responded to her mother's comment, "we are going to have to find ways to do just that. It may well fall to we Archmages to deal with them, as Emil hinted. Still, killing a dragon is going to be one tough action."

"Hey, daughter of mine, you be darn careful!" Jarka cautioned. "You're my only daughter and an Archmage and baroness too!"

Verushka grinned and gave her mother a hug. She then asked, "You know, I ought to be there with the golds when they capture the raiding dragons. As your Archmage, Tomas, I might be able to assist Emil and Renata in extracting the information we need." Jarka cringed, for this was exactly what she was hoping Verushka wouldn't be doing! Verushka added, "Besides, I am Duska too, thanks to Zoran."

At once, both Jarka's mind and hers went back to that day when she turned fourteen and Zoran had come to her offering her a gift most precious, the Ceremony of Ascension that would attune her physical body and mind, turning her into a Duska. Such was only done to those whose parent or parents were themselves Duska. She was an outsider and yet she and later her two younger brothers were given this priceless gift. She recalled Zoran explaining that he learned from the original Baron of Adapazan's journals that their first baron had discovered that anyone could become a Duska, but he had not told others of his discovery. Now she too could Shadow Walk, had lightning fast responses, had an innate sense when danger was near at hand, and much more. Couple that with having reached Archmage status, she was incredibly powerful, nearly rivaling Baron Zoran. In fact, only Zoran and Verushka and Nadia in all the Federation of Planets combined Duska with Archmage status.

Her top power spells were decidedly different from Zoran's and Zdenka's, though she shared one in common with her teacher, the ability to have foresight of future events. Rather, Verushka's talents and skills lay in more defensive power spells. If needed, she could imprison a dragon by speaking the power command word. She could erect a Defensive Sphere through which few could ever pass and remain alive. Already, she had given her husband a gem on which she had cast one of her power spells which would transport him to her room if he was ever in dire straits. However, both she and Zdenka had a good chance to be able to charm a dragon and then get them to obey their wishes. It was this ability that had caused Verushka to suggest that she tag along with the Golden Dragons.

"As much as I hate to admit it, love, you are probably right. I should speak to Emil about it," Tomas replied. Lines of worry creased his forehead; yet he always respected her, even when they were children running about Zoran's fortress.

Now Jarka *was* worried, but Chika defused the momentary silence. "Come on, Jarka, we need to work on all the other plans. From now on, all other shipments will be done clandestinely." Jarka breathed a sigh of relief. She just could not find the words to say to her daughter and was content to rely on the dual facts that Verushka was an Archmage and Duska, though she had no real subjective knowledge of either, save what she had seen in her last score of years.

"See you all later. I've got to go fabricate all of the fake quartz crystals to send along on the shipment," Verushka added. The meeting broke up and two Shadow Walked back to Brn, while the Archmage opened a Mystical Door and disappeared, leaving Baron Tomas alone. He had the physical details to handle now. He sighed and hoped this would all work out somehow.

Emil and his father, Aldrick, flew in great circles, high above Sholov Province, surveying the thin white road that led from the mines in the far north down to the new fortress. "They won't try anything too close to the fortress," Aldrick commented. "I think all dragons respect the powers of the barons."

"True, while a baron might be able to harm a dragon, it's unlikely. Rather, they have their strongest defenses and mages there. How about there?" Emil pointed a huge claw to an isolated stretch of the new road. Here, it twisted and turned, coming down from the higher elevations of the many northern mines. Riding on a wagon, the driver would be unable to see very far ahead of his position. Both dragons agreed that this area would be ideal for an interception. Now they swooped down and landed, morphing back into a human form, intent upon studying the location up close.

Aldrick commented, "Well, son, I knew that this would eventually happen. Humans and dragons simply do not get along well, on the whole."

"Well, we do, golds, that is," Emil pointed out.

"True, but we are the exceptions and only because of our higher intellect than the other dragon species, son. We value the Archmages of the humans," his father pointed out the obvious.

Emil smiled, "Yes, even though Renata and I made the Archmage level, our command of potential spells is vastly more limited than any of the human Archmages that we've met. Humans have some value."

"Yes, but I'm afraid that many of the other dragon species don't see it that way," his father pointed out. "Slave miners for gold and gems would be the fate of humans if the reds and blacks had their way. I knew that sooner or later there would be problems between our two species, son. I just hope that we can defuse this one quickly."

"We do need to protect these frail humans here on Adapazan, right dad?"

"Yes, we owe them for giving us a new chance at life. Back on Voss, we all would be dead by now if Zoran and his baron friends had not given us golds sanctuary on Adapazan, Gonda, Gladno, Terra, and Cosma. What I haven't told Zoran yet is that the reds and blacks are also raiding those other four worlds as well as Adapazan."

"Wow. I didn't know that, dad. I guess I have been concentrating too heavily on my magic of late. Is it as bad there as here? Why not tell him?" Emil asked.

"I've been staying in touch with my friends on the four other worlds, son. I've heard their reports, though the barons there have yet to realize what is going on. Only Zoran is on top of it and only because of Mage Jarka. Now that is one clever human," Aldrick commented.

Emil chuckled, "And a thief, albeit a good one. She sees deviousness everywhere, I swear."

Aldrick chuckled. "Aye, she does at that. This time, she is right. No, we need to see if we can nip this crisis early before things escalate and get out of hand. The one thing we must avoid at all costs is for the humans of the Federation of Planets to go to war against dragon-kind."

"Damn, we'd have to take sides then, wouldn't we?" Emil considered what his dad wasn't saying. "Humans are our friends and magic teachers, but we dare not side with them against our own kind, dad."

"I know, we will be damned either way, no matter what we do. Somehow, we must avoid any further escalation on the part of these raiders, son."

"Hey, those two new women from Jing — they claim to have slain nineteen greens. Do you suppose that somehow those human women could have actually done this, dad? I find that so hard to believe. They are just women, not the strong, male fighters."

"Yes, they are Duska son, never forget that. We both know that short of powerful magical spells, about the only way a dragon can be harmed really is through the use of magically enchanted weapons. Zoran told me that the women and their band all had magical blades. So yes, son, I do believe that they have slain nineteen of the Green Dragons. Dragons ought to be very wary of humans bearing magical weapons. There are just not many Archmages around for them to be a serious threat. No, it is those magical weapons that dragons ought to fear," Aldrick stated dryly.

"Say, Verushka is supposed to be coming along with us dragons. How much of what we find out from the raiders are we going to tell Zoran? Will we be able to keep sensitive information from Verushka? She is an Archmage after all." Emil probed.

"That is going to be tricky, son. Above all, we must not say or do anything to alloy Zoran's trust in us. If we betray that trust, then we too could easily become his enemy."

"But he'd be a fool if he didn't think that if push came to shove that we would side with our own kind over humans, dad."

"Zoran is not a fool. I am sure that he is well aware of this but for twenty years now, we have kept his fortresses protected. Only we stood between his freedom and an invasion from his enemies. He knows this and feels obligated to us, I'm sure. Still, we must not betray his trust, not yet anyway." Emil didn't quite know what to make of his dad's last statement and decided to let it pass for now.

"So are we going to actually kill some of the raiders, dad? We both know that they will put up a fight and not just sit down and surrender to us," Emil asked what more concerned him at the moment.

"Not if we can help it, though I suppose that such might not be avoidable, unless we allow them to escape. If we do, such must look like a bonafide escape though, especially if Verushka is present," Aldrick pointed out.

"Got it, dad. But you must know more than you are saying about these raiders. If they are raiding the other four planets too, you must know where they are coming from and why," Emil probed a bit deeper.

"Well, I am on the High Council of Dragons now. Since it was mostly my initiative which led to the rescue of all of us dragons on Voss, I was promoted to the High Council of Dragons. I have kept myself informed. Yes, I have some good ideas about who and why, but the humans will need something more tangible — something that they can relate to," Aldrick replied. He added, "If we don't handle this right, things could get very ugly very quickly."

Unknown to Aldrick, those were the very words that Jarka uttered at the same time to Zoran and his planners. "If we don't handle the raiders promptly and effectively, things could get *very* ugly *very* quickly!"

One warlord asked, "Baron, how do we kill dragons anyway? We've heard rumors that you have given sanctuary to a pair of dragon slayers. Is this true? How can mere men fight such giant beasts?"

"I just don't know yet. Magical weapons were used by the two Duska women that I gave sanctuary to here in Brn. At the moment, magical weapons in the hands of Duska seem to be the only real way and even then it is highly dangerous. One of the women lost the lower part of her left arm to the last dragon that she killed. Perhaps our Archmages will also be able to lend assistance. I sincerely hope that we do not have to begin slaying dragons. They all are not evil. The Gold Dragons have been our friends and protectors for twenty plus years now, and we've never had the slightest trouble with them," Zoran attempted to defuse the question. He just did not want his people to begin to ponder how to slay dragons. That could only escalate the current situation, especially if others began harassing the golds.

He knew well just how vital the golds had been and were continuing to be to him. Unlike the other barons, he did not have to raise, train, and equip a huge standing army to help fend off possible attacks from his many enemy barons on other worlds. Instead, for the last twenty years, he had focused all his efforts and all of the funds that he'd acquired into humanitarian projects all over Adapazan. New roads had been his first priority. Next came schools and public works, then education. Now twenty years later, no longer were the outer provinces seen as barbaric. The life of the average person had taken giant leaps forward into civilization. While he still had a long ways to go, the grim situation on the huge continent was vastly improved everywhere. True, the arts, which were so advanced on many of the other "have" worlds, were still in their infancy. Time, time, that was all that Zoran needed to bring all of Adapazan into a great civilization.

Mage Jarka's huge charts now threatened that advance. So many raids, so well-coordinated could only mean that his enemies had not been idle these past twenty years. If left unchecked, the damage they could wreak on Adapazan might well undermine all of his advances! This was his greatest fear, one that he shared only with Zdenka at night in their bedroom. Her advice, as always, was valuable. "Continue on your path. Continue to do well, improve things, flourish as never before. Make Adapazan prosperous and our enemies will fall away and give up utterly."

For a moment, Zoran wished that he could go back some fifteen years when he had held little Tomas, Nadia, and Jarmila on his lap. They were so full of life, such happy children. The future looked so bright then. Now dragons threatened all that he'd worked for, including his grown up children.

Zoran came out of his reverie, hoping that the others had not noticed his inattention. "Don't worry. We will be personally transporting all of your shipments from now on. Duskas and mages will handle it for you. As always, I will make up any loses any of you suffer. You just continue all of the public works projects. Make the lives of your people better and better."

"But shouldn't we be forming up armies to fight the dragons?" the warlord asked.

"No. Look, an army isn't going to stop a dragon. If you recall what two golds did to the Baron's army when he took out Warlord Mikolas twenty-plus years ago, thousands of soldiers were killed or injured, and Emil and Renata did not have a scratch on them. No, if we ever have to fight the dragons, an army will be of no use at all. Focus on the public works projects; help our people have better lives. Leave the dragon problem to me, please."

He didn't add, "After all, I brought them here in the first place." However, Jarka and Zdenka both "heard" what he just left unspoken. They knew that Zoran would ultimately have to deal with the decision that he'd made over twenty years ago.

Jarka ended the digression. "Okay, so when you need to ship funds or valuables, have your mage contact me and I'll arrange for its safe transport. Let's thwart these raiding dragons." They agreed and the meeting ended. Zoran gave Jarka a knowing nod of appreciation.

Barons Gang, Jie, and Li sat around Gang's private study, lounging in the plush chairs. "So what the devil are we going to do about our rogue sisters?" asked Li. Their spies had now confirmed that the two were indeed staying at Baron Zoran's fortress at Brn, Adapazan. The brothers had decided to wait until they had confirmation of this, not just their suspicions.

Jie piped up, "Well, they are out of our hair now. What can they possibly do to interfere with us now — hold up on another world? Besides, Chan lost her arm, so she's out of the fighting business anyway."

Li added, "We've put the Dragon Raiders out of business. What more can they do now?"

Gang grimaced. "Idiots. Are you both idiots? True, Chan is out of the fighting picture now, but they can foment all manner of trouble for us. Look, they have a strong backing in the marsh lands beyond our reach. They can raise all kinds of trouble for us, rebellions or worse. Besides, you forget, they are next in line for our thrones. Dad had established them as heirs until his grandchildren are of age and that's another nine years for my boy. If anything happens to one of you, you can bet Chan or Wen will demand your Circle — she has still got that right — as long as she is alive and able. Too bad the slime didn't take both Chan's arms and Wen's too. Then the whole ascension problem would be handled — incompetence. No, brothers, as long as Chan and Wen are alive and free, they pose a very serious threat of all three of us. Hell, they could hire one of Zoran's assassins to eliminate us and take our thrones. Have you even thought about that eventuality? I thought not! That's why dad gave me the main Circle here on Jing."

"So we send assassins to Adapazan?" asked Jie, rather flushed. He had always liked his sisters, while they were growing up. Still, the possibility that Chan would send assassins to kill him just to get his Circle and fortress bothered him.

"Think, brothers!" Gang chided them both. "No, first, we use political pressure. We need the whole Federation to realize that we have a righteous beef with Chan and Wen. Then, when that fails and we send in assassins; in the eyes of our other peers, we will be totally justified in the actions that we take. No recriminations against us."

"Okay. You are right. So what do we do now?" asked Li.

"First, we make a direct request of Baron Zoran to return these fugitives to us now," Gang replied.

"But Zoran is not going to do that, is he?" asked Li confused. Why bother asking? Everyone knew that Baron Zoran would do anything to upset the political balance of power. Look what he had done on Adapazan twenty years ago!

Gang laughed. "Duh? Of course he is not going to just hand our sisters over to us. Are you a complete imbecile? No, politically, this is the first step that we take. At the next High Council meeting, we can then make a formal presentation to the Federation and other barons, demanding that they make Zoran hand them over. We will be able to use his earlier refusal to help convince some of the neutral barons to back us, you see."

"Ah, then the other barons will force Zoran to hand them over to us. Good plan," Jie replied.

"Idiots! You are both idiots! Of course Zoran will defy the High Council and not hand them over. Haven't you any political acumen at all? He will refuse. That then makes it acceptable for us to send in our assassins with the backing of the High Council. Plus, it puts Zoran on the defensive and in a very bad way with respect to the other barons for refusing us. We accomplish two vital actions in one fell swoop!" Both younger brothers grinned, finally imagining Baron Zoran fighting against all of the other Federation barons.

"Okay, I am going to make my presentation to Zoran now. You hold the fort. This should not take but a couple of minutes, if I know Zoran," Gang ordered. He focused his mind and stepped into the Shadows. Soon a brownish globe appeared in the swirling grey-black masses of the Shadows, Adapazan. Gang focused on the Circle of Ascension at Brn, knowing that Baron Zoran would instantly know of his intended arrival there.

Zoran and Jarka were just walking out of the meeting room, when Zoran's Duska senses activated. He knew someone was approaching his Circle of Ascension from the Shadows! He paused mid-step and focused. *Baron Gang Meerong of Jing requesting an audience with you,* appeared in his mind.

Granted. One minute while I lower the defenses, Gang.

Jarka had seen that not-there look before and knew something was happening with the Circle. Zoran looked up and said, "Baron Gang of Jing wants to speak with me personally. He's going to arrive at the Circle. Come on." While Zoran concentrated and opened a Mystical Door to the heavily protected basement Circle of Ascension room, Jarka fired off a Message spell. She and Zoran stepped through and arrived in the basement room, dimly illuminated by magical lanterns. While he cancelled his protection spells, Jarka commanded the lights, which blazed into brilliance. Another Mystical Door opened and his daughter, Archmage Nadia, stepped quietly in beside the pair. A moment later, her husband, Dusan, Shadow Walked in beside her.

"Got to watch your back, dad," Nadia teased him, annoyed slightly that it had been Jarka who had sent her the Message. She continually felt that her dad was always taking far too many risks. She gave a nod of appreciation to Jarka, who flashed her a fast smile. The three took up a defensive position, allowing Zoran to stand before his Circle as Baron Gang materialized from the Shadows, stepping out onto the center of Zoran's Circle.

"Greetings from Jing, Baron Zoran. Good to see you again," Gang started off politely, shaking Zoran's offered hand.

"What brings you to Adapazan, Baron?" Zoran asked, though he already had a suspicion.

"My sisters. I've heard that they have taken refuge here. As you probably know, they are wanted on Jing as Master Criminals. Can you believe that they have murdered two dozen of our invited Green Dragons? Yes, it's true. We, well dad rather, gave the greens sanctuary on Jing so that they could avoid a starvation extinction. Now my two sisters are going around murdering them. We simply cannot stand for this wonton murder and violations of the dragons' sanctuary on Jing any longer. I have come to ask that you hand my sisters over to me so I can take them back to stand trial on Jing for their deeds. Everyone must he held accountable for their actions, you certainly agree with that principle, right?"

Zoran cringed a bit; he had been right about the purpose of this meeting. Further, since Gang had come alone, he hardly expected Zoran to hand his sisters over to him. What was he going to do? Hold their hands? Even if he brought the women here to Gang, they'd simply Shadow Walk elsewhere. No, Gang obviously did not expect Zoran to comply. So why was he here?

He replied, "Oh I do agree that we are all accountable for our actions and failures to act, Baron Gang. Of that, there can be no doubt. Unfortunately, I have granted the two women sanctuary here on Adapazan. When they came, I was unaware of their alleged crimes on Jing. Chan was extremely injured and in need of immediate medical attention. How could I not fail to help other Duskas in their time of great need? I am sure that you would have done the same if some Duska women from Adapazan suddenly arrived on Jing in dire need of medical attention. Since I have already given my promise of sanctuary to them, I cannot now revoke it. How about a compromise, Baron? I will give you my word that they will not again return to Jing, unless you so request their presence there. That way, you can rest assured that they will not be returning clandestinely and murdering more of your Green Dragons."

"Then you will not return my sisters to me? I will hold you to your word. My sisters must not return to Jing, except to surrender themselves and stand trial for their murdering rampages," Gang declared.

"I give you my word, Baron. If they violate it, I will have cause to cancel my granting of sanctuary and will return them to you," Zoran replied diplomatically.

"Accepted. I will, however, pursue other means of having the two murders brought to justice. For now, I accept your pledge, Baron. I must get back to Jing, business never stops, does it?"

Zoran chuckled, "No, Baron, it certainly does not. See you at the Fall High Council."

"Of course." Gang bowed respectfully and stepped back into the Shadows, smiling to himself. He was surprised that he had even gotten this slight concession from Zoran! At least his sisters would not be allowed back on Jing overtly. If they did, he would easily be able to force Zoran's hand in this business. Still, he knew that he would have a strong case to present to the High Council come fall.

"Well, I guess we ought to have anticipated that," Archmage Nadia commented when Gang had vanished.

"Idiot, what *did* he expect? We'd just *hand* them over to be killed? Boy, he sure *twisted* the facts around," Jarka added spitefully.

"Dad, will Chan and Wen agree to this new restriction?" asked Nadia, a bit concerned that this could become something of a political mess.

Zoran grinned, "For the moment, I think that they will go along with it — at least a couple more months until the High Council meeting. I suspect that there will be political repercussions then. Right now, I need those two practicing their fighting skills like mad. If they are going to survive, they must be more than able to defend themselves, especially Chan. I hope that I have been able to buy them the time that they need to prepare for the future. I guess that I ought to go speak with them now." Jarka grinned, *that he'd better do at once,* she thought.

"Eleven weeks until the High Council meets? Sure, Baron Zoran," Chan replied, "we give you our word that we will not sneak back to Jing and kill more greens just now. My brothers want us dead — you know that, don't you?" Zoran had just briefed them on their brother's visit and what he had agreed to do.

Wen added, "Dad made us next in line for any of the three Circles and thrones, should anything happen to our brothers — at least until their kids come of age. Gang's son is the eldest, so we have at least nine years. I guess our brothers are really worried that something might happen to themselves."

"Wow! Surely they don't think that we will be hiring assassins to kill them so that we can take over their thrones?" Chan suddenly realized what her brothers must be thinking.

"I got that feeling, Chan," Zoran admitted.

"Well, our brothers are paranoid! We don't want their thrones, do we Chan?" Wen declared.

"No, then we would have to really deal with the greens!" Chan agreed. "Thanks for helping us become better fighters, Zoran. I think our lives will be in danger from now on. I would not put it past our brothers to try to have us assassinated even here on Adapazan. They have long arms."

"You are both welcome. We'll do our best to keep any assassins at bay," Zoran promised.

That night in their bedroom, he brought Zdenka up to date. She said cautiously, "Zoran, things are heating up again. I've given Jarka's observations a lot of thought today. Surely our enemies are somehow behind these raids. Perhaps, they are also raiding our allies as well. I think that you should alert them to what Jarka's found out. Will there be political ramifications to our having given sanctuary to the Meerong women? Will they really send assassins here to kill their own sisters?"

"I am holding off until we see what comes of our attempts to capture some of the raiders. No sense alarming our allies needlessly, if this turns out to be just some rogue dragons looking for an easy way to get gems. Politically? There is always politics in every action these barons take, though I hope that I defused it sufficiently that Gang will let it go. We'll just have to remain vigilant on the assassin's angle, love, like we always do. Come here, my love," he whispered in her ear.

Around the same time, Archmage Karel waited patiently in his workroom for Baroness Archmage Verushka to answer his summons. Though the hour was late and she was hundreds of miles away in Sholov Province, he hoped that she would come anyway. For the millionth time, Karel rued the fact that he could not Shadow Walk between planets. He, like Jarka and Bernard, could not; they were not Duska. Oh how he wanted to be able to follow the raiding dragons back to their planet of origin! He had no means. He, Archmage no less, was totally dependent upon the Duskas to make such a journey. He cursed his futile attempts to learn such a power spell in his youth, but back then, as now, that spell remained beyond his abilities to cast, though he didn't know why.

He sensed magical energies forming and relaxed as Baroness Archmage Verushka teleported into his workroom. She'd come after all, he relaxed. "Welcome, Baroness Archmage, thank you for coming so late and on such short notice," he began politely.

Her hair was down and she'd obviously been getting ready for bed. Still that she had come filled him with hope. "Yes, Archmage Karel?" She didn't add, "Well, this had better be important." She knew that he'd not have summoned her this late if it wasn't.

"Tomorrow the plan to capture the raiding dragons begins. If I know anything about dragons, surely some will be able to escape, returning to their place of origin,"

Karel began.

"That likely depends on how well the golden dragons take them by surprise, but I agree. If there are several, one or more may well escape our dragnet. Why?" she replied.

He didn't directly answer her question. Instead he asked, "I take it that you will be going along with the golds?"

"Well, yes, that is the plan. Few know that though. Please keep it to yourself. It could be dangerous for me," she added, wondering how Karel found out. Perhaps from Chika or Jarka.

"I have made an interesting magical device on the off chance that one of the dragon raiders will flee the trap. Here, this is it," he handed her a small, gooey ball, barely a half inch across. "If you see a raiding dragon about to flee, just give this ball a toss towards that dragon. My enchantments will do the rest."

"What will it do? I am not the world's best marksman with projectiles, Karel," she protested slightly.

"No need to be. Just toss it in the general direction. The ball will home in on the dragon and rapidly fly over to it and stick itself benignly onto its hide. I doubt the dragon will even feel it or sense its presence. However, I will be able to view everything around the dragon from here. I should be able to see where it goes, what planet, others that are around it, and maybe the men who are behind the raiding dragons, giving them their orders. If not, maybe they will be some of the infiltrating spies. Its enchantments will last for one day after it is activated by your toss. We ought to get some really good information from it."

"Karel! This is ingenious! I have been worrying about dragons escaping our trap and us learning nothing at all. I don't trust these golds like Zoran does," she replied enthusiastically. Verushka took after her mother in the trust department.

"Thank you. Well, I trust Emil and Renata, but then they are dragons. I would not be surprised if when push comes to shove that they will side with their own kind. We must be prepared, I always say. This ought to give us more information, if the golds botch their plan. If you are invisible, as I surely hope that you will be, tossing this will not give your position away. It is not an attacking action, just a tossing one. I will remain here and focus on the receipt of what images my gooey ball sends back."

"Good plan, Karel. Jarka has an eidetic memory. We can all review what you have seen via our spells, and she can likely pinpoint where the raiders are located, maybe even identify some of the persons responsible, if there are some," Verushka added, becoming more and more impressed with Karel's foresight. They chatted a bit longer and she teleported home. Karel smiled and opened a Mystical Door to his bedroom where Chika was already waiting for him. He had only told Verushka about his gooey ball enchantment, no one else. If it failed, only she would know about it. If it worked, then he could share his achievement with the others in good time.

Chapter 5 The Raiders

It went like clockwork. The ten men had stopped the supposed gemstone-loaded wagon in the narrow gorge and bailed out, taking cover. Zoran and Tomas appeared beside them and Shadow Walked them to the safety of Tomas' fortress. Now the two waited impatiently. Emil, Renata, Aldrick, and seven other golds appeared beside the wagon, having teleported there in human form. Baroness Archmage Verushka appeared as well, but had already cast her Invisibility spell on herself, along with many other protective spells. She climbed into the wagon and sat back quite out of sight. She held Karel's gooey ball in her right hand. Patience, she told herself silently.

Emil and Renata climbed onto the wagon and picked up the reins. Of the many dragons, these two alone had some experience with human's horses, having been with Zoran's party so frequently in the past. Hence, they became the teamsters and soon had the nervous horses moving along the new road once more. The others carrying pole arms walked along side, providing protection for this apparently highly valuable shipment of gems from the mines to Tomas' fortress.

Renata said, "Do you think that they will really attempt to hijack this shipment?"

"I do. Everyone knows that the miners here have dug up a small fortune in gems since the snows melted in April. Common knowledge, though we were fortunate to acquire those two really big gems that they found," he added, thinking of the two whopper sized emeralds that they had acquired, trading a number of smaller ones to the miners.

"Well, I still haven't figured out just how to enchant mine, brother. It is so cool that we have such high quality gems to enchant. Why, we can put such power into them!" Renata exclaimed quite cheerfully. Emil smiled, she was right about that!

Nothing happened for most of the day. Near dark, they finally approached Hell's Switchback, a steeply descending zig-zag stretch of the road that dropped almost a thousand feet down to the lower plains below. Here was where everyone suspected the raiders would strike. The wagon simply could not move fast to flee. It was forced to follow the twisted road ahead, giving the raiders a golden opportunity to attack them with impunity. "Heads up!" Aldrick called out. Emil and Renata looked up. Sure enough, they spotted two dragons high in the sky moving their way. From this distance, their color could not be discerned. Thus, the humans would not be alarmed to see the dragons in the sky, presuming them to be the golds that were out on an antelope hunt. No, the humans would not know anything was amiss until the raiders were nearly upon them!

Verushka wondered what their attack pattern would be? How would the golds intercept them? Slowly the winged beasts drew closer. She double checked all of her protective spells, worrying most about being caught in a blast of their fiery breath. The Archmage began softly chanting her spell. Coming straight at them, the raiding dragons were able to keep their color from becoming visible until they were only hundreds of yards away. At last, the two dragons split apart. One continued swooping straight towards the wagon, but the other circled around to come in across their left side at a ninety degree angle from the first one. She realized that the one ahead of them would likely be attacking them first. Now their color became visible: red.

As the front one drew closer, Verushka saw it opens its mouth. In a flash she realized what it intended to do: destroy the horses and as many men as it could with one blast of its super-flaming breath! From the corner of her eyes, she saw the other one lowering its huge claws and realized that it would attempt to pick up the wagon once the horses and men had been flamed. Her spell detonated, an invisible wall of force appeared in front of her to deflect the fiery blast which now spewed forth from the red's gaping mouth!

A swirling, dense mass of flames enveloped the horses, Emil, and Renata, obscuring all from view. The flames pushed up and around Verushka's invisible wall, protecting her from the searing, scorching heat. She could see nothing but red flames all around her. Then, out of the flames rose the ten dragons, the low sunlight reflecting off of their golden hides, the flames adding to their shine. As suddenly as it had come, the flames dispersed and Verushka could see once more. Emil, Renata, and Aldrick swooped into the red in front of the wagon and a nasty biting and clawing battle began. She glanced to her left to see the second red swooping down, but now trying to dodge the other golden dragons, who were attempting to intercept it, mid-flight.

Verushka got a quick education in dragon fighting. The golds were heavier and larger and thus less maneuverable than the smaller reds. The one to her left successfully dodged and flew through the mass of golds who were trying in vain to catch it. The red swooped over her wagon, heading off to her right. The golds were in pursuit, but she realized that the red had gotten away. She threw Karel's gooey ball after the fleeing red and watched as the ball suddenly had a mind of its own. It flew instantly towards the red's large body and she lost sight of it. Well, that was all that she could do for that one. Either Karel's enchantments would work or not. Her attention was now focused on the remaining red that was now in dire trouble.

Emil had his claws firmly latched on to the red's body from above. Renata swooped down and latched hard onto its rear. Aldrick still clung to its underbelly, pulling all four of them down towards the ground. Bellowing like some stricken beast, the red twisted and turned, unable to free its body from the vice-like claws that dug into its hide and flesh. Down they came. At the last instant, Aldrick let go and managed to get out of the way as the red's body slammed hard onto the stone roadway ahead of the wagon. Though shaken, Emil and Renata clung to the downed red. Aldrick swooped and landed before the red's head, somewhat smaller than his own.

Verushka got out of the way as Aldrick retrieved a piece of chain from the wagon bed and proceeded to tie the red's mouth shut. Then he wrapped the chain around its chest, making the red unable to unfurl its wings and take flight again. "Got you now, red!" Aldrick finally said, as his kids let go and stepped back from their downed red.

They were speaking in their own language. Verushka smiled, thankful that she had had the good sense to cast her Understand Languages spell on herself before she joined the wagon. She listened carefully, noting the other seven golds were now landing nearby, ensuring that the red could not escape them. The other red was nowhere in sight, having fled the planet making good its escape.

"Who are you? Why are you attacking this wagon?" Aldrick asked.

"Adalberto. What's it to you?" the red replied angrily. "Let me go. You can't keep me."

"Who sent you? How did you know about this wagon?" Aldrick asked.

"None of your damned business, gold. Let me go," Adalberto said defiantly.

"You are not going anywhere until we get answers out of you. Now who sent you?"

"None of your business. Why are you siding with these pathetic humans, gold?"

Emil wisely picked up on that. "You know that this gem stone shipment is ours, don't you? So you were going to rob us!" He lied effectively.

"But Adonis didn't tell us. . ." Adalberto suddenly realized that he'd said too much. He'd reacted and not thought!

"So Adonis told you these were human's gems, eh?" Emil went along with him, hoping the red would reveal more.

"Damned humans. Can't trust them with a thing," Adalberto answered. Emil concluded that Adonis was a human.

"Where can we find this Adonis? We want a word with him?" Aldrick asked.

"Hell if I know. Somewhere on this world. Now let me go," Adalberto repeated defiantly.

"On what planet do you live? Where do you come from? Who sent you?" Aldrick asked.

"Sure as hell ain't going to tell you that! How stupid do you think that I am?"

"Dumb enough to try to steal Gold Dragons' gems," Emil continued to play his hunch.

Verushka saw that Adalberto was not about to reveal much more, and she cast her spell on him. Never before had she tried to cast a spell upon a dragon. None had, except Zoran and his group with Emil and Renata when they were getting their magic training well over twenty years ago. However, then the two dragons were quite willing to have their friends practicing their spells on themselves and each other. It was part of the learning process. Here, Verushka was attempting to cast one on an unwilling dragon, a Red Dragon to boot, one which despised humans.

Later on, she described what happened next to her fellow mages. "It was as if it and I were suddenly moved to some grey, nondescript plain. There it stood facing me and I, it. It became a matter of will power, its versus mine. It seemed to last a long time, but the instant I thought 'I am an Archmage,' the dragon lost. My magical spell finally detonated. Yet it could only have been a second or two at most for the whole thing to have happened!"

Verushka was into Adalberto's mind now. She saw at once what he was fighting to withhold! She recognized the man giving Adalberto orders! It was Baron Strom Clav of Rehor, one of their archenemies! She was now visible to the eleven dragons, and Emil moved over to her to help protect her, though the red could scarcely do much at the moment.

"Okay, I have it now. Baron Strom Clav of Rehor sent him here to rob us,"

Verushka finally spoke up, ending her spell.

"Then, we shall let him go now," Aldrick pronounced. She knew that Aldrick could not be convinced to keep Adalberto captive and turn him over to Zoran and didn't press the issue.

As soon as the chains were released, Adalberto rose and stretched his wings. His sides still ached from the pincher claws; a bit of blood trickled from several locations where their claws had pierced his tough hide. "You bitch of a human! How dare you!" Adalberto gushed. Before anyone could react, he belched forth a huge blast of flames towards Verushka. Her Duska senses kicked into high gear. She dove beneath Emil, using his body as a shield, narrowly escaping the searing flames.

Poor Aldrick. He had always intended to let any captured dragons go free once they had revealed the information that Zoran had wanted to know. But now, this was too much. Adalberto had breached all dragon protocols, attempting to slay Verushka just as he was set free. Eight lightning bolts arced into Adalberto's body, mere seconds apart as eight golds reacted defensively. Utterly electrocuted, the red died at once.

"That was close! Thanks, Emil," Verushka said, stepping out beneath Emil onto the soot covered and charred stone roadway.

"Damn, I didn't want to do that," Aldrick complained.

"I know dad, but he left us no choice," Renata replied.

With a heavy heart, Aldrick said, "Okay, go get Zoran. He and his companions will want to see this red's body before we bury it. The rest of you can go. I'll stick around and see to Adalberto's last rites."

"We'll lend you a hand," Emil added. Renata nodded. The others took flight and Verushka sent Messages flying.

Archmage Karel arrived seconds before the others, hoping and praying that he'd get to see a dead Red Dragon. He came prepared with numerous vials and sacks. Soon Zoran's whole group arrived to see the dead dragon and hear the reports. Secretly, Karel Messaged Zoran: *Keep Aldrick's attention for a while.*

Zoran took Aldrick aside and sympathized with him about having no choice but to kill the red. Aldrick related what they had learned. Meantime, Karel filled vials with the blood seeping out of the dead dragon's puncture wounds, took hide samples from around the wounds, stowing them in his sacks. Finally, he rose, satisfied that he had all the samples that he dared to take. Verushka added what she had learned and such now made sense to Zoran. His archenemy was still trying to foment troubles on Adapazan. Well, he could perhaps put a stop to this at the next High Council meeting.

"Any ideas where we can find this spy called Adonis?" he asked the key question. None had. A half hour later, everyone headed back home, except Zoran. "Mind if I stay a bit longer and lend you a hand with burying him, Aldrick? I didn't want him dead either. Killing others is not the answer."

Aldrick looked at Zoran a moment and then nodded his head. The four dug a deep pit and buried the Red Dragon. Aldrick said a few words and then they all left, Zoran bringing the wagon to Sholov with him where he left it before returning to Brn.

Jarka stayed there with Baron Tomas, giving him some ideas on how to go about finding this spy Adonis. "After all, he had to be around here to have heard your announcement of the valuable gem shipment. Want me to lend you a hand?" she gave him a wry grin. The two set to work trying to figure out how they could find the man amid all of the men in and around Sholov Province. This was a needle in a haystack problem for sure.

Meanwhile safe in his workshop on the top floor of the fortress at Brn, Archmage Karel focused on the images he was receiving from his enchanted gooey ball still stuck to the side of the Red Dragon. The dragon was just outside some castle, but he couldn't quite tell where it was. Several men were talking with the beast; it looked argumentative, and Karel cursed that he had not thought of enchanting the ball to also allow him to hear what was being said. "Now that would have been useful," he growled to his walls. "Where is this place anyway?"

The red took flight and Karel suddenly got a bit dizzy from all of the seemingly wild, random motion of the images being sent into his mind. At last they stabilized a bit and he saw rugged mountains in the distance. Much later, the dragon swooped down to a giant cave and joined up with another red. Once more they were talking and Karel cursed his lack of foresight again. Then the red took flight again, nearly causing Karel to fall to the floor from the confusing motions in his mind. Another giant cave appeared which had an idyllic lake or pond just below it. The dragon swooped down and dove underwater, which nearly caused Karel to vomit. Then the images ceased. He concluded the gooey ball had been washed off during the plunge into the lake's waters. Well, at least it had worked. Now he could go to Zoran and allow him to review the images that he'd seen. Perhaps his baron could place the world. If he had to guess, Karel supposed that it was Rehor.

Ambrogino barely made his escape. It had been a trap. The Gold Dragons were there waiting for them. Before, he had often cautioned Adalberto that the humans were not to be trusted. True, thus far they had stolen a rather large amount of gems, but this time all had gone very wrong. Obviously, the humans were not to be trusted. After barely escaping the throng of golds, he'd moved back to Rehor and then back to check on his companion, Adalberto. Arriving very high in the sky, he saw the golds burying the red's body and knew that they had killed him. Now Ambrogino was fighting mad!

"I tell you it was a vicious trap! No gems. Even the people were fake. Golds were there disguised as humans. They knew that we were coming; they were waiting for us. It was a vicious trap! Now how do you suppose that they knew that, eh baron? Well, I'll tell you. You wanted us dead, right? Well, the hell with you!"

"But Ambrogino, we want nothing of the kind!" Baron Strom protested. "I had no idea this was a trap. If I did, I sure would not have sent you two there! You have to believe me. Somehow they found out about the raid. Are you sure one of your friends didn't tip them off?" he tried to switch the responsibility of the disastrous failure onto the reds themselves.

Ambrogino stared at the ugly baron. He thought, what does he think I am, an idiot? "You haven't heard the last of this. Adalberto is dead; someone has to pay dearly for that!" With that, he lunged upwards, taking flight, leaving the baron fuming. He thought, *This is the last straw. I'm going to spread the word. These humans are not to be trusted. Hell, we might as well rob them too.*

On his way back to his cave, he decided to stop off at Adalberto's cave and let his friend's mate, Alfonsina, know that Adalberto would not be returning. He entertained the notion that now he might court her. Perhaps she would think better of him. Arriving at their cave, he landed just as the alert dragon stepped out. "Greeting Ambrogino. Where's Adalberto? Bring back lots of pretty gems did you?"

"I am the bearer of really sad news, Alfonsina. We were betrayed by these nasty humans. It was a trap. There were no gems, only a dozen Gold Dragons waiting for us. They got Adalberto. Killed him. At least they buried his body. We've been had by the baron and his men! I am so sorry for you, my pretty lady." He puffed up to his full height, hoping to impress her a little.

As he expected, she began crying over her loss, but thanked him for telling her. "We will get revenge, Alfonsina, I promise you that we will." After consoling her a bit, she wanted to be left alone and he headed to his cave. Time enough for courting her later, he thought.

As he neared it, he thought, "God, I ought to wash off all traces of that human filth and the touch of the golds!" He dove deep into the cool waters of his private pond. Chilled and invigorated, he rose out of the pond, water dripping off of his now clean hide. He walked stately into his own cave, thinking about how best to get revenge. "You can't trust these humans; that's abundantly clear now. I will spread the word."

"Great idea, Karel!" Zoran complimented his Archmage friend, after reviewing the images that Karel had shown him from the one Red Dragon that had escaped the trap. "Yes, that is Baron Strom and some of his mages talking to that red. It is outside his fortress, I think, but I can't be sure. It fits with what Baroness Archmage Verushka got out of the one that was electrocuted. The baron has been behind all of the raids here on Adapazan. Caught him red-handed, so to speak." Both men chuckled at his pun.

"Glad to be of service. I must return to my lab now. Let me know if you need more of those gooey balls. Next time, I will see if I cannot get sound with it as well. Would have been more useful to also know what they were saying. Any idea on who their spy is — this Adonis?"

"None at all. Jarka and Tomas will see if they can find him," Zoran suggested. Karel nodded, turned on his heels, and headed back to his workshop and lab. Now he had the ingredients that he had longed to have for a decade: blood and flesh from a Red Dragon. His mind reeled over all of the possibilities that this offered him. Oh, the enchantments he could now make!

Around midnight, Archmage Nadia walked the austere halls and spotted her dad pacing as well. "Dad, you still up? Can't sleep?" He looked up, from deep in thought. "You know these dragons are not your fault. You brought only the Gold Dragons who have been good friends with us all. The other barons brought the evil beasts to the Federation."

"I know, but I did and it bothers me still. You can't sleep either dear?" Zoran asked.

"No, I keep thinking about what Verushka found out today — that Strom Clav was behind the reds raiding us. Dad, I can't help but think that this runs deeper than just this. It's just not Adapazan that Strom is angry with — he hates all our allies as well. If I were him, I would be sending the reds to raid Valtr, Gladno, and the others as well."

Zoran finally smiled. "Yes, that's what has been bothering me all night. That would be the predictable thing for Strom to do. Five other worlds could well be being raided just as we have been, but what proof do we have?"

"Ah, that's what's bothering you isn't it? No tangible proof of Strom's involvement. Dad, you can at least talk with the other allied barons and see if they can find patterns like Jarka has here."

"But I've never told other barons my hunches or suspicions, dear. I always present them with proof. Without proof, it is just my word, my hunch, my suspicions. I am being a gossip, a warmonger, if I do that. I refuse to play politics."

"Dad, we know, but I had a thought. What if you and Jarka visited our allies and have her present her findings. Perhaps she can help them amass similar data on their worlds. You would then be one step closer to the truth, even if you cannot prove who is behind such raids," his daughter suggested.

"I know that you are right. I've been procrastinating, hoping none of this was so. Okay, I'll get on it tomorrow. I guess we both better get some sleep. Dusan is probably wondering where you are," Zoran teased her a bit.

"Oh, I am known to walk the halls at night, dad. You know that. Come on; let's walk you back to mom."

The first of July, Zoran and Jarka prepared to visit their allied planet's barons. "Okay, should I wear court dresses and heels and you, your suit?" she asked, hoping she'd get another chance to dress up. Jarka always attended the High Council meetings where finery abounded, as each baroness did her best to outshine her peers. Besides, she was one of his best and most astute advisors.

"This is a business meeting, Jarka. However, you are right; politics are going to enter again. We dress up. I guess I best go change. My leathers won't do at all." A half hour later, he strapped a short sword around his waist and looked at his appearance in his mirror. "I'm getting a bit old. Putting on a little weight I see. Well, that's the way it is." Jarka was not yet ready and he walked over to his wife's tower. Baroness Archmage Zdenka was busy instructing her dozen magic students, but took time to straighten his tie and give him a loving kiss. Soon, Zoran was pacing the halls, waiting on Jarka. Not like the frantic, hectic old days anymore, he mused.

Mage Jarka finally appeared wearing her fancy red ball gown, whose hoops reached twelve feet across at the floor. She wore slightly lower heels since she decided that she might not always be able to lean on Zoran for balance and support in the now standard extreme heels that most baronesses wore to the gala affairs. Still, she was armed to the teeth with concealed weapons and had all her documents nicely shrunk into a small pouch stuffed in one of the dress' many concealed pockets. She checked her appearance once more and left her quarters, where Zoran was slowly pacing the long hall. "All set here. Shall we be off?" she said ignoring the fact that he probably had been waiting for some time for her. He didn't have to get into such an outfit, she justified.

"Yes, first stop is Valtr and Baron Stefan and my sister, Baroness Rayna." He took her hand and they took one step forward, as he pulled her into the Shadows with himself. Grey-black nothingness assaulted Jarka's senses. How many times had she been on a Shadow Walk now? She'd lost count, but it was always the same eerie feeling — one of total and complete lostness, a void beyond all voids. As usual, she wondered how Zoran could possibly find his way with no visible landmarks to guide him. Still, she was eternally grateful that Zoran had performed the Ceremony of Ascension on her three children, turning them into powerful Duskas who could Shadow Walk as well as he. That gift was priceless and ensured that she'd give her life to protect and serve Zoran, no matter what.

Soon the brownish planet of Valtr appeared seemingly out of nowhere in the grey-black void. Quickly the rolling hills with their waving sea of grasslands and rocky outcropping grew larger. She saw the familiar fortress of Baron Stefan appearing, and a moment later Zoran stepped them both out of the Shadows onto the magnificent Circle of Ascension, where Stefan and Rayna were waiting for them.

As expected, Rayna wore a huge brown ball gown, Jarka noted, now convinced that they had made the proper choice of attire. From her slow movements over to hug her brother, she also knew that she was wearing the fashionable extreme heels. For a moment, she regretted not wearing hers, but soon realized she had been right. She could not lean on Zoran all of the time.

"Little brother! So good to see you again. You are gaining a bit of weight I see," Baroness Rayna exclaimed as she hugged him tightly. She wore a bright yellow dress, which accentuated her blue eyes and rich brown hair. Stefan wore a fine silk suit much like Zoran's. He too was putting on a bit of weight, but Jarka was wise enough not to comment upon it.

"Well met again, Baron Zoran, Mage Jarka! So what is all this mystery around your visit? Rayna and I have been trying to figure it out since you Messaged us," Stefan greeted him and shook Jarka's hand ceremoniously.

"You know that I dislike spreading rumors which may or may not be factual, Stefan, but this time, I have to at least alert you. Is there somewhere we four can talk in private?"

"Yes. Do you want my brothers, Baron Zdenk and Daron to attend or Zusa and Kamila as well?" he asked. He thought that Zoran might wish his half-sisters to also hear what he had to say.

"Darn, you are probably right. Let's get us all together, Stefan. I'm afraid what Jarka and I have to say is not good news at all."

While Stefan escorted Rayna on his arm, moving very slowly so she could keep her balance in her extreme heels, he Messaged the other four. By the time that he reached his private meeting chambers, Baron Zdenk and Baroness Zusa Vavrin Pavel were already there waiting him, as well as Baron Daron and Baroness Kamila Lota Pavel. Both women also wore fancy ball gowns and the accompanying extreme heels, Jarka duly noted. Still, the three women could cling to their husbands for support, while she dare not encumber Zoran.

"Hi big brother," Zusa exclaimed, moving slowly to give him a welcoming hug. Kamila was right behind her. After the perfunctory greetings finished, Stefan bade everyone sit, much to the relief of the three baronesses, whose feet and knees always took a beating when wearing their seven inch heels.

"Okay, I do not want to alarm anyone unduly. However, on Adapazan, we have a new situation that has been developing for the past six months, maybe far longer," Zoran began formally. "Some of our gem shipments from the mines to our cities have been raided by off-world dragons, reds and blacks mainly. I will allow Mage Jarka to make her presentation, since she was the one who discovered this mess."

Once again, Jarka conjured her giant display and graphs. She took her time and covered all of the details thoroughly, ending with their recent attempt to trap the raiders, resulting in the death of a Red Dragon. She outlined in detail what they had learned from the red before he tried to kill Baroness Archmage Verushka Vladislov, Jarka's eldest child.

"Oh my god! So these infernal raids that we've been having here on Valtr are not just random events as part of doing business with the dragons!" Stefan exclaimed.

"I take it you have been having raids here too?" Jarka asked.

"Yes, oh my yes. Nothing huge mind you. Until now, we thought they were merely dragons from other planets doing a bit of random thievery," Baron Zdenk inserted.

Zoran spoke up, "Please, please barons, don't jump to conclusions! We have no data that suggests that your raids were other than what you've said, random acts. I would suggest that you have your people put together charts similar to those that Jarka has made for me. Then, inspect the results and see if there is a pattern similar to ours. Perhaps you too can lay a trap and capture one or more of the raiders and weasel out of it if anyone has sent the dragons here to Valtr. Keep us posted. Perhaps we allies can get together and share findings at the Fall High Council meeting."

Stefan agreed wholeheartedly and the eight chatted for another half hour, before Zoran wanted to leave to visit Gladno and share this data with them. As they said their farewells, Rayna commented to Jarka, "Excellent work, Mage Jarka. Your daughter has become one of the most powerful women in the entire Federation, Baroness and Archmage, like Zoran. You must be incredibly proud of her."

"You bet I am. I have Zoran to thank for that. We can chat more at the council. Got to run; Zoran is a bit impatient today," she exaggerated, joining hands with him, as he prepared to Shadow Walk once more.

Once more into the void, Jarka thought as her body was pulled into the Shadows. Soon the green, heavily forested world of Gladno appeared, none too soon for her stomach which was beginning to revolt. They arrived at Baron Leo's Circle of Ascension, located in the basement level of his huge fortress complex. She wondered why Zoran was choosing to arrive in the Circles, but did not have time to ask, for Baron Leo Matous and Baroness Lida were waiting to greet them.

"Welcome little brother," Lida teased him. She wore a billowing blue ball gown, matching the color of her eyes, with a brown waist band that matched her hair. Leo wore a suit much like Zoran's, but he still looked a bit youthful, Zoran noted. After exchanging courtly pleasantries, Zoran asked that Leo's other two barons and baronesses join them for a private meeting. Again, while Leo escorted the very slow moving Lida down the long corridors and up the many stairs to his private meeting room, he notified the others, and they teleported straight to the room and were waiting on them to get there. Zoran wondered why Leo had not just opened a Mystical Door to his room, but soon realized that he hadn't so that Lida and he could chat. He hadn't seen her since the Spring High Council meeting.

Baron Viktor Pavel, Jr. had married Leo's sister Baroness Katrina. Leo's older brother, Baron Aldons and his wife Baroness Valkrie were there as well. All three baronesses wore similar gowns and heels. The barons wore suits similar to Zoran's, Jarka duly noted. Leo's sister Dusana had married Terra's Baron John Witherspoon, she recalled. Her memory was still quite eidetic.

After casting anti-scrying spells as usual, Zoran got down to the business at hand. After his introduction, he turned the meeting over to Jarka, who gave an identical presentation, ending with the results that her daughter had gotten from the Red Dragon.

"Oh good grief! This is really becoming a very nasty business indeed!" Leo exclaimed. He quickly pointed out that here on Gladno, they had been plagued with raids from reds, blacks, browns, and even whites! Once more, Zoran urged them to make a complete analysis of the many raids and graph them as Jarka had done. Leo promised to have full data available at the Fall High Council meeting.

From there, the two went to the farming planet Cosma. Cosma and Terra provided the vast majority of farming exports to the other planets. Here Baron Arcangelo Mondo had taken over for his father, Aldo, several years ago. Baroness Gabriella wore a pink gown that was at least sixteen feet at the floor, Jarka observed. His brother Baron Bernardo and his wife Berta Valtr Mondo soon joined them, as well as Baron Vincens Gervaise and Baroness Florianna, their sister. Their younger sister, Arianne, had married Baron William Weatherspoon of Terra. Yes, there was a lot of cross-cousin marriages within the ruling families of the Federation of Planets.

After the nearly identical presentation, Zoran learned that here on Cosma, they had been having raids by reds, blacks, browns, and even a few whites. The whites came mostly during the snowy winter season. All three barons also promised to gather their data and share it at the next High Council meeting.

Zoran took Jarka to Terra next, meeting with Baron John Witherspoon and Baroness Dusana Matous. As he had done previously, he asked that the other two barons of the other two Circles on Terra join them. Baron Hank and Baroness Vana Pavel Witherspoon joined them, along with Baron William and Baroness Arianne Mondo Weatherspoon. The brother's younger sister was married to Gonda's Baron Henri. Once more, Jarka noted that all three women wore the accepted fancy ball gowns and heels, while the barons wore suits. It was all business on these planets, quite unlike the laid-back attitude Zoran fostered on Adapazan. Well, these planets could afford it, she justified; after all, they were the "have" planets, full of vast wealth and crops.

After Jarka's presentation, the two learned that here they had many raids from the same four colors of dragons. All six were shocked to discover Jarka's correlations and the results from the trap. None could believe that Baron Strom was behind them and they promised to fully investigate the many raids here on Terra as well.

Finally, Zoran took Jarka to Gonda of the rolling plains and abundant herds of horses. Etienne Gervaise had passed away, leaving his son Baron Gaspard his chief heir, along with Baroness Andrea Pavel Gervaise. As before, Zoran requested that Baron Henri and Baroness Elizabeth Witherspoon Gerviase join them along with Baron Flavio and Baroness Adelphe Gervaise Mondo.

After Jarka's identical expose, neither was surprised to hear that Gonda had been suffering raids from the four colors of dragons that the other planets had been having. Gaspard promised to have the data ready by the time of the fall meeting, but added, "This is so hard to believe, Zoran. That Strom Clav would have the audacity to send his dragons to our worlds to plunder us is unthinkable! If this holds up, we will have his hide at the Fall High Council!"

Zoran smiled, but encouraged him to make certain before making such accusations. Finally, the two headed home, just in time for supper. Over dinner, Jarka speculated, "You know, Rehor might not be the only planet whose barons are sending their dragons to us and our allies, Zoran. There are no browns on Rehor. They like deserts. Anwyn, Dietmar, and Gerde could also be sending raiding dragons to Adapazan and our allies."

"I was hoping that you wouldn't suggest that," Zoran teased her. "If that is so, we have a far, far worse problem on our hands than Storm Clav."

Zdenka commented, "Well, dear, they are our enemies. Why wouldn't they use whatever means they have to harm us and our allies? With our golds protecting us, they can no longer send in invading armies, now can they? I would expect that many of the enemy planets are sending their dragons out on raids as well as Rehor."

"A dragon is almost an ultimate weapon, after all," Archmage Nadia pointed out. Zoran groaned. He'd brought the golds here for that very reason. Now what had begun as a move of self-preservation was rapidly becoming his worst nightmare.

That night in their bedroom, Zoran revealed his fears to Zdenka. "I had a most interesting day, dear. Jarka and I visited our allied planets. It's so strange. Here we are about to face a huge crisis of magnitude and all of we allied leaders are our age. Honestly, they are all between thirty and forty now."

"I remember how you used to depend so heavily on your uncles, Baron Viktor Pavel and Milan Matous. So the older generation has given way to the younger ones. Isn't that the way of things, dear, the natural order? Another twenty years and our children will take up our mantles," Zdenka replied.

"Yes, but I used to so rely on their great wisdom. I am no politician, never have been. Those two could even quote the rule book of the Federation! Now each planet has three barons, three Circles, but we're all around the same ages. Even the neutral planets are in the same position."

She countered, "Well, for that matter, our enemies are in the same situation. None of the older barons were at the last several High Council meetings, as I recall. They've left everything to their heirs, though many are now dead I'm sure. However, it sure makes for a complicated High Council meeting. I mean forty-eight barons and forty-eight baronesses all in one room, along with double that in advisors. The rooms really get packed nowadays. Still, you are not facing those older men, who were so set in their ways. That's something at least."

"I can face them as long as I have you at my side, my love," he whispered and gave her a long, passionate kiss. She extinguished her magical lighting in response.

Chapter 6 Escalation

During the early weeks of July, all shipments on Adapazan of anything that a dragon might consider valuable enough to intercept were handled by the barons, baronesses, and their mage staff. Zoran left nothing to chance. He was determined that raiding dragons would have no targets to attack. No gems, no gold shipments equaled no dragon raids — well, that was his intention, his plan and hope. For two weeks, his program appeared to be working.

By the middle of July, the five allied barons reported finding the same raiding patterns on their worlds that Jarka had found on Adapazan. They too began to implement secure transfers of anything that a dragon would covet by secure Duska or mage transport. All six barons hoped that this would be the end of the months of dragon raids on their worlds.

In the rugged mountains of Rehor, far beyond the last human outpost, the Red Dragon Ambrogino assumed the leadership role of the now deceased Adalberto. Yes, he continued to receive reports from Baron Strom, but those reports were worthless. His supposed spies on Adapazan had nothing to report: no gem shipments, no gold shipments. Ambrogino was not stupid. Humans were industrious and mining was always in full swing during the summer months. By October, the snows would be too deep to continue the mining operations. They would not reopen until late April or early May. July was prime time. Ambrogino knew this for a fact, and yet Baron Strom's spies reported no shipments. This could not be. He himself returned to Adapazan, took human form, and observed for many days in early July.

Food and produce continued to travel along the shiny new roads. Everywhere the economy seemed in working order, from what little he knew about humans. So where were the gold and gems that were used to pay for these goods? Mid-July, he finally got his answer, while pretending to hangout in a Brn pub, right under Baron Zoran's nose. Here he learned that the barons and their mages were using magic to transport the valuables from their point of origin safely into the treasury rooms! Ambrogino was furious, but held his temper.

While pretending to be relaxing outside the pub, he surveyed the Brn Fortress and mage towers. The one thing he ascertained was that it was indeed formidable; it would take an army of dragons to smash their way inside. Perhaps the gems could be stolen at their mines. He took a trip to one of the mines that he knew about in Sholov Province. Again, he was stymied. Their mine entrances were designed for humans, not dragons. He'd have to assume human form to get inside, giving up his power weapon, his fiery breath. He'd have to rely upon his more limited magical spells. "That will work only once," he said to himself as he later paced his cavern, thinking this through. "After that, they will place mages or Duskas there to guard the mines. I need another plan."

Mid-July, he came up with one. He called for a Red Dragon Coven. On the appointed morning, he watched as one by one the Red Dragon leaders from the other planets arrived, circling above his cavern before descending.

"Greetings Ambrogino," said Azzolino, who led the reds on Gerde.

"Thank you for honoring my call for a coven," Ambrogino said politely.

"Hail Ambrogino, fine day for a meeting," declared Benigno of Isi.

"Indeed, thanks for coming, Benigno. Fine day."

"What's this all about?" grumbled Dante of Maeve, as he set foot in the cavern.

"One minute, we await Dario of Alta yet," Ambrogino insisted. Soon the last of the reds landed.

"So why are we here, Ambrogino?" asked Dario, tucking in his wings, following Ambrogino inside, where the others had already taken positions in a partial circle, their heads pointing like spokes towards the center and each other. Ambrogino and Howard joined them, closing the circle. Five heads were close together, the dragon coven position.

"Look, the humans set a trap for us," Ambrogino began, outlining the treachery of Baron Strom and his spies, ending with the untimely death of Adalberto. "I have always said that you cannot trust a human. The only good human is a dead human." None disagreed with him.

"You mean they killed Adalberto? The golds did?" asked Benigno. "We should haul them to task over that at the United Council."

"True, but we are seeing pretty much the same thing," Dario interjected. "The humans have gotten wise to the spies and are now using magic to transport their gems and gold. We've not had any successful raid since late June."

Dante fumed, "Are we to start doing our own digging for gems now?" He found that distasteful. "We'd be no better than the golds if we did that!"

"The golds always try to dominate the rest of us," put in Azzolino. "I sure as heck am not going to dig for gems and gold! Those humans have tons of the stuff. Huge gems, I've heard. They have to keep them somewhere."

"He's right! I say, we should locate where they are hiding them and take them by force!" Dante added his support for Azzolino.

"Probably within those stone fortresses," Ambrogino pointed out. "I've looked one over closely and they will be darn hard to penetrate. We can fly over their puny walls, but they will likely have their valuables stored deep beneath the fortress, very hard for us to get. Plus, they have powerful mages and the Duska too for that matter."

"I have a better idea," Dario broke in on their discussion. "We mass a bunch of us and burn down one of their villages, flame all of the inhabitants, save one. Give that survivor a message to take to their leaders. The message will tell them to leave a hundred thousand in gems at this village within two days or another village will be destroyed. This way, we will get to destroy some of these worthless humans and get them to hand over their gems. We kill two birds with one flame!" The other four chuckled and quickly adopted Dario's grand plan.

The 18th of July, twenty Red Dragons appeared in the skies over the village of Curl's Crossing in Dorum Province, Adapazan, where the original Circle of Ascension lay in the city of Dorum. Home to a thousand men, women, and children, Curl's Crossing was a typical rural village, specializing in agricultural products, particularly chickens and eggs. Baron Jan Vavrin had twenty soldiers stationed there to help maintain law and order. One of these men first spotted the multitude of flying reds and sounded the village alarm gongs.

As the dragons swooped down, people fled in all directions in chaotic panic, screaming wildly. Those who were a bit on the slow side or who had a longer distance to run to their homes or who delayed for whatever reason died in the first blasts of their searing cones of flames. After a second pass, no one was alive outside their homes. Half of the homes were of wood construction. Soon these were in flames. Ten surviving soldiers braced themselves against a door in their garrison stone house.

Now more screaming voices rose above the noise of the fires, as helpless men, women, and children were forced to flee their burning homes. The dragons were waiting for them and exhaled flaming death upon them. After five more minutes, they then began knocking down the flimsy stone homes, flimsy from the dragon's point of view. The remaining soldiers attempted to fight back but were subdued with one dragon's breath shot into their garrison through a smashed window. A half hour later, the village was destroyed. In their excitement, they had forgotten to keep one alive. Ambrogino hunted around and finally found one woman who still lived and gave her the carefully written scroll to pass on to her Baron Jan. Satisfied they had done their best, the twenty dragons returned to their home planets to await the two day time allowance, convinced that their plan would work.

It was almost lunchtime. Zdenka was watching three of her more advanced magic students practice their spells. Suddenly, she felt ill and worried. One of her power spells had just activated! Somewhere on Adapazan something awful was happening, she just knew it. Zdenka slumped into the nearest chair to keep from falling down. Her three students were startled and stopped their casting. As they moved over to her to assist her, Zdenka's eyes seemed to mist over. She saw in her spell's vision the destruction that the Red Dragons were wreaking on a defenseless village.

"Archmage! Are you all right?" one student bravely asked her. All three crowded around her chair. Her face was white as a sheet. "Go get Zoran quick," he ordered his companion. Two minutes later, Zoran and Nadia stepped through a Mystical Door mere feet from Zdenka's chair. Not long after that, Jarka, Bernard, and Karel also appeared.

"Zdenka! Zdenka, what's happening?" asked a terribly worried Zoran. He'd rarely seen her looking so awful.

"Mom's spell is working," Nadia broke in. "Here, I'll cancel it." She chanted and Dispelled the Magic of Zdenka's spell, leaving her mother gasping for air.

At last Zdenka found her voice. "Zoran! Red Dragons! They've burned a whole village down! Burned every last person there! Oh my god! It's sickening!"

"Where? What village?" Zoran asked. Karel cursed. Jarka began listing what she would need to retrieve from her room in order to go after them, fully prepared.

"I don't know that. I've never seen it before. God, even the little babies and children. Oh Zoran, this is utterly awful!"

"Okay, let's get you something to drink and calm your nerves a bit. Karel, Jarka, Nadia, contact all the other barons, baronesses, and mages on Adapazan. Get them ready for a massive Mind Link. I will connect to Zdenka and via me, everyone can have a look at her premonition. Maybe one of us will recognize that village and we can get there in time to prevent this catastrophe!"

None needed to be told twice. All three began chanting, while Zoran opened a

Mystical Door and fairly carried Zdenka to her second floor kitchen area, where her staff was getting ready to serve the students their lunch. A few minutes later, Zdenka was finally back to battery, though she still looked somewhat pale. "It took me by surprise, Zoran. I wasn't expecting such a horrible premonition. Haven't had one for a long time. I even forgot I had it cast on me. I must have looked so foolish to everyone."

"No dear. Seeing something that terrible will cause any of us to react badly. Okay, here come the others. Relax and replay what you saw for me, and I'll relay it to the others. I hope someone can recognize this village before it is too late!"

Soon many minds joined with Zoran's and he then gently touched Zdenka's. She loved the gentle touch of his mind in hers, so intimate, but not today. It was horrors beyond all horrors that the two now shared. Although she could not sense the many others watching, she knew that all of her extended family and friends were seeing what she was showing to Zoran. She hoped and prayed that they would not be too late!

A bit later Karel cursed, "Damn those reds. Sorry, I've never seen that village. Looks like Adapazan though."

Zoran looked to Jarka. Secretly he was counting on her eidetic memory and his face fell when she said, "Sorry, Zoran. I have never seen that village. There are thousands of small villages scattered about Adapazan."

Precious time passed. Finally, his half-brother contacted him. *Hi, Jan here. We've discussed it here at Dorum and we think that it is one of our villages, but we cannot be sure. Damek believes it might be the village of Curl's Crossing. I'm sending folks to check it out now. If they report back that this is the village in Zdenka's premonition, we will let you know. We should be prepared for a massive battle with the dragons in that case, right?* Jan sounded very scared, Zoran noted.

Yes, good work. Keep me posted. "Gang, Jan thinks General Damek knows this place, Curl's Crossing. Jan's sending some mages out to see if this is the right village. It shouldn't take too long, I hope!"

Just then, Dana, Chan, and Wen came dashing in, armed to the teeth with magical blades. Chan gushed, "We're coming too, Zoran. If there is a dragon battle, you can count on us, even if Dana says that we are not ready."

"Your help is most appreciated. I hope that we are in time, but already we've wasted so much! I fear the worst," he replied.

Oh my god! Zoran, it's happened! Quick, here's the location! Jan sent to Zoran. Jan was scared stiff, but still managing to function, Zoran noted.

"They've found it. Yes, Curl's Crossing. Everyone, let's go, but I think that we are too late," Zoran cried out. Everyone joined hands and Zoran stepped everyone briefly through the Shadows to Curl's Crossing. He didn't realize it at the time, but he'd just transported more people at one time than he ever had in his life.

"Oh my god!" Jarka exclaimed. Many others issued similar exclamations as they arrived to see the whole village in flames, dead or burning bodies lying in the streets. Dead lay everywhere. It was beyond shocking.

Jarka's eagle eyes darted across the whole village. Then, she spotted the lone survivor and dashed over to her, summoning her case of healing potions as she ran. "Over here, a survivor!" she yelled, reaching the woman swiftly. The woman's hair was burned, her face and scalp was a mass of blackened flesh. Her dress had burned her upper legs and torso; she was barely alive, totally disfigured. A scroll lay beside her, her fingers were no longer functioning and likely never would again. Jarka tried to force a healing potion down the woman's mouth, but the flames had so seared her throat and lungs that none could enter her system, forcing her to cough it up feebly. Zoran knelt beside the dying woman, tears in his eyes. He and Jarka watched the precious flame of life leave her body. "She had this beside her. It is untouched by the flames." Jarka handed him the scroll.

While the others were dashing around looking for other potential survivors, Zoran unrolled the scroll. He read silently,

Baron,

Bring 100,000 in gems to this village and leave them for us. You have two days to get them here. If you do not give us the gems, we will burn down another village and another until you do give us the gems.

Ambrogino

Sadly, no others survived. As the solemn faced group assembled near Zoran, he read them the extortion note.

"Damn! That was the name of the one that got away!" Baroness Archmage Verushka cursed loudly.

Baron Jan spoke up, "We'll have to give them what they want. We cannot have another horrific disaster like this ever again, can we Zoran?" His face was white as a sheet; he'd never seen such destruction and death before.

"Don't worry, I'll handle this, Jan. Okay, everyone. Let's give these villagers a proper burial," he ordered.

Three hours later and dozens of Clean spells cast on themselves, Zoran and his immediate group met back in his private chambers. "You can't think of honestly giving these foul beasts our hard earned gems, can you?" Karel declared angrily, though forming it as a question.

"We really can't, Zoran. If we give in to their demands, when will they stop?" Zdenka advised him.

"Aren't our people worth a few gem stones?" Archmage Nadia countered, visibly upset by the carnage she'd seen. Like Jan and many others, she'd never witnessed such destruction.

Before Zoran could reply, Aldrick arrived. "I just heard. Is it true? Red Dragons did this?" he asked.

"Yes, here read it for yourself." Zoran handed him the scroll.

"Damn him. Zoran, I will take this up with the other dragon leaders soon. I will put a stop to this madness," Aldrick promised. He bowed to the others and left quickly.

Baroness Archmage Verushka paced the room. She, like her sister-in-law Nadia, loved to pace out her problems and worries. When Zdenka was training them, their constant pacing nearly drove her crazy, but she said nothing. At least Nadia was not pacing now, she thought. "You know, Zoran, we could use a Create Object on some quartz crystals and turn them into some crude gemstones and give that to the dragons."

"Hey, brilliant Verushka! Yes, let's do just that! They wanted gems so we'll give them gems. They didn't *specify* what kind of gems," Zoran replied. Everyone roared with laughter. Magically created gems were gems, but were not worth anywhere near as much as real gems. Besides, they would be impossible to enchant with magical spells.

Karel declared, "When they come to fetch these gems, we should lie in wait and kill every last one of the bastards!" He was extremely angry, Zoran noted, and not thinking clearly.

"If we do, Karel, we risk more villages being burned down. We need to find a better long range solution." Karel nodded, as if accepting his Baron's request. Nadia and Verushka agreed to work their magic on the quartz crystals, while Tomas agreed to find the quartz for them. Soon the meeting broke up.

As they were leaving, Karel whispered to Jarka, "Come with me, Jarka." She gave him one of her coy smiles and did so, wondering what he had in mind. She, like him, hated to see these butchers get away with their crimes. He led her up to his private lab on the top floor, just below his many falcon cages on the roof top.

After sealing the doors and casting anti-scrying spells, Karel said, "Okay, Jarka. I have some things that I want to show you. I've been a busy man. Now this baby is not your usual bastard sword. I've infused the blood from that dead Red Dragon into the steel of the blade."

"What does that do to its enchantment?" she asked becoming very interested.

"It has turned this blade from a merely magically enchanted blade into a Red Dragon Slayer blade!" Karel said proudly.

"How does it work?" she asked even more intrigued.

"Each time this blade draws blood of a Red Dragon, there is a chance that dragon will be instantly slain by this sword! Only works on reds, though. I need blood from all the other types of dragons to make similar killer swords. I aim to get some somehow," Karel explained.

"Now these are magically enchanted Red Dragon Slaying arrows. They ought to work similarly to the sword. Mind you, I haven't been able to test them yet, but I am convinced that they will work. I even made up a couple of daggers. This one is for you, Jarka. Your weight and balance. Each time you draw blood of a red, you may slay it instantly. Let me know if it works, please."

"Thank you Karel! I have been very worried about fighting these dragons. I can have hardly any effect on them at all. My spells will be almost useless, unlike yours, Archmage," she half-teased him. "With this, I have some chance, right?"

"Yes, it is magically enchanted and that alone will allow it to pierce its hide. However, the blood infusion may also magically slay it as well. We'll see."

"Fabulous, Karel! Thank you!" She gave him a hug and left him smiling smugly to herself.

Karel set to work now. He knew that Zoran was not going to counterattack these reds, but this was a golden opportunity for him to test his enchantment work. If Zoran wouldn't get revenge, he would! Well, he knew that he would get one chance at this. He took one of the special arrows and began an additional chant, adding the name of the perpetrator, Ambrogino. He finished up late that night. After sleeping in, he ate, donned his specially made Cloak of Invisibility, and grabbed his long bow and the single arrow. As an afterthought, he also took one of his special daggers and a bastard sword, just in case.

He cast his In Case of Emergency spell on himself, on the off chance that he got caught in the dragon's fiery breath. He also stowed one of Jarka's healing potions and teleported away. He arrived at Curl's Crossing completely invisible. After making sure that no one was around and observing the last dying smoke curls drifting upwards into the late July sky, he found his ideal position. A minute later, he had his bow and arrow at the ready. If this Ambrogino red should appear, he would get the revenge so sorely needed by the one thousand villagers!

"Well, there's a hundred thousand worth, more or less," Verushka stated dryly.

Nadia grinned. "Yes, but they sure aren't going to be worth that much. They radiate the magic that we cast into them. Worthless really."

"Let's hope the reds don't know that," Verushka chuckled. "Come on, we should get these to Zoran. I am a little surprised that he is not going to attack them when they come for their loot. But it does make sense. If these manufactured gems will keep the reds content and leave us alone, then it's worth not escalating this into a bigger problem."

"Right. That's dad's big concern right now. All Adapazan will be demanding protection from the reds after word of this slaughter spreads. He's hoping that he can placate everyone by providing the reds with these gems and keep the reds at bay. I wonder just how smart these reds actually are? Will they be able to tell the difference?" Nadia asked.

"Don't know. I guess we will soon find out. I doubt that many Red Dragons possess sufficient spell casting abilities to Create Objects like we can, Nadia. If so, Zoran's idea may well work for us."

"Ah, Zoran, here you go. One hundred thousand in gems as requested," Verushka smiled, handing him the bag. He looked awfully haggard this day, she noted.

Nadia saw this as well. "Want me to come with you?"

"No, this is a simple drop off. I'll just drop the bag where we found the scroll and leave at once. I sure am not about to stick around and tangle with twenty reds by myself, dear child," Zoran said with a hint of sadness in his voice. Nadia suspected that he was fighting his own desires to obtain justice for the slain villagers with the greater good of preserving the peace for all other villages on Adapazan. She was right.

Zoran stepped into the Shadows and back out, arriving at the charred remains of the small village. Smoke curls drifted lazily up into the clear blue summer sky. All was totally silent. He dropped the bag, took a last look around, and stepped back into the Shadows. As he did so, he paused in the grey-black void. He suddenly remembered how his dad had often tried to sneak up on his Circle in the night, but had seen Zoran partially in the Shadows, mistaking him for a Shadow Assassin. It had driven the evil man insane in the end. He had an idea and remained in the Shadows. He cast Invisibility on himself and waited just above the village. He wanted to see if the dragons did appear in force and if they took and accepted the gems. This way, he would know right away if they found the magically created gems acceptable. If they rejected them and headed off to attack another village, perhaps he could warn the others in time to prevent another wholesale slaughter of innocent lives.

Nadia and Verushka paced the halls nervously, much as they had when they were getting their magic training from Zdenka years ago. "Dad ought to be back by now!" Nadia complained.

"Right, something may have gone wrong, though Zdenka has not had any premonitions, nor have I. I cast that one on myself too, just to be on the safe side," Verushka explained.

Nadia grumbled, "That darn spell! I never could get the hang of casting that one. I guess I am not meant for premonitions of the future. Still, I'm going to contact dad — just to be on the safe side." *Dad, what's keeping you?*

Hush, I am fine. I have an idea that I want to explore. I am in no danger whatsoever.

Where are you?

I am Invisible and in the Shadows watching the pickup. If they do not accept the gems and then try to go after another village, I will alert you and everyone else. Maybe we can prevent another slaughter. Nothing happening at the moment.

Okay, but do be careful!

Zoran waited patiently as the hours passed. He had no idea that Karel was also waiting patiently down on the ground just behind the ruins of a building on the edge of the village. Karel was just as invisible as he. Around four in the afternoon, Zoran's senses warned him of danger, and he spotted ten reds drifting through the Shadows heading for the village. He noted that their method of travel through the Shadows was quite primitive compared to his. This he found interesting and filed it away for later reflection. Perhaps one day this would be useful. He moved a little closer to the edges of the Shadows to watch the reds sailing out above the village.

"Ah, look. The petty humans have done just what I asked!" Ambrogino called out to his companions. "There's our loot. You go fetch it. The rest of you, hover around him, just in case this is a trap. I don't see a soul around, but with these wicked humans, you never can tell. I'll stay up here where I can oversee the land all around us and alert you if I see anything amiss."

The nine others acknowledged his orders and swooped down over the village remains. Seeing nothing amiss, one landed and snatched the bag in its huge claws, then launched itself airborne. Circling to gain altitude and rejoin Ambrogino, the dragons looked totally majestic, Zoran thought. *If only they were not so intent upon evil towards us*, he mused.

Just as the nine neared Ambrogino, an arrow flew up towards their leader. It flew as if it had a mind of its own! At first, Ambrogino could not believe his eyes! An arrow shot from a pesky human's bow should not ever rise so high. Indeed, none of Storm's archers could do such a shot. He nonchalantly moved a little to get out of its path. The arrow changed trajectory, still heading straight for him! A sudden blast of fear shot through his mind and body. Such should not be happening! Now he frantically flapped his wings, moving rapidly out of the way of the incoming arrow. He twisted his head around and saw the arrow was now almost at him! Panic. He did the only thing that he could think of — he dove for the safety of the Shadows. Thud!

Ambrogino felt the impact of the arrow, a sharp pain in his rear. "Well, that wasn't so bad! Why am I so frightened?" he said to himself. Suddenly, he seemed to be on some flat, featureless plain facing what had to be a human mage. The man was glaring at him. He picked up the man's intention: Die Ambrogino! Magic flashed. Ambrogino's body died instantly but continued to float aimlessly just within the Shadows above Adapazan.

On the ground, Karel carefully observed the swarm of reds and calculated that the one hovering high above was the leader and likely to be Ambrogino. He took aim and fired his arrow. He remained completely invisible because of his enchanted cloak. To his amazement, the arrow rapidly continued its upward flight, going far higher than any normal arrow. He saw the dragon move out of its path and then grinned as his arrow changed course to match that of the dragon. Karel became even more excited as the dragon began to frantically fly out of the way of the arrow, only to have the arrow continue to close on it. "Damn, it's going into the Shadows!" Karel muttered angrily, believing that the dragon would escape. So darn close, he mused, as the dragon disappeared from view. A split second later, Karel found himself on a grey featureless plain staring at the red dragon. It was a battle between the two. Karel glared angrily, thinking of all the thousand victims. He saw magical energies flash and knew that the dragon had been slain, even though he was now back on the ground where he had been standing. A smile slowly formed as he realized that he had broken the magical resistance of this dragon and his enchanted arrow of slaying had actually worked. He teleported home. Once in his lab, he growled, "Pity that the body is up in the Shadows. I could have used a lot more Red Dragon blood! It works, though. I will have to let Jarka know on the sly."

The other nine reds circled around, but saw no one at all, just the spooky arrow. At last, they headed into the Shadows for home, but did not see Ambrogino's body in the Shadows. As far as they knew, he never made it back and was presumed slain by unknown means. This gave them pause, and they did not make further demands for some time, as many attempted to reason out what had happened to Ambrogino. Besides, there was a small power struggle over who would lead the reds of Rehor now. A couple weeks later, a crafty old red named Corrado became their new leader.

Zoran watched the nine leave and observed that although they had flown right by their fallen comrade, they apparently did not see his body. He found this even more curious. He could see the dead dragon very clearly, yet the dragons could not. Again, he filed this away as interesting information, though he could not see any use for it as yet. However, he wondered who had shot that arrow? He looked around but still saw no one at all. Zoran was quite baffled by this and at last gave up and headed for home.

Upon his arrival, everyone wanted to know how it went, and he told them what had happened. "So you have no idea who shot that magical arrow?" Zdenka asked in disbelief.

"None whatsoever. I saw no one, just that arrow coming up at the red. I say, that arrow acted as if it had a mind of its own. I've never seen anything like it, dear," he replied.

Zdenka bit her lip. "I've got to do some research. More at supper." She dashed off to her room on the fifth floor of her tower.

Before long, Nadia and Verushka joined her. Zdenka had volumes open on her table. "What's up, mom?" Nadia asked.

"That arrow. I think I know what it must have been. The key was Zoran describing it 'as if it had a mind of its own.' Here, read this. Tell me what you think." She laid the book so both Archmages could read it at the same time.

"Wow! An Arrow of Slaying! Has anyone ever seen such a thing, mom? I mean it's one thing to read about such powerful magical items and quite another thing to actually make one," Nadia declared.

"What are the ingredients?" asked an astute Verushka.

"The blood of the type of creature or person it is meant to slay and the name of the creature or person," Zdenka answered.

"Okay, that was a Red Dragon Slayer arrow and it killed Ambrogino, so whoever made it must have gotten some Red Dragon blood and also knew the name of that dragon. Mom, it has to be someone around us all! Did you make it?" Nadia asked shocked by her own deductions.

"Hardly, dear. I've never had any time left over from training all you mages. How about you two? Both of you have the skills needed," Zdenka asked pointedly.

"Sorry mom. That would have been a brilliant move, but I claim ignorance. I've been working on enchanting some gems for dad's birthday," Nadia replied.

"Don't look at me. This is the first I have even heard of such things. Honestly, aren't these things incredibly rare?" Verushka asked.

"Exceedingly. That's why I hardly ever mention such to my students. Well, someone has been making things around here. Who else has this kind of skill?" Zdenka asked.

"Dad could have made it, mom."

"Hardly, he's been preoccupied with all these goings on around here. He's not had time nor have I seen him researching such things. Who else could have the skill?"

All three women suddenly blurted out in unison, "Karel!" The three instantly cast a Mystical Door and stepped into Karel's workshop.

"My, all three of you! What brings you to my humble workshop?" Karel asked.

Zdenka put her hands on her hips. Defiantly, she asked, "We know that it was an Arrow of Red Dragon Slaying that brought down Ambrogino. We didn't make it. Did you, Karel?"

His face flushed and Zdenka had her answer, no matter what Karel would reply. "So what if I did?" he hedged.

"Well, that was one very impressive and superior work of magic, if you did," Nadia answered before her mother could.

A smile creased his lips. "Yes, mighty fine piece of work indeed. Now if you ladies have nothing more that you need, I have a whole lot more work to do here. One day, we will be fighting these infernal dragons, and we will need ways and means of doing so," he stated factually.

"You think it will come to that?" asked Zdenka.

"Don't you?" Karel answered in a non-commitment manner, though slightly accusatively.

"Well, you should tell Zoran about it. I am sure he will want to discuss such things with you, Karel. Well done, by the way," Zdenka complimented him.

Karel's Arrow of Red Dragon Slaying became the talk of the dinner table that night. Many began seeing some hope of self-defense against the dragons. "Hey, I need more dragon blood. I need samples from all of the different kinds that we may have to fight," Karel explained. Chan and Wen wished that they had had the foresight to have stowed away some Green Dragon blood. Now they had a vital use for it! However, both knew that Zoran would not allow them to return to Jing just to slay another green and bring back its blood for Karel.

The next day, Zoran relayed what the reds had done, that is, their latest extortion plot and his solution — magically fabricate nearly worthless gems to the other allied barons. He suggested that they also try this if other dragons made similar extortion attempts on their worlds. After that, he went to the fifth floor of his wife's tower and read up on Arrows of Slaying. Zdenka had left the book marked for him. After that, he visited Karel in his lab.

"Well, that was an incredible bit of magic that you created there, Karel."

"Thank you, Baron. I have not been idle. I know that I ought to have gotten your permission before slaying that vile creature, but honestly, those poor victims needed some justice done!" Karel justified.

Zoran didn't accept his justifications, however. "Isn't it more like you needed to field test your arrow?" Karel flushed and gave a slight nod.

"Well, this time, you got away with it. I was in the Shadows watching the reds make the pickup. I saw Ambrogino die there just inside the Shadows. More importantly, the other reds flew right past him and did not even see his body. So the reds will be completely mystified about the whole thing. How is it that even I didn't see you?"

"Ah, this little invention of mine," Karel smiled, showing him his Invisibility Cloak.

"We could use more of those too," Zoran grinned.

"I know. One day we will be battling these beasts, sir. I can feel it in my bones! I aim to be ready when that day comes. Only can you get me more dragon blood? I need samples from all those that we are likely going to have to fight."

"I will keep that in mind. Meantime, I am trying to find ways to keep us from having to fight them. Next time, keep that in mind too, Karel."

Karel nodded, accepting the slight chastisement. If only Zoran would bring him more blood. He thought about asking if there was any chance of retrieving some from the one in the Shadows, but decided not to press his luck. Maybe he could get his son, Milan, to help him out. Milan and his wife, Kate, were both Duskas and were working with Chika, making many off-world transfers of commerce.

The next day, Milan was back from making a run to Gonda for Chika, and Karel dropped by their room. "How was the latest trip?" Karel asked trying to make polite conversation, something that he was not known for doing well at all.

Milan yawned, "Boring mostly, dad. Brought in a load of swords this time for one of the warlords up north. Say, I just heard about the Red Dragons and the ransom. Did you really make an Arrow Red Dragon Slaying?"

"Yes, I did, I guessed right. I make it especially to kill the leader who ordered the murder of that entire village, son. I just could not let him get away with it."

"Fantastic, pop! So you just shoot the arrows and they kill the dragons?"

Karel chuckled, his son, while he knew some magic, was not an Archmage, far from it. "The usual Arrow of Slaying must be shot and actually strike the victim, drawing blood. In the case of dragons, the steel arrowhead must be enchanted or it will not even penetrate a dragon's hide. Once it draws blood, if it is the same species, Red Dragon in this case, then there is some chance that that single shot will kill him. If not, at least it wounds the dragon and the archer can shoot again. Now in this particular case, son, I knew the name of that dragon, thanks to Baroness Archmage Verushka. I added additional and very specific enchantments to that single arrow, which turned it into an Arrow of Slaying for that single beast. I shot it in the general direction of the dragon and the enchantments did the rest. If that specific dragon wasn't present, my arrow would have fallen harmlessly back to the ground. Instead, my magic won and that evil, wicked beast lives no more."

"I say good riddance. I don't think I could have kept my cool, pop, if I'd have been there and seen that woman who was burned alive — the one that Jarka tried to save," Milan admitted.

"I know, son. It was most terrible, but son, mark my words, in the not too distant future, I see us all fighting these evil dragons. Not the golds, mind you, but the really evil ones, the reds and blacks."

"Wow, you think that is a real possibility, dad?" Milan said very surprised and dismayed.

"I certainly do, son. Why do you think that I have spent nearly every day in my lab making enchanted weapons?"

"Holy molely! I had no idea. Can I help?" Milan asked.

Karel smiled; he had just heard the magic words that he had hoped to hear from his son. "Actually, Milan, there is something that you can do to help in a *very* big way. Zoran said that the dead dragon is just floating there in the Shadows. Do you suppose that you could take me there, into the Shadows, so that I could get more of its blood? If we can get more, I can make powerful Red Dragon swords and more arrows attuned to these vile beasts. Then, when the war comes, we will be able to arm those who can fight with weapons that can actually affect these vicious beasts!"

"You got it pop! Come on. I don't have to report for duty until after lunch," Milan said eager to lend his father a hand. For once, Milan saw himself contributing something of importance. His birthright was that of a Duska from his mother, Chika, who was the bastard daughter of some baron. Zoran had given him his birthright, the Ceremony of Ascension, when he turned fourteen. He could Shadow Walk. His father, though an Archmage, could not. Here was something that he really could contribute, something of value. It did not cross his mind to ask why his dad had not just asked Zoran to do this.

A half hour later, holding his father's hand, Milan pulled Karel into the Shadows, arriving just above the burned out village. Apparently, the dragon's body had shifted or floated off into the Shadows from where Zoran had reported seeing it. Milan spent an hour locating it, now quite far from its entrance point. Together, the two men began extracting Red Dragon's blood from the huge carcass. When they returned, Karel was most pleased. He now possessed nearly two gallons of the blood and some additional body parts, including claw nails, for which he now had some additional ideas for their use as well.

Once back in his lab, Karel thanked his son once more. "Say, Milan. You go off-world quite a lot. If you ever come across a dead dragon of some other color, extract a bunch of its blood for me. That will enable me to make swords and arrows for our valiant fighters against those kinds of dragons."

"You got it, pop! I will keep my eyes open and ears too. I bet that I can find ways to get you samples," Milan replied. He had a new and devious purpose, something to do while handling the mundane off-world transportation of the multitudinous trading goods. Besides, he now had numerous off-world contacts. He resolved to spread the word that he was in the market for dragon's blood. Sooner or later, he was certain that he could bring some back for his dad.

A week later, he got the chance. He had to make a trip to Isi. After checking in and discovering the load would not be ready for several more hours, he headed to his favorite Isi pub. Luck was with him, for his acquaintance was there. "Honani! Hail and well met once again," Milan called out, shaking the tall, dark man's hand.

Honani was something of a rogue, though some called him a mere thief. He had a small band and executed various actions for hire. "Got a little job for you," Milan whispered over a pint.

After hearing what Milan desired, Honani whispered back very animated, "You've come to the right man! Not all of us enjoy having those foul beasts on Isi. What you want can be very dangerous."

"Money is no object, Honani," Milan hinted. Honani grinned.

"In that case, I'll let you know when we have something!" Honani's hand received the gem that Milan secretively passed him. They chatted a bit longer before Milan left to play oxen and transport the wagon load of goods back to Adapazan. He didn't know it then, but he had initiated an interesting chain of events which would result in the obtaining of quite a lot of dragon blood.

Chapter 7 Problems

"Welcome Baron Leo, good of you to drop by," Zoran shook his friend's hand. Leo had requested a private meeting with him only this morning. It was late July now and so far, the reds' problem seemed handled for the moment. At least Zoran had not received any more ransom scrolls. He opened a Mystical Door to his private study and the two stepped through.

"Anti-scrying?" asked Leo. Zoran noted a bit of paranoia in Leo's voice.

"Absolutely. Okay, what's up?"

"I'll get right to it. Thanks to you and Jarka, we've discovered the same phenomenon on Gladno. Only it is mostly the Black Dragons who are behind the many raids. You were right, they are most frequently going after gold and gem shipments. We have spies on Gladno!" Zoran groaned, but he had expected that he was not alone.

Leo continued, "Strom must have been working on this plot of his for years, slowly but surely inserting his spies where they could do the most damage. So we've got two problems, really. One, how the devil do we stop these raids and two, how do we flush out the spies? Okay, three, how the blazes do we kill dragons? I heard that you and your forces have now eliminated two reds. Rumor has it that you are harboring two Duska heirs from Jing who have killed a large number of greens. Is this true? Any tips you care to share? We are getting desperate," Baron Leo laid his cards on the table, so to speak. He and his advisors were unable to work out effective answers to these three pressing problems, and he had come to Zoran to ask — beg if necessary — for some suggestions.

"Well, honestly, Leo, I have no idea how to weed out the spies. Here on Adapazan, we've more or less nullified their importance by making secure all shipments of things dragons find valuable. That is, gems and gold shipments are now done by teleport and Shadow Walks, from point of origin to point of destination. Thus, we are giving them no point of attack. So far, that is working for us."

"Makes sense. Viktor suggested that very thing. I ought to have listened to him."

"Well, that's understandable, Leo. He is a Pavel not a Matous," Zoran grinned, knowing he was right. Viktor Jr. had married Leo's sister Katrina to gain one of the three thrones and Circles of Gladno.

"Has that worked out? Raids stopped?" Leo inquired further. This seemed an awfully simple solution.

"Yes, and no. Yes, in that our shipments are no longer being intercepted. No, in that the reds then burned down an entire village, murdering over one thousand men, women, and children. Then, they asked for a hundred thousand in gems or they would burn down another until we gave them the gems."

"My god! Then that rumor is true. How horrible! Extortion. What will they think of next?"

"Well, my Archmages used Create Object spells on quartz, making low quality gems out of that. We gave the reds those, not real gems. So far that has appeased them," Zoran replied frankly. "However, time will tell."

"Okay, we will follow your lead on this one. How about killing them?" Leo asked.

Zoran sighed, he knew in his heart that killing the dragons was not the answer. "Well, we cannot take credit for both. The golds killed the red that was attacking Baron Archmage Verushka. However, Archmage Karel has been making weapons that are effective against dragons, reds in particular. It seems that only enchanted blades can pierce their hides. Thanks to Verushka, we knew the name of the leader of the band who destroyed the village. Archmage Karel made an Arrow of Red Dragon Slaying, enchanted to only slay that particular red, as I understand it. Mind you, I am not well versed on such enchantments. He tested it out and was successful in slaying the leader who led that murderous attack."

He went on, "Yes, I have granted sanctuary to the two sisters of the Jing barons. Chan and Wen Meerong. They used to lead a band who killed the Green Dragons that killed local villagers on Jing. I suspect everyone will be hearing about this at the High Council meeting."

"Why?"

"Baron Gang has demanded that I return them to Jing so he can try and sentence them to death for killing the greens of Jing."

"You won't let him get his hands on them, will you?" Leo asked suddenly very worried about their safety. Jing was one of their archenemies.

"Of course not. Would you like to meet them and discuss this with our dragon slayers?"

A few minutes later, Chan, Wen, and Karel joined the two barons. After introductions and Zoran's explanation of what Leo was anxious to learn, he turned the meeting over to Karel.

"Okay, Baron Leo. In order to make swords of dragon slaying, I must have fresh blood from the color of the dragon to which the blade is attuned. Here, I was able to acquire Red Dragon blood and have been enchanting a batch of Red Dragon Slayer swords. Mind you, not every time the sword draws blood will a red be slain. Rather, it is a chance. Each time such a sword draws the blood of that type of dragon, there is a chance that the sword will cause that dragon's instant death. Now with my arrow, I also knew the name of the dragon that I wished slain and I added even more specific enchantments to that single arrow. It did work as I intended."

Karel continued, "Now if you could get me a few buckets of Black Dragon blood, I could make you some highly effective Black Dragon Slayer swords."

Leo grinned broadly. "Archmage, if I can possibly slay one, you can count on buckets full of Black Dragon blood!" Karel smiled equally broadly.

Chan now took over the discussion. "We've killed nineteen greens. I wish we knew that Karel needed their blood! We could have given him tons of it. Ah well."

"But how were you able to slay these hideous beasts?" asked an incredulous Leo. He'd seen the blacks and thought they were impossible to slay.

"Greens are more like snakes than the reds and golds. We've never seen a black," Wen answered.

"They look a lot like the reds. Both are about the same size, fifty feet, not counting their long necks and tails," Leo replied.

"Okay. The greens are about seventy feet long and move much like a snake, although they do have wings and can fly," Chan took up the explanation. "When we close for an attack, we fire off a couple of spells, usually Balls of Fire or Lightning Bolts. Once in a while, our spells actually affect the greens, wounding them severely. Wen and I usually take the frontal position, because as Duskas we can get out of the way of their slime. Well, mostly we did. I lost this to the last green that I killed." She waved what remained of her left arm in the air for effect. It was not lost on Leo, who cringed.

"Our fellow members, who died in the last attack — it was a trap set by our brothers to have the greens kill us for them — anyway, they used to use their enchanted blades to chop at its sides while Wen and I kept its forward attention focused on us. Frequently, Wen or I would use our skills to jump onto its head and stab it with our magical daggers. I killed the last one that way, stabbing it in each eye until my dagger broke."

Karel spoke up. "Each type of dragon will need to be attacked differently. What works with snake-like dragons will not work necessarily with the reds and blacks. I believe that we will need to work out different attacking methods for each race of dragons."

He added, "Baron Leo, you should see if your Archmages are up to the task of making the needed enchanted weapons."

Leo sighed and ran his hands through his hair before answering. This was a sore point with him, Zoran noted. "Alas, we only have two Archmages on Gladno. One is in his seventies. He trained me, but he has retired and is not in good health. The other is in his fifties and is totally occupied training other mages. Somehow Adapazan has more Archmages than any other planet in the Federation. I wonder why that is?" This was a tease. Everyone knew now just how terrific a teacher Baroness Archmage Zdenka actually was. She was perhaps the most famous teacher in the Federation of Planets at this time.

"Well, bring me Black Dragon blood, Baron, and I'll see what I can enchant for you," Archmage Karel declared. He and Leo shook hands on that point. After that, Baron Leo took leave and returned to Gladno to see about ways and means of somehow killing one Black Dragon.

"So how many Archmages do you have on Jing?" Zoran, now quite curious, asked Chan.

"Only one. He is in the service of Baron Gang, but he too is old. He trains all the Duska," she replied.

After they left, Zoran visited Zdenka interrupting her class. "Can you do me a favor, love?" She nodded. "Check Chan and Wen. See if they are acceptable students for you. There is only one old Archmage on Jing. It would be nice if one or both of these women could learn more magic and perhaps be able to replace him." Zdenka smiled and agreed, wondering why all of this sudden, new interest in Chan and Wen.

After supper that night, Zdenka cleverly tested both women. Chan failed her test, suggesting that she would cast spells to learn who had slain the man. Wen passed, suggesting that she go to the bleeding man at once, though keeping her guard up in case there was an invisible assassin still lurking about the shadows of the room. Thus, she accepted Wen as a student, much to Wen's complete surprise.

"You go ahead and see if you can learn more magic, sis. We need all that we can muster. I will keep on with my fighter training with Dana. If and when we can go back to Jing and attack the greens again, I will protect you so you can fire off killer spells, sis." Wen grinned; she liked that idea. Somehow, she just didn't like jumping onto the beast's neck and stabbing it from there. After all, Chan had very nearly gotten herself killed doing it.

A few days later, Baron Stefan Pavel reported that he too had Black Dragons raiding for gold and gems, primarily. The reds were just being a general nuisance. Zoran quickly educated him as he had done Baron Leo. Baron Arcangelo Mondo of Cosma reported that the blacks were behind most of the gem shipment raids, though a few had been done by reds as well. After that Barons John Witherspoon of Terra and Gaspard Gervaise of Gonda reported that the reds were their biggest gem and gold shipment raiders, though blacks were also doing it in a more limited way. As July came to an end, all of the allied planets now used their Duskas and mages to handle all valuable shipments in an attempt to stop the raiding dragons. With no targets to hit, they could not raid — at least that was the agreed upon analysis of the barons. Zoran had serious reservations and cautioned all of the barons to be alert for whole villages being slaughtered in extortion plots, as had been done on Adapazan by the reds.

"No, Baron Strom, we no longer obey you," Corrado sneered at the overweight, ugly human. He'd just won the position of Red Dragon Leader on Rehor, with the mysterious demise of Ambrogino. "You have set us up and gotten two of us reds murdered. If you know what is good for you, you continue to give us a hundred thousand each month. If not, well, you know what we can do!"

Strom wanted to curse and smash this egocentric, young Red Dragon — pound some sense into him. However, his innate fear of the fifty-foot beast restrained him, but his muscles involuntarily twitched. "So be it, Corrado. There are others who will stand up and fight." He wanted to have the last word. Corrado stretched out his huge wings and lifted off of the roof of Strom's mountain fortress.

A bit later, Bardawulf circled above and came in for a landing. Right on time, Strom noted. Perhaps he would have better luck with the blacks anyway. The reds just didn't follow his orders at all well. "Welcome mighty Bardawulf! Hail and well met," Strom started off as politely as he could.

The black was nearly the same size as the red that just left. He tucked in his wings and sat down before the Baron. "I am here to do business," Bardawulf began. He hated dilly dallying around. Just come out with it, was his motto.

"Adapazan. They've taken to using mages to transport their gold and gems. The ignorant reds cannot deal with that. Now you blacks are vastly smarter than the reds. Something this simple won't stop you, right?" He played upon the dragon's ego.

"Ha, ha, ha! You have that right. What did you expect? Once the humans figured out that your spies were relaying their shipment details to the reds, they could be expected to use magical transport means. Any idiot could figure that out. So I take it you are finished with the reds?"

"Yes, they are, as you say, idiots. Now you blacks have been doing a fabulous job on Gladno, Cosma, and Valtr. I need your help with our archenemy Adapazan.

They are making secret transports of their gems and gold. I need that stopped anyway that you can do it. Are you blacks up to the challenge?"

"How much, Baron?" Bardawulf asked the key question. He was not about to risk his blacks without proper remuneration.

"How about a half million for starters. If you can bring their economy to a halt, I'll double that!" Strom proclaimed. He had little intention of doing so; the blacks could not be that strong, he thought, just greedy, dumb beasts. Well, a half million would be worth it, if that gave Baron Zoran some real problems. After all, Zoran had cheated his dad out of everything including the throne of Adapazan. Now he could get even, he thought, by bringing Zoran to his knees. One day soon, Zoran would come to him, Strom Clav, begging forgiveness.

"In advance," Bardawulf added. No way would he undertake this dangerous mission without payment up front.

Strom handed him a heavy sack containing the promised gems. He didn't mention that he had had his wizard turn worthless quartz crystals into what appeared to be diamonds. Well, they were diamonds, just not of any high quality nor could the larger stones hold any magical enchantments as real diamonds could. Bardawulf accepted the bag eagerly. "Consider it done," he stated dryly and lifted off, circling high into the mountain sky.

During the second week of August, Zoran received word from his allied planets. Indeed, the reds and the blacks attempted to run the same extortion scheme on their worlds, annihilating a village and demanding gems to keep them from doing the same to another village. All reported taking the same action that Zoran had, using mages to Create Objects, namely diamonds from quartz crystals. Zoran continued to hope that this would satisfy the dragons. He hesitated to consult with Aldrick or Emil about this, afraid of what they might say in response.

During this second week, Zoran received a frantic message from a working mage in the Chern Mine in the mountains of northern Dorum Province, some hundred miles from Castle Dorumova. "We're under attack by Black Dragons! They've entered the mine and . . ." He sensed intense pain and then the mage's Message ended. Zoran didn't hesitate, he sent out a massive Message spell, alerting everyone he could think of who had the slightest chance in combat with a dragon, including Emil and Renata.

Within minutes, he and many others began arriving at the Chern Mine, though he, Zdenka, and Jarka were the first on the scene, followed within seconds by Karel and Bernard. Many others arrived within the next couple of minutes. "Oh dear god!" exclaimed Zdenka as the pungent acid fumes billowed out of the main entrance tunnel. "Fumigate!" she chanted and slowly the deadly gasses began flowing out of the tunnels, while Zoran and Jarka kept alert for the dragons. None appeared and he soon concluded that the dragons had already fled the scene.

It took the combined mages nearly an hour to completely fumigate the mine tunnels and then to neutralize the corrosive acids that the Black Dragons had spewed all throughout the tunnels. When they entered, most wished that they had not. Here and there, bleached skulls and bones were all that remained of the hundred plus miners and mage who had been working this diamond mine for years.

Zoran was sickened by the sight, as were most of his companions. He ordered a thorough search, looking for some message from the blacks demanding something to keep this from happening again. Alas, no such note was found, much to everyone's disappointment. Baron Jan now had to find new miners who were willing to work this lucrative mine.

However, Zoran held an immediate conference with all of his top leaders on Adapazan. The topic: how to protect the miners from the Black Dragon attacks. Since mining and related activities accounted for over half of the jobs on the planet and with thousands of such mines, no one could come up with a fool proof plan to safeguard all of the mines. Zoran had no choice but to speak with Aldrick and Emil about this latest attack.

Aldrick, Emil, and Renata visited the mine, sniffing the still pungent residue of the acid. Several workers were collecting the remains of those who had died and they gave the three dragons very dirty looks. "Well, this is indeed a very bad situation, Zoran. Yes, Black Dragons did this. Why? Only they know. I will take this up with the other dragons and see if I can put a stop to this," Aldrick stated the obvious.

"I need help preventing this from happening in the future. We do not have the means to protect so many mines," Zoran explained.

"Dad, in a way, we golds share some responsibility for this slaughter. We are obligated to help Zoran protect this planet from outside attacks. This certainly amounts to an off-world attack," Emil pointed out.

"You are right, son. Zoran, we will alert all of the golds here, and we will organize protection squads for the major mines across the continent. We'll fly cover over them and discourage any blacks who make such an attempt again. I give you my word," Aldrick declared. Zoran accepted it with his thanks. Again, the golds were saving him, he thought.

During the next five days, Emil reported that the band of blacks attempted to repeat their attacks on other major gem producing mines across Adapazan. Each time, the blacks were repulsed by the rapidly swarming Golden Dragons.

However, the night of the first mine attack, Milan returned from another off-world trip, bring back several wagon loads of grain and a special sack. Triumphantly, he stepped into his father's lab on the top floor of the fortress at Brn. "Hi pop! Guess what I have for you?" he said exuberantly and triumphantly.

"I've no idea, son. What? Have you heard about the Black Dragon slaughter of the miners today?" Archmage Karel answered.

"Yes, mom's just told me. Here, have a look." He dispelled his shrink spell, revealing three large water barrels, each labeled. Karel's eyes flickered from label to label and his mouth gaped, he was speechless.

"Yep, pop. Green Dragon blood from Jing. Black Dragon blood from Alta. White Dragon blood from Dietmar. Cost me three hundred thousand gold, but I got it for you. More's a coming, I'm told."

Karel picked up his son and twirled him around the room! "You are a genius, son! Well done indeed! This is way beyond anything that I expected! More you say? Incredible. Now we have a chance! Oh," he realized the actual cost was pretty steep and retrieved some gems from his extra-dimensional safe. "This will cover your expenses, son. Keep the blood coming! Tell mom that I will likely be up all night and not to wait up for me!" He forgot all about his son and began carrying the water kegs to his workbench, talking to himself all the while. Milan grinned, pocketed the gems, and left, walking as tall as he could down the halls. For once, his father had shown him more attention and emotion than ever before. Milan knew that his father really did appreciate his off-world work.

On the second day of the continuing black raids, Zoran decided to experiment himself. He positioned himself in the Shadows where he could watch over the whole continent. After waiting what seemed to be an eternity in the grey-black void of nothingness which was the Shadows, Zoran spotted some two dozen winged forms moving through the Shadows. He grinned, he could see them, but they could not see him. He drew his Karel special short sword, magically enchanted to be able to cut into dragon hide. As one came near him, he gave it a slice as it passed by him. To his amazement, the dragon both did not perceive him and had no idea how it was suddenly hurt. When it appeared out of the Shadows over the mines, while the others swarmed down and were quickly intercepted by dozens of golds who answered the single gold's Message, the injured dragon stood back licking the long, bleeding slice to his mid-section. It looked around in vain for its attacker, but saw no one.

That gave Zoran another idea. If the Shadow Assassin idea had driven his evil father insane, maybe it would work with the dragons. When the blacks regrouped and fled back into the Shadows, Zoran again sliced the wounded dragon and also materialized an idea in that dragon's mind: Shadow Assassins. Soon the dragons were lost in the depths of the Shadows and Zoran headed back home, where he pondered what had just happened.

The next couple of days, he repeated his action as the blacks continued to make their attempted raids on the major mines of Adapazan. Obviously, they had received word of the mines' precise locations, probably from Baron Strom, he thought. Finally, the attacks stopped, and Zoran also stopped waiting in the Shadows. Honestly, it was incredibly boring, and he had the affairs of Adapazan to help run.

Friday the 13th brought the most unlucky day for Brn. Later, Zoran guessed what had occurred. Having been thwarted in their attempts to get at the major mines, the blacks decided to attack Zoran's key fortress in Brn, which was at the other end of the monetary pipeline. Once more, he was saved from total disaster by Zdenka and her power spell.

Around noon, Zdenka let out a shriek, which got everyone's instant attention. "Black Dragons will be attacking this fortress!" she screamed. She took a deep breath and let it out slowly, recovering her senses. She fired off numerous Messages to everyone she could think of as fast as she could. Spells detonated everywhere, as most headed to the roofs from where they could both see in the incoming dragons and attack them. Several rang the citywide gongs, alerting the citizens of Brn that an attack was imminent. This system Zoran had installed over twenty years ago after his father's failed attempt to storm the Wizard's Tower where he was staying along with his Circle of Ascension originally located in its basement.

A sea of chaos filled the streets of this city of some twenty thousand, as folks headed for their homes or found ways to get inside some dwelling. One by one, Zoran and his group assembled on the rooftops of the fortress and manor house and even Zdenka's Archmage Tower. He and the other Archmages cast all manner of defensive spells on themselves and the others around them. Finally, Karel handed out enchanted weapons to any that did not yet have one. At last they waited.

Zdenka stood beside Zoran, along with Jarka and Bernard. Karel, Milan, and Chika grouped themselves near his falcon cages, around which he had already cast Force Walls. Some twenty feet from Zoran, Tomas, Verushka, Nadia, and Dusan stood their ground, spells at the ready. Jan and his wife Reina along with Archmage Marek and Akira stood far to the left of Zoran's group. Dana, Chan, Wen, along with Kate and Milena stood atop Zdenka's tower. On the ground level, General Damek Kamil and a dozen mail clad guards all armed with enchanted blades stood ready to repel any dragons who might attempt to breech the entrance way into the fortress proper.

Still various servants ran helter skelter below them, pulling horses into the safety of stables and ushering others into the safety of the buildings. "Here they come!" yelled Zoran. "Watch out for the acid spewing from their mouths! Stay alert!" To Zdenka, he said, "Power spells, dear. Don't hold back."

She flashed him a very worried smile. She had no intention of withholding her wrath. This was a life and death situation. As soon as the twenty dragons reached the outer limits of the Archmage's long range spells, within seconds of each other they fired off powerful spells. Archmage Zoran shot his most powerful Bolt of Lightning at one. Archmage Zdenka formed her massive pounding, giant fist around the head of another. Archmage Nadia shot a massive Ball of Fire totally enveloping another. Archmage Verushka shot her most powerful Bolt of Lightning at yet another. Archmage Karel sent a Disintegration Beam at the head of another dragon. Archmage Marek, the Doorwarden, summoned a Storm of Meteors, firing them at three separate dragons that were unwisely too close together.

Mages Bernard, Jarka, Dusan, Milan, Chika, Tomas, Jan, Reina, Akira, Dana, Chan, Wen, Kate, and Milena — all fired off Balls of Fire or Bolts of Lightning at the incoming herd of beasts. Even General Damek down on the ground let lose a Ball of Fire at the incoming dragons.

The twenty-one spells detonated in an cacophony of sight and sound never before heard anywhere within the Federation of Planets! At the instant of detonation, each caster found himself or herself standing on a featureless, grey plain, facing the dragon or dragons that their spell was impacting. As before, Karel merely glared angrily at his beast, while the others had various reactions. Baron Jan, for example, felt a surge of fear flooding his body as he stared down the dragon facing him. Jarka tried to attack hers physically with her enchanted throwing daggers. Zdenka, on the other hand, merely stared straight into the beast's eyes. Each mage was on this strange plain for only a fraction of a second, but it seemed like an eternity to each, before they were back with their bodies, as the detonations triggered.

Eight of the incoming dragons died, dropping like dead weight from the skies. Some landed on the paved streets of Brn, some on the stone parapets of the outer walls. Two landed on buildings within the city, crushing through the roofs, descending on down into the structure, injuring those huddled inside.

Another eight took serious wounds, while four remained unscathed. These twelve belched forth streams of caustic acid towards the defenders, who now had to dive or frantically get out of the way of the incoming rain of death. Those who were Duskas simply Shadow Walked out of harm's way. Many of the mages frantically conjured Mystical Doors or simply dove and rolled out of the way of the incoming deluge of caustic acid. Some were not fast enough and the acid landed on parts of their bodies.

However, Chan and Wen did none of these things. Chan drew her dagger, Wen, her short sword. They waited until the dragons heading right at them opened their mouths to spew forth certain death and then they Shadow Walked. Both landed perfectly on the dragons' necks, just below their heads, their legs encircled the neck and clamping like vice grips. Chan began stabbing her dagger into the head of the dragon, trying to find its eye socket. Wen merely tried to sever its head from its neck. Both dragons continued their flight arcing upwards as they reached the rising mountains on the north side of the fortress.

A number of eyes spotted the approach that Wen and Chan were using, but had their own problems with which to deal. Karel, screaming and yelling, ripped off his clothes which were rapidly disintegrating from the acid he had not completely avoided. Several others followed suit, while Jarka frantically summoned forth lime, making it fall like rain over the rooftop on which she occupied. Bernard then added his summoned water to the mix, creating a seething mass of chemical reaction. Foam rose in all directions, neutralizing much of the acid around their portion of the roof. Others saw what they were doing and after struggling to get out of their disintegrating garments, duplicated their actions.

Karel, however, not to be outdone by the two from Jing, drew his short sword and teleported onto another dragon, as it turned around to make a second pass. The two dragons with the women on their necks tried to grab them with their claws, but found this was impossible while flying. They had not enough altitude to fall while doing so. Wen's beast let out a hideous moan and began dropping like a ship's lead sounding weight. She Shadow Walked back to the top of Zdenka's tower. She'd severed his spinal cord, and the beast's brain no longer communicated to the rest of its body. The body smashed hard into the side of the northern mountains. Chan finally drove her dagger into an eye socket. Her dragon twisted its neck in a weird way and then began falling from the sky. Chan pulled her dagger out and stepped into the Shadows and then back out, arriving beside Wen, breathing heavily and stepping around the still active acid. "Damn, it's eating through my boots!" she cried out. "Clean! Clean!" she shrieked.

Karel's anger rose to a feverish pitch and he sliced a bit too hard, completely severing his dragon's head! "Shit!" he exclaimed as the body he was riding and the neck around which he was holding on began to drop and fall. He barely managed to get a Mystical Door open before the dragon smashed into the side of the mountain. He came rolling out of his door, rolling through the foaming mess that Jarka and Bernard had going. Bernard directed more of his water over Karel's nearly naked body, making sure the acid didn't harm him.

Just as the remaining nine dragons had arced around to make a second pass at the defenders, who were now frantically involved with neutralizing the acid flows and scrambling for healing potions, Emil and Renata appeared in the skies above the blacks. Sunlight glistened off of their golden hides, catching the attention of the blacks. At once, the remaining blacks stepped into the Shadows, heading for home. They had lost half their numbers on the first pass, and with the Gold Dragons now here, they knew that they had no chance at all and fled for their lives.

With the dragons' exodus, the mages all focused on neutralizing the acid flows. Jarka kept yelling what to do and they followed her advice, creating both lime and water. Huge clouds of noxious gas rose from the tops of both structures, nearly asphyxiating the mages, who at last had to vacate the rooftops. Half were nearly naked as they landed on the ground; most had already lost their shoes. Jarka summoned forth her bag of healing potions and began handing them around. Hands eagerly accepted them, most gulped them down rapidly. Hands, sides, chests, feet, lungs — all had been harmed, some more than others.

Emil landed beside Zoran. "Sorry we were too late to help."

"You weren't. I think your presence convinced them to leave," he replied. "Say, I think I saw some dead dragons landing on some houses in the town. Can you and Renata lift them off? We need to get help to those trapped inside."

Emil and Renata rose in tight circles and then headed off to the two affected homes. Their enormous claws hooked onto the carcasses and with a huge flapping of their enormous wings, slowly lifted the dead off the homes, depositing them outside the city's walls.

Using a Magnify spell, Zoran called out, "Is anyone seriously hurt?" Most had minor acid burns, and Jarka's potions were already working their magic.

"Sorry, Zoran," General Damek called out. "Two of your guards took a direct hit from acid falling down from above. There wasn't anything that I could do for them." Already, Damek had covered what remained of their bodies with a blanket. He didn't want his liege, Baron Jan, to see the awful aftermath of the acid on their bodies. Already Jan was terrified of the dragons.

Damek added, "I'll take a squad of men and check on the collapsed buildings. I'll send word if anyone is hurt or killed."

"Here, take along ten potions with you, just in case," Jarka ordered, handing him what remained in her bag. She looked at Zoran and said, "Handy to have around, eh?" He flashed her a thank you smile.

"Okay, everyone, get cleaned up fast and report back here. We need to clean up this incredible mess. Thank you all. We were very lucky this time," Zoran called out. Within seconds, everyone vanished from the outside grounds. He smiled and was the last one to open his Mystical Door and step into his room to change.

Karel and Milan were already outside extracting blood from the dragon carcasses when Zoran reappeared in clean clothes. He let them go about their business while he levitated up to the roof of the fortress to inspect the damage done. There was still acid in places, slowly eating its way through the stone rooftop. Worse, quite a little had fallen down the sides of the manor house and was eating away at the thinner sides. As the others returned, he began directing them on the flushing and neutralizing actions that were needed.

Aldrick and twenty more golds appeared and demanded to be given the dead blacks. "They need to be properly buried, Zoran. I insist on this," he stated in no uncertain terms. Zoran suspected that Aldrick already knew what and why Karel was doing and he gave his assent. While Karel growled at Aldrick, he stepped back and the giant gold clutched the black's carcass and lifted it up into the sky.

"Well, we have three barrels of blood and ten claws. That's a good start!" Karel declared antagonistically, once Aldrick was out of hearing range. "Shrink! Shrink! Shrink! Okay son, let's get these into my lab. I sure as heck hope the acid didn't get into my room!" He and Milan vanished and reappeared a bit later, joining the others in the massive cleansing operation.

As the action wound down, Zdenka whispered something in his ear and Zoran announced, "Okay, when we are finished here, all of you who cast a spell when the dragons first appeared are requested to meet with us in the dining room."

"Wonder what this is all about?" Jarka muttered to Bernard.

"Don't know. Maybe he wants to go over our choice of spells," he replied, slightly bored now that excitement was over. "Sure glad my dogs are on the first floor and not up there on the roof where Karel's falcons are at. I bet those birds got quite a fright today." Jarka smiled. She'd seen the extreme care Karel had taken over the protection of his falcons. Not a feather had been ruffled on his birds.

A while later, the whole group congregated in the dining room, whispering among themselves what the meeting might be about. Zdenka produced tea, biscuits, and honey, and the twenty-one casters began helping themselves. "I asked Zoran to have us all meet. I have been researching the dragons and more importantly the phenomenon of inherent resistance to magical spells that some creatures have. I admit that all of us have been rather ignorant in this arena. Not so any longer. Let me begin by asking all of you, whether Archmage or mere mage, when your spell was about to detonate, did you suddenly find yourself on a featureless, grey plain facing the dragon that your spell was about to effect? I did."

A chorus of "Me too's" echoed around the room, as each person looked at the other. "So none of you didn't experience this effect?" she asked. "Okay, then. Now I know what that was. When we use a spell that impacts a creature which has innate resistance to magical spells, this confrontation is always going to happen. During that brief instant, which seemed horribly long to me anyway, but it could not have been but a split second of real time, you have your chance to break down that creature's resistance to your spell."

"If you win that battle, your spell will affect the creature. If you lose that battle, your spell will not affect the creature. It is as simple as that."

"So that is what that is! I'll be damned. I just glared angrily at the beast and won each time!" Karel declared, enlightened.

Jarka laughed, "I was spooked and tried to attack mine by throwing an enchanted dagger at it. I think mine flinched at that."

"It filled me with fear. I was so scared. I must have lost my battle," Jan admitted, ashamed of his failure.

"Now you know what to expect next time, Baron Jan. Next time, you hang in there and glare him down!" Karel broke in, giving him some needed advice.

"I speak for many of us," Milan spoke up. "You Archmages know that you are the most powerful spell casters in the universe, but we who only have mage status are not so confident."

"That's very true, Milan," Zdenka replied softly. "We wield great power and that helps us break down their inherent resistance to magic. Still, now that you know what is happening, your determination, your defiance, will also bring it down. That's why I wanted to discuss this with all of you. Knowledge will enhance your chances of making your magic work on these dragons."

"Magic or not, Chan and Wen proved themselves today," Dana spoke up. "Zoran, I give them both my official pass on their training."

"Hey, I learned from them too. I got mine downed, just like they did," Karel pointed out, just in case no one had noticed him duplicating their attack methods. Everyone chuckled a bit. None had missed either event.

"Well, I don't know of any better way to do it," Chan replied humbly.

"Hey, it gets you out of the way of their damnable acid spew!" Jarka pointed out. "Ruined my dress and boots!"

"Hey, Damek, was anyone hurt in the collapsed buildings?" Chika asked.

"One gal had her arm broken, but Jarka's potions has her almost healed up. It is a miracle that no one was crushed to death," he reported.

"Will they be back soon?" asked Jan, still nervous about the whole scary incident.

"Good question," Zoran replied. "I hope not. They took what must look to them like staggering losses so I am hopeful that they will think twice about assaulting the fortresses directly, Jan. In the meantime, we must continue to rely on our Archmage's Premonition spells." Everyone looked at Zdenka and Verushka. Both smiled demurely. These top power spells were only castable by Archmages and often defined an Archmage, though the other four Archmages simply had not been able to master that spell.

"Say, Chan, is it hard to learn how to jump onto the flying dragon's neck?" Dana asked what he was most curious about.

She smiled. "Like anything else, it takes practice. I didn't get it right until the seventh attempt. Do you suppose that you could get Emil or Renata to fly around and let us practice this action on them?"

Zoran already knew the answer to that one. They would not ever consent to helping humans learn to kill their own kind. Chan guessed as much.

The next morning, Zoran contacted each of his allies and relayed what had happened, urging them to exercise extreme caution. He'd escaped the wrath of the dragons primarily because there were six Archmages along with the usual mages, to say nothing of the Duskas. With only a single Archmage or two at most, the band of twenty blacks could well win the day. The situation was not only escalating but becoming far more deadly.

Just after lunch, Zoran received an unexpected Duska communication. *Baron Zoran? Good. Baron Alvaro here. May I have permission to visit your Circle?*

Of course. Give me a minute to de-activate our defenses. I'll meet you at the Circle.

A minute later, Jarka and Bernard joined him around his Circle of Ascension in the depths of his fortress in Brn. A moment later Baron Alvaro Cencion stepped out of the Shadows and onto his Circle. "Thank you for seeing me on such short notice. You are looking fit. Putting on a bit of weight I see," the mustached man of forty-five greeted the trio.

Zoran extended his hand and greeted the Neutral baron. "Afternoon, Baron. You are looking fit yourself. Been horse riding I sense."

Alvaro smiled, "Noses always give such away. Is there somewhere that we can talk in private without being overheard?" Zoran led him to his private study via a Mystical Door, leaving Jarka and Bernard to re-secure the Circle. Once inside, both men cast their anti-scrying spells. Satisfied, Baron Alvaro sat down in one of the sofa chairs, refusing Zoran's offer of something to drink.

"I have not much time, so I will get right to the matter. As you know, the High Council is due to meet on Alta on the 15th of September, a mere three weeks and a few days from now." Zoran nodded. "I've come to ask a favor of you, but before I can ask it, I must tell you a bit about what's been happening recently on Alta. It is not good, I'm afraid."

Zoran sat down, seeing no need to seem to be standing over him. He was not his political enemy and besides, he had always been treated with the utmost kindness by Baron Alvaro. "Well, start at the beginning, I always say."

"Good sense. As you know, when the Golden Dragons first appeared within the Federation, many of us also took that opportunity to bring starving dragons to our worlds, if only to not be left out with these seemingly unlimited weapons. I invited the Brown and White Dragons to Alta. For many years now, this has been a most workable union. They keep to themselves for the most part, inhabiting the regions of Alta which we find most inhospitable. We've even established trade between our races, gemstones mostly."

"Ah, but all good things have another side, it is said. Ten years ago, the Red and Black Dragons somehow found their way to Alta, settling down without my consent or permission. At first, we tried to reason with them, but to no avail. Last year, they began making demands, holding us hostage to their greed for gems. They destroyed villages until we gave into their demands and gave them some of our gems."

"Recently, their greed is exceeding our ability to mine for gems. Now I am entrusted with holding this High Council, and I am extremely worried that either the reds or blacks will do something regrettable while I am hosting all of the barons and baronesses of the Sixteen Planets of the Federation. After all, we will all be in one place at one time. What better chance to eliminate all of us in one shot?"

"So you are worried that the dragons will attack us while we meet?" Zoran asked, catching on to Alvaro's worry.

"Yes, this dragon problem is rapidly spinning out of control on Alta. I am at a total loss over what actions I can take if any. Baron, I am the longest serving baron now. All of the others who used to run things have retired or passed away. I am the senior statesman of the Federation now, but you are the second senior statesman. No one else has the twenty plus years as you have, excepting myself, of course. I am here today asking your advice. Ought I cancel the meeting on Alta and allow another baron whose lands are more secure to hold our meeting? It is not too late to change the location. What do you think? I need an honest appraisal."

Zoran rubbed his hands through his hair. Never in a million years did he ever expect to be the second most senior statesman of the Federation. Yet Alvaro was right. He had twenty-five years of service while Zoran had twenty-one now. All of the others had substantially less experience in ruling their worlds. "The situation is grim on many planets, Alvaro. Gonda, Terra, Cosma, Valtr, Gladno — all are facing similar dragon problems. Here on Adapazan it has turned very ugly." He outlined what had just happened on Friday.

"My god! Twenty blacks attacked your fortress here in Brn? Are you all right?" a very worried Alvaro asked. He had no idea it had gotten this bad and resolved to have better and more frequent communications with Zoran.

"Yes, we lost some clothing and boots to the acid and two of our guards were killed, but the rest of us survived nicely. Only nine of the twenty escaped our wrath, but six of those suffered heavy wounds and will be out of action for a time, I hope, unless dragons heal rapidly. Here's an idea that we've been trying." He outlined their use of magic to turn worthless quartz crystals into diamonds to give to the dragons. "So far it has worked."

"Amazing, those gems cannot be enchanted and are certainly not the real thing. I guess dragons may not be as smart as we think. I will do as you suggest. Perhaps that will placate them while the High Council meets. Still. . ."

"We should take further steps, Alvaro. When the blacks attacked here, by having so many Archmages present, we tipped the tide to our side. Perhaps you should request that each of we barons bring along as many Archmages as possible — bend the rules a bit. If we have a dozen to fifteen Archmages present, a horde of dragons could be stopped," Zoran suggested.

"Excellent idea. Can I count on Adapazan bringing a fair number?" he asked with a wry smile.

"Of course. After all, no planet has more of us than Adapazan. My wife does an excellent job of it," Zoran could not resist putting in a plug for Zdenka.

"I am most relieved, thank you. Yet, I am most concerned about this growing dragon problem. I have placed that topic on our agenda."

"I concur, excellent idea," Zoran complimented him. "Zdenka will be able to give us advanced warning should the dragons mount an attack while we are meeting." He didn't mention that Verushka could also do it.

"Again, I thank you. It is really up to us to lead all these young barons, isn't it?"

"Yes, if only we could pound some sense in to some of them," Zoran half teased. The two shook hands and Alvaro left, stepping into the Shadows for a quick trip home.

"Knock, knock," Jarka called out. "What did he want?" Her curiosity got the better of her. Zoran smiled and explained the difficulties Alta was having.

"Maybe you will find similar problems on other Neutral worlds," she suggested. He wondered about that. If so, the problems were rapidly getting way beyond control.

Chapter 8 Body Parts

Honani sent a Message to Milan from his hideout on Isi. Milan agreed to meet, and Honani Shadow Walked to Brn, arriving before the gates of the city. He noted the new construction and guessed that the city had been greatly expanded with these new outer walls. Shortly, Milan apparated nearby, teleporting out of his room.

"Welcome to Brn, Honani. I got your message. Why the secrecy?" Milan asked.

"Walk with me," the brownish skinned, thin, but tall man of thirty said. They slipped into the nearby forest, before Honani volunteered more information. "I can get a hold of a whole lot more parts of dragons. It seems there is quite a demand for bones, teeth, skulls, hides, and claws. I figured that I ought to see if you want in on these deals."

"Colors?"

Honani laughed, "You name it, I get it. No questions asked, eh?"

"Okay. Can I see if he needs these things first?" Milan asked. He had no idea whether his dad needed any of these. Blood, yes.

"Sure. I'll wait a while."

"Won't take but a minute." He sent a Message to his father.

"Okay, bones, teeth, hides, and claws, please. Reds, blacks, greens predominately, but any color excepting of course gold," Milan relayed his dad's answer. Karel seemed very eager to get his hands on all of these, though Milan could not fathom why he would. Blood, yes, he infused it into the weapons.

"Fine. I'll get back to you soon. Fifty thousand per set, with a set meaning hide, bones, teeth and claws. One large bag's worth, shrunk of course," Honani replied. The two shook hands and Honani Shadow Walked back to Isi. Business had really begun to pick up for this adventurer and bastard son of late Baron Hinto Yamitiwa.

It's easy to hide on the vast plains of Isi, but only if you are Duska or a mage. The inhabited continent was extremely oblong, well over six thousand miles long, but only two thousand high. Rolling grasslands with timbered evergreen forests in the northern portion and deciduous forests elsewhere formed the topography of Isi. Great herds of hoofed animals roamed freely as did most of the human inhabitants. The only one permanent city on Isi lay at Hovani Wahkan or Holy Site, the fortress and Circle of Ascension, home of Baron Chua and Baroness Alameda Yamitiwa. Hovani Wahkan was located squarely in the middle of the continent, as if someone had surveyed for this precise spot. All its grey stone had been imported from Adapazan and Rehor. He was now forty-four, inheriting the top leadership and ancient Circle from his father, Hinto.

However, within the last twenty years, two more, but smaller fortresses at the west and eastern edges of the continent had been constructed to house the two new Circles for his younger brothers. Baron Hania and Baroness Chumani lived in the Wahkan Misu, or Holy River, located at the western edge of the continent where the largest river emptied into the ocean. Baron Keme and Baroness Juci lived in the new eastern fortress of Wahkan Niyol or Holy Wind. Here, strong easterly winds blew nearly constantly in from the ocean.

Most of these nomadic people lived in semi-permanent settlements of domed huts made from saplings and animal hides. A village might house a tribe of a few hundred at most. These nature-attuned people were hunters and gatherers for the most part. The barons traded furs and hides off-world for the few essentials they needed, mostly metal tools and weapons.

Culturally, the ruling baron was expected to spread his Holy Seed throughout the land, spreading his vitality throughout his people. Hence, there were many of these "holy children" born out of wedlock, but each one was brought to the Circle of Ascension on their fourteenth birthday and given the Ceremony of Ascension making them Duskas. While these young men and women would never inherit the throne and being more able than the normal inhabitant, they were supposed to spread their vitality and strength to their tribes, thereby ensuring the tribe's long term survival.

Of course, some of these bastard Duskas didn't see it this way. Honani was one of these; he wanted more than a life of hunting herd animals. Over the years, he'd formed up a band of like-minded Duskas, and they called themselves Namids or Star Dancers, for they loved to travel the sixteen planets of the Federation. Honani was thirty-three and his soul mate was Awinita, a year older. Askook and his mate Donoma were thirty. Cheveyo and his mate Kachina were twenty-nine. Together, these six had traveled extensively throughout the sixteen planets, particularly the backwaters of the civilizations there.

More importantly, both Cheveyo and Kachina had a knack for "divination," though Kachina was far better at it. That is, they often sensed where something of value may lay hidden from prying eyes. Frequently, the Namids would retrieve that special thing. Some might call them grave robbers, but their reply would be simply, "What use is a magical sword to a dead and buried man?" Others might call them spirit wanderers, always in search of more interesting places to visit. Others might call them a pack of thieves. Opportunists might be more accurate. Honani seized this golden opportunity to vastly increase their wealth and ultimate survival in abundance. Never had they seen the kind of funds they'd already received for the blood of the dragons.

Of course, they had been very clever in obtaining that blood. Because of their wide travels, they were very familiar with haunts of many dragons off-world as well as their own. They had been patient and took key opportunities to strike when parents of smaller dragons left to hunt for their small offspring. While none of them wanted to attack a full grown dragon, they thought nothing of attacking the smaller, young ones. The needed dragon blood had thus been easy for them to acquire. The huge funds they'd received fueled Honani's further inquiries of Milan. Kachina had said that perhaps they could rob the graves of known dead dragons, who always buried their fallen with ceremony and honor.

"Kachina, your idea was brilliant! Milan went for it big time! Fifty grand per large bag! Gang, let's get this show on the road," Honani reported to his small band.

"I'll stay behind and watch all our kids," Awinta offered. "Not much danger in digging up bones." All laughed, no there was not, just easy money.

Chapter 9 The Fall High Council

During the first week of September, Zoran, Verushka, and Karel became involved with Zdenka and her training of her magic students. Why? Zdenka had three students who were at long last tackling the top power spells that any mage could possibly cast! Yes, if these three could somehow learn to reliably cast just one of these power spells, they would join the elite of the elite of mages, achieving Archmage status. She even pulled in Emil and Renata to help on the power spells that they could cast, the conjuring of a storm of fiery meteors.

Zoran's sisters, Rayna and Lida, both begged Zdenka to train their children. Lida had had a month's worth of training under Zdenka some twenty years ago and had learned more from her in that time than in years under her father's Archmage. Obviously, Zdenka could not refuse, but insisted that their children would have to pass her usual acceptance test. Curiously, Lida's two boys failed the test, but her daughter passed. Zelenka was accepted and began her training at fourteen, just after she was given the Ceremony of Ascension. This long brown haired teen had spent four long years studying under Zdenka and was now struggling mightily with these top power spells. Zdenka had watched the slow changes in Zelenka over these years.

At first, the young teen was only interested in fancy court dresses and finery, desiring to become a beautiful baroness like her mother, regal and knowledgeable. Bit by bit, Zelenka changed, becoming more and more interested in magic and what she could do with it. She was a creator type of person and took easily to the many spells that created something or some temporary creature. Now she was tackling the power spells and, as any mage did, she was having a very tough, discouraging time of it.

Rayna's son also failed the admittance test, but her two daughters passed. Her youngest, Zora, now fifteen, had only been studying with Zdenka for eighteen months, but was a mage in her own right, able to Teleport at will. Of course, as a Duska, she really didn't need this spell particularly. Zora was still growing and had a gangly frame and a gap between her two front teeth. Overly concerned with her appearance, she took to alteration spells, especially those that she could use on herself. No one could predict what color her hair would become on any given day.

On the other hand, Chesna, now sixteen, had been studying for over two and a half years under Zdenka's careful guidance. This young teen did not have her mother's good looks, but had an inquiring mind, full of curiosity. She'd become fast friends with the slightly older Zelenka, who had sort of adopted her as her little sister. After all, they were cousins. Zelenka constantly fed Chesna tips and pointers, even spending long hours with her when needed. As a result, Chesna had caught up to Zelenka, and now the two were working together, valiantly trying to learn these top power spells.

The third student was Ivana Jakuba, twenty-two years old with long black hair, greenish eyes, and a totally disarming smile. A Byn blacksmith's daughter, she knew that she could not follow in her father's footsteps. She did not want to take in laundry like her mother. She had tried sewing but simply was not good at it. For a time, she tried being a barmaid, but soon loathed how men constantly mistreated her. She was no man's thing, she often declared. Finally, she tried her hand at being a maid for the inn. When Zdenka held her spring picking five years ago, she watched all of the young hopefuls trying to get chosen. On the spur of the moment, she had decided to try it. After all, the worst that could happen is that she'd walk away smiling like so many others had. To her amazement, Zdenka chose her to learn the ways of magic!

A year later, Zelenka came and Ivana was extremely impressed with this person of royalty! Fancy clothes also appealed to Ivana. The two became good friends, especially with Ivana helping Zelenka with the beginning spells that she already knew how to cast. Later, Chesna joined them and thereafter, the three were always studying together, nearly inseparable. "Come on, you two, we just have to master one of these power spells!" she declared to Zelenka and Chesna, who were both quite frustrated at the extreme difficulty of these spells.

With the constant help of Zoran, Verushka, Karel, Emil, and of course, Zdenka, this first week in September proved the most fruitful week ever for Zdenka's students. Ivana made the first breakthrough, Stopping Time, much to the hilarity of all present. She'd tied Zoran's shoe laces together, put Zdenka's hair ribbon onto Karel, and put Verushka's staff in Emil's hands. Everyone roared with laughter at the antics when time resumed and Zoran fell flat on his face. After that breakthrough, the three began to make real progress.

Seven long days later, and Zelenka was able to cast both the Sphere of Ultimate Protection and the incredibly valuable Foresight Spell. Chesna was able to Change One's Shape — she preferred that of a white wolf, Cancel Magic like Zoran could, and Foresight. Meanwhile, Ivana could cast Crushing Fist like Zdenka, conjure a Swarm of Meteors like Emil, and Stop Time like Zdenka could.

Proudly, Zdenka announced her new three Archmages to all of her students and all of those in the fortress as well. Also in attendance were their beaming families, Shadow Walking from both Gladno and Valtr for this special celebration. "I give you Archmage Zelenka Matous, Archmage Chesna Pavel, and Archmage Ivana Jakuba!" Zdenka proclaimed, "Let the party begin." All of their parents were in attendance, though the blacksmith and his wife felt uncomfortable and out of place. Still even this could not dampen the pride that Ivana's father felt that evening.

Both Leo and Lida as well as Stefan and Rayna had come, wearing their finest dress outfits, in honor of their daughters' remarkable achievement. All four thanked Zdenka repeatedly, promising her anything that she ever desired for having trained their daughters so incredibly well.

Later that evening, Zoran made Ivana an offer that she could not refuse: he gave her an Archmage Tower of her own. Okay, it would take several years to be constructed just to the east of his outer fortress wall, but this was a royal incentive, and Ivana did not hesitate to join his staff.

The next day, Zdenka also told the three that they would need to come to the next High Council meeting to be formally presented to the Federation. Immediately, the three began to worry about what to wear, particularly Ivana who had no idea about fancy courts and the acceptable dresses worn there. Zelenka and Chesna gaily handled that for her during the week before the meeting, even going so far as to purchase the expensive apparel and accessories for her. Both knew that Ivana currently had virtually no funds of her own. "That will change soon, Ivana. You are an Archmage now and Zoran had better pay you well," Zelenka teased her.

Two days before the Fall High Council, Baroness Archmage Zdenka called all of the women who would be going together for a women's-only meeting. "Okay, most of us know well the dress code that the many baronesses will be wearing during these council days on Alta. Ivana has no idea of what to expect, though Chesna and Zelenka have been coaching her. However, ladies, there is a very real possibility that we may be attacked by a horde of dragons during this council. After all, the Federation's rulers and most of the mages will be present under one roof, making us a prime target. If an attack does come, tight corsets, enormous ball gowns, and the impossible extreme heels will make we women particularly vulnerable. Such will hinder us if we are attacked, to say nothing of hindering our men."

"What has Baroness Anita Cencion said? Has she contacted you about this?" Mage Jarka interjected. She hoped that Zdenka had some news from their host baroness. She was ambivalent. While she dearly loved these opportunities to dress up in her extremely fancy and expensive dresses, she also knew that Zdenka was spot on, such would be debilitating if an attack came.

"Yes, I am afraid that she too is worried. We've discussed this at length last night. This is the traditional time of year for us women to don our finest. If we do not do so, we would be viewed as having given in to this dragon threat. Yet, if the attack does come, we will be in trouble if we are all dolled up as usual. One can argue this both ways. Stay dolled up and show the world that dragons cannot impact us and risk possible death or go dressed for a battle which might not come. If we dress for a battle, others will see that we are taking this potential threat very seriously. If we do that, she and I both agree that can adversely affect the moral of the average person. Hence, she and I reached a compromise. Today, she is relaying our decision to all of the other baronesses," Zdenka calmly continued.

"Ladies, we wear our usual fancy court dresses, but keep the corseting to a minimum. Wear comfortable, low heels or even flats or boots. After all, our heels can rarely be seen beneath our billowing ball gowns anyway. That way, she and I feel that we will be able to react to any dragon attack and not be at a significant disadvantage. Also, each of us is to carry a magically enchanted dagger on our person at all times, just in case we are attacked. Baroness Anita insists that we have them as a last resort. In short, we dress up as usual, but be ready to fight and stand on our own if the dragon attack does materialize. Of course, we will keep our Premonition Spells activated at all times while we are there. Hopefully that will give us advanced warning and time to more fully prepare."

Jarka grinned. "I like it, devious! We give the appearance that all is well, exuding confidence, yet we will be prepared for the worst. I love it!" Zdenka smiled; she knew that Mage Jarka would have such a reaction.

After a bit more discussion, Zdenka ended by saying, "Finally, those of you who do not have a magically enchanted dagger are to go see Mage Dana immediately. He'll get you one best suited to you. Now let's get busy, ladies. We have a lot of packing to do. Thank goodness for Shrink spells!" Everyone laughed. Nothing was truer for the women at these two times of the year.

Zoran didn't want to leave Adapazan wholly unguarded during their absence. He spent part of the day visiting one of Archmages that Zdenka had trained some fifteen years ago. Archmage Jakob Hamil was in the service of the warlord of Tratky, the northernmost province. "I need to ask a very big favor of you, Archmage Jakob. We are off to the Fall High Council in two days' time. We'll be gone for four days at most. Because Baron Alvaro suspects that the dragons might take this opportunity to attack his fortress, we are bringing along as many Archmages as possible. However, I don't want to leave Adapazan defenseless. Who knows, the dragons might take this opportunity to attack us again."

"What do you want me to do?" Archmage Jakob asked solemnly. He already had suspected that Baron Zoran would be coming for his services. News of the dragon attacks had reached him here in the far north.

"Come to Brn and watch over the Fortress. If any trouble comes, Message me immediately and we'll all Shadow Walk back instantly. If you will do this for me, I will owe you a big favor, Archmage."

Jakob smiled broadly. He was relieved to hear that his baron did not want him to go to Alta with him. He hated Shadow Walking. "I accept. I'll come tomorrow morning and you can show me what's what. I'll need a Duska to actually Message you, though. This is the least that I can do for Baroness Archmage Zdenka. After all, if it were not for her, I would never have become an Archmage. I owe her far more than I can ever repay. You can count on me, Baron." The two shook hands and he Shadow Walked back to his fortress, greatly relieved.

He and Zdenka had spoken of the real possibility that the dragons might attack while they were all gone. She had countered his notion that they would not be attacking while they were gone. Her fear was that they might attack because the blacks would most likely be seeking revenge for their having killed and wounded so many blacks during that last attack. Hence, he felt better knowing that an Archmage would be on duty just in case.

"There dear, everything is all packed. One bag," Zdenka announced the morning they were to depart. She'd gotten up extra early to dress. From experience, she and Jarka knew precisely how long it took for them to get into their fancy outfits.

"You look lovely, my dear," Zoran replied, giving her a loving kiss. "What would I ever do without you?" Zdenka didn't reply but had an image of Zoran making a complete mess of his apparel.

In a nearby room, poor Ivana was dumbfounded at all of the individual pieces that had to be donned in just the proper order, but Chesna and Zelenka hovered over her, assisting her as well as each other. "Look Ivana, none of us can get into one of these outfits on our own. They are way too restrictive; another set of hands really is required." She attempted to put Ivana's worried mind at easy.

"Are you sure?" Ivana asked timidly.

"Absolutely. Jarka and Zdenka are dressing each other as we speak," Chesna explained. At last properly attired, the three women picked up their single bags which contained a whole wardrobe shrunk way down in size and headed to the Great Hall. Just as the three exited, they saw Jarka and Zdenka leaving the baroness' quarters, with Zoran trailing behind them. Ivana relaxed, apparently Chesna was right. Jarka had helped Zdenka into her sky blue gown.

"Wow, you ladies look absolutely stunning," Zoran admired the trio. Ivana blushed.

"More stunning than little old me?" Jarka jabbed back playfully.

"If I were only twenty years younger," Zoran teased the three new Archmages. Zdenka gave him a playful poke in his ribs, and all five laughed as they entered the Great Hall. Right on time, the others arrived and within a few minutes, Zoran prepared to Shadow Walk the whole group to Alta.

These sessions of the High Council of the Federation of Planets alternated among the sixteen worlds. Baron Alvaro and Baroness Anita Cencion hosted this session at their castle in Puerto on the planet of Alta, a hilly planet. Politically, Alta was Neutral, neither aligned with Zoran's group nor Clav's or as many now believed the "have-nots" and the "haves." Normally, these sessions lasted an entire week, but this session would be shorter. By mutual agreement among the barons, the dragon threat was too real to allow for the usual extended formalities.

After they all joined hands, Zoran stepped them all to the planet Alta. Since this was the first time here for some, Zoran purposefully allowed his walk to circumnavigate the world, allowing them to get a good overview look at this world, whose land masses were uniformly all very hilly. Periodically, they spied roads streaking across the green hills like gray lines a child might draw. A few towns came into view before the large capital city of Puerto appeared before their eyes. Gray stone buildings predominated as they approached, and then the giant gray stone fortress of Baron Alvaro Cencion loomed before them, growing larger and larger. Zoran focused on the giant gray cobblestone courtyard just inside the fortress gates and they arrived.

Rimming the courtyard were hundreds of orange pots, whose late fall marigolds were in full bloom, adding color to the uniform drab surroundings. On the ramparts behind and above them, a hundred fighters stood, weapons raised, ready for any trouble — Baron Alvaro took the High Council security measures seriously, though he, as did Zoran, knew these men would have no chance at all if even one dragon showed up and attacked. A tall man in a suit that looked finer than Zoran's stepped forward to meet them. He recognized the old man, recalling the first time that he'd met him some twenty years ago.

"I am Esteban, the butler. Welcome Baron Archmage Zoran," he said mostly bored, as if he had been doing this all day.

"I've been expecting you. If you will follow me, I will show you to your rooms. You are to be at the meeting room at ten o'clock for the opening ceremonies, sir. If you have a moment before then, Baron Alvaro wishes a private word with you." He then led them inside the gaping, handcrafted doors of the main manor house and down long corridors. Periodically, large orange pots hung from the walls with more flowers still blooming. After showing them to their suite of four rooms, he bowed and left them, walking crisply back down the long hall.

Inside, they found a small home, with a private bath and four bedrooms with a central living room. The women took two of the bedrooms, while the men divided themselves between the remaining two. After unshrinking their gear, they quickly stowed their things. As always, the mages executed a thorough search for scrying devices and spells. Finding none, they then setup their own personal defenses.

Satisfied, Zoran was about to visit Baron Milan when the baron knocked on his door.

The two older men hugged. "So glad that you could come. Nine Archmages! Zoran, you have an army of them!" Baron Alvaro was extremely impressed with this singular detail. "I sincerely hope that we do not need their services. Yet, I beg you; use all of your skills that we may have advanced warning of dragon attacks. I feel it in my bones, Zoran. Something awful is going to happen and on my watch!"

"You have our pledge, Baron," Zdenka's alto voice broke in on the two's hushed conversation. "Four of us will have our Foresight Spells active at all times."

"What? Four of your Archmages can cast such a power spell?" Clearly Baron Alvaro was quite taken aback. He knew that she could cast this spell, but three others? "Thank you! This is almost too good to be true! I will rest far easier now! I have put a discussion of how to best attack the dragons as the first topic of discussion, after the official opening ceremonies that is. I am so relieved. Thank you." He shook her hand and then left to greet the other arriving barons and baronesses.

Once they freshened up, Zoran led them to the huge meeting room, explaining to the three new Archmages what they should expect. Once in the room, he assisted the three into the visitor's section. This area was separated from the rest of the room by an ornate wooden baluster wall that stood two feet tall. The barrel vaulted ceiling rose some fifty feet overhead covered with highly realistic artwork depicting various landscapes representing the sixteen worlds of the Federation. "Incredible!" whispered Ivana, who had never seen anything like this before.

Out beyond them were large, magnificently made tables and plush chairs, arranged in a U-shape with six foot gaps between the two joining corners. Zoran pointed out that the neutral barons would sit along the bottom of the U, while the two other aligned groups of barons would sit facing each other. All could face the Visitor's Area. Across the way, a line of six uniformed men stood, large brass trumpets at the ready. Precisely at ten, they raised their instruments and began a fanfare. A bass voice bellowed loudly, "Baron Alvaro Cencion and Baroness Anita."

As the two walked in ceremoniously, Zdenka and Jarka saw at once that Anita must be wearing low heels or flats. Gone were her tiny steps; the couple moved rather swiftly across the room, taking their seats in the center of the section of the bottom of the U-shape. The voice then announced, "Baron Basilio and Baroness Benita Cencion, Baron Eduardo and Baroness Concha Cencion." His oldest son and daughter now controlled the two new Circles here on Alta. Slowly the forty-eight barons and forty-eight baronesses were introduced and walked ceremoniously to their assigned seats. Zoran's group was announced immediately after Baron Alvaro's group, since he was the second-most senior baron.

"Baron Archmage Zoran and Baroness Archmage Zdenka Vladislov. Baron Thomas and Baroness Archmage Verushka Vladislov. Baron Jan and Baroness Reina Matous Vavrin." Of course, Dusan and Archmage Nadia Vladislov Dragon followed them, along with Archmage Karel and Chika Ambrose, Mage Bernard and Mage Jarka Dragon, and Archmage Marek and Akira Aceda. These were both their advisors and Baron Alvaro's requested extra Archmages.

As usual, the women took careful note of each other's attire. Zoran still didn't understand why the women were so insistent upon not wearing identically colored dresses, and yet so many wanted to be wearing the latest in fashions. Jarka breathed a sigh of relief. No other woman was wearing a bright, cherry red gown as she wore, though a couple of satin gowns were close in color.

Baron Alvaro tapped his gavel, the hollow sound echoing around the high vaulted ceiling. "The High Council of the Federation of the Sixteen Planets is now officially in session. First, we have the introductions of the newest Archmages. I call upon Baroness Archmage Zdenka who will introduce her three newest Archmages."

Zdenka rose. Her mellow alto voice cut through the air, magnified by the acoustics of this special room. "It is with the greatest pleasure and pride that I give to you Archmage Zelenka Matous, daughter of Baron Leo and Baroness Lida Matous. I give you Archmage Chesna Pavel, daughter of Baron Stefan and Baroness Rayna Pavel. I give you Archmage Ivana Jakuba, daughter of Evzen Jakuba."

Zoran thought that the round of hearty applause for the three new Archmages was far more enthusiastic than he could recall others having received. Perhaps it was because of the serious dragon threat that all were now facing. Baron Alvaro rose and announced, "I call upon Archmage Abelard Brecht of Gerde to announce his new Archmage."

The aged man rose. He was sitting beside Baron Karel Ebbe, the leader of the three Gerde barons and sworn enemies of Zoran's group. "It is with humble pride that I give you Archmage Berend Deidricht of Gerde, who will be taking over for me as I am retiring soon." A thin, tall man rose. Zoran guessed that he was in his middle twenties. Again, he received an equally boisterous round of applause, and he flushed from the unexpected adoration tossed his way.

Baron Alvaro then announced, "Archmages, you may come down from the visitor's box and take your places at the High Council." Quickly, the four did as asked, the two daughters, grinning ear to ear, proudly sat down beside their mothers. Archmage Ivana sat next to Zoran and Jarka, while Archmage Berend sat beside Baron Karel.

"Now then, I have altered the usual order of business to permit Baroness Archmage Zdenka Vladislov to share a few words with us and all of the many Archmages here with us. As you all know, I am very worried about the possibility of the dragons making an attack on our High Council and have asked each of you to bring along as many Archmages as you can. She will explain why I have taken this unprecedented action. After she has finished, we will discuss how we may defend ourselves from dragon attacks. Baroness, I ceded the floor to you." He sat down, motioning for her to stand.

Again, her alto voice filled the room. For once, Zoran noticed that he could have heard a pin hitting the stone floor. Rapt attention focused on her every word. "Thank you Baron. As some of you know, not long ago, our fortress on Adapazan was attacked by Black Dragons. Some twenty attempted to destroy us. However, our Foresight Spells alerted us to the impending attack. As you may know, dragons are exceptionally difficult to slay or even wound. Normal weapons are entirely useless against them, since they cannot pierce their tough hides. Because of their inherent natures, they have a resistance to magical spells, making the usual spells cast by mages often completely ineffective."

"However, during the attack, we had six Archmages casting spells at them. We have learned a great deal from that. This is what I am obligated to share with all our fellow Archmages here. When you cast a spell at a dragon, as your spell activates, you will suddenly find yourself on a flat, featureless grey plain facing the dragon that your spell is about to affect. It is a challenge of wills. If you win, your spell will affect the dragon. If you lose, your spell will not affect the dragon in the slightest. If you flinch, if your resolve is not hardened, you will lose. Archmage Karel believes that the way to avoid this is to glare angrily at the opposing dragon. Such has worked several times for him. Honestly, I do not know any pat way to guarantee that you will win the battle of wills. Just don't flinch is the best advice that I can give you."

Zdenka tried to sit down, but was besieged with questions from other Archmages. Eventually Berend asked, "Baroness Archmage, how do we best defend our people from the dragon's breath? Can you tell us more?" Clearly, Zoran noted, Baron Karl and his new Archmage Berend were very worried. He tucked this observation away for future reference.

"Okay, I admit that I do not have all the answers," Zdenka admitted. She described the attack on the fortress at Brn in detail. "Summarizing then, Disintegrate Spells cast by Archmages are effective. Mage Jarka's counter of their caustic acid spray works. That is, conjure mountains of lime and then conjure a mass of water over the lime. The resulting chemical reaction between the acid and lime neutralizes the acid, but it also creates very nasty fumes. Have healing potions at hand. Archmage Karel used a series of Force Screens to protect his falcon cages on the roof from the dragons' acid breath. This worked perfectly. However, I do not have any experience with the other dragon breath weapons. I'm sorry."

"Surely you didn't just use Disintegrate Spells on all of them," Archmage Berend countered.

"No, Archmage Marek cast a Meteor Swarm which proved effective, especially when there were several blacks flying close together. Balls of Fire also worked against the blacks," Zdenka answered. "Please note that we began our attack at the most extreme range of our spells, giving us time to get them off and then prepare to dodge the incoming streams of acid as the dragons drew closer. Several also attacked them with weapons after that," she explained.

"What kind of weapons?" Baron Karl broke in.

"Let's save that for the next topic, baron," Baron Alvaro interrupted him.

"Are our mages going to be utterly useless against them?" asked a worried Baron Goro Yoko of the water world of Asami. "Are you saying that only an Archmage can hope to defeat a dragon?" Many other voices suddenly whispered, and Zoran knew that this was on everyone's mind. Archmages were extremely rare. Mages were commonplace. Until now, most barons depended upon their mages. Would they be completely ineffective against the dragons? Key question Zoran noted. He wished Zdenka had a better answer.

She sighed, "I wish I could say that mages are very effective against dragons, but I cannot. Don't get me wrong. A mage does have some chance of breaking down the opposing dragon's will and magical resistance, but it is not a good chance. It depends on the will power of the mage, I believe."

"Excuse me, may I add a word or two?" Mage Jarka interrupted her. She had been watching the various barons and saw precisely what their concern was: they had many mages in their service, but often one Archmage at most. That Zoran had six Archmages in this battle was so far beyond what they could field should an attack come their way that they were becoming extremely worried to say the very least.

Zdenka nodded and Mage Jarka rose. "Please relay this to all of your mages. Yes, I shot a Ball of Fire at an incoming Black Dragon. I was extremely startled to suddenly find myself standing alone on that featureless, grey plain that Zdenka told you about — the dragon that I was attacking staring coldly straight at me. I found the experience quite unnerving. However, I was not about to let a dragon defeat me and I began to toss my magically enchanted throwing daggers at it, figuring maybe I could attack it this way. I think that was what allowed my will to triumph over the dragon's. My spell took the dragon down. Now that I know what to expect the next time that I attack a dragon with a magical spell, I will be more able to focus my will power. So what I am saying, is let your mages know what to expect and what they must do when they find themselves on that grey plain. Make their will exceed that of their opponent's will. Knowledge gives us a better chance, but I will say that it is a frightening experience."

Zoran saw the relief on many barons' faces. There was some hope that their mages could help protect them. Jarka added one more detail, "However, I found myself far, far more useful in helping to undo the acid spews, helping protect others from serious injury than in actually defeating a dragon. For my money, mages ought to focus more on keeping the damage that the dragons do minimized. We are far more effective at this than in killing the beasts." This did not go over as well, but many recognized her wisdom.

"Baron Alvaro, can't we move on to how to attack these dragons with weapons? Really, we need to discuss this. It's vital," Baron Karl interrupted again. Alvaro glanced around the room; many heads nodded in total agreement with Karl and Alvaro conceded the point.

"Okay, let's move on then."

"Right. I've heard a lot of wild stories about magical weapons and such coming from Adapazan. Perhaps Baron Zoran would like to share this with the rest of us," Baron Karl said hostilely, as if Zoran was purposely keeping vital data from him.

Zoran turned to Archmage Karel and motioned for him to stand. "Baron Karl, I know little about such. I give you my expert, Archmage Karel."

Karel rose solemnly and slowly. *This is to be my finest hour,* he thought. *I will receive the recognition that I rightly deserve!* "Yes, for quite some time now, barons, baronesses, Archmages, I have been enchanting all manner of weapons. With the rise of this serious dragon problem, I have found ways and means of creating Dragon Slaying weapons, both swords and arrows. Each such weapon, however, is attuned to a specific color or type of dragon. For example, any enchanted blade will have a chance of penetrating the hide of any dragon. However, my especially enchanted blades will do far more damage to the type of dragon for which it is enchanted. For example, my Red Dragon Slayer blades will do far more damage to reds than any other type of creature."

"However, I have gone one step beyond even this. If I know the name of the dragon that I wish to slay, I can add an extra enchantment. I tested this out on a Red

Dragon, creating an Arrow of Red Dragon Slaying for one specific red who led the slaughter of one of our entire villages. One thousand men, women, and children were murdered by his band of reds. When he returned to pick up his extorted gems, I shot the arrow at him. Mind you, an arrow has a relatively short range of travel. This specific dragon was far, far beyond bow range, yet my enchantment locked on to him and followed after him, even into the Shadows, where it finally pierced his hide and slew him. Yes, I found myself on that grey plain as the arrow pierced him, but my will is power and he was slain!"

"Now as far as technique is concerned, I've learned a good deal from a pair of Duska heirs from Jing. You teleport onto the necks of these flying beasts and either stab them in their eyes with a dagger or cut off their head as I did with one of my short swords — highly effective approach, I've found."

"So our mighty armies are useless?" asked Baron Clav. Zoran noted that his archenemy looked both highly concerned and worried as well.

Zoran rose to answer this one. He had a vested interest in this topic. "Baron Clav, you bring up a key point that I wish to answer, as I have firsthand knowledge of this one. You are right; our mighty armies are completely and utterly useless if even *one* dragon attacks them. My father fielded a mighty army, shock troops and all. In thirty minutes, two dragons wiped out nearly three thousand men and had not a scratch on them. No, whatever you do when dragons attack you, do not attempt to use your soldiers. They will be destroyed utterly and likely cause no harm whatsoever to the dragons, baron. I hate to say this, but it is the truth of the matter. Dragons are at the top of the food chain, not we humans."

"Actually, only an Archmage has much of a chance with a dragon. Next come those armed with magically enchanted blades. Mere mages are probably third in line. Virtually nothing else is going to affect these powerful beasts, baron. Well, we Duska are able to dodge them fairly effectively, if that counts for anything." That sobered the entire room for a minute.

After a long pause, Baron Clav asked, "So Archmage Karel, Baron Zoran, are these special weapons of yours for sale or are you hoarding them? Obviously, many of us here would love to get their hands on such weapons to defend our own people. Can Archmage Karel perhaps share his methods of such weapon creation with our other Archmages? After all, this is a crisis that we are facing."

Again, murmurs hummed around the room. Obviously, every baron here wanted to get his hands on some of these dragon slayer blades and for good reasons, most likely. Archmage Karel knew better than to answer these questions. They were politically motivated. Baron Clav, for example, had been behind the reds attacking Adapazan. He turned instinctively to Zoran.

All eyes stared or glared at Zoran. Silence hung like an albatross around his neck. Never before had he been in such a politically sensitive arena. He knew that he had to answer these questions with great care and wished that his uncles were still alive and here — they would know just the right way to answer the questions. He sighed and said, "Look, you have to understand a few things. First, as I understand the construction of these enchanted blades, only the very finest blades are capable of even being slightly enchanted. For years now, we have been seeking out the finest blades in the Federation. Let me tell you, they are hard to find. This alone keeps such weapons from being mass produced."

"Secondly, once Archmage Karel has a blade of sufficiently high quality to enchant, it takes him several weeks to work his magic on it. Also, to make the dragon slayer weapons, as I understand the process, it requires blood from that type of dragon for which it is to be enchanted to slay. Obtaining dragon blood is no easy task. Even with the blood at hand, Archmage Karel needs more time to continue the enchantment process. In short, these blades are not only very rare but also take a long time to manufacture. The cost to him of even one such blade is quite high. It is not like we have thousands of these enchanted blades sitting in my armory on Adapazan, barons. If I did have thousands, I would not hesitate to divvy them up among all of you. Lord knows, we need to be able to protect our people."

"Further, my Master Swordsman, Dana Aceda, tells me that the blade must be matched with its wielder for a blade to achieve its maximum impact. Too heavy, too light, wrong grip — all these combine to make any given weapon far less effective than it might be if it was in the right hands. These cautions in mind *and* subject to further actions taken by this High Council on additional related matters to be discussed later on in our meetings, I am willing to share what we do have with all of you, but the blade must be matched to its wielder. I will not compromise on that detail, barons."

Barons Leo and Stefan began clapping. Soon the room echoed with applause. That he was willing to share these vital weapons was most welcomed by all. Zoran eyed his enemy Baron Karl and saw the first-ever nod of appreciation for something that he said. Perhaps, Zoran thought, the ice between us is finally breaking.

Zoran added, "I will expect those who can afford these weapons to pay for them so that we can recover our expenses and be able to make more of them. However, I am well aware that some of the "have-not" worlds may be unable to afford them. If so, I will see that you get them anyway. We all face a common foe."

"That is only fair," Baron Leo spoke up and another round of applause broke out.

"Further, I will speak with Archmage Karel about his willingness to share the manufacturing details with other Archmages. Perhaps we can offer a master class in such weapon construction." This brought yet a third round of applause.

"Okay, okay. I believe that we need to move on," Baron Alvaro attempted to regain control of his meeting. "Now then, we have a number of special requests to address. Baron Gang Meerong of Jing wishes to launch a formal protest. Baron," he motioned to Gang and sat down, checking this item off of his list of topics.

Baron Gang rose. "Yes, my father, Baron Chen, first brought the Green Dragons to Jing some twenty years ago. He made a pact with them and all has been well between our races for some years. However, our sisters, Chan and Wen, for reasons of their own, have been attacking and murdering many of our Green Dragon guests. At last count, they have murdered nineteen Green Dragons."

He was summarily interrupted by cheering and applause, which took him quite by surprise. Such was not what he either wanted or expected. Gang continued. "Over the years, we have put a price on our sister's heads for these murders. Recently, the greens and I laid a trap to finally capture our sisters and hold them accountable for their murdering rampage. However, they miraculously escaped and took refuge on Adapazan with Baron Zoran. I visited him and requested that he return them to Jing so they could stand trial, but he declared that he had given them sanctuary on Adapazan. I have come here today to request that the High Council order Baron Zoran to hand over these two criminals, Chan and Wen Meerong, to me so that they can stand trial for their murderous rampage." He sat down, counting on the High Council to approve his request. He looked smugly at Zoran, basking in his presumed victory.

Baron Leo spoke up, "Baron Gang, are you nuts? Chan and Wen have killed nineteen of these foul dragons! My god, man! No one in the Federation has slain that many! You should be giving them medals for extreme heroism!"

"You got to be kidding, right Baron Gang?" Baron Gaspard of Gonda added.

"Surely you are making a joke?" asked Baron Chua of Isi.

"This is a jest, right?" said Baron Karl of Gerde.

"You can't be serious, baron. We need all of the experienced dragon fighters we can possibly get!" declared Baron John from Terra. "Now more than ever."

Baron Gang looked around the tables at the faces of the other barons. Hastily, he retracted his request. "Yes, I made a joke." His face was beet red; his unexpected defeat, total. Zoran relaxed.

Clearing his throat, Baron Alvaro said, "Next item. It seems that many of our worlds have been experiencing random dragon attacks. However, they may not be random any longer. I have asked Mage Jarka Dragon to give us her analysis of the situation that she discovered on Adapazan. As several of you barons know, she gave this presentation to you, and you subsequently found correlating data on your planets. Mage Jarka, you have the floor."

For the first time, Jarka found herself nervous. Never before had she been called upon to address the full High Council. She rose, her cheeks turning as red as her dress. She conjured up her enormous charts. Taking a deep breath, she launched into her speech, the same one that she had delivered several times before. Soon, her nervousness evaporated as she went painstakingly through every detail. "So as you can clearly see, at first, the attacks were infrequent and basically random in nature. However, from the chart, you can obviously see that during this period here, the attacks are anything but random, targeting gemstone shipments."

She went on to describe what had been learned about them, including the role that Baron Clav had, much to his embarrassment. Next, she outlined the newest extortion attempts being made in which a whole village was wiped out and the dragons then demanding a pile of gems to prevent them from wiping out additional villages. She outlined the approach being taken of manufacturing diamonds magically from quartz crystals and that so far, these had been accepted. Some commented that the dragons must not be as intelligent as they had previously thought, but she ignored such suggestions.

"Now then, I will turn the discussion over to Barons Leo and Stefan, who have extended my research to their planets," she ended up. As she sat down, she too received a round of applause. Next, Leo and Stefan both presented similar charts to the ones that Jarka had shown, proving the attacks on Gladno and Valtr were following the same pattern as on Adapazan. Before others could add their observations, the meeting broke for their two hour lunch.

Of course, Zoran, Zdenka, Karel, and Jarka were besieged by the other barons, baronesses, and Archmages. Most barons wanted to confirm that Zoran was serious about sharing the enchanted weapons and their making with others, while the Archmages had more specific questions about the breaking of the dragon's magical resistance phenomenon. Several barons wanted Jarka to visit them and help them see if there was a pattern to the dragon attacks on their worlds. The two hours passed rapidly, with the four barely able to get the chance to dine themselves.

The afternoon session picked up where they had left off, with several other barons also pointing out the non-randomness of the recent dragon attacks. Several others had also undergone similar extortion attacks, which came as no surprise now. One by one, the many barons began to see the overall picture.

Late afternoon, before Baron Alvaro could move on to the next topic, Baron Clav interrupted. "Excuse me, baron. May I say a few words on Rehor's behalf?"

"Certainly, baron. You have the floor." Alvaro sat down, curious about just what Clav would have to say. Certainly he had a lot of explaining to do. The evidence was mounting that he had been behind some of these attacks on Adapazan and several other allied planets.

"Barons, baronesses, Archmages. I wish to confess. Yes, I was behind a number of the earlier raids upon several of your planets, just as Mage Jarka Dragon has so cleverly discovered. You all know the history between Rehor and Adapazan and Zoran, who deprived us of our allied planet. I was to have been its baron; my throne was stolen from me by Zoran some twenty years ago. Yes, there is much ill will between us, as well as several of you "haves" worlds. Rehor is a "have-not" world, a mountainous world, where we can barely eke out a living. Yes, initially I struck a deal with some Red Dragons to rob gem shipments. Please note, we only robbed gem shipments and hardly anyone was physically harmed in the process. I only wanted to get funds that our people need to purchase the high priced grains from you that we must have to survive the long, harsh winters on Rehor. That is my sole defense."

"However, I admit that I was a total fool in believing that I could hold honest deals with the Red Dragons. I too have been utterly betrayed by these foul beasts. They attack our people as well as yours. I have had nothing to do with the mass slaughter of innocent villages that have been occurring recently. We only raided gem shipments. Baron Zoran is a bigger man than I am. I came here today fully expecting him to deny me and my people any and all magical weapons with which to defeat these foul beasts from Hell. Yet, he has given us all his word to share his enchanted weapons with all of us. I would like to take this time to apologize to Baron Zoran and the others from whom I have stolen a few gemstone shipments. I am sorry that I ever stuck bargains with the red devils to do that. However, what is past is past. I urge us all to let the past be in the past. Today, we face a common enemy, the dragons. I believe that we are all going to have to work together if we humans are to survive. Thank you." He sat down. The room was silent. No one had expected or even predicted such a speech!

Baron Alvaro looked at the list of topics, drawing a line through this one much further down on the agenda, and then stared over to Zoran, unsure what to do or say. Zoran had not predicted this political bombshell from his enemy. Yet, his enemy had apologized and acknowledged his actions. True, he had placed this topic of Rehor's involvement on the agenda, but Baron Clav had already brought it up. Once more, Zoran longed for the wisdom of his late uncles. They would know the precise thing to do and say. Even Alvaro was taken aback by this sudden admission from Baron Clav. What to do? What to say? Instinctively, Zoran knew that what and how he responded was extremely vital, perhaps pivotal.

He rose slowly, sensing all eyes were upon him once more. He stalled for time, clearing his throat. "Apology accepted, Baron Clav. You are right; mere gemstones can be replaced, but human lives cannot. In the past, yes, you are right; we have been archenemies, though not by my choice. I accept your apology and I completely agree with you. It is high time that we put the past behind us and look to the future. We agree, the future looks bleak indeed. In a way, barons, baronesses, Archmages, all of this dragon problem can be laid at my feet."

Zoran decided to be equally honest. "After all, it was I who brought the first dragons to our Federation, Adapazan in specific. I admit that thus far, the relationship that we have with the Gold Dragons has been ideal. Yet, I cannot escape the singular fact that my having brought the golds to Adapazan to help defend us has forced you to strike similar bargains with the other types of dragons if only out of self-preservation goals. The record is clear, at no time have I used my gold dragons to attack any of your worlds. Yet, they are an unlimited weapon, and I can see why others were forced to strike similar bargains with other dragons. Let's ignore the fact that they were all starving to death on Voss."

"For quite a few years, dragons and humans managed to live together without strife. Now, however, that is changing and changing at an alarming rate. I have been doing all that I can to prevent an escalation of the conflict and strife between our races. We must avoid an all-out war with the dragons or countless innocent humans will pay an awful price. It is nearly impossible for me to get that haunting image of our village where a thousand men, women, and children were incinerated by Red Dragons. Their charred bodies will haunt me forever. Several of you also have similar hideous memories now."

"Baron Gang, I cannot forget the images in my mind of your valiant, brave sister, who arrived unconscious in my Circle, her hand dissolving right before my very eyes, and I was helpless to prevent it. Hideous. Similarly, one lone woman survived briefly from the inferno. Jarka tried to get her lifesaving potion into her mouth, but her mouth was so badly seared from the flames that she could not even swallow. She died in my arms. Yes, we face a formidable enemy, but we must do all that we can to prevent an all-out war with dragon-kind. If not, such images will swamp us all!"

"Our best chance is to put aside our past petty differences and unite to counter the dragons, just as Baron Clav suggests. Together, we may be able to prevent an all-out war, one that we may not be able to win, I might add. Still, we must not give in to their demands. We must maintain our own values and integrity. Without that, we are no better than the dragons. Let's not antagonize them further. Let's not force them into a war with us. Yet, if war does come, we must be as prepared as we can be."

"Baron Leo, Baron Stefan, will you join me in accepting Baron Clav's apology?" he ended up asking. Both men rose and magnanimously added their acceptance much to Baron Storm Clav's relief. For once, Baron Clav had worked out the right way to defuse a very nasty situation. He could have faced numerous High Council sanctions, debilitating ones at that.

Jarka, on the other hand, was most curious to discover who had so counseled him. She knew that he had not the wisdom or intelligence to have come up with this countermove. She covertly observed the Rehor contingent. The three barons were all Clav, children of old Bogdan. Ah, two of their wives and baronesses were Hadwig, daughters of the late Eckhard Hadwig, from Dietmar, also the archenemy of Adapazan. These two women were very bright, highly intelligent, she observed. Jarka theorized that Gisela and Greta had orchestrated this brilliant move on Baron Clav's part. She smiled as she realized this. At the same moment, her eyes met those of Gisela's across the space between the opposing tables. Gisela smiled back at her. Jarka made a note to tell Zoran about her observations: the Hadwig daughters were probably now calling the shots on Rehor, not the Clav men, Storm, Bran, or Carsten. Perhaps things were changing now for the better, she mused.

The next topic was the sharing of information on what types of dragons lived on what planets, their numbers, and locales. Baron Alvaro wanted everyone to have as accurate a picture of the dragon population and locations as possible. Everyone shared what they knew and all took copious notes, none more so than Jarka. "As it is close to dinnertime, we will adjourn until ten tomorrow. As usual, we have arranged for your entertainment. However, because of the very serious dragon threat, Anita and I have decided to bring the performers here into the fortress and not take you all out into our great city to the various theaters and halls. So tonight, we are proud to present a musical play in the Great Hall. It will begin at eight sharp. Until then, please enjoy the finest food that Alta has to offer. Meeting is adjourned." He brought his gavel down hard.

Chapter 10 Treachery

Alfonsina mourned her lost mate for several days. Slowly hatred festered in her mind. Humans had done this and she swore to get revenge for her mate. For days, the how totally eluded her. At first, she toyed with the idea of flying over the fortifications and spewing forth her deadly fires upon one and all.

Alfonsina was not stupid and quickly discarded this notion. "No, it is these barons who actually control the humans on these many worlds. The barons must be made to pay!" she swore to the walls of her cavern. How? That stumped her for some time. She took to human form and mingled among those of Baron Storm Clav's court on Rehor. There she learned of the High Council meeting on Alta, and Alfonsina now saw her golden opportunity!

"What do you make of Clav's admission? Can he be serious? Do we dare trust him?" asked Baron Leo over dinner. "Besides, have you noticed that the Neutral Baron Karl is being uncommonly sympathetic this meeting?"

"I haven't heard a word from the Hadwigs of Dietmar. Baron Cadfeel of Anwyn is strangely silent too," put in Baroness Lida. "Our archenemies are being awfully quiet."

"I think he's realized that the dragons that he allowed to come to Rehor cannot be trusted. Quite possibly are also attacking him now," Zoran suggested. "Time will tell. I trust him as far as I can see him. Still, let's accept it at face value. He is right; we must unite if we have any chance against the dragons."

Jarka spoke up, unable to withhold her observations any longer. "I think that the Hadwig daughters, who are married to the Clav men, are the ones who orchestrated Storm's speech this afternoon. Storm could not have thought that up himself. I suspect Gisela may have taken over the real control of Rehor from Strom, especially if his so called bargains with the reds have completely backfired on him." The small group discussed her observations for some time, which seemed very likely.

"Come on. We'd best get to the Great Hall. He said it starts at eight," Zdenka pointed out, noticing that many others were beginning to exit the dining hall on their way to the musical play.

They joined the throng filing into the Great Hall. At the far end, a huge stage had been recently constructed, complete with an orchestra pit below the stage. Already the place was filling up, and Zoran and his group found seats in the center middle portion of the Great Hall. Great tapestries hung from several walls along with some paintings, presumably some men and women of historical note on Alta. Before long, the room was packed with the many barons, baronesses, their advisors, mages, and Archmages. Jarka estimated the crowd at close to two hundred fifty, a large gathering of perhaps the most powerful people in the Federation of the Sixteen Planets. She felt a little uneasy. Too many key people in one confined space, she thought.

Baroness Anita walked onto the stage and the lights magically dimmed. "Welcome one and all. The Alta Players are proud to present this musical play entitled the Rise of Man." As she walked off the stage, taking a seat beside her husband in the front row, the two dozen musicians began to play the introduction overture. Zdenka rested her head on Zoran's shoulders, content to relax and enjoy the unusual sounding music.

Several minutes later, the overture finished and the flutes announced the beginning act. A portly woman in a red dress walked slowly onto the stage; the play was about to begin. Just then, Zdenka shrieked. Almost simultaneously, Verushka, Chesna, and Zelenka's shrill voices joined hers. "Dragon attack! Dragon attack!" The portly woman suddenly morphed into a mature Red Dragon. Her mouth opened up, and she spewed forth an enormous expanding cone of red hot flames, directed towards the audience. The four women saw the intention of the Red Dragon: incinerate one half of those in attendance. The cone expanded outward rapidly and would engulf at least half of the people in the room. That was just the dragon's first fiery blast!

Ivana saw the flames coming out of the dragon's mouth and cast her power spell. Time stopped for her. Frantically, she tried to think of some way to protect those in the front row from taking the full force of the flames. The only thing that she could think of was to somehow throw up an invisible Force Wall. She raced down the isle of people frozen in time. Once at the front, she cast her spell and used her hands to prop the wall at a forty-five degree angle, hoping to deflect much of the searing flames upward. As time resumed, she felt the push of the burst of flames against her wall, and she strained her whole body to hold it up and keep it from being knocked over.

In the next instant some twenty additional spells detonated and massive chaos ensued. The ever expanding cone of deadly flames surged upwards past Ivana, whose action saved Alvaro and Anita, who would have taken the blast straight on. However, a Disintegrate spell aimed at the head of the dragon took down her wall and the flames immediately expanded in all directions. Ivana dived to the floor, covering her head and praying that somehow it would miss her. A half dozen other Force Walls began appearing over the heads of the crowd, but other Disintegrate spells ran into them, taking some of them down as well.

Zoran cast his Stun Spell and found himself on the grey plain, his will versus that of the dragon. He won and the Red Dragon stood motionless on the stage, unable to launch a second devastating blast of flames. Karel knew better than to teleport onto the beast's neck. Far too many spells were heading towards the dragon. He saw one Disintegrate spell take down Ivana's incredible Force Wall, and for an instant he wondered how the devil she had gotten to the front so quickly. At last, he chose to cast Disintegrate, but first he cast his Mystical Door and stepped onto the right side of the stage. Then he cast it. Archmage Karel found that he truly enjoyed suddenly appearing on the featureless grey plain, facing down this worthy opponent. Already stunned, the dragon's will broke, but not before he sensed that she was valiantly trying to get revenge for the slaying of her mate. *I did that!* Karel planted in her mind and saw her panic and her eyes dim. He knew that he'd won. He watched as the dragon slumped dead on the stage, nearly filling the area completely. He deftly jumped off the stage to avoid being squashed.

He turned to see the room. The Great Hall, although large, was not sufficiently large enough to contain such an enormous blast of dragon fire. Already the wooden ceiling was on fire, as were all the tapestries. Although Ivana's wall had partially deflected the flames upward, still they had begun to come down upon others towards the rear. Here and there a Force Wall still held, keeping the flames off of some. Clothing was on fire. Everywhere, people were screaming, some in pain, some trying to get out of the room, some trying to issue orders. Pure chaos reined.

Jarka maintained a clear head and had dove for the floor. Sensing the death of the dragon and with so much wood on fire, she began to conjure water on the burning areas, extinguishing some of the flames. Of course, clouds of steam resulted, further obstructing everyone's vision. However, other mages followed suit and soon water and steam filled the room. The fires went out, much to the relief of everyone. Many were trampled as they attempted to flee the room. Some lay on the ground with concussions and broken limbs. Others suffered severe burns, especially among the women, many of which had their dresses go up in flames. Screams for help and screams of pain drowned out all other sounds.

Baron Alvaro finally acted. Using a Magnify spell, his voice boomed out over the chaos of noise. "It's over. The dragon is dead. Fires are out. Please, calm down. Tend to the wounded. Anyone who has healing potions come to me. Those of you who are not wounded, please calmly evacuate to your rooms. Let's tend to our fallen comrades at once."

"Well he's a bit confused," Jarka commented to herself as she got back to her feet and examined the charred lower portion of her favorite red gown.

"What's that?" Zdenka asked, thankful that Jarka had risen off of her. Now she could get up as well. Jarka had mostly blocked the flames, and she found herself in good shape.

"If everyone who is uninjured leaves like he asked, who's going to help the injured?" Jarka sneered. "You okay? How about the rest of you?" she turned to examine the others in their party and nearby friends.

"Did my covering Force Wall protect you all?" asked a worried Bernard, dusting himself off and coughing up black soot. "Are you burned dear?" He noticed that Jarka's face was blackened. She rubbed her face and noticed the soot.

"Just fine, soot I think." Quickly, they discovered that singed hair, sooty faces, soaking clothes, and slightly charred dresses were the only damage here in the center of the room. Zdenka spotted Zoran and Ivana way up front, and she ordered her group to make their way there as well.

"I got him," Archmage Karel pronounced as they made their way through the dazed throng. "Someone Stunned the dragon and I killed the infernal thing. Grey plain thing happened again. I won."

"Good thinking love," his wife, Chika praised him. "I kept putting up Force Walls, but they kept getting taken down by Disintegrate spells I think. That was a close call. Some of us could possibly have Shadow Walked out; looks like most didn't though. My god! Look at the carnage over there!" At last, they noticed that not everyone had lucked out. Those on the two far sides and towards the rear took the force of the flames, while many near the exit had gotten trampled and injured. Further, some near the front had also gotten burned, but those were few, thanks to Ivana's quick action.

Baroness Anita had taken a bad burn after Ivana's Force Wall was disintegrated, primarily because her billowing dress had caught fire. At last Jarka got to her. "Let me tend to her, Baron Alvaro. I've got six healing potions on me. I'll give her one right now. Better line up the worst cases for the other five potions. I have more in my bags in my room. Have you a workshop and the ingredients to make more?"

"Please, Jarka. She's in a lot of pain. I have some. I best get them. Zoran, you take charge while I get them. This is awful — my worst nightmare came true!" As she knelt down beside her, he vanished.

Zoran looked around and saw that half had already vacated the room, but many were still tending to the other wounded as best they could. Few had brought any healing potions with them, unfortunately. "Okay everyone, raise your hand if you have someone who desperately needs a healing potion immediately. We have five more at hand with more coming." Many hands raised and Jarka sighed. There were way more than five. She handed a potion vial each to Zdenka, Ivana, Zoran, Bernard, and Verushka. "Here. Go give these to those in need. Chika, you watch over Anita while I go get the rest of mine."

"You got it!" Chika replied and began helping Anita finish off the potion. Then she helped the burned woman rise and sit back down on a chair. The potion began working almost at once, giving her immediate relief from the sharp pain of her leg and arm burns.

A few minutes later, Zoran called out, "Mages, let's move the dead over here for now. Here comes Alvaro and Jarka with more healing potions. Be patient; we will get to the worst cases first." Others began moving the dead, and he hoped those would be few. Jarka doled out her remaining six healing potions, while Alvaro dispensed nearly two dozen, his current supply.

"Well, it's obvious that we will need three times this many healing potions. Damn. Jarka, can you whip up more? I've a fully equipped lab. I'll Message everyone and ask that all those who can make healing potions to join you, Jarka," the worried baron asked.

"You got it. Just show me where. Bernard, you come along and lend me a hand, dear."

"Hey, I'll take her, Alvaro," one of his mages offered, only too glad to get out of the filthy room. All this was a bit too much for the young man. He cast a Mystical Door, and Jarka and Bernard followed him to the lab. Soon, six other mages joined them.

"How much are we going to make?" one asked her.

"Lots! So many are burned. Make at least four dozen potions gang, maybe more. We've got plenty of broken bones to heal as well as those who were burned," Jarka replied, rather taking charge. Around ten, she sat back looking at her dozen potion bottles now cooling on the rack. "Chill. Chill," she began casting, cooling them down so that they could be used at once. "Here, dear. Take these to Alvaro. Tell him another batch is about done."

When Bernard returned, he found the Great Hall in vastly different shape. Hundreds of Clean spells had removed much of the soot and charred tapestry remains. Six bodies lay covered by white sheets over in one corner. Dozens of others were carefully arrayed on the floor, chairs moved far out of the way. "Here's a dozen more. Jarka says to expect another dozen shortly. Is it six dead?" he asked.

"Unfortunately yes, mostly advisors or wives," Baron Alvaro replied. "No baron, baroness, or mage — thank god for that! Tell her that we are going to need at least six dozen more potions." He took the rack of vials and Bernard stepped back through his Mystical Door.

Around midnight, Jarka and Bernard delivered the last of the potions to Alvaro. The other mages had returned to their quarters as exhausted as she. All told, the seven had brewed over a hundred healing potions. When she arrived with the last batch, the Great Hall had been thoroughly cleaned up and chairs neatly stacked against a far wall. A dozen more men and women were given another round of potions before they were helped back to their quarters.

"Thank you Mage Jarka, Zoran, everyone," an exhausted Alvaro said. "I'm famished. Shall we visit the pantry? Besides, I'd like to discuss what happened in here tonight with you. Thank god for the advanced warning, Archmages." A short time later, they all began helping themselves to leftovers, many guzzling mugs of ale.

"I'm sorry that we did not have much advanced warning from our Foresight spells. Evidently, they were not triggered until the dragon actually came on stage," Archmage Zdenka explained.

"We were squarely in front of the fire. How did Ivana get to us and how was it that we were spared the full force of the dragon fire?" Baron Alvaro asked.

"I stopped time, but I couldn't think of anything else to do but to erect a Force Wall in front of you all, deflecting the flames upward," Ivana explained humbly. "Someone disintegrated the wall though. I think many tried to cast Disintegrate spells at the dragon and my wall was in the way."

"Good thinking, Ivana," Archmage Zdenka praised her newest Archmage. "Your fast action prevented a mass slaughter of people. An awful lot of mages cast Force Walls as well. I believe that is what minimized the casualties. Only six dead is a miracle. Panic caused more damage than the flames really. I've never seen so many broken bones before."

"I managed to Stun the dragon," Zoran explained, "but Karel got the kill."

"Yes, I certainly did." Karel puffed up a bit, thankful that his accomplishment had not gone unacknowledged or unnoticed.

"Well done, Archmage. I am so thankful that there was only one Red Dragon this time. She must have somehow infiltrated the production crew. I sent a mage to check on the real woman, but he found her dead body in her home. Evidently, this dragon murdered her and morphed into her body's shape. She certainly bluffed her way in here well. Why though? Why did she attack us? Are there going to be more of these attacks on us?"

"Baron, I got a clue when we were on the grey plains, will-battling," Karel spoke up. "She was seeking revenge for the slaying of her mate. Somehow she held the barons responsible for that, though I don't see her line of reasoning. My theory at the moment is that this was one single dragon out looking for revenge. I don't believe that this is part of a concerted effort to kill us all, not at this time, baron."

"Revenge? Well, that would make it make sense to me. I can see that. Let's hope this is an isolated instance. However, I am canceling all remaining after-meeting affairs. It is just too risky. We averted disaster tonight, but only narrowly!" Baron Alvaro declared.

"I think that is wise, baron," Zoran agreed with him. "There is too much at stake to risk another encounter."

"Glad that we see eye to eye on this. I'm also glad that we had the foresight to request all available Archmages to attend. I'm scared to think of the results had we not had all of you here tonight. Say, we are going to need at least another fifty healing potions in the morning. We've still got some serious cases. They are stabilized now or so my physicians say, but I want everyone back to battery if possible. I'm cancelling the morning session, Jarka, and have sent off for more potion ingredients. They should be arriving by dawn."

"Excellent. Say, I could use a bath. Clean spells are just not the same thing," she teased.

Baron Alvaro personally visited with each attendee the next morning and saw that the newly made potions were distributed to those who still needed healing. If nothing else, he made sure that every baron, baroness, mage, and assistant was in good shape and did not need further healing. If they did, he made certain that they received the potions as they were made later that morning.

The High Council resumed at one the next afternoon. First on the agenda was a full explanation of what had happened with the dragon. Many wanted to know whose spell actually killed the dragon. Several others wanted to know how the flames had been initially diverted by Ivana. Bit by bit, the whole story became clear to everyone. Archmage Karel was heaped with praise as well as Archmage Ivana for her timely dispersal of the initial blast of fire. Everyone realized that had she not deflected it, the damage and carnage would have been extremely severe. Still six lives had been lost.

After that, Baron Leo set the stage for the rest of the afternoon session. "Say, when the attack came, it was an utter chaos of spells. Many countered our own defensive spells. Had someone not accidentally dispelled Ivana's Force Wall, we might have suffered far less from the dragon's breath. We need organized plans of defense and attack, should this happen again." None disagreed and they began to work out ways and means. Most plans depended upon the type of dragon attacking them along with the number of dragons and their location: inside or outside. There were so many variables to consider that the barons spent the whole afternoon working out plan after plan. Several promised to give copies of the agreed upon plans to every baron before the High Council was finished.

The next morning session again was diverted just as Baron Alvaro brought his gavel down. Baron Storm Clav asked, "Say, how the blazes to we detect a dragon in our midst? Look, she appeared to be the human singer. Surely there must be some way that we can detect a dragon that is infiltrating us! My god, anyone of us here could be a dragon in disguise!" Clearly, Baron Clav was far more shaken up than he let on to others, Mage Jarka concluded.

However, his point was quite valid. Anyone of the people in the room could be a dragon in disguise! Off went the discussion for the rest of the day!

Many of the Archmages pointed out that if the dragon used the Morph Self spell, they would appear as an exact duplicate of the person they were mimicking.

However, a Detect Magic spell, most agreed, would likely show the entire body form as being magic. Several excused themselves to test out this theory. However, Archmage Karel and Zoran pointed out that dragons could ordinarily assume human form and that this additional ability was likely not a Morph Self spell, but something inherent within the dragon species.

"Why would a dragon have an inherent ability to morph in to a human form?" asked Archmage Ivana. This then led to a lengthy discussion — pure speculation on everyone's part. No one knew the answer to that question, and Zoran decided that this was a key piece of knowledge that they needed. Somehow the answer seemed to be of vital importance, though he could not say just how or why. Many theories were suggested, but nothing came of their speculations. Still, the question of how to detect them when the dragons assumed human forms not via the Morph Spell seemed key. Zoran did share his experiences with Emil and Renata when they first met them some twenty years ago.

Soon the discussions centered on how to best tell if a person was a person or a dragon. Quickly Zoran realized that this was a futile witch hunt. Before long, everyone would be suspecting anyone who acted a little odd was a dragon! Zdenka whispered, "This is crazy talk. They will be accusing nearly anyone of being a dragon. The only true way is to attempt to cut them with a normal sword. If they are really a dragon, they won't be cut. If they are a human, they will be cut, but then they would also be wounded or killed. This is madness."

"I know dear. I know. They are afraid, scared, and frightened," he whispered back. He was only too ready for the supper break.

Zoran and his friends had no more gotten to their rooms after the hushed evening meal when Baron Alvaro came knocking. "Please, private word with you, baron." Alvaro looked thin and distraught. Nervous might also be applicable, Zdenka thought.

"Sure, come on in. Our meeting took strange turns today," Zoran said consolingly, estimating that the baron was worried about the planned agenda being thrown completely off.

"Well yes, that too. No, baron, may I speak frankly with you?" Baron Alvaro asked. His voice held a touch of desperateness in it. Zoran nodded. "Look, I know that you are aligned with the other 'have' planets even though in all honesty, Adapazan is really with us, a 'have-not' planet. Nevertheless, Zoran, I am growing increasingly afraid. This dragon problem is getting out of hand. Look. It took the combined efforts of all us Duskas and Archmages and mages to thwart this single Red Dragon. After the Council is over and everyone returns to their own worlds, what are we to do? I simply do not have the Archmages that you have, Zoran. I have a small army of some five thousand, but as you have pointed out, they will be wiped out in one small dragon attack. My garrison forces will be useless to protect us."

"We on Alta are horse breeders. Rolling hills of grasslands — that's Alta. Mind you, we here love our land, our planet. We get by trading horses off-world. We have few real mines of consequence here, few real resources. Our people are spread out far and wide — ranches are sometimes ten miles apart. If the dragons begin to systematically attack us, what can I possibly do to protect my people?"

"We have a few large cities and of course three fortresses with our Circles.

Puerto here is the largest. Yet I cannot house all of the citizens of Puerto here inside these stone walls should the dragons launch an assault on us. What can I possibly do?"

Knock. Knock. Zoran did not get a chance to answer. He was never more thankful to hear someone knocking on his door before. He had no idea how to answer Baron Alvaro. He opened the door apologetically. Alvaro nodded.

"Oh hi. Well met, baron. It's been a long time since you were vacationing on Asami." Baron Goro Yoko grinned in his usual playful manner. Zoran could not help remembering their first meeting when he and Zdenka along with Jarka and Bernard took their honeymoon on Asami as guests of Goro and his wife Kimiko. He motioned for the baron to come on inside. He nodded to Baron Alvaro. "I do hope that I am not interrupting anything. If I am, I can come back later."

"No, we're fine. What can I do for you? Is Kimiko recovering from her burns?" Zoran asked politely.

"Yes, we are all so grateful for everything that you've done for us, you too, Baron Alvaro. No, I came to ask your advice. Perhaps you can add yours too, Baron Alvaro. You see, this dragon problem has us on Asami very worried. As you know, there is no large land mass on our world, only thousands of tiny islands. We were hard pressed to even find a location for our third Circle of Ascension. No, we are frankly extremely frightened. What are we to do if the dragons attack us on Asami? We have no army to speak of and such would be totally useless as you say. We've a few mages and an Archmage, but our meager population is sprawled out on thousands of small islands across the whole planet. How can we possibly defend ourselves from a dragon attack?"

He did not expect Alvaro to chuckle and he face flushed. "Sorry. No offense meant, Goro. It is just that I came here minutes ago and asked Zoran that very same question."

"Oh, I see. Sorry. Well, I have to admit that we are extremely worried about all this. We are nearly defenseless," Goro added, recovering his momentary embarrassment. His carefree lifestyle had taken a turn towards seriousness. Zoran remembered him as more of a fun loving, carefree beach bum. Hidden beneath this was the enslavement of young women who were turned into human mermaids and forced to swim the oceans recovering pearls. Fine pearls and fish products were the planet's sole exports. Nearly all else had to be imported from other worlds.

Chika and Akira glared at Baron Goro. They had been enslaved mermaids some twenty years ago and had been rescued from death by Zoran. On Adapazan, they had established new lives and were now vital members of Zoran's group. Resentment against the ruling barons of their original home world of Asami flared up once more. Zdenka sensed this and sent Zoran a private Message. He flinched slightly as he too sensed the women's rising resentment.

Just as he was about to fumble for an answer, another knock saved him. This time it was one of his enemies at the door, Baron Cadfeel Arun of the desert world of Anwyn. "Oh, sorry to intrude, baron. I was hoping to have a private word with you." Cadfeel was obviously quite startled to find Alvaro and Goro also present.

"It's all right. Please, come on in baron. Gentlemen, if you don't mind," he said to Alvaro and Goro. "Both were just asking me about how they could possibly defend their planets from the dragons."

Cadfeel grinned and relaxed a little. Obviously he was under a good deal of tension. Making an impromptu visit to the quarters of his archenemy was not something to be taken lightly. "Thank you baron. I know that you and I have had our disagreements over the years. However this dragon mess is most troublesome. Anwyn is a desert world with few resources. This surprise attack against us all has frankly given us all a fright. Can we put aside our differences for the time being and work together against this common foe? I am not too proud to come here to ask for your help and guidance. How can we defend ourselves against these raiding dragons?"

"Yes, our differences are petty compared to the danger that all of us are facing," Zoran agreed with him. "We all must work together, baron. As I said before, I and my staff will do everything we can to help all other worlds. You have my word on that. Unfortunately, barons, I don't have any pat answer to your key question of how to defend your people. Baron Alvaro, I think that this should be the first topic that we all address first thing in the morning. Obviously, this is on everyone's mind. However, I will say this. The 'have' worlds must step in to assist the 'have-not' worlds." Zoran knew instinctively that this detail was sure to go over extremely well with the Neutral planets and his enemy planets. After all, this was the key underlying fact that had caused so much strife and dissension between the planets for centuries. The broadening grins on all three baron's faces told him that he'd said precisely the correct thing.

Zoran added, "Rather than trying to answer each of you right now, let me go talk to the 'haves' and see if I can get their agreement. In the morning session, we can all put our heads together and try to give all of the barons some concrete steps that can be taken."

"That will be a first, Zoran. If you can get the 'haves' to help us out, it will be a miracle," Baron Cadfeel proclaimed. His long standing hatred and contempt for the 'have' worlds could not be kept at bay.

"You have my word. I will get them to see reason. Expect to hear more at the morning meeting. Barons, if our meeting tomorrow is not satisfactory, please drop by here in the evening and we will talk about it more." Zoran shook each baron's hand and they left.

"Well, that was interesting," Mage Jarka commented. "Our enemies are becoming our friends. Are you sure that you can get Gladno and the others to go along with this?"

"Dunno, but I have to try. I best go see Leo and Stefan right now. Message me if anything comes up." Zoran kissed Zdenka and left hastily.

Ten minutes later, six barons met in one of the private rooms given to Baron Leo, who represented Gladno. Baron Gaspard Gervaise of Gonda, Baron John Witherspoon of Terra, Baron Arcangelo Mondo of Cosma, and Baron Stefan Pavel of Valtr joined Zoran and Leo. All were quite curious about why Zoran had requested this surprise, clandestine meeting. However, all these young men knew from experience that any really significant business of the Federation always took place at night, not during the actual Council meetings proper.

"Thank you all for coming on such short notice," Zoran began, noticing the all five men were quite attentive and curious. "I have just had three barons come to me privately and beg me for help with the dragon problem. One was our enemy, Baron Cadfeel. Two were Neutrals. They simply do not have the ways and means of defending their own people, should the dragons attack them outright. Baron Cadfeel wishes to put aside our differences and work together on this problem. Barons, I feel that we have a golden opportunity here to reach out to those who have been fighting against us all these years and form new bonds of trust. Perhaps we can end these centuries-old feuds."

Baron Leo chuckled, "That's all well and good, Zoran. What did you promise them that we'd do?" Zoran smiled. Leo had become an astute leader, much like his father.

"I promised them that you'd all help out. Look, the desert world of Anwyn simply has no resources to manufacture swords, let alone swords of high enough quality to be enchanted to be able to affect a dragon. Asami is even less able to defend its people. Even Alvaro is scared out of his wits here on Alta," Zoran explained.

"So we are to make them swords?" asked Baron Stefan.

"Right now, I think food and magical blades are needed. I know that Archmage Karel is meeting with several other Archmages, educating them on how to make his Dragon Slayer swords. I know that several of them have disposed of the red's carcass, confiscating the blood that is needed for the weapons. I think that it is prudent of us to begin making as many enchanted blades as we can. However, if the dragons attack, food is going to be a huge problem for all of us. It probably would be wise for us to stockpile supplies, just in case."

John spoke up, "True, if the dragons begin systematically attacking us on Terra, the farmers will be nearly defenseless. Farms are out in the open and cover much of Terra. They will have to be pulled back into the safety of the larger towns and cities and fortresses and there goes food production. He's right; we should stockpile as much as possible, beginning now."

"Asami is going to be in dire straits if dragons attack them. They get nearly all their food from us," Baron Arcangelo of Cosma pointed out. "Zoran has a point. If we ignore them, we will lose many of our trading partners which will create an economic disaster for us in the long run. Besides, this may well end centuries of strife between us and our enemy worlds."

"Okay, we agree with you, Zoran. Let's hope this works out, but I still say that we keep a sharp eye out for treachery. I don't trust our enemies any farther than I can see them," Baron Stefan declared adamantly.

"Thanks. Tomorrow morning, Alvaro is going to make the first topic of discussion how to defend our worlds. Honestly, I have very few ideas at the moment," Zoran continued. "I do believe that we may well find ourselves having to take in refugees from some of the worlds, like Asami. The people there have no place to hide or protect themselves — nothing but tiny, widely scattered islands."

Baron Gaspard spoke up, "One thing that I do know for sure after that surprise attack last night, we darn well better have a huge supply of healing potions and medical supplies stockpiled. Do you realize that Alvaro went through nearly two hundred healing potions?" Several hadn't and the six men chatted a while longer before Zoran yawned and headed back to his room for the night.

As Baron Alvaro sounded his gavel to start the morning session, Baron John Witherspoon spoke up. "Baron Alvaro, may I say a few words before we get started?" Alvaro nodded, hoping to hear something encouraging.

John spoke decisively, "We are facing a common enemy. We must put aside our age old conflicts among us and band together if we are to survive. I speak for many other barons. We will do all that we can to provide food and weapons to combat this threat. All normal trading payments are hereby suspended. Barons, let us know what you need and we will do our best to see that you get it. We will let you know as soon as enchanted weapons are available. Archmage Karel is working with other Archmages to get production of weapons going. I suggest that we all begin to stockpile food, medicines, and healing potions. Further, if dragon attacks do become widespread, many of us are willing and ready to accept refugees from your worlds where they cannot be protected. We want to put all of the rest of you more at ease. We will help all that we can."

"Thank you, baron and all of you. We may well need all of your help," Baron Alvaro replied. His relief was plainly visible. Jarka's keen eyes observed that nearly all of the Neutral aligned barons displayed similar relief as did their archenemies. Zoran had scored a small victory. "Now then, the first topic for this morning is just how do we go about defending ourselves? Asami is going to have a huge problem with this. I suspect many other worlds will also be in dire straits if the dragons make a coordinated effort to attack us."

Silence. Soon the embarrassing silence was broken by rustling of feet and squirming butts. No one had a reasonable answer. At last Zdenka spoke up. "Baron Alvaro, might I take a stab with this one?" her alto voice echoed solemnly around the room.

"Please Baroness Archmage, please!" The relief on Alvaro's face told all.

"I've been giving this considerable thought, ever since our village of one thousand innocent men, women, and children was destroyed. It seems to me that we have to look at this situation from two points of view. First, if dragons swoop down from the sky and use their breath weapons against a town, village, hamlet or farmstead, there is so very little that we honestly can do for them. On Adapazan, we have put mages at many of the larger villages and mines. They are under orders to Message us if an attack comes. Then, we muster all the strength that we can and head there, hoping and praying that we are in time to prevent total annihilation. Admittedly, this had not been very successful as yet. Second, if the dragons attack us and have to remain in their human forms, we have a vastly improved chance of defending against them. In this case, they must resort to using their magical spells and vast physical strength. Still, we can combat them this way."

"If the dragons do launch a war with us, somehow we must both protect our people and have a way to combat them. As I see it, we have to fight them when they are forced to assume human forms."

"How can that be done?" Alvaro interrupted her. He was following her line of thinking closely as were most all of those present.

"There is a way that we can do both. If we can build vast underground cities carved from the bedrock, then we can house large numbers of our people. By making the access to these subterranean cities narrow and constricted, we force the dragons to assume human forms if they want to attack us. If we do not have any large chambers where they could revert back to their dragon forms, they simply cannot use their breath weapons on us. We stand a chance of holding our own this way."

"I like it. We could lay in provisions and medical supplies. People could live in relative safety as long as there is an underground water supply as well," Baron Alvaro took over, already working out just how this might be done.

"Precisely. Mages and Archmages could be given the task of making such places of safety. We have many spells that we can use to facilitate rapid underground tunneling. Still, I don't know that it would be possible to house millions underground, baron, nor for how long," Zdenka admitted.

The idea took hold. One by one, the other barons added to her ideas, and the High Council soon passed a motion that each baron was to begin building just such a subterranean city near their Circles. Supplies would be brought in and stored there. At last, the barons had an action that they could do, and the morning passed rapidly as ideas were discussed and accepted. Baron Strom pointed out that even if the dragons never attacked, these underground strongholds would be a valuable asset in any time of trouble or siege.

During the lunch break, Zdenka was constantly interrupted by others dropping by to thank her for her brilliant ideas. She barely had time enough to eat. When the afternoon session began, Zoran decided to make a suggestion of his own.

"Look, we know so very little about the dragons — our enemies who have been attacking us. Where are they located? What worlds? How many of them are there? Do they work together effectively? I know from Chan and Wen that the greens do not work together at all well, for example. We ought to identify what type of dragons are where. Then, somehow we ought to ascertain their numbers and anything else that we can find out about their habits and methods of attack. Plus, I, for one, am curious about what actually was on Voss before they had to abandon that planet. Where did the dragons come from? How is it that they naturally can assume human form? Have they encountered other humans on some other unknown to us world? I can go on and on. There is so much that we simply do not know about our foe that we ought to know."

Baron Strom Clav spoke up, "On Rehor, we know where some reds live. They have caverns located high in the mountains, wholly inaccessible, except by mages and Duskas. None live in locations where I could march an army to assail them. They are not stupid beasts."

Again, the barons had something that they could do, and they began a coordinated listing of what they knew about the dragons on their worlds. They drew up an initial listing, then added more on several charts which were then magically duplicated and given to each baron, all forty-eight. That evening, Zdenka delivered the forty-eight sets of charts to the various barons.

Chart 1 Dragon Types and Locations

Planet	Predominate Terrain	Dragons Present (F-friendly; E-enemy; N-neutral)
(Allied Planets)		
Adapazan	Mountainous	Golden Dragons (F)
Gladno	Forested	Golden Dragons (F)
Terra	Agrarian	Golden Dragons (F)
Valtr	Hills	Golden Dragons (F)
Cosma	Agrarian	Golden Dragons (F)
Gonda	Plains	Golden Dragons (F)
(Enemy Planets)		
Rehor	Mountainous	White Dragons (N)
		Black Dragons (E)
		Red Dragons (E)
Jing	Swamp/Marsh	Blue Dragons (N)
		Green Dragons (E)
Dietmar	Snow	White Dragons (N)
Anwyn	Desert	Brown Dragons (N)
(Neutral Planets)		
Isi	Plains	Grey Dragons (N)
		Brown Dragons (N)
		Red Dragons (E)
Gerde	Mountainous	White Dragons (N)
		Black Dragons (E)
		Red Dragons (E)
Alta	Rolling Hills	Brown Dragons (N)
		White Dragons (N)
		Black Dragons (E)
		Red Dragons (E)
Maeve	Forested	Green Dragons (E)
		Black Dragons (E)
		Red Dragons (E)
Chana	Desert	Brown Dragons (N)
Asami	Water	Blue Dragons (N)

Chart 2 Dragon Statistics Currently Known

Dragon Race (F-friendly; E-enemy; N-neutral)	Breath Weapon	Size (Feet)	Resistance To Magic Spells	
Golden (F)	Fire + Electrical	55-70	70%	
Black (E)	Acid	50	50%	
Red (E)	Fire	50	50%	
Green (E)	Rotting Slime	70	15%	(snake-like)
White (N)	Cold	40	30%	
Blue (N)	Neurotoxin Paralysis	70	30%	(snake- like)
Brown (N)	Electrical	60	30%	
Grey (N)	Suffocating Smoke	50	30%	

Locations (estimated number, where known)
(+ means far more came than requested)

Golden (F)	Adapazan (40), Gonda (30), Terra (35), Cosma (40), Valtr (40), Gladno (40)
Black (E)	Rehor (40+), Gerde (35+), Alta (25+), Maeve (30+)
Red (E)	Rehor (40+), Gerde (30+), Alta (25+), Maeve (30+), Isi (25+)
Green (E)	Jing (50+), Maeve (30+)
White (N)	Rehor (25+), Gerde (25+), Alta (30+), Dietmar (40+)
Blue (N)	Jing (40+), Asami (40+)
Brown (N)	Isi (35+), Alta (40+), Anwyn (40+), Chana (40+)
Grey (N)	Isi (30+)

Chart 3 The Barons and Baronesses

Planet (Allied Planets)	Predominate Terrain	Rulers (Baron & Baroness)
Adapazan	Mountainous	Zoran & Zdenka Vladislov
		Tomas & Verushka (Dragon) Vladislov
		Jan & Reina (Matous) Vavrin
Gladno	Forested	Leo & Lida (Vladislov) Matous
		Alfons & Valérie Matous
		Dominik & Katerina Matous
Terra	Agrarian	John & Dusana (Matous) Witherspoon
		Hank & Vana (Pavel) Witherspoon
		William & Ariane (Mondo) Witherspoon
Valtr	Hills	Stefan & Rayna (Vladislov) Pavel
		Zdenk & Zusa (Vavrin) Pavel
		Daron & Kamila (Lota) Pavel
Cosma	Agrarian	Arcangelo & Gabriella Mondo
		Bernardo & Berta Mondo
		Vincens & Floriana (Mondo) Gervaise
Gonda	Plains	Gaspard & Andrea (Pavel) Gervaise
		Henri & Elizabeth (Witherspoon) Gervaise
		Flavio and Adelphe Gervaise

```
(Enemy Planets)
Rehor      Mountainous   Storm & Gisela (Hadwig) Clav
                         Bran & Greta (Hadwig) Clav
                         Carsten & Kate Clav
Jing       Swamp/Marsh   Gang & Juan Meerong
                         Jie & Lan Meerong
                         Li & Lian Meerong
Dietmar    Snow          Adolf & Greta (Clav) Hadwig
                         Burkhard & Cede (Clav) Hadwig
                         Conrad & Elisa Hadwig
Anwyn      Desert        Cadfeel & Catrin Alun
                         Aeron & Beanwenn Alun
                         Derog & Ceri Alun
(Neutral Planets)
Isi        Plains        Chua & Alameda Yamitiwa
                         Hania& Chumani Yamitiwa
                         Keme & Jaci Yamitiwa
Gerde      Mountainous   Karl & Madde Ebbe
                         Emil & Hella Ebbe
                         Konrad & Karla Ebbe
Alta       Rolling Hills Alvaro & Anita Cencion
                         Basilio & Benita Cencion
                         Eduardo & Concha Cencion
Maeve      Forested      Ailfrid & Breana Ahren
                         Brennan & Caitie Ahren
                         Cathal & Eithne Ahren
Chana      Desert        Atir & Aminta Makeda
                         Amal & Batya Makeda
                         Even & Degana Makeda
Asami      Water         Goro & Kimiko Yoko
                         Hiro & Fuji Yoko
                         Jurou & Mana Yoko
```

Chart 4 The Forty-four Registered Archmages

```
Planet     Archmages (Age)
(Allied Planets)
Adapazan  Baron Zoran Vladislov (39)
           Baroness Zdenka Vladislov (40)
           Baroness Verushka (Dragon) Vladislov (20)
           Karel Ambrose (43)
           Nadia (Vladislov) Dragon (19)
           Marek Aceda (44)
           Ivana Jakuba (22)
          (Emil and Renata Gold Dragons)
           Jakob Hamil (30) (Tratky Province)
           Edmund Kamil (28) (Radim Province)
           Dana Ctirad (27) (Zavou Province)
           Kate Zimir (25) (Veklov Province)
           Marjeta Dezda (23) (Vraz Province)

Gladno     Zelenka Matous (18)
           Nadezda Minik (30)
           Katerine Rickena (28)
           Josef Bedrich (63)

Terra      Ben Weatherby (28)
           Lisa Thornbird (26)
           Albert Thrace (66)

Valtr      Chesna Pavel (16)
           Patrik Rudolf (31)
           Zikmund Milan (59)


Cosma      Bianca Babiana (20)
           Alfredo Amadeo (35)
           Biagio Casimiro (68)

Gonda      Antoinette Avila (55)
           Reina Strom (25)
           Blanche Clementine (22)

(Enemy Planets)
Rehor      Valentýn Ryba (64)

Jing       Liang Don (65)
```

```
Dietmar   Dieter Eberhardt (67)
          Franz Aramund (36)

Anwyn     Byrnn Arwel (59)

(Neutral Planets)
Isi       Jaci Kaya (22)
          Chogan Hotah (66)

Gerde     Johann Kyler (39)
          Lutz Malger (59)

Alta      Bonita Blanca (27)
          Vilem Casimir (24)
          Carlos Federico (68)

Maeve     Breana Comyna (45)


Chana     Amram Mordekay (50)

Asami     Kimi Miko (33)
          Saburo Takao (64)
```

Thus ended the Fall High Council. Later that evening, Barons Leo and Stefan dropped by. Leo said, "Zoran, I can't help but think that you are on to something about us needing to know more about the history of the dragon race. Stefan and I have been discussing it, and we've decided to launch a detailed investigation. There must be records of these beasts somewhere. We've extensive libraries on our worlds. If we find out anything, we'll let you know."

Baron Stefan added, "Right, I too think that there must be more to these dragons than we currently know or suspect. Just why do they inherently have the ability to mimic human forms? Why not deer or bears or even gators, eh? Why us? Our curiosity is pricked. We're going to leave no stone unturned trying to find out. We thought you ought to know."

Zoran grinned. "Thanks. I too will see if I can find anything else on them. Let's stay in touch." The three shook hands and the two barons left, while Zoran finished his packing. Around nine, he Shadow Walked his group back home, much to the relief of Archmage Jakob who was anxiously awaiting their return. He did not like the incredible responsibility that he'd assumed. Too much was at stake, but so far, there had been no further dragon attacks while they were gone.

Chapter 11 The United Council

The last week of September, the United Council met for the first time in several years. Dragons were not known for hasty or frequent meetings. Most dragon races did not get along well with the others. However, Aldrick called for a United Council and, as he was one of the senior members, all dragons had to answer the summons. Specifically, two members from each race had to attend the meeting or sixteen dragons all told.

Aldrick and Burk represented the golds. Werner and Lothar represented the blacks. Dario and Dante represented the reds. Alistair and Frank represented the greens. Cezar and Jenryk represented the whites. Bolivar and Ernesto represented the blues. Donatello and Pietro represented the browns. Aeton and Barnabus represented the greys.

The reds, blacks, and greens were hostile and argumentative towards this whole summons. "All right, Aldrick, all right. You got us here. We can't *not* come. So what is so dang important that we have to have a United Council? This had better be good!" growled Werner, the black.

Aldrick, the gold, began, "Twenty years ago dragon-kind was on the verge of extinction on Voss. All of us were starving to death. It was these humans here in the Federation who offered us a new chance a life, a new place to live where food is plentiful. Without their help, we would have all perished by now. Yet, within the last few years, some of us have been attacking, robbing, extorting, and outright murdering our human benefactors."

He looked at the reds and blacks in particular. "I know that you have burned and destroyed an entire village of a thousand men, women, and children on Adapazan. I know that you attempted to storm the fortress at Brn, Adapazan. I know that you greens have been murdering humans for mere sport on Jing. This conduct is not acceptable and must cease immediately."

"Many of us have working relationships with the planet rulers, providing protection in exchange for gold and gems. Yet, you reds, blacks, and greens are now biting the hand that feeds you and that has saved your race some twenty years ago. You have to stop harming the humans and robbing them," Aldrick, the gold, finished up.

"The hell we do! Damn, the only good human is a dead human. You cannot trust them for anything. They've killed two of our leaders," Dario, the red, pointed out. "Plus, they've just recently murdered the wife, who was only seeking revenge for the slaying of her leader mate!"

"Hey, they slaughtered nearly a dozen of our finest fighters," Werner, the black, added. "Plus, it is these damnable humans who are sneaking into our dens and murdering our children while we are out hunting for food! We've lost three young. The reds have lost four. Even the whites and browns have had some of their children slain while they were out hunting."

Aldrick, the gold, was taken aback. He knew nothing of this and asked for more details, which both were more than ready to provide. He was shocked to hear that at least a dozen young dragons had been slain by humans in their very own homes, all while their parents were out foraging for food for their children.

"Besides, Aldrick, we reds were just obeying Baron Clav. It was he who begged us and paid us to rob some gem shipments on Adapazan. We were just doing what he asked. You can't blame us for that," Dario, the red, justified.

"The barons have gone back on their business deals with us," Alistair, the green, added. "We deserve what we bargained for, don't we?"

Barnabus, the grey, said dryly, "Well, we greys are enjoying the humans who gave us a new home on Isi. We've had no troubles with them at all. We find their company rather enjoyable, Alistair."

Donatello, the brown, said mildly, "We've had no problems on Isi with the humans yet. While we don't go out of our way to meet humans, they haven't caused us any real trouble. However, we have lost a couple of children. Say, how were you able to ascertain that the children were murdered by your humans?" The discussion digressed for sometime.

"I think that we should just dissolve our agreements with these barons and leave the humans completely alone," declared Bolivar, the blue. "That way, there are no more troubles of any kind."

"I like that idea. Just leave them alone," Donatello, the brown, agreed.

"That doesn't work. We tried that," complained Cezar, the white. "Still the humans seek out our dens in the frozen mountains and murder our young while the adults are out seeking food. We cannot allow this. After all, we only have one child about every ten years or so. Killing our offspring cannot be tolerated by we whites."

"Besides, there is something else that you do not know. The humans are passing off on us fake gems now. Yes, they take quartz crystals and use magic to make fake diamonds out of them. How stupid do these humans think we are?" complained Dante, the red.

"And another thing that we've found out," Dario, the red, added quite seriously, "their Archmages are now making Dragon Slaying Swords! If this does not show us their true intentions, nothing else does! Are we making Human Slaying Swords? Hardly!"

"Oh we don't need such things," Bolivar, the blue, said quite bored with the proceedings.

"I say call for a vote!" Dario, the red, bellowed antagonistically. "I say let's attack these despicable humans, remove them from the planets. All in favor?" Aldrick, the gold, had no choice but to allow the vote since protocol allowed any representative to call for a vote at any time. The reds, blacks, whites, and greens voted yes. The browns did as well.

"I say let's vote to leave the humans alone, abandon all trade and relationships and ignore them completely," Bolivar, the blue, declared. "All in favor?" The blues, the greys, the browns, and the whites voted yes.

"Damn you browns and whites! You can't have it both ways!" screeched Dario, the red. "Make *up* your minds! Kill the humans or ignore them. The two choices are mutually exclusive. Are you idiots?"

"Ignoring them is safer," a bored Bolivar, the blue, answered him.

"He has a point," Aldrick, the gold, pointed out. "If you escalate this conflict into all-out war, we may lose that war. The humans vastly outnumber us. They have a lot of Archmages. Besides, they also have the Duskas who are going to be extremely difficult to slay. If you go to war with the humans, you may well be signing your own death warrant. Humans are slow to forgive treachery, for treachery is what this is. They gave us sanctuary and life when we were dying. Attacking them is just that, treachery. It may take generations of humans before they forgive such treasonous acts."

"Besides, we are learning magic spells from them," the bored Bolivar, the blue, added.

"He has a point there," Pietro, the brown, agreed with him. Several others nodded.

"Quite true. Look, my own twins received the very best magical training from the human Archmage. We've never before had any dragon achieve Archmage status, but my twins did, thanks to the human Archmage," Aldrick, the gold, played his trump card, hoping for the best.

Ernesto, the blue, replied, "Yes, we must not forget that. Dario, if we attack the humans, they certainly will never again give us magical training. We can't have that, now can we?"

"That's easy for you to say. It wasn't your child that was murdered," Dario, the red, retorted.

"Well, if you escalate this into an all-out war, expect the humans to murder all of our children. They will not stop until all dragon-kind is extinct on all sixteen planets," Burk, the gold, declared. "Think about that for a minute. We are few and they are many. Yes, we are vastly more powerful than all of the humans, but they have many Archmages and Duskas. In the end, an all-out war will spell our doom."

"You are just saying that because you are a human lover," Werner, the black, countered, though he was a little taken aback with Burk's sudden prophesy. There was a ring of truth to it. "I bet that you will fight against us and with the humans if war it becomes," he taunted Burk, the gold.

"He's already done just that with us reds. He and Aldrick laid a trap for us and killed a red on Adapazan," Dario, the red, pointed out.

"You reds were about to murder the humans who were making that gem shipment. You launched a fire attack. Had they been humans and not we golds, why all ten of them would have died. We prevented the humans from taking far more serious actions against you," Aldrick, the gold, explained. "I call for a vote. We do not want to start a war with the humans. All in favor?" The golds, browns, blues, greys, and whites voted in favor with it. "At least we agree on that."

"We don't agree on that!" Dario, the red, snickered. "Count us reds, blacks, and greens out of that one."

"Oh that doesn't matter," the bored Bolivar, the blue, replied. "You know the majority wins. That was a majority vote. No war with the humans."

"For now, perhaps," Werner, the black, stated antagonistically. "Just you wait until your children get murdered. Then, we'll take another vote."

"Don't do foolish things, Werner," Aeton, the grey, admonished the black. "You know very well that the golds will come after you if you break the majority vote and attack the humans again."

"Well, we won't start a war, but we will defend ourselves," Dario, the red, finally acknowledged the voting.

"Thank you. I will speak with the humans and see if I can get to the bottom of their slaying of our young. If they have been doing so, I will see that they cease it immediately," Aldrick, the gold, then made his offer of appeasement. The others nodded and the meeting ended. However, the reds, blacks, greens, and whites stuck around after the others left, per the prearranged request of Werner, the black.

"So why do you want us to stick around? The weather is finally becoming ideal. Snow lies over much of the lands," Cezar, the white, asked somewhat curious but also rather impatiently. At last the temperatures on the white occupied planets were to his liking, bitter cold.

"Well, Aldrick's meeting went as expected. He's not facing the loss of his children and mates. Oh no, not him, the human lover. No, it is we who are suffering mightily," Werner, the black, replied argumentatively. "We blacks have adopted a new policy that is stopping the murdering of our children. One parent always remains with the young. I suggest that you all adopt a similar policy. Yet that does not address the loss of our young. We only breed once every ten years at most. Losing a child is devastating on our population. We need to find a way to make that up and I have an idea just how."

"Oh yea? How?" Dario, the red, suddenly became intensely interested.

Werner, the black, let out a long, sneering laugh. "Before I tell you, there is one other thing that we didn't bring up before Aldrick. Dante, please tell the greens what you've discovered."

Dante, the red, smiled. "We've been putting our human forms to good use, ever since Baron Clav began feeding us wrong information about the human gem shipments. We've been doing a little spying on our own here on Rehor and on Adapazan. Brace yourselves, this in incredible and terrible news."

"Ah, come on, Dante. Out with it! You always did have a flair for the dramatic," growled Cezar, the white, growing more impatient by the moment. He did not like all this delaying talk. "Just say it" was his philosophy.

Unwilling to be rushed, Dante, the red, continued, "Recently, some very large emeralds have been unearthed on Adapazan and on Rehor. Two of these are in the hands of Archmages — Jakob Hamil in Tratky Province, Adapazan and old Valentýn Ryba of Rehor, Baron Clav's lackey."

"So?" Cezar, the white, growled, growing even more impatient. The exhilarating cold was beckoning to him, and he longed to get back home and enjoy this fine weather.

"So we've discovered that these two treacherous Archmages are working on enchanting these gems."

"Why not?" Cezar, the white, growled. Dante, the red, was obviously dragging this out.

"Both are working on making some kind of Gem of Dragon Control magical items out of them," Dante, the red, finally punched in the magnitude of his spy's discoveries. "Yes, if these evil men succeed, they will be able to wave their creations about and force us to do their bidding! They will be able to control us! Force us into utter slavery!" Dante, the red, smirked. He'd just delivered the coupe de grace.

Curses filled the cavern room. When the explicatives died down, Cezar, the white, now suddenly interested, said, "This cannot be allowed to happen! Are you sure that they are actually doing this? Have they the power, intelligence, and magical skill to make such hideous devices?"

"They are Archmages, are they not? Valentýn's been at it for years, we think. No, they have not yet gotten the heavy power enchantments completed, as far as we can tell. There is still time to prevent them from succeeding. If they are successful, all dragons will be in dire jeopardy! We cannot allow them to finish."

"But killing an Archmage is most difficult," Werner, the black, pointed out.

"Quite true, quite," Cezar, the white, concurred, although he had never tried such a thing. The mere label of Archmage cast a certain awe and fear in his mind.

"What can we do about it?" asked Jenryk, the white, highly worried.

"We can slow them down a while. That is the safe route, not directly attacking the Archmages in their highly enchanted Magic Towers. No, that would be suicide on our part. Lord knows what evil, wicked, diabolical traps such powerful mages have in place there. No, we must take two approaches. First, let our people know about these and keep a sharp watch on each other. Report any strange behavior to us leaders at once. That way, the instant that they are successful, we will know about it and can then take decisive actions to stop them. Second, we can slow them down," Werner, the black, retook control of his private meeting.

"We can do two things — one to make up the losses of our children and one to slow these evil, wicked mages down," Werner, the black, lowered his voice to the barest whisper. Naturally, all the others cocked their ears intently to hear his plans.

"I love it! Brilliant, Werner, positively brilliant!" Dario, the red, exclaimed upon hearing the two ideas.

The pair of greens laughed. "Count the greens in on this one!" added Alistair, the green. "Ingenious. We'd never of thought of this!"

"Then it is agreed? We four races shall follow this path?" Werner, the black, called for a vote. He had one hundred percent agreement from them. "I'll work out the details shortly and let you know when we start." After that, their private meeting also broke up.

Later that day, Aldrick visited Zoran and told him, "I believe that I have cooled things down between the dragons and humans. However, I learned a most disturbing thing. Apparently, humans have been murdering some of our defenseless children in their home caverns while their parents were out hunting for food. Can you look into this? If this has or is happening, you must cease killing our young immediately."

"Damn Aldrick! I've heard absolutely nothing about any such thing at the High Council. No baron mentioned any such thing. The way the meeting went, I am certain that I would have heard about something like that. Nevertheless, I will spread the word and see if any of us can find out if that has been happening. I give you my word that we will try to see if that's happened, and, if so, put a stop to it," Zoran replied earnestly.

"I'm sure that you will. Good day." Aldrick left. He felt certain that Zoran was just as shocked and surprised to hear this as he had been. *No, Zoran knew nothing about the killing of our children,* he thought.

Zoran Messaged the other barons. None new anything about it, but promised to look into it. Over dinner, Zoran told the others about it. All were just as surprised as he to learn of it. However, Archmage Karel began to wonder about it. Was there any connection between these murders and the mysterious supplies that his son was providing him?

Chapter 12 The Petr Falls Affair

Tratky Province is located in the far northern portion of the main known continent of Adapazan. There in the often frozen land, Warlord Osvald ruled. Twelve years ago, he was able to purchase the services of one of Archmage Zdenka's newly trained Archmages, Jakob Hamil, who had just turned eighteen and was a nephew of Osvald. The warlord had sent him down to Brn to be trained, accepting Baron Zoran's offer of mage training for the many warlords. Luck was with him, Jakob excelled far beyond any of his expectations.

Now supported by a true Archmage of immense power, Warlord Osvald began making huge strides in bringing civilization to his people of the far north. Vastly better roads had already contributed to immeasurably better trading deals. Tratky produced high quality iron ore and emeralds along with coal. At long last, the warlord could send large shipments south, receiving large shipments of manufactured items which his people greatly desired and needed. During these past ten years, the quality of life in this far northern province had improved markedly.

The village of Petr Falls lay some five miles from his fortress and the new Archmage tower, that is, as the crow flies. The winding road took some eight miles to get there. The terrain was craggy and mountainous for the most part. However, Petr Falls was located at the edge of a fertile valley. Crops were grown there during the short growing season from late May through August. The rugged mountains with their thick cover of pines lay at the western edge of the village. Here were found a highly profitable iron mine and a vein which produced emeralds as well. Thus, the two thousand plus folks who lived in Petr Falls were mostly miners or farmers, though a few were teamsters.

"Zoran! Quick! Dragons have attacked Petr Falls! It's horrible!" Early one morning in late October, Zoran was startled to receive the panic stricken Message from Archmage Jakob Hamil who lived up in Tratky Province.

"Good god not again! Where is Petr Falls?" Zoran sent back via a Message spell.

"Five miles south of the fortress. Home in on me. Be prepared. It is a horror beyond description. Warlord Osvald was here, vomited, and left," Archmage Jakob sent back. At once, Zoran sent a Message to his ever-growing group of First Responders, as he had begun to call them. Mystical Doors flashed as they began assembling in his study, all dressed for the winter cold.

"I've got a pail of healing potions, but if this one is like the others, they won't be of much use," Jarka said sternly. "I *thought* that Aldrick said that this sort of thing was going to *stop*," she added covertly.

"Let's not jump to conclusions just yet, Jarka. Okay, grab on to me. Lord knows where this Petr Falls is at. I am homing in on Jakob," Zoran said sternly. A moment later, he Shadow Walked the large group, arriving beside Archmage Jakob, who was dressed in heavy furs and standing at the edge of the village.

"Oh dear god!" Mage Jarka exclaimed.

"Not again!" Archmage Karel cursed.

"Oh god!" Zdenka whispered under her breath.

"How many lived here, Jakob?" Zoran asked, fighting the urge to vomit himself. Smoke rose from the burning homes. Bodies lay everywhere in the snow-covered streets. The stone buildings were crumbled, as if some giant hands had taken an enormous ball bat to them. Other than the crackling of still burning fires, no other sounds could be heard in this once picturesque village.

"At least two thousand lived here, maybe more," Archmage Jakob whispered, afraid to raise his voice as if it might frighten the dead who lay everywhere before them.

"Okay, we should fan out and look for survivors," Mage Jarka took charge. Reactively, the others followed her, as she began stepping gingerly down the street, avoiding the obviously dead bodies. "Fire. Must have been reds," she called out. A bit later, "No wait, this one has acid burns. Blacks too! Wait, this one is frozen stiff! Whites were here as well! Damn reds, blacks, and whites!" Zoran's heart sank. All three types were working together — such a combination was beyond deadly. Just then Aldrick and Emil appeared flying above them.

Aldrick glided down, morphing into his human shape. "Damn them. They gave me their word that this would not happen again. Zoran, I will deal with them."

"Reds, blacks, and whites were here, we think. Take a look for yourself and verify that we are correct," Zoran said softly.

"Hey, over here! We have a survivor!" Jarka yelled. Zdenka and Verushka got to her first and saw a young woman of twenty-two lying face down in the foot deep snow. Her fur coat was blackened and burned partially, but the hood had protected her face. Both of her hands were charred, mere bones lying upon the pool of melted snow that they had melted, a ghastly sight. A foot from her was the charred remains of a one year only baby boy. To her right were the remains of a three year old girl. Her hands had been reaching for them, that much was clear. The woman was unconscious, but as Zdenka tried to lift her up so Jarka could pour in the life-saving potion, the burned bones of her hands cracked and remained frozen in the pool of ice they had made from the snow. Blood began flowing from the woman's lower arms.

"Good god!" Zdenka whispered. Jarka poured the healing potion into the woman's mouth, while Verushka used her hands to make the woman swallow the liquid. Jarka poured three healing potions into the woman, before Bernard and Chan called out.

"Hey, here's another survivor. Jarka, over here fast!" Chan yelled, excited that she had found another survivor, this time a ten year old girl.

"Verushka, get her back to our place and get her cleaned up and in a warm bed pronto. I'll get back as soon as we find the rest of the survivors. Get the infirmary ready for us," Jarka ordered, then scampered over to Chan and Bernard, who already had the young girl propped up and ready for Jarka's potions.

The girl's left arm was nearly entirely gone, eaten away by acid. She too was unconscious and blood covered the whole left side of her winter coat, which was covered in black soot and partially dissolved by the acid. Evidently, she had escaped a burning building only to run into a stream of spewing acid from a black, Jarka concluded. Hastily, she poured three healing potions into the girl before ordering Bernard to get her back to the infirmary. "Hurry up, dear and get back fast. There may be more."

"You got it, my love." Bernard gently lifted the girl and teleported away. Chan and Jarka rose and continued their search. Body by body, the group stopped and checked on the dead. After a half hour, they finished their first pass through the village and found no other survivors.

"Okay, we'd best recheck everyone and search the buildings. There could be more trapped inside," Zoran ordered. Jakob and I will start organizing the confirmed dead. Karel will dig us a mass grave. We should lay the dead out first. Jakob says that some of their relatives would like to pay their last respects before we bury them."

Three hours later, two thousand one hundred five bodies lay in a long line down the main street of Petr Falls. Several dozen relatives arrived and crying became the most common sound now. "I'll take it from here, Zoran," Jakob said softly. "I'll handle the burial. There are others on their way to pay their respects yet. No need for you and the others to stick around. It is going to be a very grim late morning, sir."

"Okay, thanks Jakob. True, there is little more that we can do here. I will let you know how the two survivors are doing. Once we know their names, you can see if they have any other relatives around here who can take them in. If not, we'll take good care of them in Brn," Zoran replied solemnly. His group quietly teleported home.

Zoran and Zdenka headed for the infirmary the moment they returned to their fortress in Brn. They found Verushka hovering over her two patients, along with Jarka. Both were now conscious, though both were sobbing.

"This is Lilia Mila. She's twenty-two," Verushka said quietly. The young woman was fairly pretty with shoulder length blonde hair and blue eyes. Her cheeks were flushed and her eyes, bloodshot from crying. Verushka had her cleaned up and tucked nicely into a bed; her two arm stumps were bandaged and resting above the covers. "Those were her two children by her. We've learned that they were attacked by a flock of red, black, and a few white dragons. She has no idea how many there were, just lots according to her. They were taken by complete surprise, naturally."

Zoran leaned over her. "Lilia. I am Baron Zoran. You are safe here in my fortress. We will look after you now. Get some rest and recover."

"My babies! I've lost my babies!" she wailed and Zoran could think of nothing comforting to say to her. Graciously, Verushka moved him over to the other bed where the young girl was sitting up. She too had been cleaned up and tucked into a warm bed.

"This is Neda Valdemar. She's ten going on eleven," Verushka said softly and the girl grinned at that last, trying to look older than she was.

"Very pleased to meet you, Neda. You are safe here. We will look after you. You have nothing to fear or worry about now," Zoran told her.

"Are the dragons gone? Will they come back? Is mommy dead too? I saw daddy burning up. He's dead, isn't he?" she asked bravely.

"I am afraid they both didn't make it. But you, young lady, you have survived and that is wonderful," Zoran answered her.

"My shoulder hurts. Will my arm grow back?" she asked innocently.

"The pain will subside soon, dear," Jarka explained. "In a little while, I will give you another of my potions and then there will be no more pain. I am afraid though that I don't know how to grow back missing arms. But that's not the end of the world. Chan lost hers to a Green Dragon. She's a dragon fighter and is now back ready to fight them again. She and her sister have killed nineteen of them. So it's not the end of the world, dear."

"Really? Chan only has one arm like I do? She's killed nineteen? Really?" Neda's eyes opened wide.

"You bet. After you get a little stronger, I'll have Chan come by and tell you about it," Jarka said.

"Promise?"

"Promise!" Neda smiled broadly.

"I'll see if we can find any of your relatives. They must be plenty worried about you, Neda," Zoran added. She smiled again and he left to do just that.

Although Jakob tried, no relatives could be found for either patient. All had perished in the attack. Later that evening, Jakob personally visited Zoran.

"Hi. Well, I have the dead buried now. However, Baron Zoran, we've come across something quite shocking. I don't know quite what to make of it," he said. From the pained expression on his face, Zoran knew that something was seriously amiss.

Jakob continued. "Thirty women are missing along with twenty-five men."

"What? Maybe they were able to flee the carnage?" Zoran suggested hopefully.

"We thought so at first. However, we scoured the edge of Petr Falls. There are no signs of anyone leaving the village. There was a light snowfall last night; anyone leaving would have left footprints or sleigh tracks or hoof prints if they went by horse. No, they are simply missing and unaccounted for — thirty women and twenty-five men."

"How strange."

"Indeed. That's why I am so late reporting back to you. I don't like anomalies so I have been checking on it further. The final results are still not completely clear, but it appears that the thirty missing women are between the ages of eighteen and twenty-five. The missing men are all similar in age and were miners, relatively burly, strong men. I'll know more in a few days. I have several men and women working on trying to put together just who is missing. None are related to the two survivors, unfortunately. I guess they are orphans now."

"How incredibly strange. Yes, we will look after them here in Brn. Fifty-five missing. Weird indeed. Where could they have gone? Could a mage have teleported them to safety someplace?"

"That is what I am hoping, baron. There were two mages living in Petr Falls, but we buried both of their bodies. If they did manage to get them to safety, we won't know from them. I guess time will tell. Still, I don't like anomalies."

"I agree. Keep on it. We need to find them and make sure that they are safe."

"I'll keep you posted." Jakob then left, leaving Zoran with a new puzzle to solve. He shook his head, what could have happened to the missing men and women? He hoped that the two mages had somehow teleported them to safety.

Late the next morning, Zoran and Zdenka visited the infirmary to check on how Lilia and Neda were faring. They found Neda was dressed in a new white cotton dress with a new pair of shoes. She was sitting on a chair while Jarka was trimming the burned hair out of her long brown hair. "Hi. Chan came to see me! She really is a dragon fighter! She promised to teach me how to fight dragons if I want to, but they scare me. I am not so sure that I want to fight them," Neda explained as they sat down beside her. "Mage Jarka gave me this new dress. It is the finest dress that I ever had and new shoes too."

"Well, if I so say so myself, you look very pretty, Neda," Zdenka complimented her.

"Thanks. She had to help me dress. I can't dress myself any more or even tie my shoes."

"Well, neither can Chan. Her sister, Wen, always helps her get dressed," Zdenka pointed out. Zoran examined her left shoulder. Jarka had removed the bandages and pink healing flesh remained. Neda still had about two inches of her left upper arm remaining, not much at all. Still she was lucky to be alive.

Neda saw him examining it and wiggled her arm. "Hardly anything is left. I can't do much at all with it except wiggle it, I'm afraid."

"True, but you are one very lucky young girl. You are still alive. I think that is a miracle." Zoran tried to put a different slant on it.

"Am I really going to get to live here with all of you?" Neda asked.

"You bet you are, unless you want to go live somewhere else," Zoran answered.

She grinned. "I like it here. Jarka says that she'll be my new mom. Is that all right?"

"Of course, Neda. Jarka's children are all grown up now, and I think that she misses having a bright young girl around," he replied and both Jarka and Neda grinned. "If you will excuse me, Neda, I should go check on Lilia now." He got a warning stare from Jarka and headed into the next room.

As he left, he heard Zdenka saying, "Neda, suppose that you walk into a room and see a dead man lying on the floor, a young woman sitting at a table. She is bleeding badly. Also on the table is a large bag of gold. No one else is in the room as you enter it. What would you do?"

Zoran grinned. He paused just outside the door to hear Neda's answer. "Oh, I should see if I can stop the bleeding like mom taught me. Only I don't know if I can do it now, not with only one hand. Maybe I can. If not, I can run for help." Zoran smiled, he knew that Zdenka just took on a new magic student. Neda was now in very good hands and likely had a bright future ahead of her.

It was quite different in the next room, where Verushka had separated Lilia from Neda. She had Lilia dressed in a new cotton dress, and the young woman was sitting on the bed as Verushka just finished feeding her some breakfast. "Good morning, Lilia. You are looking so much better today. Your arms are definitely healing up just fine." He noticed that her lower arms were quite pink where the new skin was forming up. She'd lost both hands just above her wrists.

"You two can chat while I brush out her hair. Lilia has such golden locks. Quite pretty," Verushka commented and began dealing with the woman's hair. Obviously, Lilia could do very little for herself anymore.

"Why are you bothering with me? Why didn't you just let me die with my children? I can't live like this?" Lilia raised her empty arms and dropped them in her lap.

"You are alive. That is a miracle, Lilia. Life is in you still. You are pretty and young. I am sure that soon you will be able to have more children. I am so sorry that your little boy and girl were killed by the vile dragons," Zoran tried to think of something comforting to say to her, but felt terribly awkward.

"How am I to do that? I can't do anything anymore. I have no hands at all! All I ever wanted to be was a wife, to take care of my man, keep a fine house, raise my beautiful children, and be a good mother to them, that's all I ever wanted to be. Now, all that has been taken from me. I've lost my children, my husband, my home, everything. I have no hands and am facing a life as a total invalid, a cripple who cannot do anything at all for herself, totally and utterly dependent on others for everything. I can't even feed myself. Why didn't you just let me die with my family?" She broke down and sobbed uncontrollably once more.

"You are young. You can learn new ways to do things, I think," Zoran tried his best to console her and give her some hope for the future. "Perhaps in time you will meet a new man and fall in love again. You have a long life ahead of you. Do not dwell on the past. We cannot change it, as much as I want to do just that, I cannot."

"You don't get it do you?" she wailed. "I can't change my baby's diapers. I can't cook his meals or start a fire in our stove. I can't clean our house. I can't hold my babies or fix their cuts and bruises. I can't even dress my children. I can't do a damn thing anymore! I can't even open a door! I am a prisoner now." She was off in another fit of sobbing.

"There, there, in time it won't seem so bad. I have your hair brushed out nicely. You need to rest up. I'll be back in a while with our morning tea, Lilia," Verushka said softly. She motioned for Zoran to leave and follow her.

Once out of the room, Verushka explained, "She has been like this since she recovered consciousness. She's suffered a horrible loss. Emotionally, she is a wreck; her whole family has been stripped from her as well."

"Will she recover?" he asked.

"Probably in time. Time heals all things, it is said, though I really don't believe it. Honestly, her precious children have been taken from her. How can you ever get over the loss of your own children? Plus, she is now totally handicapped. She's right. How can she do much of anything for herself now? I really don't know, but I will stay with her and see what I can do."

"Thanks Verushka. I felt so awkward around her. What can you say to her? There aren't even words. It's catastrophic for her. Still, she is young. Maybe she can make it."

"I'm keeping my fingers crossed. We'll do all that we can. Any word about the missing villagers?" He nodded no. "Well, I've been thinking about that. I have some ideas and will speak with Jakob later today. They have to be somewhere. I hope that they are safe and sound. The two mages must have somehow gotten them to safety," she explained.

Zoran saw that she was just as bothered about this disappearance as Jakob. So many things were strange about this latest attack. No gems were taken. What was the point of destroying a large village? He'd expected to find another ransom note, but none was found. He too felt worried. How could he protect the people on Adapazan for whom he swore an oath to protect?

Three days later, Baroness Archmage Verushka had a split second choice to make. Daily, she had been caring for Lilia, trying her best to help the young woman adjust to her drastically altered life. This day, Lilia seemed to be doing better and wanted to go for a walk, since that was about all that she said that she could now do. Verushka agreed and they took a tour of the fortress. Later, Verushka admonished herself for not realizing what was on Lilia's mind when she asked to go onto the roof to get a good view of the town of Brn, which she'd never seen before. Once on the roof, Lilia seemed to be in awe of the sprawling town of some twenty thousand plus, but at the last instant, she jumped off of the roof!

Verushka had but a split second to react. "I could have saved her, Zoran. I just froze. I know that she just did not want to live any longer. I can't blame her. I just didn't have the desire to rescue her from the five story fall only to have her try it again later on. We ought to be allowed to control our own lives. I know that it is very sad, but this was her choice to make. It is or was her body. God, I hope that I never have to make such a choice ever again! I feel awful."

Zoran held her close for a time. After a bit of silence, he whispered, "I'd of probably done the same as you. It was her life, though I wish she had made a different choice. Still, the barriers that she had to face are almost insurmountable."

After a brief burial ceremony, Zoran visited Jakob, partly to let him know that Lilia had died, but also to chat about the still missing fifty-some men and women. "Surely by now if they had been teleported to a place of safety, one or more would have made some kind of contact. The warlord now has guards stationed at Petr Falls night and day, buy no one has returned. Frankly, it is really bothering me, baron. What has become of them? I have tripled checked with anyone I can find who knew folks who lived there. I've confirmed the numbers; they cannot be off by more than one or two men. Somehow they have completely vanished."

"Have you considered that their bodies might have been burned in the fires or eaten up by the acid?" he asked.

"Yes, we did a ruins by ruins search. I've even made some acid tests in my lab. Given the amount of time that passed, there is absolutely no way that the dragon's acid could completely dissolve all clothing and traces of a human body. There was just not enough time, not even if the person was in the acid's direct path and took it full on. No way. I swear, baron, we have a real mystery on our hands. I'm now exploring the possibility that somewhere in the village they had a secret chamber where these people went to hide from the carnage. Perhaps its entrance was blocked by the collapsing buildings. I've sent all of my magic students out there to search for such places. I haven't heard back yet."

"Excellent reasoning," he complimented Jakob.

"If that fails, which I believe it will, since I have heard of no such hiding places from those I've contacted here who either once lived there or knew those who did, I have one other outside possibility to try."

"What's that?" Zoran asked, curious. What else could be done?

"As you know, many folks have elementary magic skills. I am going to chat with everyone who knew any of these missing folks and see if any of the missing had such skills. Perhaps one of them had a little skill, you know, even less than the adepts. If so, I will try to Message them. Of course, that may be a futile one-way action, a long shot at best."

"Say, that is a good idea. Keep me posted. I am as baffled as you are. Actually, we all are."

"I will. Here is the list of missing folks. Have your people take a look at them. Of course, it is highly improbable that your people would actually know anyone from Petr Falls. Still, I am trying everything humanly possible. I hate mysteries like this, baron. There *has* to be a logical answer somewhere, only we are just not seeing it."

"Agreed. Logic says fifty-plus adults just do not disappear without a trace. Say, is it possible that one of the attacking dragons knew the Vanish spell?" Zoran suddenly had a horrible thought that the people had been picked up and dropped into the sun.

"Even if one did, baron, they could not cast it fifty plus times. None of us can cast it that many times in such a short space of time. I already considered that possibility along with Disintegrate spells. Just not enough time."

Later that day, Zoran passed the list of names around to his people. It passed from hands to hands, accompanied by sad shaking of heads, as anticipated. Near suppertime the next day, the list, now well handled, had made it to the small group of very beginning magic students of Archmage Zdenka. She explained what the list was about and passed it around to this year's four new students, five counting Neda who had just been added. Already she could cast a Clean spell and was very proud of that fact.

Suddenly, Neda spoke up. "Archmage, I know most of these people. They were our friends. Danika Stanis, she used to babysit me when I was little. Mom chose her because she could somehow send mom a message if I got sick or hurt. I think it must have been magic."

"How incredibly stupid of us all!" Zdenka slapped herself. "Duh. We should have checked with you first, Neda." She told Neda about the spell and how it worked. At last, she decided that perhaps this young woman had the ability to cast a Message spell. Hastily, she dashed off a Message to Zoran, who came via a Mystical Door. He thanked Neda and Shadow Walked to visit Jakob with the news.

"Fantastic! Now we are getting somewhere. My students found no traces of hidden or secret hiding places, baron. We've got to try to get through to this Danika woman," Jakob exclaimed, greatly relieved as Zoran relayed the news.

"She could be a long distance away. I'll let you try first, after all, you have been instrumental in working on this mystery," Zoran allowed the Archmage his victory. Jakob sat down and cast his Message spell. He sent: *Archmage Jakob here. Danika, we are looking for you. Can you respond?* Nothing happened, in fact, the spell did not properly activate. "Well, it did not activate, so she must be dead." He looked crestfallen.

Zoran's hopes died too. Suddenly, he had another thought. "Say, what if she is off-world? The usual Message spell only works if the person is on Adapazan. Let me use my Duska Message ability. That sends the message anywhere. He focused his attention and sent off his message: *Danika Stanis. Baron Zoran Vladislov here. We are looking for you and many others. Are you there?*

He waited patiently, his fingers crossed. He sensed another's mind. Panic and fear swept into his mind, along with a twinge of renewed hope. *Yes? It's me. Help us! Help us! The dragons have us!* Zoran joined Jakob's mind with his and saw the flashing smile from the Archmage. It was working; they'd made contact with one of the missing people!

Danika. We believe that thirty women from Petr Falls are missing along with twenty-five men. Are you safe? Are the others with you?

Help! Yes, we're here. Dragons took us. Help.

Where are you being kept? Do you know what planet you are on?

No. It's cold though. We're in a cavern in some mountains. Help us please.

What do the dragons want with you?

They've raped us and made us all pregnant somehow. We are supposed to be giving birth to baby dragons. Radmilla couldn't take it and she ran out and jumped off the mountain and died. They tied us up after that, but Nadia got untied and was caught trying to untie the rest of us. They burned off her hands! Now they have put a metal collar around our necks and chained us to the walls so we can't escape. Our arms don't move anymore either. Help us please, help us.

Jakob cursed and swore angrily, but Zoran tried to keep from reacting. *Okay. Are the men in the cavern with you?*

No. We've not seen them since they brought us here.

Did they say what they were doing with the men?

I think that they are making them mine for gems.

Okay, you are doing really well, Danika. Now let's see if we can work out where you are being held. What color of dragons took you?

Red and black. Both are around every so often. Both kinds raped us.

Okay, Danika. Everything will be all right. I am coming to rescue you. Be patient. Help is coming.

Zoran asked a number of other questions in an attempt to get some idea of what planet they were on, but that proved futile. All that he had to go on was that they were in the mountains and it was cold. Well, that ruled out quite a few planets at least. He promised to get back to her soon. "Now how the devil do we find them?" asked Archmage Jakob.

"We've ruled out Adapazan. Mountains make it most likely to be Rehor, Dietmar, or Gerde. True, there are some lower mountains on some of the other planets, but the way it sounded, the woman fell a long ways to her death, implying tall mountains. Somehow we have to narrow it down."

"Even if we know they are on say Rehor, how are we ever going to find them? We're looking for a needle in a haystack." Jakob's enthusiasm melted away at the sheer impossibility of finding them.

"Okay, I'm going back home and research this further. I'll keep you posted. At least we've made contact with them and know that they are still alive. Somehow, we have to save them," Zoran replied.

Once home, he Messaged everyone about his success and then summoned everyone for a mass conference. "I believe that I will be able to follow the tiny energy line of communication with Danika while I have a link with her. Once I have her located, the problem becomes how do we rescue them from the dragons? The women are apparently chained to the wall to prevent them from killing themselves to avoid giving birth to a dragon baby. This sounds utterly wild to me, but let's leave that for later. Right now, we need to focus on how to get them back. Worse, she had no idea where the men are being held."

"Dad," Tomas suggested, "since they are being held in a cavern and are not being watched constantly, we could Shadow Walk arriving inside the cavern. Once there, we throw up Force Walls, blocking the entrance in case the dragons get wise to what we are doing. Not sure how we get the chains off of them though."

Jarka giggled, "You leave that to me, son." Several laughed. She was, after all, a thief.

Several weeks before, Amorette, Dario the red's mate, made a suggestion. "You know, Dario, the loss of several of red children has gotten me thinking about my great-great-grandmother, Alaina."

"Whatever are you thinking about, you clever wench?" he teased her. Honestly, he had no idea what she was talking about or even why. Besides, who recalled such distant ancestors anyway?

"I remember hearing stories that way back then, honestly Dario — say, that has to be nearly two and a half millennia ago, doesn't it?"

"I suppose so dear. What *are* you trying to say?" he said impatiently.

Amorette donned her peeved look. "This is important, Dario. As I was saying, I remember hearing stories that in Alaina's time, some of you virile men bedded human wenches and begat young dragons that way."

"What? Is that even possible? Human females? Bear dragon children?" Suddenly Dario was all ears.

"Yes, dear. According to what I heard about Alaina, back then, when there was a shortage of young dragons, you men impregnated your virile seed in human women, who then bore young dragon children. Of course, the women died giving birth or rather when the young dragons were born, they chewed and clawed their way out of the human women's wombs and took their first nourishment from their mother's blood and flesh. According to Alaina, that was done by the reds in order to rebuild our numbers shortly after the Gold-Red War in which nearly half of the reds were slain. After all, you know that we only breed about every ten years or so. Honestly, if we bred as frequently as these humans, why, you and I would have something like three hundred children by now!"

"Amorette, you are a genius!" Dario exclaimed, for she'd just given him the answer that he needed. "We should do this again. After all, this way, we can make the humans pay for their murdering of our young. Genius, what an idea!" Amorette beamed.

"Of course, the human females will not be willing to breed with us, Dario. I seem to recall that Alaina said that the gestation period was remarkably swift, something like sixty days or so and that the humans ate like a dragon, gobbling up food three times faster than they normally do. Of course, human eating patterns are so very strange anyway. Why, their bodies are so screwed up. We only need to dine once a week. Those silly creatures eat three times a day, though I've heard some eat more than that."

"Hum, so we are going to have to get us some human females and then keep them captive and safe for sixty days. How are we going to feed them that much? Besides, we don't even eat the crap that the humans eat. How they survive on all that junk food I surely do not know," Dario commented, mostly to himself. He was working out in his mind the details of the grand plan for revenge.

"Oh, perhaps you should make one of the human captives be the cook for the females, dear," Amorette suggested. "But I surely don't know where you will get all that crappy stuff that they will devour."

"Hum, we can infiltrate a village, find the best human cook and find where they keep their food supplies. Then, we raid the village, take the cook, take the food supplies, and take the fit women to be bred and burn the rest down. No one will be the wiser! Why, the stupid humans will not even know what we are up to! This is the best idea I have had in centuries, dear!"

"Say, it was my idea, Dario. You know, the human females might not want to go through with it. Once you have them pregnant and they realize that they will be mothers to a baby red, they might do foolish things. Humans are known to do foolish things," Amorette cautioned.

"So we imprison them in a cavern in the mountains where they cannot leave unless they can fly," Dario countered.

"Yes, that ought to do, dear, but do keep an eye on them. Humans cannot be trusted, you know."

"Of course, everyone knows that, Amorette. Everyone."

Sometime later, the raid on the unsuspecting village of Petr Falls went without a hitch. The woman who ran the inn, Bronya Casmir, was taken to be the cook. The village was ransacked and a large supply of food was taken along with twenty-nine other young women. Several days later, after they were raped and impregnated, ten were taken away by the blacks to their secret cavern, along with one to serve as their cook. Additionally, the greens wanted miners and thus twenty-five men were also taken as slave workers and given to the greens on Jing. The rest of the village was burned and the stone buildings were crushed. They made sure to leave no human alive to tell what had happened. Dario was pleased at how well this coordinated raid went. For once the blacks, whites, and greens cooperated, though he made sure that the greens followed the plan, but he did not let either the whites or greens know what they were going to do with the captive females. Not yet anyway, he wanted to increase the red and black populations first.

A special cavern was created high in the mountains of Rehor in a location unreachable by humans. Here, they had lain in a huge pile of hay to serve as bedding for the females. In a side chamber, they stored the food supplies and created a crude kitchen area for Bronya to use. Additionally, twice each day, several reds would use their breath to heat up the stone walls of the cavern which then radiated heat to keep the females warm enough.

Of course, Dario was wise enough to realize that his fellow dragons could not just bed the females directly. They would certainly protest and raise a ruckus. Hence, several reds cast Sleep spells on them first and then they had their way with the sleeping women, who woke to discover that they had indeed been raped, rather forcefully at that. Ten blacks were allowed to participate along with nineteen reds for this initial experiment.

Dario relied on the ancient information of his mate, Amorette, sketchy as it was. According to her, when the human females were with dragon child, they ate voraciously. Hence, he used this as his guideline, checking on their appetites each day. Those who did not seem to be eating excessively were again put to sleep and re-raped until they began to eat abnormally large amounts of food. After four days, the twenty-nine women seemed to be doing so and most of the dragons left.

The next day, the blacks took their ten away to their own secret cavern. However, the troubles for Dario had only begun. One foolish female ran out of the cavern and jumped off the edge, falling a thousand feet down to her death. This really annoyed Dario, who felt that she'd just murdered yet another of the Red Dragon children. He morphed into human form and stole a pile of rope. When he returned to the secret cavern, he then had his reds tie up the female's hands, allowing them to be untied only when they were being fed, which was now five times each day.

However, even this was insufficient. One guard caught a female who had somehow gotten herself loose and was going about untying the others. In a fit of rage, he used his fiery breath to burn off the woman's hands. His friend Dante was a master of the Fabrication spell. He then created locking neck collars and locked them around the women's necks and fastened them onto a long chain which was then hammered into the bedrock of the back of the cavern. Now they could not flee and kill themselves and the new young reds. He felt this would surely handle the human females. He never dreamed that they would be this much trouble.

Again, he underestimated them. The human female with the seared off hands was slain by another female, a mercy killing it seemed, since the victim continued to scream in pain all the time. "Amorette, what am I going to have to do with these darn human females to keep them from killing themselves, each other, and our new baby reds? No matter what I do, they keep on finding ways to wipe out the unborn reds."

"Let me talk to Bernardine. She has long studied the human bodies. She's been fascinated with them, ever since we came to Rehor, dear. If anyone knows, she does."

An hour later, the old red Bernardine arrived and was briefed on what was going on in the cavern. However, Dario made her swear to keep this a secret, claiming that Bernardine would be slaughtered by the Gold Dragons if they ever found out. That was enough to scare her in to keeping the secret of the human breeding experiment.

After Dario explained what the females were doing, that is, killing themselves and the as yet unborn baby reds, and explaining the steps that he had already taken, he asked, "So what else can we do to prevent them from murdering our new unborn baby reds?"

"Will they even survive the birthing?" Bernardine asked incredulously.

"Well, my great-great-grandmother, Alaina, said that they die when the baby dragons chew and claw their way out, and the newborns then dine on the mother's blood and soft tissues, before we begin feeding them proper food," Amorette inserted her views.

"Oh, so you need to keep them alive for a little while and then they will die giving birth, right?" Bernardine asked.

"It would seem so, if such ancient myths are believed. Time will tell. However, let us assume that is the case. If it isn't, why we will just kill them anyway," Dario advised her.

"Well, in that case, Dario, you need not keep them in 'mint' condition. I have studied their bodies, as you know. I rather like dissecting them, so many organs, so fascinating an internal structure. Lots to learn from their overly complicated bodies. Plus, my great-great-great-grandmother devised some very effective procedures which will work perfectly for you."

"Yes, yes, but what can I do?" interrupted an impatient Dario. Women always get off on side issues, he thought.

"Easy. Humans use their arms and hands and are doing so to kill each other's bodies and the unborn dragons. So we make their arms useless. They can still squat and pee. The can still lean over and eat like one of their dog pets, but their arms won't work. I know just how to make that happen from my exhaustive study of their anatomy. It is really fascinating, you know, so complex. So many things that can go wrong. It is a wonder that their bodies work at all, in my opinion," Bernardine rattled on, ignoring Dario's growing impatience.

"Yes, yes, what do we do?" he interrupted her again.

"You know, they might even find a way to get access to a healing potion or their bodies might even attempt to heal up. You never can tell about these humans. Okay, okay. I know just what to do, Dario. It will totally eliminate your problem and even eliminate any way around it by somehow getting access to healing potions."

"But they don't have any healing potions, we searched them," Dario pointed out.

"Yes, yes, but who knows, maybe one will conjure one up. You don't want any more surprises until the babies are born, right? Then, let's do this right," Bernardine insisted.

"Okay, okay. Make it so, please, Bernardine," an exasperated Dario ordered, thankful that she had the solution and would implement it.

"Well, you see, Dario, there are two different approaches that can be used on human bodies to make one of their appendages totally numb and useless to them. My great-great-great-grandmother passed these down to us. Neither one can be cured by healing potions — that's the key issue here, you see. The first one requires a tiny bit of very, very precise surgery on their shoulders where their arms join. I only need to use a tiny knife and sever a couple of their nerves in their shoulders. Cut those nerves and their arms lose all feeling and become 'dead' appendages. The drawback of a simple severing of the nerves is that in time some bodies heal themselves and usually a simple healing potion will also repair the cut nerves. Many years ago, I did some experimentation, and I believe that I can remove a small length of the nerves that I cut. With a piece removed, then they cannot be healed by any means. Your problems will be over. Of course, the drawback is that you must have a sterile environment or risk the woman getting an infection and dying before she gives birth."

Dario looked furious and she hastily continued. "I said that there were two ways. Yes, I certainly don't want them dying on us from an infection, which will surely happen in the unclean environment that you are keeping them in, so the second way is what I will use. You see, the alternative is to use an extraction made from Blue Dragon spittle. As you know, they spew out a highly deadly neurotoxin, which when it touches a human's skin causes paralysis. What my great-great-great-grandmother did was make an extract from it. One then simply injects a tiny portion of the extract right into the nerves themselves. Viola, instant, total, and permanent numbing of the rest of the extremity. To the woman, the arm will have no feeling, and she will be unable to move it in the slightest. It will appear to be a 'dead arm.' Thus, if they cannot use their arms, they cannot kill each other by wrapping their neck chains around each other's necks. Problem solved." Bernardine looked extremely pleased with herself.

That evening, accompanied by several Sleep spells, Bernardine performed her work on each of the seventeen women. First, she put on her magnifying lense contraption that allowed her to see enlarged images; she had to find the precise location of the nerves there at the shoulder socket. Once found, she inserted a tiny hollow needle and allowed two drops of her precious extract to slowly seep down onto the nerve. Each patient had five injections in each of their shoulders. Once done, she then verified that the patient no longer felt anything in that arm and hand. A few times, she missed getting the entire nerve covered with the extract and had to repeat the procedure. When she finished, she felt proud of her work. Her operation left virtually no signs on their bodies, save the many tiny puncture wounds that were already healing.

"There, all done, Dario. When they wake up, their arms will no longer move or operate in any way. They will merely be dangling, useless appendages. No healing potion will work nor will their bodies recover by natural means."

"Excellent work, Bernardine. Here," he handed her a small bag with a pile of shiny gemstones in it.

"Please, after the female bodies have done their work and have died, may I have them for further dissection and study?" she asked.

"All yours, all yours!" Dario replied. Now he would not even have to waste his breath disposing of the carcasses later on. He looked forward to soon having seventeen new Red Dragon children. Already, he lined up suitable parents for the as yet unborn babies. What a fabulously grand plan he had going. Nothing whatsoever could now go wrong. In fifty days, there would be seventeen new reds on Rehor, and he would become quite famous indeed. Bernardine had not, however, explained to Dario what the long term effects on the women's arms would be. That was wholly unimportant, for they would be dead in sixty days and it didn't matter the slightest.

The morning of the eleventh day since the devastating raid, Zoran had his rescue group primed and ready. Since the rescue would require a Shadow Walk to Rehor, Duskas were needed, and he was reluctant to bring along too many who were not Duska. After all, if things went ill, those who were not Duska would be trapped on Rehor. This was offset by his need for as many Archmages as possible and Mage Jarka as well. Zdenka, Verushka, Karel, Nadia, Marek, and Ivana comprised his Archmages, including himself. Jarka, Tomas, Dusan, Chan, Wen, Chika, and Akira were his added thief and Duska support. Unfortunately, Jarka, Zdenka, Karel, Marek, and Ivana were not Duska and dependent upon the others to take them to whatever planet on which the women were being held and brought back again. All armed themselves extensively, ready for a major battle.

Now they waited. Zoran again focused his Duska senses and at last located Danika. *Help please help us!*

Yes, we are now going to home in on you and find where you are located. The rescue party is on its way. Be brave a little longer, Danika.

Now came the hard part. He stepped into the Shadows, all the while maintaining his mental contact with Danika. He paused and strained his senses and began to follow, albeit slowly, the faint energy line of his connection, hoping that it would lead him ultimately to Danika. On through the swirling black void he moved, ever so slowly, being extremely careful not to break his connection. Memories of doing something similar some twenty years ago when he rescued Chika and Akira came to mind, but he hastily pushed them out, refocusing on the task at hand.

Zoran had no sense of time while in the Shadows. With nothing but grey-blackness all around, there was nothing to mark the passage of time, save his own heartbeat. At long last, he spotted the whitish-blue form of Rehor looming dead ahead, and he now knew that Danika was being held on that planet. He also had to be careful to avoid alerting the barons who lived and controlled Rehor. He had a sudden panic attack. What if they were being held in Clav's dungeons? Rescue then would be nearly impossible! Had he gotten Danika's hopes up only to dash them utterly? He forced such thoughts out of his mind, having nearly lost sight of the energy line.

As Rehor grew larger and larger, he began to relax. He was heading into the distant, uninhabited region of Rehor, certainly not towards the three Circles and their fortresses. He felt a bit of relief as he realized that the barons here were not holding the women. Still, were they involved in this diabolical plot? As bad as Baron Storm Clav was, Zoran just could not bring himself to believe that the man would side with dragons over humans. This was becoming a race issue.

Tall, craggy, snow covered mountains moved into his field of view, and he continued zooming in on the energy line, which grew more solid with each passing moment — a sure sign that he was getting close to her. At last, a dark opening appeared ahead of him. The mouth of the complex was squarely in the side of a sheer cliff, wholly unreachable overland. Only by flying, spells, or Shadow Walking could one reach this entrance. He spotted a tiny whiff of smoke, probably from the cooking fire, he concluded. He cast an Invisibility spell on himself and headed on into the cavern complex, though not before he did a hasty check for defensive spells. He found none thankfully and realized that the dragons probably thought that this secret location could not be discovered at all, so no need for defensive spells.

He moved inside and landed gently on the bedrock floor near the entrance. He spotted two passages. One led to the cook's small cave and the other to the captive women. Where were their guardian dragons, he wondered. Cautiously, he moved into the cook's area and found the disheveled woman cooking over a crude stove. She looked filthy and utterly exhausted. He later learned that she had to constantly cook from dawn to full dark just to make enough food to feed the women's now voracious appetites. There were no other exits from this cave. He backtracked and followed the left tunnel.

Within a few feet it opened into a huge chamber brightly illuminated by magical spells. There against the back wall were seventeen women chained to the wall. Each was on a thirty foot long chain. A huge hay stack provided their bedding. A long row of tables held their food bowls and water bowls. Nearby were a number of wooden buckets which stunk of urine and feces.

Danika, I have you located now. You are in a cavern high in the mountains of Rehor. The rescue party will be here shortly. Please make no sounds to attract any dragons until we get here.

Thank you. Please hurry. We need help badly. We don't want to die.

Zoran quickly Shadow Walked back to the others at his fortress in Brn. "Found them. They are on Rehor, high in the mountains. They are in a cavern complex but no dragons appear to be around at the moment. I'd like to keep it that way. Let's get in, free them, and get them out and try not to alert the dragons while we're at it. When their captors return, it would be ideal if the dragons had no clue that we were there. Leave them in mystery about how the women escaped."

Karel chuckled, that idea he liked. After they all joined hands, Zoran again Shadow Walked the group, arriving in the entrance passage. Just before he materialized the group, he checked with Danika to make sure no dragons had arrived yet. None had. He set everyone down gently. "Cook is that way. The women, this way," he called out.

"I'll put up a couple of Force Walls over the entrance and make it opaque. If any dragons should return, they can't get in or see inside," Zdenka suggested.

"Oh my!" Verushka exclaimed softly as she entered the large cavern and saw the seventeen women. At the moment, they were leaning over the tables, gobbling up bowls of food that the cook had just brought in for them. Their arms hung uselessly at their sides. Their hair was a mess of matted hair and hay. While all wore the tops of whatever outfit they had on when they were captured, everything below their waists had been either removed or cut off, thus making it easy for them to squat over the latrine barrels that had not been emptied since they arrived.

"Danika?" Zoran said, uncertain which woman she was.

"Me. Thank you for helping us. We don't want to die. None of us do. Please help us." She was twenty-two, with shoulder length black hair and dark eyes. All of the women had dark bags under their eyes, and many were bloodshot from periods of crying. Danika was a tall, thin woman, but perky. She had been the mother of two young babies before the attack. The other women ranged in age from their late teens through the mid-twenties at most, he noted, just as Jakob had ascertained.

"Jakob? Is that you too?" she called out, recognizing the Archmage of the warlord.

"Yes, we've come to get you out of here, Danika," he said boldly with an air of pride and satisfaction.

Meanwhile, Jarka took out her lock picks and went from woman to woman unlocking their neck collars. Nadia entered bringing the thoroughly exhausted cook and she gasped at the sight. "Hey, I count only eighteen women, including the cook. We are short ten women, plus where are the two dozen men?" asked Jakob, growing concerned that this rescue was only partially complete.

Danika acted as the women's spokeswoman. "They were taken away by some

Black Dragons. We don't know where. We've not seen the men since we were all abducted and flying off into the sky with the dragons after the attack."

"Damn, damn, damn," Jakob could not control his anger. "Now what, Zoran?" he asked.

"We get these women to safety and come back and do some more searching," he replied, unable to think of a better idea at the moment.

As soon as the last lock was undone, Zoran began getting the Duskas organized to Shadow Walk the women back to his fortress. However, the women's arms were just as Danika had said, useless. Apparently, they could neither move them nor had any feeling in them. As the various Duskas took hold of a woman's hand, it felt strange to them. Zoran alternated one of his people in between the women so that they all could be brought through the Shadows by the Duska. This seemed to work, so he began having the Duskas take their groups back to Brn. He and Zdenka were the last to go. Satisfied that they were leaving no trace of themselves behind and with Zdenka using her spells to make sure that no dragon was behind their opaque Force Walls, the two canceled the many spells over the cavern's entrance, and he Shadow Walked themselves back to Brn.

They arrived in the infirmary — Jarka's agreed upon location. Zoran had his two physicians there along with their four nurses. Thinking ahead, Jarka had also left two dozen healing potions there ready for use. As Zoran arrived, he overheard Jarka. "Okay, Danika, I'll have your arms all healed up in a jiffy. Drink this; it is a healing potion." She held the small vial up to her lips and poured the precious contents into her mouth.

"Tastes good," Danika commented. "We are always starving. It is so strange. After we were raped, it seems like we just cannot get enough to eat, not ever. How long will it take to get our arms working again?"

Jarka was already touching her arms, though Danika still could not feel her touch. "Hum. Strange. It should be working by now. Are you sure you cannot feel my fingers on your arm?"

"Nope, nothing. I can't move them. It's like they aren't there," she replied.

"Well, maybe it will take a bit longer. Let me look after the others," Jarka replied, quite baffled. It should be working already. Something was wrong.

"Hey, Jarka, get these three next. With no feeling in their arms, these three have somehow managed to break them, and the breaks look really bad to me," Akira called out. She had been going around getting each woman's name and ascertaining her current status.

"Oh my, those are really bad breaks. If we don't get them healed fast, gangrene is going to set in and that can be life-threatening," one physician pronounced. The two physicians and Jarka attended to these three cases immediately. Then, one by one, they administered the healing potion to all of the women.

After that, Jarka returned to Danika and tested her arms again. "Damn, still nothing Danika?"

"Nope, nothing at all," she replied bravely. "Can we have something to eat and drink? We're starving."

The cook, they learned, was Bronya Casmir, who ran the now destroyed inn in

Petr Falls. "I don't understand it. No matter how much food I cook these women, they are always complaining that they are starving!"

"Okay, let's get them a meal pronto and then let's get them all bathed and into clean clothes," Zdenka took charge, adding, "hopefully by then, the potions will have worked."

A half hour later, although the group attempted to feed the women, all of them complained that they were going too slow. Ultimately, Zdenka dumped each woman's plate into a bowl, and the women leaned over and gobbled the food frantically. "I don't understand it," she whispered. "They are eating as if they are utterly famished!"

"It's like a wave of panic is over them as far as eating is concerned," Verushka added. "At least that went quickly. Okay, ladies, time to get you cleaned up and into some new dresses."

"Will there be more food when we are done with that?" asked Danika. "We'll all be hungry again by then for sure."

While the women's needs were being handled, Zoran decided that he needed to be here and help figure out the women's true situation. "Okay, Tomas, Nadia, Dusan, and Verushka I want you to go back there and scout around some. Make sure that you are always invisible. See if you can locate the ten missing women and the two dozen men. They have to be somewhere."

"You got it dad," Tomas replied, eager to have some action. He was rather appalled at the women's situation and felt quite useless at the moment.

While Verushka wanted to stick around, she knew that Zoran wanted two Archmages who were also Duska on this scouting trip. Reluctantly, she agreed. Zdenka whispered, "I'll keep you posted via Chika." She knew that her Message spell would not go off-world, but Chika was Duska and could relay her news.

An hour later, the seventeen pregnant women looked human again, though the physicians said that they all looked like they were pregnant for forty-five days, not just ten or less. Zoran took careful note of this aspect. Somehow the dragon babies were maturing drastically faster than human ones, he found this quite alarming. Zdenka theorized that if the dragon fetuses were growing at ten times the rate for a human fetus, then that might account for the drastic intake of food. Indeed, none of the women looked at all overweight, rather the opposite.

However, seventeen women looked human once more. Dressed in clean white cotton dresses and their hair washed and brushed, they felt human as well, which raised their spirits considerably. However, none of their arms had recovered, though the three whose arms were broken were on the mend. Jarka administered two more doses of her healing potions, hoping to speed it along much faster. Bronya, the cook, however, was now sound asleep.

After feeding the women again, Zdenka and Zoran sat down with them and had the women describe what had happened in detail. They insisted the women tell them everything that the dragons had said or that they had overheard. The two needed some clues about the women's physical condition now and in the not so distant future. One woman relayed that she had overhead one of the dragons saying that when the time came for the birth of the baby dragons, the baby would chew and claw its way out and then drink its mother's nourishing blood. Of course, they all knew that would mean the death of the woman. This both shocked and frightened Zoran and everyone else. He'd rescued them, but unless something could be done about the dragons they were carrying, they'd die in spite of it all.

At suppertime, the others returned from their Rehor scouting mission. They had had no luck at all. The ten missing women and the men were nowhere to be found. Even more curious, the bodies of the two dead women could not be found as well. Jakob cursed and returned home to his new tower in the north.

Over dinner, Zoran discussed their meager findings with his entire group. Finally, he made some decisions. "Jarka, you and the physicians work on getting the women's arms working again. Verushka, Zdenka, and Nadia, you three study the women's bodies and see if you can work out any way under the sun, moon, and stars to save them from death when the dragons are ready to be born. I am going to pay a visit to Aldrick and see if he can shed more light on our serious problem and see if he can find out where the missing men and women are located. Perhaps he can get them back for us, if they are still alive. The rest of you are to help care for these women's needs, which seem to be huge at the moment."

One doesn't become an Archmage without knowing a tremendous amount of and about magic and its energies. It didn't take them long to discover that all seventeen women were now radiating heavy amounts of magical energies, quite unlike the cook who was not pregnant. Using every spell that they knew, they ascertained that there was some kind of very unique phenomenon going on between the human women and the alien dragon fetuses that they were growing within their wombs. However, they factually discovered little else. They spent all night going over every possible magical tomb in Zdenka's massive library, but found little there that could help. Defeated, they finally went to bed around three in the morning.

On a sadder note, after dinner, the women had finally calmed down enough to ask about their own families. Danika asked if her babies survived, though she had seen her husband being burned alive and held no hope for him. To help, Neda came by to visit with Danika, her old babysitter. The seventeen women cried long into the night, knowing that only Neda survived the attack. Their homes, families, and lives had been destroyed, shattered in only a matter of minutes.

"I know that I've only the one arm now, Danika, but Archmage Zdenka is teaching me magic! I am going to be a Mage when I grow up!" Neda excitedly explained. This brought the first real smile to Danika's face.

"You go ahead and do just that my Little Weed," Danika encouraged her, using the playful nickname that the two had invented for Neda, some years ago.

"I will and I promise to come and help you too, just as much as I can," Neda added. After that, Neda spent all of her free time each day chatting with Danika and the other sixteen women — all of whom knew her and she, they.

Zoran contacted Aldrick and the great gold agreed to see him in his lair with Sofie, his mate. "Well, we have a really big problem. You've heard about the dragon raid on Petr Falls up north?" he began.

"Yes, most unfortunate. I really thought that I had the dragons' agreement to stop such raids."

"Well, it is far, far worse that the mere killing of over two thousand men, women, and children. This time, Aldrick, they have gone too far. It was a band of reds, blacks, whites, and greens who made the raid. However, they took thirty young women and two dozen strong men away with them. We've managed to locate twenty of the women. It seems that the dragons have impregnated these women and that the women are now carrying baby dragon fetuses! We have no idea where ten other women are located or the two dozen men who were abducted."

"Oh good god! Is such even possible, Aldrick?" a startled and quite shocked Sofie exclaimed. "We dragons only produce an egg about every ten years. I've never heard of dragons breeding with you humans. It sounds awful. How is it even possible?"

"Probably they took human form to breed, dear. There is no other way. I highly doubt that they Morphed the women into dragons to breed. I didn't know that such interspecies breeding was even possible, Zoran. I will look into this. It cannot be good for the women."

"No it isn't. They are eating ten times the normal amount of food that we usually eat. They also paralyzed the women's arms." Zoran went through a lengthy detailed account from the discovery of the raid through the rescue and their current state. "What concerns me is what they overheard would be happening when the babies are born." He outlined what they had said.

"Oh those poor women!" declared Sofie.

"Say, I know one old gold who might know something about this. Stanislaus is getting rather old, close to five hundred sixty now and a might feebleminded. Still, it is the only thing that I can think of, Zoran. Come on; let's pay him a visit," Aldrick suggested.

A quick teleport spell later, Aldrick entered a cavern high in the mountains of far western Adapazan. After getting Stanislaus' permission, he Messaged Zoran to come on in, the aged dragon would see him. Zoran noted that the old dragon's hide was spotted and no longer golden. He moved slowly and Zoran suspected his joints ached. "We've come for some ancient wisdom, old dragon," Aldrick began. "Interspecies mating between humans and dragons. Is it even possible? If so, how does it work?"

"Interspecies mating? My, I haven't heard those words for a very, very long time. Seems to me I heard something about that. No, maybe I read something about that. No, maybe someone told me something about that at one time or other in my youth. I can't remember exactly."

"What did you hear? Is it possible?" asked Aldrick.

"Oh yes, it is possible, if I remember it right. Male dragon and female human, I believe. I don't know if it is the other way around though. Memory is not so good anymore, Aldrick. Perils of growing old, I'm afraid."

"Okay, so what happens to the human female? Does she give birth to a dragon or is it a human with some kind of unusual properties that usually associated with us dragons? I can't imagine what the baby would be like."

"My memory is a bit fuzzy, but I seem to recall something about the baby being a dragon anyway. You know, my great-great-great grandfather, he had a tomb on such things. I seem to have a memory of some kind about my dad showing me the book in his library back on Voss. Is Voss still there? I wonder what happened to Voss after we left it. No more food, yes, we ran out of hoofers, didn't we, and had to come here." His mind began wandering again. "We used to go for swims in the ocean. Now that was fun. Perhaps I ought to go for a swim here. I've seen the ocean when I am out flying and hunting sometimes. I don't think that it is too far from here. Aldrick, care to go for a swim like I used to do when I was a young dragon?"

"Not just now, Stanislaus. We need to find out more about this interspecies breeding. Some reds have done it with some human females and they are having an awful lot of troubles."

"Well, I should think so. We are not supposed to interspecies breed, you know. Why would the reds do that anyway? There are a lot of reds around. I've seen them a couple of times now. Didn't you say that the reds have their own world now and are not here with us?"

"Yes, that's right, Stanislaus. About the tomb. Any idea where it might be at? Any idea whatever happened to that tomb?" he asked.

"Don't know. Last I saw of it was four hundred years ago when I left home to make my own cavern home. I think it was on Voss, wasn't it? We did come from Voss, didn't we, Aldrick? I keep forgetting things it seems." He seemed confused again.

"Yes, we came from Voss. So it was last seen in your dad's cavern?"

"What was last seen there? Dad? Why yes, I said goodbye and he told me to live a long and prosperous life. I seem to have done just that, Aldrick. You know, that is a fine thing to say."

Aldrick was a little annoyed, but he knew patience was needed with the old dragon. He and Zoran worked with Stanislaus for several more hours, but in fact got little more useful information from him. Regretfully, the two headed back to Aldrick's home, where Sofie had prepared them a hearty drink, human style for Zoran's benefit.

"Our gestation period is sixty days, Zoran," Sofie explained. "So if interspecies breeding is possible, then I would expect that you will be having births in sixty days as well. That would make sense. What are you going to do with seventeen baby reds, that's what I'd like to know? Reds are worthless dragons anyway."

"Honestly, I don't know, Sofie. Right now, I am more interested in finding a way to save the lives of the seventeen women. Say, can I ask you both about how dragons give birth? I know nothing at all about your reproductive systems. Perhaps I can find some clues in it that will help me with our women."

Another two hours passed as Sofie and Aldrick shared the information with Zoran. Ordinarily, they'd never tell humans such intimate details, but both felt that they owed it to him, since rogue dragons had gone ahead and done this despicable action. It was late when he finally returned home, his head filled with exotic images, but no closer to a handling.

The twelfth day came with no change in the women's arms. Their voracious appetites were finally being satisfied, thanks to some astute suggestions by Verushka, who insisted that the pregnant women eat very healthy and balanced meals more frequently. Zdenka swore that she could see their womb size increasing each day, though.

Jarka, on the other hand, was terribly upset that her healing potions had not helped the women's arms in the slightest. While the three broken arms were now a thing of the past, having healed up well, the women were still in danger of breaking arms by accidentally sitting on them or other means. They simply had no feeling, no sensation, no control over their arms, which dangled about like some useless appendages. Worse, Jarka and Neda swore that Danika's arms were definitely shrinking, losing muscle tissue, and she was afraid that soon their arms might be little more than skin and bones. Atrophy was setting in rapidly, probably accelerated by their heightened metabolism.

Jarka was stumped, as were the two physicians. All three suspected the long healed little punctures on the women's shoulders might have had something to do with the arm situation, but they had no idea what. "Gang, I am afraid that I am way out of my league with this arm situation. My potions ought to have worked, yet they obviously have not."

"Let's find a corpse and do some dissection, shall we?" one physician finally suggested. For him, this was a last resort and one not taken lightly. They needed Zoran's permission to dig up a grave, and he begrudgingly gave it for the sake of the women.

Jarka wanted no part of this, however, and left the two men go their way. Instead, she visited the women and apologized to Danika and the others, "I am so terribly sorry that my healing potions have not helped your arms. I have failed you, and I am so sorry that I have. I cannot fathom what the dragons did to your arms, and I am at a complete loss about how to heal them. Please forgive me. I will keep on trying, but right now, I have no more ideas at all."

"That's all right, Mage Jarka. We are more worried about what's going to happen to us in a few more days when these foul, evil beasts want to be born. I really don't want to die. Maybe you can work on that for us," Danika suggested bravely. The other women agreed with one pointing out that having their arms working again would do them no good if they died giving birth to these evil, wicked beasts growing rapidly inside them. She agreed with them and began helping the Archmages with their research.

"I wish that we could actually see what the developing thing looks like," Verushka declared somewhat exasperated. More days passed and the various Archmages were no closer to understanding the situation than when they started. There simply were no records, no hints, and no ideas about dragons interbreeding with humans. For that matter, about the only item on dragons was old Archmage Oldrich's treatise that they'd read when they were magic students of hers well over twenty years ago.

The women's bellies were growing almost daily or so it seemed. The only data that they had was the fragments of comments the women had picked up from their captors — not much to go on. Still, they refused to give up all hope.

On the other hand, the two physicians were having a marvelous time dissecting several corpses. While they saw much that they did not understand, they had no real sense of what they were actually trying to find. The only conclusion that they reached was that the human body was awfully complicated, far beyond their knowledge and means.

Lacking any real progress, Zoran finally decided to see if his allies could find out anything that might help. Besides, he was overdue in informing them of the latest treachery on the part of the dragons. Shocked. That is the best way to describe the reactions of the other allied barons and baronesses when they heard what had happened. After the horror reactions and anger subsided, Baron Leo made an interesting suggestion. "You know, if we are going to find anything written about dragons, it is going to have to be in the most ancient records that we have. Obviously, there have not been dragons on our worlds ever, since their founding, but our founding barons came from somewhere else. If there is going to be any records or data on dragons, it would have to come from that era, if such even exists."

His suggestion triggered a new wave of research by the barons of the allied planets. Zoran still had the many ancient volumes penned by the original founder and baron of Adapazan, Baron Valentýn Vladislov. Further, the Zars also had volumes and volumes of the ancient writings of Bandar Zar, the creator of the Circles of Ascension from those founding days. Zoran Messaged his daughter, Jarmila and her husband Miroslav Zar. Both came for an extended stay and began searching through the huge number of volumes that were stored in the secret extra-dimensional room near Zoran's Circle of Ascension.

Further, following another suggestion of Baron Leo, Zoran sent all those who could be spared over to the main ancient Castle Dorumova and the original Circle of Ascension here on Adapazan, where Baron Jan Vavrin reigned. The mission: perform another exhaustive search for ancient books and scrolls and to look for hitherto for unknown secret chambers which might hold more records. Baron Jan, however, was hoping to discover more gold and gems hidden away in these forgotten hiding places.

Day thirty came, bringing Aldrick by to report. "Damnable reds anyway. Blacks too. I swear that they are lying to me. Both leaders claim that they know nothing at all about any raid on Petr Falls. They know nothing about any captive women or men and tried to sound appalled at interspecies breeding, claiming it was news to them as well. I don't believe a word that they said! Yet, I can find out nothing for you, Zoran. I've decided to send out spies. I haven't done that for nearly two hundred years now, but this is the vilest treachery imaginable. We will see if we can locate the missing women and men somehow. I must apologize for my failure, Zoran. Such has not happened to me in hundreds of years. This is not going to turn out pleasant, I am afraid, especially if we catch those dragons responsible."

"Thanks, Aldrick. I know that you are doing all that you can to help out," Zoran said gracefully and the big gold left, teleporting away.

Later that day, Baron Leo dropped by to personally show Zoran what they'd found. He was excited. "Look, we've been going through all the most ancient documents that we can find. Lida has been a big help with this. She is working tirelessly on the project. We came across this one passage written by our founder, Baron Leopold Matous himself. Here, the writing is pretty faded, but you can read it for yourself."

Zoran read:

The conflicts with the worms have escalated to the point where we could no longer live together. I chose, with many others, to follow Bandar Zar's suggestion and have led the exodus of the Matous clan to this, our new home, free of all worms.

"What's a worm?" Zoran asked.

"We honestly don't know, but it sounds promising. Perhaps our ancestors called dragons worms. Some of the snake-like dragons could be called accurately a worm. Lida thinks so anyway and is now cross-checking everything looking for anything written about worms. I think that we might be on to something vitally important here, Zoran." Baron Leo was very animated and excited.

"Okay, I'll see if we can find anything here about these worms of yours. It sounds plausible. There is no reason that the ancient word for the beasts has remained the same. After all, as far as we are concerned, dragons are a recent arrival." Since Leo was so excited about this finding, Zoran summoned everyone else to come have a look for themselves, which pleased the young man. After he left, everyone hit the records once more, this time looking for anything that mentioned the word worm.

Several days later, four such passages appeared in dis-related documents. Essentially, all four suggested that the original founders were fleeing from worms, backing up Baron Leo's discovery.

By day forty, the seventeen women's problem grew worse, requiring the Archmages' full attention, and Zoran had to drop this research project to help out. The growing dragons were now kicking and moving around within the women's wombs causing them terrific discomfort and pain. "Good god, imagine one of those four legged creatures with huge claws and enormous wings and giant tail inside them moving around," Archmage Verushka explained. "I am amazed that the women are not being seriously injured by the baby dragons! We have got to start to do something, Zoran, we just have to."

Mention of the form of the babies got Zoran to thinking or rather imagining what was going on inside the women, just as Verushka had intended. However, it also got him thinking along an entirely different line of thought. "Say, Verushka, if the babies are moving around and actually have a basic Red Dragon body form, what would happen if we cast a Morph Other spell on them, turning their bodies into a human form? Wouldn't that settle them down and make it more like a regular pregnancy?"

"Brilliant Zoran! Yes, it just might work. If we can force them to assume their human shape, the pain and discomfort ought to alleviate almost at once! You are a genius. Now then, how do we do it?"

"In this case, we will be morphing dragons into human forms. Since a dragon has this ability natively — say, it just occurred to me — why would a dragon have this as a native ability — to morph into human form any time it desires? Anyway, there is a good chance the spell will fail with these highly intelligent dragons. So we must be prepared to cast it several times just in case. Then, if it works and the women get relief, we can keep at it. Probably at some later point in time the dragon may well revert back to its dragon form again. We may have to keep on casting the Morph Other spell frequently," Zoran explained.

"Hey, I wrote that one down to research later, Zoran. Just why should a dragon be able to inherently morph into a human form? Okay, let's get all the Archmages together and have a go at it," Zdenka suggested.

Ten minutes later, they all gathered in the infirmary. "Okay, ladies, we are going to try something that we hope will alleviate the pain and discomfort that you are experiencing," Zoran explained to the seventeen women who were moaning and groaning, holding and rubbing their large bellies rather awkwardly with their feet. Their arms still hung uselessly at their sides. "Danika, we'll use you as our test subject." She managed to flash a slight grin. Obviously, she was in great discomfort and being unable to use her hands only made things far worse for the brave young woman.

Verushka cast her first Morph Other spell. As the magical energies flashed, Danika felt immediate relief! "Oh, that is *so* much better! Thank you!" she exclaimed, greatly relieved. All the Archmages grinned and set to work on the other sixteen women. Several times the spell had to be repeated, but within ten minutes all felt the enormous relief of having a normal human shaped baby in their wombs.

Zoran then explained what they had done. "We cast what is called a Morph Other spell. It allows us to change the recipient's body into that of any other species we can think of. In this case, we morphed the dragon body into a human body. Now the problem is that dragons can do this anytime that they so desire. So don't expect them to stay this way. It is likely that sooner or later the baby will of its own accord morph itself back into its dragon form. When that happens, let us know and we will morph it back into human form again."

"Thank you. Just having this much relief is wonderful," Danika replied.

As the time of birthing was rapidly drawing near, the group thought it wise to start preparing. Somewhere around twenty days or less remained. "When the time comes, we could cut the foul beast out of them," suggested one of the physicians.

Zoran rejected that idea, except as a very last resort. The vast majority of women who had to have their babies cut out died as a result of the operation. Surgery was in its barest infancy within the Federation at this time. Zdenka pointed out another consideration which also moved this idea to that of very last resort, "Look, it is a dragon after all. If we go cutting it out, might it not feel threatened and let loose a blast of its fiery breath on us all?" That sounded terribly grim, particularly to the physicians who would be doing the surgery. None knew at this time that a baby dragon's breath weapon was not fully developed at birth.

Verushka made the best suggestion. "Say, since this morphing is working, when it is time for the birth, why don't we continue to keep the dragon morphed into human form until it is out of the woman? That way, it would seem to be a normal birth."

Lacking any other viable idea, they decided to follow this approach. Zdenka insisted that between now and the time of birth that they keep accurate records for each woman, noting each time that that specific baby dragon had to be re-morphed back into a human form again. That way, when it was time, they would have a better idea how this would work out. All were worried about pulling out a flaming dragon with their hands.

A day later, they began to have a good idea of how long a dragon baby would stay morphed into human form. On the average it was six hours per spell, some longer, some shorter. On the sixth day of this, Archmage Karel came up with an improved variation. He also cast the Make Permanent spell on the morphed dragon. Of course, he knew that it would not really be permanent. After all, on anything other than a dragon, the morphing would be permanent anyway until the magic was dispelled by a mage. However, this extra push extended the average time by four hours, giving everyone a nice break — ten hours, more or less, between re-castings.

As the sixtieth day approached, Verushka had another fear. "Look, what are we going to do if all these women go into labor at the same time? We're going to need seventeen spell casters here just in case the spell has to be re-cast over and over while the baby is being born." That was a sobering thought and Zoran commandeered all of the other Archmages on Adapazan who were in the employ of the warlords. Zdenka had trained them many of the younger ones and now she called for their help. Jakob and four other Archmages joined the throng in the infirmary, all patiently waiting for the women to go into labor.

November 25th came and Verushka's worse fears materialized. That morning, woman after woman went into labor! Worse, the babies continued to attempt to morph themselves back into their natural dragon form, but the Archmages continued to re-cast their morph spells and adding to it their Make Permanent spells. However, the duration now ranged from a half hour to an hour at most. The casters and the women had a very long, arduous day of it all. Each had to stay alert. By now, the women could tell when their baby dragons were about to morph back into their dragon forms and alerted the casters who intervened before it could fully take place. It was a race between dragon and caster and woman.

Late afternoon, the sounds of a newborn baby's cry echoed off the stone walls of the infirmary! Danika's dragon was born. At once, Zoran cast his Vanish spell, depositing the dragon just above the sun. The physicians immediately began examining her and Jarka poured three healing potions down the woman's throat as fast as she could. A huge round of applause from the Archmages, mages, and others accompanied the physician's pronouncement, "Hey, I do believe that Danika is going to be just fine. Everything looks absolutely normal with her now! Incredible!" The relief on the young woman's face told all. She would have clapped too if her arms would have been working.

One by one, during the next two days, the other women gave birth to their baby dragon, without mishap. Zoran, Jarka, and the physicians repeated their actions sixteen more times before everyone breathed a sigh of relief.

After the last woman was pronounced fit, Zoran said cheerfully, "Ladies, congratulations. With your help, we've done it. We've saved your lives. Way to go ladies! I am extremely proud of each and every one of you. You never gave up hope and neither did we. Well done! By the way, I would be honored if you would all consider staying here in my fortress in Brn. However, if you wish to return to Tratky, that is fine too. Either way, I will see that you all never want for a thing for the rest of your lives. Never have I seen such bravery in the face of certain death!" Now that they knew that they were going to live, he desperately wanted to help them continue to survive and to perhaps establish new lives here.

Danika said to the other women, "See, I told you that Baron Zoran would save us." She had never doubted him these past fifty or so days and had constantly worked to convince the other sixteen women, keeping their morale up as well.

"Yes, but what about their arms?" asked Neda, who had come to watch and hold Danika's hand, even though she knew that Danika could not feel her hand.

"Ah yes, that," Zoran sighed. "As you ladies know, getting you through this birth process took priority. As Danika pointed out to me days ago, 'What use are arms if we die when the dragon is born?' We've necessarily have put that on the back burner so to speak. We will all get onto that now that you are all safe and sound. However, in all good faith, I must say that we are at a complete loss about what they did to your arms or how to repair them. Still, tomorrow we will get back onto that project. Ladies, how about a bath and a move into real bedrooms for you all?"

The women were all for that. While the others began handling the seventeen women and Neda lending her single hand, Zoran, Zdenka, Jarka, and the two physicians met in his room to discuss the women's arm problem. He had not told them the full truth, not just yet. While their full attention had been on trying to save their lives, they had also been working on their arm situation, gathering more data and making more observations. At this point, none of it was good. As expected, their arms continued to atrophy due to zero movement and exercise and their highly escalated metabolism. Worse, their arms continually got in the women's way and several more fractures had occurred.

One physician pointed out the rather obvious conclusion, "Look, it is way too dangerous for us to leave their arms as they are. If they break them accidentally, which has already happened five more times, then they risk getting gangrene or worse. With no feeling in them whatsoever, they can be broken and the woman won't even know it. They could get a cut and bleed profusely, and unless they spot the blood, they'd never know it had happened. Honestly, these arms are going to be incredibly dangerous for them. They will have to keep healing potions with them at all times and have someone ready to dispense it at the first sign of trouble." Although Zoran, Zdenka, and Jarka hated this line of thought, this was a rather obvious conclusion that they had more or less seen for themselves these past weeks.

"What are you saying? If we can't restore their arms back to normal, then what?" asked Zoran.

"If we exhaust all options and cannot get them back to normal, the only safe thing to do is to remove them," he replied. Jarka groaned.

The group continued to try all manner of ways and means and even wild spells during the ensuing days. Nothing made the slightest difference. In desperation, the physicians wanted to dissect the women's arms to see if they could learn anything that way. This was going too far, Zoran decided, much to Jarka's relief. After all these women had endured, she didn't want the men cutting up their bodies. It didn't seem fair or right.

At last in mid-December, Zoran finally had to make the decision. "As you know, we've tried everything imaginable as well as some pretty wild things, but nothing has made the slightest difference to your arms. It is like they are dead."

"Hey, they look almost dead!" Danika interrupted, stating the obvious. Her arms were so thin now that they looked like mere skin covering her bones, a rather sickening sight.

"We can't leave them like they are. Already, a couple of you have broken your arms several times. It is way too dangerous for you, since you cannot feel then when they get hurt."

"Well, I don't mind that," Danika joked. "I broke my toe when I was a girl and man did that ever hurt! I've broken my left arm here and didn't feel a darn thing.

That's dangerous, isn't it? If you can't get them working again, can you get rid of them? After all I've been through, I don't want to die because my arm got infected or something and I didn't even feel it. Besides, even if you got them going today, there's almost nothing left of them. I don't think that they would be able to even lift a spoon."

"Yes, Danika. That is the conclusion that we have all reached. Since we simply cannot undo whatever the dragons did to your arms, the only safe thing to do is to remove what little is left of them so you don't risk life-threatening injuries later on," Zoran explained as gently as he could.

"Fine with me. It won't hurt a bit, will it?" The others agreed and the operations began. The very instant the physicians finished their work on a woman Jarka poured her healing potions down her throat. The women had a full recovery in only a single day, thanks to her potions. However, Zoran did permit the physicians to hang on to the removed arms for further study. As it turned out, in the long run, this was a brilliant move, though at the time, Zoran thought this was particularly gruesome and macabre.

Of course, during this time, Zdenka and Verushka both worried about what kind of life these women could now have. Thus, they continued to observe and study them, making notes of what each woman seemed to like to do or had done before this had happened. Until the women had finished giving birth, their attention had been forced onto satisfying their craven hunger and somehow hanging on. Once they were taken to their new bedrooms and out of the infirmary, their massive losses began to surface. More than once, they sobbed over their lost families and lives. Their suppressed grief surfaced at last, compounded by the reality of what their lives had become because of their arms. None of this was missed by Zdenka and Verushka.

Long hours they discussed the women's future and their plight. Then, Zdenka noted, "Say, they are still radiating enormous amounts of magical energies."

"Are you thinking what I am thinking?" asked Verushka.

"Let's see if they can learn to cast spells."

"Like minds think alike," Verushka joked. "Or is it because you were my teacher?" Both women laughed.

They picked on Danika first, a day after the operation and after Jarka pronounced her shoulders were fully healed. Zdenka placed a little pile of dirt on the floor. "Now then, Danika, I want you to concentrate on the dirt pile." Ten minutes later, Danika's first spell detonated. Clean. The dirt had vanished. Of course, she then asked where it had gone.

"How would you like to learn to cast magical spells, Danika?" Zdenka asked.

"What? Me? Cast spells? Become a real Mage? Whoopee!" The Archmage had her answer.

One by one, the two worked with each of the other sixteen women. It took between ten and fifteen minutes for each one to learn to cast the Clean spell, fantastically rapid for a total beginner. Immediately, Zdenka added seventeen more magic students to her school. Verushka was pulled in to help with their training, and Zdenka twinned all of her other students with one of the seventeen to be their hands as needed. When Zoran heard the news at suppertime, tears of joy trickled down his cheeks. He finally relaxed; the women could start a new and valuable life.

Around the same time, ten new baby Black Dragons were born in the mountains of Gerde and were immediately given to ten families to raise. The dead women's bodies were drenched in acid and disposed of, leaving behind no trace of their existence.

Dario was furious when he was told of the disappearance of the eighteen women. He sent out scouting parties to scour the mountains, looking for any trace of the women. None was found. He personally inspected the cavern and saw that the locks around their neck had been picked. At last, he came to the only conclusion that seemed plausible to him. Somehow they had picked the locks with their feet. The cook was not bright enough to have done it, that he knew. Besides, the poor woman was totally exhausted from constant cooking. One of the women must have picked the locks and then they tried to escape and had fallen down the thousand foot cliff to their deaths. Probably wild animals, bears likely, had then carried them off and dined on them. This was the story that he told to the seventeen expectant sets of parents.

Later, when Aldrick visited him, he denied it all, but began to wonder why the gold suspected that he might be trying to do interspecies breeding. Perhaps no other conclusion was possible, since they had taken thirty women. He resolved to be more careful in the future.

In the high, snow covered mountains, the whites monitored the interspecies breeding of their neighboring blacks. In late November, they saw for themselves that such was feasible. Cezar, the white, sent Dario a word that the whites were now interested.

Chapter 13 A Long Winter

Yuletide came to Adapazan, the traditional time of celebration. For five days, folks partied and exchanged small gifts. Song and dance, often aided by a bit too much ale, predominated at all the inns. On the night of December 25, Zoran hired the Stodgy Inn and held his usual come-one, come-all Yuletide Dance. All food and drink was on him and the place was always packed with folks from Brn. Of course, the Archmages cast all manner of spells on the entrances beforehand, guaranteeing that no thief or assassin could enter without a loud alarm going off.

Danika and her friends had been learning to cast magical spells for two whole weeks now. Amazingly, all had this very day completed all of the Adept Spells and were ready to begin their study of "real spells," as the women began to call them. That is, they could cast the three dozen useful, helpful spells, such as Clean, Mend, Tie, Wipe, Polish, and Light a Lamp. Normally, those whom Zdenka accepted into her school required three months to learn all of these, sometimes more in the case of those who would only ever reach the Adept level of magic use. Neda, although now eleven, had also just finished up learning all of them, but she was bright and young. Zdenka had expected that she would pick these up quickly for Neda had an inherent knack for them. These seventeen were adults and as such ought to have taken three months to learn them. Hence, she and Verushka were shocked to see the incredible rapidity with which they learned them. Both attributed it to the women's altered bodies, having carried a magical creature full term. Somehow that had altered the women's sensitivity to magic in ways neither Archmage understood.

So this night, Zdenka promised Neda, Danika, and the others a celebration for their impressive achievement: party time at the Stodgy Inn. She and Verushka had taken them all to dressmakers earlier in the week and bought them each a new fancy dress just for this occasion. Naturally, the women had to have their partner help them get dressed and ready for the party, though Neda always did her best to help Danika as well. In actual fact, it was becoming difficult for the two to be parted now.

The two Archmages had an ulterior motive behind the celebration and the fancy dresses. This would be the first time that these young women would venture out into the public eye since their abduction, rape, and loss of their arms. They worried about how the women would deal with it. "We've got to know, Zdenka. Are they going to adapt or are they going to have nervous breakdowns or totally introvert, never venturing into the public again? We have to know and we have to help them adjust, you know," Verushka stated factually.

"Wow, you look beautiful, Danika," Neda admired her close friend.

"Oh, I don't know about that. I have no arms anymore, Neda. I need others to help me with everything now. I feel so nervous and awkward. Everyone will be looking at me."

"I think that they should, Danika. You look very pretty. I have all these pimples which just won't go away and the gap between my teeth is really large. I think I look goofy," Neda admitted.

"No, you look like a pretty young girl should. Hey, I had them when I was your age. When you get older, they will go away. Maybe there is a spell that will fix your teeth. We should ask Archmage Zdenka or Verushka. Do you really think that I look okay? I feel so nervous and funny."

"Oh sure. You look great. Here, let me fix your hair a bit. Say, I have wanted to ask you something, Danika. Since mom and dad are dead, will you be my mom? At least for a while, please? Jarka is always way too busy."

Danika grinned. "Of course, silly Little Weed, though I can't do a whole lot for you, no arms anymore. You have to help me now."

"Thanks! I will, I promise," She hugged Danika with her arm. "Come on, we best get going. I hear the others gathering in the hall." She opened the door and Danika walked out into the hall, growing more nervous with each step. She glanced at her comrades, the other sixteen like her. They looked really nice in their new dresses, but she knew that they were just as nervous as she was.

One whispered to her, "I'm really scared! What if I get bumped and fall? I have no arms to catch myself. I am going to make a complete fool of myself."

"Me too, I'm so nervous I can barely walk. We have to go though, after all Archmage Zdenka has done for us, but I'm really scared."

"Me too," another added, overhearing them. "We all are. We are so helpless. I think it is folly that we go out into the world like this. Maybe we should just stay here. What if we have to go pee? How can we even eat or drink anything?"

"Hey, that's what I'm here for," her twin broke in on their conversation. "I'm supposed to be your hands, though if you want to dance with some young fellow, please go ahead," she added.

Danika frowned, "Get real, what guy is even going to be with us, we're. . ." She didn't get to finish her sentence because Zdenka came out into the hall with Zoran on her arm.

"Okay everyone, it is time to relax and celebrate. Eighteen of you have just mastered all of the Basic Adept Spells. So I want you all to have fun and enjoy the night. Merry Yuletide to one and all. Follow us, off we go. A dancing we will go, a dancing we will go," her voice trailed off as she stepped out into the main street before her Archmage Tower, two blocks from the Stodgy Inn.

"Aren't you overdoing it a bit dear?" Zoran whispered.

"Have to. The women are frightened to death of going out. We have to make sure that they really do have an enjoyable time *especially* this first time out. It's critical to their well-being. I can't imagine what they must be feeling right now, but I am trying my best. It has to be awfully scary for them. If all goes well, it will give them a huge boost of self-confidence which they absolutely must have. Now promise me that you will dance with each one of them at some point tonight."

"Yes dear. You are right as always." He leaned over and planted a quick kiss on her forehead.

As they reached the doorway, a voice called out, "Make way for Baron Archmage Zoran and Baroness Archmage Zdenka!" The room was packed as it always was, but somehow an opening formed and the pair strolled inside, glad for the warmth. No one bothered to wear a coat; it was just two short blocks. Her forty magic students followed right behind them. Each twin had his or her arm around their partner, ensuring that they didn't slip on the snow packed road or have any trouble getting inside. Once the last of them entered, the opening somehow vanished and the musicians stuck up a lively dance tune, one of Zdenka's favorites.

"Everybody's staring at us!" whispered a very nervous Danika. Her legs felt suddenly very weak.

A voice nearby called out, "You bet. You look beautiful. You must be one of her new students. I haven't seen you around Brn before." Danika turned and saw a young man in his twenties. He had black hair and a matching moustache. He was well dressed, but the suit was well worn. He also had big hands. "Rafael's my name. I'm a blacksmith and work in the fortress for the baron. What happened to your arms anyway?"

"I'm Danika. Yes, we are her new students. Only been studying for two weeks though. The dragons got them," Danika fumbled about, uncertain just what to say or reply.

"Mind if I have this dance, Danika? They always play this one first because it is the Archmage Zdenka's favorite."

"Well, I don't know. I don't have any arms to hold you back," Danika replied, trying hard to find an acceptable way to get out of this without turning him down. Surely he can see that I am completely helpless. There are so many other women in here for him to ask to dance, she thought.

"Go ahead, Danika," Neda whispered encouragingly. Rafael's arms slipped around her waist and then over her shoulder and he gently moved her into the dance pattern.

Meanwhile, a boy came up to Neda. "How come you only have one arm?" he asked.

"Cause a dragon got it when they attacked and destroyed my village up in Tratky. I'm Neda and I am going to be a mage too," she replied.

"Cool. I'm Dragan Zikmund. My dad runs the Stodgy Inn. One day I'm going to run the inn. Wanna dance?"

"I don't know how," she replied honestly.

"Hey, no problem. I'll show you. It is not hard at all."

While nearly everyone took note of the seventeen women — word of their situation had long ago spread around Brn, by the second dance, the newness had worn off and folks were back to chatting, dancing, drinking, eating, and enjoying themselves. Long ago, Mr. Zikmund had purchased the building behind his inn, had it torn down, and doubled the size of his main floor. Tonight, he reaped a huge profit, best all year, as over four hundred men, women, and children crammed into his inn for the dance. Zoran paid for everything with a huge tip to boot. Mr. Zikmund was very pleased with this long-standing arrangement at Yuletide.

By the third dance, Zdenka began looking around for her special students. She'd gotten lost in the dances and rather forgotten them. She said a silent curse for her negligence. She spotted Danika dancing with a stranger — no he was a blacksmith she recalled. One by one, she located the others. All were at least dancing with someone and she relaxed a bit. So far so good.

"You dance well, Danika."

"My husband and I used to. . ." her voice faltered.

"I'm sorry is he here? I don't mean to . . ."

"Oh no. He was murdered by the dragons that kidnaped me. They murdered my two little children too. I watched him get burned to death by a dragon. It was horrible."

"I'm so sorry for you! That is just horrible! If that would have happened to me, I don't know how I could go on living. Your children even! How awful." Rafael seemed very sincere and she relaxed a bit further.

"Well, then I was raped by the Red Dragons, but I wanted to live. Zoran found me. He can talk directly into your mind somehow. After hearing his voice inside my head, I just wanted to live somehow."

"Well, I am so glad that you did. Were you a stay at home mother raising your children?"

"Yes, I took care of our house and all that. I wanted to be a good mother, but I also made quilts to sell. It brought in much needed extra money. When I was a kid, times were really harsh. No one had hardly anything. Then, Zoran became our Baron and after that, why everything changed for the better."

"You can say that again. I was six when his evil father invaded Sholov Province and wiped them all out. Here in Brn, we were scared that soon he would be marching his Shock Troops into Brn and wipe us out as well. Then along come Zoran and the Gold Dragons. Everything changed after that. Do you realize that Brn has now more than doubled in size since then? Pretty amazing times that we are living in, isn't it? Say, would you like something to drink? All this dancing has made me a bit thirsty."

"Well, yes, an ale would be great, but I . . ." she faltered, her helplessness came flying back into her mind.

"Of course, I will help you drink it. Come on, old Mr. Zikmund has a very special dark ale that is just incredible. Come on. Let me be your hands for tonight, okay?"

"It is so utterly embarrassing," she admitted.

"Of course it must be, but hey, the Archmage knows what she is doing. If she thinks you can learn magic, you must be incredible able and powerful. She only takes the very best students, you know."

"I didn't know that."

"Oh yes. She has made more Archmages in the last twenty years that she's been running the magic school than have been made throughout all of the rest of the whole Federation! Who knows, maybe one day you will be an Archmage too. Two of your dark ales, Mr. Zikmund, the special one. Zoran is paying for it," he teased.

The innkeeper grinned as he filled two mugs. "Right he is. Enjoy. A gold a mug usually," he added.

Rafael held the mug up to her lips and she took a frothy sip. "Wow, this is the best tasting ale I've ever had. Thanks."

"Told you. Let's move over there where we have a bit more room to drink and chat."

A bit later, the music stopped and one of the musicians raised his voice. "Okay, it is that time again. The Zoran Dance. All you ladies, this is your chance to dance with Baron Zoran himself! One, two, three, four." The next lively dance began. Danika, still sipping her ale with Rafael, watch as everyone made an open space in the middle of the large room. The ladies moved closer and Zoran appeared. One by one, he danced with each woman who came up to him. So many wanted a dance that he could only do a few steps with each. Rafael explained, "He does this every year. The ladies really go for it. After all, nowhere else can you get the chance to dance with your very own baron! Go on, get out there and dance a few steps with him," he encouraged her.

"I don't know if I should," she hesitated. Before long, Zoran began spotting the seventeen women and cleverly moved in each one's directions. As he got close to one, he purposely pulled her in for a few steps, before moving on to the next woman. Suddenly, he was right before Danika and, before she could say anything, he'd swept her up and twirled her around for a few steps, then gently moved her back to Rafael before moving on to the next woman. The crowd clapped and cheered all the while.

"Why, you're flushed!" Rafael noted as she came back beside him. "Here, you'd better have another sip," he teased her.

Their ale done, the two headed back for more dancing. A bit later, Rafael whispered in her ear, "You are nervous about being out here among all of us, aren't you?"

"Is it that obvious?" her voice trembled.

"No, but I rather picked that up from you. I know that I would be scared to death if I were in your shoes. But you needn't be. Honestly, Danika, you are pretty, very smart, and a good dancer. You've nothing to be afraid of here."

"I'm helpless," she replied. "I can't do anything."

"Ha! Now that is a fib if I ever heard one! You can dance. You have just drunk a mug of the finest ale in Brn. You can talk and you are learning magic. I think that is quite a lot of doing."

"You know what I mean," she retorted, a bit miffed with Rafael.

"So you need help holding the mug, opening doors, probably getting dressed. So what? Everyone needs some help from someone for some things. It's just that you need help with things that others usually do not, that's all. I need help with magical things. Can't cast even the dinkiest spell. Not a magic bone in my body. Come on, let's dance instead."

"Say, how come you aren't married?" Danika asked, realizing that she still knew very little about this blacksmith.

A flash of grief flickered over his face, but he recovered quickly and answered. "I was, but she died in childbirth five years ago. Our boy somehow got stuck and her heart gave out. I lost everything that night."

"I'm so sorry. I didn't know. How awful," Danika fumbled for comforting words.

Rafael sighed, "Life goes on. She was a fighter, you know, never gave up. Tonight, I see in you some of what I once saw in her and I just had to meet you. You never give up, neither do I."

"I never thought of it that way. Come on, dance with me," she whispered.

At midnight, the dance finally ended. The six hours had passed rapidly for everyone. As the music ended and the folks who remained began filing out, heading for home, Rafael said good night to Danika. "Say, can I see you on Sunday?" he asked.

"I'm always studying," she blurted.

"Yes, but the Archmage always gives her students Sundays off to do whatever they want. Can I drop by Sunday afternoon, say around one? We can do something, maybe go for a sleigh ride or I can show you my shop."

"Well, okay. I suppose that it will be okay with the Archmage. I'll have to ask her," she answered tentatively.

"Good. See you at one on Sunday then. Thanks for the dances." He turned and left, while Danika waited for the other students and the Archmage to lead her back to the tower.

Neda came rushing up to her, face flushed. "Danika, I think that I have got a boyfriend! It's the innkeeper's youngest boy. Over there by his dad. He's called Dragan. He's kind of cute don't you think? Do you think the Archmage will let me have a boyfriend? I am only eleven. Maybe you can talk to her about it for me."

"Of course you can have a boyfriend, Neda. You don't need her permission for that. He is cute, isn't he?" The two chatted as the other students finally congregated together, the twins taking up their positions once more. The last people to leave, Zoran and Zdenka led them back the short distance to her tower. Although neither she nor Verushka said anything, both were highly pleased with how the evening had gone for their newest students. All had integrated with the locals very well, although some better than others. The ice had been broken for these women.

The next day, it was back to studies once more, though Danika did ask about Sundays. "Yes, that is your day to do whatever you desire. Some locals take the time to go visit their families. Some sit back and relax. A few use the time to get in extra studies. Okay, now let's get cracking. Your check sheet for the Beginning Mage spells is vastly longer than that of the Adept List."

With things back under control and running smoothly once more, Zoran decided to continue his researches into ancient history. He now had several clues to follow. However, he did make planet-wide security changes as the new year began. He doubled the pay for the Gold Dragons and had them flying routine security patrols near the larger outlying towns. He established a Lookout Stipend for any mage who pledged to spend three hours each day checking on other larger towns. If anyone spotted a flock of dragons coming, they were to personally Message Zoran immediately. He estimated that he now had coverage of a third of all the likely targets on Adapazan, at least partially. Somehow another Petr Falls had to be avoided.

In January, Barons Leo and Stefan came by to discuss all that they had found in their lengthy researches into the ancient history of their worlds. His sisters came with them, Lida and Reyna, but they spent time with Zdenka and Verushka. Besides, they wanted to meet the eighteen survivors about whom they had heard so much. Before long, the three men invited Miroslav and Jarmila to join them, since Bandar Zar's records proved to be far more extensive than theirs.

"Well, we know that all of our ancestors were once together on a single world," Leo pointed out. "They apparently left that place because of the worms, which may well have been the dragons, but as yet we can't prove that, can we?"

"Not really," Stefan concurred. "Still, from all we can find, apparently Bandar Zar was the key man who led all of the original barons to these sixteen planets."

"Yes, that seems to be supported by what we have found in Bandar's writings. What we don't understand yet is just how is it that Bandar learned to create the Circles of Ascension or how it is that he knew of the location of the sixteen planets," Miroslav agreed.

Zoran's youngest daughter, Jarmila, added, "We've also discovered that there is a missing batch of Bandar's journals. He was the most meticulous person we've ever encountered. He kept very precise records, though Brother Jiri rather made a mess of them. He got them all out of order. I put them back in the right order, but that took me three weeks! There is a journal whose number is six. That's the oldest one. Then, there is a gap. The next one is number ten and they continue on up from there through the last one, twenty-four. So we are missing volumes seven through nine and one through five."

"Say, one through five might contain the key data that we need to know now," Zoran theorized.

Both Zars grinned. "Yes, dad, that is precisely what Miroslav and I think. So how do we find those missing journals? We have no ideas at all."

"Well, we went over Castle Matous with every possible spell looking for other secret chambers or hiding places," Leo broke in. "Found a few secret stashes of gems, but no other books or records unfortunately. Lida and I have concluded that those journals are not on our world, because they would most likely have been stored in Castle Matous if Bandar had left them on Gladno."

"Same with us on Valtr," Stefan added. We found some interesting secret chambers that we did not know existed. Found some cool magical armor and weapons and gems, but no journals or books. Bandar Zar must not have left them on Valtr either."

"Well, Warlord Miklos discovered them in a secret chamber in the basement of his old fortress in Sholov Province," Zoran replied, although everyone knew this story already. We've been all over the main Castle Dorumova here. Nothing there. However, as you know, we found the Valentýn's journals hidden in a secret location on a nearby island, which the Yellers now occupy. I'm sure that we found everything that he had hidden there. Yet, Bandar chose to hide his precious journals in Sholov Province. Maybe there is more to be found there. I don't know what else to suggest. I wish our predecessors had kept better records of such things."

"Say, I think that is an excellent idea," Miroslav spoke up. "It stands to reason that Bandar would have kept all his journals together. I bet that they were just not found by my dad and the warlord. Any chance that we can conduct an extensive search there at the ruins in Sholov Province?"

Complaining, Jarmila taunted, "In the middle of the winter with all this snow?"

"I'll put together an expedition once the snows have melted in April," Zoran promised. "Right now, it is buried under the snow pack. Tomas has rebuilt the fortress a little east of the ruins. I think he is planning to restore it and make it a museum. Okay then, I guess that there isn't much else we can do along this line until then."

"True. Say, how is the subterranean construction coming along?" Stefan asked.

"As crazy as this is going to sound, it is paying for itself," Zoran teased them. "Actually, slower than I wanted. We've had so many other more critical things to handle of late. We chose to extend out from our two under-the-fortress mines, since much tunnel work was already in progress there. I have to heap the praise on Archmage Marek Aceda, the old Door Warden of Zdenka's Tower. It was he who took charge and developed the spell alteration. He took advantage of the fact that we were extending the gold and gem mine tunnels. He tweaked the mining spell — you know, the one that turns stone into mud or dust. He adjusted the spell so that any gold or any gemstones which may be lying in the current volume of stone to be removed by turning it into dust remains unaffected by the spell."

"He alters the composition of a section of solid stone of the desired shape on the master drawings. After the spell detonates leaving behind a massive dust pile in place of the bedrock, workers then sift through the dust as they carry it outside and dump it. The gold nuggets and raw gems are trapped in the netting of their sifters. So far, the gold and gems recovered more than pays for the construction of the subterranean work. Pretty amazing."

"Damn," Stefan teased Zoran, "leave it to Baron Vladislov to make a tidy profit while digging an underground relief center for his people." Everyone laughed.

"Yes, but we should have gotten far more work done. We would have if that dragon attack had not occurred up in Petr Falls," Zoran admitted. "How goes yours?"

"Making headway," Stefan answered first, since he'd just picked on Zoran. "We've concentrated on making subterranean corrals and granaries. If the dragons do attack us, we want all of our food reserves and stock to be beyond their reach as well as our horses. If things go bad, we want enough horses to both help the rebuilding efforts as well as to re-breed our herds without having to go off-world to get them. Already, we have that part mostly completed and our fall harvest is safely underground. Now my workers are tackling the city part. If you don't mind, I'll send Chesna back here so she can learn Archmage Marek's spell variation. I'd like to make money digging my subterranean city too." He grinned. So did Leo, who promised to send Zelenka back to pick up Marek's spell variation as well.

After joining their wives for a social lunch, Archmage Karel and Dana had the two barons drop by the armory. Karel had a half dozen of his newly enchanted weapons ready for each baron. "This one is merely an enchanted blade. However, these two are Red Dragon Slayer blades, these two are Black Dragon Slayer blades, and the last one, a White Dragon Slayer bastard sword. May they serve you well," the Archmage said proudly.

Both barons were very much impressed with the blades and with Karel's work. He, on the other hand, was much impressed with the weight of the two bags of gemstones they gave him. Once the barons left with their prized new weapons, Karel handed one bag to Dana. "Okay son, I am turning this project over to you and the blacksmith Rafael. I've moved what you two will need into an unused room next to my lab on the top floor. What gets made out of what and for whom and their distribution I am officially turning over to you. When you two are ready for the next spell incantation on a blade, Message me and I'll come and cast it. Meanwhile, I will be free to work on my next project, one which may well ensure us total victory over the vile, wicked dragons!" Karel snarled as he spoke the accursed noun.

"Thanks!" Dana replied enthusiastically. Now he would be playing a far more important role. So many barons wanted to buy or get some of the Dragon Slayer swords that just dealing with the many details had become almost a full time job. Already, they had gone through half of their stock of recently purchased weapons of sufficiently high quality to undergo the enchantment process. More had to be obtained. Quite a lot of prep work was needed on each blade even before the actual spells were to be cast. The metal had to be heated to just the right temperature, only then could the infusion of the appropriate dragon's blood be made. Dealing with the heating process would be Rafael's task. Archmage Karel only needed to be involved in the actual casting of the power spells that both enchanted the blades and infused them with their special properties, making the enchantments permanent. Thus, Karel now expected to have at least six hours each day freed up for his newest project.

In fact, both he and Archmage Jakob were working together on very secret projects, known only to the two of them. I say working together, but that is not entirely true. Yes, they originally got the idea together and they did share information and they did help each other out of the myriad problems each had been encountering, but the two men were also competing with each other, a friendly Archmage rival to see just who was the best. At the moment, Archmage Karel's name was widely known among all of the barons as the producer of the best enchanted weapons money could buy. Archmage Jakob's goal was to get his own name just as widely recognized as Karel's. A friendly competition had evolved between them since early July. Each was following a different path, however.

Karel's approach centered upon the acquisition of numerous body parts from various types of dragons. Jakob's approach focused on the huge gemstones found in the mines of the northernmost province of Adapazan. Although the two approaches were vastly different from each other, they both had similar goals in mind: the control of attacking dragons.

Archmage Karel needed the services of a blacksmith and thus he made use of young Rafael, who was pleased to do more useful work than making another set of horse shoes. Of course, there were plenty of horses to shod, but it was boring work for Rafael. He leapt at the chance to help out the Archmage.

For both men, the problem was how to confront head on the attacking dragons and somehow control them, while not at the same time being destroyed by the blasts of the dragon's breath. Chan was visible proof that this was not an easy problem. She'd lost her hand to the ever so slight mistake of catching a bit of rotting slime on it. Had she taken the full blast on her whole body, Chan would have been quite dead — a mere skeleton within minutes. Yet, the two Archmages knew that if humans were to have any chance in a battle with the dragons, they had to somehow become impervious to the dragon's breath. Karel took the approach of constructing forged rods infused with body parts from the dragons, while Jakob took the approach of utilizing powerful spells infused within a hugely expensive gem to be worn on one's chest, protecting its wearer.

"But gold rods will be weak, Archmage," Rafael had cautioned Karel when he'd come to him for advice and assistance in the forging of a test rod. "Gold is highly malleable. It will bend way too easily."

"Hum, very true, and yet it conducts magical energies so very well. What kind of compromise can we make?" Karel asked the young blacksmith.

In time, Rafael had come up with an ideal alternative. Essentially he forged a steel casing to enclose the golden rod that was the heart of the magical item. That then gave Karel additional ideas. If he could infuse the dragon body parts between the steel outer casing and the golden rod core, he would have the best of both worlds: strength and magical power. Of course, the final product had to be altered. The steel was hard and cold to hold in one's hand. Rafael then wrapped the rod in a fine leather sheath.

He commissioned Rafael to then make a dozen such rods, paying the lad handsomely. Rafael was extremely pleased with the arrangements, more so when he began helping Dana with the magical blades construction. True, his part was mundane; still it was more rewarding than making horse shoes.

Karel was methodical, if nothing else. As the rods were made, one by one, he tested their enchantment capabilities, logging each one carefully in his notes. Not until he had determined the exact quality each rod could hold would he actually begin their enchantments. He saved the most powerful one for last, hoping to gain valuable experience on the lesser rods.

Meanwhile, he began working out the needed enchantments that the rods would have to hold. Because the dragon's breath weapons were so vastly different, each rod would have to be attuned to a specific type or perhaps types of dragons. Days stretched into weeks during the coldest part of the year. Karel hardly noticed though, but his wife, Chika, kept him apprised of the rest of the world.

To be effective and protect the wielder, each rod would have to hold one portion of one of the top-most power spells that only an Archmage could know and cast. Few Archmages ever mastered this massive protection spell. Essentially, he needed the rod to cast at will the Sphere of Breath Weapon Protection, a sphere twenty feet across, centered on the wielder of the rod. If he could somehow infuse that one part of the power protection spell into each rod, then the wielder would be able to stand before the oncoming dragons and make use of the rod with impunity. That was the first step. Once he'd gotten that accomplished, then he could move on to the much needed offensive capabilities to combat the dragons. All told, this was an enormous task that Archmage Karel had set for himself and he spent long hours into every night working on it.

By late January, he had one rod holding the proper protection spell, but now the question became: how can it be tested to see if it works? He needed to hold it and stand before a dragon that would shoot his or her breath weapon at him. Of course if the rod failed to work properly, he'd become the late Archmage Karel. On the other hand, he could not proceed until he proved that the rod would protect the wielder from a dragon's breath weapon.

He chose Renata as his test subject. Why? He figured that Emil might be more reluctant to help test a weapon that may ultimately be used against dragons, though certainly not against golds. Besides, he and Renata had trained together under Archmage Oldrich. The other aspect for choosing her was her age, she was still a young dragon, as dragons go. As a dragon ages, the strength of their breath weapon, such as a cone of fire from a red, increases. If he asked Aldrick to shoot his flaming breath at him and if the rod failed to work properly, he would more than likely be burned to death. However, he coldly calculated that if it failed and he got burned from Renata's flames, he just might not be killed.

Carrying his precious rod and an entire bag of healing potions just in case, he visited Renata in her cavern high in the mountains. "Wow, you sure have a spectacular view from your entrance, Archmage Renata." He began by complimenting her view. The snowy peaks were quite breathtaking, rugged and jagged. "You are looking well."

"Karel, what is this that you need my help with? I've known you long enough to know that you are not big on social pleasantries. Out with it," she chided him and he grinned. She certainly knew him well.

"Okay, I need you to breath your fire onto me. You see, I need to test the new rod of mine. As you know, the reds have been wiping out entire villages with their flames. Baron Zoran is reluctant to have all of us stand and fight them because we can be killed by their flames and such. So I'm trying to make a simple device which they could hold and have it provide them some protection from the red's flames. If I can get it to work properly, then Zoran and the rest of us can stand up to the reds when they attack again. I've brought along a stash of healing potions just in case it doesn't work. You should have seen the carnage at the Fall High Council when the red shot its flames out towards all of us in the audience. If we had not had those few seconds of forewarning, hundreds including ruling barons would have died, not just six Advisors. Please, will you lend me your breath?" He teased her a little.

She readily agreed if he would tell her all about what had happened at Petr Falls and what had happened to the abducted women. Renata wanted more facts than Zoran had relayed to her father, Aldrick, and thus to her. Karel agreed. He conducted three tests. First, he stood at the extreme limits that her fiery breath would reach. His rod activated properly and he felt nothing. Next, he stood in the middle of her cone of fiery breath. Once more, he was fully protected. Encourage and excited, he then stood directly in front of her, taking her breath fully on him. Once more, the rod fully protected him. Karel was elated and Renata was very much impressed, vowing to tell her dad about this interesting new magical invention. Karel then told her the full story about the dragon attack on the village and the rescue of the kidnaped women. She was keenly interested in the interspecies breeding, though, and asked him numerous questions, most of which Karel couldn't answer. He didn't know. Thus, in a roundabout way, Aldrick learned that magical items that could protect the wielder from the power attack of dragons were being made. This unnerved him a little and he thought long and hard about this new twist.

That night, an elated Karel picked up his wife, Chika, and twirled her around in circles. "It works! It works! I stood right in front of Renata's fiery breath and didn't get the slightest burn! I wasn't even hot! With this, we can stand and fight the raiding dragons!"

"Incredible, dear! Make me one, please. Now if it could only help me attack one, that would be great. As you know, I only have mage status and hardly ever can best the dragons on that grey plain, unlike you, my love," Chika both replied and hinted.

"Coming up, dear. That's the next step. Here's the problem. If I have these rods shoot a Disintegrate spell, there is always a chance the dragon will dodge it. If I have the use a spell that causes some damage to the dragon, as strong and powerful as some of these are, it may take a bunch of those attacks to actually kill it."

"Well, I'd prefer the certain route, dear. If it can't harm me with its breath, then I can hold my position and strike it many times, knowing that with each strike it is slowly being wounded and will eventually succumb," she pointed out. He took her opinion to heart and opted to install damage causing spells instead of the chancier die or no effect type spells.

However, he was limited in what he could cast. Of all the Archmages, he had actually mastered the fewest of the more powerful spells. Karel's pride prevented him from asking other Archmages to join him and cast their spells into the rods for him. No, these rods were his masterpieces and his alone. Karel hated to have to share the limelight with other Archmages. He always had.

Now came hard research. One of the topmost power spells and Zdenka's favorite was the Crushing Hand. The giant magical hand appeared around the head of the victim and began pounding on it. At first, the amount of damage inflicted was small, but it increased each minute that the spell continued to operate. After a few minutes, it reached its full power and continued to deliver crushing damage for many minutes after that. Karel estimated that if the dragon did not attempt to try to dodge it and took the full amount of damage each minute, even old Aldrick could be slain within say six or eight minutes! Though, it would deliver a certain kill, something that Chika greatly desired, still, in terms of the battles, six minutes was a *very* long time indeed. He rightly figured that anyone who was not an Archmage would likely feel the same way. Unfortunately, only one of the rods was going to be able to hold such a powerful spell in it.

Hence, he backed down to lesser power spells. He rejected the Stun spell at first, but later came back to it. After all, if they were in a fight and the dragon was stunned for even a couple of minutes at most, that would give the blade wielders enough time to hack it to death. Over half of the rods could accept this spell.

In the end, he reverted back to the tried and true damage causing spells, Ball of Fire, Bolt of Lightning, and Magical Missiles. The rods simply could not hold the same levels of power that he could conjure when he cast such spells. For example, when he cast his Magical Missiles spell, he could conjure into existence ten of them simultaneously. The rod would only be able to shoot six at the same time. Similarly with his lightning bolts. The rod would only be sixty percent as effective as he was. Still, these spells will cause damage and eventually, after enough were cast, kill the dragon. While there were numerous other variations of damage causing spells that could be used, Karel decided to keep it simple. These spells could easily be stored in the rods.

Just as he was about to commit to the spells that he chose, he realized that the dragons could just as easily be casting spells at the wielder of the rod. "Duh! I forgot all about that! I will have to put some defense against other magical spells into the rod as well." After a good deal more study and calculations, he decided to infuse the rods with the defense spell that blocked all Balls of Fire and Lightning Bolt spells and those of even lesser power. All of the rods were good enough to hold that enchantment; few could hold even more powerful defensive spells. "The rod's no good if it can't protect the wielder," he declared to himself.

The rods would have to be specifically tailored to the specific type of dragon it was meant to kill. For example, if the target was a Red Dragon, shooting a Ball of Fire back at it was utterly pointless. They loved fire; it would cause them no harm at all. Similarly, shooting a Lightning Bolt at a Brown Dragon would be useless, since the brown's breath weapon was a bolt of electricity. However, only the browns and golds could breathe out these bolts of electricity. All other types of dragons would be severely harmed by such spells.

He also had to consider the playing field. If the rods were shooting out their own balls of fire, then the wielder would have to make certain none of his friends were in the area to be affected. Thus, he ruled out putting Ball of Fire in the rods, too dangerous.

At last armed with just what spells to use, next came the question of just how much magical energy could one rod hold? With each use of the rod, some of that initial energy would be drained off. Of course, later on, a mage could cast magical energies back into it, recharging it to its original full potential once more.

The topmost power spell that provided the wielder his or her protection from the incredible breath of the dragons would consume ten percent of the total charge that a fully charged rod could hold. That is, if the wielder did nothing but use the rod to protect himself, he could take ten such dragon attacks before the rod needed to be recharged. The defense against magical spells used only six percent of the full charge with each usage, similar to all of the attacking spells, which also used up six percent each time. Thus, if the wielder did not need the breath weapon defense and used the rod solely for attacking, the wielder could get off seventeen such attacks before the rod would have to be recharged again.

Finally satisfied, Karel began the arduous work of enchanting the ten rods. It took him until mid-April to get all ten finished. He decided to call these Rods of Dragon Slaying. His intention was to present these to the other ruling barons at the Spring High Council meeting.

Archmage Jakob spent the long winter on his inventions as well. He and Karel had conferred about the need to enchant the protection from the dragon's breath weapons into any of their inventions. His giant diamond received this enchantment first. However, from this shared starting point, Jakob chose to follow a different path. A diamond did not make a rechargeable device, because it had no gold core within it. Rather, this diamond would retain its singular powers and each could be used but once per day, recharging or rather recovering its potential energy overnight via vibrations of its crystalline structure.

Unlike Karel who wanted dragons dead, Jakob wanted to control the horde of incoming dragons, thereby deflecting them from their original purpose. He spent long hours choosing just the right spells for his gem. When it was finished in April, it could Charm a Dragon easily and had a good chance of Charming up to five at one time. It could temporarily Blind a dragon or Stun him or her for a few minutes. The wielder had a good chance of being able to totally Dominate a Single Dragon, forcing it to the wielder's will. It could Stupefy a Dragon for a few minutes. The wielder could make a Group Suggestion of a horde of dragons and via the spell alter somewhat the original purposes of those dragons.

However, it's most powerful action was to permanently Imprison a Dragon by placing it in suspended animation some hundred feet under the ground. Jakob had an expensive but secure golden chain made so that the wearer could display it on his or her chest, much like a necklace. He named his new item the Gem of Dragon Control. He too secretly tested his invention on the nearby golds, but was careful to only ask those whom he controlled to do some slight things for him, just enough for him to know that it was working.

Jakob planned to show this to Baron Zoran and then take it to the Spring High Council and demonstrate it to the other barons. If he could get orders for more and could get such exquisite gems to use, he would both become famous and wealthy at the same time, as well as helping the overall fight against the dragons.

Archmage and teacher Zdenka had her own problems to face. Normally, she kept around twenty students in her tower, training them to become Adepts, mages, or Archmages. Each year at the Spring Picking, she added eight more new students, carefully chosen. Four were chosen to become Adepts, that is, they had the capability of learning all the really useful introductory type spells, such as Clean and Polish. Normally, these folks would take nearly the whole term to learn some three dozen such spells. Certainly by early spring, these men and women would then take positions in the city as Adepts and make a good living using these spells.

The other four that she chose each spring were real mage candidates. They would usually pick up these three dozen useful spells in short order and spend most of their first year learning real spells, as they always called them, such as Sleep and Magical Missile. In January, she had these usual eight students whom she'd picked last spring. Additionally, Zdenka had four second year students, four third year students, three fourth year students, and two who were in their fifth year of studies. These last two were struggling with the higher power spells. All of the fourth and fifth year students were already officially mages and had their sights set on becoming an Archmage. Of course, she knew that possibly one of the six might actually achieve that power ability. These were the students who had been twinned with the seventeen women who needed so much help in daily life.

Now suddenly her conservatively arranged world had been turned upside down. She'd added Neda easily enough. The young eleven year old had learned the useful Adept spells far more rapidly than the usual student of magic and here in late December had joined up with those other four who had started last spring, learning as they said, the "real spells." No, her world was flipped by the addition of the seventeen armless women who had been abducted by the Red Dragons, raped, and whose lives had just been saved.

Oh it was just a simple matter to twin each of her other students with one of these women. That easily solved the physical handicap of the seventeen women. No, that was not Zdenka's problem or real concern. Rather it was the incredible rapidity with which these seventeen had mastered the basic useful Adept spells: two weeks! She was extremely thankful the Verushka had volunteered to lend her a hand with these women. It was almost impossible to keep up with their incredible rates of learning.

True they all didn't learn at the same rate of speed. So far, Danika was going the fastest, but the slowest was only a day behind her speed! Somehow their carrying a dragon fetus to full term had infused them with an incredible ability to master magic! Alarmingly so, Verushka continually claimed.

Of course, these women had to have an enormous amount of physical help as they tried to learn to live with and adapt to their unfortunate situation. Verushka speculated more than once that if these women were not learning magic and learning it so well and fast that they might succumb to their situation and become depressed or suicidal, living without any hope for the future. Magic was giving them a new purpose in life and new goals — stellar goals for these once simple village women. "Look, they are so excited about learning magic and doing so incredibly well with it, that they are paying very little attention to the fact that they've lost their arms and are so physically handicapped now," she pointed out to Zdenka.

"Right. And that is going to allow them to adapt and eventually live useful, productive lives, to flourish and to prosper," Zdenka added.

However, there were limits to the twinning approach. She could not pull these other students off of their studies just to be the constant arms of the seventeen. That would be unfair to them. Instead, the other students helped the seventeen get dressed in the morning, to dine, and to deal with the mundane things that needed to be done from time to time. During the long study hours, the seventeen were basically on their own. Verushka assisted them, retrieving the next book a woman needed and helping them with the occasional restroom needs. Right from the start, she insisted that they use their feet to hold the books and flip the pages. From the beginning, of necessity, she was forcing the seventeen to adapt and use their feet as much as possible. Thus far, it was working out. The other students didn't mind helping the seventeen as long as that didn't detract from their own studies.

However, now that they hit the "real spells," both Zdenka and Verushka were kept constantly busy helping them. Four students on these spells were about all that Zdenka could easily handle, along with all of the other students. With seventeen more added and with those going at an alarming rate, the two women were swamped. They desperately needed help.

Zdenka knew that she dare not attempt to pull others off of their work to help her out. Zoran needed every last one at this point. On the 1st of January, she at last told Zoran about her problems. "Dear, do you suppose that I could impose on your two sisters? Would it be acceptable for me to ask Lida and Rayna to come here for several months and help me with the seventeen?"

"Oh I don't see why not. Look, you trained their daughters to Archmages. They owe you big time, my love. I think that they would look upon this as a way to pay you back for all that you have done for them. Plus, Rayna would also likely consider this a humanitarian aid situation, helping those particular women. Come on, let's find out," he suggested, happy to have an excuse to visit with his two sisters once again.

Lida's response was, "Zdenka! I am so thankful that you thought of me to help you with them! I would love to help them. Thank you. When do I start?" Her surprise enthusiasm took Zdenka by surprise. She'd expected to have to make a real pitch to get Baroness Lida to volunteer. Rayna was even more thrilled to help out. On the 2nd of January, the two arrived and were introduced to the entire student body. All thirty-nine students were buzzing over the fact that they now had two baronesses helping them out as well! They were most impressed. Lida and Rayna were put to work with the seventeen that very day. Zdenka and Verushka alternated their days with the seventeen and the regular students. That way, each could keep close track of the progress of the seventeen and Neda.

By the end of that first week, Lida and Rayna both commented on how pooped they were. Lida added, "I've never seen students picking these spells up so quickly! It is so hard to keep up with them. If you only had four of them, why, I could manage to keep up with them. But we've each got six and boy do they ever keep us hopping!"

Rayna added, "You know, I've noted that when they are studying and practicing, they completely forget about their handicaps. Yet, when mealtime comes, they seem a bit embarrassed or something."

"Yes, we've noted that as well. How are the alternate methods of casting working out?" Zdenka asked. The group had just gotten to the Magical Missiles spell. Usual casting had the mage pointing his or her finger at the intended target. These women had no fingers with which to point. Hence, the teachers had to devise alternative ways. This is what was keeping Lida and Rayna so busy.

"Head nods are working well," Rayna replied. "Verushka suggested it. So far, so good. I guess they'll have to use their feet when a spell requires them to touch the recipient of the spell."

"Say, can I ask a question?" asked Lida. Zdenka nodded and she asked, "What are we going to do with the Flaming Hands spell? They have no hands from which to emit the flames. That one is coming up shortly."

Inspired, Zdenka suggested, "Let's alter it to Flaming Mouth. Have them cast the flames from their mouth, much like a dragon. I bet that they will go for that variation in a big way."

"Great idea! You know, they all tried very hard to make the Change Oneself spell give them back arms. Every last one of them tried to do that. It was heart wrenching, but Rayna and I let them experiment anyway. When they get to the Morph Self spell, then they can alter their forms into a person with arms, though such will only be temporary," Lida pointed out.

"Right, then they can really help themselves and they won't feel so utterly helpless at other times when they aren't working on their magical studies," Rayna added.

"Right, that spell usually comes in a student's third year, just before they learn to teleport and become mages," Zdenka answered.

"Somehow, I don't think these women are going to take that long to get there," Verushka joked and the four chuckled.

"Say, who is the Door Warden now? Archmage Marek is off on other duties I see," Lida asked.

"Blanka Kornel is our Door Warden. She's achieved Mage status and I have hopes that she may well make it all the way. She's a bright mind and quite intelligent," Zdenka answered. "Oh yes, Sunday is their day off. Time for us to recover. Boy do I ever need the day off!" Again all four laughed. Indeed, change was occurring at a rapid pace. Some changes were good ones.

The first Sunday in January, Rafael knocked on the tower's door. The tall, thin, but quite imposing Mage Blanka Kornel opened the door. She stood six inches taller than Rafael, "Yes?" she said dryly, as if Rafael should not be here. She recognized him as one of the blacksmiths who worked just inside the baron's fortress walls.

"I've come to meet Danika. We have a date," he said timidly, somewhat taken aback by the taller woman.

"Are you *sure* about this? You *know* that she doesn't have any arms and has recently lost her whole family and kids as well," Blanka did her best to discourage this young man. After all, what could he possibly want with such a woman when Brn was filled with normal women?

"Sure, we danced all night at the Stodgy Inn dance at Yuletide," he explained.

"One minute. I'll see if she *wants* to come." Blanka shut the door, leaving Rafael standing outside in the cold and snow. A bit later, the door opened. Blanka had Danika with her.

"Hi Danika. It's Sunday. Ready for a walk?" he said politely.

"Well, I guess it won't hurt. Blanka, can you. . ."

"Of course, I'll get your coat for you. Now you be careful. Message me if you need anything. I am sure glad that you've learned that spell," Blanka chatted away, hovering over Danika like a mother hen, Rafael thought. Once her heavy cloak was fastened, Danika thanked her and stepped outside.

"Hi, I am glad to see you again, Danika. I want to show you my humble shop." He put his arm around her to steady her as they walked through the packed snow there inside the fortress walls. "Plus, I have some exciting news. I am now helping Archmage Karel make his new magical items and weapons!"

"You are?" Danika replied, very much surprised. "We don't hear much news inside."

"Well, I'm really doing the blacksmithing part, the heavy pounding, heating, and forming work. Nothing magical about that, but still to know that I am helping make these things — well it makes me feel really good, you know."

"I can see how it does. Congratulations. Say, I am learning new spells too. I can change my appearance now. We tried to make our arms come back with it, but I guess the spell isn't that powerful."

"I am sorry that it didn't work. I can't imagine how hard everything is for you and the others. Still, I am impressed with your becoming a real magic user! That is really terrific. Here's my shop. Pardon the messy floor. I didn't have time to clean it up yet."

Danika grinned. "Clean!" she said. All of the accumulated bits of dirt on a section of his floor suddenly vanished.

"Wow! That's fantastic," Rafael exclaimed, truly awed by Danika's spell. She cast it four more times, leaving his blacksmith shop's floor sparkling clean.

"You are hired! Thank you, my pretty mage," Rafael complimented her. She beamed. Next, he showed her some of the fine quality swords that he was working on as well as the shells of the dozen rods that he was fabricating for Archmage Karel. In turn, Danika was impressed, but she was totally enamored by his iron grillwork adorning one wall.

"Yes, I am making myself an iron fence to go around my future home. I am putting butterflies on top of it spaced every six inches. When it is done and painted, it ought to look really unusual," he explained.

"Now that is incredible. You made that from those chunks of metal?" she asked in disbelief. Rafael was more than willing to explain how it was all done and she was a good listener. Later, the two took a long walk around the sprawling inner grounds of the fortress. Danika was getting her first good look at it all. Thus far, she'd mostly been in the infirmary and then inside the adjoining Archmage tower. After that, the two headed over to the Stodgy Inn for mugs of hot cider to warm themselves up.

"Hey, want to go ice skating next Sunday afternoon? The freshwater pond out back which supplies the fortress when it is under siege is all frozen over. Everyone goes skating on it during the winter. How about it?" he asked.

"I used to skate a lot before I was married. Oh, I don't know if I can possibly skate anymore, not like this," she replied shrugging her shoulders.

"Hey, we can give it a try. I bet you can; only keeping your balance will be a bit more tricky than before. Please, let's give it a try, shall we?"

"Well, maybe. I don't want to fall down and get hurt though."

"I will make sure that you don't. I sort of tired it with by holding my hands behind my back. I could still skate, though I will admit it was trickier, but I think you can do it."

Later when he returned her to the tower door, she leaned over to him, pressing her body against his, frustrated. "Sorry, I wanted to give you a hug to thank you for a really nice afternoon, Rafael, but I can't hug anymore."

"Sure, you just did." He pressed their bodies close again and she flushed. He knocked and Blanka appeared.

She didn't miss the flush on Danika's face as the two said goodbye to each other. Once inside, Blanka asked, "How did it go? Did he embarrass you too badly?" She assumed that Rafael would have done that.

"Oh no. We had a really nice time. He's asked me to go ice skating with him next Sunday. Blanka, do you think that I can really skate anymore? Like I am now? I used to skate well, but now I doubt that I can."

"Well, you won't know unless you try, but do be careful, Danika." Blanka was rather surprised that this afternoon's date had gone well for Danika. She'd predicted that it would have ended in a disaster for the young woman. Her opinion of these new students began to change.

As the cold days of January continued to pass, the four teachers continued to see amazing progress from Neda and the seventeen young women. By the end of January, the seventeen had already surpassed Neda in terms of the number of beginning "real spells" that they knew how to cast. Neda was going perhaps twice as fast as other normal beginning students due in large measure to her youth and willingness to learn, but these seventeen were going at least four times faster! Zdenka had no choice but to re-twin Neda with others who were at her level, for Danika was going far too fast for Neda to keep up with her, no matter how hard she wanted to keep up. However, Neda still remained Danika's hand for many other things and still shared a bedroom with her adopted mother.

In February, the seventeen finally encountered their first spell that slowed them all down, primarily because of their inexperience with magic in general. It was the spell that identified the magical properties of a magic item. "Just explain what it seems to be able to do," Zdenka coached woman after woman. They were frustrated because they had not the vocabulary and knowledge to be more precise about what they were detecting in the items.

"Well that slowed them down," Lida commented as the four met on Sunday while the many students took the day off.

Laughing, Rayna added, "Sure did. They took a whole week at it. Damn, I remember when I was dealing with that spell for the first time. I took nearly three weeks to get it all sorted out."

"Yes, but we had a crappy teacher, sis," Lida pointed out.

"At this rate, they are going to be into the second level of spells long before spring comes," Verushka pointed out.

"I told you they are an incredible batch of students," Zdenka teased them all.

"Hey, I heard that one of them went ice skating. Is that true?" asked Rayna.

"Yes, Blanka watched over her a couple Sundays ago. Danika was a bit nervous about it and had some very awkward moments, but by the end of the afternoon, she was skating very well indeed. I think that she used to skate a lot when she was younger," Zdenka pointed out.

"That is encouraging. They are adapting well, I'd say, far better than I ever imagined that they could when I first heard about them," Lida admitted.

Due to the weather, Zdenka rearranged her usual order of covering the second level spells. For safety's sake, some of these really needed to be cast while outside. Thus, she moved other spells, such as ESP, up sooner than she normally taught them. By early April, the seventeen fully mastered this most interesting spell.

Danika decided to put this spell to good use. Every Sunday afternoon, Rafael came by and took her out for the afternoon. More and more, she began to look forward to these times, but she was also pragmatic. What was his real motivation for seeing her? She could see that some around the fortress area pitied her and the other women. Was he doing all this out of pity? If so, she wanted nothing more to do with him. Maybe he really liked her, she thought, but quickly abandoned that notion. After all, if she really took a good look at herself, she was nothing more than a helpless cripple now, wholly dependent on others for most things. She hated the fact that someone had to feed her like she was a baby. It was embarrassing for her to have to have someone help her use the chamber pot. The list went on and on. Only when she was doing or studying her magic did these feelings vanish entirely. She resolved to find out this Sunday.

As Rafael came to the door to pick her up, Danika cast her ESP spell upon him. Danika was totally surprised to discover that it was not pity for her that he felt. Instead, he was in love with her. He not only admired her but also had a tremendous respect for her. She flushed when she picked up his worried thoughts about whether or not he should kiss her. *Will she be offended if I did? Will it embarrass her? She is a magic user now. God, I don't want her to suddenly dislike me because I am so forward. Maybe I best play it safe a while longer. She is so beautiful and so powerful.* She picked up some further thoughts and then silently canceled her spell. She decided to make the first move. She leaned over and gave him a passionate kiss. After that, their bond of love grew stronger with each passing week. Danika also knew that she was making good use of her magic skills. Without her spying on Rafael's thoughts, she would always have had doubts about him and his true intentions towards her. Now she had none. During their afternoon strolls, she opened up and shared more about herself and her feelings than ever before. The two found that they shared many the same future desires. Both wanted to have children and a home, for example.

Chapter 14 Elsewhere, Winter Turns Bad

For Adapazan, the long winter dragged onwards but it took a turn for the worst on several other worlds. On the 10th of February, Zoran received a panic message and summons from Baron Arcangelo Mondo of Cosma, the agrarian planet. *Help! An entire village of ours has just been destroyed by dragons! Please, can you come at once and lend us a hand? Please.*

Zoran agreed and sent for Jarka, Bernard, and his son Tomas. Everyone else was really extremely busy with all of the teaching, underground construction projects, and guard duties. He left orders to be Messaged at once if any dragon attacks came while he was off-world. "Bring a stash of healing potions, Jarka, but I suspect we will be too late, as usual."

She grimly nodded. To Bernard, she growled, "Here we go again. I hope to heaven they didn't abduct women again!" A few minutes later, Zoran Shadow Walked the four to Arcangelo's Circle of Ascension, where he found a very shaken baron waiting for them.

"So glad that you could drop everything and come. Honestly, I just can't believe that this has happened here on Cosma. We're farmers, for heaven's sake. We grow food. Come on. I'll take you there. Barons Bernardo and Vincens are there along with our three Archmages and fifty of my best soldiers." He took hold of Zoran's hand and teleported the five to the smoldering ruins of Pieta, a rural farming village of some two thousand people. The destruction instantly reminded the four of Petr Falls. Wooden structures had been burned to the ground, stone structures smashed by the might of the dragons. Burned, frozen, and acid eaten bodies lay everywhere. The soldiers were in the process of going through the rubble searching for more bodies and any survivors.

"It is quite similar to the raid on our village of Petr Falls, baron," Zoran said softly. The three Archmages walked over to greet the four arrivals. Zoran recognized Archmage Bianca Babiana at once; she was a recent graduate of Zdenka's, but he'd only seen the oldest Archmage once and had watched the other one when he was announced at the start of a High Council meeting some years back. Bianca looked greenish; the destruction had unnerved her.

"Archmages Biago Casimiro and Alfredo Amadeo," Baron Arcangelo briefly introduced them. Both men nodded respectfully to Zoran and his companions. He nodded to Bianca and the two men.

The elder Archmage explained, "I got word from Mage Celia. She lives in the next hamlet. A farmer was hauling wood into the village when the dragons swooped in from out of nowhere. It happened about an hour ago. He hid and saw reds, greens, blacks, and whites. Worse, he saw them carry off thirty women and two dozen men as well. After the dragons left, the farmer headed to the next village for help and Celia notified me. We are still combing the ruins for possible survivors."

"Ah ha. Then this attack, baron, is exactly the same as the one at Petr Falls," Zoran said grimly. Jarka sighed and then cursed.

"What does it mean?" Baron Arcangelo asked, though he had a good idea.

"They intend to breed the women. In sixty days, the women will give birth to baby dragons, which will kill them as the baby dragons chew and claw their way into the world. Exactly what they are doing with the men we still don't know as yet. If, however, we can find where they are keeping the women, we can rescue them. We've worked out a way to save the women and destroy the foul creatures within them," Zoran explained.

"Oh good god! You mean they are . . . Oh hell! They can cross-breed?" Baron Arcangelo exclaimed in a violent mixture of shock, surprise, and bitter anger bordering on rage.

"Yes, I am afraid so. If we cannot get to the abducted women before they give birth to these bastards, the women will die giving birth," Jarka added, quite graphically.

"How — how can we possibly find them?" asked Archmage Biago, hanging his head. "I am getting too old for these things. I should have retired years ago."

"You are just shocked as we all are," Archmage Alfredo consoled his former teacher. "Come on; let's put our heads together and see if we can locate the women. Baron, if we know the names of some of the women, then we can Message them and home in on them."

"I'll see what I can find out," Baron Arcangelo said, the first faintest hope appearing in him. He headed off to talk with Mage Celia and the farmer.

"Baron Bernardo, if the Archmages are unable to Message the women, it is highly likely that they have been taken off-world. In that case, it will be you barons who will have to try to locate them by establishing a Duska Mind Link to them and then following the communication's energy line to the person. Have you ever done anything like this? I know that Arcangelo can't because he inherited your father's Circle. You and Vincens are bonded to your two new Circles, like I am. We have a stronger bond with the Circles and our Duska senses than the others."

"I've seen the energy line once, but that's all," Bernardo admitted. "All this is new to me, really, Baron Zoran."

"I'll stick around and help you both," Zoran suggested to their great relief. "Also, we were only able to rescue eighteen of our abducted women. Alas, we never did find another ten women or the two dozen men who were taken. More than likely, the ten women are dead, but we've no idea about the men. The key is if you can find out the identity of those who were taken and make contact with them either by magic spell or Duska senses. If you can't, then more than likely there will be nothing further that you can do for them."

"Hey, at least you had a witness to the abductions. In our case, we didn't. It took some clever work on Archmage Jakob's part to even determine that some had been abducted," Baron Tomas pointed out.

Just then a soldier yelled for help. He'd found a survivor and Jarka reached the wounded man before anyone else did. The man's right leg was still smoldering foul fumes; acid had eaten away most of the flesh, leaving black goo over the major leg bones, a grizzly sight. She poured a healing potion down the unconscious man and stabilized him. Bernard conjured lime and water over the acid covered, mostly destroyed leg, neutralizing the acid and washing it off the man. As the soldier then picked the man up to carry him out of the battlefield, most of the leg simply fell off.

"I'll take him to your infirmary, baron," Archmage Bianca quickly spoke up. She teleported both the soldier and the man he was carrying directly to Baron Arcangelo's infirmary. Bianca reappeared a few minutes later. "He's stabilized and the physician says that he will survive." The soldier thanked her.

During the next hour, they identified three women and one man who had been abducted. Methodically, the Archmages attempted to Message the four but had no success. Of course, this meant that they were likely now being held off-world, beyond the range of the mage spells. Now the Duska barons attempted to make their Mind Links to the four. Unfortunately, they did not know the four victims and had little reality on making such connections to people with whom they didn't know. Thus, there was little more that Zoran could do and they returned home. He did promise to return the instant that they established contact with any of the abducted men or women.

Once back home, Tomas pointed out, "Dad, we sure had more luck than they did."

"We're used to dealing with tough situations, son. Cosma has not had such conflicts in centuries. They are a bit soft, so to speak," Zoran noted. He kept in touch with Baron Arcangelo during the next few days, but nothing more came of it. The baron had scratched those who had been abducted off; there wasn't anything that he could do for them.

On the 10th of March, the raiding dragons struck again. This time, the allies got a break. Fifty dragons swarmed over the town of Valtr Hills, some fifty miles from Baron Stefan's Circle and Fortress. The carefully laid plans of Baron Stefan, based on Zoran's advice, paid off. In these larger towns, he'd stationed a mage whose job was to provide early warning of attacks. Luck was with the mage, he just happened to be out walking when he spotted the dragons just arriving from the Shadows, several miles above the sprawling town of some three thousand. Instantly, he Messaged Baron Stefan and then cast his Magnify spell and shouted an alarm to warn the townsfolk. His voice was so loud that everyone heard it. "Dragons are about to attack Valtr Hills. Take cover immediately!"

Baron Stefan had drilled his Duska, Archmages, and mages on just what to do in the event of a dragon attack. Such an attack had never occurred before and despite the drilling, confusion reigned for a few minutes. At once, Stefan sent Zoran the frantic call for help and then got his staff to the outskirts of the town. Already, the dragons were swooping down, shooting flames right and left, along with slime and acid flows. However, almost no one was outside, much to their surprise, and the dragons began to torch wooden homes, the easier targets. Terrified inhabitants then fled their burning homes, falling victim to the acid and slime flows from the greens and blacks.

Five minutes after the initial warning, Baron Stefan and his group arrived. Barons Zdenk and Daron, Baronesses Zusa and Kamila, Archmages Chesan, Patrik, and Zikmund surrounded him. Five other Duskas and ten mages circled around them, forming a battle squadron. Just as Stefan was about to issue his attack orders, Zoran stepped his group out of the Shadows, landing them nearby. He had spotted Stefan as he zoomed in on Valtr. Zoran brought his usual Archmages, barons, baronesses, and all the Duskas that could be spared, leaving Baron Jan in charge of

Adapazan. Lida and Rayna had also come, unwilling to be left behind.

Stefan glanced at Zoran and the huge force that he'd brought and grinned. Zoran nodded and the two groups launched their counterattack. Stefan took his forces to the northern entrance to the town which sat on a tall hill, while Zoran took his to the southern edge. Chaos reigned.

Circling dragons suddenly found themselves under a very serious counterattack. They greatly feared the Archmages and here were way too many of them. Deadly spells flew in all directions, enormous cones of flames, freezing cold, caustic acid, and rotting slime likewise flew all around, landing eventually upon the ground or roofs of the many buildings, adding to the wild random chaos. Dead dragons fell from the sky like falling locomotives, shattering whatever they happened to land upon.

Amid all this frantic chaos, Zoran spotted Archmage Karel and paused to watch the lunatic, or so Zoran thought at first. Had Karel gone mad? Berserk? The man stood squarely in the middle of the street, totally oblivious to the flames and acid being hurled at him. He did hold some small stick in his hand, but otherwise, he was merely casting his spells of death right and left. Somehow the man seemed immune to the flames and caustic acid. Zoran's Duska senses triggered and he made a frantic drop and roll to get out of the way of a blast of searing fire from a red who saw that he was distracted and attempted to wipe him out. Zdenka shot her Disintegrate spell at the red, covering for Zoran. The spell took the left side of the red's head off and the huge beast came plummeting to the ground, crashing through the roof of an inn. Zoran got back on his feet and nodded her way. She flashed him a smile and headed after another black.

Streaks of Lightning, Crushing Fists, Balls of Fire, Magical Missiles, Spectrum Sprays, Stuns, Disintegrate beams, Blind, Blasts of Frost, and many other spells flashed through the skies above Valtr Hills. This was the biggest display of magical spells that had even been seen at one time anywhere in the Federation of the Sixteen Planets! The noise was deafening.

Five minutes later with half of their attacking force destroyed, the remaining two dozen dragons suddenly fled the battlefield, stepping quickly into the Shadows, leaving the carnage behind them. At last, Zoran relaxed and signaled his group to regroup. "Injuries?" he called out to everyone.

"Over here, Jarka. I took a bad burn," Bernard called out. Six others had minor injuries and needed her healing potions as well. Karel had not a scratch on him, however.

"Hey, I got seven of the beasts! Not bad," Karel bragged to his wife, Chika, who had only slain one. She'd spent most of her time dodging the flames and acid.

Stefan used his Magnify spell to notify the townsfolk that the dragons were gone, but to stay inside until further notice. He ordered his mages to conjure water to douse the flaming roofs. Archmage Chesna also ordered the conjuring of lime to help neutralized the streams of acid running down the sides of the buildings and flooding through the paved streets. They dare not enter the town until the acid and slime had been nullified, otherwise, it would eat through their boots! Meanwhile, Zusa and Kamila tended their wounded, doling out their healing potions right and left. Stefan's group suffered more injuries than Zoran's, though neither had lost any of their people, unlike the two dozen dead dragons that lay scattered about the streets and upon crushed buildings.

An hour later, the fires were out and the slime and acid neutralized. Now they could at last enter the town and remove the dead dragons. "My god, they are heavy," he noted. It took several mages working together to lift the carcasses and move them to piles outside the town proper. Their working spells got quite a work out. Meantime, Stefan, Zoran, and several others joined up and discussed the event and how to proceed, going door to door checking on the possible wounded inside.

"Hey, Archmage Karel, I thought that you were a total goner. Did you go sort of berserk there?" Stefan asked.

"Nope, I got seven of the beasts. Anyone kill more than that?" the prideful man replied.

"Well, I got three," Zdenka replied. Several other Archmages also had slain three. No one was close to his tally.

"Okay, Karel, out with it. How the devil did you not get killed six times over? I saw you getting the full blast of flames and acids several times," Zoran asked, becoming a little annoyed at the arrogance of Karel.

He waved his small rod and Chika grinned. She knew that Karel was about to tell the world of his new super weapon. "Just combat testing my latest invention, baron. This here is my Rod of Dragon Slaying!" His voice was louder than normal; he wanted all within hearing to take notice, which they did. Everyone around stopped and stared at the small rod that he held up for curious eyes to see.

He added, "Makes you immune to the breaths of the dragons, leaving you free to destroy the foul beasts. Works rather well, wouldn't you say?" he teased his audience.

"My god, man! We need them immediately! How soon can you deliver me a goodly supply of them? Name your price!" Baron Stefan took the bait.

Karel smiled. He tossed the baron his rod. "Here, you can take this one now. It needs to be recharged. After we get this mess cleaned up, I'll tell you all about it. Don't worry, Zoran, I have eleven more back home, one for you too." He quickly alleviated the worried look on his friend's face.

"My god, man! Thanks! Do you realize what you have invented?" Stefan effused. "With this, we actually stand a chance against the dragons! Wow, seven slain and not a scratch on you. Unbelievable! I would not have believe it if I hadn't seen it with my own eyes. You really did get blasted many times! I figured you were a goner!"

Karel accepted the praise. "Yes, totally immune. Gives us a chance. The rod also can attack the dragons as well, but this time I used my own killer spells. If the battle had lasted longer, why I might have tied Chan and Wen's kill total."

"Hey, we are up to twenty-two dragons now," Chan boasted, punching her good hand into the air.

Wen added, "Give us one of those rods, Karel, and you'll never catch up to us. We're the Dragon Slayers, after all." Everyone laughed at their taunts.

After spending an hour going door to door, miraculously few of the townsfolk had been killed, only those who had been forced from their burning homes. Another two dozen suffered broken bones from collapsing houses but these were quickly helped with liberal doses of healing potions, doled out this time by Baronesses Zusa and Kamila.

Finally, leaving his mages in charge, Stefan had everyone accompany him back to his fortress. Everyone wanted to examine and hear about Karel's Rod of Dragon Slaying. Archmage Karel grandly explained the details of his invention. He cautioned Stefan, "Remember, if you do not use the rod's attack powers, you can withstand ten dragon breath attacks before it needs recharging."

"Simply amazing, Archmage Karel! You are to be highly commended. Are you going to tell the other barons about it at the Spring High Council? If you do, expect to receive many, many orders for these. I am incredibly honored to receive this, Karel." The Archmage basked in the limelight and also returned home with a hundred thousand in gems in his pockets. At home, he then gave a rod to Chika and one to Zoran. He was still in the process of finishing up the last enchantments on the remaining rods.

Of course, that very night Stefan told the other allied barons all about the attack and the powerful new weapon that Karel had invented. Baron Leo was drooling with envy that Stefan had gotten the first of these new magnificent weapons. Lida and Rayna teased their husbands about this before they returned to continue to help Zdenka with her students. "They are like little boys with a new toy and they don't want to share," Rayna joked. Lida laughed.

In bed that night, Zoran said, "Dear, for once, we all got a lucky break there on Valtr."

"Yes, your idea of stationing mages around the land finally paid off. I am sure thankful that more women were not taken. I feel so badly for those women of Cosma. There is still no word on them, is there?"

"Nope, they've had no luck in locating any of them, but there is still time to save them, if they can be found. It hasn't been sixty days yet. So there is still some hope."

On the 10th of April, Zoran sighed. Now there was no hope for the abducted women of Cosma. Probably they had given birth to thirty new dragons and died for their efforts. Zdenka did not need him to tell her why he looked so glum at breakfast that morning. She knew what he was thinking.

Two days later, Baron John Witherspoon roused him just before dawn. The man's mental voice was shaking. Fear and terror fought to gain control over his logical mind. *We've been attacked by dragons too. I just got word this morning that a farming village of Westumbria was attacked around midnight last night when everyone was sleeping. The mage there died in his bed. So much for my early warning system. Can you come and lend us a hand? I beg you.*

No need to beg. We'll be there in a few minutes. I'll home in on you there at the site.

Thanks Baron Zoran. I never believed it would happen to us. It is beyond awful. It just makes me sick at my stomach. The carnage, the destruction. We're just farmers.

"What's up?" a sleepy Zdenka asked, as she realized he was up and getting dressed rapidly.

"Another attack. Terra this time. They are getting smarter. The dragons attacked at midnight when everyone was in bed. Damn them anyway!"

"Want us all to come?" she said getting up and rapidly dressing.

"No, I'll take Tomas, Jarka, and Bernard. There is probably nothing that we can really do now. It's been six hours since the attack. I'll keep you posted. Will you inform the others please?"

True to his word, five minutes later, Zoran Shadow Walked his son, Jarka, and Bernard to the site, homing in on Baron John. Westumbria was in ruins, much like the other destroyed villages. Homes were still smoldering; stone buildings lay half crumbled. Soldiers were going from building to building, hauling out the dead and searching for survivors.

"Thanks for coming. No survivors as yet. This is just appalling," the pale faced Baron John said softly.

"The thing to worry most about, John, is this. How many women and men were abducted this time? That is the pattern that we've seen several times now. They are going to interspecies-breed the women, and the women will later die when they give birth to the dragon babies," Zoran advised, keeping his voice low as well.

It took a moment to fully register with him. "So many dead. How are we ever going to know how many were taken? There were thousands living here. My god, breeding our women? That's, that's, that's the most despicable, hideous, vile thing that I've ever heard." Now it fully registered with Baron John.

"Well, you might consult those living near the town. Have them identify the many dead and see if they can spot anyone that they knew who lived here whose body is not among the dead. That's how we did it at Petr Falls. It took days, but we finally got a pretty good idea. You are looking for missing strong, burly men and young women between say eighteen and twenty-five."

"I see. Yes, if we knew the name of even one who was taken, we can try to make contact with them and rescue them. Makes sense. I'll get on it," Baron John replied. He quickly left them to issue new orders.

There was little for the four to do and they helped the others arrange the dead in long lines, ready for the outlying neighbors to view with the hope that they would be able to discover if anyone was missing. While it was quite shocking for these farmers to walk along the long lines of the dead, Baron John desperately needed to know if some had been abducted. Around ten, Zoran returned home to await John's report.

"Vile beasts are getting smarter," Jarka commented, as Zoran prepared to Shadow Walk them home.

"Dragons are formidable foes, my dear," Bernard replied.

Three days later, Baron John contacted him again. *We're in luck. Abigail Westwood is missing. Apparently, she is widely known for making superb quilts. That's how they spotted that she is missing. If you don't mind, I could use you help now.*

On our way! Be there in a few minutes. Zoran Messaged his group with the news and called for a quick conference to decide who ought to go with him. He decided to take Karel, Tomas and Nadia, along with Bernard and Jarka, of course. The others were on standby in case they needed more firepower. "Here you go, Zoran. Remember, if you do not use it to cast spells or to absorb spells shot at you,

you can take ten dragon breath hits before the rod exhausts it charge." Karel handed him a Rod of Dragon Slaying. Then, he gave another to Tomas and one to Bernard, allowing the men to decide if they should wield it or let their wives use the rod. Both men passed the precious rod to their wives. Jarka gave Bernard a quick thank you kiss.

Just as they were about to go, Archmage Jakob teleported beside them. "Excuse me, baron. I wish to come with you this time. I need to test out my new magical gem on the dragons. It could prove to be more powerful than Karel's rods." Karel gave him a snarled look, which the tall man ignored.

Zoran grinned. "Okay, grab a hold of each other. I'll take us to where Baron John is waiting for us." Once more Jarka's stomach did a violent lurch as she was pulled into the grey-black Shadows, totally disorienting her. She focused all her intention on holding tightly to Bernard's hand, praying that he was doing the same with Archmage Nadia. Soon, the bluish orb took shape and then the white snow covered the plains of Terra appeared and she began to reorient her senses. She disliked this Shadow Walking.

"Ah, here you are. Thank you for coming on such short notice," a worried Baron John Witherspoon said as the small group materialized beside his larger group. He had his fellow barons and baronesses with him along with his two younger Archmages. Old Albert was too infirm to make such a trip as this. He also had six other mages with him. Karel noted that John was now wielding one of his magical Dragon Slayer bastard swords and smiled.

"We still are not totally sure just how many were abducted, conflicting opinions. Some suggest as many as a hundred men and women are missing, other believe it is more like sixty who are unaccounted for. However, we finally got a break. Abigail Westwood is a prominent local woman who makes beautiful quilts that are in high demand. I had Archmage Lisa attempt to Message her, but as you suggested, she must now be off-world. Zoran flashed the young woman a smile. He'd last seen her when she graduated as yet another of Zdenka's Archmages five years ago.

"Zoran, I have never really done this kind of tracking before," John admitted.

"No problem. You make a Duska Mind Link with her and I'll follow the energy line."

"Big brother, we'll pay close attention to how he is doing it," Baron Hank added. Zoran nodded; the two younger barons would soon learn how to do this tricky, but useful action. John focused and reached out for the woman. His communication line arced through the Shadows and at last latched onto Abigail. *Baron John Witherspoon here. We are coming to rescue you now.*

Help! Black dragons have us. They've raped all of us! It's horrible! The woman's panic and terror nearly overwhelmed John, but he fought to maintain his link to the woman in spite of this. Zoran spotted the faint energy line and stepped the group into the Shadows. Zoran noted that John's two younger brothers were also able to see the faint line, and he purposely moved them slowly through the Shadows, hoping the two could keep up with him. They did. Before long, a whitish world appeared and everyone recognized Gerde. Snow covered the mountainous world, which had almost no plains or lands on which to grow crops. Life here was tough.

Before long, Zoran led them high into impassible mountain ranges, far from the civilized portion where the barons dwelled. Zoran appreciated this, since that meant he would not need to contact the Ebbe brothers and clear this visit with them. Finally a dark cave entrance loomed ahead and Zoran sent, *In that cave. We should go Invisible and check it out before we go charging in there.*

I'll go; they are my people, Baron John sent. He cast his spell and vanished from sight. Meanwhile Zoran and the others hovered near the entrance still in the Shadows and thus invisible to anyone on Gerde. A bit later, he sent, *One Black Dragon is standing guard over fifteen women. If we attack, the women will be in the way and likely be harmed!*

Let me have at the dragon first, please, Jakob Messaged John, as they stepped out of the Shadows, scrambling for footing on the narrow entrance ledge. A fall of over a thousand feet awaited the slightest misstep. John looked at Zoran, not daring to agree unless Zoran approved of this.

Be careful, Jakob! Go ahead, Zoran sent. Jakob cast his Invisibility spell. However, he also knew that he could not mask his human smell and that the dragon may soon smell his presence. He counted on the presence of so many women to mask it long enough for him to activate his Gem of Dragon Control. He moved as silently as he could into the cavern. Ah, the dragons had cast Permanent Light spells aplenty around the whole cavern so it was well illuminated. He spotted the women lying on crude mattresses against the back wall. The black was lying on the floor between himself and the women. He approached the dragon and activated his gem. He found himself on a grey, featureless plain, staring down this dragon, who was totally shocked to find himself in this place. The mental battle ended abruptly as Jakob won.

You are my friend. You will do everything that I tell you to do. I want you to go into a very deep sleep. You are overly tired and must have your rest. You will not wake up for several days. He waited. Would it work? He listened and soon heard snoring and smiled.

The dragon is in a deep sleep. If you don't make a lot of noise, he will be sleeping for days now. Come on in, he Messaged the others.

One by one the others entered and cautiously moved around the huge form of the sleeping Black Dragon. This was incredible, but none dared say much. Karel with his rod at hand stood guard in front of the beast in case it woke up. If it did, he'd handle it personally, allowing the others to deal with the terrified women. They were filthy and their clothing torn, but they were otherwise fit. One by one, the Duska began Shadow Walking the women to freedom arriving in John's Infirmary. The last to leave, Zoran and Karel took hold of Jakob, but only after making doubly sure no others were hidden around this complex. A minute later, the three stepped into the Infirmary where the others were already cleaning up the women and asking them what had happened. More to the point, John wanted to know where the other women and men had been taken.

"We're always hungry now. They said that we are going to die when we give birth to their baby dragons! How can this be? We feel sick," Abigail wailed.

"Trust us, Abigail, we have a way to prevent that from happening to you women," Zoran consoled her. "Baron Zoran Vladislov. We saved seventeen women on Adapazan who were raped by the Red Dragons too. They all survived the ordeal just fine.

"Okay, calm down now. We need to know how many of you were taken and where the others are at," Baron John took control of the interrogation.

One woman spoke up, "We don't know. The reds took fifteen women away with them. The whites and the greens each took ten. The greens also took away at least twenty strong men. We don't know where they are."

The lucky streak ended abruptly. While some of the rescued women had seen some of the others around the village, they did not know their names. Without their names, a Mind Link could not be established. "Well, at least you were able to rescue fifteen," Zoran tried to make the best of it.

Meanwhile, Archmage Nadia explained in detail to John's Archmages and others just what to expect as they days progressed. More importantly, she outlined in detail what they would have to do to save the women's lives when the sixty-day gestation period ended and the dragons were due to be born. Considering the sheer number of morph spells that would be needed, Zoran offered to take these fifteen to Brn until their ordeal was over. Baron John thanked him profusely and later sent significant financial support for the women. Their due dates were around the 15th of June.

That settled, John invited them to take tea with him. "We all want to know about just how Archmage Jakob got that dragon to go into such a deep sleep," he added.

This time, it was Jakob who reveled in the admiration and praise for his Gem of Dragon Control. Karel glared at him, eventually muttering, "The only good dragon is a dead dragon." Jarka chuckled. She knew that Karel was rather annoyed with Jakob for stealing the limelight from himself and his rods.

Before leaving, Zoran pointed out, "Look all isn't over yet. You still have some fifty plus days to locate the other women. I say keep at the detective work, John. Holler if you find another name and we'll come help out."

After many thank you's, Zoran's group returned home. Now Jakob again had to explain all about his invention, much to the annoyance of Karel. Still, in the right situations, Zoran saw many uses for such gems. The problem was finding large gems capable of holding such powerful spells. Later, Baron John and his brothers Shadow Walked the fifteen women to Brn and they were given beds in the infirmary.

The next day, Milan received a visitor, Honani. "We meet again, Duska Milan. Now that the snows are melting, I thought I would drop by and see if you need more of our special goods." He never spoke outright precisely what these were, not after that one initial bargain. Secrecy required such and he knew that Milan knew what he meant.

"Not really. We've been killing many dragons of late." Milan was only too keen to tell Honani all about what had been going on, particularly about the abduction and interspecies breeding of more dragons. He ended after relating all that his dad had told him about yesterday's rescue of fifteen women. "There are still a bunch of women unaccounted for and some men." Again, he told Honani about what Karel had said that the women had said.

"So the greens have a lot of men and ten women; the whites, another ten; and the reds, another fifteen?" he sought clarification.

"Exactly Honani. If we don't get the women rescued in fifty days, they will die when giving birth to these foul beasts!"

"Hum, do you think that Baron John Witherspoon will pay a finder's fee if they can be located in time?" he asked, sensing another way to pull in some funds. He was a bit disappointed that they didn't need more dragon blood. Killing the baby dragons to get it was easy.

"I am sure of it."

"Thanks. We will see if we can locate them. I have to be going. Catch you later on, Duska Milan." The two men bowed and Honani teleported away, before going invisible and then Shadow Walking back to his group on Isi.

Chapter 15 The Fall of Jing

Li Shan fought to control the intense pain shooting through his left arm, pain unlike any that he'd even known. To fight it, he imagined finding ways to use the Green Dragon rotting slime to torture his victims into talking. Talk they would, that he knew, as he fought to keep from screaming. He was an assassin, always had been. As a nine year old boy, he knew what he wanted to do: kill. The feeling of power and control was addictive, gained at that time by killing his villager's pets, one by one. No, he had to get to the safety of his liege, Baron Gang. He had to report; he had to get healed. Gang had to know. Healed? He hazarded another glance at his left arm and involuntarily gagged. Already his hand had rotted and fallen to the ground, lost somewhere behind him. Now his lower arm was about to drop off as well. Pain, excruciating pain.

Now he was far enough away that he could hazard a spell. Could he concentrate enough to do it? Somehow, he just had to. "Focus, focus," he whispered, shocked to hear the awful raspiness of his voice. Had the slime affected his lungs too? Was he rotting from the inside out? "Focus!" he commanded himself. His spell detonated and Li Shan dropped two feet from the air onto the outside paved entryway into Gang's fortress in Nanchan. A gate guard saw him and rushed to his side. "Take me to Gang immediately!"

Two minutes later, he stood before his master. "My god, Li! What happened to you? Guard, get the physician and tell him to bring lots of healing potions with him. Run man, run! Hang in there a bit, Li. No, don't try to talk. Wait for the healing potions. My god, slime! The bastard greens!" Shortly the aging physician came running behind the guard. He saw Li and set to work, forcing a healing drought into the man's mouth. From behind the man, the physician shook his head and Gang picked up his intention. Li was dying and all the potions in the world would not save him from the rotting slime.

"Okay, tell me what happened?" Gang ordered, hoping that Li could live long enough to report. On the marsh planet of Jing, there were few locations which had solid bedrock ground. Three of the largest patches had become the locations of the three Circles of Ascension and the huge stone fortresses of the barons. Beyond these three, there were only a few other smaller areas of solid ground.

"I went to Xiaosheng just as you requested. It is far worse than we suspected! The greens have totally taken over that entire complex. They've turned our homes there into their own dens. Worse, they have got some women prisoners there, pregnant ones. I don't believe what I heard though, that those women are carrying green dragon babies in their wombs. That can't be."

"My god, then the rumors are true. We've lost the small fort at Xiaosheng. You are right; obviously humans and dragons can't breed together. They must have something else going on there." Gang felt crushed. The greens were most definitely now out of control, having broken all of the agreements they'd made when offered sanctuary here on Jing while they were starving on their own world of Voss.

"I barely escaped from there. I dropped by our secret mine at Baozhai next.

You wanted to know what the holdup was. Well, the greens have taken over the mine there! We've lost that entire mine. They spotted me poking around and tried to slime me. I nearly killed one, but another came out of nowhere and caught me with its slime. I thought that I was a goner, but I fled on foot into the marshes. They gave chase, but I lost them." Suddenly, his throat felt like he'd swallowed a pile of dirt. He coughed and gagged. Up came a pile of rot and blood, which spewed across the baron's fine rug. Pain! His chest now throbbed. He tried to breathe, but even that hurt. His legs felt weak and he slumped to the ground. Li tried to ask for more potions, but only blood mixed with rotting slime came out. His eyes opened wide as he realized that he was not going to live. He looked at his baron, who turned away from the grotesque sight of the man. Rot had appeared all over his body, most noticeably his face. Li gagged again and fell forward; life left him.

"Get his body out of here. Clean up this mess. I have to get to work," he ordered. The news could not have been worse. He stepped over the dead man and the pile of slime slowly eating away at his own carpet and added, "Dispose of the carpet too."

In the safety of his plush study, he summoned his brothers. Somehow they had to do something. "What's up?" asked Jie, who arrived seconds before his brother, Li.

"Li Shan is dead. Slimed. However, he did bring me the news. It's far worse than we ever imagined. Sit down." They did so and he told them what Li had reported and what other news he'd gathered before.

"My god. They have taken Xiaosheng and are making it their den? Damn!" Li cursed.

"Hey, that's not anywhere near as vital as the loss of mine at Baozhai. Without the gold and gems from Baozhai and Honghui, we have zero income! All will be totally lost, brothers, lost completely! No revenue, save the paltry taxes we collect from our pitiful citizens," Gang muttered.

"Well, we still have control of Honghui. Half the income is better than none," Jie tried to make light of the mess.

Just then the booming voice of their father caught their total attention. Chen Meerong, although retired and quite lame in his right leg, came into the room, moving slowly, each step nearly too painful to take. "So what the devil are you going to do about it? Do I have to repeat everything? I give you control of Jing and what do you three idiots do with it? Lose our fourth fortress — lose our number one secret mine which provides us with the funds to survive! Idiots! Incompetent nincompoops, that's what you three are. I would have been better off leaving Jing in the hands of your rebel sisters!"

"Dad! Li Shan is dead, slimed while trying to find out what the greens are doing," Gang said flustered. He wished the old man would have died when his mother had. "What are we supposed to do?" He regretted saying that. He'd put his foot in his mouth and his dad would surely lecture them for hours now. Jie gave him a dirty look.

"Sons, it is plainly obvious what you must do immediately: take back our mine. Forget the fourth fortress for now. That mine and the one at Honghui are the most important places on Jing. We lose them and we've lost everything! What have we got an army for? Use them. Summon all mages too. Put old Liang Don to work too. High time he earned all the pay we've been giving him for the last forty years. Storm the mine and retake it immediately."

"But those are dragons, dad," Li protested, becoming a little worried that his dad actually meant every word that he just said.

"Dragons can be killed. How many did your sisters supposedly kill? Eighteen? Nineteen? Something like that. If your feeble sisters can slay that many, surely you powerful sons can vastly top that count. Let's show these greens that they cannot mess with the Meerongs."

The three brothers had little choice but to follow their father's suggestion. While Chen really was no longer the baron of Jing and had given up the throne, still many supported him. He was still an influential man around the courts. He could easily embarrass all three boys and turn public opinion against them, making their jobs even more difficult. If the army mutinied, they'd lose control of Jing. Chen could easily step back in and retake control of the planet.

The three brothers summoned their generals. Originally, Chen had three generals commanding each of his three mighty armies. Some thirty thousand men guarded the three fortresses and other vitally important locations. How many had died at Baozhai and Xiaosheng none knew at the moment, but it had to number a few thousand. After all, the two secret mines were critically important to Jing. Further, the soldiers who were sent there to protect the mines were never allowed outside contact after they were posted there. When they grew too old to soldier any longer, they were executed. Beyond Chen, the three barons and their wives, a few mages, and a general, no one even knew of the existence of said two mines. Any local person who accidentally stumbled upon the mines was captured and executed on the spot.

An hour later, their wives, the generals, a dozen mages, and Archmage Liang Don had assembled in Gang's private study. Philomena, his servant girl, went from man to man, filling their cups with the finest wine on Jing, and then she sat in the back of the room, awaiting further orders. Many nodded or spoke to old Chen, whom they still respected. He had been a kindly tyrant, at least to them.

Gang began outlining what had recently happened. "General Tingfeng. You take half of your army and secure the secret mine at Honghui. Li will go with you to show you the way. The other half of your army will join with General Zedong here. All of us will march on the mine at Baozhai and re-take the mine from the greens."

"Against dragons, my liege?" General Zedong asked, startled.

Gang didn't quite know what to say. It was obvious that they were going to attack the greens. However, his father, who had been sitting silently watching his sons, spoke up, "General, let all of the soldiers know that the barons will pay a one thousand gold piece bounty for every green that is slain. All those who partake in its slaying will get their share of the bounty. Tell them that this is a golden opportunity to become very wealthy soldiers." General Zedong grinned. Old Chen had not lost his touch. Chen added, "Plus, everyone here will get a five thousand gold bonus for the holding of Honghui and the successful re-taking of Baozhai." Now the smiles broadened. The men saw that there was something in this risky venture for them.

"Er right. Now how long will it take to muster your soldiers and prepare for the greatest battle in Jing history?" Gang asked, getting into the act and not wanting to be outdone by his father. They agreed upon marching tomorrow at ten in the morning. On a large map of Jing, Gang then showed them where the two secret mines were located and asked how long it would take for the armies to reach them. Luck was on their side. After a full day of marsh pole boating, the army would be in position to attack them at dawn. Everyone shook hands and the meeting broke up. Many stuck around to chat with old Chen. Philomena was dismissed and soon only the three brothers remained. Their father had finally hobbled his way out of the study.

"Well, that went better than I expected," Jie commented. They chatted a while longer.

That evening when her official duties ended, Philomena went for a walk outside the fortress walls. Once out of sight, she cast Invisibility on herself and morphed back into her true huge, green form. Then, she teleported to Baozhai to report in to Axelrod, who commanded the greens at the mine.

Gang and his brothers and their wives gathered at the appointed rendezvous point the next day, the 13th of April. The combined forces were incredibly impressive. Fully thirty thousand men, many wearing armor, stood on the patches of dry ground, their pole boats beside them. The generals looked resplendent and the barons and baronesses wore their finest armor as well. The mage pool stood close to the three barons and observed the horde of soldiers. Everyone's morale rose to a fevered pitch and the generals barked their marching orders. Action. Men boarded their crafts and off they went. Gang felt confident that this action would be successful. How could dragons survive this mighty army?

General Tingfeng and Baron Li arrived at the secret mine of Honghui, some hundred miles from Nanchan, long before the main army was to reach the captured Baozhai mine. Three thousand men strong, the force moved into the mine's area. The entrance to the mine was easily missed in this vast marshland. A low stone, circular wall whose height was barely three feet above the surrounding marsh waters was the actual entrance. It was barely twenty-five feet across. Ordinarily, the security guards, several thousand strong, ought to have been encountered already. They were supposed to be patrolling the marsh waters around the entrance, keeping out locals. None had thus far been seen.

Inside the opening, a spiraling stone staircase attached to the wall led downwards far underground. Some hundred feet below, Chamber One sprawled out, nearly a mile in diameter. Here were the living quarters for everyone. Three dozen additional shafts angled downward from Chamber One, following the many ore veins. This mine had been worked for centuries. An incredibly extensive set of additional tunnels and smaller chambers stretched out for nearly a mile in all directions.

Li, the general, and the three thousand soldiers moved up to the entrance, surrounding it, pole boats packed in tight. Just as General Tingfeng was about to give the orders to unload and head down the stairs, Baron Li's Duska senses flashed him a dire warning of extreme danger. "Something's terribly wrong, General," he whispered his warning.

Just then, four green dragons flew up and out of the circular hole in the ground, their seventy foot long, snake-like bodies twisting and turning as they flew.

All four let loose a volley of rotting slime which completely covered the general and Li, who dove off the boat into the shallow marsh waters, but not in time. As the four cleared the entrance, four more flew out, and then four more. The battle was on in earnest. The soldiers had no choice but to attempt to fight the dragons with their pole arms and swords.

Although covered in the slime, Baron Li managed to get off a Disintegrate spell, bringing down the green that slimed him. He collapsed from the intense burning pain, slumping into the slime covered marsh waters. He died shortly afterwards. Twenty minutes later, the last of the greens had finished their mop up action. All of the invading force was now dead, a massive pile of bodies floating on the shallow march waters. Three greens had died. A couple of soldiers had somehow managed to spear two greens, running their pole arms into their eye sockets, quite by accident.

Able ordered his greens to now get rid of the rotting bodies and to clean up the place. He left one green on guard duty just outside the circular entrance. He went back down inside to make sure that the captured humans were still mining as ordered.

At dawn, although Gang and Jie had not yet heard from Li, they attacked the secret mine at Baozhai. This mine was a hundred twenty-five miles from Nanchan. However, its design was pretty much the same as Honghui. Its main chamber was octagonal and double the area of Chamber One at Honghui. Mined for nearly a hundred years longer, Baozhai was far more profitable, yielding quality gems, not gold.

The twenty-seven thousand soldiers, the two generals, the two barons, their three wives, the ten mages, and Archmage Liang Don moved in to retake their precious mine from the greens. Axelrod had summoned all of the greens on Jing to help defend the mine, leaving only fifteen to guard the recently taken mine at Honghui. Seventy greens lay in wait, eager to put an end to the human control of Jing. According to Axelrod, they would be the first dragon race to take total control over their new planet home. That they also now had the highly profitable mines was even more important to them.

Axelrod had made precise plans for the coming battle. According to Philomena, the two barons and three baronesses had to be taken out first, followed by the mages. Once those were gone, the army posed no threat at all. In fact, they could probably capture many of them and use them as slave labor along with the men they had taken in raids on other planets. Axelrod made sure that his seventy greens all knew the battle plan. Kill the Duska first. Then kill the mages.

The problem with the greens is that they rarely follow orders, as each thinks that they know best. While all seventy greens nodded to Axelrod, hardly any would actually do as he asked. He had twenty greens out a mile from the entrance, supposedly hiding beneath the marsh waters. They were to rise up and attack the army from its rear, who would then be totally encircled. Others would rise up out of the entrance like a roman candle, spewing forth rotting slime on the barons and baronesses, then the mages. If Axelrod's plan had been executed as he outlined it, the battle would be over and swiftly.

Of course the opposite occurred. As the thousands of pole boats slipped past the submerged greens, several rose up and began to slime the trailing boats. In the lead boats, the barons and mages were still a half mile from the mine's circular stone entrance, likewise barely three feet above the marsh waters. Hearing the sounds of battle coming from behind them, the leaders turned to see a number of greens attacking their rear. All launched volleys of deadly spells at the greens. Axelrod was peeved and ordered his remaining greens to spew forth from the entrance and join the fray. Thus, his quick kill of the barons and mages failed at first. Against the original ten greens, the combined spell power took a deadly toll, ten were killed before Gang screamed, "Look out! Behind us!" They turned to see countless greens spewing up out of the entrance, their tiny wings working like mad to support their huge, snake-like bodies. Greens disliked flying, but had little other choice to get into and out of the mine.

Streams of slime flew in all directions, instead of directly at the Duska and mages. Although they had to dodge some streams, they continued to fire off killer spells as fast as they could. To their credit, each of the baronesses managed to kill a dragon themselves before they were slimed. Jie got two and Gang, three. Just when Gang thought that they might yet have a chance, Axelrod managed to sneak his slime stream on the two barons. Jie dove out of the way, but took slime directly in his face, before plunging into the murky waters. Gang was not so lucky; slime covered his body before he was able to reach the protection of the foul waters.

Searing, intense pain, unlike any that he'd ever felt before enveloped Jie. It was all he could do to prevent himself from exhaling and then drowning. With the last of his will power, he attempted to Shadow Walk to Gang's fortress, where he knew his father sat waiting news of their victory over the dragons. Somehow, Jie managed the maneuver, but stumbled and fell onto the floor not ten feet from where his father was sitting, fretting and worrying over the lack of news.

"Good god son! What happened to you?" Ignoring the crippling pain in his leg, he moved over to the prone man and turned him over. His hand went to his mouth, covering it. Jie's face was slowly rotting away! Hastily, he began casting spells to neutralize and cleanse the deteriorating flesh. He yelled for the physician. By the time the old man arrived, potions in hand, Chen had gotten most of the active slime off of his son's face. The physician poured four vials of healing potion into what remained of Jie's mouth, in a valiant attempt to keep the man alive. It actually worked, Jie would live, but he was ever after completely blind; his eyes were long gone. His face was hideous to look at, a mass of twisted, scarred flesh. His mouth was totally mutilated. Few ever dared to look directly at him. He no longer had lips and his speech was difficult to understand. But he lived.

An hour later, his son stabilized and being looked after by the physician, Chen began to attempt to make Mind Links to his other sons, their wives, the mages, even Archmage Liang Don. Nothing. Nothing at all. He could contact none of them. Frustrated, he attempted to contact the three generals next. Nothing. Panic flooded over the old man. After taking a long drink of wine to steady his shaking nerves, he cast every protection spell that he knew on himself, adding Invisibility last. He then Shadow Walked to Honghui and saw the greens disposing of thousands of dead men. Shocked, he moved over to Baozhai, remaining just within the safety of the Shadows. He vomited thrice. The carnage was beyond anything he could have possibly imagined!

Twenty green dragons lay in crumpled masses in a huge random pattern around the entrance of the mine. He spotted the rotting remains of Gang floating on the foul waters. Nearby were the three baronesses. All were dead. Twenty-seven thousand men — he just could not fathom what had happened here. He did not know that many of the soldiers had been captured; some hundred of them were still alive, but had been taken into the mine and forced to work for the greens until they died. As he watched, he mechanically counted the greens and reached forty-four before he believed he had seen them all.

"We got a third of them," he whispered to himself, "that's something, at least. My god! The greens now can control all of Jing! Dear god, what has happened to Jing?" The realization that the greens now controlled his whole world sank into the old man. Nothing stood between the greens and anything on Jing. At any time they could walk into the defenseless fortresses and Circles of Ascension and do anything they desired. Gone were all of their possible defenses. Only he remained. He sank into a deep depression and headed back to the fortress at Nanchan.

"He is going to live, Baron, but I am afraid his face will be permanently disfigured. How goes the great battle?" the physician asked.

"We lost it all. They are all dead. Barons, baronesses, mages, generals, soldiers — all dead!" He slumped into a chair, his old bones and joints aching as never before. He lived to see his world overthrown by the Green Dragons, betrayed by them, destroyed by them. *My daughters saw my folly and tried to stop them,* he thought. *What have I done? My daughters! They still live! Maybe it is not too late!*

"Physician, look after Jie. I am going to get help if it is the very last thing I ever do," Chen barked out. He nodded and Chen focused his mind and slipped into the Shadows once more. Soon the blue-white world of Adapazan appeared before him. Snow still covered much of the higher country. He headed for Brn and Messaged Zoran. *Baron Zoran, this is Chen Meerong. I beg to meet with you and my two daughters. The greens have wiped us all out. Please, I beg you.*

Damn. Sure. Arrive at my Circle. I'll lower the protections. Zoran hastily did so and Messaged his large group, including Chan and Wen. He stepped through a Mystical Door and arrived just in time to watch Chen Meerong materialize in the middle of his Circle of Ascension. "Welcome to Brn once more. It's been quite some time since I last saw you," he began, offering the old man his hand. Other Mystical Doors opened and the room quickly filled up. Both Chan and Wen arrived and saw that their father really had come.

"Please, is there some place we can all go? My leg can't take much walking or standing," Chen asked. Zoran looked at a totally beaten man. He put his arm around Chen and stepped him into his study. Everyone else followed them. Zdenka sent for refreshments as Zoran helped Chen to sit down in his comfortable chair.

"Greetings daughters. Forgive me, for I have been an utter foolish old man. I have brought total ruin to Jing. I am afraid that I bring hideous news. The greens now control all of Jing; they are all dead. Only Jie still lives, barely, but he will never be the same. I should have listened to the both of you twenty years ago. All is lost, but I have come to beg you to lend a hand and try to save Jing from the total ruin that it now faces."

"Please, Chen, start at the beginning. Tell us all what happened, please," Zoran asked.

Slowly, Chen outlined all that he knew, withholding nothing. "What? We have two secret mines that produce lots of gold and gems?" Chan interrupted.

"Yes, closely guarded secret for all that did." He went on.

"Wait, you say that the greens are holding women at this place called Xiaosheng?" Zoran interrupted him this time.

"Why yes. The assassin who went there and lost his life suggested that somehow the greens were breeding with them, but that's utterly preposterous, utter fantasy."

"Oh no it isn't! That is precisely what they are doing, using human females to make more baby dragons. It seems they only breed every ten years. With all of their losses, they are getting frantic to produce more greens," Zoran answered. "But please, continue."

Chen did so, but was obviously highly unnerved by Zoran's comments. He talked for an hour. At last, crying too badly to continue, he Mind Linked them and replayed what he had seen while lurking in the Shadows. Wild curses and exclamations echoed randomly through the room. No one had ever seen such carnage before. It dwarfed anything that they had ever seen, far worse than the destroyed villages. Thirty-thousand men gone!

As he finished up, Chan and Wen picked up on his dragon count. "Say, you counted only forty-four there and perhaps a dozen at the other mine? Their numbers must be drastically lower than when we were there hunting them down. Maybe we have a chance yet," Chan suggested.

"Right sis, only fifty or so. Maybe we can strike back. Zoran, we are going to have to go after the women and soon. If we kill enough greens, we might be able to retake Jing from their clutches," Wen added.

"Daughters, you two are the last official rulers of Jing. Jie — well he will be an invalid the rest of his life. Please, take back our world if you can. I have so failed you, my daughters."

"Well, you certainly have, dad. Failed us and the people of Jing, but we'll do our best to retake Jing from the wicked, vile greens," Chan declared.

"Thank you. There is much that I must tell you, the secret pass codes, the location of our treasuries, many such things. If I don't so much will be lost forever," Chen added, a slight hope in his voice.

"I'm going to let the other barons know that we've located some of their missing men and women. We'll put together a coordinated attack as fast as possible. The women may not have much time left before they give birth and die," Zoran said quickly.

"You are worried about those women?" asked Chen.

"Of course, dad, their lives are precious. That is what ruling is all about, helping our people live better lives, not about our comforts and finery. That's where you went so very wrong," Chan could not resist chiding her father. "We've been rescuing folks right and left since Zoran gave us sanctuary in our time of great need."

The others then returned to their duties, leaving the three alone to discuss what they needed. Obviously, the two women had a lot to get off their chests too.

Besides, everyone now had serious plans to make, preparations to handle. None had the slightest doubts that Zoran would not take this opportunity to attack the greens of Jing.

Chapter 16 The New Rulers of Jing

Zdenka joined Zoran in their small, private study. "We are obviously going after the women being held at Xiaosheng. Probably there will only be a few greens there. Are we going into the mines after the whole mass of greens?" she asked.

"Well, Chan and Wen certainly will want us to eliminate all the greens possible, but I am going to leave the fate of the men up to their barons. If John, Arcangelo, and Stefan want to make an attempt to free them, we'll back them with all we have. If they do not, then we'll not go it alone. Instead, we'll do what we can to help Chan and Wen secure the rest of Jing. That makes sense, doesn't it, dear?"

She agreed and Zoran summoned the three barons to Brn at once. Five minutes later, he explained, "I summoned you here because I have some good news at last. We've located a number of women being held by the greens. They are on Jing. We've also located the many missing men from your lands and perhaps ours too. It seems that Jing has lost all of its barons, baronesses, mages, Archmage, and its entire army of thirty thousand."

"What? Gang, Jie, Li, all dead?" asked Stefan in total disbelief. Zoran then explained what Chen Meerong had just related to them all. "He shared his images of the aftermath of the battles with me. Beyond all imaginable horrors, barons. Sickening. At least we now know where the women are and likely all the men — slave workers in the mines there. I will point out, Baron Arcangelo, some of the women might be from Cosma. If the greens didn't impregnate them as soon as the others did, they may still have a few days at most before they give birth and die as a result. I really can't say, but there is a chance. I've asked you here to find out what you want to do about it. Adapazan will back up you with all that we have."

"If there is even a remote chance, we must make the attempt to rescue the women. I've pledged my life to protecting my people," Baron Arcangelo replied. Stefan and John backed him. "Do you think that we can possibly take on that many in the mines?"

"We have to try," Stefan countered. "If Archmage Karel has more of his Rods of Dragon Slaying, we would have a good chance against that many of them."

"He has made ten of them so far that are operational. Okay, then let's get this rescue going as swiftly as possible. I believe that we should get to the women even today, if possible. No telling how much time they have left. I suspect resistance there should be minimal," Zoran advised.

"Right. Tomorrow we can organize a major strike force to go after the enslaved men," Stefan proposed. "Give us an hour to get ready. Shall we meet back here then?" The barons agreed and promptly left.

Zoran then summoned all his people to the Great Hall. "In an hour, we are going to help the other barons launch a rescue of the captured women. Tomorrow, we will join with all of their forces and make an attempt to rescue the enslaved men. That means going after some forty dragons possibly. We'll need everything we can throw at them and all the protections we can get. Karel, I think that the remaining rods would best be used by the Archmages, who stand the best chances of delivering killing blows, if they are not distracted by the dragons' attacks."

"Right. I will dole them out. Ours get them first, though," he replied.

"Okay, go make your preparations. The Duska who are not Archmages will be primarily responsible for Shadow Walking the women out of harm's way as fast as possible. We are going to use our infirmary here as the initial arrival point. We have the most experience with this situation. We will examine the women and make recommendations to the other barons. Make sense? Any other ideas?" he asked.

"What we need is a suit that can withstand dragon slime a bit," Verushka commented. She still saw the hideous face of Jie in her mind. That gave Karel yet another idea, but it would have to wait until he had time alone in his lab.

Promptly an hour later, the other three barons arrived with their forces. They brought their baronesses with them, primarily to help evacuate the women. That made nine more couples. Additionally, they brought along their Archmages, another nine. Zoran left the four northern Archmages in charge of Adapazan, though Jakob insisted on coming along. Zoran's group numbered twenty, as Dana insisted on coming along with Chan and Wen.

Stefan had his precious Rod of Dragon Slaying. Karel loaned one to Barons John and Arcangelo. Zoran, Zdenka, Verushka, Nadia, Marek, and Karel had the others, plus Chika loaned hers to Ivana so that all their Archmages had a rod and could withstand ten slimes while delivering their killing blows. Also Jakob wore his gem and could fight with impunity as well.

Since Chan and Wen both knew where Xiaosheng was at, Zoran allowed them to handle the large Shadow Walk. However, tomorrow, old Chen would have to take them to the secret mines; his daughters had never known of their existence. Five minutes later, the large group stood in the Shadows just above the solid ground which held the small fortress of Xiaosheng. They surveyed the area for a few minutes, but saw no signs of life. A small town ought to have been here with people going about their daily lives. It appeared deserted, but they knew better. Somewhere inside the stone fortress women were being held captive. Just where and how many dragons remained a mystery. At last, the large group materialized on the outer ramparts near the main entrance doors.

Chan whispered, "We are familiar with the city, though we haven't been here in years. Let us go invisible and scout things out. We'll maintain a constant Mind Link with you." Zoran agreed and the two cast their spells and vanished. However, Zoran could just barely hear their footsteps on the stone floor and hoped that would not give them away.

Once inside the two women split up to cover more ground more quickly, Chan taking the left side while Wen, the right. The others grew impatient. As the women pronounced these outer rooms clear, the large party moved in after them, leaving Jakob to act as a rear guard in case some greens arrived here. While he didn't like this idea, he saw its wisdom and didn't protest his assignment. *Kitchen. One dragon.* Wen sent along her observation. Apparently, the greens were doing the cooking for the women. This one was called Philomena, Wen later learned.

Dragon blocking the hall. Can't get past him. Chan sent. *There ought to be many rooms down there that could well be housing the women,* she suggested. Chan added, *Say, the space is very narrow for a dragon. If there are more further on down, they will have to be in human form.*

Pantry clear. Nothing else down this way. Must be on Chan's side, Wen sent, heading over to where she thought Chan must be waiting.

Chan, wait for us. I have an idea, Zoran sent. The Archmages with the rods went invisible and headed to meet up with Chan. Following his orders, the two women quietly laid down on the floor as they heard the soft steps of the approaching small group. "Now," Zoran's voice broke the silence. Simultaneously, seven Archmages cast their Disintegrate spells aiming for the head of the green, that suddenly lifted up its head at the sound of Zoran's voice. Of course, the Archmages immediately became visible to the dragon, but that was only momentary. Taken by surprise by seven ultra-powerful Archmages, the green lost all seven battles. Its head completely disappeared; the rest of its snake-like body slumped lifeless to the floor. "Okay continue," Zoran whispered. Chan and Wen got up and continued their silent movement down the hall.

At last they arrived at the doors, ten on each side of the hall. All were closed. Now came the moment of truth. They would have to open them one by one. If dragons were inside, the battle would be on. Zoran whispered again, "Let's play it safe. A couple of you go back and take out the dragon in the kitchen first. We don't want it wandering in on us. Then, let's have those with the rods open the doors. Safer that way. Verushka and Karel headed off to take care of the cook. They returned a couple of minutes later; smiles told of their complete success.

Nine rod holders moved to the first nine doors. On Zoran's signal, they opened them together and looked inside. Several of them called out, "Women in here." "Clear." After checking on the last five doors, no further dragons were located. All told they uncovered fifty women. Ten from Cosma, ten from Terra, thirty from Jing. While the Duska-non-Archmages proceeded to Shadow Walk the fifty women to Zoran's infirmary, the rest fanned out to thoroughly search the fortress. One other dragon was found sleeping in the basement, surrounded by ten newborn baby greens. These were quickly dispatched!

"That ought to set them back further. I bet these came from our women," Zdenka speculated. "Come on; we best get to the infirmary and see how far along the Cosma women are. Could be a long night for us."

Satisfied the place was dragon free, the large group returned to Brn and followed Zdenka to the infirmary, where the baronesses and Jarka were already working with the women. They were filthy beyond belief, starving as expected, terrorized, and emotionally numb. Those from Cosma were very pregnant and were in a good deal of pain from the movements of the baby dragons in their wombs. Quickly, the mages worked their magic, giving the women the first relief they'd had. They were due any day now. "It's going to be a long night," Verushka commented to Zoran.

The thirty women from Jing were in worse shape and in various days of their enforced pregnancies. A few were also due within a few days. Most had lost all sense of time, having given up all hope of living. After the women were cleaned up and fed, Chan and Wen worked with their fellow countrywomen to figure out when they were due. With some coaching, each woman was able to fairly accurately tell them the day that they were abducted and how long after that they were raped by a green. The two then worked out the due date for each woman, placing a card with her name on it beside her bed. "We're going to be constantly busy for over a month," Wen pointed out. Verushka made sure that plenty of Duskas and mages would be on duty at all times of the day and night for the next month, establishing doable schedules for the women helpers. Men could be called in if the task became too much for the women to handle.

"What do you want us to do?" asked Baron Arcangelo.

Verushka and Zdenka began instructing them on what needed to be done. While she would have preferred that only women handle these poor victims, there were too many for them. A bit reluctantly, she allowed the barons to lend a hand as well. Certainly, their Morph Others spells would be needed soon. However, they did get one break. The ten women from Terra had not yet been raped and impregnated. Gang's attack on the secret mines had forced Axelrod to postpone the breeding night. Had they waited another day, these ten too would have been impregnated. Baron John breathed a huge sigh of relief. However, now Baronesses Rayna, Zusa, and Kamila would get firsthand experience in handling the birthing process with the Cosma women. They'd be prepared for the future.

It turned out to be one very long night. The baby dragons had to be re-morphed into human form nearly every hour. Around one in the morning, the first woman went into labor and the others were not too far behind her. At this point, the spells had to be recast nearly every twenty minutes and the greatest of care taken. One false move and the dragon would begin ripping the woman apart from her insides out.

As one baby green was born, either Zoran or Karel used a Vanish spell on it, depositing it near the sun. The last woman delivered hers around nine the next morning. All ten women survived and began the long road to recovery. At last the group headed off to bed, dead tired.

When they arose the next evening, Verushka and Zdenka began examining the ten, looking for the latent magical energies that they had discovered in their seventeen young women. They found the results intriguing and triple checked their findings, then conferred. "While there is that same residual magical energies in their bodies, it is nowhere near as strong as it is in Danika, for example, drastically smaller, I'd say," Verushka stated. "I wonder why?"

"Well, the greens are the least magically inclined of all the dragons. Perhaps that's why. Still, we are going to have to tell Baron Arcangelo about this phenomenon. We've not mentioned this to the other barons before now. Guess we owe it to the women to do so now," Zdenka declared.

"What? They are magically energized somehow?" Baron Arcangelo gushed when Zdenka explained what she and Verushka had found.

"That's not the half of it," Verushka grinned. She began telling the barons about their rescued seventeen women and their incredible propensity to learn magical spells at a phenomenal rate. "These women are highly likely to be able to pick up magic spells rapidly. My advice is to get them all into magical training with one of your Archmages immediately. You may well end up with ten strong mages as a result. Besides, it goes a long way to help them regain their lives and self-respect."

"I'll do it," Archmage Bianca volunteered. She didn't want the women to study under Alfredo, who had learned under old Biagio. She would use Zdenka's techniques, which were far gentler on the student and, she thought, far more productive. As expected, the ten women were quite surprised that they were going to be given the chance to study magic under Archmage Bianca. Their road to recovery was assured, Verushka concluded, wondering just how the ten would take to learning magic.

Months later, Bianca told her that the ten were some of her brightest students. However, they did not progress any faster than her normal students, quite unlike the seventeen. Verushka began to wonder what would happen to a woman if she were impregnated by a Gold Dragon, but quickly put that thought out of her mind.

Now all thoughts turned to the massive assault on the mines to free the enslaved men. As they group discussed ways and means, Karel pointed out that the rod's protection was a sphere twenty feet across, of course centered on the wielder. "Look, if another person stands to the right of the wielder and a third stands to the left, they will be protected as well. That gives three spell casters unlimited freedom of action for around ten slime attacks. We should take advantage of that."

"Archmage Karel, you are a genius!" declared a most impressed Baron John.

"Right! Thirty of us can be protected and cast our spells or fight them. That does give us a chance, if there are fifty of the beasts there," Baron Arcangelo added, growing more confident by the minute. Chan smiled, thinking maybe there was some hope after all.

"Okay, then let's work out our trios of attackers," Zoran suggested.

Chan spoke first, "Jakob, Jarka, and I will make one team. Wen, Dana, and Karel can work together. Dana insists on going with Wen." She made darn sure that Dana was included. Wen and Dana were now lovers and she wanted to keep them together and safe.

Old Chen said, "I'll go too. I'm the only one who knows the mine's layout. I may be all crippled up, but this is the least I can do. I want to be a part of cleaning up the hideous mess that I created. I brought these vile creatures to Jing and I never listened to my daughters. Please, I must do this."

"Okay, Chen, you're in. You tag along beside me. Bernard, you are with me. We have eight more trios to arrange," Zoran replied.

Archmage Verushka took her husband Baron Tomas and her brother Evsen with her. Archmage Nadia took her husband Dusan and Milan with her. Archmage Zdenka took Baron Jan and Baroness Reina with her. Archmage Marek took his wife Akira and Chika with him. Archmage Ivana took Valtr's Zdenk and Zusa Pavel with her. Baron John took his Archmages Ben and Lisa with him. Baron Arcangelo took his Archmages Bianca and Alfredo with him. Baron Stefan took his Archmages Chesna and Patrik with him.

Finally, the remaining barons and baronesses from Valtr, Cosma, and Terra, all Duska, also came. Their tasks were primarily twofold: act as rear guards and evacuate the injured or rescued men to Baron Stefan's infirmary. Zoran's was already too crowded with the women. Further, these were entrusted with the numerous healing potions that the barons brought with them, though they hoped and prayed that they would not need them.

Around ten on the 15th of April, the large band of rescuers took a deep breath and began their Shadow Walks to Jing and the secret mine of Baozhai. Following Chen's lead, the group hovered just in the Shadows high above the low circular entrance of the mine. Chan saw that he was right. The twenty-five foot circular wall only reached three feet above the marsh waters. However, the sight was anything but serene. For over a mile around the small opening that led to the subterranean mine, dead and rotting bodies of men and dragons floated on the shallow waters. Many were bloated. Gators were active around the perimeter and ten greens were mechanically moving the bodies further out into the nearby marshlands.

Zoran sent, *First, we ten attack groups take out the ten dragons. Let's get which group is attacking which dragon straight. We will attack simultaneously. Use silent spells so we don't alert those within the mine.* This took some doing and several minutes passed until Zoran was sure that everyone knew who was to attack which green. At last, he gave the order and the ten groups stepped out of the Shadows and into the incredibly foul smelling marsh waters. All thirty nearly gagged from the awful stench of slime-rotting and decaying bodies. No wonder the ten dragons were trying to disperse the dead.

Taken by total surprise and being attacked by so many Archmages at the same time and with such powerful spells, the greens had no chance whatsoever. It was totally lopsided. Sixty seconds after they materialized in the foul waters, the ten greens were dead, their bodies adding to the surreal mess around the entrance. *Less than forty to go,* Chan sent to Wen and Dana, encouraging them.

As the remainder of their party materialized into the reeking waters beside the circular stone entrance, only one person here knew the layout of what lay far below them, old Chen, who was being supported by Zoran. He could barely walk because of his throbbing leg and hip, but he was determined to see this through.

"This shaft goes straight down a hundred feet to the floor of Chamber One. It is octagonal in shape, at least a mile across. There are some thirty shafts that lead down to lower smaller chambers and the working ore face," Chen explained.

"Okay, the strike forces will go down, while the rest stand guard here. Message us if more dragons arrive. We'll Message you when we have men who need to be rescued. Cast Invisibility and then Levitate. We'll float down in eleven groups, spaced a minute apart. Once you land, each group fan out so that the others coming down don't land on top of you. Let's maintain our element of surprise as long as we can," Zoran ordered. His group headed down first.

Below, Zoran saw an incredible sight. The Chamber One's ceiling rose some fifteen feet overhead. Every twenty feet, a three foot square column of bedrock supported the ceiling. High atop each side of these columns a pair of Permanent Light spells had been cast. The illumination was as strong as daylight, though they were a hundred feet below ground.

Far off to the right, he could see rows and rows of squalid bedding. Perhaps here the slaves slept, he guessed. None were in sight. To the left, he spotted over a dozen greens, many were organizing a vast pile of gemstones. He headed his group towards the unsuspecting dragons. He heard the soft footsteps of others arriving and hoped that the dragons would not hear them. In the extreme distance, he could hear the sounds of picks on stone, probably the men mining down the many tunnels further underground. Sounds really echoed in here, he also noted.

Suddenly, a green looked up and stared at them. "Intruders?" he said questioningly. Although he couldn't see them, he heard them and smelled the unmistakable scent of fresh humans, not the foul smelling slaves working far below. Several other greens looked up. "Now," Zoran called out. Spells began to fly. This time, they didn't have time to coordinate who was attacking which dragon. As a result, during this first volley of spells, several dragons were double and triple teamed and several were not attacked at all. The battle for the mine began in earnest. Rotting slime flew from those who were not attacked. However the eleven groups flinched as the wicked slime came their way, but the rods worked perfectly. The slime dripped off the spherical shells surrounding the eleven groups.

"Invaders! We are under attack," screamed one dragon. In the deepest recess of Chamber One and lying on his own private pile of gold and gems, Axelrod was roused. He cast Invisibility on himself and headed off to see what was going on. Who could possibly be attacking them? They'd killed off every mage and baron on Jing. This could not be.

He saw thirty-three mages, men and women, attacking all his dragons with powerful spells! He grinned as four spewed their deadly rotting slime all over four of these trios, but his mouth opened wide as he saw the slime dripping off of a sphere some twenty feet around the trios! How can this be, he thought, his fear growing. Their spells were deadly, Disintegrates, he assumed. Rather than cast one of his own, he began sending Messages to his twenty mates who were below guarding their slave miners. He watched the eleven groups more closely as they fanned out, leaving behind the dead greens.

One by one, his other twenty greens came up out of the side tunnels, prepared for battle, spewing forth slime at those they saw nearest them. Axelrod watched with growing fear and dismay as their slime continued to have no affect at all. Then, he spotted the rods that one of the three was holding. Quickly, he saw similar rods in each of the groups. Panic set in as he watched all of his arriving dragons being slain. Magical Missiles and Disintegrate beams were killing his companions right and left. Even a Crushing Hand was pummeling one to death, eventually pulverizing its head into a soggy mass of brain matter! After watching twenty more of his greens succumb, Axelrod panicked utterly.

Zoran heard the sound of a dragon behind him and turned in time to see Axelrod spread his wings and Shadow Walk out of Chamber One. "One is getting away!" Hastily, he Messaged the others outside to be alert. One had fled the battle.

Outside, Milan stepped into the Shadows in time to see Axelrod leaving the planet. He followed the Green Dragon a ways until he was satisfied that the dragon was indeed leaving Jing and not attempting to counterattack from behind. He then returned and Messaged Zoran that the dragon had headed off-world, much to Zoran's relief. Those waiting outside had no protection from the dragon's rotting slime.

A half hour after it started, Chan killed the last of the greens that were in Baozhai. "Okay, now let's go down the shafts, but stay alert for more dragons." Chen told them to use five specific shafts, the ones that were still producing gem stones. Down they went. Periodically, they encountered smaller chambers. Finally about a mile below ground, they reached the sites of the current digging. Here they found the men who had been taken and turned into slave miners for the greens.

"Oh my," Zdenka whispered to Verushka when she first saw the slaves being forced to mine for the greens. Poorly fed, if at all, tattered clothing, lack of sleep and sleeping on the hard stone floors, the men were in uniformly very bad physical shape with raw, festering, and infected wounds, to say nothing of their mental condition.

"Okay, men, we've killed all of the dragons. We are going to heal up any wounds you might have or illnesses and then get you back to your planet and homes. When one of us comes to you, please tell them your home planet. Right now, you are on Jing. Oh, I'm Baron Zoran Vladislov. With me are Barons John Witherspoon, Stefan Pavel, Arcangelo Mondo, and others from those worlds." Several men cheered a bit, but most were beyond exhausted. Many just fell to the ground, dropping their picks and shovels.

Zoran had those who had been waiting outside the mine join them and they began sorting and handling the rescued men. He took the attack force and they completed a total search of the entire mine complex, rooting out any other greens that might be hiding. They found none, even though they carefully searched for Invisible dragons as well. Next, Zoran had the large group put their heads together to find a way to clean up this awful mess of dead. "We need a bright idea and fast."

"Normally, the dead are cremated," old Chen explained. "There is so little dry ground in which to dig a grave, but so many dead. . ." His voice trailed off, intense sadness loomed heavy on his mind. So much of this dead was his own doing.

The thirty-three discussed the problem. Cremation seemed the only viable route, but the sheer number of dead men was staggering. No one had any effective ideas. Finally, Zoran did. "Gang, keep a sharp lookout for greens coming back and Mind Link to me if they do. I have one possible thing that I can try." He gave his rod to Bernard and Shadow Walked back to Adapazan.

"Aldrick, I have come to ask a huge favor of you and a number of your golds," Zoran began after the usual welcoming words one must say to a dragon when arriving unexpectedly. "On Jing, we have a really big disaster to handle." He outlined what the greens had done, what the barons had done in reaction, and what his group had done a short while ago. "Honestly, the carnage is beyond all description for both our species. The dead must be disposed of properly and I know that you desire that all dragons get a proper burial. Could you possibly lend us a hand with this?"

A while later, a dozen Golden Dragons appeared over Baozhai along with Zoran, who landed and explained what his dragons were going to do. Aldrick swooped down, morphed back into his human form, and stood balancing on the top of the circular stonework. Emil quickly joined them. "My god Zoran! It is worse than you said, so many lives lost," Aldrick said softly.

"Many dead greens are down in the mine, a hundred feet down below too," he added. "It is incredibly grim. Can you help?"

"Of course, we will handle our dead first," Aldrick said, visibly upset, far more than Zoran had ever seen before. Emil was also. Never before had they seen so many dead dragons in one place. Yet, the nearly thirty thousand dead humans also made an permanent impression on these golds. Zoran could not tell if this was good or bad, only that Aldrick and Emil were quite emotionally upset over the massive loss of life. He hoped and prayed that his decision to ask the golds for help would not come back to haunt him later on.

When the golds entered the Chamber One, they also saw the pitiful condition of the slaves that the greens had taken, further adding to Aldrick's upset, confusion, and internal turmoil. "Sir, we greatly appreciate the help that you and your friends are giving us," Chan spoke up. "I just don't know how we can possibly clean this disaster up by ourselves. Here, we usually cremate our dead because as you can see, there is hardly any really solid ground on which to bury them. I understand that it is also the custom among your kind to bury your dead, but I just don't know where you could do that on Jing."

"You are the Duska, who lost your hand to a green, aren't you?" Aldrick asked. He'd been told about her, but had not met her before.

"Well, yes. My sister and I are now the rulers of Jing and we are going to try to establish peace here if we can," Chan replied diplomatically, hoping that the gold would not be too offended with her. After all, she'd now killed quite a number of dragons. My late brothers foolishly tried to retake our mines back from the greens who stole them from us, driving us from our ancient mines. The greens were housing their interspecies breeding women here and abducted many men from our world and several other worlds to be their slaves working the mined for them. The men you are seeing being evacuated are those."

"Yes, Zoran has told me about this mess — a fiasco on both races. We will deal with the greens first and then see if we can assist with the human dead," Aldrick replied. His tone was rather morose, perhaps even sad.

"We haven't yet gone to our second mine which the greens also took from us. Perhaps you could convince any greens there to return our mine to us peacefully," she suggested. "I'd like to avoid any further loss of life if I can."

"Admirable. Yes, perhaps some of you can take me there now," Aldrick said what she wanted to hear. Old Chen, though, was the only one who knew its location. Zoran, Chan, Wen, and Chen led Aldrick to Honghui.

Aldrick entered the mine but returned a half hour later. "It seems that the greens that were here have already fled. I give you back your mine, Chan."

"Thank you. I am glad that we did not have to have any confrontations here. Thanks, Aldrick. I owe you one. If you need something sometime, let me or Wen know and we will try to help as we can, sir."

"Just Aldrick, please," he said solemnly. He then returned to the burial detail.

"We'd best put the mine's protection spells back in place," old Chen advised. "Always, we kept an Invisibility spell on the stone entrance and a Go Away spell on the whole vicinity. It might be wise to put a Force Wall over the entrance as well, until you can get a strong force here to defend it, Chan." Quickly, they did just that.

"We get about five hundred thousand in gold from this mine each year," he explained to his daughters. "We usually get four times that in gems from Baozhai."

"Well, if we get that much, think of the good we can do for all our people," Wen said becoming more enthused about now being in the position of running Jing.

"Yes, but without the army to guard things and no mages and so few Duska, perhaps we are already doomed," old Chen said gloomily. He could not see any way to guarantee the survival of Jing. It all seemed so hopeless at the moment.

A couple hours later, all of the men had been evacuated to Baron Stefan's

Infirmary on Valtr. The golds had already removed the dead dragons from inside the mine. "Okay, what do we do with all the gold and gems that we've found in here?" asked Milan. "I think the greens may have stolen it from your treasury or perhaps it is their personal horde. Be careful of those massive piles of slime. How are we ever going to clean that up?"

Old Chen spoke up, "Chan, there is a secret treasury in the fortress and Circle at Nanchan. You ought to take the valuables there where they cannot easily be stolen again. I will show you its location and the codes to use to operate it. I have much to tell you about the Circle, its protections, and the fortress. Actually, you will have to know about all three of them now. I keep forgetting about the Chaohu and Zhouhan Circles. I am afraid that Jie will be unable to do much of anything any longer. I left your brother with our physician."

Zoran and his group volunteered to help them transfer the treasure, an offer that was very much appreciated. He estimated that there was about ten million to transport, an enormous sum. Once that was completed, Chan and Wen decided to remain there in the fortress at Nanchan and start to re-establish some government.

"Hey, mom, dad, Baron Zoran, I am going to stay here with Wen and help out," Dana piped up. "They are incredibly shorthanded now." While Zoran didn't like to lose his top swordsman, he knew better than to say no.

Archmage Marek added, "Okay son. I am going to ask your sister Kate and her boyfriend Milan to stay with you for the time being to lend you more help. Don't hesitate to come fetch me if you have need of an Archmage."

"Thanks dad."

"Oh, that would be great of you. We will. There is also the late Archmage Liang Don's tower to open, de-trap, and search. I am really hesitant to enter his place myself. Think of all the traps and protections he must have in there," Chan replied. Marek smiled, thinking she is right about that!

Zoran and the rest then Shadow Walked to Valtr to help out with the rescued men. Milan made a quick trip back to Brn to fetch his sister and their things. Meanwhile, Chan, Wen, and Dana looked in on their brother Jie in the infirmary. Involuntarily, all three gasped when they saw his face. It was hideously deformed from the rotting slime. His empty eye sockets really spooked the trio. "Chan? Is that you? I can't see any more." Jie tried to speak, but with no lips, his words were difficult to understand.

"Yes, it is me. Wen is with me and her boyfriend Dana Aceda. We've just killed all the green dragons and retaken both mines and the small fortress at Xiaosheng. None of us got hurt. We've got to run Jing now. There is so much to do and almost no people to do it. You try to get well, little brother. We'll check in on you later on."

"Am I awful to look at?" he whispered.

"Well," Chan faltered. What could she say?

"Please, don't lie to me, not like this. Please?"

"Well, yes, your face is frightful to look at, Jie. Maybe the physician can do something to help. Maybe we can work out some spells to help you. Give us some time, brother. Right now, just rest up and get well," Chan attempted to instill some hope in her brother's mind, though she honestly didn't see any at all.

The palace cook had diner ready for them and the four dined together. This was the first time that old Chen had dined here in his old palace in ten years. Gang never invited him for diner of late. "Well, daughters, we have some hard decisions to make. There are three Circles of Ascension which by Federation Law must have caretakers, barons and baronesses or at least a steward and someone to handle the Circle and its protections. If we cannot figure out any other way, I will lend a hand with one of the Circles, but I am so lame that I am almost useless anymore."

"Well, dad, Nanchan here is the largest and most important Circle and fortress, our only real palace. I think that Wen should run it. I only have one hand and need help with any number of things now. I can take the closer one, Chaohu. Who can we possibly get to watch over Zhouhan?"

"You see the problem that we face. The Spring High Council comes soon and you must be prepared to formally announce how the three Circles are to be protected. If you don't, the Council will appoint caretakers. Lord knows who they will pick, but they have to be Duska by law."

"Gang has a son, only I don't know where he is at right now. He is only nine and thus would have to have an adult be his official regent. If that person is not a Duska, then you'd need one to guard the Circle," old Chen added.

Chan thought a moment and then with a slightly flushed face said, "Dad, I have to ask you this. I don't mean anything derogatory by it. Did you father any illegitimate children or did mom? I don't want to go off-world to fill these positions if I don't have to do so." She tried to soften the embarrassment of her question and hoped that he would answer truthfully. Chan wanted to give their closest relations an opportunity to perhaps gain power and respect that had been denied them.

Old Chen grinned, "Mischievous and devious, are we, Chan? Honestly, no. I miss your mother terribly. I see where you are heading. You will make a good leader, daughter. I guess that we have no choice but to consider your aunts, uncles, and cousins. I bet they never expected to gain power on Jing." Chan grinned, her opinion of her father rose slightly.

He continued, "As you suspect, there will likely now be a power struggle for control of the Circles, fortresses, and rulership of Jing. I have proven that I make very bad choices. I will stay out of the decision making process, Chan. However, I will back whomever you and Wen choose."

"Thanks dad. Wen, we'd best put our heads together and make some key choices very fast. News of this disaster will spread rapidly," Chan suggested.

"Hey, I know the perfect choice," Wen blurted out. She'd just remembered their cousin who had begged them to be allowed join the Swamp Raiders, when she and Chan had become famous as Dragon Slayers, fighting the dragon oppression on Jing. Despite her pleadings, she and Chan had rejected their cousin because she was only fourteen at that time. Now she was nineteen. "Our cousin Zong Ying would be perfect."

"Say, you are right. She would be," Chan concurred, relieved.

Old Chen sighed, "I might have known." Both daughters gave him a questioning and sharp look. "She has been a constant thorn in court politics for Gang for at least the last five years. He never could stop her protests against many of his decisions. In hindsight, I can now see that she was right more than she was wrong about those issues. She's into making leather clothing for women." He gave them her home-shop address here in Nanchan and the three headed off to find her. Although it was still early evening, her shop lights were on, but her Closed sign was on the door. They knocked anyway.

After a few minutes, they heard the door being unlocked and presently saw the scowled face of Zong Ying peering out at them in the early dusk light. Zong's frown quickly changed to surprise and then worry. "Wen, Chan! Wow! Oh, come in quickly. Did anyone see you on the streets? There's a huge price on your heads now."

"Hi Zong. Not anymore. Oh, this is my boyfriend, Dana Aceda. He's from Brn, Adapazan. Zong, we need to talk," Wen replied, trying to ease Zong's fears and introduce the stranger to Zong. She'd definitely matured since she'd last saw Zong some five years ago. She wore a well-made leather top and pants, suitable for a fighter or one who needed durable, rugged clothing. However, she didn't get very far with easing the young woman's fears. Zong saw Chan's missing left hand.

"Oh my god! Chan! What happened to your hand?" she exclaimed, growing even more worried.

"Green Dragon slime got me, not quick enough once. It's okay, really, Zong. We have to talk." Chan tried to defuse Zong's fears, but Zong continued to stare at her arm for several more minutes as she began to explain what had happened in the last few days.

"So that's what it was all about! We all saw all the soldiers leaving, but I figured they were after you guys. Dead? Really? Gang, Li? Jie mutilated? The Archmage too? The whole army? There had to be at least twenty-five thousand men in it!"

"Thirty thousand men, all dead. All the mages and the baronesses as well," Chan added.

The shocked expression of Zong gave way to a look of fright. "Then who is running Jing now? The three fortresses, the Circles of Ascension? Are we leaderless now? Have the dragons taken over?"

"Dad is now backing Wen and me to take over leadership of Jing and two of the Circles. Wen is going to control the fortress, palace, and Circle here in Nanchan. I'm taking nearby Chaohu. We need another Duska to take over the third fortress and Circle, the one at Zhouhan. Zong, how would you like to become Baroness Zong Ying of Jing?" Chan popped the surprise question. Zong shrieked.

"Me? Be a ruler? With you two? Control all Jing? Are you serious?" Her surprise sublimated into doubt. Perhaps the two were teasing her or this was some kind of joke. Never in a million years had she ever expected to inherit the throne of Jing!

"Yes, you are a Duska and you have been fighting for many of the same things that Wen and I have all these years. Now you have a chance to put things right and truly help our people on Jing. What say you? Ready to join us?" Chan asked.

"Yes, oh yes! Wait! If we are the three baronesses, then who will be the powerful barons?" she asked.

"Excellent point, Zong. As of this moment in time, we have no barons and won't have until we three get married, if we ever do," Chan replied. "Wen and Dana are in love, perhaps they may be the first to marry." Wen flushed and Dana shuffled his feet about. "Dad says that a baron is not specifically required, as long as the baroness is a Duska and can handle the protection of the Circle, the palace staff, and the fortress security. This is especially true if we are not yet betrothed. Dad is backing us and has also told us that he will back you if you agree to become baroness of Jing. What say you, cousin?"

"Okay, I agree. Wow! Hey, I don't know anything much about the Circles and their protection spells or anything," Zong protested slightly.

Wen laughed, "Neither do we, Zong. Dad is going to teach us what we need to know, starting tomorrow. We have a major crisis on our hands. Soon now word is going to spread of the terrible tragedy that has struck us. The loss of the entire army, our rulers, and mages, could lead to wide spread panic or worse. We have to act quickly. We have the backing and support of Baron Zoran and several other barons as well. Can you come with us to the palace now? Dad can begin educating we three this evening yet."

Zong hastily closed her shop and followed them to the palace, using teleport spells to avoid any trouble in the streets of Nanchan. Milan and Kate were both already working with the many palace guards, setting up new security protocols when the three arrived. "Hi, got some semblance of security going again," Milan spoke up. "Oh, and Archmage Ivana will be joining us tomorrow. She will stay a while and help with magical enchantments. Later on, Zoran and the other Archmages will come to help open up the late Archmage tower, defusing his traps and such. Who is this pretty young woman?" he finally spotted Zong and gave her a good look. Chan thanked Milan and Kate and introduced their third baroness to the two.

After that, old Chen went over the basics of Circle security with the three women, but he tired easily and cut the evening's session short. It was enough so that between the three and Milan and Kate, they managed to put new security arrangements around the three Circles of Ascension — enough for the immediate moment at least. All three women began to realize the enormity of what they did not know and yet had to know. That was what had caused Chen to become so tired. He too realized how much the three didn't know about the fortresses, palace, and Circles. Much of it was entirely his own fault, for he had never educated them in such, only his three sons. By neglecting to give them even the basics, he'd sold them short on their birthrights. Now he needed time, lots of it, and patience too, he figured.

Aldrick and his golds worked far into the night. They took the green's bodies back to Adapazan and gave them a proper funeral. Then, they began the grim task of picking up the remains of the soldiers, piling them into massive mounds and setting them ablaze with their fiery breaths. In the process, they also collected massive numbers of cheap swords, daggers, and armor. These, they put into piles just inside the mine. However, they also discovered a number of magically enchanted swords and daggers, along with several magical rings, gems, and amulets, along with mundane coins and gems. The coins and gems, they left on the floor of the mine near the huge mound of weapons. The magical items, however, they divided up among themselves. Aldrick looked upon them as payment for their services. After all, dragons prize magical items as much as their large gems.

Thus, when Milan came by the mine to check on things in the morning, he found that the golds had worked through the night and were now gone. Dozens of pyres were still smoldering however. He entered the mine and found the numerous piles and brought the gold and gems back to Nanchan, along with his report.

That day, the three new rulers issued a lengthy proclamation. It outlined what had happened to the former rulers and army. It told of their actions in retaking the mines and their assumption of the mantles of Jing's baronesses. The proclamation also said that there would be no taxes on anyone for at least a year or more and that each town should send them a report of what aid and assistance the town needed to further its survival. Additionally, they advertised for new guards for the fortresses, stating that the pay would be quadruple what it had been under their father's and brother's rule and that the guards would never, ever be ordered to attack or fight dragons. The lengthy proclamation was duplicated and sent out to all towns and villages with at least a thousand inhabitants, with a request to forward it along to the smaller hamlets and farmsteads.

Archmage Ivana came as promised and they discussed how they could deal with the huge, debilitating shortage of mages on Jing. She promised to help train others until a more permanent solution could be worked out. Yes, the three new baronesses were constantly busy from dawn to dusk until the Spring High Council came. By then, they had some semblance of a proper government going once more and were prepared to stand before the High Council and defend their right and skill to be the official rulers of Jing.

Mage Jarka pointed out to Zoran that now another of his enemy planets had joined his allied planets. Only three planets remained in the enemy category, while the allied planets now numbered seven. "This is *sure* to be pointed out at the High Council meeting," she declared flatly.

Chapter 17 Honani Makes Waves

"Dragons can breed with us? How hideous!" thirty-four year old Awinita, Honani's wife, exclaimed. He'd just returned from visiting with Milan. The weather was tending towards spring and his group had expected him to return with easy-to-fill requests for more dragon blood and body parts. This past fall's easy profits had quadrupled their funds in just a few months before the heavy snows came to many worlds. His group had anticipated more of the same now that the harsher weather was moderating.

"The Great Spirit must be in great turmoil over this," Cheveyo, the Spirit Warrior. added his exclamation to the mix.

"Why are women always the victims anyway?" put in Askook's wife, Donoma. "It's bad enough that we carry ours for nine long months, but carry a dragon's? I cannot think of a more despicable, horrid, abhorrent, repugnant, and repulsive thing!"

"It's monstrous!" Cheveyo's wife, Kachina, the Spirit Diviner, exclaimed, spitting into the pit fire in center of their hide hut. They were encamped out on the vast plains of Isi, far from any other nomadic settlements.

He went on to describe what Milan had said, particularly about the time factor. "If we are to locate any of these women alive, we have to move soon. Reds and blacks are our prime targets," Honani continued. "We should focus our attention onto Rehor, Gerde, Alta, and Maeve. That's where all the reds and blacks dwell, well also Isi, where a few reds live."

"I would suggest that we focus on the reds first, since according to Milan they are doing the most and are being the nastiest about it," Askook suggested. The other five agreed.

"I will see what I can to tonight when the children get to sleep," Kachina, the Spirit Diviner, announced. She was their principle diviner, though Awinita also did some. Kachina was the youngest of the six at twenty-eight. She was also the frailest, a weak constitution. While Duska born, her body was thin, short, and not physically strong by any measure. She had a knack for raising children and usually the others relied upon her skills to watch their children while the five were off on their "adventures."

On the other hand, her divination skills were unmatched by anyone within the Federation of the Sixteen Planets, though no one even knew of her, save these five. In fact, many years ago, it was Kachina who got this band together. She'd seen that together, they were to do many great things. Thus far, she'd been right and none of the others ever doubted her in the slightest. Her predictions and "guesses" had always been right.

After dark, the men tossed another log on the fire, sprinkled several herbs over the flames. The sweet scent soon filled their domed hide hut and Kachina sat down on her deerskin mat, crossed her legs, closed her eyes, and began to focus her Duska senses. Ever outward she reached, out into the Shadow Lands. She approached Rehor and took up a monitoring position. After what seemed like an eternity to the anxious men, she moved on to Gerde. She was being methodical in that they already knew that there were more reds on Rehor than any other planet. Then came Gerde, Maeve, Alta and Isi, their world. If these women were being held on Isi, Kachina felt that she would already have sensed their presence. She intended to thoroughly search Isi last because of this.

Two hours after she apparently entered her trance, her body's voice spoke, though she was hovering over Gerde at the time. Her voice sounded hollow and distant, "Terror, death, birth, fear, helplessness. Some are on Gerde." Honani nodded to Askook and Cheveyo, who return his gesture. A few minutes later, her ghostly voice added, "High in the mountains. A cavern, unreachable by land. Birth and death, terror and pain. Go, go now!" Kachina's body suddenly re-animated, her face twisted from the horrors that she'd just felt from so many women.

"I've never sensed such a horrid and repugnant-repulsive thing before. The women's pains are almost unbearable! I saw the place. Touch me and go find it now. Get them help, but it may be too late, I fear." Quickly, the three men and two women Mind Linked to her and saw her image of the mountainous cavern in which the women were being held. That's what she meant by touch her.

"Well, no time like the present. Will you be all right here with all the kids?" Cheveyo asked.

'Yes, I will imbibe some herbs and relax my nerves. I will be fine. You be careful. These are adult dragons that you will be handling, not infants as before," she advised. She need not have. None of the five had any intention of fighting an adult dragon. They were not dragon slayers, just collectors of dead dragon body parts and infants who were too young to deal out much damage to them. The five packed their few things, donned heavy winter hide and fur coats, and Shadow Walked out of their large hide domed hut, appearing over Gerde together. It took them a few minutes to move around and spot the correct mountain peaks and a bit longer to find the actual high alpine cavern entrance, far above the tree line. Many feet of snow still covered the jagged rock of these mountains, on which it was treacherous to even set foot.

Honani cast Invisibility on himself and stepped out of the Shadows onto the stone floor of the entrance. His moccasins made no sound as he quietly slipped inside. Already, he'd rubbed a rag covered in red dragon musk over himself to disguise his scent, a trick all of his people on Isi used when hunting game. Invisible to sight, sound, and smell, Honani was confident that he could get in and out undetected.

Barely! He had to dodge out of the way as a female red came swooping into the entrance, very nearly landing on top of him! He followed her inside. The sight nearly caused him to gag and vomit. What was left of several human females lay discarded against a side wall; their bloody abdomens had been ripped open from the inside and their soft organs devoured by the newborn baby reds! The arriving red was given one of the newborn babies and she made quite a fuss over the small dragon, eventually taking it back to her home with her.

Honani saw many other women chained to walls. All looked pregnant to various degrees, though the terrified look in their eyes told him that they had witnessed the births and the deaths of their fellow women. He counted three adult males and a female red and then quietly left, following the mother red and her new infant out of the cavern. He stepped back into the Shadows, but was a bit reluctant to show the others what he's seen. He sent, *We best notify Milan and get our reward now, before it is too late.*

The five waited until morning to contact Milan, being too risky to attempt to contact him in the middle of the night. They Shadow Walked to Brn, stepping out of the Shadows in the nearby pine forest to avoid being seen. While the others waited, Honani entered the gates of Brn and went in search of Milan. He sent him a Message, but the spell failed to activate. "Damn, Milan must be off-world. There is no time to wait. Best see if someone else will see me," he muttered to himself. It was 17th of April and Milan was on Jing, not in Brn, Adapazan. Hence, Honani asked the gate man if he could have an audience with Baron Zoran.

A bit later, a guard escorted him into the Great Hall, where Zoran was having breakfast with his family and friends. "A Honani of Isi to see you, baron," the guard said formally. Honani was a bit shocked to see Baron Zoran causally dining with his family and friends. Ordinarily, a baron would have made him wait until he sat upon his throne to conduct the business of the day. He felt a little at ease.

"Welcome, Honani of Isi. Care to join us? Come, have a seat. Is all well on Isi?" Zoran asked. Many eyes focused on the leather clad, man, who was holding his enormous leather and fur parka.

"Yes, Milan came to me with a proposition. If we could locate the women the dragons had abducted, he said that we would get a substantial finder's fee. We've done that, found a cache of women being held by the reds, but I can't Message Milan, as we agreed."

"Ah, he is on Jing at the moment, helping the new rulers there get the planet salvaged. You've found women who have been abducted from other worlds?" Zoran both explained and asked. "If so, I will see that you are handsomely rewarded."

"Yes, but I warn you, it is beyond description. Women are giving birth to baby red dragons, but they die as they do. It is monstrous beyond description. I can show you what I saw when I was in the cavern," Honani answered. "If you want to save many of the women, you will have to act swiftly." He allowed Zoran to Mind Link with him and he forced himself to replay the grizzly sights that he'd seen in the cavern.

Zoran's face both grimaced and turned white. Zdenka knew that this tall stranger from Isi was telling the truth. At last, the location where the reds were holding the captive women had been uncovered. "Reds apparently come and go from the cavern, probably as the women give birth. Four adult reds seem to be running the show. I don't know how you can possibly attack all four of them, but that's the score. Have we earned the reward? If so, we will get on with looking for where the blacks are holding their captives."

"How does fifty thousand gold sound?" Zoran asked.

"Most acceptable. Can you find the place on Gerde from what you've seen or do you need us to accompany you there?" Honani asked.

"How about you take us there, but you don't have to step out of the Shadows if you so desire. However, if you and your companions wish to help us transport the rescued women after we take out the dragons, we'd appreciate your help. We need all the Duskas that we can get to help move the women, at least that has been the case so far," he replied. "Right now, we're short five, what with Archmage Ivana off on Jing with Chan, Wen, Kate, and Milan." He wrote out a note instructing his paymaster to give Honani his finder's fee. While Honani was obtaining the gems, Zoran contacted his ever-growing team, including the barons from Cosma and Terra, since some of these women may well be the ones abducted from their planets.

Last time, Zoran took old Chen and Bernard with him. He was short one and he asked Jarka to join him. Likewise, Archmage Nadia was short one, she took her husband Dusan with her, but Milan was off-world. They were short Archmage Ivana and the Valtr contingent. However, the other groups remained intact. Namely, Archmage Verushka took her husband Baron Tomas and her brother Evsen with her. Archmage Zdenka took Baron Jan and Baroness Reina with her. Archmage Marek took his wife Akira and Chika with him. Baron John took his Archmages Ben and Lisa with him. Baron Arcangelo took his Archmages Bianca and Alfredo with him. Baron Stefan took his Archmages Chesna and Patrik with him. Finally, the remaining barons and baronesses from Cosma, and Terra, all Duska, also came with them. All had high hopes that more of their women would be saved somehow. None of them were prepared for the ghastly, grizzly encounter that they were about to have.

Around ten, the group assembled, weapons and potions ready, particularly so with Archmage Karel's Rods of Dragon Slaying. He personally checked the charges in each rod and that they were in good shape. Honani brought his companions into the Great Hall and they received many compliments and thank you's from the barons for having located the abducted women. Just how they had done this feat none dared ask, though Zoran decided to ask Honani later on, once the critical situation was handled. Following Honani and his group, the large attacking party stepped into the Shadows, leaving Adapazan behind them.

God! I hate this, Jarka thought as she found herself nearly dumping the contents of her stomach as her tidy universe vanished into nothingness, disorienting her completely. She gripped Zoran's hand hard.

As before, when they reached Gerde and the high altitude cavern, Zoran had those who were not being protected with Karel's rods remain in the Shadows, close to the entrance. They were charged with Messaging the others if another red suddenly came to the cavern. After each cast Invisibility on themselves, each trio materialized out of the Shadows and onto the stone floor of the huge, gaping cavern entrance.

Unlike Honani, they were ineffective at hiding their footsteps or their odor. Zoran's group only got some twenty feet inside when one dragon who was on guard duty started sniffing the air and listening. "Intruders! Intruders at the entrance!" he called out. He did not need to see them to know that humans were invading the cavern. Further, considering its prime location, he also knew that it had to be powerful Duskas at the very least or perhaps mages. The cavern was wholly unreachable on foot by humans, which was precisely why this spot was so carefully chosen and the enormous cavern dug from the bedrock of the mountain.

The red belched forth a huge blast of his fiery breath, and from its size and intensity Zoran guessed that this was an older adult, capable of extremely hot, killing fires. Jarka found it hard to keep from flinching as the huge wall of searing flames came straight at her! It took every ounce of willpower to keep from fleeing from the flames, to stand still and trust in the rod in Zoran's hand.

The attackers had the compounding problem of not knowing precisely where the women were being held further back in the cavern complex. Thus, they dare not cast area of effect type spells for fear of harming those whom they came to rescue. Zoran cast his Disintegrate spell hoping that it didn't miss and accidentally cause harm to any who might be behind the red and in the line of sight. Bernard also realized this and cast his Hold spell, hoping to freeze the dragon in its tracks so that they could hack at it with their swords while it was motionless and couldn't blast them with another fiery cone of searing flames. Jarka merely tried to hold her location against the flames as they rushed around the protective sphere around them. She was fascinated with how the flames were forced to follow this unnatural path, thanks to the rod.

Again, Zoran found himself on a grey plain staring at the old dragon, who glared back at him, evil hatred flowing from his very beingness towards him. He didn't particularly hate this red. He'd never seen it before, nor did he know what, if anything, his role in these abductions and rapes had been. He held his position and didn't react to the red's hatred towards himself. Bernard appeared beside him now, also staring at the red. Likewise, Bernard didn't react to the flow of hate coming from the red, rather he was merely bored as usual. All this time spent fiddling around on this grey plain seemed a complete waste of time to him. That was the last straw; the red's will cracked. He could not cast fear into the minds of these two opponents.

Both spells detonated. The red was fast, dodging the Disintegrate spell. A chunk of the ceiling carved out by the spell dropped harmlessly onto the stone floor. However, he could not avoid the Hold spell of Bernard, since it covered the entire area in which he was located. The red found itself frozen to the spot to which it had dove to get out of the way of the deadly beam of destruction.

This gave the other two adult male reds time to get into position behind their motionless comrade. One opened his mouth and sent a second huge cone of fire out and over Zoran's group, expanding ever outward, striking several other groups who were joining the attack. The second chose to cast his Lightning Bolt spell, aiming for Zoran's head. Once more the rod activated, sucking into itself the spell's energy, the bolt fizzled.

By now, Archmage Karel and his group had moved into position behind Zoran's and they also tried to ignore the intensely hot flames flowing over themselves. Karel cast his Disintegrate spell at the motionless red directly in front of Zoran and this time, the red took the beam directly in its head. The enormous, lifeless body slumped slowly to the stone floor. Bernard countered with a second Hold spell, hoping to freeze the red that had cast the spell at them, while Jarka finally cast her first spell, but failed to win the battle of wills. However, from behind them all, Archmage Zdenka's huge, Crushing Hand appeared around the red that cast the spell and began pummeling its head, sending bits of the dragon's saliva right and left.

With so many in front of her partially blocking her view, Archmage Verushka could only dare cast her huge volley of simple Magical Missiles, significantly wounding the red that had just sent its fires towards them all. Several others took their cue from her and sent various volumes of their Magical Missiles towards it as well. While some lost their battle of wills with the dragon, too many succeeded and the red, severely wounded attempted to Shadow Walk out of the battle and the cavern.

"We're on him dad!" Archmage Nadia called out. Towards the rear, she and her group had yet to get into the fray. Instead, she moved her group back into the Shadows after the dragon. As she moved her group close, her husband, Dusan, fatally stabbed it with his magically enchanted bastard sword. The red's body ceased all movement and floated off in the Shadows, carried along by its previous momentum. Nadia then moved her group back to the cavern.

By the time that she returned, Zdenka's Crushing Hand had beaten the red's head into a mass of crushed bones and brains, and it too slumped onto the floor. Between the two dead reds, their passage into the cavern complex was rather blocked. As they began trying to climb over the huge forms, the female red stuck her head around a corner, peering out at the battle. The three guards were dead or gone and she made her choice. Their searing fires had not stopped the invaders nor had spells. Thus, she did a huge jump over the two dead and began clawing and biting at Zoran, who was in the lead.

"Potion Jarka!" Zoran yelled, fighting the intense pain in his leg. She'd nearly bitten it off; her teeth marks gouged into his leg bones! Jarka responded, while Bernard took a hold of the rod which Zoran dropped while holding his leg.

Verushka fired off a Disintegrate spell along with Karel, while Zdenka blasted the female red with a huge volley of Magical Missiles. Against all three, the red had no chance and her body joined the two guards. "I got him," Jarka yelled, motioning for the others to pass them by and head further inside, looking for more reds.

"God, that looks bad," whispered Baron John as he climbed over the carcasses, passing the prone Zoran, who was guzzling Jarka's healing potions like water. The red had nearly bitten his left leg completely off, just above his knee!

"Bet that hurts," Baron Arcangelo teased him as his trio passed them. Zoran gave him a glaring stare.

Soon, he heard various voices calling out, "Clear." Shortly after that, he heard various gasps and exclamations of horror and revulsion, followed by, "We have some in here." He relaxed a little, apparently they had killed the dragons and the others were now dealing with the women. "I feel a little giddy, Jarka, but the pain is subsiding."

"You drank way too much at one time, silly man. It is working now. I can see the wound closing. Don't try to stand for a while," she ordered, digging out a wrapping bandage from her med kit that she'd just un-shrunk. "Never forget that a dragon *is* a formidable foe even if it doesn't breathe fire on us or cast spells," she chastised him. He groaned but knew she was right. He'd gotten too dependent upon the rod making him invulnerable and lowered his guard.

Archmage Verushka and her group were the first to enter into the deeper part of the complex and came upon the ghastly sight. The bloody, mutilated bodies of six women lay heaped in a pile, ready for disposal. The cold stone floor around them was covered in blood and quite slippery. The women's internal organs were mostly gone, leaving a shell of their former bodies, ripped open for all to see. She fought hard to keep from gagging and vomiting, pressing on deeper inside instead. Her companions did likewise, though one muttered, "Oh dear god!"

Deep inside the cavern, four side chambers held the women and the crude pantry. Apparently, the female red had been handling the cooking and heating of these internal caverns, thus keeping the women warm, she concluded. One chamber held only four remaining women, all in labor. Her group and Nadia's group stopped here and began their usual treatments, Morphing the baby dragon fetuses into human form, easing the terrible pains of the women, at least temporarily.

Archmage Zdenka's group and Archmage Marek's group explored the second side chamber, while Baron John's group and Baron Arcangelo's group took the third chamber. As the last group came up to Zoran, namely Baron Stefan's group, Zoran asked him to return to the entrance and keep watch for other reds who might come to help defend the cavern complex. He agreed and took his people back to the entrance.

Zoran hated not being up front where the action was, but he dare not and could not stand on his injured leg yet. The bleeding had ceased and the healing potions were working, though not as fast as he wanted. He resigned himself to missing the action. "Bernard, move on up there and report back to me what they have found. I need to know what's happening."

He grinned, "Okay, boss. Here, you are well enough now to hold onto the rod yourself." He handed him the rod and headed on over the fallen dragons and disappeared from view.

Before long, Baron Arcangelo returned. "What incredible luck. We found our ten missing women. They are not due for a few more days! What luck, Zoran! I'm fetching our Duskas now. Zdenka has ordered us to take them to your infirmary at once. John's found ten of his women, but they are not due until the 15th of June, according to what the women were told by the female red who was caring for them. Apparently, another ten were taken from Rehor. Old Clav probably doesn't even know they are missing. Six have already died giving birth. We found their bodies — grizzly sight. Never seen anything as horrible before. The other four are in labor. Verushka and Nadia believe that they are going to have to deliver them right here in the cavern. Yes, over here gang," he spotted the small army of Duskas materializing near the entrance. "Got twenty-five women from Terra and Cosma to rescue immediately."

"What happened to you?" one asked Zoran as he passed him.

"Got bit by the red. Nearly took my leg off with one bite!" he replied glumly. Jarka smiled.

Bernard returned as Baron Arcangelo led the large Duska group deep into the complex. "Boss, it is really bad in there. I've never seen women in such awful condition. Their clothes, if you can call them that, are in tatters. They have more filth on them than clean skin. More than a few have been severely beaten. It's a wonder that they are still alive. All are so emotionally drained that they appear zombie-like. I don't think that they even realize that they are being rescued, boss. Four are giving birth now. The Archmages are keeping the babies Morphed into human form, so that's something anyway. I think they are from Rehor, if you can believe that. It's pretty grim in there. Spotted four piles of vomit along the way. Guess that's understandable. Otherwise, not much is going on," he yawned.

"Their arms. Bernard, how are their arms?" he asked.

"Oh, they seem to all have working arms, not like our batch of women. They are not chained either. I believe that they learned from that first batch and this time they kept three dragons watching over them at all times so the women couldn't do anything — you know, like jump off the side of the mountain there at the entrance. Not sure what else might be wrong with them, though. It's pretty chaotic in there."

"Well, that is good news. I feared the worst, Bernard. Thanks." He relaxed a bit more. If the women survived, at least they would not end up like those from Adapazan had.

The Duskas Shadow Walked the women out of the cavern directly. Thus, Zoran didn't get to see them go by him as he lay with his back against one of the fallen reds. Before long, the distant noise died down somewhat. Baron John returned to check on Zoran and to report. "Only the four who are in labor are left now, baron. We are going back to the entrance to help guard it, just in case. Verushka says that we will have to remain here until the four give birth. Too risky to try to Shadow Walk them at this time. You hanging in there?"

"Yes, pain's gone, but I can't stand on it yet. Thanks, watch the entrance. Sooner or later I expect more to be coming. Honani says that when one is born, a red female comes to take it away and presumably raise it as her own."

"Why do they need to use our females for this?" he asked.

"I think that their females are fertile only once every ten years or so."

"Ah, I see. Cheap and easy way to increase their population rapidly then. Makes strategic sense," Baron John replied, before following his group to the entrance, joining the others there. "I owe you a big thank you for not only finding them and helping to rescue them, but saving their lives when the foul beasts within them come forth. I'll send along my Archmages when yours tell me that it's time. These reds are just plain vile, wicked beasts that deserve to be extinct! I'm going to vote for that at the next High Council. I think that Arcangelo is going to second it."

As he left, Zoran grimaced. Such talk was exactly what he was trying to prevent: an all our war against the dragons. He heard the sounds of a baby crying. At first, he thought it was a human child, but realized that it was just another Morphed Red Dragon. Quickly, the sound disappeared, he knew that one of the Archmages, probably Karel, had Vanished the beast. Mentally, he calculated only three more to go.

"Heads up! We have company coming!" someone yelled from the entrance. "Throw up a series of Force Walls!" another voice called out.

"Damn! Jarka, Bernard, help me up. We have to get to the entrance and back them up," Zoran ordered, struggling to get onto his good leg. Leaning on Bernard with Jarka holding the precious rod, the three made their way slowly to the entrance. Archmage Karel came flying past them, rod in hand.

Marek stepped back to Zoran. "A few females are hovering outside, probably expecting to pick up new infant dragons. The Force Walls are holding for the time being, but sooner or later, they are going to break through them. I anticipate a whole army of reds to show up any moment. We ought to consider evacuating as soon as possible. I'll go see how the ladies are doing."

"Right. We don't really want to take on a flock of reds. Some of the rods are getting low on charges," he replied, continuing to make his way to the back of the group holding the entrance. Already one dragon was casting spells at the Force Wall. "Keep putting up more walls, stall them a while longer," he ordered.

"Damn. Just what we don't need right now," Archmage Verushka cursed upon hearing Marek's report. "They could Shadow Walk inside the caverns. I would not put that tactic past them if they can't get the Force Walls down. However, moving these three women through the Shadows at this critical point — well, I don't know what's going to happen to them."

"If they break through, it will be the end of us," Marek countered.

"Okay, tell the others to evacuate. Come on, let's get these three back to Brn if possible, ladies," she ordered.

"Has anyone ever taken a woman in labor through the Shadows before?" asked Archmage Nadia. She too was worried about this aspect. If the dragons Morphed back to their true forms while they were in the Shadows, the mages could do little to prevent it, she thought. Everyone shrugged, but they had little choice. Sacrificing their lives for these three Rehor women was not an option; far too many others depended upon them.

"I'm taking you and your group through," Baron John insisted. "Zoran, you can't walk on that leg yet. Let me pull you through." Zoran had never allowed anyone to pull him through the Shadows before, but he wasn't about to crawl on his hands and knees, though he thought that he might be able to move through the Shadows that way. He agreed, much to the relief of Jarka and Bernard. Soon, Jarka felt her usual total disorientation accompanied by the strong urge to vomit, but she valiant fought to control her gagging, especially with Baron John doing the Shadow Walking. Her imagined humiliation of having him see her empty her stomach during the Shadow Walk out weighted her nausea and she survived the trip once more.

Nadia and Verushka, on the other hand, ran into some startling events. Dragons natively can Shadow Walk. Somehow, while still in the mother's wombs, the infants detected that they were moving in the Shadows. All three had been fighting a losing battle with the Archmages and their Morph spells. Although they were far to young to actually Shadow Walk on their own, they attempted it anyway. All three reds burst out of their wombs, escaping into the Shadows, leaving behind the dying mothers. The Archmages gasped but could do nothing about it. However, the now free infants were confused and lost utterly, drifting off aimlessly in the Shadows. Soon they would die of starvation, a small consolation for their human hosts.

Upon arrival, the bloody dead bodies shocked everyone. "My god, what happened to them?" asked Zdenka. Nadia and Verushka explained what they had seen and were powerless to prevent.

"Well, I think we Duska learned something from this. Don't take women in labor through the Shadows," Baron John proclaimed. "I will spread the word to other Duskas about this startling discovery. I don't think anyone has tried to do this before now and we sure won't after this!"

"Ladies, I'll see that they get buried. You go attend all the other women," Bernard volunteered. Jarka went with them, while Zoran sat down, rubbing his leg.

"It is itching fiercely," he commented, as John stared at his antics.

Karel gathered up the rods to recharge them and the women went straight to the Infirmary where the other Duska women were already tending to the rescued women's huge needs. Several of the previously rescued women from Jing were now in labor along with two who had just been rescued, which only added to the complications of handling twenty-six new arrivals. At least the men they'd recently rescued from the Jing mine were in another wing and required little attention at the moment.

By supper, Zoran was at last able to stand on his rapidly healing leg and he joined the others for dinner, receiving a full report from his wife. "Well, we've saved six more women — three each from Cosma and Jing. Three more are likely to go into labor this evening. We've got the women cleaned up, clothed, and fed, but we are facing a new problem. It seems that the reds have worked out a new method of torturing their captive women. Perhaps this was for the best."

"What do you mean, dear?" he asked. His feeling of accomplishment suddenly vanished.

"Well, it seems that the reds cast Blindness on the women, shortly after they were brought to the cavern. Thus, the women were unable to see the rapes occurring or the horrors their companions were suffering as they gave birth and died. In a way, that may have been an act of kindness to the women. However, in the case of the Rehor women who were first ones brought to that cavern, the reds removed their eyes after three others tried to escape and chose to fall to their deaths rather than bear the dragon babies. Apparently, that did not go so well and two got serious infections and died before giving birth. That's when they came up with the idea of using the Blind spell. The lone survivor, Andrea, will be permanently blind, obviously, and unable to learn magic spells, even though magical energies are strong in her body now."

She continued, "The fifteen from Terra were also Blinded, but we've been able to dispel their blindness, though not without many re-castings of our counter spells. They are going to be just fine, physically. Emotionally, I doubt if any of these women will ever be just fine again," she said with a hint of anger and disgust in her usual conservative mellow voice. "Now apparently the reds were in the process of permanently blinding the ten Cosma women. Half of them have lost their eyes permanently, while the other half we were able to salvage and they are now able to see normally. The Cosma women backed up Andrea's story. From the snatches of talk that the women overheard, I think that the reds are still in the process of working out the best way to handle the women that they capture and breed. A simple Blind spell works well enough, since they anticipate the women to die at childbirth. Perhaps in the future, we will only encounter a simple Blind spell on the captured women. I certainly hope so."

Zdenka added, "I sure am glad that at Spring Picking a few weeks ago that I chose to add six new Adept students and only two normal beginners. Soon, I will have extra hands around the tower to help out. This is becoming quite a mess."

"As always, dear, you are rising to the challenge and doing a superb job of it," he complimented her. "All of you, thank you all for your help today. I'm proud of the way that we are helping so many other barons out. We are becoming the Federation leaders." Many grinned and all were pleased with the praise.

"Well, next week is the Spring High Council meeting. This time it is being held on Dietmar, the snow planet. Remember to dress warmly and bring along winter parkas," he gave everyone formal notice. "Tomorrow I'll decide who will come with us this time. I know that this is one of our enemy realms where assassinations rule, but also the threat of these dragon attacks while we are gone has me as worried as well as dragon attacks on us all while we are there. It's going to be a tough call this time, not to mention the many are going to be needed here just looking after the women who are due soon."

"Now *that's* an understatement, if I ever heard one," Jarka teased.

Chapter 18 The Spring High Council

Jarka looked out the bedroom window, finally satisfied. Their accommodations on Dietmar were nice enough, but the large window was a security breech. True, it had a permanent Force Wall instead of glass panes so that one could have a view and yet feel secure. She didn't. Any caster could dispel the Force Wall at any time and an assassin would have easy access to the sleeping party. Hence, she'd added two more of her own plus several Alert spells as well. Now she took the time to examine the view of Dietmar.

The Castle Hadwig was a huge affair, resting on Knob Hill. Craggy slopes dropped off all around the castle proper. Far below the hill lay the sprawling city, with rolling hills going off as far as she could see. Snow, however, lay still several feet thick on the grounds, although it was late April now. By the middle of June the snows usually had melted except in the high country, where glaciers predominated. The short growing season normally ended around early September with the first snowfall. In the distance, she spotted several groves of pine forests, though most of the nearby forests had been felled for firewood. Dietmar was a cold planet, a harsh, hostile place to live.

Yet it had mines. Gold, silver, iron, and copper predominated, thought in several locations diamonds had been found. Few people were out of doors. Those that were looked more like enormous bears. Layers of coats made a thin person appear quite rotund.

Zoran had brought along Zdenka, Jarka, Bernard, Karel, Chika, and Jakob. Barons Tomas and Jan brought their wives and a couple of advisors. The other Archmages and Duska had their hands full dealing with the rescued women who were either in labor or darn close to it. Nadia had promised her dad that she'd let them know if they really needed anything and he'd promised to head home prematurely if they did.

Baron Adolf and Baroness Greta Hadwig were hosting this High Council. They were in their thirties. The baron took after his father, Eckhard, a robust, powerful man, and ruled with an iron vice equal to the harshness of the planet around him. Rugged pioneers, one might say about the people who lived on this world. Although claiming to be a "have-not" world, Dietmar was rich in minerals and ores, shipping vast quantities to other worlds in exchange for grain and food supplies, because their short growing season yielded only marginal crops. A variety of winter wheat was about the only grain produced in any quantity here on Dietmar.

In addition, the other two barons, Burkhard and Conrad were secondary hosts as well as their wives, Cede and Elisa. Both men were also burly and had thick, black beards and moustaches. Cede and Greta were Clav's and were anything but pretty looking women. Both were also very heavy set women, suited for this world, Jarka thought.

Baron Adolf gave each arriving party his full assurances that no dragon could possibly get into Castle Hadwig, that they would be safe here. He had many strong guards posed everywhere one looked, and several assassins, Jarka noted. "We might be safe from dragons, but are we *safe* from the assassin's blades?" she said snidely to Zoran when they were alone. "I think *not*."

"Keep all your protection spells on yourself at all times," Zdenka cautioned, heeding Jarka's advice.

Promptly at ten, the Grand March began. Accompanied by trumpet fanfares, each Baron and Baroness was announced and marched in to their seats, their advisors following behind them as usual. Once the processional was concluded with Zoran's group the last to be announced, which is what he had expected from his archenemy, Baron Adolf rose to begin.

"Welcome to the Spring High Council here on Dietmar. As you can see, the snows of winter are still deep and will be so until at least June. Of course, the snows will be back before the fall council meets. Such is the hard life here on Dietmar, but we don't complain." Zoran had heard this same speech once before delivered by the man's father, the late Baron Eckhard.

"First order of business is the introductions of the new Archmages. Seeing none this time, Baroness Archmage Zdenka must be slipping," he slid his dig in at her. He had been behind the enforced testing of many of her Archmages, claiming that they did not know their spells and were fakes. He'd been proven wrong but he still held a grudge against her. His Archmage had yet to produce any.

"Moving on, the next order of business is the seating of the Jing delegation." Zoran suddenly realized that Chan, Wen, and Zong had yet to be announced. "Retired Baron Chen Meerong of Jing wishes to address the High Council concerning the recent affairs on Jing. Baron." He gave the floor to his ally, but he already knew the full story.

Old Chen rose, apologized for not being able to stand long and sat down for most of his speech. "Woe indeed has come to me and my family and all Jing." He slowly related all that had happened on Jing in the last few weeks. Gasps of horror and disbelief punctuated his lengthy narration for many had not yet heard the full story. "So yes, two of my sons and their wives are dead. My other son Jie is unfit for much of anything at all. Thus, I am here to announce my new heirs and Baronesses. Wen will become the Baroness of Nanchan, Chan will take over at Chaohu, and my niece Zong Ying will run Zhouhan. True, as yet, they have not married, though Wen is engaged, I'm told. In time, there will be Barons as well. I certify that all three women are in complete control of the three Circles of Ascension and the fortresses. They are trained and ready to take their places as the rulers of Jing. I ask the High Council to validate my choices. I am rapidly running out of children," he added injecting a small bit of humor.

"No Barons?" asked Baron Storm Clav, a bit annoyed, but seeing an opportunity.

"Not at this time." Politically, he had no choice but to add, "Suitors are welcome to court the three baronesses at this time." Storm grinned mischievously, as did the Hadwig group. Now if they could only arrange a marriage with the Meerong women, they could regain control of Jing, or so they thought. Years ago, such might have been possible, but now all three were securely behind and supportive of Zoran's group. Their allegiance and alliance had changed, though the Hadwig's and Clav's had yet to fully realize this. Baron Cadfeel of Anwyn, the remaining enemy planet already knew better. Jing was lost.

"I move the baronesses be accepted and seated," Baron Bran Clav spoke up. The vote was unanimous and the three were announced to a trumpet fanfare. Many gasped when they saw that Chan Meerong was missing her left hand though. Archmage Ivana, Dana, Milan, and Kate, walked in behind them as their temporary advisors. Storm Clav groaned and the three Hadwig barons grumbled that they'd been hoodwinked. Their advisors were all from Adapazan, their enemy.

Once seated, Baron Arcangelo and Baron John each gave a vivid and lengthy account of the devastating dragon raids on their worlds. Baron Stefan then told how his mage alert system prevented a similar raid on Valtr. "What is this interspecies breeding that you keep mentioning?" asked Baron Cadfeel. Many others wondered too.

Zoran rose to address this aspect, with Zdenka adding additional facts from time to time. First, they outlined what the reds had done to the seventeen women they managed to rescue and what happened to those who gave birth to the dragon infants. Several other barons backed up their vivid descriptions. "You mean they all lost their arms?" asked Baroness Greta Hadwig, quite moved and shocked by what she was hearing.

"Yes," Zdenka explained. "Whatever the reds did to their arms, healing potions could not undo, nor could any spell that we could find, nor could our physicians. After a lengthy period, their arms atrophied to merely skin and bone. Worse, they often began breaking them without even knowing it. To avoid gangrene and other mishaps, their useless arms were removed."

"My god! Those poor women," Baroness Greta exclaimed, genuinely sorry for the seventeen women.

"Well, there is more to the story, baroness," Zdenka continued. She described their observations that their bodies now somehow had huge magical energies within them. She explained their incredibly rapid advancement in learning to use magical spells at an unheard of rate. "That alone had given these poor women hope for the future. After all, they lost their homes, husbands, and children all at once, to say nothing of what they endured." She then continued with the women abducted from other worlds, including Rehor.

"What? We've lost no women!" Baron Storm protested, then thought better of it. "Have we?" he looked at his advisors, who whispered something in his ear.

"My theory at the moment is that the reds are working out ways to keep their abducted and raped women under control so that they do not commit suicide, thus ending the fetus dragon's life. They've backed off from removing their eyes to merely blinding them with the Blind spell, which can easily be undone. Now they seem to be having at least three reds watching the women at all times." She also explained the observed differences between the women who carried reds to full term versus those who carried a green. "We suspect their bodies are absorbing magical properties from the fetuses. Greens are weaker than reds, so those we've rescued from Jing are picking up magical spells at a slightly better rate than normal students do."

"But why are they doing this?" asked Baron Goro of Asami.

"Apparently female dragons only are fertile about every ten years. With their population so small, they are doing this to rapidly increase their numbers," Zoran gave his best guess. It was accepted, since it did make sense, but only fueled the fires of hatred.

After more discussion, Baron Adolf retook control. "At this time, I would like to call upon Archmage Karel Ambrose to explain his incredible invention. When he is finished, would Archmage Jakob Hamil explain his invention as well? I am sure that we all want to hear about them. All this is so unbelievable. Yet we've heard several of our barons and baronesses witness or use them."

This was Karel's finest hour. He rose and began a lengthy discussion of his Rods of Dragon Slaying. The arrival of lunchtime ended his speech sooner than he desired, but many chatted with him over the dinner table, unwilling to let him end his explanations. Nearly every baron wanted to order dozens of them from him, but since it took him nearly three weeks per rod, such was not feasible.

By contrast, Jakob began the afternoon session, explaining how his Gem of Dragon Control worked. Although it did make the wearer immune to the dragon's breath, its main power was to control them, to make the dragons do his bidding. Many eyes opened wide and he too received many potential orders for similar gems. His drawback was finding large gems worth five hundred thousand a piece. That gave the barons pause.

Next, the group discussed how it was possible that thirty thousand soldiers had been slain by the greens at the mines. Old Chen actually Mind Linked everyone to himself and replayed the images of horror that he'd seen firsthand. That did it.

"I move that we declare war on these dragons!" Baron Arcangelo cried out.

"I second it!" Baron John followed suit.

Zoran's worst nightmare was coming true! "Wait a second!" he rose and fairly yelled over the many others who were shouting their agreement and calling for a vote. At last, Adolf had no choice but to give him the floor.

"Look. Has anyone of us had any trouble with the Gold Dragons? No, we've been helped time and time again by them. Further, what about the Blue Dragons, the Brown Dragons, and the Grey Dragons? Has anyone had any trouble with or from them?"

"No, but they are still dragons. I say kill them all! Golds too!" yelled Baron Strom, not to be outdone by the other barons.

"Well, I don't know about that," Baron Alvaro spoke up. "Zoran's right. On Alta, we've not had the slightest trouble from the browns."

"Same with us," put in Baron Cadfeel. One by one, the other barons who had browns, blues, and greys on their worlds pointed out that so far they had had no trouble or problems with those.

"Okay, then I'll amend my motion. I say let's declare war on the reds, blacks, greens, and whites for massive crimes against humanity," Baron Arcangelo declared. It was seconded and before Zoran could say much else, it passed. Only Adapazan, Gladno, and Valtr voted against it. Barons Stefan and Leo followed Zoran's lead. Baron Alvaro of Isis nearly voted with Zoran, but seeing the overwhelming majority voting in favor of the declaration of war, he voted for it.

At last, Zoran got the floor. "Look, have you given any thought at all as to what the neutral dragons will do if we go to war with their kin? Or the golds, for that matter? Besides, how are you going to actually fight them? You've seen that conventional armies are completely useless against them. You'd think that Gang Meerong would have learned from my late father, who sent his shock troops against two golds and lost it all. Thirty thousand men, soldiers, all armed to the teeth failed to kill even one green dragon and there were only around fifty of them." He lied a little, a couple dead greens had broken shafts of pole arms protruding from their heads and possibly another few had been slain by spells from the mages before they died. He had to defuse this talk of war and fast.

"Think of that: fifty to thirty thousand, and those were the weakest of the dragon species! My god, I almost lost my left leg to one bite from a red female days ago. We should think this through before we do something we might regret."

Zdenka spoke up, "He's right. These dragons are highly intelligent and have been adapting to our moves. Look, the only way that we have been having the successes that we have is by combining large numbers of Archmages, Duskas, and the magical rods. The reds have adapted to human actions, even with their treatment of the captured women. Several from the first batch that they abducted and impregnated found ways to take their own lives. Later, the reds removed the women's eyes to stop that and then backed down to lesser Blind spells to keep the women from taking their own lives. In our last battle, the female red saw that dragon's fiery breath was doing nothing to us, likewise their spells. She adapted and used her claws and bite. Had she been one of those adults that we'd just previously slain, Zoran would be minus his leg, that's for sure. These reds will adapt. The next time that we face them, you can count on the fact that they will have developed a different strategy for battling us. Besides there are just not enough of us Archmages. There are only forty-four, I'm sorry, forty-three of us, against hundreds upon hundreds of dragons. How can we go to war with them? So far, we have only succeeded because we had surprise on our side." She finally said her piece and sat down, leaving them thinking hard.

"But we cannot do nothing," Baron Arcangelo pointed out. "In just the six months since we discovered the dragons were raiding us, we now have them destroying whole villages, abducting women, and attempting interspecies breeding with them. If we wait another six months, what will this all have escalated to? Annihilation of one of our worlds? If old Chen is right, it almost happened on Jing! We can't sit back and do nothing."

"If we declare war," Baron Stefan spoke up at last, "how can we possibly protect our people, our towns, and our infrastructure? The dragons can raid at will, stepping to our worlds from the Shadows at any time and at any place. We cannot possibly defend against such attacks. Our own people will rebel and demand that we protect them somehow."

"He has a point," Baron Arcangelo conceded. "So what *do* we do?"

"The hour is getting late," Baron Adolf broke in. "I suggest that we break early for supper. Baroness Greta has some light entertainment for us after dinner. Let us all think this over on a good night's sleep and tackle it in the morning session." Thus ended the first day of the council.

As anticipated, the real bargaining occurred during the evening. Yes, the baroness had a small group of musicians playing local folk dances, but everyone's attention was on the awful situation facing the Federation. For once, the many baronesses were not interested in the latest fashions or fine arts presentations. Rather, they hovered around Zdenka, Jarka, Chika, Chan, and Wen. Many expressed total disbelief that dragons could fertilize a human woman, yet it was happening. They wanted to know how it was possible, but Zdenka had no clue. Many asked about how the abducted women were managing and several wanted to know specifically how to handle the birthing nightmare and yet save the woman. She suspected that they were gathering the information just in case they found themselves dealing with similar situations, as well as for their husbands.

Stefan and Leo met briefly with Zoran. Stefan asked what both were thinking, "Zoran, I think that we now have them realizing that it will be a mistake to declare war on them, but how do we answer the 'what do we do now' question?"

"I haven't the faintest idea. The only offensive option that I can see would be to continue to make the kind of superpower raids that we have been doing, lowering their numbers gradually. We haven't heard anything from the greens since the battle. If nothing else, they must be off licking their wounds. There cannot be that many greens left, so maybe they will leave Jing alone for the time being. Lord knows the women there need that," he replied.

"Yes, but it is getting more and more dangerous to attack them," Leo pointed out. "You almost lost your leg there. All the rods in the world can't prevent them from biting us or even simply dropping down upon us, squashing us flat."

"Ah, it is my own stupid fault. I failed to cast my usual battle protection spells. Skin of Stone would have protected me from her bite, I hope. I just didn't think of it," Zoran admitted.

"Yes, that is precisely the point that we must make," Stefan added. "Always, there will be some detail that we've overlooked that the dragons will use to their advantage."

"So how can we protect our people, towns, and mines?" broke in Baron Alvaro. "Don't mind me, barons. I haven't a clue. While we can muster all the top forces of Alta at once fortress and perhaps withstand them nicely, that would sacrifice the rest of the world to the worms."

"Funny that you just called them worms," Zoran broke in. "Ancient writings my friends here have uncovered also talked of creatures called worms. I wonder if there is any connection?"

"Oh, I meant that as a derogatory, slimy, vile dig at the dragons," Alvaro explained. "Any ideas?"

"Not as yet. You are right. Each of us has probably enough force and weapons to protect one fortress and Circle from the dragons. That means we sacrifice the rest of our worlds to them. About the only thing that I can think of is to continue working on making our safe havens underground. Perhaps if each major town had its dragon shelter, that might help save lives."

"It might, but they would come out to find their town destroyed, their livelihoods gone," he countered. "Still, they would be alive. People can always rebuild," Alvaro pointed out.

"Yes, but we've no place to go 'underground,' Baron Goro of the water world of Asami interrupted them. "So what do we do? We can cast Breath Water and go under for limited period of time, but then what?"

"Have you tried making some subterranean areas?" asked Alvaro.

"Yes, but there are so little land masses on Asami that we were not able to do more than make a nice place to store food for a time," Goro explained. His face told all; he was frightened of what the future may hold for everyone.

Baron Cadfeel paced back and forth, trying to decide if he should talk to his enemy or not. When Goro and Alvaro moved off to talk with Arcangelo, he made his move. "Excuse me, baron, a private word?"

"Sure," Zoran replied, waving his two friends away with his fingers. They stepped away, but were most curious about what Cadfeel wanted. They were not above eavesdropping but Baron John took this opportunity to chat with them.

"On our desert world of Anwyn, we only have the browns, like I said at the meeting. However, as you pointed out, the other dragons are raiding many different worlds. Our safe haven is not as safe as many think. At any time, we too could suffer a horrific raid. I have taken your advice and had my mages construct underground safe havens at our three fortresses. However, there is one significant detail. Food. We have little with which to pay for such in the quantities that a siege demands. Perhaps you could be of assistance to a fellow 'have-not' world?"

"Yes, of course. Come on. Let's grab Baron John right now." After pulling him aside, Zoran explained Cadfeel's situation. As Zoran had anticipated, all of the recent happenings on the agrarian world had shaken up Baron John.

"Yes, baron. In times like these, we must stick together and help each other out. You make up a list of what supplies you need and get it to me. I'll see that you get it as soon as we can raise it. Some may come from our own stockpiles, while others may have to wait until harvest comes. No charge. Just use it wisely and save as many of your people as you can. That will be thanks enough."

For a moment, Baron Cadfeel was speechless. Never before had the 'haves' been so generous! "Thank you, thank you. The desert people of Anwyn thank you for saving them."

"Let's hope that you actually do not need the food. God, this dragon situation is totally out of hand. You should have seen those women! If it were not for Zoran and all his people giving tirelessly their aid, I'd have lost them all. We have to stick together, baron," John replied, glad that he could begin to return help to others. He'd been receiving it now for some time from Zoran and his people.

"Indeed, it has. We on Anwyn will be in dire need if the dragons attack us. We have so few mages and only one elderly Archmage, who is only able to teach these days. His health is failing," Cadfeel replied.

"Hey, if you are attacked, you only have to Message us. We, all of we barons, ought to sign a mutual defense pact — you know, promise to come to the aid of each other when called. I think I should make just such a motion tomorrow, baron," Baron John added, pleased with his bright idea. It was an answer to the question: so what do we do now? Cadfeel praised him, but thought that Adolf was right: the real business was conducted outside of the council room.

Jarka was bored by all this political talk, though Bernard mingled, always asking about the breed of dogs that were available on each planet. He doubted that he'd find one dog on Dietmar, but he continued to check. She slowly found herself moving towards the dozen musicians who were playing in the background. Unlike all of the other councils, this time no one was dancing. The musicians didn't seem to care, but they were not playing loudly. Perhaps their softer touch was what attracted her attention. Or maybe it was the room which was overly hot. Great pine logs crackled in three huge fireplaces strategically located around the rim of this Great Hall. As she drew closer, she noticed that the musicians were also perspiring and she smiled. It wasn't just herself that was hot.

Perhaps it was her basic distrusting nature. Perhaps it was just her early training as a thief, albeit a good one. No matter the motivation, Jarka noticed the perspiration dripping down one man's face was discolored and she focused her attention on this anomaly. *His face is somehow painted?* She thought to herself. No, beneath the fleshy color of the man's face a ruddy reddish hue shone through the perspiration streaks! Her eyes rose up and met the man's eyes, ignoring the fiddle what he was playing. "Dragon! Dragon in our midst!" Jarka screamed as loudly as she could. Her eidetic memory called up her first look at the strangely cold black eyes of Emil and Renate, the gold twins. The man's were similar as were all of the other dead dragons that she'd subsequently seen.

Her screams got everyone's instant attention. After all that was the sole topic on absolutely everyone's mind this evening. She backed away from the man as the other musicians ceased playing mid-note. The man stood up as the entire room of people suddenly looked his way. Before anyone could act, the man stepped into the Shadows as his form slowly Morphed into that of a Red Dragon! Everyone caught a glimpse of his huge form as he melted from view into the Shadows. A chaotic uproar followed at once, with hundreds of defensive spells being cast right and left. Zoran tried to form a ring of defenders, using the five rods that Karel had with him. Those with magically enchanted swords drew them as everyone fully expected a surprise attack similar to what had happened at the Fall Council meeting.

Although everyone dashed about taking up defensive positions, changing their minds and forming new positions, nothing happened. After a few minutes, the chaos began to subside, though few let down their guard. "I thought you said no dragons could get in here," Baron Arcangelo cried out to Baron Adolf, who was so angry and upset that his veins throbbed visibly along his neck and temples. He barked orders to his staff right and left. Soldiers raced about, but nothing came of it. The shocked musicians were roughed up by the soldiers, but none of them turned into dragons and several received bloody lips instead.

Right in the middle of the chaotic scene, Honani made a Mind Link to Zoran. *Hey, we've located where the blacks are holding more women hostage. They are on Maeve in the eastern uninhabited mountains. We are too late for some of the women, their bodies lie at the base of the a steep mountain side among the huge boulders by the tarn. There are still quite a number of other women there who are still living. We should act now.*

We'll rendezvous at my infirmary in Brn. Meet you there soon. Casting a Magnify spell, Zoran's voice boomed out above the frantic chaos of the Great Hall. "May I have your attention? We have located another group of abducted women. While some are already dead, many are still alive. They are being held by some blacks in a cavern in the eastern uninhabited mountains of Maeve. The Adapazan contingent will be leaving the council for a short while to lead the rescue efforts.

Baron Ailfrid, you and your Archmage Breana Comyna may accompany us, since it is your planet on which they are being held. If you would prefer not to come, that is fine too. Baron Arcangelo and Baron John, bring along an Archmage. These may well be your missing countrywomen. We will leave here in say five minutes. My advice for the rest of you is to get out of this room. The dragons may well attempt to Shadow Walk into this room, since they now know where we are all located in one place. Until we get back, the safest action is to avoid being all together in one room where a large attack could wipe out all of we rulers in one battle."

"Damn! Not again," Zdenka cursed as Jarka and Bernard hastily moved to her side, forming a minor protection squad. Chika, Karel, Jakob, and Barons Tomas and Jan were on the other side of the room. Karel spotted Zoran and Zdenka and opened a Mystic Door to their sides. He and the others stepped through, jostling others standing nearby as they stepped out, adding to the protection squad. Others were doing the same thing as well, forming up protection barriers around their barons and baronesses.

"Jan, Tomas, you and your advisors stay here and keep me informed. Let me know instantly if the reds attack here. Jakob, you stay with them and protect them with your gem. Chika, Karel, you are with us." Tomas conjured a Mystical Door and his party left the Great Hall safely. Baron John and Archmage Ben Weatherby quickly took their places, followed shortly afterwards by Baron Arcangelo and Archmage Bianca Babiana.

"We need to change and rearm ourselves," Baron John advised.

"So do we. Let's meet in the hallway outside our room in say five minutes," Zoran suggested. Mystical doors opened and most stepped through, leaving Zdenka and Zoran alone. He needed to talk with Baron Ailfrid and Archmage Breana. The baron, shocked by the dual events, had finally gotten his own orders issued, and Breana saw the others leaving Zoran and opened a Mystical Door to his side. The two stepped into the door on the far side of the Great Hall and stepped out beside Zoran and Zdenka, a far faster mode of transportation than walking the couple hundred feet.

Baron Ailfrid was perhaps twenty-five, a youthful fellow with yellow hair and goatee. He was a handsome fellow, cutting a dashing figure, a ladies' man, Zoran thought, ill-suited to fighting dragons. Archmage Breana was forty-five, mature, and educated. She had that stern matronly look about her that told all around her that she would tolerate no monkey business. She was definitely not comely and the two made a startling contrast, Jarka thought.

"I want you to know, baron, that we have never been able to explore the eastern mountains. There is no overland passage beyond their foothills. Extraordinarily rough terrain," Baron Ailfrid began to explain, justifying that he knew nothing of these blacks and the abducted women. "I am not sure of what use I will be fighting dragons."

"You and Breana will be with me. Always stay within ten feet of me and the rod I carry will protect you from the black's caustic acid sprays and any magical spells they might shoot at us. In return, cast Disintegrates, Magical Missiles, or perhaps Hold spells on those in front of us. Careful not to use area spells, like Balls of Fire. We don't want to harm the captives if we can avoid it. Meet in four minutes in the long hallway just outside my room. I believe yours is down at the far end of the hall. Okay?"

Archmage Breana spoke up and Zoran smiled. Here was another mellow alto voice. "It will be my greatest honor to fight at your side, baron. Four minutes. We will be ready. Come on, baron. This way." She opened a Mystical Door and the slightly annoyed baron stepped through to their rooms.

As Zdenka opened a door for the two of them, she commented, "I don't think Ailfrid is going to be of much use."

He grinned and whispered, "But it will be a good education for the baron." She chuckled.

In their room, they arrived to hear Jarka chastising Bernard, "*See*! I *told* you it wasn't silly to bring along twenty healing potions with us." He faked a moan. Both had changed and were ready.

"We'll get everyone here together and then meet Honani and the rest of our Archmages and Duskas at our infirmary in Brn. From there, Honani will lead us to them," he hastily explained while using useful magic spells to quickly change into his fighting leather clothing. His fancy magically enchanted short swords seemed to fasten themselves around his waist. Likewise, Zdenka used spells to rapidly change into her leathers as well. He added, "Very well done, Jarka, spotting that red spy, by the way." The short woman smiled.

Four minutes later, they left their room while Tomas recast protection spells on the door. He was taking no chances with the others left under his care. Shortly everyone assembled in the hallway. After joining hands, they Shadow Walked to Brn, arriving just outside the infirmary. Zoran was pleased; the rest of his group was already there.

Archmages Nadia, Verushka, and Marek were standing by along with Dusan, Evsen, Akira, and Chika's daughter, Katerina, who insisted on coming along in her mother's place. She was eighteen now and Zoran consented, pleasing the young woman. The more Duskas the better. Once again, Karel handed out his precious rods and they formed up their trio teams, with at least one Duska in each trio. After issuing a few orders, they followed Honani's group of five into the Shadows. They were off to Maeve, the forested world, though some claim it is more of a jungle.

This time, Jarka and Bernard were with Nadia, acting as Zoran's rear guard, right behind him. She fumed that Zoran would have the "dandy" baron at his side. He'd likely do nothing to protect him. Well, she'd make that right, she swore as she felt her body being pulled once more into the Shadows. Her stomach fought to release its contents as usual and her hand gripped Nadia's even tighter. Oh how she hated Shadow Walking!

Before long, the blue-green orb that was Maeve loomed ahead of them. As it grew larger, the blue oceans gave way to the lush green of the heavily forested main continent on which the baron's people dwelled. Honani led them on beyond the inhabited regions off to the east. Ahead loomed exceedingly tall and rugged granite peaks whose tops were still snow covered. All could see why this region was uninhabited. It was formidable even to Shadow Walkers.

Honani led them high into these mountains, where glaciers fed tarns below them. At last, he took them in closer. As they approached another tarn, they spotted dozens of women's bodies lying smashed upon the giant boulders near the edge of the lake. Some wolves were fighting over bits of bodies, a wholly disgusting sight. It was the living that concerned Zoran at the moment. Honani led them upwards on a nearly vertical grey mountain side. Then, he spied it: a gaping black hole right in the middle of the sheer granite face two thirds of the way up to the craggy peak. Zoran guessed that they must be well over two miles high, maybe more, far above the timberline.

Honani pointed out the watchers to everyone. Perched high atop the peak above the cavern entrance lay a huge black dragon. He was bored, but nevertheless was keeping an eye on the entrance far below him. Across the vast space between this peak and the one to the north, another pair of Black Dragon eyes was watching the entrance as well. Unlike the reds, the blacks were taking no chances at all with their new breeding program. Zoran wondered if the reds and blacks shared information. Did the blacks know how they had raided the red's dens? Would the blacks have alternate plans in place? He decided to make that assumption since the sole entrance was being carefully watched.

As they halted in the Shadows just before the entrance, Zoran made sure that everyone had Skin of Stone spells on their bodies as well as Spheres of Magical Protection, which would ward off all of the lower spells, such as Magical Missiles and Bolts of Lightning. This time Zoran would be taking nothing for granted. He took a deep breath and continued moving heading into the cavern's entrance.

The other trios were right behind him. Honani and the Duska groups remained behind, waiting in the Shadows. Their task would be to transport the victims to safety and to alert those inside if more dragons arrived. Katerina kept watch on the distant black while Akira watched the one resting on top of the peak above the cavern's entrance.

Zoran's trio materialized inside the cavern's entrance some distance inside, leaving room for the others to set foot inside without being seen by the two watchers. No sooner had he materialized than an Alarm Warning spell detonated. "Intruders! Intruders! All hands, intruders!" This was followed by a long gong sound. Almost at the same time, a Force Wall went up over the opening of the cavern and a second one appeared some twenty feet ahead of Zoran, blocking their forward progress as well as their retreat. "Damn, we've set off a trap!" Jarka yelled. "We should be looking for traps now. What's next? Arrows from above?" She, of course, was referring to the murder holes many of the barons had installed in the key entrance gates into their fortresses. The enemy would be trapped in the long, narrow halls, while the defenders rained arrows down upon their heads from arrow slits in the ceiling. She looked up, half expecting to see arrows raining down upon them.

Instead, she saw several large holes. "Damn! Look out, above us!" she cried out. All heads looked in time to see great blasts of Black Dragon Acid pouring down on them from above — a certain death, Baron Ailfrid was certain. He covered his head with his hands in a hopeless attempt to prevent his own death — his body eaten by acid. He didn't even think to Shadow Walk out of the trap.

The rods worked to perfection, ten great spheres surrounded all of them, keeping the acid completely off of them, rather like umbrella in the rain. Unfortunately, the acid's volume continued to build up. Soon they would be in a swimming pool of extremely caustic acid. Archmage Zdenka quickly shot a Disintegrate beam at the rear Force Wall, dispelling it. The acid began flowing to the lower elevation, on out the cavern's entrance, drooling down the mountain's steep side, creating a caustic cloud of fumes rising into the clear sky as it ate its way into the bedrock while it dripped on down towards the tarn far below. Zoran did the same to the Force Wall blocking their further passage into the chambers ahead. "Okay, off we go. Stay alert!" he ordered and they moved on into the cavern very slowly. The acid began eating into the soles of their boots, unfortunately. Jarka yelled towards the rear, "Someone back there, conjure lime and water over the floor or our boots are history!"

Ailfrid glanced ahead and to the rear, trying to absorb what had happened so quickly. He was still alive and unharmed, much to his amazement. Archmage Breana, on the other hand, grasped the scene and said, "Fast thinking. I will be more alert." Zoran smiled, the Archmage would be a valuable ally.

Ahead, the long entrance tunnel gave way to an enormous cavern. Zoran saw why instantly. Five adult blacks had already moved from their positions above them and were now lined up just ahead of them. This huge space had a smaller exit to the far right, but was otherwise empty, perfect for the dragons to battle their intruders. This place had been well thought out. Zoran suspected very strongly that the reds had shared their information with the blacks who had prepared their defenses accordingly.

Knowing that their acid had done nothing to the invaders, the blacks resorted to using their spells next. As Zoran and the others set foot in the huge underground room, the five blacks cast their spells. Great Balls of Fire encompassed the trios; Caustic Gas Clouds filled the air around them; a Forked Lightning arced towards them, threatening to hit the front three. Once more, Zoran's foresight prevailed. All these deadly spells were lower level ones and their Protection spells detonated, negating or countering the five deadly strikes, much to the chagrin of the five blacks.

The two guards are swooping down by the entrance. I think they are going to attack you from the rear! Katerina Messaged Zoran and Zdenka, distracting them, and causing them to have to delay their spells. Verushka and Nadia fired off their spells as did Karel and Breana. All had shot disintegrate spells. Unfortunately they had no time to coordinate their attacks and ended up with overlapping attacks. Two blacks died as the four beams eliminated large portions of their mammoth heads. The other three acted, leaping into the air and dropping down on top of the large group of invaders! Tons of dragon weight bore down upon them. Baron Ailfrid bailed out, Shadow Walking back to his own fortress! *If Zoran wants to get killed, let him!* he justified his cowardice.

Duska senses warned those who had them and their lightning fast responses allowed them to duck and roll out of the way of the crushing bodies of the three blacks. Similarly, the Archmages long used to lightning moves to dodge attacking spells just barely managed to avoid being crushed by the dropping massive bodies. Bernard and several others didn't, due in large part to the confined space that they were in. One black landed squarely on Mage Bernard. While the Skin of Stone protected him and he took no actual injuries, he was knocked unconscious. The wind also knocked out of him and he suffered several broken ribs and internal injuries.

Jarka leapt to the side of the dragon lying on top of her husband and began to stab it with her magical dagger. The conflict turned to one of physical blows now. Zoran reacted, drawing both of his enchanted short swords, cutting into the dragon resting atop poor Bernard.

Zdenka calmed down and cast her usual Crushing Fist around the head of a second one. Verushka and Nadia shot huge, devastating rounds of Magical Missiles into the third one, while many others began hacking at the dragons with their enchanted blades. One black's huge gaping mouth with its razor sharp teeth found its target, Verushka, and it bit down hard, hoping to sever her head from her body. Once more, the Skin of Stone spell activated. Although shocked and stunned by the severity of the massive strike and bite, she was not decapitated as the black expected. The Skin of Stone kept its teeth from actually puncturing her flesh, but the force of its bite crushed her neck. She passed out. Another black tried to rip Zoran's right arm out of his body, but the Skin of Stone activated, once more saving him, although he dropped one of his deadly short swords as that arm went numb on him. His left arm was dislocated, throbbing in pain.

Things were not looking too well for the group, as two more blacks came rushing up from their rear. "Oh this is just great!" Jarka cursed, wholly unable to get the black off of her husband, whom she figure was now quite dead, crushed by the huge black mass.

Just then, they heard other voices. "Need a little help?" It was Chan and Wen. Both had materialized upon the rear blacks necks, plunging their enchanted daggers into their eye sockets. Dana had come with them and was stabbing his huge enchanted bastard sword into the belly of the black that Wen was attacking. It moaned and swooned, collapsing on the ground, causing Dana to dive to get out of the way or be crushed as it fell. Wen teleported off it, landing nearby.

Again, Chan, holding onto the dragon's neck, struck its other eye, plunging her dagger deep into its brain. Her dagger snapped and the dragon fell. She too teleported off it landing beside Wen. "Damn, there goes another dagger!" Dana handed her his.

Zoran took a hint from Wen and Chan. He teleported to the dragon's neck and plunged his short sword into its eye, driving it deep into the dragon's brain. It let out a hideous wail and slowly slumped to the stone floor, dead. However, it was still on top of poor Bernard. "Bernard's under it! Help!" Jarka screamed, figuring the worst.

"Verushka's in trouble!" Zdenka yelled to anyone who would listen.

As the chaos spread, several Archmages, including Breana, joined together and cast multiple Lift spells, moving the heavy dead weight off of the unconscious man. Zdenka suggested they dump it off the edge and the group continued to push the levitated mass on out and off the cliff, whereon they cancelled their many Lift spells. The carcass dropped like a rock, smashing into the huge boulders below, joining the dead human bodies.

Meanwhile, Nadia reached the unconscious Verushka and began pouring a healing potion down her crushed throat, praying all the while. Dana saw Zoran leaning against a carcass of a black, his left shoulder dangling at a strange angle. He rushed to him. Taking a hold of Zoran's arm, he said, "This is going to hurt a little." He gave a huge pull. Zoran bellowed in pain, but the arm snapped back into its socket. Someone handed him a healing potion and he guzzled it and finally began looking around at the scene.

One by one, the remaining six huge dragon bodies were similarly disposed of, clearing out the cavern and entrance area. "Okay, recast protections. Our rods are about out of charges, so be careful! Let's see what else they have in store for us. Jarka, you stay behind and look after our fallen."

"He's alive! I don't know how, but he is!" she exclaimed, tears of joy streaming down her face. She poured a healing potion after healing potion into his mouth and forced him to swallow them. Then she moved on to several others who could use a bit of healing and repeated her actions, holding their heads and pouring her special potions into their mouths.

"Oh my head! What happened?" a moaning Bernard finally roused and spoke, his hands grasping his head. "I ache all over. Oh! Dragons!" he suddenly remembered the fight.

"We got them all. You are safe! I am so glad that you are unhurt, dear," she exclaimed as the other three regained consciousness as well. "I think that we got them all and the others are exploring the cavern now, probably rescuing the women." She then outlined the battle to the four.

"I am not okay! I feel like someone dropped a mountain on me," Bernard complained. "My whole insides ache beyond belief!"

"They did drop a mountain on you — a huge black one," she teased. "I'd better go throw up a Force Wall over the entrance in case more blacks arrive. It'll slow them down a bit. Honani and Katerina haven't said more are coming, but I don't want to take any chances."

After they all regrouped, Zoran led the way further into the complex. The tunnel soon branched to the right. Zdenka took her group that way, figuring it led to the murder holes above the entrance. It did and she quickly rejoined the others who had now entered a large chamber with four side chambers. They'd just finished checking the one on their right, which turned out to be a pantry-kitchen to feed the captive women.

"We have three more. Let's divide up and check. Yell if there are traps or more dragons," he ordered.

A minute later, Zdenka entered the middle chamber of the three that remained only to see a female black dragon working on cleaning up a newborn baby black. The dead human woman's body lay nearby, a blood pool was nearly four feet around what remained of her body. "You beasts!" the black screamed. Before they could react, the black, still holding the newborn, Shadow Walked out of the underground room. She yelled "Dragon!" She then added that it had left with a newborn.

"Oh dear god!" Verushka whispered as she and her group came upon the women in the right chamber. She'd recovered from her crushed neck, thanks to the healing potions, but her voice was funny and weak still.

A woman was obviously about to give birth. The woman called out, "Alfreda, I think it is time for me, but it is hurting so! Please, help me, I can't take the pain." Verushka rushed to the woman's side to assist, casting her Morph spell. "Oh, that is so much better," the woman said.

The sights that the trios saw were far worse than they'd yet witnessed. "Why are they acting that way?" Jarka asked as she finally joined the others.

"The blacks have made good use of their Charm Person spells," Verushka replied. "Here, lend me a hand with her." She grimaced as she realized her voice still sounded strange.

Meanwhile Zoran finished explaining to everyone standing just outside the three chambers in which the women were housed. He'd brought them all in from the Shadows to help transport them all to safety. "Okay, we have two women in labor right now that we dare not move, not after what happened last time. The blacks have apparently learned from the mistakes of the reds. They cast Blind spells on the women and then Charm Person, thus the women willingly do what is asked of them. From what little we've learned from a few of them, shortly after they were Blinded, they were put to sleep, probably by a simple Sleep spell. They awoke missing their arms, with aching shoulders. As you will soon see, the blacks used their acid on the women, dissolving their arms near their shoulders. Jarka guesses that they then used some form of healing potion on the women. The blacks wanted to guarantee with absolute certainty that these women would carry their baby dragons to term. Prepare yourselves for the awful sight. All of the women are naked. We've left most of the Charm and Blind spells un-dispelled until we get them to our infirmary. Jarka says they will have less trauma that way." Many gasps and groans echoed in the huge chamber.

He continued, "Based on skin colors and the little that we dared communicate, it appears that eight are from Jing. Eight are from Terra and Baron John has confirmed those. One is from Rehor; four are from Adapazan; and two are from Cosma."

"But how?" Bernard asked. "Didn't we find all our missing women?"

"It seems they have taken a new approach. With our four women, Bernard, they went to bed in their homes and woke up here as captives. I am theorizing that the dragons came in the middle of the night and abducted the sleeping women from their beds. We must now alert our people to anticipate such things and to begin reporting isolated disappearances. Not even I would have made the connection, Bernard, but we will now! That is also the story on the eight Terra women. Okay, you can now transport them to our infirmary. One from Cosma and one from Adapazan are currently in labor and we'll have to wait on those, I am afraid."

"Baron," Archmage Breana spoke up, "we could teleport them to my tower down in the forest. I don't like hanging around here. They could come back in force."

"Okay, let's make it so. Zdenka and I along with Jarka will remain with the two. Everyone else, head to Brn now."

A few minutes later, Zoran, Zdenka, Jarka, and the two women allowed themselves to be teleported by Breana into her tower within Baron Ailfird's fortress and Circle at Dunharrow Caern, deep within the forest, where it was springtime and warm. While Zdenka and Jarka attended the two women, Zoran stood by ready to do whatever was needed. Breana summoned Baron Ailfrid and forced him to witness the women's plight. So stern was her countenance that the frightened baron could not help but do as she asked. He turned green and rushed to the bathroom. "Serves the coward right," Breana chastised him as he left. Zoran grinned. "What do we do with the newborn dragons? Vanish spell?" He nodded.

"Little help, Zoran. It's not accepting my Morph spell anymore," Jarka called out. Both Breana and Zoran recast the spell much to the relief of the poor woman from Cosma. Shortly after that, the black dragon appeared, though it was still forced to be in its human form.

"Allow me," Archmage Breana said, just as Baron Ailfrid reappeared. He saw it turn into its tiny Black Dragon form as it suddenly vanished from sight.

"My god! It was a Black Dragon in her!" He hastily left once more, very sick at his stomach.

Breana grinned. "What some of we Archmages have to live with," she commented dourly.

An hour later, the other woman gave birth and within a few minutes, they all returned to Brn and the over-crowded infirmary there.

"Our first decision, Zoran," Verushka explained, though her voice was still not fully recovered, "was whether or not to cancel the spells of blindness and charming. You see, they are totally calm, relaxed, and do whatever you say in spite of their awful condition. In some ways, having them calm really helps the care givers. However, we opted for truth. These women need to know the truth. Thus, one by one, we have been undoing the spells that the blacks put on them. You can tell when we are successful. Ah, there, that woman's screams indicate the last of her spells have been undone."

"Well, I'd scream too if I woke up and discovered all this had been done to my body and me," Zdenka agreed.

"Yes, we then talk with the women, getting their names and stories, logging them as Jarka has ordered. Once that's done, it's off to get them bathed and their hair washed. When we finally get them into clean dresses, they are usually hungry. Once fed, we've been assigning them specific beds, putting their names and due dates on a card over their bed heads. Jarka, perhaps you can take a look at their scarred shoulders where the blacks used acid to burn off their arms. Can anything be done to improve the look of their shoulders?"

"On it," she stated and left to do just that.

Verushka continued her report. "We saved the two who just gave birth. We expect two more will be due in the morning, with another woman due the next day and then another the day after. Those are from Cosma and Adapazan, by the way. The blacks have been smarter than the reds. They've planned the due dates cleverly. Instead of all the women coming due at the same time, they've staggered them at least a day apart. Around the 4th of May and continuing for eight days, the Jing women are due. Around the 15th of June and for eight days after that the Terra women are due. Clever, we will not be so swamped. Oh and one more thing, the women who have just delivered are also radiating the same level of magical energies that our seventeen women are. We should begin their magic training as soon as they've recovered from the birthing. Once they have mastered the Morph Self spell, they can then have arms as long as the spell lasts and that will help them immensely."

Archmage Nadia added, "Dad, we have run out of helpers for the armless women. Can you see if you can obtain some helpers from Cosma and Terra to lend a hand with them?"

"Okay, but let's have the fifteen women from Terra who have their arms and are not due until June lend a hand to the blind women and the new arrivals. Let them help out. Meantime, we're going to need at least a dozen mages and or Duska trained women to help with the maternity problems. Too many are due at nearly the same times in June." He set about to see what could be worked out with the other barons.

"Dad, we've got six permanently blind women. There must be something that we can do to help them learn to live again," Nadia complained bitterly.

"Say, I know of a blind woman in Brn who gets around really well. Her name, as I recall, is Eva," Zdenka spoke up in a flash of recognition. "I am going to see if she will be willing to work with the six and help them adjust to life. I know that later on if their magic training goes well, they can then use Morph spells on themselves to recover their sight at least temporarily. Of course, if they run into a Dispel Magic, their spell would be cancelled and they'd be sightless again. Still, this may well help them in the long run."

"Right, while they are studying magic, we can Morph them ourselves, otherwise, they won't be able to read," Nadia traced her mother's line of thought further on down the line.

"Say, the blind woman from Rehor, Andrea, she refuses to go back to Rehor. She wants to stay here with us and get her magic training from me," Zdenka volunteered since they were discussing the futures of the women. "I've agreed, dear. I hope this will not become a political issue."

"What Storm doesn't know won't hurt him. Mum's the word then," he replied with a wide grin. "Okay, although we've not heard from Tomas, I think I ought to get back to the High Council meeting. I'll take Bernard back with me, the rest of you can stay. I don't envy the work load that you are facing. I'll try to get some volunteers to return with me as well." After a pair of loving embraces, the two men Shadow Walked back to Castle Hadwig on Dietmar. By now, it was suppertime and they were just in time. Bernard didn't feel much like eating. His insides still ached and Zoran favored his left arm, still sore at his shoulder.

"Hi dad. Glad you are all safe," Tomas welcomed him back. "Just heading off to dine. We're dining in shifts now just to play it safe. Baron Adolf has suddenly gotten extremely paranoid. His nice tidy world was turned upside down by the appearance of the dragon among the musicians. He swore that no dragon could possible get into his castle here. He's had to publicly eat crow. Now he's going overboard on new security routines such as eating in shifts. Well, that one I kind of agree with — no sense in having us all together in one spot unless necessary."

Over diner, several other barons dropped by to thank Zoran for having taken charge. Already Tomas had spread the word of the rescue. He loved telling the story over and over to keenly interested men and women. "Say, we still have to meet tomorrow. I plan to call for a vote on the mutual defense pact," Baron Cadfeel declared. "Any other bright ideas for what we actually can do now?"

"Keep on building the underground towns where they can't get to us," Zoran answered. "Perhaps other bright minds will supply some more tomorrow."

In the morning, they finished dining and were in their room preparing for the morning session when another Mind Link message came. Almost at soon as Zoran acknowledged it, his daughter, Nadia appeared bringing Jarka with her. "She insisted and we agreed. Bye dad, got babies to deliver and women to save." She vanished leaving Jarka collecting her physical self from the unnerving Shadow Walk.

"I wish a teleport would work. I hate these Shadow Walks. Anyway, glad to see me?" she finally returned to her old self. "Had to come back. Nothing more I can really do for the women at the moment. I am working on some new potion ideas though."

"Glad you're back, but Nadia said you had to see me?" he inquired.

"Yes, before the meeting starts. I'll explain as we walk. You see, I got to pondering the motives of that dragon yesterday. It did not attack us or make any such move, unlike that red did last fall. I asked myself why?"

"How did you answer yourself, dear?" Bernard jested her. He was feeling better this morning, though his ribs still hurt if he took a deep breath.

"Spying, my love. Yes, you see, it was really keen on getting out of here fast. I didn't detect any real fear from it, though it ought to have been very scared — what with all the Archmages present. No, in fact, it didn't even morph to its dragon form before it Shadow Walked or whatever it calls what it did. Why? The only answer I can handle is that it was spying on us for the dragons! It had collected a lot of information on what you barons are planning and it had to get that back to the other dragons! Now that makes its behavior understandable, don't you think?"

She rattled on, "Besides, if it was able to so infiltrate this Castle Hadwig, it might have done some other things as well before playing music. Considering the magic usage that we saw being employed with their captured women, I am suspecting that it used more while it was here."

"What are you saying, Jarka? That it was spying on us before while we were in the meeting room?" Zoran asked, finally seeing where she was headed with this.

"Precisely! I'll make a good thief out of you yet, though you are still a little slow on the pickup," she teased him.

"Well, there was no one who is unaccounted for that I could see, yesterday at the meeting, I mean. I've seen all those advisors before. So have you."

"Oh sure. I always double check their current faces with those in my eidetic memory of pervious sightings. I agree, all checked out down to their eye colors and no one has reported any of their advisors having gone missing or such. No, I don't think that it impersonated an advisor. What if it planted a magical listening device somewhere in the meeting room?" There, she'd finally gotten to the key point that had so driven her to come back so quickly.

"My god! I think you have a valid point! Come on. Let's hurry up and check this out." He sent a quick Message to Baron Adolf, asking him to meet him just outside the meeting room by the huge doors.

Adolf's eyes looked blood shot. He'd been up all night worrying about nearly everything, checking and rechecking everything around his Circle of Ascension and Castle Hadwig. "What's so important now?" he growled.

"Find a clever excuse to get those who are already in the meeting room to quietly evacuate it. We think that the dragon might have planted a scrying device or worse in there," Zoran came right out with it.

"Crap! Well okay, I see your point. We've search it, but found nothing. I will concede this request, if it will make you happy." Using a loud voice, Baron Adolf called out, "Barons, Baronesses, and staff. Would you all please follow me to the dining room? We have some very special morning tea for us all before we tackle our monumental problems." Several wanted to decline, but saw Adolf frantically waving at them and the followed the others out, wondering what was going on? Another dragon attack? Once in the long halls, Adolf explained what Zoran had just suggested. They stood around talking in hushed voices.

When the room was empty, Jarka and two of Adolf's men, assassins she was sure, entered the room. She began casting her detection spells, while the men redid the search that they had done yesterday, grumbling in low voices that this was pointless. After a few minutes, a big smile replaced Jarka's intense look of concentration. She walked over to Baron Adolf's table and cast another spell and then walked straight out of the room and up to the baron.

"I say, did you know that you were drinking out of a magically enchanted mug?"

"What?"

"Yes, it has been enchanted to act as a sort of microphone, broadcasting what was said in the room to its listener, probably that dragon who fled yesterday. I believe that it is safe to say that the dragons now know absolutely everything that was said within that room yesterday," Jarka pointed out.

"My god. They know about the magical rods, how they work, all our preparations!" Adolf said flushing red.

"Worse, they know that we are declaring war on dragons," Zoran pointed out the very worst detail that had been revealed. "Now they know what we are planning and will be taking strong countermeasures."

"Dieter! Vanish that foul thing!" He fairly screamed at his aged Archmage, who shuffled into the room and did just that. The water mug vanished from sight.

Five minutes later, the room had filled and the morning session of the High Council finally began, ten minutes late, but now secure. Many mages cast Anti-scrying spells. Paranoia now ran high!

As promised, Baron Cadfeel made his proposal for a mutual defense pact. "When any baron or baroness needs help, they are to send a Mind Link Message to other barons who will relay it to all of us. We will come at once to their aid, bringing our Archmages with us. I call for a vote." It passed, though not unanimously. Several barons abstained, including Ailfird. All of the Archmages present swore that if they were notified of the request for help that they would answer it promptly. Zoran took that as a very good omen indeed. After all, the best defense against the powerful dragons were the Archmages, who of all people stood the greatest chance of breaking down the dragon's inherent resistance to magical spells.

Zoran repeated his call to continue the construction of subterranean towns and to stockpile food and water, just in case. All agreed, but Asami needed additional aid and the barons discussed their unique situation the rest of the morning. Asami had the smallest population of any of the sixteen planets due primarily to the distinct lack of land on which to survive. Still it was the vacation planet of the federation and many wanted to offer them a helping hand. Just at lunchtime, the council passed a resolution that if the dragons attacked Asami, all of the barons would join together and work out a mass evacuation of the people to other worlds. Baron Goro was pleased with this and promised them all free vacations — after this whole dragon mess was finished, that is.

During the afternoon session, many barons wanted to assemble an attack force to go after the dragons, to carry the fight to them by going on the offensive. "Look, all Zoran has done is fight reactive, defensive battles. We need to *strike* these dragons in their hearts! Put some *fear* into their oversized minds!" Baron Strom Clav argued. Many barons agreed with him and such a resolution passed by a narrow margin. Of course, who would make up this attack force was problematical.

"Look, Strike Force One will use tactics that have been developed by Baronesses Chan and Wen. Move around, locate an isolated dragon here or there and wipe it out!" Storm slammed his huge fist hard onto the table for emphasis, cracking the polished mahogany. Adolf gave him a very dirty look before quietly casting a Mend spell. By late afternoon, the council voted to fund and supply Strike Force One, to have Zoran equip them with enchanted blades, and for each planet of the Federation to supply one hot Duska fighter to man up the force.

Chan pointed out that she would be hard pressed to meet that requirement. Jing had just lost thirty thousand soldiers, all their mages, and many of the court Duskas. The council agreed to waive Jing's requirement to send one Duska, but asked her to help train them in her methods of combating the dragons. This she could handle. Zoran voted against the whole concept, but lost. Far too many barons were totally paranoid now and frightened. They saw this as a way for them to somehow be seen as doing something against the dragon threat but without putting themselves in danger. Baron Ailfrid was a prominent supporter of this motion, as Zoran expected.

The whole of the third day was spent on working out where the Strike Force One would be based and who would be responsible for their maintenance, supplying them with food, for example. Barons John and Arcangelo volunteered to supply all the food they could desire. Baron Gaspard of Gonda volunteered to supply all the horses they might need, should they need them. He didn't want to be seen not supporting the Strike Force One. Naturally, Baron Storm Clav insisted that Strike Force One be based on Rehor, claiming many of the dragons that had to be fought lived on Rehor. Zoran wondered if he merely wanted to get rid of the dragons that they'd asked to come to his planet in the first place. Evidently their trading agreements had completely broken down.

Zoran at last raised his protest. "Look, if you are insisting that I provide the sixteen fighters with enchanted blades, then all of you who have been promised enchanted blades will have to wait quite some time until we can acquire more blades to enchant. We simply don't have that many weapons to just give out fifteen without giving them some of those we've promised to you barons."

This had the desired effect. Jarka worked hard to keep from smirking at the barons. Quickly one moved and called for a vote, passing an amendment that said Zoran would provide an enchanted weapon to those fighters who could not be so supplied by his ruling barons. Zoran hoped that would lower the total number he'd have to give up on what he saw as a lost cause, ill thought out at best.

The fourth and last day was spent on more mundane trading arrangements. Zoran was very glad to finally head home. However, Karel was none too pleased about the weapons loss and Zoran now had a hard decision to make. One of his Duska would have to join the Strike Force One, which was more than likely a death sentence. Whom should he send?

A day later, Evsen, Bernard and Jarka's youngest son came to chat with him. "Look, I heard about the Strike Force One and that you have to send a Duska member. I want to volunteer. I am eighteen and have some experience already helping fight them and I have my own enchanted bastard sword as well. I can always keep you posted on what's going on and all that. I'd be a valuable spy for you as well, especially if we are based on Rehor. What do you say? Please?" Evsen begged.

"Son, this is likely a foolish mission, a death sentence. What have your parents said? Have you discussed this with them?"

"Well, no, but I am sure that they want me to do my part. After all, you gave me the Duska gift and this is one way that I can repay you for that. Please, baron."

"Well all right, but only if Jarka and Bernard agree." A half hour later, Evsen headed off to find his fiancé Katerina and tell her that he was Adapazan's official member of Strike Force One!

Chapter 19 The Spring United Council

Aldrick once again summoned the leaders of the dragon species together for a parallel Spring Council. He was furious with the green's slaughter of thirty thousand plus men and women on Jing. He knew that the barons would most certainly take some kind of retribution on dragons, though he did not know just what. He still held out hope that a war between their races could somehow be avoided. To that end, he called for the United Council once more.

He made his arguments first, outlining the devastation caused by the greens on Jing. "What do you expect from the humans when you burn down their villages, steal their valuable mines, and abduct their women and breed them and mutilate their bodies? Of course, you are forcing humans to attack you!" Aldrick, the gold, argued.

Alistair, the green, countered, "We greens have been hunted to near extinction on Jing! Do you realize that among all the planets there are only thirty of us greens left? We were only trying our best to preserve our race." He didn't mention the many male slaves who were forced to mine for their gems and gold. "The humans are committing genocide on us greens. Are you going to stand for that?" Many supported him, particularly the reds, blacks, and whites. However, now the browns tended to agree. The idea of genocide bothered the brown representatives, Donatello and Pietro.

After more discussion, Werner, the black, played his Ace card. "We sent in a spy to their High Council meeting. The barons have now declared war on dragons!" This sent a shockwave of growls through the entire group, as he expected. When it died down, he continued, "There can now be no doubt about the *true* intentions of the humans: *extermination* of all dragon-kind! Worse, their Archmages, who the golds so love, have now produced two hideous weapons that have already been used against us!" He described in detail the Rod of Dragon Slaying and the Gem of Dragon Control.

"Yes, you may well one day soon become a puppet to the human who wears the Gem, doing his bidding as his dragon slave!" This created even more of an uproar, for a dragon fiercely loves his freedom of action and choice. Aldrick began to see the neutral dragons sliding over to the reds and blacks and greens.

"Look, thus far, these power weapons have only been used by the humans when they went to rescue the women that you had kidnaped! Not once have they launched a war against you. The greens cannot argue that the retaking of the mines that they stole from the barons on Jing was an attack. The humans there were merely defending their mines. If the humans truly wanted a war with us, they would send out attacking forces, which they have not done as yet," Aldrick attempted to persuade the neutrals, having given up on the others. "Please, please, we need calm here. Stop provoking the humans by burning their villages and stealing, breeding, and mutilating their women."

"He does have a point, Werner," Bolivar, the blue, pointed out. "It is clear to us that you and the reds and greens have been seriously provoking the humans on many planets. After all, Werner, if someone stole my mate, I would go after them with all I could muster to get her back. I would be very angry indeed if when I got her back I found that her wings had been cut off or her legs. I am sure that you would be too. If we do not provoke them, perhaps things will settle down and remain quiet and peaceful. After all, we have so much food here that life is quite enjoyable now."

Donatello, the brown, and Aeton, the grey, both agreed with Bolivar, the blue. Aldrick wanted to call for a binding vote, now that he'd regained the support of the neutrals, except the whites. However, he knew that it would result in a tie vote. If only Cezar, the white, would see reason and side with his fellow neutrals could Aldrick hope to win such a vote.

"I call for a vote," Werner, the black, seized the initiative from Aldrick, the gold, knowing that at least it would be a tie vote and thus non-binding. His attempts to sway the neutrals had almost succeeded.

"Wait a moment, Werner. Cezar has not voiced his feelings and opinions," Aldrick, the gold, barely managed to avoid the vote.

Cezar, the white, one of the smallest dragons present, cleared his throat, rather enjoying his pivotal role, seldom experienced by the whites who were always considered the lesser dragons by the others. "I say that Werner should be commended for his efforts to learn just what the true intentions of the humans toward we dragons actually are. I am appalled at these horrific magical weapons they have invented, whose use is solely and only against we dragons." Werner, the black, thought that Cezar was finally going to side with him. However, the white's next sentence blew all such thoughts away.

"Yet, I can also see the wisdom of Donatello. We would do what the humans are doing if our females were stolen, impregnated, mutilated, and ensured of death when they give birth. We would do the same thing if the humans burned our villages and murdered all its inhabitants. We whites would most certainly counterattack to retrieve our mates and obtain justice. I see now that the role that we whites have played in interspecies breeding has been the wrong path to follow. We have been antagonizing the humans who are merely reacting to our own ill-conceived deeds. It is the opinion of us whites that the humans have thus far been entirely justified in their actions against we dragons. We should do as Aldrick suggests, cease and desist, allow peace to return."

Werner, the black, grumbled mightily. All his planning with the whites just crumbled, but Cezar, the white, was not yet finished. "However, I am worried about this declaration of war against dragon-kind. I would like to add a stipulation that, if in the future we obtain evidence that the humans have gone on the offensive against us even though we are not continuing our ill-conceived actions against them, then the whites will side with you, Werner. War it must then be." Werner relaxed, the cause was not as hopeless as it seemed. Cezar, the white, had just given him a key concession!

Now Aldrick, the gold, called for a vote and it passed by one vote. He summarized, "From this day forth, dragon-kind will no longer burn and destroy human villages, murdering the occupants, and abducting their women. No more interspecies breeding. No more antagonizing the humans."

Werner, the black, spoke, "We blacks will no longer attack their towns and destroy them. We will not murder whole villages. We give you our pledge." He cleverly did not mention interspecies breeding however. Dario, the red, picked up on Werner's words, realized what hadn't been said, and repeated them. Alistair, the green, somewhat confused, duplicated what the others just said, not realizing Werner's intention at all. He was just glad that Aldrick had not come down harder on the greens.

With the compromise passed, Aldrick dismissed the council and left to inform Zoran of the results. He hoped and prayed that this would appease the many barons and avoid an all-out war.

After the neutrals also left, including the whites, the others held their own council. "So what was that all about, Werner?" Dante, the red, asked.

"Yes, clever wording," Dario, the red, added.

"Perhaps we did overdo it a bit by destroying whole villages just to get some appropriate females to breed. We blacks have been doing some experimentation of our own. There is a far better route. Go into an unsuspecting village in the middle of the night. Cast Sleep spells to ensure they don't rouse while we search each house for suitable women. We take only one or two from any given village. No one is the wiser and no one comes looking for them. It is a far better solution. We've also found that there is no need to pull out their eye balls. Rather a Blind spell is highly effective and less damaging to the female host. We are also using a Charm spell on them and thus they become docile and obey us fully. However, we are still removing their arms as a precaution. We don't want to chance one of them killing themselves. Three did just that in spite of our spells. So their arms have to go. However, burning them off with our acid has caused other problems, and we've had to follow that with healing droughts of our own. Wasteful, wasteful."

"Ah, fantastically good idea. We will follow this new approach," Dario, the red, replied. "Say, we reds have a better solution to the arm problem. We'll have to show you. Meanwhile, what about these constant raids by Zoran's group? How in the world are they able to find our secret caverns on so many different worlds? How do we stop those raids? If they keep on raiding us, we are getting nowhere in our breeding program."

"Good point. I suggest that from now on, we keep only a few human females at any one secret location. We won't have all our babies in one nest. However," Werner, the black, added, "I suggest that we also focus our attention on discovering just how Zoran is able to locate our nests. Let's use this breather to work that one out and then take countermeasures. I am certain that sooner or later we will get our way and be able to outright exterminate the humans on these worlds."

"Excellent. You can count on us reds," Dario, the red, replied. "We should spread our abductions out over more worlds and not all from the same general area. Mix things up a bit."

"Good idea, Dario. Let's work on that now. We just lost a pile of our babies and there is no way that we can get them back. Zoran's fortress is too heavily defended at the moment. Besides, they have the despicable magical rods with them. We blacks are in a complete mystery over how Zoran found our secret cavern on Maeve. We find it incredible that he found it!"

"Same with us, he keeps on finding our secret locations where the women are being held. Perhaps we are leaving behind some kind of trail that he is able to follow," Dario, the red, suggested. For an hour, they discussed this idea and similar ramifications before they headed back to their homes.

Meanwhile, Aldrick visited Zoran. "I've just been blind-sided by the barons. Have they really declared war on dragons?" he asked antagonistically.

"Yes, old friend, they have done just that. I failed to keep that from passing. However, Aldrick, their declaration is mere words. They have not the means to seriously back it up. It was done more for their own morale and that of their people. The only real action they took along those lines is to form up Strike Force One, fifteen fighters who are to attack the evil dragons wherever they can find them, but only single dragons. Obviously, they are not strong enough to fight more than one at a time and they will not be carrying the magical rods. It will be swords only for them. I doubt that they will have much of an effect. However, I will do all that I can to slow them down."

"Well, that is a relief. I just barely carried the day. The blacks almost won a declaration of war against humankind! We simply must keep this from becoming an all-out war. So many humans will die. So many of us will die," Aldrick pointed out with a sigh.

"I couldn't agree with you more, old friend. We must continue to keep this war from happening. Say, can I ask you something?" Aldrick nodded. "Have you dragons ever been called worms?"

Aldrick gave Zoran a funny look. "Why, I haven't heard that name in many centuries! Yes, our ancestors were called worms. Why do you ask?"

"Curiosity. We've come across some ancient records of ours that mentions fleeing from worms. Although we can find no description of just what a worm actually was, I kind of got the feeling it might be dragons. Strange."

"Very. I am not much of an historian. Perhaps Burk might know more. I will get back to you on it. Farewell." Aldrick left and Zoran had to tell the others all about the meeting. Everyone wanted to know what the gold had to say. These days, if a dragon was involved, everyone had to know all about it. How times had changed, he noted.

Early May, Physician Bedrich came to see Jarka. "Excuse me. I need you to look at my fingers here, Mage Jarka." He held out his right hand.

She looked them over. "I don't see anything. They look fine to me." Jarka looked a bit baffled. What was wrong with them?

"They are numb on this side, but not on their back sides. Try it. Stick a needle in one of them." He insisted until she did so.

"Wow! You didn't feel that at all?" she asked incredulously. She'd stuck one in almost a quarter of an inch before he began to feel the needle.

"Precisely. My fingers are numb and so are those of Physician Kamil. Most strange. Can you do anything for them?" he finally asked what he'd come here seeking.

"Have you tried a healing potion?" she asked the obvious. He had and the two chatted for a bit, discussing a number of lesser possibilities.

"Well how long have they been numb like this?" she asked finally, giving up on immediate cure possibilities.

"Nearly five months now. We've been trying various cures and hoping that in time, feeling would return to them. However, they seem to be permanently numb."

"Five months? Say, what happened to them in the first place?" Jarka finally asked the key question.

"We are not sure at all. You see, we have been dissecting all those women's arms that we had to remove last late fall. You know, from the seventeen women that were first rescued, the withered, numb arms. At first, we could find nothing at all, but then I noticed a small amount of a thick bluish liquid on one arm, near the shoulder ball. Of course we extracted samples of it and examined it thoroughly, but we have as yet to identify what it is. Our fingers went numb right after we were examining it, though. Physician Kamil has now discovered this same substance in nearly all of the remaining intact limbs that we still had. It is our theory that somehow this bluish stuff was injected into their arms, causing their arms to become dead to the women. Of course, we cannot prove this. I was hoping that you could perhaps find a cure for our fingers."

"Wow! Fascinating, Physician Bedrich. This stuff might just have been the cause that we were looking for, but of course I will need samples to work with," Jarka exclaimed, eager to have a new research project.

"Follow me to our workroom, Mage Jarka. We have two arms intact so you can see where it was originally inserted. Physician Kamil and I have extracted a small vial of the stuff from the remaining arms. I'm afraid the quantity is so very small. It's sticky and gooey, do be careful not to get any on your fingers or they will become numb like ours."

Jarka held her nose as she entered their workshop. Severed arms lay all over the tables, each one tagged and labeled. Physician Kamil looked up as they entered. "Any luck?" Bedrich shook his head. "Here, Mage Jarka, you can see the foreign substance right where it was somehow deposited. We've cut away the tissue above the stuff so you can see it. Have a look."

Gruesome, Jarka fought for control of her stomach as she looked closely at the withered arms. She saw a tiny spot of the bluish stuff there near the rounded ball of the arm. "What are those things that it is covering? They are not blood vessels, right?" She knew little of what lay inside human bodies. Furthermore, she didn't really want to know. Both men shrugged their shoulders; they didn't either.

Taking the vial, she promised, "Okay, I will get on this. I have no idea what this stuff is either. I'll see if I can find out."

"Don't forget to find us a cure," Physician Bedrich called out as she left their workroom.

Chapter 20 Summer's Respite

Daily life chores continued to be a huge challenge for Danika and her sixteen friends, for friends these seventeen women abducted by the reds had become. Companions in misery, some often jested at their helplessness. Every day, they were forced to face the sharp reality of their lack of arms, requiring many others to assist them with the mundane things of life. Yet the moment that they set foot in Zdenka's classroom each morning, all that changed, for they knew that they were true mages in the making. They had no doubts about their ability to cast magical spells. Any lingering fears that their armless state would hinder their studies had long ago vanished entirely. All seventeen continued to make utterly phenomenal progress in their training.

While standing on the roof top of Zdenka's tower and casting lightning bolts at the distant mountains using their feet as pointers of direction, all traces of doubt vanished forever from the seventeen minds! With a simple chant and point of their toes, great arcs shot forth from them — to say nothing of the massive Balls of Fire also cast harmlessly at the mountains. All seventeen knew that they were on the route to greatness as mages. If only they had the time to continue their studies.

During the late spring and early summer, the seventeen were elated with each new spell. At last, they were casting really power spells, from their point of view, spells that could really kill or help them. True, these were only at the third level, far from the true Archmage spells at the ninth level, but for these humble women, the casting of a Ball of Fire or an Immobilize Person was vastly beyond their former realities.

By the middle of the summer, all seventeen were now tackling the next level of spells, fully a year or more ahead of Zdenka's usual students, who themselves were often far ahead of other Archmage teachers on other planets. They had reached the spells that Zdenka had been hoping and praying for: Morph Others, Morph Self. If her students could master these, they could Morph themselves into a woman with arms, partially removing their awful handicaps. True, the spell could easily be dispelled, reverting them back to their armless state. Still, it would give them additional options and abilities, however temporary that might be.

On the 10th of July, Danika's Morph Self spell detonated for the first time. Suddenly, she looked perhaps a year younger, but she now had arms! She jumped and screamed, waving her arms around for her companions to see. "Oh my! It works! It works! We can have our arms back again!" All sixteen others cheered her.

Zdenka rose and cautioned, "Excellent, this is just what I had been hoping for all along, ladies. However, I must caution all of you. Soon you will all be able to morph yourselves and regain arms. Yet, it is only temporary. If a Dispel Magic is cast, the Morph spell will be undone. Thus, I cannot impress this upon you hard enough: do not ever depend entirely upon having your arms in your morphed state. In combats, Dispel Magic spells are frequently encountered, and right in the middle of a life and death battle, you may be armless once again, dropping anything that you are holding or falling if you were hanging on to something with your arms." That brought the spell's reality home to the seventeen. Yes, once they learned the spell, they were no longer dependent on all the others for their daily living, and that meant everything to these seventeen. Within a day, they all were able to cast that spell.

Zdenka then estimated that by fall, the seventeen would be tackling the level five spells and of course, the Teleport spell. As soon as that spell was mastered, the seventeen would officially be recognized as mages throughout the Federation. She had no doubt that all would progress much farther than that, though how far she could not anticipate.

Archmage Bianca on Cosma had already taken on the ten women rescued from the greens, and they were making the progress that normal students did. As the 1st of May came, Zdenka and Bianca now had to tackle the training of an additional dozen women, made all the more challenging because these dozen were similar to the seventeen in that the magical energies within them were as potent as the seventeen. If the pattern held true, these dozen ought to progress as rapidly Danika and her companions were, posing a terrific challenge to the Archmage teacher. The first ten were attuned to Red Dragons while the last two, blacks. Five of these women were whole and in good health, Concetta, Edda, Ermina, Ginevra, and Marta. However, five had no eyes, though with Jarka's help they now had attractive glass eyes which greatly aided others who looked at them, though it did nothing for the five. These were Daniela, Drina, Gabriella, Ines, and Luisa. Lacking sight, studying magic would be impossible. Thus, special actions were needed with them. Finally the remaining two had their sight, but lacked their arms and thus were similar to the seventeen Zdenka was already training.

Because these were women and had recently undergone severe emotional trauma to say nothing of the physical abuse, Zdenka and Bianca were against having Cosma's other two Archmages take over their training because they were men. Enough said. Bianca explained, "What with the ten I already have, I may be able to handle the incredibly rapid progress of the five that have no physical limitations, Zdenka, but I am just starting out teaching others. I lack the experience that you have."

"Point taken. Why don't I take on the seven with physical limitations here at my school? Is that acceptable? Can you persuade your baron to go along with this? They are his people," Zdenka asked.

"Yes, consider it done. Actually, I don't really care what Baron Arcangelo desires. We must think of the women's welfare first," Bianca stated flatly. That settled it.

Already, Zdenka had hired the blind woman named Eva to help the five blinded Cosma women and Andrea of Rehor learn to deal with life. She was good with the women, spending ten hours each day with the six, coaching them, leading them, and sharing what she found workable with them. Already, Zdenka saw forward progress; the six were now being far more independent than when they first arrived.

Once she and Bianca reached their agreement, Zdenka took Andrea, Daniela, Drina, Gabriella, Ines, and Luisa aside. "Ladies, as soon as you learn to get around better on your own here on the first floor of my tower, then we will begin your official magic training. As you probably have heard, you women had an aftereffect of carrying the dragon fetuses. Intense magical energies now flow within you. With some hard work on your part, I expect that each of you may well become an official mage."

"Really, real mages?" asked Andrea.

"But we can't see to read," Drina protested slightly.

"Ah, I have a plan to temporarily restore your sight. Magic can do many useful things, but I must caution you not to depend upon the magically restored sight. It can very easily be dispelled by other magical spells. So take the time to learn all that Eva can teach you now. When you are ready, we will begin. Just remember that at times you will be unable to see and you must be able to still function and recast the spells needed to restore your temporary sight."

"That would be a miracle in itself. Count me in," Drina replied.

"We have a number of other women who will be giving birth during May and June, so we may have to either delay starting your magical training or go slower than you might like. Bear with us, we have so many women that we have yet to save when they give birth," Zdenka explained. All six agreed and Drina began to smile again, a subtle thing, but not missed by Zdenka.

Next, she met with the other group, those who were lacking arms. These included the two Cosma women, Marcella and Marzia, the Rehor woman, Bronislava, and the four women from northern Adapazan, Zora, Luba, Chesna, and Mila. These had all been carrying blacks and had the same residual magical energies as the original seventeen. Since their arrival, Zdenka had assigned her six new spring picking students to be their twins, assisting them with their many physical needs.

"We were hoping and praying that we'd get chosen!" Zora exclaimed when Zdenka explained that she would be teaching them magic as well. "We can't help but see how fantastically well the others are doing — you know Danika, Eliska, and the others. We were all praying that we could get the chance to learn. Like we are, we can have no lives at all, but with magic we can live full lives again."

"Yes, that is very true. However, I must caution you seven too. You must learn to find alternate ways to do the things of life, just as the Danika and the others have. It is hard, I won't say otherwise, but you must. Magic cannot ever give you back your arms and hands permanently, but if you study hard, practice diligently, and are patient, in time you may be able to cast spells that will give you both arms and hands on a temporary basis. Always, though you must be prepared to have the spell canceled and be able to get by as you now are."

She went on, "I am going to have Danika and the others work with you during the next few weeks teaching you the many tricks and ways that they have found useful. As you know, we have many more women who will be giving birth here shortly during May and June, half are armless as well. We must focus our immediate efforts on saving their lives. Once that is done, then we'll begin your training hot and heavy."

"Couldn't you just cast the spell that gives us arms now?" asked Marcella. "Then, we would not be such total burdens on everyone."

Zdenka smiled, anticipating this question. "You are right; we certainly *could* cast that spell on each of you, giving you both arms and hands. However, we will not, unless it is a dire emergency. Why? Remember, the spell is temporary and at any moment it can be dispelled. You simply must learn to get by on your own as much as possible so that when such a thing happens you will be able to manage and eventually recast that spell."

"So we have to learn to do things with our feet?" asked Zora.

"Yes, I made the seventeen use their feet to study magic. In fact, they still do so, but soon, I hope that they will all learn the Morph spell and finally be able to have arms and hands once more, at least temporarily. Remember, you must be able to get by as you are, even if you should become an Archmage." That satisfied the seven.

A few days later, Zdenka changed her mind a little and started the seven off on the extensive reading of the basic background materials. She watched them plunge in with total abandon, just as Danika and the others had. Even though their actual spell casting training would be delayed for a time, at least they were getting a start. She didn't do so with the blind women, since they had to learn to get around on their own and that was far more difficult and challenging, facing a world of total blackness.

While Zdenka continued to focus on the training of her many students, she left the pregnant women under the care of the other Archmages, mages, and Duskas. Verushka and Nadia led that group which included Jarka, Chika, Akira, and her youngest daughter, Milena. High Priestess Jarmila, Zdenka's daughter, joined them along with Baroness Reina Vavrin, and Zoran's sisters, Reyna and Lida. When too many were approaching birth at the same time, Archmage Ivana returned from Jing to help out as well as Archmages Kate and Marjeta from the other warlord provinces. At several points, the men were also asked to help cast the frequent Morph spells as well. Verushka didn't wanted to have to pull in others from off-world unless they simply could not handle it.

During the first weeks of May, the eight armless women from Jing were saved. These included Mei, Lin, Fan, Hualing, Meili, Ning, Jinjing, and Qing. Of course, Zdenka met with Archmage Ivana and Baroness Chan ahead of time to discuss their future training, since these were Chan's countrywomen. All had the powerful magical energies within their bodies now and would likely progress as rapidly as the original seventeen had. Ivana knew that she simply could not handle them. This was her very first months as a teacher and she had her hands full with the other thirty Jing women who had been victims of the greens. Zdenka had no real choice but to accept them under her tutelage, much to Chan's great desires.

As soon as they recovered from their harrowing birth experiences, she got them learning to deal with life using their feet and had them join the others studying the basic magical background materials, much to their joy as well. Comradery blossomed.

The real test of everyone came in June when the eight Terra women who also had lost their arms gave birth followed within a couple days with the fifteen other Terra women bearing blacks and another ten with reds. At least the twenty-five had their arms and eyes. That was a welcome break, Zdenka thought. Yet, how to train all of these was her problem. Once more, the difficult cases fell to Zdenka, who anticipated this happening. Thus, during the middle of June, she added Jane, Betsy, Ann, Milli, Sally, Janine, Mary, and Beth to her group, once more setting them to work on a study of the basic background materials.

As the last of the women were handled that third week in June, Zdenka now had far more students than she could possibly handle alone. Hence, she and Verushka and Nadia met to see how they could handle the women by dividing the students between the three of them. "I'll keep the original seventeen because we are blazing the trail for all the others," Zdenka suggested. "I'll handle the six who are blind and the Rehor woman, Bronislava , and our four Adapazan women, Zora, Luba, Chesna, and Mila. That gives me twenty-eight tough ones, plus my dozen regular students."

"Okay, I'll take on the other armless women, the eight from Jing, the eight from Cosma, and the seven others from Cosma. That gives me twenty-three tough cases," Verushka volunteered.

"Great, I'll take the women who don't have any physical disabilities. That means the fifteen from Terra who have just given birth, five from Cosma, and ten from Terra. That makes thirty women for me," Nadia volunteered. "That is probably the best for me, since these will be my first real students and my tower is almost done now."

Having decided on a division of students, the three Archmages discussed this with their students and all their helpers. All three were very pleased when Reyna and Lida announced that they would stay here through the end of July, helping out wherever needed.

After that point in time, the seventeen were able to use Morph Self spells and immediately volunteered to assist many of the others with their daily living needs. Nadia moved her thirty new students over to her tower which was newly built on the opposite side of the Fortress from Zdenka's tower.

Verushka now shared Zdenka's tower with her and space was at a premium. Archmage Verushka's tower was at the Fortress and Circle of Ascension in Sholov Province where she was the baroness. Since Verushka's students were also armless, she and Zdenka thought it was wiser to keep them all together here in one location. Verushka also liked that idea, since she really needed Zdenka's guidance and experience in training these women.

By the end of July, a very strong bond had formed between these many women, a bond that would never be broken in years to come. Yet, other bonds formed during that time as well. In many ways, Zdenka felt that these bonds were nearly as important as their magical training.

"Good afternoon, Door Warden Blanka. I'm here for Danika and Neda, please," Rafael said politely to the stern faced woman who always answered the tower door. He was sure that she must be at least a mage, but he had no way of knowing. For some unfathomable reason, he always felt cowed when he spoke to this woman who held the love of his life hostage. One word from her and he'd not get to see lovely Danika this week. Thus, he always held his breath after he made his request of her. It didn't help that she stood six inches taller than him. She nodded and closed the door. Rafael always hated this part — the uncertainty — would she fetch them or would she leave him standing in the doorway? He never knew which.

It was the first Sunday in May, the snows had melted and spring flowers blossomed. Behind his back he held a spring bouquets of daffodils, cradled in a pair cloth pouches with a long strap. He smiled as he felt them in his hand as he rocked impatiently on his feet. While working on a sword for Karel, he'd suddenly gotten the idea of how his love could carry flowers. Women, he knew, always liked flowers — at least his late wife had.

The door opened and the flushed, smiling face of Danika met his. His heart leapt for joy once more. "Hi Rafael. Glad you've come." Behind her, eleven year old Neda poked her head around Danika's shoulders, flashing him a grin.

"Now you two be careful out there," the stern voice of Blanka called out as the two stepped out onto the cobblestones.

"Oh don't worry so much. She's got me with her," Neda replied, waving her arm at Blanka.

Two months ago, Danika had attempted to again dissuade Rafael from taking a romantic interest in her. "Look, Rafael, Neda's lost her parents and home. I used to baby sit her when she was little and I am all that she has left and I couldn't refuse her request to be her mother. I can't just leave her."

"No you certainly can't, Danika. If you do, I will have to disown you. She'll just now have to also have a new dad to depend on — me," he replied. Danika had suspected that Rafael would now abandon his interests in her, since he would certainly not want an eleven year old girl. Thus, her heart fluttered when he accepted her as well. Ever since then, Rafael always took both of them on their Sunday outings. He did explain to Neda that he'd never had a young daughter and wasn't sure what Neda might need, but he'd always be there for her. That was enough for Neda, who began to see that she might have a new family here.

"For my fine, lovely ladies," Rafael said, producing the flowers from behind his back. "Daffodils. I've made each of you a little carrying cradle. Here, it goes over your heads like this and the pouch dangles down like this so you can see them and smell them." He placed one on each, stood back, and saw how they looked.

"They're beautiful, Rafael!" Danika fought to keep tears from coming. "You know I love flowers. If I can ever get a new home, I want to have hundreds of spring daffodils in the front and hundreds of marigolds around the sides, for they bring in the new year and later keep the summer alive far into the fall." She gave him a loving kiss.

"Dad, what are we going to do this afternoon?" Neda asked after she gave him a hug and a kiss on his cheek.

"Well, for my little Neda and her gorgeous mother, this afternoon, we have a really big surprise." He purposely teased her a little.

"Come on, out with it! What are we doing?" Neda insisted, pulling on his arm with hers, while Danika smiled at her playfulness. It was so good to see Neda opening up like this once more. She was the old Neda that she had baby sat years ago, full of life and vibrance. She'd been so solemn and withdrawn since the dragon attack that killed her parents and destroyed her home. Of course, it was the same dragon attack that cost Danika and the others so dearly as well.

"Jiri knows this perfect spot in the Dark Forest. We are all going on a picnic! But there's more."

"What more?" Neda giggled.

"You'll see soon enough," Rafael replied, as they walked a short distance to the Stodgy Inn. "I've a fine buggy waiting for us. Neda, I think someone is sitting in our buggy!" He feigned a little surprise. "Why don't you run ahead and see who it is for us?"

She did so and let out a little squeal. It was her boyfriend, Dragan, the innkeeper's son. "Hi Neda. Rafael said that I can come with you on the picnic, that is if it's okay with you," he said. It was, of course.

"You've made her day," Danika whispered lovingly to Rafael, who was smiling over his little surprise.

"Now I have to make yours, my love," he whispered back, giving her waist a slight squeeze. "We're going with the others. I hope you don't mind," he said in a normal voice.

"Oh, that's fine. We are all so close now." She knew that he was referring to the Gang of Six, as they now called themselves. During the early part of the year, Rafael discovered that five others were quite serious about dating some of Danika's companions. Some were widowers. One had a five year old daughter, but two were merely bachelors who'd never met quite the right woman for one reason or another. At the Yuletide Dance, they'd met some of these seventeen new women to Brn and had been smitten.

During January's Sundays, they had occasionally run into each other as they went to pick up their dates at the tower, the only day that Zdenka's students had off. The six had discovered that they were all getting to know these new women and a special comradery formed between them. By May, they all worked together to plan enjoyable outings for their dates and themselves. This Sunday, they were following Jiri, the miller's, idea of a picnic among the soft pine needles of the Dark Forest, at the edge of Brn.

Jiri was dating Kate. Viktor, a fortress guard, was dating Eliska. Bedrich, the cooper, was dating Marjeta. Veko, the bootmaker, was dating Byrona. Zdenek, the stone mason, was dating Svetlana. A widower, Zdenek had a five year old daughter, Chesna, to raise, and Svetlana took an instant liking to the shy young girl. By May Chesna was hanging on to her as if she was her mother already.

The six saw these women not as helpless cripples but as the beautiful young women that they were, highly intelligent, strong willed, and powerful. The raiding dragons had kidnaped the prettiest of the young women of the village. Further, all of Brn was now talking about the fabulous progress these seventeen were making, claiming these would soon be Archmages. Of course those doing the talking had not the faintest idea of just what this all meant beyond knowing that an Archmage was almost as powerful as a baron. Beauty and power attracted the young bachelors, but the women themselves had won their hearts.

Weeks ago, Rafael had actually proposed to Danika. This was what she had feared would happen. Rafael had said that they simply had to wait to get married until she'd finished up her magic training. "I simply will not marry you until you finish up. I cannot keep you from that. I couldn't live with myself if I did." No, it was not that she might have to terminate her magic studies in order to say yes and marry Rafael. No, it was not that she didn't love him. Her heart had opened up to him at last. The loss of her own husband and two babies had finally returned to the past, though she was occasionally reminded of them. Her hesitancy came from her physical situation, her lack of arms and hands, which made her so utterly dependent upon others for the most mundane actions of life.

"I — I can't marry you right now, Rafael, even though my heart yearns to do just that. It would not be fair to you. I cannot uphold the duties of a wife anymore. I can't cook or take care of our household things that must be done. I can't get the groceries. I can't even pick up the dirty clothes, let alone feed myself well. How can I cook our family's meals? I can't care for Neda; she is caring for me. If we have more children, how can I change their diapers or even feed them? Rafael, I feel awful. I could not uphold my side of our marriage. I would be making you do all of the things that I ought and should be doing if we were married. I would be a leech on you. I love you too much to do that to you."

Rafael was not about to give up. "That is true, my dearest, but you are only looking at the things that you can't do, not at all the incredible things that you can do. My shop has never been so clean and orderly since you came into my life. Each Sunday, you cast a few of your powerful spells and everything is spotless. We simply have to work out all the other ways you can help me and let me do what I can for you. We just have to juggle things around a little."

"Well, that's true, but a Clean spell is nothing compared to all that you'd have to be taking on. Let me think about it," she finally conceded and that he accepted. She just needs time, he thought.

As the days passed and May rolled around, one by one Eliska, Kate, Byrona, and Svetlana chatted with Danika during their private hours of the evenings. Their new boyfriends had asked to marry them as well and they wanted to get Danika's advice before replying. It was responsibility kicking in for these women. As they progressed in their magic studies, gaining ever increasing powers and skills, so also came their own personal responsibility. Danika's reasons for stalling Rafael's proposal were really real to these women at this time. All six realized that six months ago, they would probably not have hesitated a second in saying yes and marrying their loves. Yet they all knew what was likely to have happened after that. Once the newness wore off, their new husbands would soon tire of the constant care they would be needing, ultimately ruining the relationship, because they had so little that they could give back, so little that they could do as a wife.

Zdenka overheard them discussing this and smiled, knowing that these women were becoming more and more responsible. She knew that this was paramount if they were ever going to master even more powerful spells. Failure to assume the responsibility that comes with magical powers always kept one from mastering such spells.

Although the six asked for more time, the Gang of Six continued their weekly dates, not taking no or even a stall. As the women picked up their power spells, Ball of Fire, Lightning Bolts, and so on, they effused excitement each Sunday afternoon, eagerly telling their boyfriends about their incredible new spells. More than ever, the six men wanted to marry and support these powerful women.

Then came the breakthrough in July. Rafael swore that he would never forget that Sunday afternoon. When Danika came out to meet him, she had arms and hands again! She threw herself on him and hugged him tightly! As Rafael's tears of joy trickled down his cheeks, she explained this powerful new spell she'd just learned. "This is what I looked like just before the dragon's attacked. Of course, it is only temporary. I can cancel my spell at any time and go back to my old armless self, and other mages can also dispel it as well. But I can recast it. Now I can uphold my half of our marriage. So yes, Rafael, I will marry you as soon as we want, only I have to continue my magic studies." Six men and six women were extraordinarily happy and exuberant that Sunday.

Their breakthrough with the Morph spell also worked wonders on the morale of all of the other women as well. Hope surged through out Zdenka's tower like never before. The seventeen women were now able to operate fully independently and assist the others taking a huge burden off of the normal students and the adepts who had stuck around after graduating to help care for the armless students.

Further, at the Midsummer's Ball, more of the seventeen met eligible bachelors and more friendships blossomed, though none were as strong as the Gang of Six, who planned fall weddings. True, while the brides would still remain in the tower, they would have Sundays to spend with their new husbands.

As August drew to a close, the seventeen achieved yet another milestone. Eliska was the first to successfully cast the new spell, but Danika was only minutes behind her. The group was outside Brn standing in a small open meadow. Zdenka had set up red cloth X's a hundred feet away from the group of seventeen students. Eliska suddenly vanished from where she stood beside Danika and appeared just above a red X. Her first Teleport spell had activated and everyone cheered her. Soon Danika appeared there as well. By the end of the afternoon, all seventeen were Teleporting all around the meadow, thoroughly elated with their success. All knew the implications: they were officially mages! They were among the elite of Adapazan and the other worlds as well. They were mages!

"Now then, it's back to the tower, ladies. Again, I caution you. Teleporting into and out of my tower is tightly controlled. Unless you contact the Door Warden Blanka first and have her lower the protection spells, your Teleport spell will fail to activate. This is done for all our security, we cannot have assassins teleporting into the tower while we are sleeping or studying. Further, there are similar protections on the Fortress and grounds. Brn proper is unprotected, so you could teleport from here to our front doors. Message Blanka if you need to teleport in or out and you must abide by her decisions. Sometimes emergencies arise and we don't have time to notify you students. The Door Warden is always kept informed first, so trust her judgment in these matters, my new mages."

That evening as usual, all of her students joined Zoran's whole group for supper in his Great Hall. This evening, the six proud husbands joined them and helped to celebrate the women's incredible achievement. Within days, all of Brn was talking about the seventeen. Having so many new mages here in Brn was looked upon as fantastic new security by the local townsfolk. Such a quantity was unheard of before in any town or city on Adapazan. The local would-be soothsayers, who had complained all along that their Archmage was being foolish in attempting to train armless women in the ways of magic, all had to eat crow that week.

Politically, Baron Zoran, Baron John, and Baron Arcangelo now saw things in a whole different light. Zoran now had seventeen more mages to help defend Adapazan with perhaps another six on the way before too long. Baron John hoped to eventually add thirty-three mages to his employ, while Baron Arcangelo hoped for another twenty-two. Baronesses Chan and Wen now anticipated that their eight armless women would also become mages for Jing and within a few years, maybe thirty more would become mages as well. The two baronesses were in desperate need for mages at the moment. After the celebration was over and Zoran was alone once more, he pondered the significance of this. He explained to his walls, "The dragons have just given me an enormous gift of mages. Perhaps they have planted the seeds of their own destruction." Then he began to wonder if these women would progress even further in their training. When Zdenka finally crawled into their bed beside him, he asked her, "Are they nearing their maximum? The seventeen?"

She knew that sooner or later he would be asking this question. "To be honest, dear, nothing about these women surprises me any longer. No, I have seen no signs that they are nearing their maximum. However, we should soon begin seeing missed spells cropping up here and there between them, just like it did with our group when we were all learning magic under Archmage Oldrich."

"Keep me posted, please. Security and all that."

"Ha, you just want a whole bunch more Archmages, I know politics, baron," she teased him.

"Well?" he teased her back.

"We will just have to see," she returned her conservative tease.

Chapter 21 Countermoves

Werner, the black, and Dario, the red, wasted no time in getting together to work out new plans. "We must take advantage of the supposed lull in our relations with the humans," Werner suggested.

"Indeed. This Baron Zoran always seems to be at the crux of attacks against us. We need spies in his court," Dario pointed out.

"Failing that, we need someone in Brn gathering information. After all, what happened to all of our babies that they stole when they took away our women?" Werner questioned rhetorically. Both knew the answer: they murdered the babies. Early May, Schultz, the black, and Elmo, the red, were chosen to infiltrate Brn and set themselves up in positions to gather information on Zoran and the Archmages.

That settled, the two began discussing just how Zoran always seemed to be able to find their secret caverns. "Look, until we figure this out, what's the point in abducting and breeding? We'll just lose them again as before," Dario, the red, pointed out the obvious.

"Let's approach this logically," Werner, the black, sighed. There just had to be logic behind it. "What about See Through Another's Eyes or Hear?"

"Don't be silly. Those spells have a very limited range," Dario pointed out the fallacy in those spells. "He is an Archmage. I've heard of a powerful Vision spell, but I only have rumors of what it can do. That is a possibility, a long shot, but it probably doesn't go off-world."

"Maybe we are going about this backwards. Maybe Zoran is using one of his Duska skills," Werner suggested. "We know next to nothing about them."

Dario scratched his head and replied, "Hum, good point, but why haven't the other barons used it as well? Baron John and Arcangelo ought to have been able to locate the caverns where we were holding women taken from their worlds. No, it is only Zoran who is doing this. What's so unusual about him?"

"Well, he is an Archmage and a Duska baron," Werner pointed out.

"Hum, well so is Verushka and Nadia but they are not doing this, only him. Do you suppose that it is someone else entirely who is discovering the locations of our secret caverns?" Dario suggested.

"Perhaps you are on to something, Dario. We should exercise far more care in the choosing and security of our new bases. And I know just the perfect thing to do! I don't know why we didn't think of this before! It's brilliant, Dario, brilliant! I know where we can be totally immune to the Duska and their Shadow Walking," Werner exclaimed in a bout of brilliant thinking. "Voss! We take our captured females to Voss. They can never find them there. They don't know where Voss is located. Only we dragons know that!"

"Brilliant, Werner, positively brilliant!" Dario exclaimed grasping instantly the totality of the suggestion and all that it implied. Total security for their breeding program. No more interference whatsoever.

"We must be careful to keep Aldrick off our backs. We take only one woman from a given village and spread them out among the various planets," Werner continued. "We should abduct say a dozen at most each week. We were too greedy before, acting too hastily. Let's be more deliberate this time. Make sure that pretty women are picked; we want handsome young dragons from them," Werner continued. Dario agreed wholly, but wondered if having a pretty human mother yielded handsome baby dragons.

Dario then added, "Perhaps we ought to insert a spy in many of the other baron's cities. Sooner or later, someone will learn key information about their plans."

"Yes we should. However, we ought to work out new defense plans. This Zoran keeps thwarting every move that we make. I thought that we had a sure kill defense at our Maeve cavern complex. Yet they survived nicely while we lost many," Werner complained.

"Well based on what your spy at the High Council reported, those wicked rods are only good for at most stopping ten breath attacks. After that, they are totally vulnerable. With so many Archmages, you can bet our spells will be countered," Dario pointed out the obvious.

"Yes and that also means they can have some immunity to attacks. There is such a spell that does that I'm told. This just means that when we next get attacked, we are going to have to really let them have it so as to use up their rod's capacities and their spell's capacities to protect them. Once that is done, we kill them," Werner growled and banged his huge tail on the stone cavern floor.

After a long pause, Werner began again, "You know, perhaps we could lay a trap, one that might help us figure out how they are finding our secret hideouts so easily."

"Ah, I like that idea, but come to think of it, they have not found a single one of our habitation caves and caverns, only those where we were holding our new breeding stock," Dario pointed out.

"You have a point, Dario. "Had they gotten to our habitation sites, think of all the gold and gems that we would have lost! Hum, I still want to lay a trap though. I just have to know how they always seem to know what we don't want them to know. Let's think on that one, shall we?" Werner asked and the red agreed.

"Well, I can always bring in Old Sniffer, Gustavo. I know that he is five hundred sixty years old, but his nose in unequaled," Dario suggested. All this talk of trying to find out how Zoran knew of their hideouts had set him thinking.

"Who is Old Sniffer?" Werner asked rather annoyed at having his train of thought interrupted.

"Tracker. He can pick up scents and follow them anywhere. Keen nose, best one of our kind. I'm going to have him nose around the sites where we lost to Zoran's group. Can I bring him to those of yours as well? He might just pick up some clues."

"I don't see how, but give it a try." After they broke up, Dario did just that.

Old Sniffer was a huge, ancient red, who spent a lot of his time sleeping these days. "Hey wake up, Sniffer. Got a job for you. We need your sniffer."

"Huh? Really. Oh I suppose so. I was having such pleasant dreams you know. All you young folk are in such a hurry these days. All right, all right, don't get your tail in a tussle. I'm coming. What's the job?" the red asked finally, drawing up to his full height. Dario felt dwarfed by him, but quickly outlined what he wanted done.

Although days had passed, Dario took the old red from raided cavern to raided cavern. "This one belongs to the blacks. You sure they won't mind me sniffing around here?" he asked.

"No, cleared it with Werner. Sniff away." He did. He sniffed around the outsides, the entrances, and the insides. After finishing up with the last one raided by Zoran's party, he asked, "Okay so what can you tell us? What's the old nose saying?"

"Complicated. That's what it's saying."

"Of course it's complicated. If it wasn't, why would I bother you?" Dario replied a bit testily.

"Mostly the same humans at each site, but you already knew that, didn't you?"

"Of course, it's that nasty Baron Zoran and his crew. We need to know how they located these places. Ideas?"

"These things cannot be rushed. Nose picked up all sorts of things." He snorted and blew out a rain of dust particles, many of which landed on Dario who then sneezed too. Gustavo ignored Dario's nasty look and closed his eyes. They were sitting on the peak above the black's cavern most recently raided by Zoran. He closed his eyes and began moving his mind over the accumulated odor memories, correlating them, identifying which ones were at which locations. He discarded those scents which did not appear at all of the sites or at least a majority, unless they were faint. The heavy scents he also passed over, those had obviously been the ones present attacking and killing the dragons. Someone had obviously been scouting out these locations and the scent he wanted was a faint one. If humans behaved as he expected, they would not risk valuable scouts, who could somehow find these locations, on a deadly battle to capture them — far too risky of such valuable resources. Hence, he focused on the faint traces.

After an hour, during which Dario also fell asleep, he stirred. "Hum. I think that you are looking for five humans, they smell strange. I've not smelled their smells before or have I? Wait, yes, yes, I have smelled that before. It was when I was surveying all these new worlds looking for a fine place to settle down. Yes, where was it? Oh I know, the one you call Isi. I didn't like it there — too much open land for me. Yes, your spies come from Isi."

An hour later, Dario revisited Werner with his news. "Ah, so we are looking for spies on Isi. Interesting. Strange humans live there. Nomads for the most part, living in crude hide huts. Ah, makes sense now. Those humans are hunters! Yes, Zoran has sicced a bunch of hunters to sniff out our secret hideouts! Well done, Dario. Yes indeed. Now we are getting somewhere."

"How is this going to help us?"

"Well, we've narrowed it down to one planet out of sixteen. I'll let those who live there spy around some and scout around. Don't suppose your Old Sniffer could track them on Isi and find where they are located, could he?" Werner asked.

"Probably, I'll check and see." He left once more. Unfortunately, it took him two days to rouse Old Sniffer from his deep slumber. The ancient dragon had overdone it physically and was quite tired.

"Well, I suppose that I can sniff them out, but Dario that is a whole planet to search! After all that exercise a couple days ago, I need my sleep."

Dario got Old Sniffer to agree to spend a day sniffing and then sleep as much as he needed before starting out again. He ignored the fact that it might take the old one many weeks to sniff the planet and there was no guarantee that his nose would find the scent that he was looking for anyway. Still, it was all they had at the moment.

Mid-May, Werner and Dario met up again. "Okay we are all set on Voss. We've a perfect location established there for our breeding human women. While it is highly unlikely that Zoran and his group will be able to find us there, we are not going to take any chances. Have you got your list of volunteers ready? We will have twenty dragons on duty at all times. We've tripled the number of traps and alert spells. I've written out specific order of battles to be followed. See here," he pointed out his copy of the orders he'd plastered all over the walls in the new hideout on Voss. "No one does anything until they reach Point A. Then, twenty fire at the same time. Acid comes at them from their left and right, while your flames come at them from the top and front sides. That ought to reduce their rods to useless. Next, they are all to cast their attack spells, designed to reduce or eliminate their defensive spells. Then, they fire a second volley of acid and flames. Finally, they charge and go head to head with the few that will be left alive."

"Of course, that is not all I have planned. I've set my best trap designers to work. If by some strange quirk of fate they get by all twenty guards, the traps lie between them and our female hosts, who will be behind Force Walls once they activate the first trap. Further, if they activate the last trap between them and our host females, my final contingency spells will activate, teleporting our breeding stock to a second location. Zoran will have undergone all that for nothing!" Both dragons laughed heartily. No one could withstand this trap!

"Now it is time to acquire new breeding stock," Werner went on.

"What about all that human food they will need?" asked Dario. It had been such a pain gathering up all that human food.

"Taken care of — plenty is growing on Voss. I've sent out a few to forage and fill up the pantry. Even got one who has some experience cooking for humans. She's going to deal with all their needed cooking. Now one other thing, Dario, we all agree that the breeding stock must not be allowed to retain the use of their arms. With them, despite our spells, they can do many wicked things, killing each other and such. Last time, we used our acid to burn them off, but that then forced us to have to dole out some of our own precious healing droughts. All suffered physical trauma which might have bothered the fetuses. We've seen your breeding stock. Would you care to share just how you can immobilize their arms like that without giving the breeding stock such trauma?"

Dario grinned. "Well, I believe that can be arranged. I will instruct him to show your representatives at the cavern how it is done. Yes, it is clean and effective and the humans cannot undo it, not even the almighty Zoran can." Dario chuckled. At least this action worked well and could not be undone.

"So the plan is starting tomorrow night, we find sixteen pretty and prime human females, one on each of the planets, and take them to Voss. Then, we wait a week and do it again. We follow that pattern, never striking the same section of the planet a second time. Spread the abductions out far and wide. Make it seem random, which it should be. Each month from now on, we will begat another thirty-two of our kind. Think of it, Dario, a year from now, you will have a hundred ninety-two new reds!"

Dario chuckled, he liked the numbers. "But what about the greens? They've lost far too many already. The whites have backed down, so they don't get to participate, right?"

"Right. The greens totally botched it. They had Jing in their hands and lost the whole planet. Idiots. Well, greens are morons anyway. No, we leave those imbeciles out for now. Later on, when we blacks and reds totally dominate these worlds, we can allow the greens to breed a few more of their kind, and the whites will one day come begging to us." The two chuckled and left to issue the orders. It was the 20th of May.

Chapter 22 Strike Force One

Evsen Dragon, the eighteen year old son of Jarka and Bernard, a mage and Duska trained, sheathed his enchanted new broadsword. Already his new enchanted dagger was stowed at his side. Jarka carefully stowed six healing potions in a special bag that would withstand rough handling and submersion. Shrunk down, it fit nicely in his shirt pocket. She fastened its button, making sure it could not accidentally fall out. "You remember everything that I've taught you, Evsen," Jarka fussed over her youngest son. She hated to see him go off with this Strike Force One. It had little chance of succeeding and was more like a suicide mission.

"Mom, I'll be all right. I get to do my part now. Trust me," the embarrassed tall, thin lad whispered, hoping that his fiancé, Katerina, who was nearby waiting to see him off, wouldn't see or hear.

Bernard added, "Message us or whatever it is that you do when off-world. Let us know if you need anything and we'll come running. You'll do fine, I'm sure." Evsen smiled; at least his dad hadn't embarrassed him in front of Katerina.

At last, he was able to move to her side. They whispered to each other and she gave him a parting kiss. Katerina, Marek and Akira's daughter, was also Duska and that meant they would be Mind Linked each night just before Evsen turned in. She would relay anything useful to Zoran — that was the plan the two hatched.

Zoran entered to see him off and shook his hand, "Evsen, you will do well, but just play it safe."

Evsen agreed, focused, and stepped into the Shadows. Destination: Rehor. Place: Roskoy Castle, Eastern Sector. Roskoy Castle was a small garrison fortress where a hundred soldiers were stationed. Their charge was to protect the nearby mines. One whole wing was empty, and Baron Storm donated it to be the home base of the Strike Force One. True, the accommodations were Spartan, but the food and ale flowed freely. There were plenty of women in the town of Praha five miles to the south, if that was one's wont.

With the exceptions of Asami, the water world, and Jing, each planet provided the force with one of their skilled fighters, well-armed of course. Fourteen fighters were supposed to arrive at Roskoy Castle by ten on the morning of May Day. Evsen pictured the map he was given and tried his best to follow it. Unfortunately, he entered Rehor from the wrong side and got turned around. He arrived just at ten, stepping out of the Shadows onto the arrival stone platform. Several others appeared at the same time and he relaxed about possibly being the last to arrive.

A thin woman in leather with a large longbow stepped out beside him. She had long brown hair, her braid falling to her waist. "This must be the place. Kaya Kasa from Isi," she introduced herself. Evsen estimated her age at twenty-four and quickly introduced himself. A strong man and another woman stepped out of the Shadows behind them. The two turned to see the new arrivals.

The woman had long blonde hair also braided and equally long, but she was extremely well-muscled. Evsen knew that she had to be significantly stronger than he! She certainly was anything but shy. "Anwen Alun, from Anwyn," she shook

Evsen's hand. His hand felt like it was in a blacksmith's vice grip. She carried a bastard sword and a short sword. He carried two short swords, emulating Zoran. She was twenty-three. "And you must be our tracker," she said to Kaya.

"Yes, Kaya Kasa, from Isi." Kaya was shy and seldom said much, Evsen quickly discovered.

"Viktor Denek, Gladno. Pleased to meet all of you. This promises to be an exciting and worthwhile adventure. Glad to have an Isi tracker with us." He was twenty-four and Evsen sized him up correctly — he was diplomatic. "I think the others may be waiting on us. Shall we?" he gestured and they entered the castle's side door, where a guard led them to their barracks, explaining that this whole west wing was theirs to use as desired.

Upon entering the bunk room, the four discovered that they were the last to arrive. Ten other men were already stowing their gear, after unshrinking it, naturally. "Well, look what we have here!" a burly strong man bellowed. It was Boris Clav, nephew of the baron. He was a huge man and thirty-eight, their designated leader and quite opinionated and bossy. He was referring to the two women.

"Looks like we are the only women, Kaya," Anwen said, ignoring the loud Boris. "Anwen Alun of Anwyn. Kaya Kasa of Isi, our tracker. Evsen Dragon, Adapazan. Viktor Denek, Gladno." She introduced the four. Evsen was very impressed that she remembered all their names so quickly. He soon learned that she had an eidetic memory just like his mother, Jarka.

"Your leader, Boris Clav. Men, looks like we can have some fun when we are not out fighting." He leered at the two women.

Anwen put her hands on her hips and faced Boris. "I will tell you all this only once. Lay a hand on me or Kaya and I'll cut that part off!"

Boris did not like to be challenged by a woman, no less. With all these male fighters in the room, the two women stuck out prominently. "Whoa, did you hear that men? Ten gold says I can subdue her in two minutes or less. Any takers?"

Viktor spoke up, "Look, we are all supposed to be working together to kill these infernal dragons, not bickering among ourselves. I am sure that she is a competent fighter otherwise her baron would not have sent her." Evsen sensed that he was trying to defuse the testosterone filled atmosphere.

"I say it will take you three minutes, Boris," yelled the second largest man in the room, Bernd Hardt from Dietmar.

"I think that we need a new leader," Anwen challenged him right back. Boris drew his bastard sword. Anwen pulled hers off her back in an easy draw. Everyone else backed away, giving them room. Brute strength headed for agility, strength, and intelligence. Boris took one mighty swing at Anwen. She ducked, parried, spun his sword out of his hands, caught it mid-air, and pointed hers at his throat. "Gee, you didn't last ten seconds, big man." The other men roared with laughter, while Boris fumed and his face crimsoned.

"Come on, she's obviously a great fighter. I'm Tom Leadshire from Terra. This is Vladimir Milla from Valtr. Henri Huges from Gonda."

The others introduced themselves rapidly. Fino Fione came from Cosma. Klaus Stantin was from Gerde. Federico Milano was the Alta fighter. Farrell Ahern came from Maeve and Yada Shem was from Chana. Evsen was the youngest here at eighteen. Most of the others were between twenty-two and twenty-five. Klaus was only twenty-one and Boris was the oldest by nearly ten years at thirty-eight, handpicked by Baron Strom to lead the group and serve the baron's own ends, if possible.

The two women took an adjoining room for their quarters. Once settled in, everyone headed outside to practice and see how well each other fought. "The tracker is going to be a liability, Boris," Bernd complained loudly so all could hear. "I don't want to be the one having to always protect her."

"Don't need protecting," Kaya said softly.

"You don't even carry a sword," he continued putting her down. He'd sized her up as their weakest link.

"Don't need one," Kaya again replied quietly.

"Oh yea? What if someone comes after you like this?" Bernd drew his sword and made a lunge towards her. To everyone's surprise, Kaya moved like a blur, stopping some ten feet from him. As he tried again, she flashed a hundred feet from him, only this time her bow was out and an arrow notched.

"Try that again and I'll put this arrow through your right eye," she said quietly again. Kaya was incredibly swift. Evsen had never seen someone move as rapidly as she. He began to respect her more than the others.

Boris asked, "Well, how far can you shoot accurately? We ought to know that."

It was a bit windy out here on the practice field. She looked at the trees in the distance and replied. "I can put this arrow in yonder wasp nest."

"That's three hundred yards if it's a foot!" Boris retorted. Twang! She let her arrow fly and it pierced the wasp nest. That ended that challenge. The woman could shoot.

"Say Boris, it is wise of us to have a keen archer with us. She can protect all of us while we are in close combat. She's obviously a dead shot. We need her," Viktor said politely and diplomatically, hoping to defuse the air a bit. "Shouldn't we pair up and go a few rounds to see how we all fight? We have to work together if we are going dragon slaying."

By lunch all had a chance to go a few rounds with each other. Evsen was barely able to hold his own with most of the older men. He used every trick that Dana had taught him and he was pleased with the results. He doubted that anyone could take Anwen, though. She was just too skilled and quick for the men. Kaya merely stood and watched the others with their swordplay.

After lunch, Chan, Wen, and Dana arrived. Per the High Council's orders, they were to share all of their experience in dragon hunting and slaying with the group. After all, these two women had more "dragon kills" than any other person in the Federation at this time. Admittedly, most of theirs were the weaker greens, but they were nonetheless deadly. Chan's missing hand was testimony to that.

During the ensuing days, Viktor managed to obtain a concession from Boris. The fighter from whichever planet they were on would be the group's temporary leader. Obviously, that person knew their own planet far better than the others. Boris grumbled about that, but could see the logic and wisdom behind it. He'd seldom been off-world and then only to Dietmar.

By June, Boris decided they'd done enough training and it was time to "go kill dragons!" At once the how raised its head. Boris decided that they should ride the countryside looking for a dragon to slay. They did so for a week without any success. True, occasionally, they spotted one flying high in the sky, but it was miles upon miles of rugged terrain away from them. Secretly, Boris was trying to lead them deep into the mountains where Baron Storm thought that the leader of the reds had a cavern home. He wanted that red eliminated. After a fruitless week, most were complaining that this was totally useless.

When asked, Evsen explained, "Well, Chan and Wen always began their hunt at the sight where the dragons attacked their people. They tracked it down and killed it."

"But we don't know about any dragon attacks," Boris protested. "We know they are up there somewhere." He pointed into the nearly impassable high peaks, a few of which still had snow packs on them.

For days, the men argued about how to proceed and Evsen was content to sit back and relax and allow them to waste time. Finally in utter frustration, Boris asked, "Kaya, you are our tracker. What would you suggest?"

"I'm not on Isi."

"Well, no matter, what would you suggest?" Boris insisted.

"You want to kill red?"

"Yes, yes!" he fumed. "Find me a damn red!"

"Okay. Kaya will find you one." She either teleported or stepped into the Shadows, Evsen couldn't tell. It happened too fast. Several hours later, Kaya returned. "Join hands. Kaya lead you to red." Suddenly everyone got excited! At last they could fight a dragon! Evsen felt uneasy about this, but joined the circle. Kaya was a Duska, he noted at once. She was Shadow Walking them all high into the far distant, uninhabited mountains. She deposited them at a small tarn. Blue-grey ice from a permanent valley glacier contrasted with the orange-red granite of the mountainside. Boulders lay everywhere, like some giant's play toys, long overdue to be picked up. "Up there in the side of the cliff. Dragon den. At least one red lives there."

"Okay, we charge into the entrance and slay this beast!" Boris ordered. Some Shadow Walked, some teleported. All but Kaya arrived at the large cavern's stony entrance. Swords drawn, Boris led the charge into the dragon's den. Valiant, Evsen thought, but foolish. He hung back, watching the party's rear as ordered.

Evsen's Duska senses triggered, eminent danger! "Intruders! Intruders! Thieves!" a loud, disembodied voice screamed as Boris ran past an Alarm spell, triggering it. So much for surprise, Evsen thought. The dozen continued their forward charge, while Evsen warily looked for a dragon coming at their rear or for additional traps. Suddenly, his senses screamed and he dove for the floor. Just in time, a huge wall of searing flames came rushing at him. He heard screams from those ahead of him. The flames vanished almost as suddenly as they came, typical of a red's breath, he thought, and he picked himself up. Anwen came running back towards him. She was untouched, he noted. Out of the smoke he saw others running.

"Retreat! Get the hell out of here now!" Anwen yelled at him. He didn't wait for further instructions and teleported back to where Kaya was waiting. She had an arrow notched and was aiming upwards.

"Silly men," she said softly, as he landed beside her, his sword still drawn. One by one the others appeared nearby. Several men were badly burned, some limping, dragging their swords behind them.

"Where's Boris?" Anwen called out.

"Took it full in his face! Dead most likely," Bernd yelled, visibly shaken to his roots.

Just then, the dragon soared down from on high. His huge wings fully extended, sweeping down for the kill. "Damn, evacuate, retreat!" Bernd yelled.

Hastily, the fighters began to chant or Shadow Walk. Evsen saw that the dragon would likely get off one more blast before they could fully get away. Just then, he heard the twang of Kaya's bow. He saw the arrow fly true and to his amazement, it struck the dragon in its chest. The huge beast let out a hideous bellow, veering away just enough to allow them to retreat back to Roskoy Castle and the landing platform.

"Thanks, Kaya!" Evsen complimented her as she was the last to arrive.

"Well done, Kaya!" Anwen added. Hastily, the men also thanked her, and they raced inside to tend to their wounded, that is, burned men. All of the fighters had been given some healing potions by their barons and many were quickly consumed. A half hour later, the intense burn pains were gone and the men began cleaning up. Half threw their old outfits away, destroyed by the dragon's fire.

Over dinner, Anwen said, "Well, that didn't go so well, did it? I think that we need better leadership."

"And better plans," added Viktor. "Look, we can't just go charging into a dragon's den. Fighting dragons is vastly different than fighting men."

"That was foolhardy, I admit it," Fino put in. "We best work out some vastly better ways or we will all be toast soon."

"We didn't check for traps the instant we arrived," Evsen spoke up. "That ought to have been the second thing that we did."

Many nodded, but Anwen asked, "So what was the first thing that we should have done, oh young one?" She taunted him about his age.

"We should have gone invisible and stayed mostly in the Shadows and gone inside to see what we were facing, the layout of the cavern, where the dragon was located, how many were in there and so on. Then, we appear at the entrance and check for traps, disarming the ones we find," Evsen replied.

"I like the young one. He is smarter than he looks," Anwen praised Evsen. Others began to change their opinion of the youngster.

Uncharacteristically, Kaya spoke up, "He is right. That is what we should have done, not charge in there and get killed. I don't have a death wish. I have nothing to prove to anyone."

"Why didn't you do all that?" Bernd challenged her.

"Boris did not ask that. He told me to find him a red and I did what I was ordered to do. He was the boss. Hope next boss is smarter." Bernd flushed.

"Well, one thing is for sure, we need a new leader. Any takers?" Viktor asked. Several grumbled.

"You should ask Evsen to lead. He's fought dragons before with Zoran," Kaya spoke up. She'd reached a decision. It was time for a real leader to step forward, one that would not get them all killed.

All eyes turned to him. "Why didn't you say something about that?" Viktor asked.

"If I had, would any of you listened? I am only eighteen and Boris was a score older than me."

"Touché. Point taken, Evsen. You're right; we would not have," Viktor said diplomatically. "So tell us about your dragon fights."

The evening passed rapidly as he retold his few encounters helping Zoran rescue the kidnaped women. After that, he was unanimously appointed the new leader of Strike Force One.

The next day, everyone agreed that they needed to return and get revenge for the slaying of Boris. Evsen had everyone out watching the entrance, Invisibility spells in full force. After a day of reconnoitering, they discovered that only one dragon lived in the cavern. "Dragons leave to feed at least once a week. Here's what we do. We wait and watch. When it leaves to go feed on an antelope, we enter its cavern, disarm its protections, and prepare a surprise attack when it returns. We must be spread out widely so that its fiery breath can only get one or two of us at the same time. The others use the time that it is blasting out its fire to close to close quarters combat. Then, we have a chance. Not a good one, mind you, but we have a chance. If the dragon's breath comes your way, do everything in your power to get out of harm's way, even teleporting or Shadow Walking away. Stay alive, that is your first order. Stay alive to return to the fight."

Four long boring days later, the red finally left to hunt for food. Evsen stepped out of the Shadows and onto the entrance that he'd left in such a hurry before. Now he carefully checked for traps as did the other Duskas behind him. They all spotted the Alarm Warning spell and deactivated it. A bit further inside, they disarmed an Explosive Symbol, which would have detonated had they passed it. Even further inside, Evsen found a trip wire which he deactivated, pointing out that, if triggered, it would have dropped a one ton slab of granite on top of them. At this point, everyone was convinced they had their leader chosen well this time. No further traps were found. Now they laid theirs for the unsuspecting dragon, but not before they found the charred remains of Boris. Bernd collected the bones and put them respectfully into a small sack.

Several hours later, the red returned, carrying the carcass of an antelope. It walked into the long entrance way where it had laid all its traps. Although it sniffed the air noting something was amiss, by then it was too late. Their trap sprang. Several cast Bolts of Lightning at its head. The casters were standing far back from the dragon, but became visible the moment that they attacked it. While Evsen didn't think that they would be able to have their spells succeed, only the Archmages stood much of a chance, the casters' job was to draw the dragon's attention to them, most likely getting it to breath a blast of fire at them. What the dragon didn't know was that all of the others were standing Invisible against the sides of the entrance. The moment that the dragon responded to the two spell casters in front of him, they were to close and attack it with their swords. Evsen made sure that the two casters were Duska, giving them a good chance in this situation to get out of the way of the dragon's fire. He was one of them, Viktor, the other.

The dragon reacted as expected, though Viktor's spell somehow detonated, harming the red a little. It shot a fierce blast of fire at the two Duska, who dove out of the way, landing and rolling as fast as they could, narrowly avoiding the flames by mere inches. When they got to their feet, the sword hacking was already in progress. Bodies were thrown right and left, but the eleven continued to land deadly blows. Dragon blood covered the floor, making footing slippery. At last with a hideous groan, the dragon succumbed to the dozens upon dozens of sword wounds to its chest, sides, legs, and neck.

Six of the eleven close quarters fighters had broken bones. Several had very nasty bite wounds and some had claw puncture wounds as well. Only Anwen was unwounded of that group. Quickly, healing potions were doled out and the wounded stabilize. Kaya then joined them and she and Evsen made a search of the lair.

"We've hit the jackpot. Loot, plenty of dragon treasure," Evsen called out. An hour later, the few unwounded got the wounded back to base along with bags of gold and gems. By suppertime, the wounded were on the road to recovery, though it took most of their healing potions to make that happen.

The next day, they sorted out their treasure and divided it up equally. Evsen now had the equivalent of close to thirty thousand gold! He was pleased but now it was time to review what they had done.

"Okay, we've gotten our first dragon and you all know just how challenging and dangerous this is going to be. We've used up our entire supply of healing potions on just this one dragon. Nearly all of us got wounded slaying a solitary one, even when we took it by complete surprise *and* on our own terms. Think how it is going to be when we have to take it on *its* terms," Evsen pointed out. All were quite sober now and listened to their proven leader.

"One thing is clear to me now. We are each going to need dozens of healing potions per dragon attack. We'll need to get that worked out with our sponsors before we try this again." They agreed fully and sent word of their action and needs. Over a week passed before another batch of potions arrived. Evsen saw that although they might be successful, at the very best, they might tackle one dragon every couple of weeks, hardly the offensive that the barons had in mind when they setup this Strike Force One. Zoran, on the other hand, was quite pleased with the initial results.

Chapter 23 Detection and Action

Word of the dragon raids spread like wildfire across many worlds, including Adapazan. By late June, even the smallest of villages had heard about the destruction of Petr Falls. Zoran had the various warlords relay the facts but wild rumors still carried weight in the smaller villages. Some said that the dragons were breeding with young women. Some said that the dragons were stealing away little children, though many thought that was just a way to get the children to obey their parents. Some said that their baron rescued some of the women, but they were horribly disfigured, even blinded or worse. So the rumors went.

Zoran had a few reports coming in from his Archmages of the north and knew how wild these rumors were becoming. "Aren't you going to try to set them straight?" asked Jarka. "Most are half-truths or outright lies."

"No, Jarka. I've come to realize that there is no way at all that I can have mage watchers in every town and village on Adapazan, not even remotely. We need an early warning system. If the villagers believe that dragons are raiding and stealing women and children, so much the better, because they will report on missing women, I hope. In that way, we may become alerted to kidnap victims, if the dragons wise up and snatch one here and there. Instead of wiping out a whole village which brings instant attention, a snatch here and there could well go unnoticed. I am hoping these wild rumors will aid us. If not, well I can always issue a document outlining the true facts and get it to all towns and villages."

"Sneaky, baron, sneaky," she teased him. Jarka liked his motives now.

What Zoran had not yet realized is that from these distant provinces, there is a long delay in communications in reaching him in Brn or one of the other two barons. Around the end of July, he began receiving messages stating that a woman was abducted or at least gone missing from this village or that one. Many of these had follow up messages stating that it was all a mix-up or mistake. The woman had gone to care for a sick relative or such. However, at the end of July, he had five messages that remained mysterious. Specifically, he stared at the five messages he'd received. Acedia of Dobro, Tehov Province was missing since late May. Anezka of Sobin Creek, Kin Provence, Kamila of Kusor, Radim Province, Katerine of Velen, Zavou Province, and Reina of Dratsy, Orlova Province were missing. As he reread the documents, he noted a disturbing similarity. The women had apparently disappeared in the middle of the night, right from their own homes. The reporting mage, Archmage, or baron verified the story before sending it along to him. It fit the pattern of pervious dragon abductions and he decided to take some action.

Sitting in his study, he focused his mind and reached out through the Shadows in search of Honani. At long last, he made contact. *Honani? Zoran here. Say, I believe that we have had five women from various locations on Adapazan abducted by dragons during the last ten weeks. Can you see if you can locate them for us?*

Yes, of course. We thought that all was going to be quiet now. Oh well, they are dragons. I'll get back to you if we can locate them. Zoran relaxed. There was nothing much more that he could do. Adapazan was huge, no matter how hard that he wanted to protect everyone, there was just no way to do that. He toyed with the idea of installing night watchmen in every village and town, but that could easily be overcome. Dragons possessed spells, a simple beginning level Sleep spell and there go the night watchmen. No sense in getting the populace frightened any more than they already were.

Out on the rolling grasslands of Isi, three hide domes marked the current homes of Honani and his friends and family members. "Well, Zoran thinks more women have been abducted," he announced.

"Does he want us to find them again?" asked Kachina.

He smiled, "Right as always. Think you can do it?"

She shrugged and agreed to see what she could do that evening. After the children were tucked in, she sat before their campfire and relaxed. She focused her mind and began to work her divination magic. She flowed out into the Shadows, searching for traces of terror or panic and found numerous traces, though some were quite faded. Kachina could not date them, but knew that the faded ones were older.

It was different this time, she observed, much more difficult and confusing. Before, she picked up the combined terror from a whole group of women who were being transported from their homes by the abducting dragons. Easy. This time, it was only a single woman here and there. Just as she was about to give up, she realized that if she took them all together, they would become a group, just as before! One by one, she began to follow them and was rewarded with the discovery that they all joined together in one group somewhere over Isi, of all places!

Her joy in that discovery quickly faded. Again the group had moved, now as a group off into the Shadows. Undaunted, she attempted to follow them as she had done before, expecting them to arrive on one of the other worlds. Suddenly, she stopped! Now she was frightened. She'd reached the very edge of the known Shadows. There were no more known worlds beyond this point! Hastily, she returned to her body beside the late evening fires, which had now died down to undulating red coals.

"Any luck?" Honani asked. Askook and Cheveyo watched her closely as well. Her face had shown a variety of expressions during the last few hours.

"Most strange. Most. Scary too, I'm afraid that I am at a loss. Yes, I found isolated traces of frightened, terror filled women in the Shadows, but each one was coming from a different world. I followed them and they all joined up right here on Isi!"

"Where?"

"On the High Plains before the foothills, the boulder field area. What is strange, Honani, is that after that, they all then traveled together as a group, I think."

"Well, that's good. Probably picked up a woman from various worlds and brought them together and then took them to their secret cavern," Honani speculated.

"That's what I thought."

"So which planet do we search?"

"That's just it. They left all known Shadows. I have no idea where they went, but it is not any of our sixteen planets!"

"Incredible. That's a setback. Well, let's sleep on it. Maybe an idea will come."

The next day, Honani decided that the best thing to do was to go check out the boulder field. Perhaps there they would find some traces of the women or some clues. The five took off, leaving Kachina watching over the three family's children.

Within a few minutes, they hovered over the High Plains and the boulder field, famous for its gigantic sized boulders that covered ten square miles. They set down and began looking for clues on the ground. After some time, they spotted dragon dung in quantity. "Hey, over here. I found a woman's shoe!" Askook called out. Several other items were located in the same general area.

"This must be their staging area," Honani concluded. "We might not have found the women, but this is likely where they all met up and then took off together as a group. It's something to go on anyway."

"Think we'll get a reward for this discovery?" asked Cheveyo.

Suddenly, their Duska senses tingled. "Danger!" Honani called out, though he need not have. The other four already felt the same warning. "Up there! A huge Red Dragon — circling us!"

Awinita exclaimed, "Let's get out of here fast! Shadow walk back to the huts!" The five stepped into the Shadows, safely out of the reach of the enormous red. They stepped back onto the plains of Isi near their hide homes. Their children ran up to them, welcoming them back, as Kachina walked slowly to greet them.

"Found the spot. It was definitely the rendezvous location. We found discarded women's apparel, shoes and the like," Honani reported.

"Yes, and the largest red that we've ever seen also spotted us. We got out fast," Awinita exclaimed rather excitedly.

Old Sniffer doggedly kept at it, making detailed search patterns over the plains of Isi, just as Dario had asked of him. It had been weeks now, well days actually, he needed to sleep most of a week after flying about all day. This day, he flew over the boulder field area and spotted five small humans below. Just as he was about to move on, he caught a faint whiff of their odor and his nose did not fail him. "Hum, that's them! Ah ha." He fired off a Message spell to Dario and was surprised at his response.

They are over the boulder field! My god, they've found our meeting place! Don't lose them! Am sending a flock of reds to intercept them! Surprised at the request, he began spiraling down after them. One by one, they Shadow Walked away, but now Old Sniffer had really acquired their scent, quite strongly. As twenty reds appeared in the sky, he flew up to meet them.

"Where are they?" asked Dario.

"Shadow Walked as soon as they saw me circling, but now I have their scent. Follow me." He slipped into the Shadows after them, his nose guiding him unerringly through the nothingness of the Shadows. Dario and the reds followed right behind him. For once, Old Sniffer really felt alive again. He was on the hunt. Oh how he used to love the hunt! Old memories came back to him, fun times, those days of the hunts. At last, he followed the trail out of the Shadows and back onto the rolling grasslands of the plains of Isi. Below him, he saw three domed huts and a number of people. The scents he was following led straight down to them. One by one Dario and the reds appeared from the shadows and he pointed out the group.

"My god! The red has somehow followed us here! Quick! Children, run to your parents. We have to — my god! Look at all those reds!" Honani screamed. He grabbed his children and Awinita, while Askook and Donoma rounded up theirs and Cheveyo and Kachina grabbed a hold of their three children. Just as the horde of reds swooped down to fry them all, Honani stepped them all into the Shadows and then out again, five hundred miles further north. They relaxed and tried to make sense of what had just happened. Honani only had time to ask a question when that huge dragon also stepped out of the Shadows a thousand feet from them. He didn't wait to see if the horde followed the enormous red. He stepped them into the Shadows once more, this time arriving a thousand miles to the south.

"This is unbelievable!" Awinita exclaimed as they landed on the empty grasslands with a large patch of pines not far away. "God! Here it comes again! How can it follow us?" Honani reacted and stepped them all back into the Shadows again. This time, he kept them all there for a time, before appearing five hundred miles further east.

No one said a word. All eyes stared at the skies around them. "Mommy, there it is again. Make it go away," Kachina's littlest daughter exclaimed, frightened by the dragons coming after them.

"This is ridiculous!" Honani yelled and stepped them all into the Shadows once more. This time, he took them off-world, arriving out in the middle of the deserts of Chana. "Let's see them find us on Chana. Kids, this is the desert planet of Chana." He was about to tell them a bit more about this strange land devoid of grasses when Awinita pointed out the huge red had again appeared above them!

"This cannot be happening!" Honani protested, but again quickly stepped them all back into the Shadows. This time he took them to the outskirts of Puerto on the hilly planet of Alta, close to the baron's fortress and Circle of Ascension. Within a minute the giant red appeared, followed shortly by the horde of smaller reds!

"What are we going to do?" his wife, Awinita cried out, becoming terrified. No matter where they went, these dragons were relentless in their pursuit! Honani stepped them again into the safety of the Shadows. He paused and tried to think. Where could they possibly go and yet be safe?

Zoran! Help! We have a large band of reds after us! They are following us everywhere we go through the Shadows even! This cannot be, but I swear it's true! Can you help us, please?

Zoran was more than a little startled by the sudden Mind Link and message from Honani. *I am lowering my protections. Land on my Circle of Ascension — the sky blue circle. We'll take it from there.* He sent frantic Messages to his crew and then headed for the roof of his fortress, using a Mystical Door. Verushka appeared beside him, and then one by one all of the others in his usual fighter group joined him. Karel rushed about handing out his precious rods, hoping they still had time. Suddenly, the largest red that they had ever seen appeared in the skies over Brn. Townsfolk began screaming and dashing into any available building. Chaos hit the streets. Then twenty more reds suddenly appeared close to the ancient red dragon. All circled, but stayed well out of spell range.

"Come on. I'm ready to kill you!" Archmage Karel screamed angrily up at them, as if that would somehow provoke them to attack.

"Well, well, well. Old Sniffer, you have certainly earned your pay this time!" Dario exclaimed as he observe Zoran and the many Archmages just waiting for the reds to get too close.

"Pay? What pay?" he asked.

"I'll bring it by this evening. You can head home now. We have learned what we needed to know. Thank you, Old Sniffer! Thank you. Okay, home everyone."

"Hey, come back here and fight!" Karel yelled as the dragons vanished as suddenly as they had appeared.

"What was that all about?" asked Verushka, greatly relieved that the certain battle had been avoided.

"I am not sure but they were chasing Honani. Karel, keep watch for a while up here. Everyone, thanks for the fast response. I'll see if I can figure out what the devil is going on here." He opened his Mystical Door and stepped out far below ground near his Circle of Ascension. Honani was explaining all about the Circles and what a great honor it was for them to be standing on Baron Zoran Vladislov's Circle.

Zoran noticed that the children and women looked half scared out of their wits. Something had been going on. "Okay, we've chased the reds off. Wow, that one was huge. Positively the largest red that I've ever seen, almost the size of a gold. Welcome one and all to Brn and the Circle of the Free Peoples of Adapazan. If you will follow me, let's get some refreshments. Cookies kids?"

A few minutes later, the nine children were merrily eating cookies and milk, their fright now forgotten. Honani and the others explained in great detail they had discovered on the boulder field and then the huge red. After his detailed explanation, he asked, "Zoran, I swear that red was after us like a blood hound dog tracks a fox!" The others concurred with his observation.

"Well, this is certainly a new and startling discovery about the reds. I don't think anyone knew that they have such a fantastic sense of smell that they can even follow you through the Shadows. That is most disturbing and distressing," Zoran stated, thinking hard.

He continued, "I don't think that it will be safe for you to return to Isi. They are on to you and could come after you at any time, even when you are sleeping. That is, if this is some kind of blood hound dragon."

"What are we going to do?" asked Awinita.

"That's the easiest question I've had all day. Simple, we'll go back and get your things and you can stay here in my fortress for the time being until it is safe to return to Isi. After all, I got you into this mess by asking you to help find our missing women. It is the very least that I can do for you."

After accepting their profuse thank you's, he, Honani, Askook, and Cheveyo headed off to retrieve their possessions. "I guessed that this is what we'd find," Honani said sadly as they arrived to find their huts smoldering ruins. After casting a few Extinguish and Chill spells, the men salvaged what they could, including all their gems.

"Don't worry. I'll see that everything gets replaced. The kids will need new toys — all on me. I can't thank you enough for what you have done and the sacrifices made by you and your families. We'd best get back in case the reds show up again," Zoran volunteered.

Once safe inside the fortress, he had Bernard take over for him. Bernard then got the three families settled, gave them a tour of Brn, and set them up an open account so that they could purchase what they now needed, especially things for their children.

Meantime, Zoran summoned his whole group together, filling up his private study. Quickly, he outlined the basic new fact. Yes, their women were being abducted but were being taken to some other world beyond the Federation. Further, he related the fact that apparently the reds could follow the scent of someone through the Shadows. This they all found most disturbing. After the short meeting, Zoran then Mind Linked to his key allied barons, joining Stefan, Leo, John, Arcangelo, and Gaspard of Gonda with him. Once more he outlined the new discoveries: that the dragons were still abducting women, but following a different pattern. All were highly disturbed to learn that the women were all brought to a staging area on Isi and then taken to some unknown world beyond the Federation. They were also extremely worried about the latest development that the reds could follow someone's scent through the Shadows.

I urge you all to do what you can to find out if women are or have gone missing on your planets. Keep me posted. Somehow, someway, we must find a way to rescue them, though it may be too late for some. All promised to do so.

That evening, Zdenka invited Honani and his group to dine with them all in the Great Hall. Each evening all of her students joined Zoran and his group in the Great Hall. With so many needing assistance, everyone found this far more practical. Thus, Honani and his group finally met some of the women that they helped save. They were appalled at the sheer number of armless women and the six who were blind. Kachina's heart went out to these women, some of whom she now recognized as the ones whose terror she had followed to locate the caverns in which they were being held.

After the meal, the students returned to their respective towers and rooms. Zoran felt this was as good a time as any to make key inquires and he began chatting with Honani and his people. "You know, I have wanted to ask you for some time now how it is that you folks have been able to locate our captive women? It is all right if you do not wish to divulge that information. It's just that I am curious."

"It is my doing," Kachina volunteered. Cheveyo tried to stop her as did Honani. "It's okay guys. We have no need to keep it a secret from him. He's saved us from the dragons." They frowned, but she looked at Zoran. "It is my doing. I can sense the women's terror while they were in the Shadows and can follow those energy lines which lead to where they are at on some planet in the Federation." She went on to explain it in greater detail and Zoran listened quite fascinated. He was getting some key information that he needed.

When she finished, Honani spoke up, "You can see why we keep this a secret. She is the only person in the Federation that can do such divinations. If word got out about her abilities, not only would everyone come begging her for help, but ruthless barons would try to force her to do their bidding as well. We have to protect her."

"I give you my word that I will keep this to my most trusted staff and not tell the other barons. Your secret is safe with us. You have my word on that. I hope that you will not find life too offensive here in such a large town." They thanked him and chatted about how to adjust to life in a big city, for to them Brn was just that. The children, however, loved it.

A week passed before he heard more unwelcome news. Here on Adapazan, a young woman named Zusa had just gone missing from Vole in neighboring Ves Province. The warlord's mage notified him two days after her mysterious nighttime disappearance. Not long after that, the barons began reporting that they too had uncovered women missing from seemingly random locations throughout their planets. He then asked them to relay all this news to the Neutral Barons for him. He figured that it might be taken more seriously by those barons if the news didn't come from him. In a way, he was right.

That night, he had Kachina make another of her divination scans for these new women. She quickly discovered that again there were sixteen taken and the rendezvous was at the same boulder field on Isi. "They probably laid a trap there, just in case we went there to intercept them," Zoran concluded. He had no idea just how right he was. Sixty dragons had lain in wait all that night, hoping that Zoran would show up and try to retake the women.

Chapter 24 The Strange Case of Adrianna Whitehall

Adrianna Whitehall just turned twenty. She had long raven hair, just like her mother, and charming blue eyes. She was extremely pretty and highly sought after by the young men of Westfarthington, Terra. Her unmarried mother owned the only inn in Westfarthington, a small farming village some hundred miles from the capital of Terra and its primary Circle of Ascension. She had never known who her father was, though she begged and pleaded with her mother on many occasions. All her mother would ever say about this mysterious man was that he had given her this inn and livelihood and that Adrianna should be thankful for even that much.

Well, she wasn't. True, she helped her mother run the inn ever since she could walk or so she claimed to the boys who would listen to her. Still, she often wondered just who her father had been. Why had he not married her mom? Why had he abandoned them? Perhaps he didn't abandon us, she thought, since mom says that he gave her this inn. We do all right with it. Still. . .

Adrianna felt different somehow. During her childhood, she believed this was because, unlike the other children of Westfarthington, she had no father, no dad. When she turned thirteen and entered womanhood officially, all that changed. Things changed. At night, she began to see strange things, things that were not there, unreal things, shadowy images. At times, she felt as if she could somehow reach out and touch these illusory images, if images they were. She had no other name for them and dare not talk about such things, not in conservative Westfarthington! She'd be labeled a crazy teen. Besides, such would surely ruin her mother's business.

Adrianna tried to not see these things, but that never worked. Then, she buried herself in work and rather forgot about the strange visions. Last year, even that ceased to work. Now she was seeing things again — this time more clearly. She imagined there was another universe calling out to her, for that might explain it. She asked her mother if there was such a thing and that idea was promptly dispelled. Still as she grew older, it seemed more and more real to her, like she ought to be able to reach out and touch it or feel it or go to it, somehow. It was because of this that she rejected all of the many suitors that begged for her hand or a date at least. How could she deal with boys when this so demanded her attention all the time? Maybe she was insane or crazy after all, she concluded. That thought was of no comfort to her either.

On the 2nd of August, she closed up the pub portion of the inn for her mother as she always had done since turning eighteen. She counted out the day's receipts and put them into the safe. She wiped down all the tables, checked the front doors: locked as they ought to be. Finally, she retired for the night, letting her hair down from its usual attractive bun. She brushed out her long raven locks and admired her beauty in her hand mirror. "If only I could stop seeing these things," she muttered to herself. She blew out her lantern and crawled into bed. Tomorrow she'd have to scrub the pub's floor. Able had puked on it again tonight. If only he'd learn not to drink so much, she thought as she drifted into sleep.

Six reds came out of the Shadows over Westfarthington, hovering in the air above the small village. Seeing no one about, they flew over to the large inn, the largest building that wasn't a granary. They had sent in a spy last week and he'd located a perfect host. The six morphed into human forms and walked up to the inn. One chanted briefly and the door unlocked. The six slipped quietly inside, shutting the door behind them. Based on the spy's data, one headed to the back room and chanted, ensuring the older woman would not awaken.

Three others headed up the stairs, while two stood guard, just in case. Werner was most insistent that no one knew that they were here. Secrecy, secrecy, secrecy, he'd drilled into their heads. One of the three cast another spell and a zone of complete silence followed the three as they climbed the stairs and opened the bedroom door. Another cast his spell and the young woman fell into a deep sleep and was not aware of the man picking up her body out of her bed. She had on only her summer nightgown. The early August days were hot, reaching ninety at least.

Again, the zone of silence followed the three as they descended the stairs, rejoining the other three. After a quick check, one opened the door. All stepped outside, while one cast another spell and the door locked itself. Satisfied, the six morphed back into their true black forms. One gently picked up the young woman in its claws, flapped its huge wings, and became airborne.

Adrianna began to have a most pleasant dream. She was somehow floating high in the sky above Westfarthington. She could see the homes getting smaller and smaller, as if she was rising up somehow. She felt the cool late night breeze flapping against her gown. However, she felt a gripping pressure around her and tried to move to reduce it. Suddenly she was fully awake! She was flying! She saw that she was in the claws of a dark dragon that was flying higher and higher into the nighttime sky. Five other dark forms were flying close at hand. Adrianna screamed as loudly as she could! Over and over she shrieked, but the dragons totally ignored her. Stark, utter terror filled her and she screamed even harder.

Then it happened. She began to see the strange things again. Suddenly, she felt herself moving straight into what she had always thought were mere images! Although she didn't know it, she'd just entered the Shadows. Adrianna became disoriented. Which way was up? Everything was grey-black shadows and yet she felt like she was still somehow moving. Her terror crescendoed and she sent out mental screams in all directions.

Zoran awoke in a cold sweat! "What's the matter dear?" Zdenka's sleepy alto voice broke the midnight stillness of their bedroom.

"Bad dream or something. It felt like a woman screaming from somewhere in the Shadows or something. I kind of woke up and it all drifted into mush. Sorry to wake you. Best get some sleep." He rolled over and she did too. Soon, he was asleep once more.

Adrianna's terror only grew, but just as suddenly land appeared, real land, though filled with enormous boulders, light grey in the silver moon light. Adrianna screamed once more! More dragons, lots of them. She heard other women screaming and twisted about to peek in their direction. She saw other women being clutched in the great claws of dark dragons, all circling around this strange land of monster-sized boulders. She screamed even louder, adding her voice to the many others about her.

It did no good, of course. After a time, the whole group of dragons once more stepped into the Shadows. Again, Adrianna's terror grew far worse. She was moving into those awful images that she'd seen all her life. She screamed and screamed.

It was around two in the morning. Zoran again awoke, terrified and flying uncontrollably through the Shadows! Sweat poured down his chest. "Bad dream again?" Zdenka's voice sounded a bit annoyed, this being the second time that she was awakened.

"Yes, bad dream. I haven't had such nightmares since I was initiated into Shadow Walking when I was a teen. Ah well. Back to sleep. Sorry dear."

The dreams didn't go away, but he managed to ignore them and fall asleep once more.

Daylight! The dragon stepped out of the crazy, insane images into daylight! Adrianna felt slightly better. At least she could see a little. Where was this place? What did these dragons want with her? Hers was a black one, she saw, but there were red ones flying alongside too. A dark hole appeared in the side of a russet colored cliff. Soon the dragons flew inside, landing carefully, avoiding harming their captives. By now, Adrianna had stopped screaming. Her throat hurt and her mouth was parched.

Her dragon finally let her go but pushed her back against the wall. She looked around and saw a lot more young women like herself, all were shivering and scared. Adrianna looked out at the huge dragons staring at them. She assumed that her life had ended. They were probably going to eat her soon, she guessed, and her fear left her as she accepted her certain death. She stared back at these enormous beasts.

One began chanting and then touched the woman next to her. The woman screamed and her hands went up to her eyes. "I can't see!" she screamed over and over. Adrianna was still trying to understand what had just happened to that woman when the same dragon touched her. Suddenly, everything went black, blacker than the nighttime, where starlight turned things into ghastly shapes. No, this was a total, complete blackness. She screamed as well, rubbing her eyes with her hands. Vaguely, she heard the other women screaming.

Then came a sort of sharp, stabbing pains in her left shoulder. She instinctively tried to rub it with her right hand. Stabbing pains came into her right shoulder too. Then another wave of panic flooded over her. Adrianna could not move either arm. A voice said, "Can you feel this?" Was that her own voice saying no? She couldn't feel either arm or her hands. She tried and tried to move them to rub her blind eyes, but nothing happened, nothing, as if she no longer even had her pretty arms and hands. Terror filled her and she screamed once more. Worse, the blackness and the shadow images now seemed to blur. What is real? What is not? She could no longer tell. She heard other chanting and voices talking. What are they saying? She tried to listen and was even more horrified. She could not feel the dragon touching her as it cast its Charm Person spell on her. Thus she didn't know that it had happened nor did she know that it had failed to work on her.

"There now, my pretty. You will do as we say and you will be fine. Soon we will breed with you and then you will become pregnant with a baby black dragon. You will grow ravenously hungry, but if you do as we say, we will feed you all that you desire. Of course, we will release you when you give birth to our baby dragon. Do you understand? Nod your head if you do?"

Adrianna didn't know if she was being talked to or not, so nodded anyway. Anything. Why can't I see? Why can't I move my arms or hands? Pregnant? Baby dragons? How can this be? Wild ideas flashed through her mind. Then, she recalled two men chatting over ales in the pub. They were talking about all these women who were abducted by the dragons. "When they give birth, the baby dragon eats its way out of her womb and then dines on the dying mother's blood and internal organs. Leastwise, that's what I've heard," the man said.

"Am I going to die?" her voice said. Did I say that? She wondered. Reality and unreality merged.

"Of course, but you will have a beautiful baby black to carry on your legacy for hundreds of years," a sympathetic voice said. "Now drink this." Something was touching her lips. Liquid. Tasted funny, but Adrianna drank, doing as she was told, though she continued to try to move her arms and hands. If only she could get them to work, maybe she could feel her way out of this chamber and somehow escape. Unconsciousness overcame her.

When she awoke, she felt violated and knew that she had been raped while she was unconscious. Yesterday? Was it only yesterday that she would have been totally crushed if she had been raped? She was reeling, dizzy, unable to tell which way was up. She heard only silence and she dared not move or scream for fear of falling — or was she falling and couldn't see that she was? Instead, she continued to try to get her arms to move — all her life she depended upon them. If they would just move, maybe she could grab on to something. Nothing, nothing at all, as if her arms and hands were never there. Just like her eyes. Total darkness. No, there were those strange grey shapes or images or whatevers there. Again, she freaked out in utter panic, screaming for help. She had no idea that she was halfway into the Shadows when she was screaming and thus her sounds were not heard inside the cavern. All the women appeared relatively calm to the dragon woman who was in charge of them at the moment.

Zoran was eating breakfast when he felt the utter panic of the Shadows swelling over himself. He nearly upchucked his breakfast. However, no one noticed him and he quickly took a drink of tea and calmed down. Maybe he was coming down with something and he decided to pay a visit to one of his physicians later on this morning.

A voice said, "Here, eat, drink. Bowls are on the table." Another voice, a young woman's said, "But where? I can't see! Help me." The original voice answered, "Use your feet. Find your chair. Sit down. Use your nose. Eat. Water is to the right of the food bowl." Adrianna heard sobbing noises — no, shuffling feet, that was it. Food. Water! She wanted water in the worst way. She rose unsteadily, flailing her arms to steady her in her total blackness. Nothing. Was she spinning, falling? Adrianna could not tell which, if either.

Ouch! Pain! Her toes touched a chair perhaps. What had the voice said? Sit down, yes. Adrianna's mind reeled flickering from one bit of confusion to another, wholly out of control. Insane! That's it. Has to be. I've gone mad. This is all some madness that has swallowed me. No, I am feeling a chair. Yes, it feels like a chair. Sit, maybe that will be better. How? I can't see where I am sitting! Another wave a panic swept over her and her legs gave out. Adrianna found her body sitting down. Now the odor of food, stew perhaps, reached her senses from somewhere in the blackness or was it coming from the grey cloudy images? She lowered her head to see if she could smell it better and landed her face in something warm. She licked and tasted stew and strange spices. No, I want water. Go right, her memories said or were they even her memories? Did she even have memories anymore? Water entered her nose and she tried to use her hands once more but nothing happened and she blew hard. Water! Her parched throat demanded it. Her face was in the water, yes. Drink, she told herself.

Never had water felt so good. She desperately needed the good, long drink, but her mind asked, Is this really water? A disembodied voice answered, "Can't tell." Is that my voice? She belched and felt hungry. Food. She licked at the stew and then waves of hunger took over. Chew your food. Yes, there she was three years old and her mother was telling her to chew her food. "Okay mommy." Was that my voice?

Time passed, though she could not tell that it had or could she? Adrianna decided that she couldn't. She heard that disembodied voice again. What was it saying? Something about finding a pee bucket. Pee! She knew she had to go badly, but where was it? So confusing! Everything is so confusing. She nearly slipped wholly into the Shadows trying to find the bucket. Relieved, she heard that voice again, this time telling her to find her bed and take a nap. Lie down! Yes, that would be good, she thought.

Adrianna again tried to walk, but once more felt herself turning upside down or was it spinning or perhaps she was just falling. Nausea came over her and she panicked as her arms failed to flail about her as she fought hard to keep her crumbling balance as she slipped slightly into the Shadows once more. She screamed involuntarily. "Help me! Help me!" An arm pulled on her body, pushing it down, down onto a bed? Yes a bed. Her mind screamed as the body pushed hers down onto the bed, while her arms did nothing at all.

Zoran was walking to his study just after breakfast when waves of dizziness came over him again. "Help me! Help me!" Words screamed in his mind, his hands reached out and held on hard to the door frame as he steadied himself.

Now awake, he knew. It was a woman's voice, calling for help, but not just any woman. She was Duska-born, experiencing the disorientation and nausea upon first entering the Shadows while undergoing the Circle of Ascension ceremony which activated her special gland. He was somehow connected to this woman through the Shadows. He headed for his easy chair and sat down, collecting his wits.

Just then, his daughter appeared, stepping out of her Mystical Door. Nadia looked trouble, he thought. "Dad, I am experiencing the strangest things this morning."

"Come sit. It helps. Are you hearing a woman calling out for help?"

Nadia suddenly looked her dad straight in his eyes. "How did. . ." She didn't finish her thought. No need to.

"Yes, it is almost as if she is about to undergo the Ceremony of Ascension, but her priestess is failing to give her the proper instructions," Zoran said.

"Yes, dad! That's it precisely! I don't know why I didn't realize this sooner!"

"Well, I've been there before — with Akira and Chika." He didn't get to say more because another Mystical Door opened and then another. His son, Tomas, stepped out, looking quite upset. Verushka stepped out of her door, a perplexed look on her face as well.

"Don't tell me that you two have also heard this young woman calling for help? A young girl undergoing her Ceremony of Ascension but her priestess is failing to give her the proper instructions," he repeated himself. Nadia smiled, how could she have missed this?

Both Verushka and Tomas stared at him. "But how? Well, yes, that's it exactly," Tomas gushed, thoroughly impressed with his father.

"Akira and Chika. I went through something quite like this some twenty plus years ago with those two."

"Dad, she needs our help," Nadia declared.

"Of course she does. Okay, you stand by. I am going to see if I can reach her and find out why her priestess is failing to assist her. I'll strangle that priestess," Zoran half-teased. Well he would certainly tell that priestess a thing or two. Zoran stepped into the Shadows and then reached out for the voice. Nothing. All traces of the woman were gone. Reluctantly, he returned to his study. "No luck. Nothing."

"Yes, dad. I sensed that too," Nadia said. "Maybe the priestess finally got through to her."

"Yes, that must be it. Okay, everyone, we best get back to our duties," Zoran declared, sending for a strong cup of black tea. The others left him and he pulled out his papers and began studying them again. So many women were being reported as missing from all over the Federation. Where were they being taken, he mused for the thousandth time. His tea came and he nearly gulped it down. "Thanks."

Am I sleeping? I must be, Adrianna thought. Well, I need it, don't I? Such a weird, strange dream that I had. Soon, I will wake up and have to go scrub up Able's dried puke on the pub's floor. I know, I ought to have done it last night, but I was tired. Guess I will have to pay for that in the morning. I wish morning would come soon. This is such an awful nightmare that I'm having. Her mind drifted into sleep — a welcomed, refreshing, much needed sleep. Vaguely she'd heard that disembodied voice chanting something before she drifted into sleep.

Zoran looked over Chika's reports that had come in just after lunch. He smiled, she'd found three more high quality weapons that she though Karel might be able to enchant. One had been a family heirloom on Gonda. She'd paid a pretty steep price for it, but she thought it stood a very good chance of holding powerful enchantments. Good girl, he thought. He looked over the grain reports. Already his workers had built up a nice stockpile in the ever-growing subterranean city he was having constructed far below his Circle in the basement. This was encouraging. If need be, Brn could be evacuated and survive down below. At least he'd not let these people down, he thought.

Now he went over Tomas' report. Good, he could now support his entire group below ground. Baron Jan's report was not so good. Well, Jan's city was vastly larger by orders of magnitude. It had been the seat of power on Adapazan for centuries. He made a note of some suggestions for Jan to follow. Zoran finished the day wrapping up these administrative details. He smiled; he hated these duties and had long ago worked out this system whereby he did the whole week's administrative duties in one long boring day. Satisfied that he now had six days of freedom from these mundane tasks, he headed off to the Great Hall, where everyone was congregating for dinner. He smiled as he thought of all the excited chat the many students would be doing, going over all their new spells that they had worked on today. It brought back fond memories of his days in training here with Zdenka and the others. "Having us all together for dinner has been one of my brighter ideas!" he said as he rose and headed down the hall, stretching his legs.

"Productive day," Zdenka told him as she sat down beside him and the two looked out over the many tables at everyone. The seventeen mages had Morphed themselves and were using their hands to help all of the others. Her Adepts were assisting the six blind women as well. Conversations were bubbling and cheerful, great morale and spirits, he thought. All is well with the world.

"I can't thank you enough for your training of these many women, dear. You are giving them their lives back."

"Yes, that I am. So rewarding and fulfilling. That's why I do it."

A Mystical Door opened and Miroslav and Jarmila stepped out. Both were covered in dust, but highly animated. "Zoran, we've found them! Bandar's missing journals!" Miroslav called out. They'd just Shadow Walked from the old fortress in Sholov Province, where they were on site as the construction crews continued to both restore the old fortress as a museum and build Tomas' subterranean city retreat.

"Dad, the construction crews found another long hidden chamber. Found a few gems, but we found the missing journals! We are going to stay here and see if we can translate them, starting tomorrow. Maybe we can learn more about where Bandar came from and what the worms actually were. Do you suppose the worms really were dragons like the ones we have here?" she asked. Now they had a new topic of discussion over dinner.

Afterwards, the three headed down to his Circle of Ascension where the Jiri's kept their secret, prized journals, one of which gave the detailed instructions on how to build a Circle of Ascension. The three poured over the journals all that night. He enjoyed this diversion, besides he was keenly interested now in the Federation's most ancient history.

"Listen to this, dad," Jarmila said excitedly, she read:

Today, old Vladislov discovered my secret. I had little choice to but to confirm it. Any human between puberty and twenty-one can undergo our Ceremony of Ascension and become a Duska themselves. Yes, it is not limited to the ruling class. I was forced to tell old Vladislov that he was right. However, I pointed out to him in no uncertain terms that this must remain a secret. I appealed to his vanity. "Look, if anyone can become a Duska, how will you ever be able to hand down your throne to your sons? Our natural procedure for inheritance will become a chaos of infighting. May the most skilled Duska win." He agreed with me. If word of this got out, we'd have Duskas everywhere and that would bring down our monarchies. We all agreed on establishing individual monarchies on these new worlds. We all agreed that would be the best, most stable form of government. Democracy broke down completely on Home World and that led to all the problems in the first place. He has agreed to keep this to himself.

"Dad, isn't that just incredible?" Jarmila asked.

"Explains a lot, dear. I wonder if he makes any more references to Home

World? Where is it? What was this Democracy that broke down? What problems did they face that so drove them to abandon their Home World?" Zoran asked. All three shrugged their shoulders and continued reading the journals, hoping to discover more data.

The hour drew late and at last they abandoned the project for the night. A bit later, he crawled into bed and told Zdenka what they'd learned. She was impressed and asked the same questions that he had. He smiled; they were so attuned to each other. He gave her a passionate kiss.

"Time to wake up and eat again." There was that same disembodied voice. Adrianna complained to herself. It must be morning now. Why is it still black outside? Where's my lantern? Oh I do wish this night would end! I am so tired of this awful nightmare anyway. Why am I so hungry? Have I missed breakfast? Couldn't of, it's still pitch black outside. Best get up and light my lantern. She felt her body struggle to get up. My arms aren't there? Suddenly, it all came back — the dragons, her abduction, her rape, her blindness, her vanished arms, the mysterious shadow images! She was trying to get to the table or was it to light her lantern? The grey swirls offered illumination, unlike the total blackness around her. Confusion. Panic. Chaos.

Focus! She told herself mentally. I will light my lantern. That should pull me out of this nightmare dream. Yes, that's the ticket, Adrianna, that's just the thing to do to end this terrible nightmare dream! Light my lantern. Ouch! She had banged into the side of her bed. Her lantern table had been moved somehow. She tried to feel her way over to her table and lantern, but her arms did not seem to be there at all. As she moved, however, she found herself more readily moving into the semi-visible grey Shadows, which were more inviting than the total darkness around her. Yet, when she did that, her whole world turned upside down. Waves of nausea swept over her, she was falling and yet not falling. Her arms didn't work to help her regain her balance. Terror and panic won. She screamed and screamed. "Help me! Help me! Please, someone help me!"

Zoran awoke in a cold sweat. This time, he knew what was going on! He focused his Duska senses. Yes, I have her now. He reached out and found her mind. *Hello. I am here. I am Baron Zoran Vladislov. I have come to help you. It will be all right. You are partially in the Shadows. Where is your High Priestess who is performing your Ceremony of Ascension?*

Huh? Who is this? Baron? Where am I? Shadows? Ceremony? Priestess? No! Dragons have me. I can't see anything but these grey images. It's better than the utter blackness. My arms are gone, I think. Maybe this is all a bad dream and I somehow can't wake up. I can't seem to pinch myself awake or find my lantern. Where has it gone to now? I keep banging into things. There are a whole bunch of us or maybe they are just a part of this awful dream too. I don't know. Nothing is real anymore, except that I am falling and very sick at my stomach. Help me!

Zoran flew through the Shadows. Now he realized fully what was going on. The dragons had made a huge mistake this time. They'd accidentally abducted a woman who was Duska born! That is, at least one of her parents was a full Duska, probably a baron or baroness at least. The native power in her was strong. Long ago she should have been given the Ceremony of Ascension, if only to preserve her sanity. She could see the Shadows even without the proper indoctrination! Criminal, he thought, as he flew through the Shadows, homing in on her, just as he'd done with Akira so many years ago. Out right criminal of them, he swore under his breath. *I'm coming to you. Relax if you can. Help is on the way. Won't be but a moment. What is your name?* He tried to get her mind focused on something other than the swirling, disorienting Shadows. Where the devil is she? He just left all the known Shadows behind!

Adrianna Whitehall. I live with mom. We run an inn in Westfarthington, Terra. Yes, now I remember. I was sleeping and some dragons came and took me away in the middle of the night! Oh god! They've done terrible things to me. I can't see and my arms are gone I think. They raped me, I know it. I am to die, they said so. Something about a baby dragon living on for me. I don't understand it. Help me. I am falling and falling and falling! Please hurry.

Zoran spotted the naked woman with raven hair. She still had her arms, but her eyes were cloudy. He recognized the Blind spell immediately. He touched her arms, but she didn't feel it and he suspected that whatever the reds had done to the seventeen, they also had done to her. He put his hands on her shoulders, steadying her. *I am here with you. There, that's better. Now you are not falling. You are halfway into the Shadow Lands.*

Thank you. I am not falling anymore. Please, don't let go of me. I am really, really scared.

I will not let go of you. Let me see what is going on here and where we are at.

Okay. How are we talking without using our mouths? I don't understand.

It is something we Duska can do. You are Duska born and should have long ago been given your birthright. I will see that you get it. Give me a few minutes, please, Adrianna.

Zoran peered out into the unfamiliar cavern. It was russet colored. He spotted sixteen women in the room lying on their beds. Adrianna's body appeared quite thin as she was partially in the Shadows. One female black dragon was cleaning up the messy table and periodically casting a Sleep spell on those women who seemed disturbed. She then left the room. *I am going to bring you back to your bed. Please lie still for just a while. I need to see where we are located. So many other women need help too. Can you be patient a while longer, Adrianna?*

Yes, this is much better, but I don't like the utter blackness. I can't see anything.

I know. Relax. I'll be right back.

Zoran remained in the Shadows partially and moved out of this cavern room. He saw that the walls were radiating heat, so evidently the reds were here too. He found five other chambers, each held sixteen women. Some were being watched over by reds, others by blacks. He moved on and discovered these chambers led to a single huge one. Here dozens of dragons lay snoozing on the floor, guards evidently. He moved on, looking for the entrance. His Duska senses tingled and he checked for traps. Half of the entrance way flashed. They had a half dozen different traps set. These, he avoided by remaining in the Shadows, moving on down the entrance tunnel. At last he left the tunnel and looked at the world before him. He'd never seen this planet before. Everything looked strange. Oranges and reds predominated in the rocks of the mountains. They were at a relatively high elevation. He'd seen enough that he knew he could find this place again and he appeared back above Adrianna. Now how to rescue all these women?

There were too many dragons and traps guarding the cavern. We dare not attack them, he thought. Then, he had an idea. Why should we give away the fact that we now know of this secret hiding place? He chuckled at his own deviousness. He focused and began making a large Mind Link.

One by one, he joined with Verushka, Tomas, Nadia, Jarmila, Miroslav, Dusan, Chika, Akira, Jan, and Reina. He was short five and so he added Rayna, Lida, Leo, Stefan, and his half-sister Zusa to the huge Mind Link. *Okay. I've just located all our abducted women. I have no idea what world they are on, but I can now get you all here with us.* He explained all that had happened and what the situation here actually was. *Now here is the plan. Under no circumstances do we want to alert the dragons that it is we who are doing this. We need complete secrecy. Keep the dragons in a total mystery.*

One by one, they all stepped into the Shadows and homed in on Zoran, arriving in the Shadows beside him. He gave them all time to familiarize themselves with the scene. *Where is this place? It is so strange,* Jarmila sent. No one had that answer.

Zoran waited patiently. The care-giving black finally left to fix the women their next meal, but not before she looked each one over, satisfying herself that they were all asleep. *Remember, their arms do not work and they cannot feel them, so put your arms securely around their shoulders when you lead them back through the Shadows. Now, everyone and be quick about it.*

Adrianna, I am with you. I have you secure and we are going to get you away from these dragons now. We're going to my castle first. Just relax. I will go as fast as possible. He felt the young woman take a deep breath and hold it, as if it were her last possible breath. One by one, the other fifteen appeared in the cavern beside the sleeping women. Each put their arms around the women who were under a Sleep spell and stepped them into the Shadows. Zoran moved as rapidly as possible and soon stepped lightly into his infirmary, where Zdenka, Jarka, Bernard, and others were already waiting for the new arrivals, water barrels warmed and ready. Plenty of towels lay close at hand.

"Here we are, Adrianna. You are now safe in my fortress in Brn, Adapazan."

"Thank you. I can't see and my hands are gone, arms too. What's happened to me? I don't understand. I still see the grey images, the Shadows you call it. I am pulled to them cause I can sort of see. It's better than this other total blackness," she gushed out all at once.

"You have had a Blindness spell cast upon you. We will get it undone pronto," Zoran answered her partially. He knew that it was top priority to get her sight back, otherwise she would continue to be drawn into the Shadows, understandably so. He chanted and cast his Dispel Magic.

"I can see again! Wow! So bright in here! I'm naked? Oh, I do have arms! Why can't I feel them? Who are all of you? Oh, so many of us." She now saw fifteen others like her and many other men and women around as well.

"Incredible, Zoran, just incredible," Baron Leo commented. "Oh, yes of course, cancel the Blindness spells." He and the others quickly cast their spells as well, though a couple of them had to be recast after the first attempt failed.

"Ladies, you are all now totally safe. No dragons will ever get you here. You are in my fortress at Brn, Adapazan. I am Baron Zoran." He introduced the others and the women were very much impressed — surrounded by so many barons, baronesses, Archmages, and mages. He explained that first they would get bathed and any wounds looked after. Jarka would be examining their arms to see if they could be healed as well.

"I know this sounds cruel, but we may not be able to do anything for your arms. Don't panic. We will always look after your needs here," he tried to soften the blow which he suspected would soon be coming. "Now then, we men will leave you women to bathe and dress. You may have your privacy back from now on." Quickly, the men left and Zdenka issued bathing orders.

"My god, Zoran, you've done it again!" Leo praised him. The men had gathered in his study.

"I should have realized what was going on, dad," Tomas chastised himself.

In detail, Zoran explained how he'd found them and shared his memories of the other four cavern rooms with their captive women. "We have sixty-four more women to get out of there. My idea is to keep the dragons wondering just how the women are disappearing on them. If they don't get wise to us, we can keep recovering the women that they abduct. I don't know if we can do it fast enough to prevent them from being raped and their arms damaged, though. I think that we ought to rescue those who are showing their pregnancies the most next. We don't know their due dates yet and I don't want to risk their lives now that we've found them."

"We still don't know what the dragons are doing to the women's arms, do we?" Tomas asked.

"No, but let's hope Jarka's potions will work on them this time," Zoran replied.

"Say, this Adrianna — she's Duska born, isn't she? How come she's not had her Ceremony of Ascension?" Stefan asked.

"I don't have the full story yet, but I think that she is an illegitimate daughter of a baron on Terra, most likely the late Tom Witherspoon. Downright criminal of him not to have given her the Ceremony of Ascension at the very least. She is so attuned to the Shadows it's not funny. I will have Jarmila perform the ceremony as soon as possible."

"I hate to point this out, dad, but you are running out of helping hands in the infirmary. If Jarka cannot fix up their arms, how are you going to handle eighty more women?" Tomas pointed out and asked.

"Simple," Stefan replied before Zoran could say anything. "We are going to have to lend a hand. After all some of these are likely our women too, right Leo? Zoran, we'll get together a bunch of Adepts and all the Duska we can spare. We'll see that you have all the helping hands you need."

"Right, after all, your people are the only ones skilled enough to handle these women properly," Baron Leo replied, also getting himself off the hook. He could not fathom how his people could possible help and train the potentially armless women. "There is only one Zdenka," he teased.

"All help is welcome. Gentlemen, I'd rather focus on the women still there and the dragon problem further. One of us ought to hang out there, hiding in the Shadows observing them. As long as from the dragon's point of view the women simply vanish without any visible cause, we can keep them stalemated in their vicious breeding program. If we checkmate them, as we have done before, they will just invent new ways and means. Let's keep them guessing."

"You got it, dad. I will return and take the first watch. How soon are we going to 'vanish' the next batch of women?" Tomas asked.

"Later today, I hope. I'll keep you posted. Honestly, the trauma being inflicted on these women is beyond description," Zoran declared.

Just then, Jarka's Mystical Door appeared and she stepped into the room. From her glum countenance, Zoran already knew what she would report. "Failed again. Whatever they are doing to those poor women's arms is beyond me. Nothing works to restore feeling or sensation in their arms. It is like their arms and hands are just dead."

"I assumed that would be the case, no failure on your part, Mage Jarka," Zoran said formally because of the presence of the other barons.

"Well, I have one last thing that I'd like to try," she continued. "Verushka told me that you are able to sit in the Shadows and observe them. Can you actually see the dragons and what they are doing?"

"Yes, we can. Why?"

"Well, whenever they bring in another sixteen women, I'd like to be there, as much as I hate Shadow Walking. I want to see exactly what they are doing to these women's arms. They have most peculiar little puncture marks on their shoulders and I don't have any idea just what they are doing. If I could somehow see that, maybe I can find a way to undo it properly." She didn't yet tell him about the mysterious blue gooey substance which the physicians had found. It had thus far totally eluded all her detection spells and chemical tests. Jarka hated to be baffled. Seeing what was done to the women might give her more ideas of ways to help them.

"Makes sense, Jarka. I'll tell you what. If and when one of us sees that happening, we'll open a Mind Link directly to you and you can be here and observe it directly through one of us. That way, you will not have to hang out long hours in the Shadows. I'm sure that would make you very ill," Zoran replied. She was satisfied and returned to help the newly arrived women.

Tomas then left but Mind Linked to Zoran not long after. *Say, the women in this one room seem awfully pregnant. I swear they could go into labor anytime. You'd better be prepared. Give the others a head's up on this one.*

Zoran was afraid of this from his own initial inspection of the cavern complex earlier. "Okay, Tomas says we have to retrieve another sixteen who are likely due anytime now. I'm going to the infirmary to help get it ready. You can take care of whatever you need. We'll head back there later today." Leo and Stefan headed home to arrange for more Duskas to come lend a hand with the expected women.

His daughter met him at the entrance to the infirmary. Jarmila said, "Dad,

I've examined Adrianna. She's just got to have the Ceremony of Ascension and soon, but she is definitely pregnant with a Black Dragon. Her body is now beginning to suck up all kinds of magical energies. I think that we'd best wait until she delivers it before I give her the ceremony. If I do it now, there is no telling what that will do to the fetus that she is carrying. I know it is still small, but I am worried that somehow it could harm her or somehow alter the dragon too. I sure don't want to do something that will aid dragons, dad."

"High Priestess, I will abide by your wisdom in this. I think that she ought to be stable enough to get by until then. That Blind spell was probably what triggered her bout of Shadow Sickness. Now that she can see, I think we can keep that at bay."

"My thoughts exactly. Let her sleep at night with a lantern on. Okay, we have them bathed, their hair washed, and gotten them into clean dresses. Jarka's probably told you that their arms are still useless."

"Yes, we need to prepare for another batch which will be delivering at any time now — that is, if we can find a way to get them out of there without being seen by the dragons," he replied. The two headed on into the women-filled room. Zdenka had brought all her dragon-harmed women into meet and discuss the situation with the new arrivals. Yes, many including Adrianna were sobbing. They saw the armless women and truly didn't want to lose theirs. However, the seventeen then eased their misery and feelings of hopelessness by demonstrating their Morph abilities.

"See, once you learn the Morph spell, you can have arms any time you need them," Danika explained. Zdenka left her students alone with the newcomers and moved her group into the next room with Zoran.

"They are taking it hard, but I believe they will be able to handle it eventually," she reported. "I promised them that we would leave their arms alone as long as possible, in case Jarka can somehow find a cure. You said some are near their due dates?"

"Yes, we are going to have to fetch another batch yet today. Tomas is there keeping watch over them. He and I both think that sixteen are due anytime now. Leo and Stefan are going to send more Duskas to help."

"Bout time," Lida retorted. "Men, honestly," she added exasperated.

"Right. Being raped is horrible, but what these poor women are forced to experience is beyond description," Rayna added. "If Stefan doesn't send along a bunch, I'll hang him out to dry!" Zoran chuckled. His sister just might do that.

A while later, Baron Stefan returned with six of his relatives, some as young as sixteen, all were Duskas. Additionally, he introduced an older woman. "Baron Zoran, this is Izabela Alfons, a distant cousin and Duska. She is also a Potion Maker. Izabela has heard of the situation facing the women and came to me with some ideas. I thought that you ought to hear her and make your own decisions."

Izabela was a matronly looking woman, with sharp eyes and a confident demeanor. "May we speak of this in private or perhaps with a few of those who are dealing with the intimate details of the birthing of these women?"

"Yes, of course. Rayna, get your helpers acquainted with everyone and the infirmary. We'll be right back. This way. Verushka, Nadia, Zdenka, Jarka, if you will join us?" he replied and requested, not so much as asked. He knew that he was out of his league in this area. A minute later in his private study, they sat down and Izabela spoke frankly.

"I don't wish to offend anyone. However, in my line of work, Potion Making, I receive many unusual requests. Sometimes a woman needs to have a pregnancy terminated prematurely. Usually, it is for medical reasons, but not always. Over these many years, I have developed potions which do just that, if taken within about the first couple of weeks. Beyond that, the risk factor to the woman steadily increases. I've only recently heard of what the dragons have been doing. At first, I thought this was utter nonsense. How could they possibly interspecies breed? Last week, I had to come to the Fortress on business and wisely stopped to see young Stefan. I asked about this business and he fully briefed me on it. I decided that I may be of some assistance. It may be possible to terminate some of these pregnancies, if they are caught early on. However, if I understand Stefan, carrying them to term somehow turns the women into 'super-fast' magic students. Is this really true? If this is so, perhaps they might not wish to terminate their pregnancies early."

"We just rescued sixteen women not six hours ago! Good timing. Yes, these were raped only a day or so ago. We are not precisely sure, since they were Blinded beforehand and had no way of telling time after that," Verushka explained. "The gestation period is not nine months, but a mere sixty days. And yes, those who have delivered are now able to learn magic but at an alarming rate. The first seventeen are already Mages and all that in less than a year."

"You're kidding? That makes them superwomen. I spent years getting to Mage level!" Izabela was most impressed.

Zdenka continued, "Yes, here's the thing. It's kind of complicated and depends on how badly the woman has already been physically hurt. If they have lost their arms or eyes, then we've discovered that carrying the fetus full term allows them to learn magic and at a rapid rate. It gives them new hope, self-reliance, and likely a way to use Morph Self to gain arms or eyes when needed. Failure to do this for them leaves them with destroyed lives and little or no hope. On the other hand, if they have not lost body parts, then it is their call. Some may want to do what's needed so that they can learn magic, others might not and will want the potion."

Izabela agreed, "Yes, that makes sense. Have you worked out how long a woman must carry the dragon for her body to become filled with magical energies?"

"No, only some raw facts. We can begin examining these current women. This first batch has been pregnant a very short time, a few days. Others that we will be rescuing have been so for varying times. We can attempt to work it all out."

"May I lend a hand and help out?" Izabela asked. She was welcomed with open arms. Zoran return to the others while the women headed off to check on magical energy levels of the new arrivals and consult the long ledger that Verushka had been keeping on each woman that they treated here. They quickly saw that these recent arrivals did have magical energies flowing in their bodies, but at a fairly low level. Verushka then sat down with the sixteen and explained in great detail the future track for the women and also presenting the termination route and its potential effects, particularly acute if no cure could be found for their "dead arms." As she expected, all wanted to wait as long as possible to see if a cure could be found. They did realize that those who came before them had had no choice but to have the "dead" appendages removed. The sixteen clung desperately to the faint hope that

Jarka had offered them, which was better than losing their arms.

On his way back to the other men, Zoran found himself wondering what planet this new one was. He knew that dragons had limited abilities to Shadow Walk between planets. He also recalled Aldrick said that they all lived on Voss. Could this be Voss or was it some other planet known to the dragons only? How could he tell?

Around four, Zoran issued his orders to the fourteen who would come with him to rescue the women, joining Tomas who was still there observing. "We have to exercise extreme caution with these women who are near their due dates. We tried Shadow Walking two who were in labor. Although we Morphed the dragons into their human forms, when we hit the Shadows, they morphed back and clawed their way out, killing the women. If we do nothing, these sixteen women will die giving birth. If we attempt to Shadow Walk them here, there is also a chance that they will die, but I say we have to try."

"If you Morph the dragons before you Shadow Walk, how long do they stay Morphed?" asked Stefan.

"Ordinarily, when they are that close to delivering, less than a half hour between Morph spells. The dragons keep trying to prepare themselves for birth. We lost the two because we didn't know that would happen. We do now. Ideally, I'd like an Archmage with each Duska who is transporting a woman. The Archmage can constantly monitor the dragon and recast the spell as often as needed. However, we simply don't have enough Duskas and Archmages to do that. I thought about the Duska bringing along a non-Duska mage with them. The idea being that person could monitor and recast. However, the snatching of the women is going to be tricky and must be a fast action. The non-Duska would be in serious trouble if the Duska let go of them while materializing and snatching the woman. So I think we must discard that idea."

Jarka had dropped by to see how soon they were planning on leaving, and had overheard his suggestions and chose to speak up, "My advice is to do your Shadow Walking as fast as you possible can, but also talk to the woman and have her tell you if she is sensing any activity from the dragons. Usually, the woman has a bit of advanced warning that it is about to morph back into the dragon form; she gets a lot of pain and motion before it actually morphs. If you use this as a guide, if and when it happens, you can pause and recast it before continuing." Zoran adopted her plan.

"Okay, here's how it must go. When the coast is clear and I give the signal, materialize before your woman. Snatch her up and step into the Shadows. At once, cast the Morph Other spell. Then Mind Link to her, I guarantee you that she will feel an enormous relief when you morph the dragon. Tell her to let you know if the pain and discomfort start up again. Travel as fast as you safely can back here." Zoran felt he had all bases covered. After briefly notifying Tomas, they all joined with Zoran, and he Shadow Walked the fourteen and himself to this secret cavern, joining up with Tomas.

Tomas, via a large Mind Link, quickly outlined the situation and took everyone to their positions. Essentially, each Duska was in the Shadows beside a specific woman, ready to materialize and snatch her up. The women were lying on crude beds against one wall. A short ways from the bed was a small barrel, their makeshift potty. Further away was a long table with a chair for each woman. Here was where they were fed, he explained. There were several female dragons, both red and black, who visited the women or checked on them periodically. The women that they wanted to snatch were close to birthing and were being kept under a Sleep spell most of the time. The other women were only given Sleep spells when they grew too upset or frightened.

We have about a five minute window when no one is in the chamber with them. Timing is critical if we want to avoid detection, Tomas sent. *By the way, it is working. The disappearance of the sixteen women has caused quite a stir among the dragons! They've been coming and going all over the place. Speculation is running rampant. They've rechecked all their traps and drilled all of the guards, but the leaders are becoming convinced that no one entered the cavern. They are completely mystified over the disappearance. This should further confuse them, but I think that they may decide to move the others to a new location, so we ought to snatch the others as soon as possible as well.*

Zoran signed, it was going to be a long night. Tomas was probably right. They could well spook entirely and move the women elsewhere. He dare not risk that happening. A red entered with a steaming pot of what appeared to be a stew. After filling the sixteen bowls, the red roused each sleeping women and made sure she got to the table and ate. Those with Zoran who had not seen how these women were forced to eat were shocked and appalled, but could only bide their time. Once fed, the women struggled to find their beds and whereon they laid back down. A black entered and cast a Sleep spell on each in turn, while the red cleaned up the table. Presently, both left the cavern room.

Now! Zoran gave the signal. Each Duska instantly stepped into the cavern beside their sleeping woman, lifted her up, and stepped back into the Shadows. Zoran double checked that they had not been seen. So far so good. He cast the needed Morph spell, roused his woman, briefly explained she was to tell him if she felt the baby moving or was hurting her, and then flew as fast as he could through the Shadows, stepping her out in the infirmary. Although he left last, he arrived first. Zdenka took the confused woman from him and began working with her, recasting the Morph spell and then dispelling the woman's blindness. That alone helped the woman immensely. She could see again.

One by one during the next ten minutes the others arrived. Tomas was last, he had to stop and recast Morph. "We did it. We didn't lose one this time!" Zoran cheered the group as Jarka took the woman from Tomas. Then, they all headed back, led by Tomas, who took them to the next most critical batch of women. These were not likely due for a couple of weeks, Zoran thought, based on the many women he'd seen these past months.

Indeed, the caverns were in an uproar. The red and black caretakers were being grilled. "Of course we fed them. Yes, we cast Sleep on each one and they were out like a light. I swear it," the poor red said defiantly. "No I don't know where they went. They just vanished utterly. No, no one but we two have been in here all day. You know that's not allowed. You need a woman here to handle the delivery of our babies."

They slipped over to the next cavern room where the next batch of women was held. Two dragons were lying on the floor, their heads watching the sleeping women.

They were extremely bored. Now they waited, these two would have to leave before they dared rescue the women. An hour later, another dragon came by to check on them. "Yes, sleeping like babies. Nothing going on at all. I tell you this is a complete waste of time."

"Okay, okay. Go get something to snack on," the new arrival ordered. The two didn't waste time and beat a hasty retreat from the cavern room. The remaining one checked on the women. Satisfied that all sixteen were sound asleep, he too left. At once, Zoran acted. A minute later, these sixteen were in the Shadows. A minute later, Morph spells cast, they were on their way back to Adapazan and the infirmary.

Zoran had the rescuers cast Dispel Magic to undo the women's blindness. He briefly explained where they were and that they were safe. Soon they would get the necessary attention they needed. Zdenka entered and took over and they headed back for more. This time, they found that the missing women had not yet been discovered. Further, none of the remaining two groups were being watched, the women were sound asleep. Zoran had reservations and Verushka cast her Premonition spell. *We should take both groups with us this time,* she advised via Mind Link.

He decided the best way was to divide into halves. Each half would take one set of sixteen women. Each Duska would have to snatch two women from adjacent beds. He allowed them time to get into position and to work out in their minds how they would get both women and then gave the signal. Essentially, the Duska grabbed each woman's hand and physically pulled them into the Shadows. However, this turned out to not be such a good idea. More than half of the women suffered broken arms, though no one knew this until Jarka examined them later on in the infirmary. Their arms had atrophied significantly. With the last of the women safely now in the way over crowded infirmary, he sent Tomas back to keep an eye on the dragons. He wanted to know what the dragon's reactions and responses might be. All eighty of their abducted women had simply vanished into thin air. How would the dragons react and deal with this?

Although it was midnight, he arranged for other Duska to relieve Tomas, setting up a two hour shift among those Duska who could be spared from handling the women who were close to giving birth. Meantime, Zdenka put all of her magic students to work assisting the new arrivals. Dispel spells flew right and left, returning sight to the women. Next, a brief explanation was given to them, followed by a bath and physical inspection. Jarka discovered the broken limbs and doled out healing potions to sixteen women. It was four in the morning before the last woman was clothed and helped into a clean bed.

Two women were assigned to closely monitor the sixteen and were to rouse everyone if they went into labor. The rest headed to bed themselves. The next day became a nightmare for the caretakers. All sixteen went into labor around eight in the morning. Morph spells had to be recast every half hour or so and the sixteen constantly watched. Zdenka's students were of great assistance. They took over the feeding of the many other women, caring for their needs as well. When a dragon finally was born, Zoran cast his Vanish spell on it. In the meantime, he helped out as needed with the women, usually casting Morph spells. Finally around six that night, the last dragon was Vanished and the exhausted care givers finally got a well-deserved rest.

Meanwhile, Stefan, Leo, and the other men took turns monitoring the dragon's reactions to the disappearance of all their breeding stock, as they called these women. As expected, speculations ran the gambit. However, one dragon's idea began to take hold. According to him, he suspected that there was some kind of physical incompatibility with Voss and these women from the Federation. Yes, they finally learned that this was indeed the planet Voss. The dragon suggested that this magical incompatibility caused the women's bodies to disintegrate rather rapidly. Of course, he couldn't explain the time factor. Already, sixteen women had given birth to eight reds and eight blacks and they had not disappeared. Plus, the new arrivals had only been there two days before they vanished. Still, his idea met with increasing support.

Dario and Werner arrived and grilled everyone yet again. Many continued to suggest that there was some kind of physical incompatibility between Voss and these women. At last Werner reached a decision. "Okay, let's test out that theory. We'll move up the next abductions to tomorrow night. We'll bring in another sixteen. Then, we'll monitor them closely. Either they too will disappear or they will not. We'll see. Incompatibility? How can that be?" he muttered to himself. His grand plan was crumbling.

Baron Leo was watching from the Shadows around one in the following morning. He had slept in and volunteered for the late shift, which pleased Lida. She'd said, "I am really pleased that you are taking such an active role in all this." As he watched from the Shadows, he still felt pleased by her validation of him. He was the first to see the new arrivals, when suddenly sixteen reds and blacks swooped in carrying their latest batch of kidnaped women. He fired off his Mind Link messages as ordered and prepared to carefully observe just what these dragons did to the women. He correctly determined that they were currently under the influence of a Sleep spell.

Not long after that, Zoran arrived beside him and quickly made a Mind Link to a sleepy Jarka. *Okay, I need to see very closely just what they do to the women's arms. What is the purpose of those small punctures that they make in their shoulders,* she sent back.

Under Sleep spells at the moment, Leo sent to Zoran. Now they watched, just a little frustrated that, though they were here, there was really nothing that they could do to prevent what was about to happen to these innocent women. They simply could not take on over two dozen dragons at one time.

Werner arrived to personally supervise the operation this time. Four dragons went methodically down the line of women casting Blind spells on them. Most of the women woke up at this point and the cavern was filled with their screams of shock and horror. Their hands rubbed their eyes mechanically. Zoran could feel their terror and wild emotions. He felt rather sick at this point, Leo too.

A red dragon Morphed into her human form and a large medical bag suddenly appeared in her hand. *Summons spell,* Zoran mechanically noted. The woman opened the bag and took out several items. *Pay close attention now!* Jarka sent. She watched the woman pull out a long hollow needle, an eye dropper, a large bottle of what appeared to be that bluish gooey substance similar to what she had been analyzing for months. She pit a contraption over his head. The device had a sort of magnifying lense that she pulled down over her left eye for close work. Jarka thought that this was a clever invention. She walked up to the first terrified and struggling woman.

All three recognized the spell at once. Immobilize. The woman froze, unable to move a voluntarily muscle. True, all her involuntary muscles worked, she breathed and her heart pumped. She was just unable to move or talk on her own. Another dragon helper at once removed all the woman's clothing, generally just a nightgown. The morphed dragon in human form moved up to her left side and Zoran focused his full attention on the woman's shoulder, knowing that Jarka desperately needed to see just what the dragon did to the woman.

Using the magnifying apparatus, the dragon inserted the hollow needle in her shoulder at very precise locations. The dragon stopped pushing it into her shoulder when the woman's arm jerked slightly. Zoran estimated that the needle was maybe a quarter to a half inch beneath the woman's skin. A small funnel was then attached to the hollow needle. How strange, Zoran thought. What was he doing? Then, the dragon measured out two drops of the bluish liquid and dropped it into the funnel, watching it slowly seep down the hollow needle and into the woman's shoulder. After doing four more spots on that shoulder area, she pulled the needle out and moved over to the right side and repeated the entire process. Once done, she then cancelled the Immobilize spell and took the needle and poked the woman in her lower arm with it. The woman had no reaction at all. The dragon then tested the other arm with similar results. Apparently done, she moved on down to the next woman, leaving the one she'd just finished screaming about her arms no longer working.

Zoran adjusted his position in the shadows to try to get a better look as the dragon performed the same action on the next woman. The procedure was precisely the same, only this time the woman had a reaction to the needle puncture test, and the dragon redid that shoulder a second time. *Well, that explains it. My potions only heal a body's wounds. It does not remove that bluish stuff that it is inserting in them. Now we know what to look for!* Jarka felt somewhat vindicated, in that there was no failing on her part in concocting her potions. *I will get to work on it!*

After he finished this second woman, she moved down the line to the next woman. Another dragon came up to the one she'd just finished. The woman reacted as expected, when she suddenly could no longer feel or move or even sense the presence of her arms and hands. She screamed and shrieked even louder. This ended abruptly after the dragon then cast a Charm spell on her. He suggested that she felt fine and that she should lie down on the bed behind her. Unable to see, unable to use her arms and hands, the poor woman made a valiant effort to find the bed and lay down, though as Zoran already knew, their dangling arms sometimes got in their way and bones cracked as they sat or lay upon them. Worse, the women could not even tell it had happened.

Zoran almost could not stand what happened next. It took all of his will power to prevent himself from doing something foolish. Werner said, "Okay, Dario. We want to create only the best and smartest offspring, so let's do it now." He Morphed into human form and proceeded to rape the first woman. Dario did the same to the next one. The virile pair of dragons continued on down the line of women, impregnating them with their seed. After the last was finished, the two Morphed back into their dragon forms, just as the red finished putting his tools back into her bag.

"Thank you doctor. Now we shall see if these vanish like the others. I just do not see how anything that we are doing could possibly create this so called incompatibility and dissolve their bodies, leaving not a single trace of them," Werner stated dryly.

"Well, it took a couple of days for the last ones to vanish, but I don't get why the first batch was not affected at all and why four batches disappeared at nearly the same time. It doesn't make any sense at all," Dario complained. "Maybe it is the food that we are feeding them. Perhaps something about Voss food that is dissolving the humans' bodies."

"We are not going to take any chances with these," Werner added. "Guards, I want every trap double checked and a guard it to stand watch every fifty feet from the entrance to the hall out there — twenty-four-seven. Now then, Dario, are your dragons ready with the collars?"

The red sent for his workers. In came four reds, who were in their human forms. They carried locking neck collars and proceeded to lock one around each woman's neck. Next, they brought in long chains, fastening them to hooks bolted securely to the cavern's stone wall behind the beds and then snapped them onto a loop on the neck collars. The chains would allow the women to reach the long line of tables but not much beyond that.

Satisfied with this new arrangement, Werner said, "Now that's better. The women cannot get up and walk out of here, and no one can slip in and carry them out either, not without dealing with those locks. Leave nothing to chance, Dario, remember that. These women are not going to vanish on us, not this time!" He walked out of the cavern room, followed by Dario, leaving the red female caretaker alone with the women. She went down the line casting a Sleep spell on each woman. Then, she headed to the kitchen to begin fixing the women's breakfast. Another dragon quickly entered, sat down, and watched the sleeping women. Soon, he was quite bored.

Leo sent encouragingly, *Won't be a problem. We cast Silence, then Unlock, and then snatch. When do we do it?*

Best wait and see when the women are left alone for a couple of minutes. See what the pattern of observation is, Zoran sent back. By dawn, they finally realized one fact: the women were never going to be left wholly alone. Every two hours, another dragon came in to relieve the one watching the women. Periodically, the red dragon that was caring for the women's needs came back, sometimes with a huge pot of what appeared to be stew. Zoran let Stefan take over for them. He and Leo returned to Brn.

"It's hopeless! How can we possibly sneak them out of there now? They are watched every minute," Leo complained. It was ten the next morning and Zoran had assembled his staff to work out how the women could be rescued. He'd explained the situation and Stefan continued to report no change. One dragon was on duty at all times, the women were never out of sight of at least one dragon. There seemed no way that they could continue their charade. They'd have to charge in there with all their attacking spells and hope for the best.

While many ideas were tossed about, one way or another, all involved blowing their cover and attacking the dragons. Finally, Archmage Nadia spoke up, "You know, I have been mulling all this over in my mind. It seems that the dragons are thinking along the lines of some kind of incompatibility, one in which their victims' bodies dissolve into nothingness. I have an idea that will take advantage of that and perhaps solidly re-enforce that mistaken belief. Of all of us, I have more skill with illusions. What about this idea?" She outlined her plan.

"That's down right devious and incredibly ingenious! Leave it to my daughter to come up with such a plan!" Zoran effused praise on her. "I think it might well work! If no one has any better ideas, we go with it. How long do you need to prepare, Nadia?"

An hour later, the rescue group of Duskas was again in the Shadows, hovering just over the cavern room where the captives were being held. *We wait until they are fed and put back to sleep,* Zoran ordered. That way, they would have the longest period of time available for their magic. Yes, all sixteen were thoroughly upset watching the miserable way that the women were forced to eat. Disgusting and revolting and downright inhumane, Nadia thought, but she continued to restrain herself from breaking their cover and murdering one or two dragons. Oh, how she wanted to ring their necks!

An hour later, the red recast a Sleep spell on each woman, then cleared off the dirty bowls and left. A replacement guard dragon entered and the very bored one left. Zoran waited until the new arrival became bored, which was not long. Watching nothing but sixteen sleeping women quickly bored the dragon, his eye lids began drooping. Zoran gave Nadia the go ahead, and then gave the others their signal.

The dragon suddenly opened its eyes, blinking several times. He saw thin, ghostly images of small dragons rising up out of the wombs of the sleeping women! They moved around the sleeping bodies as a thin fog appeared in the room, partially lowering the visibility of the women. Now the little ghostly dragons began flapping their wings and flying upwards towards the ceiling. The guard's eyes followed their flight. Many Silence spells detonated, followed by Unlock spells. With Invisibility cast upon themselves, the rescuers stepped out of the Shadows, arriving beside the beds. Each quickly snatched up their woman, cast Lock spells, and stepped back into the Shadows.

As the ghostly dragons seemed to float on through the stone roof of the cavern room, the guard's eyes returned to the women's bodies on their beds. He saw their bodies begin to dissolve into thin wisps of grey smoke. Bit by bit their bodies seemed to thin until there was nothing left at all, save the locked collars lying on the beds. Like the ghostly dragons, the wisps floated up and out through the ceiling. By now, the women were actually well on their way back to Brn traveling rapidly through the Shadows. A while later, Stefan returned to continue monitoring the dragons and their reactions. He was in time to see the tail end of Werner and Dario's extensive questioning of the guard, complete with many detection spells cast on the poor guard. Fortunately, nothing could shake the guard's story. Both Werner and Dario looked rather pale, if dragons can be said to pale, Stefan thought. He returned to Brn after he heard Werner issue the orders to abandon this entire complex. They had to rethink their entire strategy, he'd complained bitterly.

Jarka and Izabela conferred for over an hour. She went over in detail the operation she'd just witnessed for the benefit of Izabela, a fellow potion maker, in hopes that a second viewpoint would yield a solution. Neither woman had any idea what the substance was that the dragon had carefully inserted into the women's shoulders. Jarka began drawing up a chart. "Look, we know that a hollow needle was used. We know that the dragon took extraordinary care to insert the needle at very precise spots and at very precise depths. We know that he put two drops of a bluish substance into the needle. We can assume the purpose was to get the bluish substance to an exact internal location close to where the arm socket meets the shoulder. We know that within a very short time after insertion, that tiny amount completely numbs the arm. We know the women cannot move their arms or fingers or sense anything in them after that, not even if they break their bones. Their arms are basically 'dead' to them. We also know that healing potions have no effect on them. We know that within some sixty days, the arms have atrophied to nearly skin on bone."

Izabela added, "That tiny amount must be extremely potent, whatever it is. Add that please."

Jarka did so. "Now then, there is something else that we can very likely assume."

"What's that?" Izabela asked, her face stern with reflection upon their assumptions thus far.

"Our physicians studied the dead arms that they removed from the original seventeen women. They discovered some bluish, gooey substance at about the same locations that where we saw the dragon making the insertion. While accumulating samples for me to analyze, they got some on their fingers and their fingers went numb, just the surface of their fingers, one side only. No matter what we've done to their fingers since then, feeling in them has not been restored and it's been eight months now. I'd say that the stuff is pretty darn permanent," Jarka explained.

Back to her chart, she then added, "We surmise that the bluish drops the dragon inserted into these women is the same as the bluish substance our physician's recovered. Thus, we have a sample, albeit in a very small quantity. It seems to be extremely potent, whatever it is. I've tried to determine what it is, but so far I've only been able to determine what it isn't, I'm afraid."

"Incredible! We've a sample. We ought to be able to figure this out then. What have you tried?" Izabela asked, becoming keenly interested. Jarka listed a very lengthy list. With each one, Izabela's enthusiasm faded a wee bit more. "Gosh, you've tried everything! What *is* this stuff?"

"That is the question. Since we cannot identify it, chances are good that we cannot find a direct counter-agent to dissolve and remove it," Jarka concluded.

"Well, then, Mage Jarka, we should investigate what other avenues are available to us. Let's see, jot these down. If we do nothing, in sixty days, the atrophy almost certainly dictates amputation. Correct?"

"Absolutely, the bones have also gotten so brittle that they break extremely easily, which can lead rapidly to very serious health risks. They can get a serious cut and bleed to death before they even feel it. You are right, at that point, they should be removed if possible," Jarka agreed with her.

"So, what other choices do we have? Now that we know that there is this substance inside their arms and we know its approximate depth, what about making a surgical attempt to remove it? Cut them open around that spot, dig in a bit, find the blue stuff, and remove it," Izabela suggested.

"We ought to try that for sure. However, the two physicians have barely gotten the stuff on their fingers and it numbed them. They've washed their hands with everything imaginable. Surely there cannot be more of that stuff still on their skin, yet they are still numb. So if we cut them open and remove the stuff, I wonder if their arms will still be totally dead, like the physician's fingers? We ought to work on other possibilities as well," Jarka suggested.

She frowned and added, "I suppose that I can add another column called speculations."

"Sure go ahead, I'm all ears," Izabela replied encouragingly, out of bright ideas herself.

She produced the Chart 2 Dragon Statistics as Currently Known that was created at the High Council meeting. "Look at this line here: Blue Dragons — breath weapon: Neurotoxin Paralysis. I admit that no one here has ever even seen a Blue Dragon, let alone dealt with its supposed breath weapon. Just from the sound of it, it sounds somewhat similar to what we are dealing with here, don't you think?"

Izabela agreed. "You know, this might be the best avenue to explore. If we can find out what the substance actually is, it might lead us to a cure. Only trouble is that we have so very little time. Already sixteen women's arms are perilously close to being needed to be amputated."

"Come on. I know just the one to ask about this!" Jarka was suddenly inspired. She sent a Message first and when the reply came back affirmative, she teleported Izabela and herself to an isolated cavern high in the mountains.

"Er, hello Aldrick, sir," she called out. "We're here, sir," she added timidly. The great gold stood up to greet the two women. As always, Jarka was a little frightened standing before a huge dragon. His seventy feet dwarfed her five-five frame. "This is a fellow potion maker, Izabela. Thank you for seeing us, sir."

He chuckled, but it sounded more like a hurricane racing through the trees to the two women. He morphed into his human form, and Jarka visibly relaxed. "Sir, we need to know more about the Blue Dragon's neurotoxin. Can you describe it and what it actually does?"

"When they are hunting, they snort out the toxin. It is a thin bluish spray. When it hits living tissue, it numbs and paralyzes the surfaces on which it lands. The antelope then collapse onto the ground and the blues then merely pick up their dinner."

"So they blues are not affected when they ingest an antelope that's covered in the stuff?"

"Not in the slightest. Why all this interest in their toxins? Have the blues been attacking as well?"

"Oh no, sir. Nothing like that. In fact, we've never even seen a blue before." Jarka then explained her complete findings to Aldrick. "So those seventeen women's arms that you removed contained a tiny amount of a bluish substance? The physician's fingers went numb after touching it? Hum, that sure does sound suspiciously like the blue's neurotoxin at that. My humble opinion, mages, is that this would be a fruitful line of investigation."

"Thank you, sir. We will do that. Thank you, sir." Jarka repeated herself and prepared to leave.

Aldrick chuckled again. "Just Aldrick, mage. Just Aldrick." Somehow Jarka just could not bring herself to omit the 'sir.' He was far too important and impressive to do otherwise.

Back at the infirmary, Jarka and Izabela decided that they had to pursue this new lead. The problem was how? A quick check with the Archmages yielded no information on this topic whatsoever.

"Oh here you two are," Verushka interrupted them. "Been looking for you, Jarka. Have you worked out any way to heal the women's arms yet? I am going to have to address this issue with the ninety-six women today. They keep asking about it, especially Adrianna Whitehall."

"We've finally made significant headway," Jarka reported. "We need to do further research. If that fails, we want the physicians to see if they can cut out the bluish gooey substances from their shoulders. That might end the paralysis, but we both are highly doubtful that will work. We need more time. Tell them not to give up hope just yet, please. I know, sixteen are in dire need of a cure immediately."

"Okay, thanks, Jarka, Izabela. Say, would you mind looking in on three of those who have just given birth? I am afraid that they sat on their arms accidentally and broke them. We all heard the cracks this time. Otherwise we would not have known about it for some time."

"Yes, of course, right away."

"I see the magnitude of the problem," Izabela said as the two headed for the infirmary. "After sixty days of carrying the dragon fetus, their arms have withered to mere skin and bone. I suspect the fetus also leeched material from their arm bones as well. I took the liberty of examining some remains that the physicians had. It is like you said. The bones are very thin and brittle, as if half of their mass had been removed. I am surprised one or more have not gotten gangrene yet."

"We keep a close eye out for that! Have to," Jarka replied, thankful for the assistance of another healing potion maker.

A while later, Verushka assembled the ninety-six women together for a frank and honest conference. "We've at last observed what the dragons have done to your arms." Many women nodded and smiled, hoping against hope for encouraging words, especially the sixteen who had just given birth and whose arms looked more like matchsticks now. Adrianna glanced over at them and shuttered. Hers were still in good shape, just as if nothing had happened to them, only she couldn't use or feel them any longer.

"Unfortunately, the dragons apparently know more about the human anatomy than we humans. Cleverly, they've injected some tiny substance into your shoulders, where those pin pricks are located. While it was a very tiny substance that they inserted, its effect on your arms and hands is catastrophic. I am afraid to say that it is beyond the healing potions that we currently have to repair the damage that they've done. However, our two potion makers have told me that at long last they have some key clues and wish for time to explore them. Of course, there is no guarantee that they will discover a cure, but they want some time to try. It would be cruel of me to tell you to count on the fact that they will be able to find a cure. The reality that we must all face is that this may well be permanent. You have all seen how the arms so rapidly atrophy. In a mere sixty days, they have become skin and bone, all muscle tissues mostly gone. Worse, many of us heard three women's arms break earlier today when they accidentally sat on them. At least they felt no pain, but you all know just how life threatening this is going to be for you."

"So what are we to do?" asked Adrianna.

"Yes, what are we to do?" asked Anezka, who was one of those who'd just given birth and whose arms were frighteningly thin and frail now. Worry lines creased her forehead and she definitely was withholding a mountain of grief.

Verushka sighed, "I wish that I had better answers for all of you. First, let me point out that we've verified that each one of you who have just given birth does have now a strong potential to learn magic. Yes, it is true, if you study hard and practice diligently, we Archmages believe that you all can learn to use magic. I cannot guarantee you that each one of you will be able to achieve the skill levels that the seventeen have, but you all have a very bright future as users of magic, very likely as official Mages at least. We are offering you a new chance at a very worthwhile and remunerative life, if you so desire it. The rest of you also have that same magic energies now running through your bodies as well."

"Let me explain further. After carrying the dragon for sixty days, the build up of magical energies in your bodies is as high as it is in the original seventeen who have already become mages in less than a year. Those who have only just become pregnant, while that same energy is in your bodies now, it is very weak. The longer you carry the dragon, the stronger the energy level becomes and the more likely it will be that you can learn to use magic."

Verushka shrugged, "So what are you to do? I cannot answer that for you. It must be your own personal decision. I can give you my recommendation."

"Please," Anezka asked.

"Okay, here is my best suggestion, but please, it is only a suggestion. Those who have already given birth, it is time to have our physicians remove the atrophied arms. Once that is done, your life is no longer at risk. Immediately after that is done, we will begin your magic training, handling and caring for your personal needs all during your training period, however long that may take, usually several years. There is no cost at all to you. It is the least that we can do for our fellow women. If you wish, you can rest up and give the mages time to do more research, but please be exceedingly careful."

"But what about the rest of us? We heard rumors that we can have this wicked beast in us somehow removed," put in Kamila, who was not due for another two weeks.

Verushka smiled, these were observant women. "My recommendation for the rest of you is to continue on as you are until you give birth. After that, when your arms are then a serious threat to your survival, proceed as I've already outlined and get on with your magic training. That is, I am asking you to build up as much potential to learn magic as possible and at the same time give our mages the time they need to work on a possible cure. While the cure may never come, at least we Archmages believe fully that after birth is done, you will be able to learn magic and learn it swiftly."

She went on, "Now it is true that we now have the skill, thanks to Izabela here, to force that evil, wicked thing out of your bodies even today."

"Why don't you do it?" asked Kamila, who was not due for about a month yet.

"Because remember the longer that you carry it, the greater your chances of learning powerful magical spells become. If we remove it from those of you who were raped just last night, you would find that your ability to learn magic would be perhaps enough to reach the Adept level, if at all. Worse, you would in all likelihood still lose your arms in a few months and then you would be doomed to a terrible existence for the rest of your lives. I know how badly you want to be rid of the foul beast growing inside of you, but think of your future. Endure it and you have the greatest chance to become Mages yourselves and overcome it, as you've seen how the seventeen have."

"When you put it that way, we don't really have much choice, do we?" Kamila retorted. "Spend our lives as a helpless cripple or bear it and become a Mage who can conjure arms and hands."

"Bluntly, Kamila, that is correct. I am not going to pretend otherwise with you. Besides, this gives the mages a bit more time to find a cure, if possible."

"But what about me?" asked Adrianna. "Shadows and stuff. I have to sleep with all the lanterns on brightly in my room."

"Your situation is wholly unique among all of the women that have so far been abducted, Adrianna. Let's talk about yours in private, shall we?" She nodded. The women asked a few more questions and they agreed to follow Verushka's recommendations. As Kamila had said, what real choice had they?

A bit later, Zoran, High Priestess Jarmila, Archmage Nadia joined Archmage Verushka, Jarka, Izabela, and Adrianna. "Your situation is a most unusual one, Adrianna," Zoran began a lengthy explanation. He wanted her to know the full details.

"When a child is born to a baron or baroness or other Duska members, then when they reach puberty, somewhere between ten and twenty-one, it is their birthright and is vitally necessary for them to be given the Ceremony of Ascension. This special ceremony activates something within us and gives us many very special and unique abilities. Among these is the ability to Shadow Walk and to move through the Shadows, which you have seen many times, though you did not know what it was. It also gives us lightning fast reflexes, a sort of second sight or early warning of imminent danger. Plus, it also gives us the ability to learn magic rather swiftly, even if we had no chance to learn it before the ceremony. When it is not given, as in your case, the child often gets Shadow Sickness, which is what you have. It is cured by giving the person the ceremony, of course."

"Barons are often unfaithful to their wives, it seems, fathering children in secret affairs. Ordinarily, the baron would make some provision to see that such offspring are given their birthright, the Ceremony of Ascension, when the child reaches puberty. Failure to do that can have terrible repercussions on the child. You have experienced such things already, and yes, they are extremely scary! In your case, Adrianna, I suspect that your father was the late Baron Tom Witherspoon, though I will research it as soon as I can and give you a better idea who was your father. I owe you that much."

He went on, "Your case is unique, Adrianna, in that you need this Ceremony of Ascension. All by itself, it will give you the ability to learn magic. That means that you could take advantage of Izabela's potions to abort your pregnancy at once. True, unless we have a miracle in fabricating a cure for this stuff that they injected into your arms, you will likely have to get rid of your atrophying arms in some sixty days or so, if you continue to carry the dragon. If you abort it, we don't know if your arms will take far longer to atrophy or not. We've no idea on that situation. However, by virtue of your birthright as a Duska, you will still be able to learn magic, like my sisters, Rayna and Lida have. Once the ceremony is completed, I give you my word that I will see that you are fully trained as a full Duska ought to have been trained."

"What I am saying is that you could take the potion of Izabela's today and get started on everything else tomorrow." She brightened up considerably.

"However, Adrianna, there is something else to consider before doing that. Ordinarily, a Duska will spend between six and ten years learning magic and how to best use their special Duska skills. My two sisters are prime examples. Furthermore, until I came along twenty-one years ago now, never in the entire history of the Federation of the Sixteen Planets has a Duska ever become an Archmage. I was the first to be able to join both together. Since then, my dear wife Zdenka has been able to train Duskas Verushka, Nadia, Chesna, and Zelenka to this ultimate Archmage level, an incredible feat unheard of even within the Federation."

"How does this affect you? Simple. As Verushka has already told you, we have observed that the longer a woman carries these foul beasts, the more that their bodies now inherently have magical energies permanently within them. Those that go full term have shown incredible ability to learn magic at nearly triple the rate of ordinary students, perhaps more! It is our shared belief, that if you chose to go full term, you will have the very best chance to also become not only a Duska as is your birthright, but also an Archmage. We cannot guarantee that you will actually achieve that. It all depends on you and how well you take to magic, how well you practice it, how well you learn it, and so on. What we are asking you to consider here is to give yourself the best possible chance to become the very best that you can be, Adrianna. That's all."

"Incredible. I never knew any of this. So I can't get this ceremony until the beast is out of me?" she asked, considering his words carefully.

Jarmila answered this one, "It would be exceedingly difficult and possibly life threatening for you to undergo the ceremony while carrying the dragon within you."

"I'm going to lose my arms either way, right?" she asked timidly.

Verushka answered her. "More than likely. Although we will do our best to find a solution in time, I am doubtful such can ever be found. I honestly do not hold out much hope that a cure will be found in time, but Jarka will do her very best to try. The dragons were too good at what they did to you."

"If I get rid of the dragon today and then get the ceremony and start in on learning all these things, does that mean I have to also lose my arms or can I wait until later," she asked, still clinging to the slightest hope for her arms.

"Yes, you can wait until keeping them becomes life threatening to you," Zoran answered.

"I have to consider mom too, in all this. You see, it is just her and me. She has the inn and without me, how's she going to manage? She probably is wondering what happened to me. The sooner that I can get back to life and help her run the inn, the better. Two whole months is a long time to add on top of everything else. I don't know a darn thing about magic and Archmages or even Duskas, for that matter. I just know that I want to get back to helping mom run our inn as soon as I can. Sitting around for two months doing nothing seems foolish to me. I could be done and back to her sooner if we get started today."

Damn, we forgot all about their relatives! Zoran thought. These ninety-six all have relatives who are alive and wondering what happened to them! Now we've got to handle them too. He mentally sent these thoughts to Verushka and Nadia, not wanting to alarm the others. Verushka rolled her eyes as she got his message, Nadia frowned. Everyone had been so busy that they had not even thought of this aspect.

Verushka then said, "Okay, Adrianna, we will abide by your decision. If you will go with Jarka and Izabela, they will get you the potion. Assuming that you are recovered enough, High Priestess Jarmila will give you your birthright ceremony tomorrow. After that, we will meet again and work out a daily learning schedule with you. Thank you for weighing all the options and making your choice." Adrianna looked both relieved and hopeful. Smiling, she rose and followed the two women out of the room.

"Well, honestly, Zoran, we've been way too busy with these women to realize that they have families to consider in all this," Verushka justified.

"Dad, how can we keep up our subterfuge with the dragons if we let these ninety-six women's families know what's happened to them?" asked Nadia.

"Let me worry about that detail. You handle the women." Both women smiled, more than willing to let him deal with this hot potato. "I'll start in on that after the ceremony. I need to make sure that Adrianna is okay and is safely on her path."

That evening, Adrianna, closely monitored by Jarka and Izabela, complained, "Oh, I've got these awful cramps and I can't even rub my belly!" Jarka quickly began massaging her. An hour ago, Izabela gave her the special potion. It was the worst tasting thing that Adrianna had ever tasted or so she claimed. Now it was working. The dragon fetus was being rejected from her body.

"This is normal, Adrianna. In a little while, you will start bleeding and then it will be all over," Izabela explained softly. It had worked this way many times in the past for her. No one expected what would happen next, however.

Zdenka had just finished working out the next day's lessons for her top level students, when her Premonition spell activated. Startled, she jumped up and opened a Mystical Door to the infirmary room where Adrianna was now sitting on the edge of the bed, complaining of cramps. Jarka and Izabela looked up in surprise as Zdenka's Door appeared. All most at once, so did Verushka's and Nadia's. The three Archmages stepped into the room, saw each other and nodded. Evidently, all three had just had the same vision.

"Jarka, Izabela, please leave this room immediately and shut the door behind you," Zdenka ordered sternly. Something was up, Jarka knew at once, but she hastily obeyed, though she kept looking back over her shoulder to see if anything was happening until Izabela shut the door. Both put their ears to the door. Curiosity got the better of the two.

"How do we handle this one?" Verushka asked rapidly, slightly scared. Nadia looked very pale and said nothing.

"Roman Candles through the ceiling," Zdenka replied. Already she had raced through all her spells in search of an answer. She found none, but did recall reading about something similar in one old, dusty volume. "Prepare to absorb and shoot it out through the ceiling."

"Oh! It's really hurting now! Something's wrong. I can't move my arms. Oh god!" Adrianna began to panic.

"Put your hands on her body. Whatever we do, we must not let go," Zdenka said rapid fire.

"What's happening to me? Am I dying?" Adrianna wailed, becoming terrified again. She felt the three women's hands upon her shoulders, forming a sort of human pyramid around her. Without warning, it began.

Enormous quantities of magical energy suddenly surged up and out of Adrianna's body. She lit up like a giant bonfire. The three Archmages absorbed the energy and released it upwards towards the ceiling, like some gigantic Roman Candle, shooting fire and flames skyward. All four women's hair rose up into the air. Each strand of their hair fought to get as far from each other strand as possible. For a moment, Zdenka felt like her own body might explode.

A minute later, the energy flow vanished, as suddenly as it had come. Lying on the floor was the remains of the dragon fetus. The four women looked at each other's hair and they started to laugh. Soon all four were roaring, their hair looked absolutely wild, in a dire need of brushing. At least it had fallen back down. "What happened? I feel a whole lot better. The pain is gone, but I still can't feel my arms," Adrianna asked, very confused.

"When the dragon fetus was ejected from your body, it caused a massive release of magical energies, which likely would have killed you, had we not absorbed it and released it harmlessly into the air," Zdenka explained.

"Mom, look, she's got the same energy levels now as those who have just given birth!" exclaimed Nadia. All three examined Adrianna carefully, verifying that was indeed the case.

"Well, *this* is an interesting discovery. It seems that you have the same huge energy potential within you as our seventeen women have," Zdenka explained. "Perhaps you will be learning magic at an accelerated rate as well. I wonder if this is unique to you as Duska born or if it will happen to the other women as well?"

Jarka knocked on the door and asked what was happening. The three now let them return and explained what had happened. "You should have seen our hair!" Adrianna cheerfully described how wild it had been. After making sure that there were no ill effects and making her drink a healing potion just to be on the safe side, the three left her in the care of the two potion makers. They had to discuss this new phenomenon immediately.

After much discussion, the three agreed that they needed to repeat this with one of the other women. By the next morning, everyone had heard about the Roman

Candle Phenomenon as everyone was now calling it. Zdenka again got the ninety-five women together and explained what had happened. She ended by asking, "We would like to have one volunteer who wishes to end her pregnancy now and take a gamble on this, realizing that you might be jeopardizing the speed with which you will later be able to learn magic. If it fails, you could go slower in your studies, probably like one of our normal students. If it works, we have a solution for all of you."

Zusa volunteered. Two hours later, she too went off like a Roman candle. Magical energies shot through the ceiling — this time witnessed by Zoran's whole group. When it finished, Zusa was carefully examined, and they discovered that her body now also held the same level of magical energies as the original seventeen had. Embolden by this incredible discovery, though clueless about the reason for this phenomenon, the Archmages decided to go ahead and treat all of the remaining pregnant women. If nothing else, they would not have to deal with ninety plus births and the women could get started on their magic training significantly sooner.

The various mages and Archmages teamed up in trios and began treating all the remaining ninety-four women. It took them two days, but by suppertime the next day, no pregnant women remained in the infirmary, much to the relief of everyone. Further, all of the women were feeling very much alive and attuned to magic, eager to begin learning! Izabela got quite a workout preparing so many potions in a big hurry. Also, to be safe, Jarka made each woman drink one of her healing potions as well. Hastily, she worked to brew another large quantity of them. Never in her life had they gone through so many healing potions in a single year.

The following day, the Archmages met to discuss just how they could possibly train so many women. Already Zdenka was training twenty-eight of these women in addition to her dozen regular students. Verushka had twenty-three. Nadia had thirty, but hers all had their arms. Now they had to deal with an additional ninety-six more whose arms were likely going to be lost. Sixteen were matchstick arms already and another sixteen were only a few weeks behind them. Nadia had not taught magic before and Zdenka did not want to overload her. Verushka had taught a few, but not many. Likewise, Zdenka wanted to keep her load low, especially since they were all armless and required special handling. Zdenka had room for one additional student in her tower, all available bedrooms were now occupied and then some. She gave the last room to Adrianna, who now needed special treatment. What to do with ninety-five more?

Zoran came to their rescue. He turned the nearly unused fourth floor of his Manor House over to the ninety-five women. Zdenka had no real choice but to have Zoran request Archmage Kate Zimir of Veklov Province and Archmage Marjeta of Vraz Province to come to Brn and assist in the training of these women. While Zoran promised to help as well, she knew that he needed to be free to handle everything else in the world. Hence, she asked Archmage Marek to begin teaching some. Additionally, Lida and Rayna decided to also stay on and help. Further, Zdenka had to ask Mage Jarka to lend a hand. The three mages would be able to help train some on the Adept useful spells as well as many of the lowest level "real" spells as well, though the Archmages kept their eyes on them to make sure all went well.

Teaching magic was totally new to Jarka, but Lida and Rayna had already been helping with this and now were given even more responsibility. Essentially, the three Archmages were given thirty-two students each along with one of the mages. Their first action was to use their spells to duplicate enough materials for the women to use. That took them a couple of days to accomplish. On the 10th of August, the ninety-six began their studies of magic in earnest.

The day after Adrianna recovered, High Priestess Jarmila performed the long overdue Ceremony of Ascension on Adrianna. Dressed in her fancy white robes with shimmering bands, one for each of the forty-eight Circles of Ascension, Priestess Jarmila began her special chant. Zoran stood by his Sky Blue Circle and observed, ready to assist if something went awry.

Adrianna, quite nervous, stood beside her wearing a new white cotton dress, her arms hanging lifeless at her sides. Jarka had brushed out her hair and declared that she was going to be the prettiest Duska ever, which pleased Adrianna, though she didn't really believe that because of her arms. At the correct time, Jarmila took Adrianna's hand even though she could not feel the priestess' hand, and they slowly began walking around the Circle, stepping on the forty-eight colored threads. Suddenly, Zoran was connected to his Circle and was a silent observer of the actual Ceremony of Ascension. This phenomenon was not new to him. He'd discovered that always happened, way back when he had insisted Akira and Chika get their birthright Ceremony of Ascension here.

Priestess Jarmila instantly realized that he was present but did not otherwise react. As expected, Adrianna got dizzy, disoriented, and nauseated. Still, the two continued to walk the Circle. At last, the two entered the Shadows disappearing from the Circle of Ascension.

Jarmila led Adrianna to all of the sixteen planets in the Federation of Planets, one by one, following the ancient rites. After the trip was done, she repeated it, only this time, Adrianna began to understand. Her special gland now fully activated. Gone was her dizziness, her nausea. The third trip around, Adrianna thought, *Well this isn't so bad now, is it?*

When they stepped back out of the Shadows, Adrianna was all smiles. Per Zoran's request, Jarmila then, while still holding on to her, had Adrianna repeat the process, pulling the priestess to all of the planets. Finally, she and Adrianna practiced stepping into and out of the Shadows many times until Adrianna felt completely at ease with the Shadows. Gone was her lifelong fear of the Shadows. More importantly, she understood what the Shadows were and her relationship to it.

When the two finally stepped back into his Circle, Zoran said proudly, "Welcome Duska Adrianna Whitehall. Welcome to the Circle of Ascension of the Free Peoples of Adapazan." Adrianna beamed with pride and self-confidence.

"I have much to learn — I can see that! Whoever my father was, it was criminal of him to not have seen that I *got* this ceremony! All these years, I have been so terrified of this that I did not understand but yet saw so clearly."

"Yes, it certainly was, Adrianna. You are right. We have to hone your Duska skills and senses, as well as get you trained in magic use. Part of the Duska training involves diving out of the way of certain death. You know, when someone attacks you. However, all that is going to a problem with your arms. If you dive to the floor, you are likely to break them in many places by landing on them. They are going to be nothing but a huge hindrance to you from now on, unless by chance we can undo what the dragons did to you."

"I sense that you are right. I desperately do not want to lose them. I've been clinging to the tiniest hope that they will find a way. Now, I see things differently. I need to learn much and fast. I feel so different, so, so powerful. Perhaps I can get by somehow without them. The seventeen sure are doing fine and I hate to hold up this training for two months. If I get them removed now, can we begin my training really soon, Baron Zoran?" she asked.

"Yes, just as soon as Jarka pronounces you healed, likely a day at most. I am going to personally see to your Duska training. Zdenka will handle your magic training," he replied.

"How can I ever thank you for what you have done and are doing for me?" she asked. He smiled. Her responsibility level had already risen far above what it had been only yesterday. Becoming a Duska had a tendency to do just that.

"Become the best that you can; then help others. I'd like you to consider staying here on Adapazan with us when you are done. I am going to visit your mother later today and let her know that you are safe and that we are giving you the training that was your birthright." She thanked him repeatedly and the three chatted a while longer. In the end, he convinced her to get started on her magic training and give Jarka a little time to find a cure. Duska training could wait a little, besides, Zoran had quite a lot to do fairly soon. He needed a bit more time as well.

That afternoon, armed with directions from Adrianna and insisting that he go alone, Zoran stepped out of the Shadows and onto the main street of Westfarthington, Terra. Quaint stone buildings lined the street of this small farming town. The inn was easy to spot; there was only one. It was small and he readily saw that Adrianna was right — they were just barely able to make ends meet. He estimated that they could take in ten boarders, but the main pub area could hold perhaps fifty. Upon entering, he saw a forty year old woman sweeping the floor. She had long raven hair, just like Adrianna, and blue eyes that missed little. Even in middle age, she was quite attractive and Zoran guessed that had drawn the baron to her some twenty years ago.

"Pub doesn't open until five. Rooms are available now, if you need one," she spoke politely, but in a no nonsense manner.

"Are you the owner of this inn?"

"Yes, stranger, I am. Beth Whitehall. Why?"

"You have a daughter, Adrianna, who has recently gone missing during one night?"

She nearly dropped her broom. Her face flushed. "Yes! Adrianna. How did you know that? What do you know about it? Did you kidnap her? Out with it or I am calling the sheriff!" Her face grew more and more flushed; her near constant worry was no longer suppressed.

"Please sit down. I have a long story to tell you. Yes, Adrianna is now safe and is doing extremely well. Please, Beth, sit down." He slid a chair out and sat down himself. Mechanically, she duplicated his action, sitting across from him.

"Adrianna was abducted by dragons, but we've rescued her and ninety-five others and she is now doing well. Might I ask you why you've never told her who her father was? He was a baron, right?"

"Who — who — who are you? Dragons? Oh my god! She's alive? They didn't kill her?"

"I am Baron Zoran Vladislov of Adapazan. Yes, black dragons. She is alive and fine. Now then, why haven't you told her who her father was?"

"Baron? Well, I can't. Really, I can't. He gave me this inn free but he told me that if I ever told anyone, even her, who he is, then he'd take the inn back and throw us out in the gutter. I just can't tell you or her. Don't you see? This inn is *all* that we have. Without it, we're penniless. I just can't." She fidgeted and toyed with her skirt.

"Yes, you can tell me. In fact, I have a pretty good idea who he was. If I am right, you are no longer bound by that oath. He's dead."

"Dead? I had no idea. He's never been back here, not since he learned I was pregnant with Adrianna. That's when he swore me to secrecy and gave me this inn to support her."

"It was the late Baron Tom Witherspoon, wasn't it?"

She crimsoned. "He's dead? Really?" He nodded. She visibly relaxed, "Well, then I guess there's no harm in it. Yes, he came into town and back then I was the prettiest young girl in town. I was so taken with his charm and demeanor and apparent wealth — well, you must know how it goes."

Zoran smiled, "I understand. Also know this, Baron Tom has denied his and your daughter her birthright."

"Birthright?" she asked confused. "What birthright? Money? Dowry?"

"No, nothing so mundane as that. He was a baron and a Duska. Your daughter has inherited this from him. She should have been given her Ceremony of Ascension and been trained as a Duska, to say nothing of learning to cast magic spells. All this, he denied her, just to keep his dark little secret from the world."

"A Duska? A mage? My Adrianna?"

"Precisely. I have had my High Priestess perform her Ceremony of Ascension. Your daughter is now officially Duska Adrianna Whitehall. She is at this moment learning her to use her special Duska skills and is learning to cast magical spells at my Fortress in Brn, Adapazan."

"You are kidding me? A real Duska? My little Adrianna? One of those super powerful people? Casting magic spells? My Adrianna?" Clearly, she didn't believe it or was totally overwhelmed by this news. He couldn't tell which yet.

"Yes, all those. True, she has perhaps a couple of years of training ahead of her to master all that she ought to already know at her age. I am covering all of her expenses until she is fully trained and able to make her own way. She will be a most powerful young woman when she finishes her training."

"If this is so, I cannot possibly thank you enough! Can I see her? I miss her terribly. We've never been parted since she was born. I've been heartsick ever since she just vanished a few days ago. I've been sick with worry. Please, can I see her?"

"I have a better idea. What would you say if we sold this inn and I help you purchase a much better, far more profitable inn in Brn? Then, you could see your daughter every day, though it would have to be in the evenings when she's done with her studies. I know that she misses you very much and would really love having you close to her."

"If I can see her and verify what you are saying is true, then I would give anything to do what you say. You must understand me. I've been on my own supporting and raising Adrianna all these years. I have learned not to trust men, if you take my meaning."

"Absolutely. I certainly do know what you mean. That is agreeable with me as well. Shall we go now?"

"Well, I can get Amos to run things tonight. Sure. Need a few minutes. Does she want me to bring her some of her things? Dresses? Hair brush?"

"No, we have already provided her with the things that she needs." Beth quickly summoned Amos, who was working in the basement, lugging ale barrels. She issued her orders and then returned to Zoran, straightening her dress and undoing her bun, allowing her hair to fall naturally.

"I guess I am ready now."

"Okay, please sit down for a minute. There is a bit more I must tell you before I take you to her." She did and stared at him. "The dragons have been abducting quite a few young women from many of the Federation planets."

"Why would they do this? We've heard all sorts of wild rumors, but we don't know what to believe."

"They are doing interspecies breeding, impregnating the women so that they then give birth to baby dragons. It seems the dragons only breed every ten years or so."

"Oh my god no! My poor Adrianna! Did they. . ."

"Yes, I am afraid so. However, it is far worse than mere rape. They blinded the women and somehow paralyzed their arms in a permanent manner, such that nothing any of us Archmages have been able to undo. We've managed to remove their blindness, except for six women whose eyes were physically removed. The women's arms are atrophying and quickly become mere skin and bone. Yes, Adrianna is among those many women who have lost the use their arms. She is still hoping that we can find a cure for her and ninety-five others like her. If we cannot, it's pretty grim. Their arms eventually atrophy, becoming skin on bone, extremely dangerous to the women's lives. At that point, the physicians have little choice but to remove what's left of them."

Beth looked absolutely crushed. She began crying as it fully registered. Zoran continued softly, "Take heart. As a byproduct of their ordeal, all of these women now have an uncanny ability to learn magic and at an unbelievable rate. Last November, we rescued seventeen women who lost their arms. My wife has been training them for almost a year and every one of them can now cast spells that give them their arms back. So it is not going to be utterly devastating for her in the long run. We will do everything possible to help her learn to cast the spells which she can use to have arms again. Right now, she is fully healed and quite healthy and is extremely eager to start learning her magic spells, but she desperately wants to see you. I know that it would be a huge help to her if you were nearby for support. That is one reason why I would like you to move to Brn to be close to her."

"But how can she survive without arms or the use of them? Others are like her? How many are you talking about? Ninety-five more?"

"In the last few days, we have rescued all of the still living women that the dragons have been abducting over the last several months. In her group alone, there are ninety-six women.”

“ Ninety-six! Oh dear god! So many will need help with everything! I absolutely *must* move to Brn today! I can help many of them with everything.”

“I understand. Your help will be most welcome. I would also like to let you know that Adrianna is responsible for our even locating her and these women. We had no idea where they were at until Adrianna tried so hard to contact any other Duska to help her. She reached me across the Shadows and, because of her reaching me, I was able to find her and all the others. The ninety-five women owe Adrianna their lives. If she’d not tried to use her untrained Duska senses to reach someone, we’d have never found them before they died giving birth to the baby dragons. You can be immensely proud of your daughter. She saved not only herself, but ninety-five other women.”

“She did that? My little Adrianna? Well, she always did want to help others.” Beth did look extremely pleased. Zoran then took her hand and stepped into the Shadows. He moved swiftly, minimizing her extreme disorientation, but hovering briefly over Brn, giving her a birds-eye view of the thriving city, some ten times larger than her town. His castle with the Archmage towers was also quite impressive. He took her into his private study, where Zdenka brought Adrianna. He had sent her a Message in advance.

“Mom! You came! I am so glad to see you!” Adrianna rushed to greet her mother, who gaped at her daughter’s lifeless, dangling arms, then threw her arms around her, hugging her daughter tightly. Both began to cry. “Mom! So much has happened to me. I am a Duska now, a real Duska, just like the baronesses! I’m learning magic too.”

Zoran allowed the two some private time together. A while later, Adrianna asked if she could show her mother around and have her meet some of her new friends and other women. Since it was dinner time, they headed to the Great Hall where everyone congregated. Beth was visibly shaken seeing so many women in such dire need, but she also met Danika and several other women and began to see what Zoran meant. Later that evening, Beth asked if she could stay here permanently and help the many women with their personal needs. Her help was accepted and he arranged for her inn to be sold.

The next Sunday, he took Beth and Adrianna on a tour of Brn and suggested a couple of inns that might be purchased. To his surprise, Beth made an entirely different offer. “I mean no offense, baron, but I would be far more useful in your kitchen. With so many mouths to feed and so many women to help, I would dearly love to help cook for them, help them dress, wash and brush their hair, things like that. I am a good cook.”

“You are hereby hired, Beth Whitehall!” He put her on his payroll that evening. To her surprise, she found herself making four times what she had been earning from her inn. More importantly, she was contributing something that she saw was needed and valuable.

Zoran was now convinced that arrangements had to be made for all the other ninety-five abducted women and their loved ones. Just what this would entail, he didn’t know at the moment, but he knew this was vitally important for the human aspect of the women and their families.

Chapter 25 Repercussions

Zoran knew that he had to notify Aldrick of what the reds and blacks had been doing. However, he mulled this over for several days, while assisting Adrianna and the others. He knew that Aldrick would be furious that they had broken their word to him. He'd tried hard to put a stop on the abductions, knowing full well that if it continued, the humans would do far more than declare war on dragon-kind. Yet, they had continued. Still, Zoran was pleased that he had left the dragons in complete mystery over the disappearance of the women and had put a temporary halt on their abductions for the time being. He had little doubts that the dragons would eventually hatch up another plan to continue their interspecies breeding. For now, the abductions had ceased.

If, however, Aldrick went to the reds and blacks and confronted them about the abductions and told them that Zoran had rescued the women, then they could easily go right back to it again, probably using another location on Voss that was wholly unknown to them. This time, they had been phenomenally lucky that Adrianna was able to send out her message through the Shadows. Had she not, these ninety-six would be dead and many more abducted, sixteen every couple of weeks. If they resumed their abductions, Zoran knew that the barons would have no choice but to take far more drastic actions against the dragons. Just what that might be, he didn't want to speculate at the moment.

Hence, notifying Aldrick was fraught with peril. He debated the issue for several days, considering other aspects. The loved ones of these women needed to know that they were alive and well, that they were really on their way to learning powerful magic, but also the terrible price that they had paid. Some, he now knew, had their own children at home and some were married. The only thing that kept these new women from a total emotional collapse was their driven desire to learn enough magic to be able to overcome what had happened to them, at least at this point in time. He suspected that in due course, they would also develop a love of magic. Some already knew that mages on their planet were extremely important people, wielding power and wealth. One could not overlook the fact that this also was playing a role with these women.

They were confronting a personal physical disaster, shared in common by nearly a hundred of them and that also helped them keep their own previous lives on hold while they frantically learned magic. Yes, they were doing everything possible to learn everything in one day, valiantly trying to go as fast as possible. Well, the original seventeen had behaved much the same way. That would soon wear off as they actually began casting spells. Nevertheless, their families ought to be notified.

That notification in and of itself would further complicate matters. Upon hearing the full story of her daughter, Beth had insisted on seeing her daughter. Once she saw Adrianna, nothing else mattered but her desire to be there and help Adrianna anyway that she could. Would not other women's families and relatives feel much the same way? How could he deny them the chance to visit? What could he do when many subsequently begged to stay and help their loved one? What about the women's babies and young children?

Then, there was the inevitable political fallout. His and Zdenka's original plans were to train the women fully and then return them to their home planets. As either Mages or Archmages, the ruling barons would certainly hire them on the spot! He knew that the barons were desperate for more of these powerful magic users and would recompense the women more than likely beyond the women's wildest imaginations. Yes, the barons would help them develop rewarding careers. Certainly Jing was in dire need of mages.

His mind drifted to Danika and these original seventeen from Adapazan. As their baron, he really appreciated having seventeen more powerful mages on his world and he could not help but wonder if some might achieve even higher abilities, Archmage perhaps. Already the other barons drooled over the sheer number of Archmages on Adapazan and this was allowing him to deal far more effectively with the dragons than any other world. Yes, any baron would dearly love to have these women returned to his world as fully trained mages or better.

Prior to the recent arrivals, the tallies were very lopsided, in that Terra had thirty-three women in training, Jing had eight, and Cosma had twelve. This didn't count the lesser possibilities, that is, those who had been impregnated by the greens and were learning at a normal student rate — the ten on Cosma and the thirty on Jing. That didn't include the twenty-one total from Adapazan or the two Rehor women who begged him to never send them back to Rehor, not ever. He had agreed to their wishes. That left the other rulers out in the cold and left Terra anticipating an unbelievable influx of new mages, thirty-three!

Now the game had shifted, the ninety-six came pretty much evenly divided among fifteen of the sixteen worlds. None of the women came from Asami, the water world. Baron Goro would be totally left out of this huge influx of potential new mages. The political ramifications were huge. Even Duska Adrianna Whitehall was going to be a problem. Zoran strongly suspected that she would not desire to return to Terra when she was fully trained. Yet, she ought to be recognized as the half-sister of the ruling barons! In fact, she ought to be in line for one of the thrones, should something happen to one of the barons. But would they accept her and give her her proper birthrights? He doubted that very much and she, in turn, would not return to work for them. Politics would definitely become a thorny issue.

On the other side of the coin, only Aldrick stood the slightest chance of reining in the treachery of the reds and blacks. Only he could potentially stop them from their continued abduction of women and their wicked interspecies breeding plans. Aldrick had to know. If the reds and blacks once more promised to cease and desist, what would prevent them from secretly doing just the opposite as they had been doing all summer? Worse, had it not been for Adrianna, they would not have known where any of the women were being held and almost another hundred would have been dead by now. If the reds and blacks merely found another secret place, the whole game could begin once more. At this moment, he had them stymied under the false belief that something had gone horribly wrong with their breeding program on Voss. That meant no more abductions, at least for a while. Zoran faced a tough decision.

On the 12th of August, he finally visited Aldrick in the dragon's cavern high in the northern mountains north of Brn. Sofie had gone on a hunt and the two of them sat down to chat. "Aldrick, I don't know how to say this best, so I will just tell you the full story. Perhaps, we can work something out."

The old dragon merely said, "Hum!" Zoran explained in vivid detail what had been happening on the sixteen planets during the summer months. He told how Adrianna had somehow reached him with her frantic cries for help. He told him about the cavern complex on Voss, which startled Aldrick noticeably! Aldrick grinned when he heard how Werner and Dario had bought into the illusion that the Archmage created and had thus terminated the program on Voss, ending the abductions for the time being.

"Let me get one thing clarified, Zoran. The reds and blacks have now given you nearly two hundred women who are going to rapidly become mages and perhaps some even Archmages?"

"Absolutely, Aldrick. The original seventeen are full mages already and are working on the advanced spells now. I am hoping that by winter they will be able to cast Disintegrate spells as well. When I add that many more mages to my arsenal, I will have a deadly strike force against the reds and blacks. That's something they ought to consider. Within a few years, the reds and blacks will have helped create the strongest attacking force anywhere in the universe and you can count on those women seeking revenge against the reds and blacks," Zoran play his final card, making the only move he could see which Aldrick might be able to use to persuade them to stop their interspecies breeding program.

Aldrick pulled his mighty chin. "Now that is a powerful argument that I can use with them. Yes, yes indeed."

"Please, may I ask another thing of you? When you discuss this with them, they are going to know now that the hundred women didn't dissolve and perish and that they are now in Brn getting trained. I'd rather that they didn't know that I and my staff were the ones who found the women and rescued them. I'd appreciate it if you told them that you were behind the locating of their caverns on Voss and that you and your golds rescued the women and left them with me. That would seem very believable to them."

Aldrick chuckled. "That will leave you off the hook. All right, I will do this. It may also give me more clout over the reds and blacks if they think that I have such powers. Agreed. I will meet with them and do all that I can to get them to stop. Even though you are building up a powerful attacking force, Zoran, we both know the consequences of a war between our species. We are few, but immensely powerful. Humans are many, but weak. Millions of humans will die and hundreds of we dragons as well. Who can say what the outcome will be, save an enormous and tragic loss of life. We must keep this from happening, old friend."

"Yes, Aldrick, somehow we must. I will continue to try to keep the mages in check. As far as the Federation's Strike Force One, while it has killed a few dragons, my man in it has been keeping it from doing much more than that."

Later that day, Aldrick summoned Dario and Werner before him. His summons carried an enormous weight and the two decided to play along with the human-lover gold. "So what do you want? Have you seen reason now? They have fighters out hunting down and killing us dragons now," Werner, the black, fired the opening salvo.

"Minor, Werner, hardly worth mentioning. No, I want to talk about you two breaking your pledge to stop abducting human females and breeding them. I know all about your latest attempts back on Voss. Who do you think found your secret caverns and got those poor women out of there, eh? You believed there was some kind of incompatibility with Voss that made the women seem to dissolve and vanish. Clever of me, eh? We golds are not to be trifled with!" He bellowed, causing both smaller dragons to involuntarily jump nervously.

"What? You? You stole a hundred of our women with our babies inside them?" Dario exclaimed shocked. Until now, neither dragon had even considered that Aldrick, the gold, would ever interfere with them. He was a dragon, after all, not a human.

"Yes, with a little help of my fellow golds. We dropped the women off in Brn, Adapazan. Zoran's people are now caring for them. When I told you I wanted this stopped, I meant it!"

Werner's mind raced to absorb this new and startling revelation, which cast an entirely different picture on everything. Dario, the red, was merely befuddled, trying to grasp the significance of it all. "Well, it's stopped now," Werner, the black, decided to speak the truth.

"It had better stay that way. Do you two realize what you have done with your ill thought out plans?"

"Yes, we are trying to increase our dwindling populations," Werner, the black, replied, wondering if Aldrick had become senile. It was obvious that they needed to increase their numbers. So many had died of starvation on Voss and here in these new worlds many had died.

"Fools! Utter fools! Your idiotic attempts have nearly brought the total destruction of all dragon-kind upon our heads!" Aldrick, the gold, bellowed.

Now he has lost it! Werner, the black, thought. "What in the world are you talking about, Aldrick? These petty, weak humans can easily be wiped from any planet."

"You are fools then! Your impregnating of these normal humans has infused their bodies with huge magical energies, which is allowing them to learn magic which otherwise would have been completely beyond them. On top of that, they are learning spells at triple the normal rate. Those women who Zoran rescued from you last November have already become full mages and are about to master Disintegrate spells! Within perhaps a year or so, thanks to you two, Zoran will have trained up over two hundred mages and Archmages out of those women! Can dragon-kind withstand an attack of two hundred Archmages?"

Werner and Dario turned pale. They had no idea this was happening. "Two — two hundred, you say?" Dario, the red, muttered, visibly shaken.

"Yes, every one of those women who has been rescued and who you had impregnated is now rapidly becoming fierce mages and Archmages!" Aldrick exaggerated, of course. "My guess is that within a year or two at most, these petty humans as you call them will have the power and ability to slay us all. Furthermore, thanks to you two, they will also have the *motivation* and *drive* to do just that! *Revenge* for what you've done to them."

Werner, the black, wanted to say, "But we didn't know," but he thought better of it. Instead he simply said, "Oh. I give you my word that we will not pursue this any longer."

"It had better stop. If I catch you doing this even one more time, I will personally kill you myself. I hope and pray that I can talk sense into the humans who are now out to get revenge. You have all sixteen planets seeking revenge for what you have been doing. I have my work cut out for me to cool down this hatred before we all get exterminated. Now get out of my sight!"

Werner and Dario made a fast exit, Shadow Walking to Werner's cavern. Once there, both dragons calmed down. Dario, the red, asked, "Do you believe him? I mean about Zoran making those women into Archmages? I mean so many of them cannot even use their arms. How can they even cast spells? I think he is bluffing us."

"I don't know. He seemed serious enough. We should put a spy in Brn and have him see if he can find out if this is true or not. No, what bothers me is that the golds are now siding with the humans and not with their fellow dragon-kind. Most unsettling, Dario, most."

"Well, yes, I suppose so, but are we really going to quit? I mean this breeding program is really working, if they stop stealing our pregnant women that is."

"For now, we best put it on hold. Not because Aldrick said so, but because he knows where we have been holding them. We'll need to figure out a fool proof location before we resume. Next time, we simply cannot allow Aldrick or the humans to steal away our unborn babies before they are born. Let's find us a spy, shall we?" Werner, the black, suggested.

A week later Rolf, the black, returned from his mission to Brn, Adapazan. His news startled both Werner and Dario. "Yes, boss, these women are being trained and rapidly so. It is the talk of the town. Their useless arms have been cut away for the most part, but even armless, seventeen have already become full mages. I saw some with my own eyes around the city on Sunday. Rumors say they have two hundred women there training to be mages or better. The humans claim once that happens, Brn will be invincible."

"Oh my, this is most unfortunate," exclaimed Werner, the black, thoroughly shaken up. He had not anticipated this. Perhaps Aldrick was right about this unexpected side effect of the breeding program. Well, it would not have happened if the humans had not been allowed to steal back those women, he thought. But what to do now?

He knew a direct attack on the fortress at Brn was out of the question. They had tried just that last year and lost far too many dragons and accomplished nothing. There were just too many mages and Archmages there and now with so many more present, it would be suicide to attack it again, not without marshaling a huge army of dragons. What to do?

The two discussed the situation for a while. Presently, Werner, the black, said, "It is becoming clear to me, Dario, that we have two choices really. If we do as Aldrick says, sit back and do nothing, in a couple of years, they will have an army of two hundred mages and Archmages. At that point, we dragons are doomed. We will become second-class citizens, slaves to whatever the humans demand of us. How can we hope to stop two hundred of them? We can't. I say that path leads to the subjugation of all dragon-kind. It is even worse than this. Every month that we delay, their Archmages make more of those evil Rods of Dragon Slaying and Gems of Dragon Control. In two years, heck, they won't even need their Archmages to wipe out dragon-kind. Their weapons will be able to do just that!"

"We could always go in search of another uninhabited planet," Dario suggested.

"Why? These here are perfect for us. No, I have no intention of becoming a second-class species! A slave to human demands, never! There is only one real choice, Dario."

"What's that?"

"We must strike first — now, before Zoran gets those two hundred women fully trained as Dragon Killers. We must take control of these worlds before he can take over all of us dragons. We have to act before he can get those women fully trained. It's that simple."

"But they are too strong for us — you just said so," Dario, the red, protested, growing concerned.

"Yes, for merely we reds and blacks. But what if we had all the others except the golds on our side? Let's not attack the Brn Fortress. Rather, let start wiping out their villages all over the planets. That will force them to spread their mages out far and wide and then we can kill them, reduce the number of their mages until Zoran is so weak that we can take his Fortress and win this war," Werner, the black, explained his reasoning.

"Ah, brilliant. Pull their mages out of one big group, thin them out, and then we can overpower them all. I see. But how? How will we get the foolish Neutrals to join us? They were not about to do that at the last council."

"We will just have to be more persuasive this time, Dario, that's all. I believe that we can, thanks to Aldrick. He may have just given us the ammunition that we need to sway the Neutrals to join us! Come on, we have dragons to meet!"

Chapter 26 Jarka Makes Waves

For a week, Jarka mulled over all that she'd learned about the presumed neurotoxin that the reds had used to deaden the women's arms. True, she was kept busy assisting Archmage Marek with the training of his new students. She marveled at the wisdom of Zdenka who had very cleverly organized these new ninety-five students.

Archmage Marek was male and had not taught before and these were women who had undergone a massively traumatic experience and were still fighting its consequences with their "dead arms," many of whom held onto little hope that they would even be able to keep the severely atrophied appendages. She'd given him the women from their enemy planets to teach. He had nine from Rehor, nine from Dietmar, and seven from Anwyn, the desert world. She also gave him six from Chana, the other desert world. She'd assigned Jarka to Marek so that she could keep an eye on the women. After all, most came from their enemy planets. Jarka smiled as she realized this and that Zdenka was giving their allied planet's women and the neutrals the two female Archmages with Zoran's two baroness sisters as their helpers. Biased? You bet, Jarka grinned.

Archmage Kate Zimir and Rayna were teaching the eight women from Adapazan and six each from Gladno, Terra, Valtr, and Cosma. Archmage Marjeta and Lida were teaching seven women from Gonda, seven from Isi, and six each from Gerde, Alta, and Maeve. Jarka felt that the allied and neutrals were getting the better deal, but then that was as it should be, she felt strongly.

After the first week, she and Marek had the women heavily embroiled in their beginning studies, the broad survey of what magic is all about, its history, what it could and could not do, and so on. Even though these were going to be super-fast students, all this reading would take them a fair number of days. Now she could afford to take time off to research a cure for their arms. Sixteen women were getting quite desperate, though she doubted that even if she cured them today, that their matchstick arms would ever be really usable again. She got Marek's sixteen year old daughter, who was about to have her birthday, Milena, to fill in for her for a few days.

Armed with every weapon she had and two dozen healing potions, Jarka was ready to set out on her expedition. Goal: discuss the neurotoxin with a Blue Dragon. Her problem: blues were found only on Jing and Asami, the swamp and water worlds. Off-world. She had to go through the Shadows and thus needed a Duska to take her. Who should she ask? With so many women to train and help with their daily needs, everyone was quite busy. Then inspiration struck.

"Honani, I need a little help and I hear you are just the man," she said coyly, having tracked him down. He and his male companions were standing on the roof of the Manor House both admiring the view of the towering mountains to the north and Karel's fine collection of falcons housed on the roof.

He bowed, "I am known for helping others acquire what they need," he replied just as mysterious as she sounded. Both grinned.

"I have need to either speak with a Blue Dragon or to examine a recently deceased blue. I understand that they are to be found on Jing and Asami. I am not Duska and have no way to get to those worlds," she admitted.

"Ah, yes, we have only seen the blues on those two worlds. Their bodies are quite long, much like a snake, and they are fabulous swimmers. We've seen them mostly on Asami, where the waters are deep and pure, though we've always kept our distance from them. Burns, acid, cold, and shocks — these we can deal with and usually cure, but not their paralyzation spray," Honani replied.

"Indeed, no!" Askook added. "Once we saw one of their fishermen trying to pull in a fish that a blue had decided was its. The man was sprayed by the blue and was completely paralyzed. He lived but he could not move his arms, head or legs after that. Grim."

"Yes, we think he purposely fell overboard to end his life after that," Cheveyo added. "Grim. We've heard the stuff doesn't wash off. Once you've been sprayed, man, that's it. You are done for, much like these women you have rescued. Oh, I see where you are going with this!" His eyes brightened up and a coy smile creased his lips.

Honani caught it as well and grinned. "So you think there is a connection between these women's dead arms and the blue's spray weapon?"

"Yes I most certainly do. That is why I need to talk to a blue or examine a recently dead one," Jarka replied. These men were sharp on the pickup, she thought. They'd make excellent thieves. She grinned back. "Can you assist me with either?"

"Well, as far as we can tell, both worlds have about the same number of blues living there. That is, in our explorations, we've seen about equal numbers on either world. Jing, however, is nastier to explore. Its swamps are filled with snakes and 'gators and foul smells. We prefer Asami with its vast oceans of pure waters. Of course, you'll need a yacht to get around. There are almost no solid land masses on that world. We know where you can rent one, for a price. The captain will take you *anywhere* you desire, for a price," he hinted. "There are even mermaids on Asami, bet you didn't know about that?"

Jarka grinned, thinking of their rescue of Chika and Akira well over twenty-one years ago. "Of course I do. I know two of them *quite* well."

Honani grinned, "Well, I'll be! Is there anything that you don't know, Mage Jarka?" She knew that he'd make an excellent thief, a man right up her alley.

While Chan and Wen would be glad to help her, Jarka knew that those two were already overwhelmed with the process of regaining control of Jing. Besides, she hated marshes and the dense mosquitoes there. "Asami will be perfect. I'll need the yacht and need to find a blue willing to talk to me. Can that be arranged?"

"Yes, leave that to us. Consider it our contribution to the cause," Honani replied. "First, let us visit with Kachina and get her advice in this matter. This way. She has taken the children out to the pine forest south of the city where there is at last Nature underfoot." The four teleported, arriving at Needle Crest, a favorite hangout for Brn lovers. Here the ground was dense with the soft needles, an ideal spot for picnics and other romantic interludes. The odor of pine was strong and the gentle breeze played songs through the dense evergreens. Kachina and the nine children were playing running games, though she was mostly watching them.

"Hello Mage Jarka. Come to play? This is such a lovely spot amid all that harsh stone of Brn," Kachina said, welcoming her with a wave of her arm. "Come, sit a spell."

Jarka sat down on the soft needles. Kachina then said, "So Honani tells me you need to speak to a blue or examine a dead one on Asami. Is this so?"

"Yes, I think that somehow the reds used some of the blue's neurotoxins to cripple up the women's arms. I need to find out if what we've found inside the women's arms is the same stuff or if the blues know anything about it," Jarka explained.

"I will see the best path for you to follow then, Mage Jarka," Kachina replied. "Cheveyo, you watch the children for a while." Her husband moved over closer to the nine youngsters dashing madly among the trees. Tag was their game.

Kachina unrolled her deer hide mat which she had strung across her back and sat down on it. She crossed her legs, held her hands out before her, palms up, and began chanting in her native tongue. Jarka was about to cast a spell that would translate what Kachina was saying, but thought better of it. Soon the woman's eyes took on a distant look, as if one could see the stars of the whole universe in them. Her voice fell away and only the wind's song and the laughing of the children could be heard.

Jarka finally sat down, her legs grew tired of just standing there. How long had she been in the trance-like state, she didn't know, a half-hour? Maybe more. Almost as suddenly as she had gone into the trance, Kachina's eyes returned to the present location. She spoke, "The one you seek is called Bolivar. He will not speak with you unless you get Baron Goro's permission first. Blues on Asami have little dealings with humans. You may get that which you seek but there will be a price to pay. Baron Goro may not wish to pay. You will have to choose. I cannot say more, but I sense much hangs in the balance. I can say no more."

"Thank you, Kachina. We will speak with Goro first. Okay, then, Honani, I'm ready whenever you are. Please, don't get me lost in the Shadows. I hate Shadow Walking — makes me sick."

Honani chuckled, "As it should, Mage Jarka. I will not lose you. I give you my word. Kachina, who should go with Mage Jarka?"

"Only you, Honani. The blues will not speak with her if there are more than two. They see more humans in a party as threatening," she replied. Jarka wondered just how Kachina could possibly know all these things. Still, she had little to go on if she didn't follow Kachina's advice.

"Since you are ready to go, wait here. I'll get my things and be with you in a couple of minutes," Honani advised and teleported away.

Kachina saw that Cheveyo was still playing with the children and decided to speak with Jarka. "It is a miracle, you know — these women that you've just rescued. Ordinarily, I would have expected many to have jumped."

"Huh?" asked Jarka, not following Kachina's train of thought.

"The woman whose hands were lost. She jumped from the roof to end her misery. Her emotions are still strong there. I felt them. Traces of what happens at a place remains at that place, if only you open your senses to them. Yes, of these hundred women, many ought to have also jumped. Yet, they have not."

"Oh, well, yes, yes she did jump. She'd lost her two babies, her husband, her home, and her hands. I'm sure that she felt that she had nothing more for which to live. It is understandable. Our hundred women, well ninety-six new ones, their bodies have been infused with a tremendous amount of magical energy which is allowing them to learn and pick up magic very quickly."

"Yes, that is what I sense. It has given them an overriding new purpose in life. Yet, I warn you Mage Jarka. They must see it through to the end. If they do not, the goodness will turn to badness."

Jarka wondered just what Kachina meant, but she didn't have time to pursue it further. Honani reappeared, armed to the teeth as she was. "All set. Shall we be off?" he said, offering her his arm. She grabbed it and held on for dear life, muttering to herself how she hated Shadow Walking. Waves of nausea flooded over her as Honani took her to Asami, the water world and the vacation paradise planet. Soon the blue world appeared and Jarka began to calm down as she spotted the island and fortress appearing before her. The sandy beaches were just as she remembered them when she and Bernard took their honeymoon here twenty-one years ago. She focused on these memories as Honani landed them on the beach, well beyond any of Goro's protection spells.

"I will leave you here to obtain the baron's permission while I hire us that yacht that I mentioned. Back soon," Honani said quickly. She picked up the distinct impression that Honani did not want to see Baron Goro. Perhaps they had had some differences in the past, she thought. He stepped back into the shadows and she headed up the beach to the Fortress and Circle complex. Halfway there, Baron Goro came out to meet her. He wore shorts and little else, the temperature was a balmy eighty degrees, the sun shone brightly, and the waves rolled in and out behind her, an idyllic scene.

"Hail Mage Jarka Dragon. It has been a long time since you visited our world. Welcome indeed. Pleasure or business? Have time for a swim and a beach party?" Goro said as he closed the distance between them, his arms open in a welcoming gesture. He also glanced about to see who had brought her here. He knew that she was not Duska and could not have gotten here without a Duska's aid.

"I am afraid that it is a business trip this time, baron. I forgot how wonderful it really is here! I love it. I sure wish I could spend a month here basking on your beaches! No, it's business this time."

"Well, come on inside and at least have an ale with me," Goro replied, still glancing about half expecting to see the Duska.

"No time. I'd love to but no time. You've heard about the recent abductions of women from all of the planets of the Federation except here, haven't you?"

"No! Really? All of them? The dragons! On no! I thought that the problem was supposed to be solved!"

Jarka didn't know how much she really ought to divulge to Goro. This was politically sensitive information and Asami was not technically involved since none of the ninety-six women came from here. "Can you keep a secret? This is all extremely sensitive information, for your ears only!" she lowered her voice, glancing around as if looking for eavesdroppers.

"Oh my goodness! Yes, a secret it will be! What has happened this time?" he was suddenly keenly interested and also made sure that they were not being overheard.

"The reds and blacks have been at it again. Ninety-six women this time. Diabolical, I say. They somehow have paralyzed the women's arms, you know, like those original seventeen women that we told you about at last fall's High Council meeting."

"A hundred? Dear god. Will they also lose their arms like the seventeen? This is most alarming news! How awful. Is it really that bad?" Goro looked extremely trouble and shocked, Jarka surmised, either that or he was extremely good at hiding it.

"Some women's arms have atrophied to matchsticks already. I am here to make a last ditch attempt to save their arms."

"Here? On Asami? What can possibly be here that could help those poor women?" Goro asked, completely surprise by her statement.

"I need to talk with the Blue Dragons, one called Bolivar. I've heard that I would need your permission to speak with him. I don't quite understand that at all, but that's what I was told."

"The blues? Oh!" Goro was not a stupid beach bum as she had always suspected. He instantly made the connection. "You think it was the Blue Dragons who somehow paralyzed these women's arms? The blues are in cahoots with the reds and blacks!"

"No, you are jumping to conclusions on their complicity. No, I think that the reds are using something similar to the stuff that the blues exhale, their neurotoxin stuff. I want to discuss this with this Bolivar fellow, whoever he is. I am trying to find a cure before it is too late for these women, that's all. I'm not sure why I need to have your permission to talk to this Bolivar, though."

"Whew, that's a relief! Yes, the only dragons who find Asami a fine place to live are the sea loving blues. Dad made a deal with them and so far it has been upheld. In general, the blues leave us alone and we leave them alone. Once in a while there have been some slight problems, but overall, it has been a fine arrangement. We don't bother them; they don't bother us. They live far out in the oceans, far from our small islands. By agreement, when communication between our species is needed, I have to send a formal document requesting the meeting. Bolivar is their representative who deals with us, though I really don't know if he is actually their leader. Honestly, we know almost nothing about the blues, except they are fun to watch swimming in the ocean. They are terrific swimmers."

"Good plan. Keep the contact between the dragons and humans small and only go through official channels. I like that idea. Minimizes trouble and confusions," Jarka replied, figuring all this was merely more politics at work.

"I'll make you that document right now. I should warn you. He's a little aloof. I don't think he likes us much," Goro admitted and chanted. A scroll appeared in his hand and he handed it to her. "Present him with this and he should speak with you. Of course, the problem will be finding him. They apparently don't have permanent homes like we do. Last I heard, he was in the far south quadrant. You'll need a yacht. Tell the captain far south quadrant and he'll know where to sail. Can I get you a yacht?"

"No, my Duska friend is getting us one. On behalf of all the women, we thank you, baron for your help. I hope that this proves fruitful. The women are so depending on me to save their arms."

"I simply cannot imagine how they must feel. To lose one's arms is to be almost completely helpless," Goro replied sincerely. "Ah, that must be your yacht coming in now. Be careful with that one. The captain is something of a rogue."

"Thanks, I certainly will. Talk to you later. Thanks again, baron." Jarka shook his hand and used her Mystical Door to step out to the incoming yacht without its having to dock, much to Honani's pleasure. He'd sent her a Message to that effect.

"Did you get what you needed?" Honani asked. Jarka waved the document. "Good. This is our captain, Hachiro. Captain, this is Mage Jarka Dragon from Adapazan, Baron Zoran's mage."

She looked the man up and down. He too wore only shorts. His fit body was nicely tanned from long hours in the sun. He saw her glancing at the ship and quickly spoke up, "She's a bit old, but she's sea worthy. Honani has paid me well to enter dragon waters. What is our destination? No questions asked."

"Far south quadrant," Jarka replied. "I have a document from Goro. It will allow me to speak with this Bolivar dragon. Somehow we need to find him."

"Off we go then. Honani has said that time is of the essence. Normal sailing time to that zone is a week. For an additional ten thousand, we can be there later today," Captain Hachiro explained. Jarka had no choice — a week was way too long. She handed over a couple of gems. Hachiro grinned as he accepted them. "Excellent, excellent. If you will please go below to your cabins, Honani will show you the way. I will arrange for our speedy journey, Mage Jarka."

Honani led her below deck. They shared a cabin. Two hammocks served as beds. "Best get you into one of these contraptions," he suggested. Neither had been in one before and it was a rather comical scene before she finally was securely in hers. She laughed as he struggled into his. "Crazy way to sleep!" Honani commented, frustrated with the awkwardness of just getting into one. No sooner had he gotten into his when the entire yacht slipped slightly into the Shadows.

Jarka called out, "Oh no, not again!" Nausea and disorientation struck her once more! Fortunately, it lasted only a couple of minutes.

When the universe finally seemed stable to her once more, a deck hand knocked on their door. "We are there. It is safe to come back on deck and search for your blue."

Honani rolled over and fell out of his hammock and Jarka laughed. He returned the favor when she crashed into the floor trying to get out of hers. Still chuckling, the two walked back on deck. The sails were billowing in the wind, and the yacht was cutting through the ocean waves. The motion began to take its toll on Jarka. Soon, she leaned over the railing and emptied out her breakfast. Not long after that, Honani followed suit. Captain Hachiro roared, "Land lubbers, mates, land lubbers. Keep your eyes peeled for a blue," he ordered his lookouts.

Jarka looked out at the waters. Water was everywhere. No land was in sight in any direction. She was thankful that she did not live here on Asami! An hour passed before they spotted their first blue. "Wow!" exclaimed Jarka. Ahead off their port the huge, blue, snake-like dragon's body was undulating in and out of the waters in a rhythmic pattern. It had to be at least seventy feet long, though its wings were currently folded back forming a streamlined shape.

As the yacht approached it, the dragon unfolded one wing and dipped it into the waters. The breaking action of the right wing caused the dragon to suddenly make a ninety degree turn in the water, now making for them. As it approached, it raised its enormous head up out of the waters, some fifteen feet tall, looking down upon those standing on the deck. "These are our waters," it said menacingly.

"Speak to him," Captain Hachiro whispered to Jarka.

"I wish to speak to Bolivar. I have a document from Baron Goro allowing me to speak to him. Where can we find him, please?" The dragon's black eyes glanced at the document she held up and nodded its head slightly.

"Very well. You stay here, Bolivar will come to you." The dragon dove back into the water, its head disappearing before the bow of the yacht. All ducked to avoid the following ocean spray. Jarka guessed the dragon had done that on purpose.

They didn't have to wait long. Soon an even larger blue appeared in the waters just off their port side. Jarka guessed that it had either teleported there or Shadow Walked. It raised its head and called out, "Unfurl the document." The voice sounded cold and inhuman. She did as asked and the dragon appeared to be reading it. To her surprise, the document vanished from her hand. "Can't keep it. Don't want it to be reused." He morphed into human form and appeared on the deck beside her, all in one swift motion. "We talk back there where we are not overheard. I am Bolivar, the blue." Wearing only shorts, he walked back to the stern and Jarka followed after him. He was impressive. If he'd been human, the sunlight glistening off of his wet, well-built body would have really pricked her interest.

"Mage Jarka, you may speak now. Why have you sought me?" Bolivar said. She detected either annoyance or possibly a twinge of hostility in his tone, if dragons had such.

"This is going to take a bit of explaining first. The reds and blacks have continued to abduct human females and impregnated them. This time, a hundred women have been recovered, though we do not how many others died while giving birth to the baby dragons. Again, to make sure that the captive women did not try to kill themselves or each other, the reds injected something into their shoulders which has made their arms totally numb, useless. Their bones can even be broken and the women do not even feel it. Worse, over time their arms atrophy and become mere skin on bone."

"So it is true? There are a hundred of these women in your care now?" he asked, displaying a bit of interest she thought.

"Yes, but some of their arms are more like matchsticks now."

"May I ask what you are doing with these women?"

"Well, because of their carrying the baby dragons, their bodies have been infused with magical energies. All are now learning magic and at a very rapid rate."

"So it is true? They will become mages?" he asked even more interested.

"Yes, very likely, though some may well become Archmages."

"Then what Werner says is true. You are making hundreds of mages and Archmages on Adapazan."

"Yes, that is true. These women have been abducted, their families murdered, their arms mutilated and in a few cases their eyes ripped from their sockets. We are trying desperately to give them the means to live a worthwhile life after all that they have endured. After all, I am sure that you would be upset if humans abducted your mate, raped her, tore out her eyes, and paralyzed forever her legs and wings. Surely you would do all that you could to help her gain new skills so she could live a worthy life."

"Hum, point taken. What has this to do with Bolivar?"

"Ah, now we get to the reason for my visit. We observed the reds inserting two drops of a bluish gooey substance into the women's shoulders. Once inserted there, their arms became dead to them and have remained so ever afterwards. I have heard that your race sometimes breaths out a neurotoxin that perhaps acts in a similar manner."

"Yes, it immobilizes our food for us so that we can easily pick up the shark or fish. It beats the red's approach of diving down from above like some silly bird-like creature." She detected a bit of hostility towards the reds.

"Mind you, I have never had the honor of meeting a Blue Dragon before, nor have I ever seen your neurotoxin. Yet, I was wondering if you could look at a sample that we took from some women's arms and tell if it is somehow similar to your neurotoxin."

"Are you suggesting that we blues had something to do with these abductions?" his voice raised up a notch. Anger was definitely present.

"Oh no sir! No sir! Nothing of the kind! I am looking to find a cure only. I do not mean to suggest that blues were involved in this in any way!"

"Fair enough then. Blues do not like reds. Let me see this stuff that you have." She produced her precious vial, though its meager contents were half gone now, used up in her many experiments. Bolivar opened it and carefully sniffed it and then frowned, he looked terribly annoyed, she thought, if dragons could look annoyed. She wasn't too sure about that.

"This is most distressing, Mage Jarka. While it is not exactly the neurotoxin that we breathe out, it is made from it. I find this most distressing indeed! It came from their arms?"

"Yes, our physicians collected it from many withered arms that had to be removed. They got some on their fingers and their fingers have been numb ever since."

"That is to be expected. It is a permanent toxin to human flesh."

"Yes, that's what I wanted to discuss with you. If you blues spray this on your food to paralyze them and then you eat the food, how come you do not paralyze your own selves? As I said, I am trying to find any way possible to neutralize this toxin so that the women do not have to have their arms cut off."

"Our digestive juices neutralize the toxin. While this vial contains a definite neurotoxin quite similar to ours, I do not know if it can be neutralized. May I examine some of it?" Bolivar asked. He poured a few sticky drops out onto the wooden deck and then he spat on it. Immediately, a chemical reaction took place. After a slight fizzle, not dissimilar to pouring vinegar on baking soda, the bluish hue was replaced by a greyish color. He sniffed it again. "Ah ha. Yes, it is neutralized. Test it yourself." Hesitantly, Jarka touched the grey mass, but found nothing happening to her finger.

"Now this is encouraging, Bolivar. Until now, nothing at all even remotely neutralized it. Your spit did the job, incredible!" Jarka exclaimed, but thought, *now comes the hard part. How am I going to bargain for a bunch of his spit?*

To her surprise, Bolivar said, "So now I suppose you want me to give you a bunch of my spit."

"If you wouldn't mind."

"So you can perhaps cure these hundred women whose arms have been paralyzed by the reds when they were abducted and forced to bear their children?"

"Yes."

"And these are the women who are now extraordinarily gifted? The ones who are learning magic so swiftly and may well become mages or even perhaps Archmages?"

"Yes."

"Have not your Archmages and mages been killing many of the reds and blacks within the past year?"

"Yes, but. . ." she admitted. He interrupted her mid-sentence.

"You want me to help you cure these very women who will mature into Dragon Killers?"

"Yes, but they won't bother you, sir." Jarka grasped the reason for his hesitancy. He was a dragon after all. "If they have any beef at all, it is only with the reds and blacks who kidnaped them, did this to their arms, raped them, force them to bear their dragon babies, and if not for us, would have died when the baby dragons were born."

"This is most serious, Mage Jarka. What you ask is that I betray dragon-kind."

Jarka knew that what she said next could well be the most important words that she ever uttered in her life. The fate of at least a hundred women rested on her shoulders, may be countless more in the future as well. Yet, her devious mind saw an opening. "Yes and no. I give you my solemn word that the women will be fully informed that the Blue Dragons were coming to their aid and restoring their arms. If it were not for the blues, they would be armless. That, sir, will be a most powerful incentive for these women to never harm a blue. Further sir, you would not really be betraying dragon-kind. These women, whether they retain their arms or not, will in all likelihood become mages and perhaps Archmages. Casting of magic has little to do with one's arms. On the other hand, they will be most thankful for their arms in their daily living, as you would be if you continued to have the use of your wings and legs, sir. See my point?" She certainly hoped so.

"Well, Mage Jarka, you have a sharp mind. Yes, I do see your point. I will agree to a one time only trade of blue spit for something of vital importance to us blues."

"Oh thank you, sir, thank you. What can we give to you in return?" Relief swelled through her body. Gems, she thought, would be his reply. Never in a million years did she expect what she heard next.

"We want Baron Goro to give us the island known as Orochi. Bring me the Baron Goro's document ceding that island to the blues and I will provide you with a jar of spit," Bolivar stated. He guessed that she would be unable to procure the island and thus he would be seen as offering to help with the cure while not actually doing so. He was still mulling over whether there would be any significant differences between an armless Archmage and one with arms. It seemed to him that lacking arms would make the Archmage vastly more vulnerable. If he lacked his wings or his legs, he knew that he would be extraordinarily handicapped.

"Oh! An island? Oh my. What on earth do you want an island for? I thought that the Blue Dragons were a sea faring creature," Jarka replied. Her mind staggered from the seemingly off-the-wall bargaining request, one she could not hope to obtain. Why did he need an island?

"Orochi has many ideal caves in and around it, perfect breeding grounds for we blues. Bring me that document and we will trade. I must be off now." He bowed to her and dove into the water, morphing into his huge serpent-like form just as he hit the waters. He went under and, though she watched, he didn't surface again.

Honani walked back to her. "Well, how did it go?"

"Good and bad. Good, in that we now know of at least one substance which neutralizes the toxin. Bad in that Bolivar wants me to get Goro to give the dragons one of his islands, Orochi. What *am* I going to do now?"

"Any chance of faking Goro's signature on such a document?" Honani asked.

Jarka smiled, "Well, if I must, I must. First, I suppose that we should talk to Goro about it."

"You want me to give the Blue Dragons our island, Orochi?" Baron Goro exclaimed. Jarka had Messaged him and then teleported to his fortress. Honani sat back on the yacht and enjoyed the warm sea breezes along with the captain. She'd explained that his saliva neutralized the neurotoxin that was used in the women's arms.

"Yes, they seem to need its caverns for their breeding grounds, it seems."

"You don't know about this southern island do you?"

"No."

"It is one of our secret pearl sites. We obtain a fair number of pearls from the oyster beds around there. That is a most expensive piece of real estate on Asami, Jarka."

"But I can tell all of the other barons that their women regained their arms solely and only because you gave up a valuable island to obtain a cure for their women," Jarka began to play politics. "The other barons would be deeply in your debt, Goro."

"Yes, I can see that, but we have a colony of mermaids there."

"I know all about your mermaids, Goro — how you Duska impregnate women and then when the girl children reach the age of around ten, you use metal rings to clamp their legs together so they cannot move them or ever walk again and then force their legs into a mermaid tail. You use them to procure your oysters, using them until they die. If that isn't totally inhumane, I don't know what is. I could let the other barons know about that little dicey thing." Jarka played the last card that she had.

"You wouldn't! Zoran wouldn't let you."

"I would. I am not Zoran."

"This is blackmail."

"No, this is helping a hundred women avoid living a life without arms. You are giving these women their lives back, not to mention gaining great favor from all the other barons in the process," Jarka put the emphasis back to where it ought to have been.

Goro squirmed. He could ill afford to have his mermaid scheme widely known. The only off-worlder who knew about the mermaids of Asami was Zoran and Jarka, and of course their spouses, unless they already told others. He doubted that, since no one else ever mentioned it. This was a steep price to pay for the goodwill of the barons.

Jarka had another thought, "Look, Goro, if the blues ever begin attacking your people, we will have the antidote to their paralyzing breath and I give you my solemn oath such will be readily available to you. The reds went against Rehor and Dietmar. The blacks turned against all the worlds they inhabited. What's to prevent the blues from one day going after you and taking over all the islands they desire?"

"But they've not bothered us yet."

"Key word: *yet*." She punched in that bit of doubt, knowing that Asami had almost no way to protect itself from any dragon attack.

"Does Zoran know about this?" he asked.

"Nope. Should I tell him?"

"No! All right. Let's keep this between you and me. I will agree if you will put it in writing that you will ensure that all of the recipients of this cure of yours knows that they are getting it because of Asami's gift to them and that all of the barons are also told that their women are being cured only because I gave up a huge fortune to the blues to obtain the cure on their behalf. We'll keep the mermaids between us."

"Perfect. Thank you, Baron Goro. I'll write it up now and you can look it over and make any changes you wish." Jarka felt a huge weight lifting. Hastily, she conjured pen and paper and wrote out the declarations. Goro looked it over and suggested a few word changes and she made them. When he finally agreed, she then signed it, with Kimiko acting as their witness.

Once that was done, Goro wrote out another document, ceding Orochi to the Blue Dragons. He needed a couple of days to evacuate his mermaids. She agreed and after thanking him again, returned to the yacht in the far southern quadrant.

"Got it!" Jarka waved the new document in front of Honani.

"How in the world did you manage that? Incredible! He gave up a prize island for spit of a dragon?" Honani replied flabbergasted.

"I am a shrewd negotiator," Jarka replied with a wry grin. No way was she divulging what she had done, not even to Zoran. She'd merely relate the agreed upon generosity angle of Goro's.

Having met Bolivar, she was then able to Message him. *Sir, I have Baron Goro's document that you requested.*

A few minutes later, Bolivar rose from the ocean once more. He delayed a bit, recovering from his total surprise. He had never really considered that Mage Jarka could possibly obtain such a deal for mere spit! After he regained his composure, he surfaced and morphed into his usual robust human form.

Bolivar looked over the document seeking to find any hidden clauses or exceptions or loop holes. He found none at all. Goro simply turned the island over to the Blue Dragons, but requested they not take possession for two days so he could get his people off the island. When he seemed satisfied, Jarka said, "I need this filled, sir. We don't know how much we are going to need for the women and will have to do some experimentation. Neither of us wants to repeat this — well maybe you might, just to obtain another island." She couldn't help interject a little teasing jest.

For the first time, Bolivar cracked a slight grin. "This will take a while." An hour later, he had filled her gallon container with spittle. They bowed to each other and Bolivar dove back into the ocean. Honani and Jarka thanked the captain and he Shadow Walked her back to Brn.

Zoran was there to meet them. "Jarka, you went off world on your own! Don't you realize just how dangerous it is? Honani has a bloodhound Red Dragon that is out there looking for him. You could have gotten both of yourselves killed. Why didn't you ask me for help?"

"Cause you and everyone else are busy, really busy. We had no trouble at all," she smiled waiting for the chance to announce her bombshell. He saw her carrying a gallon container.

"What is that?"

"A gallon of Blue Dragon spit, baron. A couple of drops will neutralize the neurotoxin in the women's arms. Bolivar demonstrated it for me and it works."

"What? You found a cure? Incredible, Jarka!" Zoran forgot all about her going off-world without telling her. "Where did you get that much Blue Dragon spit?"

"Bolivar gave it to me. We made a deal. Baron Goro paid a very steep price to the blues to obtain this cure for all of the other barons. It cost Goro a fortune, but now we have a cure for all the women. I do hope that you will let the many barons know that they owe Goro a huge favor and thank you. He gave up a prized oyster island just to get this cure to the afflicted women. Of course, I do believe I have got tons more than we need right now. Just thinking ahead, Zoran. We've got enough for future needs as well."

Zoran picked her up and twirled her around. The relief he felt was tremendous. "If this works, I will make sure that all the barons know how much they owe Goro. Incredible. Go, get this cure going!"

She smiled. "Need to do all sorts of tests and such. We have to find ways to inject it at just the right spots. I have no idea whether it will be of any use on those with matchsticks for arms though. We'll see." She skipped out of the room and off to her small lab, summoning Izabela on the way.

After some discussion, the two potion makers agreed. Injecting dragon spit into a woman's arm could well cause all manner of other unpredictable things to occur, infections being the least of them. The two decided to do some experiments first. Izabela pointed out that spit contained a lot of water. Perhaps they could distill some of it down and concentrate it while also killing any infectious things that might be in the dragon's spit. They did so and tried putting a drop on a drop of the bluish gooey substance. Once more, it worked and the chemical reaction neutralized the toxin. That took a day.

Another day was spent fabricating a delivery system, using a hollow needle and syringe system the two conjured up, based on the needle that she'd seen the red use to insert the blue toxin. Now came the real problem: how to know where to inject it and how deep it had to be?

Adrianna became their first test subject, primarily because the pin pricks in her shoulders were still barely visible. Using that as a guide and a rough estimate of the depth, Jarka inserted a couple of drops of the extract into each of her shoulders. They waited.

"I feel a burning sensation in my shoulders," Adrianna said. "Something is happening."

"You bet it is! Look, her fingers just moved!" Izabela pointed out.

Within minutes, Adrianna had partial sensation and mobility in both arms, but it was far from complete. Instead of making a second injection, one of the physicians suggested massaging the injection site; perhaps that would spread the extract around some. They did so and more and more feeling returned to her arms and hands. An hour later, Adrianna had fully recovered and began to cry. She was that relieved. So was Jarka, for that matter. Adrianna returned to her magic class waving her arms about — stopping the whole class. Zdenka beamed, this was the most welcome interruption ever!

"We'd best get this cure to the most needy first," Jarka declared, and then began planning how she and Izabela would handle the remaining ninety-five women. That meant the matchstick cases, whose arms looked almost dead.

Physician Bedrich shook his head. "Here, look at these samples that we've saved. He and I have been doing some further studies on the remaining arms of the original seventeen women." They'd cleared away most of the flesh around an elbow and then the wrist. "You see, one of the reasons the women were breaking their arms so easily after they gave birth is that their arms were like this is — the joints were extremely stiff and didn't bend much. Since we could not figure out any cure, we decided to see if we could see why that was happening. See for yourselves. The bones have begun to fuse together." Jarka and Izabela looked at the grizzly sight. He was right.

"So you think that even if we inject the cure, the women's arms may be beyond the recovery stage?" she asked.

"Yes, we thought that we ought to point this out to you. We could be wrong. Maybe the process can be reversed, but maybe it is too late. We just don't know, but you need to know this before you begin," Physician Bedrich explained.

"You sent for me?" the timid voice of Anezka got their attention. She had been summoned from Kate's class to the infirmary. She was one of the worst cases, having gone weeks beyond giving birth. Her arms were extremely thin and brittle. She'd broken her arms three times now in the last two weeks.

"We have finally found a cure, Anezka. It worked on Adrianna. Now we are going to give it a try on you," Jarka explained. They tested her arms and hands first. As the physicians anticipated, her elbows barely moved. Her wrist was almost immobile. Her fingers didn't move at all. Jarka looked for the injection site, but could not find it. Physician Bedrich held up one of the preserved arms, pointing out where they'd uncovered the bluish toxin. Jarka used that as a pattern and performed the two injections. Now they waited. "It shouldn't take long to see if this works on you." She kept her fingers crossed.

"I can feel them! It's working!" exclaimed the young woman. However, not long after that, Anezka began crying. "God! It hurts! My arms, they hurt really badly!" Soon, she was shrieking in pain and agony. While they had restored all feeling in her arms, now the poor woman was enduring the terrible consequences! "Make it stop! I can't stand it!"

Quickly, Jarka cast a Sleep spell on Anezka. The physicians raced to retrieve some pain killers and slipped the liquid into her mouth. "We should keep her sedated and on pain killers a while. Give her arms time to heal, perhaps," Physician Bedrich suggested. They all agreed.

Instead of doing all the worst cases first, they began doing all of the easy ones, handling two dozen each day. Sometimes, a second injection was needed. All of these women responded well. Sixty-four women regained the use of their arms. True, the last sixteen had very stiff arms and needed a long period of recovery and daily warm massages, but they made it. Sixty-four women were elated, overjoyed that Jarka had found a cure for them. The remaining thirty-one were on hold, waiting to see if Anezka could recover.

During these three days, Anezka was constantly monitored, but the excruciating pains didn't abate nor did her arms improve. After the sixty-four were handled, Jarka looked the remaining women over. Fifteen were more than three weeks beyond the sixty day point, while another sixteen were about a week beyond their sixty day point from the time of the injections. At last, Jarka decided to experiment on one of the sixty-day plus one week women, Kamila of Adapazan. Her joints were stiff but there was still some flex remaining. Like Anezka, when feeling and sensation returned to her arms and hands, Kamila was in intense pain and also had to be kept on heavy pain killers, a morphine derivative drug.

The final thirty women visited Anezka and Kamila daily, hoping and praying that the horrible pains they were experiencing would begin to subside and their arms would begin to recover. Oh how these women wanted just that. After a week, Anezka said, "Please, Jarka, please, just take them off me. The pain is intolerable and they aren't getting any better. My arms are just plain dead. Please, I beg you."

With a sad heart, Jarka relayed her request. As soon as the other fifteen in her group heard of Anezka's decision, they each asked for theirs to be removed as well. The next day, Anezka was cheerful and ready to resume her magic studies. Jarka's healing potions worked wonders on her now empty shoulders. Anezka commented, "Look, I have had eighty plus days without them and I am getting used to life without them. Besides, if I work hard at my studies, I will be able to morph just like Danika and the other are doing. It's for the best, Jarka." Two more days passed and the rest of her fifteen women were back into their studies, their shoulders properly healed.

Kamila was also monitored during these busy days. Physician Bedrich attempted to wean her off of the pain killers with some small success. Finally after more than a week in recovery, Kamila, Jarka, Izabela, and the two physicians met to make a final decision. "Look, it has worked some. While I am still taking morphine, it's not as much. I am able to swing my arms around like so. I can sort of bend them a little at my elbow, see?" She bent her lower arms up perhaps ten degrees or so, but that was all. "I can wiggle my fingers."

Kamila sighed. "Take them off me please. If this is all the recovery I get, it's pointless. I can't do anything with them and it is totally delaying my magic studies! At this rate of recovery, it may take a year if they really did ever recover. I am far better off without them and as soon as I can get to the Morph Self spell, I won't need them anyway. I know you did your best, but I want to get on with my life and I can't like this."

To be on the safe side, Jarka asked her fifteen like companions to visit with her and discuss the situation among themselves. After all, the fifteen had been visiting her each day since the experiment began. A half hour later, they all agreed and two days later they were back in their classroom studying away. Their shoulders were nicely healed up, again thanks to Jarka's healing potions.

"Well, we saved sixty-four of them and only lost thirty-two of them," Izabela pointed out as Jarka and the physicians picked up their things. Besides that, Archmage Marek really needed Jarka back in his classroom. "We don't always get what we want, but I think you worked a miracle anyway, Jarka."

That evening when Jarka walked into the Great Hall for dinner, quite exhausted from all the running around she'd done to help Marek's group of thirty-one students learning to cast their Clean spells, the room erupted into a huge round of applause and cheers. Jarka had never had such an outpouring of thanks sent her way before. Her own emotions got the better of her and tears trickled down her cheeks. All her work on their behalf was acknowledged by the women themselves.

Later, she overheard Anezka and Kamila chatting. "I actually did it, Kamila. I cast a for real Clean spell! The dirt really did vanish!"

"So did I! It's fantastic, but I wonder where the dirt actually went? Did Kate tell you that?" Jarka smiled, knowing that the women were now on their way to becoming Adepts, the first step on the road to greatness.

With the successes confirmed, Zoran fired off Messages to all of the barons telling them of the terrific news and the role that Baron Goro of Asami had played. Goro began receiving many thank you's from the other barons, which pleased the beach bum considerably.

Chapter 27 The Problem with Neutrals

During the fourth week of August, Werner, the black, and Dario, the red, began their attempt to rally the neutral dragons to their side. Now they were armed with exciting new data and plans. Why?

Wenzel, an ancient Black Dragon, had just given Werner another brilliant idea. Wenzel was Werner's mentor. Of all dragons, Werner respected old Wenzel's opinions the most. So far, his ideas had worked out, for the most part. Of course no one could predict the constant interference of Baron Zoran. Wenzel had stated factually. "We need to raise far more blacks. The breeding program is crucial, if we blacks are ever going to survive and take our positions as the leaders of all dragon-kind as we were meant to be."

"Yes, but Zoran keeps interfering, finding our secret locations and stealing away our unborn baby dragons," Werner, the black, complained bitterly.

"He is a Duska and they are to be respected. Still their powers are not unlimited. He's made use of that Tracker Honani from Isi to locate some of your secret sites. We now know that for a fact, thanks to the red Sniffer and your spy in Brn. It was blind luck that one of the abducted women was a latent Duska. How could anyone have known that? No one could. Alas, Zoran and his Duska now know where Voss is located. However, they only know about that single location and Voss is large. Pick another location. I have some additional ideas that may keep these Duskas from finding the breeding stock. The Duska use mental communications to reach through the Shadows. Werner, it takes two to communicate. So we use a No-detect spell on each woman. That will handle that part. However, Werner, the real solution is so simple that you are going to bite your own tail when I tell you. I can't believe that I didn't suggest this in the first place."

"What, Great Master? What is the real solution?" Werner, the black, asked. He was nodding as his mentor made his points. He grasped their having overlooked the No-detect spell. True, they were using Blind, Charm Human, and Sleep spells, but this one would eliminate the detection in the first place. What had they overlooked that was so simple?

Wenzel, the black, chuckled to himself. "After you have impregnated the breeding stock, Morph them into a dragon, black or red. When Zoran or anyone comes looking for them, they will only find more dragons, not humans. Make sure they are impregnated first or you will have to wait ten years or so. Blind and Charm should also be kept on them as well as Dominate and No-detect to ensure that they remain under your control."

"Brilliant! You are right! I ought to bite my tail! This also solves the frailty of their human bodies. We feed them normal dragon food. They will not die when they give birth. Once done, we can reuse them by Morphing them back to human form, re-impregnating them, and Morphing them back into dragon forms once again. We'll have an unlimited supply of new dragons coming from them! Brilliant indeed. Thanks Master Wenzel, thanks!" Werner, the black, was ecstatic. So simple, so effective, so fool proof, as long as the morphed humans were kept blinded. No more need for the exotic neurotoxin extracts of the reds.

"Now then, about the Neutrals. We must get them on our side at all costs," Wenzel, the black, continued. "Visit them and see if you can now convince them. If not, then here is a last resort which should work." He outlined his next plan.

Werner, the black, grinned, "Master, it shall be done! I will return with good news this time."

After visiting Dario, the red, and outlining just how stupid they both had been with regards to their breeding program, the two issued new orders to get another secret site constructed on Voss. It would be ready in two weeks' time. In addition to the existing traps that they had used previously, Werner, the black, added a couple more of them. Now it was time to convince the neutrals to join up, rally time.

First stop, Cezar, the white, on Rehor. His cave was high in the forbidding alpine region filled with year-round glaciers. Snow perpetually covered his peak. While the red and black hated the infernal cold, the personal visit was crucial. As always when conferring, the dragons lay in a circle, their heads facing each other at its center. Werner, the black, did most of the talking, while Dario, the red, tried to keep from catching a cold.

"Cezar, the time for action has come. As you know the barons have declared war on dragon-kind. Have you not seen their Strike Force One in action here on Rehor?"

"Well yes, most pathetic excuse for an attacking force. Wholly useless for the most part," Cezar, the white, replied. Werner's statement had not even gotten a rise out of the old white.

"This is just the very beginning of their war against us. Each month that goes by, their Archmages are pumping out more and more of their enchanted Dragon Slayer swords. Dozens are made each month. Another year from now and you will be facing a dozen more strike forces as they slowly get armed. In two years, two dozen strike forces."

Cezar, the white, replied, "Hum. Point taken. Is that all?"

"Oh no, only the tip of the iceberg, old friend. Do you realize that at this very minute Zoran and his Archmages are making more of their Rods of Dragon Slaying and Gems of Dragon Control? Have you seen what they can do? The rods make the humans totally impervious to your frost breath, my acid spew, Dario's flames. Our biggest weapon is nullified by these enchanted rods of theirs."

"Yes, that is serious, Werner, most," Cezar, the white, noted, becoming a bit more worried about the time line.

"It gets worse, Cezar. Each month, another of these foul, wicked, evil rods comes into existence, again made by the Archmages themselves. A year from now, another dozen at least will be in the hands of the humans. Two years, why two dozen or more will be used against us. Further, we've seen firsthand that even one rod will protect three fighters. So you are looking at dozens of nearly impervious fighters and mages attacking us at one time."

"Well, if we don't provoke them, surely they will not use them against us," Cezar, the white, suggested. "Good reason to leave the humans alone."

"But they have already declared war on we dragons, Cezar. The only reason that you have not yet been attacked is that they are waiting for more of these rod and enchanted blades before they have sufficient strength to assail you."

"Point taken," Cezar, the white, admitted.

"Cezar, it is far worse than you can ever imagine! Zoran and his group of Archmages are now training all those women who we tried to have give birth to our new dragons — all those he stole back from us and slaughtered the unborn dragons within their wombs. We gave them life and now Zoran is using even that against us. These women are learning magic an unheard of rates, even for humans. Those seventeen he stole almost a year ago are now officially mages and are well on their way to becoming Archmages! He has hundreds of these women in training at his fortress in Brn, Adapazan. If you do not believe me, send in a spy to Brn. If you are like me, you will be terrified of having to fight against an army of Archmages!"

"Yes, that is precisely what will be happening within just a couple of years. Two hundred Archmages will come marching out of Brn to kill off all dragon-kind! You've seen what just a few Archmages in a fighting group can do, they decimate our forces. Imagine what two hundred can do to us. Who knows if he will be training up even more than this? Two hundred in two years. Cezar, do the math. In two years, dozens and dozens of enchanted Dragon Slayer blades in the hands of the fighters, accompanied by hundreds of Archmages, all immune to our powerful breath weapons — Cezar, there will not be a dragon anywhere in these sixteen worlds that would be safe from that. The end of our whole race is at hand."

"Two hundred? Archmages? Impossible." Cezar, the white, replied, though Werner, the black, sensed the white had serious doubts about his statement of "impossible."

"Go send in a spy and see for yourself. Zoran has two hundred in training at this very minute. Have your spy see for himself the incredible progress these killer mages are making."

"I will do just that, Werner. Yet, let us say for the moment all that you have said is true. What are we to do?"

"Fight! Fight the humans now, *before* they complete their massive buildup of insurmountable forces. That's what we must do. Old Aldrick just doesn't see what's coming. True, he'll probably be the last dragon to be killed. He is so blind that he won't see the sword strike coming until he's hit with it."

"You mean to go up against Zoran at his fortress in Brn?" Cezar, the white, asked, somewhat taken aback. He feared Zoran and his army of Archmages already.

"No, that would decimate our forces too badly. No, we start wiping out whole outlying towns and villages across all the planets. We force the barons to spread their, as yet not fully equipped and manned forces, out over wide areas. Then we smash them. Get a single Archmage alone, like the greens did, and we can defeat him. Allow seven Archmages to join forces and we are doomed to massive losses. It can be done, but only if all we dragons work together."

"Well, Werner, if what you say about their massive buildup of Archmages and rods is true, then we are left with little choice but to attack them before they can become fully prepared to slaughter all dragon-kind. Let me send out some spies and learn of this myself."

Werner, the black, could get no further commitments from Cezar, the white. Still, he was certain that once the white's spies reported back, Cezar would be on board with the attack plans. He and Dario then left to visit the next neutral leader. "Let's go-o-o to the desert. I am freezing to death," Dario, the red, suggested. They did just that, visiting Donatello, the brown, on the desert world of Anwyn.

Werner , the black, made basically the same presentation to Donatello, the brown, as he had to Cezar, the white. Donatello's reactions were vastly more subdued.

"Our relations with the humans have given us no cause to harm them. They are puny and we are strong. Have you and the reds not provoked them into this? I certainly think so," Donatello, the brown, countered. "We browns have no desire to fight your wars for you. Would you let a brown lead the attacks? I thought not."

After hearing about the two hundred Archmages, which ought to have filled the brown with fear and trepidation, Donatello, the brown, answered, "Yes, if I had been the ones provoking the humans, I would be frightened and rightly so. I am sure that the humans will leave us alone, just as we leave them alone, Werner. Blacks and reds are famous for biting the hand that feeds them, literally in this case."

Clearly, Donatello, the brown, would not be siding with the proposed war. He would need Wenzel's further inducements. Worse, with the near annihilation of the greens, Donatello, the brown, now commanded the largest force of dragons of any color. It was critical to get Donatello onboard. Originally, the reds and blacks had the largest numbers, but having suffered so many losses in the past year, the browns now outnumbered them. This was another factor spurring them into the breeding program.

The two dragons next visited Bolivar, the blue, on Asami. The total number of blues was about half of those of the reds, blacks, browns, and whites. Further, they preferred a watery existence. Still, a dragon is a dragon and the two delivered their pitch to Bolivar, the blue. His reactions were nearly the same as Donatello's had been. He chided Dario for having used Blue Dragon Extract to paralyze the kidnaped women, however, annoying Dario, the red.

Finally, the two visited Alistair, the green, who had abandoned Jing and was now living on Maeve, with the final remnants of the greens, barely forty all told. He was all for the war, but pointed out that his greens were almost extinct as it was. Hence, Werner, the black, outlined their new, foolproof breeding program.

Alistair, the green, still smarting over having conquered Jing only to lose it and nearly all his greens, declared, "Okay, Werner, here's the deal. You get the breeding program going. Capture dozens of human females for us. We will come and breed them. Once we actually have fifty baby greens in our hands, I will commit the remainder of our males to the war. Our remaining females must care for the new young ones."

Werner, the black, saw his point and agreed with Alistair, the green. "Okay, once we have the breeding program going, I will come get you to partake. Fifty it shall be for starters." Alistair, the green, nodded, confident that he'd made an incredibly good bargain. The blacks did all the work and he had to do nothing to repopulate his greens. Werner must really be desperate, Alistair thought after the two left.

Back at his warm cavern, Dario, the red, complained, "Werner, we've accomplished nothing. It is still four to four in the voting, assuming Cezar gets aboard with his whites."

"Well, the greens are nearly useless anyway and there are so few of them that it isn't going to matter much, except for their council vote. Same with the greys, too few of them to amount to much. No, it is the browns that we need to convince. I have a plan for that too, old friend.   We need to get fourteen of our most trusted dragons together and at least two have to be able to cast the Morph Other spell. Here's what we are going to do to get the browns on our side. Once it is five to three, the blues and greys will have no choice. They always follow the vote." Both dragons chuckled at his jest.

Chapter 28 Love Lost, Love Found

Wen, Chan, Zong, and Dana were swamped. With the entire ruling body and the entire army of their world suddenly eliminated in one day, Jing entered very uncertain times. They had scraped together a dozen palace guards for each of the three fortresses, woefully inadequate. True, they still had the domestic staff that their late brothers employed and they retained them by immediately doubling their salaries — Chan's idea.

With no mages handling the usual communications and court details, the three new rulers were forced to deal with every issue personally turning long days into near nightmares for the three women. They had little choice but to offer various court positions to many of their cousins, though they tried to keep their power hungry uncles out of the picture in so far as that was possible.

Outside of the three main cities with their fortresses, palaces, and Circles of Ascension, the common folk accepted the change in rulership. Many proclaimed that this was for the best, especially since the greens seemed to have deserted Jing. The three women knew that opinion would change the instant the greens made a reappearance. No, their greater security problem came from the very cities in which they now lived. At last tax time, Nanchan residents tallied one hundred fifty thousand, while Chaohu and Zhouhan tallied around a hundred thousand residents each.

Here in these cities dwelled most of Jing's assassins and thieves, some of which in the past had been frequently employed by their brothers. Many of the deceased soldiers' families lived in the cities too. Some of these relatives were demanding compensation for the lost men. A dozen palace guards were ill equipped to really maintain security over the large palaces, fortresses, and Circles. Hardly a day went by without the Dana or the baronesses having to stop everything to handle a robbery attempt or even an assassination attempt. The occurrences of the latter forced the three women to keep Skin of Stone spells on themselves nearly all the time, especially when they were asleep. Few nights went by without at least one Alarm spell going off, rousing them all to deal with some kind of break in.

A week after the High Council had accepted them as Jing's official new rulers, the three were routinely only getting three or four hours sleep at a time. Enter politics — Federation politics, to be precise. Duke Bogdan Clav was the first suitor to put in an appearance at Wen's court in Nanchan. "Greetings Baroness Wen Meerong. I've come to offer you my hand in marriage. Obviously, you need a strong man to rule at your side, to enforce your will on your people. I am that man," he declared boastfully.

Per Federation Rules, she had to accept his offer and genuinely consider it, even though she found him repugnant. At least she had another strong sword hanging around the fortress. Not long after that, Chan had to welcome a suitor from Dietmar, followed within days with a suitor from Anwyn. As Dana pointed out, the enemy planets were moving swiftly to attempt to bring Jing back into their group of planets.

Zoran knew that this would be happening, but he could do nothing about it, save allow Dana to remain with Wen. He knew that the two had fallen for each other but he also knew that the rulers of Jing were facing monumental problems that he really could do little about, except provide advice when asked.

Barons Leo and Stefan, on the other hand, saw the overall political implications. For centuries, Jing had been solidly in the enemy planet alliance. Overnight, its allegiance had flipped, thanks to Zoran. At the High Council meeting, these two barons saw that if Jing were going to remain in their camp, they would have to act. "After all, Zoran has done all the hard work for us. It is up to us to secure what he's done," Leo pointed out. The two agreed to do so.

Each baron kept in touch with either Chan or Wen at least twice each day, answering key questions the baronesses had and subtly analyzing the new rulers' current needs. They did their best to assist, sending many loads of supplies at way below going prices. Thus they learned of the arrival of the various suitors and knew that they had to take an even larger role if they were to keep Jing from falling back into the enemy camp. They would have to provide suitors as well.

Both barons had married for love, having carefully avoided the usual arranged marriages that their parents' generation had done — frequently executed for political gains. Indeed, it had been Zoran's split from his father that had allowed Leo and Stefan to marry for love, breaking the long standing tradition of arranged marriages. True, there was still quite a bit of that still going on as witnessed by their own sibling's marriages, Dusan and Andrea, for example.

Stefan pointed out, "Look, we're going to have to have our suitors bring something more to the arranged marriage than just their own good looks and skill. Barons Storm and Adolf will raise an awful stink if that is the sole criteria for choosing. We need to have our suitors bring what the baronesses really need: soldiers, Duska assistants, and mages."

"Yes, but the tricky part is that the Meerong women want and need to be the real rulers. Whoever we choose must not be power hungry and usurp or override Chan and Wen's desires. That is the tricky part. We know that they will not accept anything less; they are powerful, strong willed baronesses," Leo argued.

"Granted, that makes our choices more difficult. Another thing to consider is that Jing is mainly marshes and swamps. We cannot turn to Baron John or Baron Arcangelo for help; their people are used to good black-dirt farms. Their men would not adapt to swamps at all well. Here on Valtr, we have great rolling hills that are often heavily forested and your Gladno has dense forests. Our people would have an easier time adjusting to the marshlands and swamps than the farmers," Stefan suggested.

"True, but we dare not risk sending three suitors. What about the plains of Gonda? Would someone from there be able to adapt to the extremes of Jing?" Leo wondered.

"Have to try. It is going to be tough finding an available cousin in their early twenties who is not married already and who is willing to go to Jing and yet be subservient to the women there. Though what man would not jump at the chance to become a baron? Still, we have our work cut out for us," Stefan replied. "We have to do this very carefully otherwise Chan and Wen may reject the whole thing. Ought we also work with old Chen as well? Does he have any influence left with his daughters?"

"Certainly not much, I'll wager. Still, if we have his backing, he might be able to lend an extra push, if needed. We'd best get busy and find our three beaus," Leo advised. "The enemy barons already have suitors on Jing."

It took the two men nearly two weeks to find three suitable bachelors. Baron Gaspard of Gonda readily cooperated and on the 5th of May the three barons took their bachelors to Jing to meet the three available baronesses. They were to meet at the fancy palace in Nanchan and Wen was to be the primary host.

"Dana, what about us? I love you, but. . ." Wen fought back her conflicting emotions, unable to finish her sentence.

"I know, I love you too, but — but," he faltered, "you have to think of your whole world, Wen. At least see these men and hear their offers."

"If only my stupid brothers had not gotten themselves killed, we could get married," Wen shifted the blame over to Gang and Li.

"I know, I know, you didn't ask to be the main ruler of Jing. Yet, you are and there is no one else. That's certainly clear enough. So many have died!" He had dark bags under his eyes from lack of sleep. He'd been awake much of each night standing guard over her quarters. At least twice, an assassin had attempted to reach her while she slept. Possibly they were sent by Rehor or Dietmar in an attempt to remove the women and regain control of Jing for the enemy camp. He couldn't prove such assertions, but few had other plausible ideas for the attempts on Wen's life.

None of the three women chose to dress up or even wear fancy dresses to meet the arrival of the three barons and their three bachelors. Instead, they wore their new leather outfits that Zong had made. These were highly practical and reflected their positions and personalities. Right on time the group of six arrived. Dana stayed in the back of the room, his heart grieving already. He knew that Wen was going to have little choice now. Six suitors had come already, but these three new ones would likely win the day. He'd carefully outlined to Stefan just what the women desperately needed. If Stefan and Leo provided that, he knew Wen would have to accept. Old Chen sat in a chair beside Dana. He'd been kept appraised of the suitors and had wisely decided to keep quiet for the moment.

The barons wore their finest suits and the three suitors also dressed well, but also carried their prized enchanted swords. "Welcome to the Royal Palace of Nanchan," Wen greeted the six arrivals, stepping forward and giving a perfunctory hug to Leo, Stefan, and Gaspard. Chan nodded politely as did Zong.

"Hail and well met again, Dragon Slayers and baronesses," Baron Leo began, setting the tone by emphasizing the fact that these were not ordinary baronesses. "It is my great privilege to present my cousin Wenceslas Radink to you, Baroness Wen. He is twenty-three and a master swordsman on Gladno. He carries his enchanted bastard sword with him everywhere he goes." Leo knew that Dana was Zoran's master swordsman and thus he had to at least equal Dana. Wenceslas was tall and fit, but not extremely handsome.

The young man bowed to Wen, "Most pleased to meet one of the most famous Dragon Slayers in the Federation and one so fair as well." Wen returned his bow respectfully. At least he isn't an ugly pig like the one from Rehor, she thought.

Baron Stefan stepped forward towards Chan and announced, "It is my privilege, Baroness Chan to introduce my cousin, Radek Ves, a proven fighter. Alas, he's a young widower raising his three year old daughter, Vesna. His wife died in childbirth two years ago. Terrible tragedy."

Radek was fairly attractive, tall and blonde, with piercing eyes. "It is my great honor to meet the most famous Dragon Slayer and Baroness Chan Meerong at last. If nothing else, I would dearly enjoy discussing your techniques for slaying the foul beasts which are ravaging our worlds today." He had been coached to play to her skills in this arena and her fondness of small children.

"Well met, Radek. I would love to do just that. The more who know ways and means of slaying these fell creatures the better. It must be hard for you to raise your daughter all by yourself. Surely you have a nanny to look after her." Chan bought the dangling bait, Stefan mused.

Baron Gaspard introduced his cousin next. "Baroness Zong, this is my cousin, Edmond Douard and proven leader of the Tenth Regiment. He is twenty and a most able fighter and Duska."

"Very pleased to meet you, Edmond. We surely do need fighters around here," Zong replied.

"I am your humble servant, Baroness Zong. I must admit I admire your leather outfits. So very well made, so appropriate for the hard times that have befallen all of us," he addressed Zong for the first time.

She flushed, "Thank you, I made our outfits myself." Again, Dana guessed the three men's initial remarks were very well rehearsed and the three women had accepted them, establishing an instant affinity for the three beaus. Well, that first impression would be critical, he thought.

"We should sit down and discuss what these men have to offer you three baronesses," Baron Leo suggested, wasting no time. Chan and Wen had expected this and led them into Wen's private study.

"This is the most secure room at this time. We have so few security forces now and this is the best that I can offer," Wen admitted. Dana took up his guard position at the door, protecting the three barons, the three suitors, and the three baronesses. "Oh, do you need refreshments?" Wen asked. "You must forgive me. Our whole days have been focused on regaining control of Jing, not on such formalities."

"We are good. We fully understand, Baroness Wen," Leo answered. "We are here to help. Now then, Baroness Wen," he continued.

"Please, just Wen. We really are not used to such formalities. Just Wen," she suggested.

Smiling, Leo said, "Wen it is. If you accept Wenceslas as your husband, he will bring with him one thousand soldiers, four mages, and two Duska. This should go a long way to helping you get firmly established here."

"Right. Radek will bring a thousand soldiers with him, Chan," Stefan added, "and five mages and three Duska workers."

"Edmund comes with my support as well, Zong," Gaspard spoke his proposition. "He'll also bring a thousand soldiers, four mages, and three Duska helpers."

Leo added, "That should help you three out of the most difficult positions that you are in at the moment. We dare not offer these men outright, baronesses.

Politically, other barons would raise strong protests that we were interfering in the affairs of another planet. Old Chen can back this up, if you doubt me."

"You sure do know precisely what we are most desperate to have at the moment," Chan replied. "Lord, knows this help will save the day. We've been having at least two assassination attempts on us each week. Security is almost nil around here, what with the loss of almost everyone who was in the government. But Wen and I have one huge problem with this whole marriage proposal thing."

She didn't see any of the barons reacting as she thought they might and so she continued, "It's this way. Wen and I are the rightful rulers of Jing. We don't want to suddenly give that away to a husband who is not even from Jing. On your worlds, barons, you rule, not your wives. Here, we are the true Dragon Slayers, the true and rightful rulers of Jing. We've earned that along with the respect of the common folk who we've tried to protect over the years from the tyranny of our brothers and the dragons. We are not about to give that up and become window dressings. Besides, with this," she waved her left stump, "I am hardly fit for such. I can't tie my own shoes without using magic spells."

Baron Leo chose to reply, knowing this was the most critical point of the negotiations. "You are absolutely right about that, Chan, Wen. We six have discussed this aspect in depth. All three men are more than willing to let your rule stand and not usurp your power and authority. Yet, that is mere words. Instead, we've taken the liberty of drawing up three official agreements, one for each of the men. In essence they state that each will always follow your decisions and wishes, excepting in those areas in which you give them full control. In essence, they will be your window dressing and protection as well. In time, they may come to earn your full trust and respect as well as that of your people on Jing. These will be binding pledges, breakage of which will void their marriages, freeing you if they fail to back you all the way. You can't lose and each of you will retain full control of Jing, not the men."

"Damn, Leo, you've thought of everything," Chan replied, somewhat surprised.

"We have to, Chan. These are hard times. This dragon mess threatens to destroy us all. We have to help each other out or the dragons may well win," Leo declared.

Stefan added, "We've taken up too much of your time already. We three barons will return to our worlds and duties. If you need anything, we will be in regular contact as always. We'll let you take time to get familiar with one another. If you find our choices not to your liking, let us know and we'll see if something else can be worked out and soon."

After the barons left, Wen asked Zong to show the three men around the palace and fortress. She and Chan wanted a private word with their father. After they headed out to inspect the buildings and security arrangements, Chan said, "Dad?"

"I know, you both want to marry for love not politics. Yet, you could do far worse. Their offer is not to be taken lightly. It is a kingly offer. Never has an arranged marriage come with such arrangements. You two must be very highly thought of by Leo and Stefan. When you were young, I always told you what to do and I was wrong to have done that. I won't tell you what to do now. I can only share what little wisdom I have learned the hard way at times. As rulers of our people, you sometimes have to place the welfare of the many above that of your own. That is the awful mistake that I made for so very much of my own life. I put mine and your brothers ahead of our people. Here I am at the very end of my road and have had my own daughters teach this to me."

"At least you finally learned it, dad," Chan replied, warming to him somewhat.

"I had my heart set on marrying Dana, dad," Wen fought to keep from crying. All her life she had sworn that she'd not take an arranged marriage, that she would marry for love instead.

"There is far more at stake here, dear, than your love for one man. Look at it this way, while you have been fending off a couple assassination attempts each week, it will only take one successful one to end your life and perhaps that of Jing. Their offer will ensure that the assassinations cease. You need mages now and guards and Duskas. Yes, Archmage Ivana will likely come through with some mages for Jing a few years down the road. Your job is to keep Jing here for them. There's no reason that you and Dana cannot be lifelong friends. If you insist, he could even be your consort. Many barons are unfaithful to their wives. You could do the same."

"No, I couldn't do that to Dana. I'm not like that," Wen sighed, seeing that really she had no choice. Dana's eyes told her that he had been up most of the nights watching over her. She could not keep on having him do that. It wasn't fair to him or her.

"You are better so much better than I ever was, Wen, Chan. I am very proud of each of you. Go now, get acquainted with the men. Realize that they too are giving up their worlds and lives to come here and marry a strange woman as well. You will each have that much in common initially," old Chen hinted.

After they left, Dana slipped in beside the old man. "Well, did they accept it?" he asked.

"My daughters are so superior to me and my sons that I am ashamed of myself, Dana. Time will tell, but the barons presented a kingly proposal, one that they desperately need right now. I hope that they do, but I am sorry for you and Wen, though."

"I know, I had such high hopes. She is a fantastic young woman," Dana sighed, knowing that the love of his life was likely lost forever to him.

During the next few days, the other suitors heard of the proposals and contacted their respective barons for help. However, after much juggling and dealings, they simply could not match or exceed Stefan, Leo, and Gaspard's proposals. A week later, the three agreed to the arranged marriages and the promised support personnel arrived shortly afterwards, much to everyone's relief. Now at last, the three baronesses could really begin to get Jing back on the road to recovery.

Dana stuck around for several more weeks, helping the new fiancés get familiarized and helping them set up proper security for all three fortresses and the Circles and particularly Wen's palace. He also spent time with Archmage Ivana and several others, helping them de-trap and clean out Jing's late Archmage tower inside the fortress at Nanchan. He also assisted Ivana with her new magic students which allowed her to do a little advanced planning for her students. This was her first batch of students and she was just a little frazzled by it all.

That last night, Dana and Wen held each other tightly. "What will happen to us?" she asked, fighting to keep from crying. She didn't want his last memories of her to be watching her bawling.

"You will be the best ruler that Jing has ever had, Wen. I just know it. I will always be your friend. Call on me for help anytime and I'll come as fast as I can. Remember everything that I taught you and stay alive," Dana whispered in her ear, smelling her hair and scent for the last time.

"I never wanted to be the baroness."

"I know, I know, but your people really need you. You and Chan have been fighting for what is right for Jing for a decade. Now you have the chance to really make a huge difference. You have to do it. I know it and so do you."

"I know, I know. But I will miss you."

"Same here, my little Dragon Slayer." They kissed and at last Dana tore himself away. He picked up his bag and waved as he stepped into the Shadows heading for home with a heavy heart, arriving late on the 12th of August.

Akira welcomed him home with a late birthday cake. She and Marek knew that he'd just lost his first real love and wanted to cheer him up a little. "Mom, don't you think that I am a little old for birthday cakes?" he grumbled.

"Well, you are still my little boy, even if you are all grown up now. You can lend us all a hand with the new magic students. You heard that Jarka found a cure for the women's deadened arms, didn't you?"

"Yes, but some didn't make it?"

"True, thirty-two to be exact. Tough break for them, but they are all displaying the same spirit as Zdenka's original seventeen, so we are all hopeful," Akira answered positively.

"Damn dragons anyway. Well, it is good to be back. Jing is nothing but a swampland, everywhere you go. Mosquitoes are murder."

"I know. I bet you really miss her, son."

"Yes, but you know, I think it is for the best. I really don't want to be a baron. I got a taste of what it is like this summer and honestly, mom, I don't want any part of it. I surely don't know how Zoran can stand it."

Archmage Marek laughed, "Son, I've watched him. He doesn't like it either and puts a whole week's worth of administration duties off and does them on one day only. Kind of funny or maybe sad. You keep your eyes open. There are plenty of other fine women out there in the world. I was fabulously lucky to come across your wonderful mother here." He gave her a hug. It was his best attempt to sympathize with Dana's lost love.

The next morning, Dana reported to Zoran. "I'm back baron. What is needed to be done?"

"Good, Dana. I've really missed you. Sorry about the way things turned out for you and Wen. Planetary politics can make a mess of personal lives. At least this way, Jing is relatively secure and can begin to recover properly and move forwards. I am surprised that Storm or Adolf didn't try to physically invade and take the planet by force of arms."

"Sent in enough assassins," Dana replied.

"I heard. Good job, Dana. Say, I have another critical job for you, my master swordsman." Zoran just had another idea.

"Name it, sir. As long as it involves swords I am more than willing and ready," Dana answered. He was prepared to thoroughly drown himself into his work.

"You have heard about out latest Duska, Adrianna Whitehall?"

"Not fully, just what mom's sent me once in a while. What's her story? Did she really have Shadow Sickness?"

"Yes, worst case that I've ever seen." Zoran spent a half hour relating her complete story, particularly her key role in their discovering Voss and the rescue of ninety-six more victims. "She is beginning her magic training now and from Zdenka's reports, she is flying through the useful Adept spells. We really do owe her the Duska fighter training that she's been denied."

"No chance that the Witherspoon barons will acknowledge their half-sister and provide for her?" Dana asked.

"Nope, I already went to them. Not a chance, so it is up to us."

"So how far do we want to take her training? Get it up to the baroness defensive level?" Dana figured that would be the case. Most Duska women only wanted enough skill with blades to be able to defend themselves.

Zoran rubbed his hands through his hair before replying. "Dana, I don't know. After what she's been through, she might desire more. I can't say that I blame her either. Let's at least get her up to the defensive level of most baronesses for sure. Beyond that, Dana, I will leave it to your best judgment. She may have no desires for more. She may not have the physical ability for more. You call the shots. She is limited in the time that she has for training though. It will have to be after suppers each night and perhaps on Sundays, if she wants to use her day off from studies."

"Okay, that will free up your time, right? Mom told me that you had agreed to train a new Duska. I just didn't make the connection. Been gone too long," Dana replied.

"Right, Dana. I really do appreciate this. There is so darn much going on right now, but I have promised her the best Duska training that we can give, and there is no one better than you, except perhaps Zdenka's father when he was younger." Dana grinned, for he'd learned a whole lot from him.

After supper that night, Zoran introduced the two. "Adrianna, this is Dana Aceda, eldest son of Archmage Marek and Akira. He is my Master Swordsman. There is no one as good as he is. I am putting him in charge of your fighter training. After dinner each night, he'll work with you for a couple of hours. He is free on Sundays too, if you wish to use your day off. Your call on that one. Once you have your Duska fighter training, I'll work with you on other aspects myself. It is critical that you learn what to do with your lightning fast reactions."

"Hi, great! I'm ready, Dana. Let's do it," Adrianna said enthusiastically.

"Follow me. I have a well-padded training room all set up for this," he said and led her to the room. He noticed two things about her immediately. One, she was one of the prettiest women he'd ever seen and two, she was his age, twenty. She noticed three things about him. One, he was attractive and well-built and confident. Two, he was a Master Swordsman, Zoran's best, evidently. Three, he was about her age, she thought. Already she'd heard the circulating scuttlebutt that he had been in love with Wen Meerong of Jing, but that she had accepted an arranged marriage instead. She noticed that he was a little blue. Her many years of tending bar had taught her to read people accurately. It had also taught her more, as Dana was soon to find out.

"All these mats are to soften your falls when you get knocked off your feet. The first things we must learn is to be able to effectively dodge and get out of the way of any attack coming your way. This will be extremely valuable to you when you begin to study the attacking spells, Adrianna. If an enemy shoots a Disintegrate beam at you, your Duska senses will alert you that it's coming, and you must react instantly to get out of its way. Same thing with Balls of Fire and Lightning Bolts spells. Likewise, sometimes you will be unarmed when someone attacks you either with blades or even their fists. You have to be able to effectively dodge and get out of the way and land so that you can take effective counteractions against your attacker. Got it?" He thought, well, she probably has no idea what's coming next. Ah well, few actually ever do.

"You bet. Okay, dodge and reposition to take effective counters. Got it. Let me tie up my hair first." She hastily did so tying up her long raven hair. "Okay, ready."

Without warning, Dana attempted to slam his open hand into her shoulder, intending to knock her off her feet. He really didn't want to actually punch her with his fist. She wouldn't be ready for that for perhaps a week, he thought. Adrianna reacted, moving her shoulder back and down, brought her left arm up hard against his head, flipping him off his feet, and landing a surprised Dana on the mats. "Oops, sorry, I didn't mean to hurt you. Are you okay?" She bent over offering him a hand up.

"Well, that was a pleasant surprise. No, you did extremely well. Let's try some more moves." Dana began running through all his usual training hand to hand attack strikes. Although he had to use his own Duska senses several time, he still found himself landing hard on the mats four more times.

"Okay, okay, Adrianna. You win. How the heck do you know how to counter these moves?" Dana was very impressed with his new student.

"Tending bar at our old inn. I got all kinds of action there, mostly overly pompous teens and drunks. I had to take care of myself. Am I doing okay?"

"Hey, better than okay, Adrianna. Most beginners don't get this good for at least a week. Okay, I can see we are going to have to speed this up some. Did anyone ever threaten you with knives or daggers?"

"Sure, several times. Never swords though. I am nervous around them. They are so deadly."

"Okay, let's see how you do protecting yourself from knife and dagger threats." Once more she was quite good at deflecting an incoming thrust. He finally found her weak points and began to show her better alternate moves.

Near the end of the session, she asked, "Are you still holding back on me, since I am new at this? Or is this the best that I should anticipate running into out there?"

"I'm trying to get a feel for what you know and don't know — what your strengths are and your weaknesses. Yes, I am holding back some. Why?"

"Give me your best shot, really your best shot. I want to see how much more I really do have to learn, Dana."

"You sure about this?"

"I need to know. How else can I judge my progress?"

"Okay, here goes." This last time, he used his full hand to hand skills on her and quickly flipped her hard onto the mat.

"Ah ha. I was thinking that I was pretty good, but I can see I have lots to learn yet. Thanks, little help up, that hurt. You are good."

By the end of the week, she asked, "Can we really go at it on Sundays? I don't want to take away your time, if you have personal things to do, I mean."

"No, work is good for me. I love teaching the fighting arts, Adrianna. Sure, let's meet say at ten."

Adrianna was a very fast learner, Dana soon discovered. Within a week, she had passed the unarmed defensive actions portion of her training. Now came the more difficult and likely very lengthy period of learning to defend with a blade. Of course, they would begin with daggers. Only when she really mastered the dagger would he suggest moving up to a full sword. For a full week they sparred with wooden daggers and wooden swords, in his case. Then, he took her to the huge, secret display case to match her with her first enchanted dagger.

"Wow! All these are magical?" she asked, blinking twice.

"Yes, we can't keep up with the demand, but we always have some in reserve for our own defense. It is my job to find the perfect dagger for each person."

"Aren't they all the same?" she asked.

"Heavens no! Okay, let's show you." He gave her one that was too heavy for her and then one that was way too long for her reach. Finally, he gave her the one he thought would match her best.

"Wow, this one feels very different, sort of comfortable."

"Yes, this is the one for you." He then explained more fully.

Adrianna was impressed with his knowledge and skill. "You seem to be able to size up a person and know just the right blade for them."

"Astute observation. Yes, I rarely make a miscalculation in that department. I know my blades well and the right fit is mostly dictated by the body who will wield it."

"Wow. Say, I bet that sword can really dole out the damage!" She pointed to the huge two-handed monster.

Dana laughed. "Yes and no. Yes, if the fighter actually hits solidly with it, it can inflict substantial damage. However, it takes enormous strength to wield it and as Zoran always says and which I often prove, in the time that the fighter can get in one strike with the monster, he and I can get in two to four hits with our short swords. He and I are firm believers in using short swords. They are fast and deadly effective."

"Well, I want to be deadly effective too! You are just going to have to get me there, Dana." Adrianna nodded to punctuate her declaration. Dana grinned. He liked this spunky young woman. As they wrapped up the evening's session, Adrianna asked, "Say, do you really play the harpsichord at the dances? I've heard all the Seventeen talking about your return to Brn and that you play."

"Yes, I play in the first and third sets each dance. The viols play on the second and fourth sets so I can get a chance to dance too. So they like my playing eh? Are you coming to the dance? If so, perhaps we can get a chance to dance a bit. Do you play or sing?"

"I like dances, though I haven't been to many. I don't know how to play anything, but I can sing along to all the bawdy bar songs that the men always belt out — all manner of 'get the bar wench.' Well, they never got this bar wench!" She laughed and Dana did too.

At the dance, Adrianna discovered that indeed, Dana played the harpsichord and saw why the Seventeen raved about it. Further, she found that Dana was also a good dancer as well. Slowly she really began to enjoy being around this man. On the other hand, Dana found himself becoming quite attracted to this incredibly spunky and beautiful young woman. Could love strike twice, he wondered?

Chapter 29 The Abbreviated Fall High Council

During the days and weeks leading up to the Fall High Council, Zoran used his free time to track down the relatives of the recent Adapazan women, namely Anezka, Kamila, Katerine, Reina, Zusa, and Ryba. His plan: see how it goes with these families. Then, he could better advise the other barons who would have to contact the other eighty-nine women's families. He began with the families of the two armless women, Anezka and Kamila, figuring these would be the hardest to handle.

He found Anezka's husband, Alan, and her year old daughter Vanda. He was a carpenter in Sobin Creek, Kin Province. His reactions were even stronger than Adrianna's mother's had been. "My god! I've *got* to go to her. She needs me now more than ever. So does Vanda. Baron, you must let me go to her. I can help, really I can. I must."

"I can always use another carpenter. What say you move to Brn for at least as long as Anezka is getting her magic training? You can work for me and earn good wages," he suggested. Later that day, he watched as the tears of joy flowed from both. Anezka really missed her daughter, even though now she was so helpless to care for her infant. That deal worked out well.

Kamila's husband, Krystof, in the village of Kusor, Radin Province, was also insistent on seeing her. They had two daughters, two and three, Xenia and Jolana, who missed their mother very much. He was a barrel maker, and Zoran also gave him a job at his fortress in Brn, making barrels to store their supplies in the ever growing subterranean city.

The other husbands were thankful their wives were okay and extremely pleased that they were learning magic now. They decided to remain in their villages and let their wives learn as much as possible, though they all visited them first before reaching their mutual decisions.

Thus, Zoran became convinced that not all of the women's families would have to be moved to Brn. Now he concentrated on the upcoming High Council meeting which was scheduled to be held on the desert world of Chana, Baron Atir hosting. A week before the meeting, Baron Atir visited Zoran to personally discuss the upcoming meeting.

Baron Atir Makeda was in his mid-twenties, Zoran estimated. He looked much like his father who Zoran had known. He was tall and thin, sporting a full brown beard and moustache. "Thank you for seeing me. Chana is a desert world and we do not have the resources of the other worlds. We cling to our ancient heritage and ways. Yet, I am breaking our traditions and coming to ask your advice."

"Understood, baron. I'll do my best and respect your traditions as always."

"Thank you. Hosting the coming High Council has my brothers and me very worried about security and the dragons. While the browns and we have not had any problems, I am worried about having all of our rulers on Chana. If the reds or blacks try something, I won't pretend to say that we on Chana could prevent an attack. We can't. At each of the last two councils, dragons have been involved. Worse, you have been right every time. We have discovered that a number of our young women have simply vanished without a trace. Before I go, I would like to see those that you have managed to save."

"Yes, of course. I will address this issue at the council. Perhaps I should give the first report at the start of our meeting."

"Would you? That would be much appreciated. I'll put you down as the first speaker. What I wanted to bounce off of you is this: how about limiting this meeting to one baron and baroness from each planet? That way, if trouble comes and we are wiped out, each world will still have a pair of barons to carry on. Further, if dragons attack the other worlds while the council is meeting, the home worlds will not be left defenseless."

"Now that one I really like, baron. Don't put all our dates in one basket." Atir chuckled at the old Chana saying. "We should be alert for more trouble. While I managed to put a halt to the latest dragon abduction plot, they are sure to try something else. They've been awfully quiet for a month now. Zdenka will be with me and we will do our best to give you as much advanced warning of trouble as we can."

"Thank you. I will rest a little easier. I am glad that you approve of my caution. I was worried about going to the other barons, who might just say that I was being paranoid."

"I think a little paranoia about the dragons is a good thing, baron. Never ever take a dragon for granted," Zoran declared. "How are your subterranean cities coming along?" The two chatted a while longer and then Zoran took him to meet with the six Chana women he'd rescued. Atir nearly cried as he hugged the two who had lost their arms to the dragons. He promised them high paying positions just as soon as they finished their training, which pleased all six, but especially the two who had suffered the most. He also promised to take back their messages to their loved ones.

"It really is criminal — what these dragons are doing to our women," Baron Atir commented sadly to Zoran as he said farewell. "Thank you for all that you are doing for us. I admit, we on Chana would not be able to give our women the care and training that you are able to provide. I owe you one, baron. I will not forget it."

Archmage Karel cast his top defensive spells after unpacking his gear and magical rods. He, Jarka, and Dana accompanied Zoran and Zdenka to this High Council at Arad, Chana. Zoran wanted at least another Duska present, in case anything happened to him. Karel had brought a rod for the remaining barons who as yet did not have one. So far, he'd successfully made twenty-five of them, with Zoran retaining ten of them.

Jarka looked out at the city from their second story window. Brown sands of the distant desert crept up to the brown stone buildings of the city proper and even seeped up to the foundations of the fortress itself in which they resided. True, dates, figs, and palm trees broke up the relatively dismal landscape, adding a bit of color to an otherwise monotonous scene. The large oasis in the center of the city added the only touch of blue, unless one counted the seemingly endless sky overhead. Already, she'd experienced the intensely hot sun here and didn't much appreciate it. They'd arrived on the outdoor platform and by the time she entered the cooler fortress, she was sweating. "Inhospitable," she commented to Dana, who agreed.

"Okay, let's get these rods delivered now," Karel declared, "that way if trouble comes, more will be protected. Besides, I worry about someone trying to steal them."

"And I worry about having to protect you," Dana teased the Archmage, who frowned.

Zoran agreed and began Messaging the barons. For the next hour, Karel was bombarded with thank you's and many blessings. He was divided on whether he appreciated the funds that some barons donated or their undivided attention and praise. Jarka thought the latter, but wisely said nothing.

The next morning's opening ceremonies were very subdued. Instead of the usual trumpet fanfares that many of the other barons used, here Baron Atir chose to use simple drum rolls. Of course, he was announced first, followed by the other Neutral barons and baronesses. Next, came the allied groups with Zoran and Zdenka being announced first. The Rehor delegation was announced last. After everyone was seated, all eyes glanced at the visitor's section. No new Archmages were waiting, though some had hoped that there would be more of them, since only the Archmages stood much of a chance battling dragons.

Zoran rose to speak first. Slowly and carefully, he outlined the summer's dragon abductions focusing on the pivotal role that Duska Adrianna Whitehall had played. He presented each baron with a list of the names of the women from their worlds and their status, including which Archmage was training them. He detailed Jarka's amazing work to create an antidote to the reds neurotoxin used to deaden the women's arms, but pointed out that after sixty-seven days, the antidote could not be effectively used, the arms were simply too atrophied to be saved.

He also pointed out that the planet on which the women had been kept was called Voss. However, he continued to credit Aldrick with the women's rescue. Why? He did not want any word to get back to the reds and blacks on just how the women had been recovered. He suspected that the dragons had spies in many of the barons' courts. He ended with, "Continue to be vigilant. Stay alert for more abductions, especially random ones here and there. As always, report these to me."

"So you expect more, even though they shut down their operation on Voss?" asked Baron Strom Clav.

"Absolutely. The whole point of their interspecies breeding program is to quickly increase their population. We've pretty well blunted it thus far."

"Are these women really all going to become Archmages within a few years?" asked Baron John, who had the largest number of women currently being trained in Brn. Many of the Neutral barons were keenly interested in this answer, for Archmages were exceedingly rare on their worlds.

"Who can say? So far, the women are on track to very likely make mage status. How much further they can progress we do not know."

The barons wanted a more complete report and Zdenka was called upon to discuss the progress of the women and also their new procedure to abort the dragon fetuses without harming the women. All were amazed at her vivid description of the Roman Candle Effect. That used up the morning session.

In the afternoon session, the entire Strike Force One was introduced and Evsen presented a detailed report of their actions. They'd managed to kill four dragons during the summer, with only the single loss of one fighter from Rehor.

However, the incredible drain on healing potions was duly noted. Evsen pointed out that on the average each dragon slain required fifty healing potions and a couple weeks of recovery time for the fighters. That this was a steep price to pay for so little results finally registered with the barons.

The rest of the afternoon, they discussed ways to improve the effectiveness of the force. If they had one or more of Karel's rods and a handful of Archmages, they would be a significant fighting unit. However, when asked who would be willing to give up their precious rod and their Archmages, none of the barons volunteered, just as Zoran predicted. The first day of the meeting was spent on all these many reports, bringing everyone up to date.

There was no entertainment planned for the evening. Baron Atir did not want any repeat of what had happened before. Instead, the barons held private conversations, while the baronesses did likewise. Zoran heard nothing new from any of the barons, just same old questions.

They had just assembled for the next morning session when Baron Atir's guards came running into the meeting. "Dragons! Dragons are coming!"

Donatello, the brown, strode into the meeting room, throwing several guards who attempted to block his way across the room. He was angry, fuming in fact. He strode up to Baron Atir and tore up a document. "Our agreements are now null and void, Baron Atir. Your Strike Force One attack on our defenseless young shall not go unanswered!"

Baron Atir nearly fainted. Hastily, Zoran moved to face Donatello, standing in front of the shocked Atir. "Excuse me, Donatello, is it? I am Baron Zoran Vladislov. What is this about an attack on your young and women? Our Strike Force One is here with us. They have not been out in the field for at least the last week. When did this attack occur?"

"What? You deny that your fighters did not do this heinous crime?"

"I do not believe that they did, but, please, when did it happen?"

"Yesterday afternoon! Three infants are dead along with one mother!"

"Sir, there must be some mistake here. Yes, we do have a Strike Force One, but all of those fighters were right here in this room all day yesterday, giving us a report yesterday afternoon on just how little they had actually accomplished. Every baron here can vouch for them as well as everyone else. Please, if you have any means magical or otherwise to discern that we are being truthful with you, do so. Our force most definitely did not do this deed. There must be another explanation; it could not have been them."

Donatello's anger subsided a little. "Perhaps your fighters being here was merely some illusion created by your Archmages."

"No, our Strike Force One members were and are really here. They have not as yet ever slain a pregnant mother or any young or baby dragons of any color. All summer long, they have only slain four adult reds and nearly gotten themselves killed four times. I can bring them forward and you can question them yourself if you desire."

"But we had two browns who witnessed the fourteen human fighters doing this wicked deed. How can that be?" Donatello countered.

"I don't know. Do you have any enemies? Could the reds or blacks have been behind it? Some of them have seen our Strike Force One." Zoran wracked his mind to figure out a viable alternative.

"I suppose that might be possible," Donatello finally admitted.

"Look, sir. As far as I know, humans and Brown Dragons have never even had a quarrel, let alone any reason to harm each other, have they? I admit that I do not know how your relations with the humans on Chana have been, but I've heard nothing but kind words about the browns from Baron Atir here. What could we hope to gain by murdering your children? Rather, our problems are with the reds and blacks who continue to abduct our women trying to breed them to create more of their kind," Zoran elaborated a bit.

"You are the one who is training all those hundreds of new Archmages?" Donatello asked. He realized that he was facing the man whom Werner, the black, claimed was doing just that. He was curious to see if what Zoran answered agreed with what his spy in Brn reported.

"It is true that the women who carried the reds and black's offspring and who we saved have an unnatural ability to learn magic. Yes, seventeen of them have reached mage level after about a year of study. However, not one of them is even close to making Archmage and most of the women are just beginning their magical training, learning the useful Adept spells. Whoever is claiming that we are making hundreds of Archmages is grossly exaggerating the situation. Yes, in time we do expect many of these special women to perhaps reach mage level. We all know that achieving Archmage is an extreme rarity in all the Federation. There are only forty-three Archmages in the entire Federation and some of those are old men."

"Interesting. Okay, then at this time I will tentatively accept your explanation that your people were not responsible for the slaying of our children. I will call off the many raids planned for your villages, Baron Atir. However, I may be too late for some. You must understand my position in this. Good day." He turned and walked out of the room, followed by a shocked silence.

"What just happened?" asked Baron Atir. "Are our villages being attacked by the browns?"

"We should adjourn and at least check on your people. If there has been an attack or two, we all should lend a hand helping the survivors," Zoran spoke up before anyone else could. His suggestion was accepted. The meeting adjourned and Baron Atir rushed off to issue orders to his men and fellow barons. A long afternoon followed. Three villages had been attacked by the browns. However, their deadly breaths consisted of bolts of electricity which impacted a relatively few people, compared to the scorching flames of the reds, the cone of slime or acid from the greens or blacks. A number of healing potions salvaged several lives. At the end of the day, twenty had lost their lives, but ten thousand people were now terrified of dragons, much to the dismay of Baron Atir, who was unable to calm their fears.

That evening, Zoran let the others in Brn know what had happened and had Verushka relay it to Aldrick. At the time, he had no idea just how critical that message had been. He would learn of that later on.

The third day was spent trying to work out what had happened the day before and its consequences. Zoran was relieved in that once again he'd prevented an escalation of conflict between humans and dragon, but he wondered just how long he could do it.

The fourth day, they finally got back to the business at hand. Each baron outlined how their advanced preparations of subterranean cities were coming and their level of supplies. Then, they quickly handled their routine trading deals, the boring part, as far as Zoran was concerned.

As Zoran prepared to leave that evening, Baron Atir came to his room. "Baron, once again, I owe you my eternal thanks. You saved the day with the browns. I thought for sure that we'd just gone to war with them. I wanted to give you a little something to show you just how much we on Chana appreciate what you've done and are doing for us. It is called the Tara Diamond." He handed Zoran the largest diamond that he'd ever seen.

"Thank you! What an incredible diamond."

"Yes, it comes from our northern diamond mine. It's value can only be estimated at a half million. May it adorn your incredible wife or perhaps you wish to enchant it. God speed."

Jarka ogled over the diamond after the baron left. "Look at the *size* of it!"

"Dear, I can't possibly wear something that expensive. Perhaps we should enchant it, maybe see if Archmage Jakob can enchant it," Zdenka suggested.

Chapter 30 Foiled Again

Donatello, the brown, was shocked to hear the report. The humans had just slaughtered several of their young and a mother? He could not believe it. He sent word to his counterpart on Anwyn, Pietro, and headed off to inspect the site himself. The grizzly sight of dismembered young caused an anger to rise in Donatello, an anger he'd never felt before in his four hundred years!

He questioned the three browns who had witnessed the slaughter but had not been able to get to them in time. "Fourteen humans with mighty weapons — they appeared here and began hacking the children to death. The mother who tried to defend her young was not even given a chance to fight back. They chopped her head off and left. It happened so quickly."

"Hum, how quickly? We fly fast. I can't understand how you could not have gotten to them before the humans could get away," Donatello asked. He was angry, but also confused. Had he not been angry, he might have detected the discrepancies right there, but the viciousness of the attack was sufficient to raise anyone's anger, even his.

Pietro, the brown, appeared and was equally dismayed. "We cannot let the humans get away with this!" he declared, hatred building in his large frame.

They discussed what retribution actions they should and could take. While others handled the burial details, Donatello, the brown, said, "Tomorrow, I want you to go summon the United Council. Tell them what has happened here and ask for a declaration of war against the humans. Call for a vote, Pietro. Meanwhile, I will launch some retaliatory raids on some of their villages. However, we should sleep on it, Pietro. In anger, we often make gross errors in judgment. Our strikes must not be made from anger, but as coldly calculated strikes."

After sleeping on it, Donatello, the brown, ordered three villages to be attacked. However, he wanted to personally visit the baron and tear up the contract, the agreement under which they were both living. He wanted to let Baron Atir know just how angry he was at the wanton murdering of their children. He did just that, however he returned with huge doubts in his mind. Thus, he sent a messenger off to the United Council meeting that he'd requested.

Donatello, the brown, then returned to the scene of the crime and studied the area. He re-questioned the three witnesses. It still didn't add up. "I want you to go back to where you first saw this happening and fly here just the way you did yesterday. I'll raise and lower my head as a starting signal." The three obeyed their leader.

"Hardly a minute had passed. You three got here in less than a minute, I swear. How could humans have done all that you say they did and depart in less than a minute? Duska are swift, but not that fast. Something is very wrong here. Dig up the mother's body, please."

Later, he examined her head and neck. "Hum, this does not look like a sword cut. Not even their huge swords that they wield with two hands could so sever her head in one clean cut. It's blade is hardly long enough. Besides, the strength needed has to be far beyond that possessed by these puny humans. This is making even less sense to me. Okay, re-bury her. I am going to the United Council myself. He lifted off and stepped into the Shadows.

Around nine, the many dragon representatives gathered for the surprise United Council meeting. "Why have you called for a special session, Pietro. This had better be good," growled Werner, the black.

"Yes, it had better be good!" declared Dario, the red, acting as annoyed as he dared.

"The humans have just slaughtered three of our infants and murdered their mother! That's what. On Chana. Donatello ordered me to request this council. He is off leading retaliatory raids on the humans of Chana as we speak!" Pietro, the brown, stated hostilely.

"Calm down, Pietro. Tell us the full story," a shocked Aldrick, the gold, ordered. Pietro, the brown, took a deep breath and then described what he had seen. He told of the three eye witness accounts that claimed the crime was done by the human's Strike Force One, the fourteen fighters who had been on a crusade of dragon slaying all summer long.

"There must be some mistake here," Aldrick, the gold, tried valiantly to defuse the rapidly escalating emotions. "Some things do not add up. Donatello visited Baron Atir and found the humans were holding their High Council meeting. Further, everyone there swears that all of the members of their Strike Force One were present at the meeting both the day before and the entire day of the attack. In fact, they were addressing the council members at the time of the attack. Something is not right here. We should delay making judgments until all of the facts are in."

Pietro, the brown, disagreed. "Donatello ordered me to ask for a declaration of total war on the humans of the Federation. I am to call for a vote on it."

"Yes, of course, it is your right to do so, Pietro. None of us would dare say otherwise," Burk, the gold, responded. "However, we ought not act in anger or in haste. If Aldrick says that something is perhaps not as it seems, we, as the superior beings, ought to investigate first."

"As bad as this is, Pietro, I believe that Burk is right. We should examine the discrepancies before we vote," Barnabus, the grey, cautioned.

"I agree. It may be crucial to discover how these humans can be in two places at the same time. This sounds like a hideous new weapon or magic the humans have created. We should study it before we act," Bolivar, the blue, added.

"How many crimes against dragon-kind will you all suffer before you finally act?" growled Dario, the red. "We reds love our children and would strike back at anyone who harmed them. I don't care what magic they may or may not have. I say let's vote and get on with it."

Cezar, the white, was a bit unnerved by what Aldrick, the gold, stated. "I think that Burk has a valid point. We need to know how it is that these humans can be in two places at the same time. Can both of them attack at the same time doing double damage? Are we then to face them twice? What if we slay one of them, will the duplicate one also die or not? It seems to me that we must know this before we act. It could be critical information for us to have when we battle the humans."

Werner, the black, wanted to groan, but kept a straight face. Somehow this was all working out wrong yet again! He'd been purposely silent, hoping that the vote would come and he could simply vote yes and not be seen at the center of the declaration this time. Once again, the damnable Neutrals were making a complete mess out of what should have been an open and shut situation. Hence, he kept unusually quiet and let the Neutrals carry the discussion for some time.

Alistair, the green, finally spoke up, "Werner, you've been uncharacteristically quiet. What do you have to say?"

"Vote and be done with it," Werner replied sarcastically.

Just as they were about to vote, Donatello, the brown, arrived. "Sorry for being late. I have gathered more facts." He then outlined what he'd observed and what had been said by the barons. At last he said, "I move that we study this in more depth. We need to find out if the humans have some new magic that allows them to be in two places at the same time. Do they have some new super weapon that can cleave the head of an adult dragon with one strike? Do they have some new super spell that allows them to move at least ten times faster than they normally do in a battle? We must know the answers to these questions before we can make an informed decision. I call for a vote on this." It carried unanimously and the meeting adjourned.

The browns, blues, and greys hung around after the other dragons left. Donatello, the brown, spoke up, "I have more news for you. I talked with this Baron Zoran human about the supposed hundreds of Archmages that Werner claims that he is making. I sent in a spy to Brn to learn what he could about them. Both are in agreement. While these nearly two hundred women are learning magic at a rapid rate, their progress is the normal one followed by all magic students. Only seventeen have even reached the mage level and most are barely on the useful Adept spells. It is my opinion that Werner is exaggerating the threat a good deal. However, we ought to continue to monitor it ourselves." The others agreed and all returned to their planets and homes.

Werner, the black, and Dario, the red, landed on a huge boulder in the middle of an alpine lake, not far from Dario's cavern. "Well, that went awry. Damnable Neutrals. They never have the guts to act," Dario, the red, complained bitterly. He had so hoped this would be the beginning of the war which would wipe out all of the humans.

"Something must have gone wrong. No matter, Dario. Our new breeding program is ready for execution. We begin tonight. Let us focus on increasing our numbers for the time being. We still have another plan to try, but winter is almost upon us. I'd rather wait until warmer weather. I hate the cold," Werner, the black, replied.

"Agreed. I hate it worse than you do, old friend. Agreed. We begin tonight. This time, *nothing* can *possibly* go wrong. Is it to be fifteen or sixteen this time?"

"Asami folk are not worth taking. Fifteen. We can alternate who gets the odd one each time. Spread them out over two weeks as usual," Werner answered. The two departed to see to the execution of their new breeding plan.

Chapter 31 Discoveries

By the end of September, Zoran finished arranging suitable housing and temporary employment for another thirty families from the various planets who insisted on being there to help their wives or daughters. He simply could not refuse them and their emotional reunions spoke volumes. Additionally, he had the mages schedule trips home for all of the others to visit their families as well, staggering them during the fall. Every one of the women personally thanked him for making this happen for them.

As October came, Zoran began to relax, feeling things were finally settling down and under control. That feeling lasted one day, for the following day, word reached him of another missing young wife from one of the northern provinces. Her age fit the pattern as well as the circumstances of her disappearance. He sighed and set to work once more. This time, he went straight to Kachina to ask her if she could sense the abduction of the woman, perhaps giving him some clues as to where she was being held.

For Kachina, all this seemed frighteningly similar as she worked her divination magic. As before, she was able to isolate the terror of the young woman as the dragons kidnaped her from her bedroom and Shadow Walked her to the rendezvous location. Kachina counted fifteen women all told this time and as before they met at the boulder field on Isi. However, this time, all traces of the women completely vanished after that. "It's as if their minds were wiped clean of all emotion and fright, as if they had never even been abducted," she explained.

Zoran then Shadow Walked to Voss and checked the cavern complex where the ninety-six were held. Deserted. Dust was slowly settling on the stone floors, no foot prints were visible. His conclusion was simple: they had built yet another secret hideout. Frustrated, Zoran visited Aldrick to again ask his aide. Furious, Aldrick promised to investigate immediately. However, when he reported back, he said, "I grilled them, but both Dario and Werner swear that they do not have a single human female in their maternity caverns, only their own dragon mates. Considering how he answered, Zoran, I believe that he is being truthful. He does not have humans this time. I am truly sorry."

At this point, Zoran knew that he really had a problem and continued to monitor the situation. Relaying the data to the other barons, he asked them to keep him informed on any missing women on their planets. He could find little else to go on and felt frustrated. He needed a break, but didn't get one. As September turned into October and then November, more abductions were reported. Each one he tried to trace, but came up with the same results. Worse, there was no discernable pattern this time. Before, the abductions occurred every two weeks, precisely to the night. Now it seemed random, but at least three women were disappearing from Adapazan every four weeks or so. Worse, the rendezvous locations were never at the same place as they had been before. Each time Kachina worked her divination magic, she lost them all right after they merged into one flock. "I need a break!" he cursed and pounded his own desk.

Duska Adrianna Whitehall continued to make extremely good progress learning her Duska defensive fighting skills and really wanted to move on to taking the offensive with her twin short swords. "She has the knack for it, baron, but I would like your opinion if you think she's ready," Dana gave his weekly report on his student.

"Okay, I'll test her tonight, Dana, though I am sure that your judgment is a sound one. When has it ever been otherwise?" he replied, more worried about the recent clandestine abductions.

Dana flushed. Dare he say why he distrusted his own observations? Zoran detected his slight flush and put his attention on Dana completely, causing the young man to squirm slightly. "Okay, okay, I want your opinion on Adrianna because mine may be biased, colored."

"How so?" Zoran asked without thinking. Had he thought a bit more, he ought to have known. As it was, he embarrassed his Master Swordsman further.

"She and I — well, we've sort of fallen for each other. I didn't intend for it to happen. It just did. I mean I never thought that I'd get over losing Wen, but I can't help it. I can't tell if I'm putting what I want to see in her there or if she really does have what it takes," Dana blurted it out, realizing that he never could withhold anything of importance from Zoran. His baron had that all-knowing air about him.

"I'm sorry. I haven't been paying enough attention to things up close to me of late. All these women being abducted has unnerved me. I understand, Dana. She is quite attractive and has more potential than most — spunky woman who doesn't give up. Reminds me of Zdenka. Sure, I'll test her thoroughly and give you an honest appraisal tonight." Dana relaxed, he felt quite relieved that at least Zoran knew of his feelings for Adrianna.

That evening, Dana explained to Adrianna that Zoran would be giving her a defensive fighter test to make sure that he had not overlooked any holes in her defensive reactions and responses. "Oh my! The baron himself? What if I get all nervous and goof up, Dana?" Worry lines creased her forehead and chin.

"Hey, relax, dear. Think of him as just another one of your pub's slightly drunken men. Trust your training patterns and you'll do fine. Honestly, hardly anyone has ever beaten him, so don't worry about that," he attempted to calm her down. He began helping her into all of the thick protective gear needed when practicing combat with real enchanted short swords. One miscalculated move could result in a very serious injury or death. The padded armor protected them from the worst of it, though a blade could still cut through it if one was not careful.

Zoran showed up in good spirits. For him, this was a pleasureful diversion from his many problems. Dana quickly helped him into another padded outfit and he strapped on his twin short swords. "Adrianna, this is simply a test to see if you have your defensive actions down. We Duska never know when an assassin may strike us. When I was eighteen, I managed to survive three assassination attempts on my life and they came when I least expected them. That's why we place such an emphasis on fast reactions to dangerous threats. Our goal here is to train you to be able to survive whatever may get thrown at you. Shall we?"

"Yes, sir," she said, still quite nervous about the surprise testing. Any nervousness she had vanished almost at once. Spinning, twirling short swords coming at you tends to force you to focus immediately. Thrusts, lunges, fakes, Zoran threw the book at her, though on a gradient, beginning with only one of his swords making the attack at one time. She countered, dodged, and feinted herself. He noticed that unlike most fighters, she did not favor her strong side, usually the right. That is excellent, he noted. At last, he upped the ante and began using both short swords in his attack.

Adrianna sweated, concentrated, and watched her opponent's moves. God, he's good, she thought, bringing her left sword up to parry and deflecting his right sword's thrust. Expecting a left side follow through, she brought hers up to block his and steel clashed. She'd anticipated it properly and met his. Both pairs of blades slipped off of each other and each stepped back a step, as Zoran began to make his next move. Short swords are really a battle of speed and dexterity, quite unlike the attack modes of the much heavier weapons. This was a style that Zoran loved. For once, he was getting a good work out, one that only Dana could give him in the past. Well, that was not entirely true; Zdenka's father could too, before age took its toll on him. She's good, he thought and picked up his tempo even more.

My god, how can he go this fast! Adrianna thought, barely able to deflect his whirling blades. She found herself having to constantly back up, unable to parry or deflect his flashing swords at this speed. As she neared the back wall, she thought, darn it anyway! Trip! She cast one of her useful spells on Zoran. His feet tripped and for the first time in the test, Zoran felt challenged. He had not expected this twist but he was not going to allow her to win this easily. Although falling forward, he added to it, tucking and rolling as he hit the mat, bringing his left short sword in a sweeping arc around to his backside, while he thrust his right one straight behind him. It was a calculated move, one designed to protect his rear while he regained his posture.

Adrianna saw him duck and roll and was hesitant to simply take the bait and rush up behind him. As a result she saw his left arm swinging around and met his sword with her left one. At the same time she saw the stabbing right one and knew that she had been right. If she had rushed him, she'd have taken it in her stomach. Instead, she dodged and put her right sword at his neck.

Zoran felt cold steel at his neck and promptly stopped and dropped both swords. As he felt her back off, he turned and removed his protective head gear. "Incredibly well done, Adrianna! You are only the third person ever to best me in a sword match! That was a really good, unexpected move you made. Honestly, I can't believe I fell for a Trip spell. Well done!"

Adrianna removed her head gear, sweat pouring down the sides of her cheeks. She was breathless. "I did it. Wow! Say, who else bested you? I can't believe I did it. I am sorry. I got a little pissed there at the end. I know I am not supposed to go on the offensive, but I was not about to get backed into the wall."

"Sometimes, the best defense if a good offense, Adrianna. That was one of them. Dana here often bests me and Zdenka's father used too when he was my Master Swordsman many years ago. You really do have a knack for this. Dana, the only flaw that I could find is the inherent flaw with all beginners. She backs off when the action of two attacking swords becomes too great. Just more practice and experience is all she needs for that. I agree with your judgment. Adrianna, you are ready to tackle the offensive side, if you desire to learn more." He offered her his hand, surprising her even further.

"Yes, I want to learn more. It is quite a workout, but I think that being able to handle swords is a great compliment to using magic spells. To defeat dragons, I think I need both worlds," she declared her own opinion.

"I won't debate that one," Zoran chuckled, extricating himself from the padded armor. "I'll leave you to it. Got some pressing problems to handle." After both thanked him, he left the two alone.

"See, I told you that you were good, dear," Dana said, helping her out of her gear.

"I can't believe I bested him. You are a great teacher." She planted a passionate kiss on his lips. The two embraced and then continued with her first theory lessons on offensive fighting.

Of course, the buzz around the fortress and magic towers was the Adrianna had bested Zoran in a dual short swords contest. Over lunch, Jarka whispered to Zoran, "Did she *really* best you? It's going around, you know."

Zoran laughed, "Yes, she did." He saw many eyes glancing their way. He rose and called out loudly, "Yes, she did. Adrianna bested me last night in a practice session. And yes, she's only the third person to ever do that to me." Giggles and chuckles echoed around the room, along with many whispered voices.

Jarka later added, "That was a good morale booster."

"I know and it quieted the silly rumors," he teased her back.

Zdenka continued to give him weekly reports on how the Seventeen were progressing. That was now the name officially given by all of the other students to those original women, who were blazing the trail for all of the rest of the women.

"They are progressing just as one would expect of normal students, only more quickly. Each is discovering there are some spells that they simply cannot manage. Yes, they are taking it rather hard — griping that they must be stupid or something. In many ways, they are reacting much like Karel did. I am helping them overcome their frustrations. Also I am greatly relieved. I was worried that these women would actually be able to learn every darn spell in existence. Now I am seeing that they are just like the rest of us. We all have spells that we are keenly interested in, our specialties, so to speak. I can't tell you how relieved I am over this."

"Right love. I too would be spooked and unnerved if the Seventeen learned every spell in the book! Think they will make Archmage?" Zoran asked her.

"Honestly, my love, I just don't know. It is too early to tell for sure. You never can know precisely who is and who is not going to make it. If pressed, I would say that the Seventeen are all good prospects, though."

"Great. Keep me posted as always. I could use seventeen more Archmages," he grinned. Who couldn't?

"Dear, there is one other thing that is bothering me. It's Danika. She claims that she can sense when a dragon is around. She and her husband Rafael spend Sundays together, often out in Brn. That's where she claims she is sensing them, though neither she nor Rafael has actually seen the flying beasts. Could you look into this for me?"

Sunday afternoon, Rafael knocked on the tower door. As always, he was intimidated by the sternness of the Door Warden. "My wife and daughter please?" he said.

"Well, it's about time. They've been waiting a couple of minutes," she replied just as sternly, as if he'd just committed a huge offense against the two. Danika and Neda came bouncing out to meet him.

She threw her arms around him and they hugged and embraced, while Neda found herself between them, being hugged by both. Danika was, of course, morphed so that she had arms and hands. Rafael explained, "Sorry I am late, but Baron Zoran wanted a word with me. He is going to meet us at the Stodgy Inn today. Something about dragons, but I surely don't know what. Come on, my lovely ladies. It's our day once more!"

At the inn, Neda, now nearly twelve, ran off to chat with her boyfriend. Zoran motioned the two over to his table. He wore a disguise and Danika didn't recognize him at first. "Greetings, Mage Danika. Zoran here. Have a seat please." After ordering the pair mugs of the most expensive ale, Zoran explained.

"Zdenka has said that you can tell when a dragon is near. I want to fully explore that today, if we can. I will follow you both around today, staying in the background. Message me when you sense the presence of a dragon. Okay?"

"Then, you think this is real? That I am somehow able to sense them?" Danika whispered back. "I thought that maybe I was just imagining it or something."

"That's why I am here. Let's see if we can prove it or disprove it, shall we?"

"Sure, but I am sensing that a dragon is in this inn right now, Zoran. It is somewhere in this pub area."

"Okay, act normally. Let me meander around, please." Zoran rose and casually moved around the spacious pub area, where the Yuletide dances were always held. Some fifty men and women were here, sipping ale or dining out on a late fall Sunday early afternoon. Smoke from pipes drifted towards the sooty ceiling. Conversations buzzed — all the normal chatter one would expect from one of the nicer inns and pubs in Brn. Nothing seemed out of the ordinary to Zoran. Still, anyone of these people could be a dragon in human form.

Although it took him a while, in his nonchalant wanderings, he managed to get a good look at most everyone present, except one man sitting alone near the rear. He wore a cowl over his head and Zoran couldn't get a good look at the man. He slowly made his way closer to him, pretending to have had a wee bit too much ale. As he approached, he dropped a coin and bent over to pick it up. As he rose, he looked up and finally got a clear view of the man's face under the cowl. He nodded and hiccupped, then moved on, eventually returning to the table where an anxious Danika and Rafael were sitting whispering about this whole business.

"Here, have a seat, old man, ale's on us," Rafael said loudly to Zoran, who had just sent him a Message telling him what to say. After sitting down, Zoran whispered his findings.

"Danika, you are not dreaming. That solitary man in the back corner is not a man, but a brown dragon. I got a good look at his eyes, coal black. His skin has a brownish hue to it. Somehow you are able to detect the presence of dragons! This is an incredibly useful skill that you have. Well done."

"Well, it's not just me, Zoran. All of us Seventeen have been having these strange feelings too. Eliska, Dusana, all of us," she replied. "What does it mean?"

"It means that somehow you are natively attuned to the presence of these creatures. Now why don't you get on with your Sunday afternoon? Let me know if you detect other dragons and where they are located. Thank you, Mage Danika. Oh, on your way out, let me know how far away you get before you can no longer sense this one, please." She smiled and Zoran wandered out of the inn, opening a Mystical Door straight into his study.

He summoned all his staff at once. "Sorry to bother you all on your day off. I will be quick. The Seventeen are able to detect the presence of dragons nearby when they are in human form. We've long suspected that the dragons have sent in spies to Brn. Danika spotted one and I've verified a brown is in the Stodgy Inn observing quietly."

"Incredible! This is a breakthrough," Karel exclaimed. "Want us to go get him?"

"No, it is far more valuable to us if the dragons don't know that we have a way to detect them when they are in human form. We need to test the women and see how accurate they are and how close they must be to detect them. This really is a breakthrough for us."

Jarka commented, "Now *we* can feed *them* disinformation!" Everyone chuckled. She was so right, many thought.

He advised, "Caution, this skill is limited. Danika can sense the dragon's presence out to about a hundred yards away from it, but can only give you its rough direction. Still, this is a major breakthrough. We will need to test the other women later on."

The next day, Zdenka surveyed her Seventeen and all had at one time or other thought a dragon might be lurking around Brn when they were out on Sundays. After relaying this to Zoran, she got them back into their magic studies.

Jarka, on the other hand, was waiting for Zoran in his private study right after breakfast. "Boss, we have a major security problem on our hands. Since we now have proof positive that there are dragon spies in Brn, we cannot allow the women to wander the streets of Brn on their day off. At any time, a dragon could snatch up one of them and take off through the Shadows!"

"I know, but we cannot keep them locked up all of the time. You and I both know that they have to have at least one day to relax and get out of the cramped tower rooms. The married ones have to have family time. I am open to suggestions, Jarka. If I let Brn know that there are dragons walking among them, I will only be causing panic and witch hunts."

"Quite true. How about establishing the policy that no woman goes out alone? She always must be in the company of another or several. We ought to try to identify the dragons and keep an eye on them, don't you think? Or would that raise their suspicions?"

"Yes, it would. Right now, I would like the dragons to think that we are not aware of them. Then, I can 'feed' them the information that I want them to have."

"Oh, you are getting as devious as me," she laughed and returned to helping the students with their spells. Zoran then issued orders that none of the magic students were allowed to leave the towers or fortress alone and why.

As always, October was a busy time, harvest time. Loads of grains and many other necessities poured into Brn. Some were distributed to the town granaries, some to the fortress-towers complex. Additionally, a good deal was also packed into air tight caskets and stored in the subterranean supply pantries. He was kept busy with overseeing the emergency supplies and their proper storage. Zoran disliked this aspect of his position, but could not avoid it. All his mages and Duskas were already overworked dealing with the many magic students and the off-world transport of even more supplies coming into Brn.

Near the end of October, his daughter, High Priestess Jarmila came to see him. "Dad, we've finished going over every darn one of Bandar Zar's journals. That was quite a chore."

"I'll say, he was quite the documenter."

She continued, "Yes, he was. Anyway, Miroslav and I came across one strange page that we'd more or less skipped over before. We still don't know what to make of it. Part of it is damaged by water, part, by mold. We've Cleaned the mold off, but still can't make much of it. We think it might be some kind of code. Have a look."

V~~~ ~~stor~ ~our~~~~

Pacov ~~rtr~~~

Sublev~~ 5

A52C96

Vols: A-~ (T maybe)

"That last bit might be T, we think, dad."

"Looks pretty garbled," Zoran replied.

"Well, true. However, dad, knowing that Bandar was a stickler for writing everything down in his journals, surely he did not start doing that when he came here to our worlds. It only makes sense that he wrote journals of everything he was doing before he came here," Jarmila suggested.

He replied as she anticipated, "Well that is an assumption that I would make. Yet, we've not found any of his writing which seem to predate his arrival here."

"True. Either we have yet to locate that secret stash or it is stored elsewhere. Now what Miroslav and I find particularly interesting about this page is that last line: Vols: A- and then probably a T, we think. All of his journals that we have are numbered from 1 to 26. Perhaps he originally designated them by letters. That last line could mean volumes A through T."

"Reasonable assumption. Then this might be directions telling where he stored them," Zoran suggested.

"Precisely our thinking, dad. We both believe this is a map to his earlier writing, predating the founding of the Federation. However, we can't make anything out of the rest. V, stor, our, rtr. It is indecipherable. I mean, dad, rtr? What can that be?" Jarmila was quite frustrated at her inability to truly decipher the message.

"You want me to have a look at it?"

Relief gushed out, "Oh would you dad? Please? It could be important, well, maybe. It sounds really interesting."

"Okay, leave it with me and I'll see what I can do with it. Yes, rtr? Strange indeed. Pacov sounds like a town's name. I think we even have a Pacov up in one of the northeastern provinces. Probably not the right Pacov though. Let me see what I can work out." She hugged him and gave him a kiss on his forehead. He patted her rear as she left and then stared at the cryptic page. "At least I have something to occupy my mind besides barrels of wheat," he said to his walls.

He looked at it off and on for a couple of weeks but really hadn't made any progress in deciphering it. He wanted it to start off saying Voss. That would fit, but then so would Veca, Vela, and many more possibilities. Wishful thinking, he acknowledged.

Mid-November, while staring absent mindedly at it, Jarka entered to report on the progress of the women that she was helping learn magic. "Say, what's that you've got there?"

"Oh a partially destroyed page of Bandar Zar's early journal. Jarmila wanted me to see if I could make out what is missing. It is possibly a map to his journals written before he came to our worlds here. Who knows?"

"Can I see it?" He handed her the page. "Oh, I do love maps and mysteries. Can I hang on to it a while and see what I can make out?"

"Sure be my guest. I've spent a couple weeks on it, getting nowhere really. I'd like the first word to be Voss." Both chuckled. "Well, that would be interesting," he added.

"Sure would be. I'll let you know," she stated. Then, she gave him the report. All ninety-six women were well into their grade two spells now, making very rapid progress. "I wish it had been this easy for us way back when we were studying." Both laughed, recalling their endless hours of studying under Archmage Oldrich.

Jarka worked on the page at night in her spare time. There were two kinds of damage to the page. One was water damage; the other was caused by mold, probably the mold resulted from the page getting wet, she theorized. The water damage was in the upper left corner only impacting that first word and part of the second. She decided to see if she could bring out the washed out ink. Under a magnifying glass, she detected that there was still a tiny residual ink present, just not enough to make out the letters.

She conducted some experiments on ordinary paper and ink, unwilling to touch the actual document until she had the procedure worked out. If she damaged it, the message could be lost to them forever. A week later, she exclaimed, "Eureka! It works." She'd applied a special dye to the affected area and now the dye reacted with the residual ink and she read:

Voss H~stor~ ~our~~~~

"Now we *are* getting somewhere!" She summoned Zoran to her lab.

"What's up? Got it all figured out?" he teased her.

"No, but look at this! Voss. You are right, it is Voss. And I can guess at the next word, History. Voss History, then something."

"Excellent work, Jarka. Jarmila is hoping this is a map to the whereabouts of a bunch more of Bandar Zar's earliest journals. Makes sense, Voss History."

"Hey, journals. That third word could be Journals! Voss History Journals," Jarka stated formally.

"I do believe that we are definitely on to something that may well be fantastically interesting. Don't know if it is really important, but could be interesting to know our ancient history, Jarka. Keep on it."

"Oh you couldn't pull me away from this with a herd of dragons!" she replied, exaggerating a bit. One dragon could pull her away from it. Both laughed.

It took her another week to work develop a moldy paper on which to experiment. However, after only another two days, she applied an acidic solution and turned the invisible writing back to a dingy yellow, but it was readable. She sat back and said, "Duh. It's obvious. I should have figured this out weeks ago!"

Voss History Journals

Pacov Fortress

Sublevel 5

A52C96

Vols: A-T

She summoned Zoran, Miroslav, and Jarmila. When they arrived via Mystical Door spells, she said, "Ta da! Your old Mage has done it again. Care to read the full page?" All three dove for the page.

"We did it! We found the map to his earliest writings! Yahoo!" Jarmila exclaimed.

"This is interesting," Zoran added, "our ancestors originally came to the Federation planets from Voss, where the dragons are also from — what an interesting fact. This raises far more questions than it answers!"

"We absolutely *must* find those journals, Zoran. I bet they contain tons of useful facts," Jarmila broke in, still excited about the discovery. "Maybe they will give us some ideas on how to handle the dragons, dad. We have to find this place."

"Okay, okay. I can take a hint. We will have to visit Voss, but don't get your hopes up too high, Jarmila. It is likely a large planet about which we know nothing. Finding something millennia old, this Pacov, may not be possible. Besides, Voss may be dragon infested as well. Still, we have to try."

"I'm going, dad. Miroslav too," she insisted, not waiting for him to begin to organize an expedition there.

"Of course, unless your mother objects," he replied, putting the final decision onto Zdenka for the moment.

"Damn!" Jarka exclaimed.

"I know, you want to go too, but you are really needed here helping with the training of the women. Tell you what, if and when we actually find this place, we'll come get you. I would not think of entering a strange fortress without my thief with me. I don't want to get crushed in some diabolical trap, now do I?"

Jarka laughed and relaxed. He was precisely right. "Thanks, you know I am your best trap detector and finder of secrets." He grinned, for she certainly was that and more. "So who can you get to go with you?"

That was his immediate problem. Nearly everyone was quite busy. He certainly could not pull any of those teaching the hundreds of magic students off their positions. Yet, going to Voss and exploring necessitated bringing along members who could handle tough situations. At last, he decided upon Archmage Karel, though he would have to pull him off of his magic item fabrication projects. If they had to fight dragons, he wanted at least two Archmages present. Thus Karel would have to come along. Duskas were crucial. Yet, who was left that he could ask?

Since this was likely an uninhabited planet, that is, sans humans, they would either have to bring along their own food supplies or gamble on finding edible food there. Since he had no idea what was there or what might be poisonous to eat, he opted to bring along food. Were there strange wild animals? So many variables had to be considered. Certainly the living conditions would be rather primitive at best, unless they opted to return to Brn each night, limiting their searches to the daytime only.

He wanted to bring his son Tomas along, but that would leave only Baron Jan on Adapazan. Should anything happen to them, Jan was ill-equipped to run the whole planet's affairs. Besides, Tomas was swamped with overseeing all the construction in Sholov Province and the northern provinces as well. He thought about asking his off-world friends, Leo and Stefan. Both might be interested, but they were dealing with their own world's problems. Besides, the two were devising a scheme to try to find their planet's missing women by catching the dragons in the act of snatching more women and then following them. Since they now each had one of Karel's Rods of Dragon Slaying, both men felt more comfortable going on the offensive. No, he'd best allow them to do their own independent actions instead of relying on him. Who to take?

Honani had heard of the message and its implications. The group of Star Dancers drooled over the prospect of seeing first hand a new world, though they were not much interested in ancient history. He caught Zoran in the hallway as the baron headed to his study after breakfast. "Excuse me, baron. Rumor has it that you are planning an expedition to the dragon world of Voss."

"Morning Honani, yes, Jarka's translated what appears to be a map to some ancient writings of Bandar Zar. They are on Voss, so we've decided to see if we can possibly find them."

"Well, we Star Dancers would like to join you in your search. Kachina will remain behind and watch over the children during the daytime, but we'll bring her to Voss for a brief time each night so she can see the Star Universe too. We five will lend you a hand, if you'll have us," Honani suggested.

"Hum, not a bad idea, Honani. Help accepted. I'm bringing Archmage Karel along so that we have at least two of us in case we have to deal with dragons, but he's not Duska. I need to make sure that, if something happens to me, Karel has a way back home and doesn't get stranded on Voss."

"Thanks, we will make our preparations. We are good at surviving off what the lands have to offer us. We will not need much in the way of supplies," he suggested.

"Okay. I've just not worked out yet who else is coming, so it will be a few days yet. I'll keep you posted." Later in his study, he smiled. Honani and his group would be perfect — all Duska and excellent trackers. Still, this could be very dangerous, if there were still dragons on Voss. Sitting back in his chair, he thought of Evsen and Strike Force One. "Brilliant! Why didn't I think of them before? They would be perfect for this, fourteen strong, able fighters. Besides, then they would not be aggravating the dragons by killing a few of them this winter. Defuses a sore point with Aldrick."

The question now was how to get the force to veer off their assigned orders to slay dragons and come help him search Voss. Ah, that was it. Search Voss, the original home of the dragons. That would play well with all of the other barons when they discovered what he'd done with their strike force. He Mind Linked to Evsen and asked him to bring his group to Brn for a special meeting.

An hour later, the fourteen fighters, heavily armed and well supplied, though their supplies were Shrunk, arrived on his sky blue Circle. Zoran thought these brave fighters ought to have a bit of honor shown to them. Yes, many were impressed to be allowed to actually set foot on one of the Circles of Ascension. Normally, the barons kept these under tight lock and key. This bit of honor also put them into a more acceptable frame of mind. Zoran had planned well.

A bit later, settled into his War Room, Zoran outlined what the mission would be and why. Anwen Alun of Anwyn responded first. She said enthusiastically, "Hey, I like this. We can take the fight to Voss, where they came from in the first place."

"We might gain some valuable clues that we can use to defeat them," Viktor Denek of Gladno proposed.

"Even if there are no dragons left on Voss, we might find all manner of valuable things there which we can make use of in our battles with the dragons," concluded Vladimir Milla of Valtr.

"If our ancestors did come from Voss, we might find things of great historic value for my people of Chana," Yada Shem added, taking a different approach.

Evsen had yet to say anything. Of course, if Zoran wanted them, he would go, no questions asked, but he'd rather not have to order the group to go. Seeing the others nodding their approval, at last he said, "I think I speak for all of us, baron, count us in. We'd all love to go on this expedition. Who else is coming?"

"Archmage Karel. I want at least two Archmages along, just in case. Plus, I will bring along a few of his rods to help you all out a bit. Honani of Isi has also volunteered to bring his band of Star Dancers along to help," Zoran replied.

Kaya Kasa of Isi, their tracker and archer who spoke infrequently, said quietly, "That is good. They are rogues, but highly competent in such matters. You could do far worse."

"How soon can we get this expedition going?" asked an impatient Bernd Hardt of Dietmar. "We have been idle too long for my tastes."

"Let's get supplies together and leave first thing in the morning. I'll get the others here now so we can meet and finalize everything. Then, you all can raid our supplies for what you think we're going to need."

"Ah, Kaya, we meet again," Honani reverently addressed the thin archer the moment that he and his group entered the room with the fighters. It was obvious that he greatly respected the woman, Zoran noticed, a good sign the two groups would get along. Karel, Miroslav, and Jarmila arrived and the introductions began.

"Okay, undoubtedly Voss is a large world. My plan is to divide us up into three scouting parties with each taking a specific quadrant of the planet to search. We map it as we go. If nothing else, let's at least produce a map of this world. It might help us in the future. Between Karel and I, we have five of his powerful rods. He and I will each have one on us and we can protect two others if they stay on either side of us and within ten feet. They will protect us fully from around ten dragon breath attacks. I will give each leader of the three groups a rod as well, though I hope and pray that we don't need them."

"Unless anyone objects, Evsen, I'll take Kaya and Anwen with me along with Honani's group and Jarmila. That leaves a dozen of you and Karel and Miroslav. Evsen, you divide the rest of your force into two groups anyway you desire and put Karel with one of them."

"Will we be coming back here each night or camping there?" he asked.

"I'm open for opinions on that," he replied. After some discussion, Honani and Kaya's views ruled. They would wait and see what they found on Voss. If conditions were acceptable, camping was preferred. They then broke up to pack more supplies, on the assumption that they might be camping out.

Evsen took Karel and Miroslav with him, along with Tom, Vladimir, Viktor, and Berndt. Karel insisted that Evsen carry the extra rod for his group. Evsen then insisted that Miroslav carry the rod. "Look you are the only person in the Federation who knows how to build Circles of Ascension. You have to be protected." He couldn't deny that point.

Yada took charge of the third group that included Fino, Henri, Klaus, Federico, and Farrell with himself. He was given the fifth Rod of Dragon Slaying. On the 15th of November the explorers set out for Voss and the great unknown.

Chapter 32 The Exploration of Voss

Zoran led the expedition to the only known location on Voss, the cavern complex where they had rescued the abducted women. They stepped out of the Shadows on top of the peak which held the caverns and took a look. Russet colored mountains with snowcapped peaks stretched as far as they could see. Picturesque. First, they stepped partially into the Shadows and moved out for an overview of Voss, circumnavigating the world, getting an overview.

They saw three large landmasses. One was roughly circular, centered on the north polar region. Here, the terrain was snow and ice, though rugged. It did not show promise of much. Ice flows predominated at its south pole, but no land masses. Two huge continents, roughly on either side of the globe, were the obvious choices for habitations. They called one of these the Zucchini Continent, because of its unique shape. From its narrow crooked northern most portion, the continent swept southward, crossing the equator with its rounded bottom in the far southern hemisphere. They guessed that it was perhaps seven thousand miles north-south, but only three thousand at its middle near the equator.

The other continent they called the Rectangle. Again, it was roughly centered along the equator, but was at least ten thousand miles from east to west and six thousand north to south. Dividing the Rectangle in half was a huge north-south range of mountains. Smack in the middle lay the russet peaks in which the caverns were located. In the vast oceans, they spotted a fair number of island groups. Now the question was where to begin their search.

Evsen took the Zucchini continent, while Zoran took the eastern half of the Rectangle, leaving Yada to search the western half. This first day, their sole objective was to rapidly sweep across these land masses and see roughly what they were facing and if there were dragons in the areas.

Zoran swooped over a vast arid plain which covered the northeastern section of his half of the continent. Further inland, cradled against the Russet Mountains, as they began calling the peaks, lay a vast desert land that stretched from about five hundred miles below the northern coast to an equal distance from the southern coast. Evidently, the Russet Mountains blocked rainfall here. In the southeastern corner lay a dense, sprawling forest region.

Zoran spotted numerous antelope and other herd animals roaming the arid plains and the edges of the forest. The only dragons his group spotted were a number of reds and blacks high in the skies over the Northern Russet Mountains. He saw no signs of human survivors — no smoke clouds curling into the blue skies. The rendezvous location that evening was the southern coast where the forest met the foothills of the Russet Mountains.

Yada's group swept across the western half. In the far north, they encountered a vast marshland, which gave way to rolling hills. In the southern portion, another great forest stretched from the Russet Mountains down to the sea. Vast plains covered the entire western half of this half of the continent. His group too spotted the reds and blacks in the far northern Russet Mountains, but nothing further south or west, just desolate lands devoid of people, though teaming with wildlife.

Evsen's group started in the north of the Zucchini, where plains predominated. Archmage Karel enjoyed himself immensely. He used his power spell to change into a giant falcon and spent most of the day circling high above the lands, his now keen eyes searching for clues. Further south, a thick forest took over, though it gave way to a marsh land and swamps on the eastern coast. The forest only grew denser the further south they went, until it became a thick jungle before thinning out as the Dividing Mountains — their name for the mountain range with sliced the Zucchini into the northern two thirds and the southern third. Another vast plain covered most of the southern third which gave way to another desert at the northeastern edge of this lower third. They spotted no dragons at all but much wildlife. No signs of human dwellers were seen.

At camp they discussed their findings. Two things were clear. Nearly all of the dragons of Voss had migrated to the Federation of the Sixteen Planets, only a few remained, unless they lived on the islands or oceans. The decimated herds of antelope and other wildlife had recovered during the last twenty-some years. Honani told everyone that this proves that Nature always wins in the long run.

The next day, the real work began, low level reconnaissance. The goal was to find traces of the lost human towns and cities. Once one was found, they were to search it for any clues to the location of Pacov. Pacov could be a fortress, a Circle of Ascension, a town or city, or even some special geographical feature. To their credit, no one suggested this was looking for a needle in a haystack.

As they prepared to begin their day, Zoran pointed out, "Our ancestors founded the Federation eighteen hundred years ago. If all of the humans on Voss left at that point, time and Nature will have taken its toll. Cities and towns may well be overgrown, perhaps not even recognizable."

He began his search here in the dense southern forest. After a couple of hours, he halted. "Time for a new plan," he suggested to everyone's relief. The thick foliage prevented them from an aerial search. They couldn't see through the green canopy. On foot, they encountered brown bears, black bears, poisonous snakes, and even wolves.

"Dad, if Pacov is in here, we'll never find it," Jarmila complained.

"Okay, let's head back to the extreme northeastern corner and try the plains," Zoran suggested. Now they had more luck. Here and there, they came across the ruins of a town or village, but they were little more than distinctive raised patterns on the ground. Time and the elements had worn the dwellings down to rubble. Try as they might, they could get no real clues from these finds. However, they were spotted several times by high flying dragons of the far north, several who came closer to get a look at the party. However, they did not seem threatening and left quickly.

Yada encountered similar findings on the vast western plains where he'd begun his low level searching. Evsen reported the same, since he too began systematically back at the extreme northern plains of the Zucchini. After a fruitless week, they concluded that the adobe dwellings found so frequently in the plains simply could not withstand time. "We need to look for stone buildings and forts. Forget these cities of adobe mounds," Zoran ordered.

"Stone is more prevalent in the hills and mountains," Kaya pointed out. "We should look there first." Zoran agreed and the next day, Evsen took his group into the Dividing Mountains. Yada headed for the vast central western hills.

Zoran, on the other hand, had another idea. "Look, let's check out the desert. There, dwellings may well have survived longer. The worst we might find is the sands have flowed over the towns, burying them. If we have no luck, we'll start in on the Russet Mountains down at the southern edge of the Rectangle. I'd like to stay clear of the known dragons as long as possible."

As they searched the sand dune covered central desert, once more the reds and blacks observed them from a high altitude. Evidently, they were content to merely watch and showed no signs of hostility, for which Zoran was thankful.

Kaya was the first to point out the significant signs that people used to dwell in this desert land. "Look. That is a road, paved at one time."

"What's it mean, Kaya?" asked Jarmila. "I didn't know that there were actual paved roads in a desert land."

"Ordinarily, we desert dwellers use well-worn paths and seldom build paved roads," she replied.

"And that can mean only one thing, Zoran," Honani added. "This road must have played a very significant role in these people's lives. This route must have been so important that they went to a huge amount of work to make this a paved roadway. That means it must connect one or more very, very important sites. Of course, is it this way or that way," he pointed in the two directions along the faint outlines of the tract.

They decided to head south away from the dragons. Near dusk, they were finally rewarded. They were about halfway through the desert land and midway through the continent where the Russet Mountains veered out into the desert land some three hundred miles, before returning back to its usual north-south line. Cradled against the rocky foothills of the Russet Mountains was most definitely a city and fortress built out of the russet colored stone! Sands had nearly covered the streets and many of the buildings had been knocked down as if some giant's hand had played dominoes with the stonework. The outer walls of the fortress were unmistakable, though within the walls many of the building had crumbled. Still it was their first hopeful site to search.

Yada returned to camp enthused. They had come across three caverns which had once been occupied by dragons. They had recovered a large pile of loot, gold, gemstones, and jewelry. It was obvious that much had been looted from humans. Additionally, they had located four towns worth further exploration.

Evsen was equally enthused. "Look what we found," dumping out a large sack of gold, jewels, and necklaces. They too found four dragon dens, long empty in the high mountains. Likewise, they found two cities to search.

Bernd suggested that once they finished the mission, they ought to search all of the dragon dens they could find. "We could be fabulously wealthy!" Everyone chuckled, this was so true.

The teams headed out the next day filled with excitement. The hunt was on, ruins to explore, and amazing things to find. "It sure is eerie walking these streets, imagining what this city would have been some two thousand years ago," Jarmila broke the silence as the party walked over the thick deposits of sand covering in small drifts the paved streets of this once great desert city.

Anwen, who came from a desert planet, replied, "Yes, a city of this grandeur must have been a most important site for these people, rather like our fortress and Circle on Anwyn. We should look for a pair of statues whose arms form an arc over a doorway."

"Why?" asked Jarmila.

"That would mark the entrance to the Holiest of Holies, where the High Priests carried out their religious duties for the people — that's if they were anything like we Anwyn," she answered. "If anything will tell us where this Pacov is located, it would be with the priests. They maintain our records on Anwyn."

"Is that what you're looking for?" Honani asked pointing to a pair of bronze relief statues etched into giant stone walls and surrounding a pair of rusted iron doors. "The paved road that we are following leads straight to these doors. Must be important."

They had found the Holiest of Holies temple entrance. It took a number of Strength spells cast on everyone for them to finally pull the rusted doors open, breaking their hinges in the process, much to Anwen's dismay. She felt this was somehow sacrilegious.

After casting a number of Light spells and placing them on the tips of their swords, the group entered the dark, but cool temple. None saw the Invisible red sitting on the remnants of the fortress wall watching them enter. After the last human entered, the dragon quietly took flight, heading north.

What had once been a great and holy temple had long ago been sacked, presumably by the dragons. Anything of value had either been smashed or taken away. However, none of that mattered to Zoran. What was left did.

"Wow! Look at that!" he exclaimed. All eyes and lights turned to examine one wall. Here a hundred foot long, fifty foot tall mural was etched into the wall, with gold inlays outlining inscriptions and lines. They quickly realized this was a map of Voss! The golden dots represented principle cities and the lines, territorial markings. They quickly used their spells to translate the huge lettering across the top and the smaller words scattered about the mural.

Democracy of the Sixteen read the title. "Now we are getting somewhere," Jarmila exclaimed. "There must have been sixteen different groups or countries or kingdoms here, all united as one. See here. This is the mountain group; we're standing in one of the two desert ones."

"Interesting, so our founding fathers resettled on planets that were similar in nature to where they had lived on Voss," Zoran concluded. "That makes sense. Look, there is even a dot out there in the ocean. Must be the Asami ancestors."

"Oh my goodness! Cast your spells on the fine printing!" Anwen called out, terribly excited. "We are right in the Republic State of Anwyn! There is the Republic State of Adapazan! There is the Republic State of Gladno!"

"I'll be! Our ancestors were not very inventive!" Zoran exclaimed, rapidly scanning the finer printing.

"Dad, there is not the slightest doubt that our founding fathers came from Voss!" Jarmila declared. "So they were here along with the dragons. Was there a war here too? What happened to all the people? Did they all migrate out to the sixteen planets leaving the dragons behind? I've got more questions than ever before!"

Zoran laughed, "This sure casts a whole new light on everything. I think it is even more important that we find those journals now. Look at the rest of the fine print and see if we can find city names or something. Dear, make a good drawing of this mural for future reference. We have our first map."

While they spent the rest of the day searching the temple and the surrounding areas, they found nothing more. The fortress keep would have to wait until tomorrow. That evening they all shared notes. The other two groups had returned loaded with magical weapons. They had found stashes of them here and there in some of the ruins. They had found plenty of totally rusted normal weapons however. Evsen described one interesting room that he'd entered. He opened a door deep within a fortress keep. Inside the roughly twenty-foot square room, he saw tables, chairs, tapestries, books, a scroll, and wooden cups — all perfectly preserved, as if someone had just left the room. He sneezed from the dust. Right before his eyes the entire contents of the room collapsed into one giant dust cloud. He'd had to teleport out of there fast. Somehow the very molecules had retained their perfect balance for millennia before he opened the door and disturb their delicate balance.

"If nothing else, Zoran, we are finding enchanted blades that we can use to arm more fighters against the dragons," Evsen stated what his fighters had declared.

The next day, everyone headed back to see the mural in the temple. All were impressed. Then, they searched the keep and uncovered a few gold coins and several enchanted weapons, including two daggers. However, they found nothing that identified any city by name.

A week later, the group was forced to make a return trip to Brn. They had accumulated so much gold, gems, jewelry, and enchanted weapons that they could not continue to keep them with them as they explored Voss. Dana was given charge of the new weapons and was extremely pleased with suddenly receiving so many ancient blades. After sharing all that they had found, the large group returned to Voss the following day.

Back on Voss, Zoran suggested, "Gang, during this respite, I have been doing some thinking about all this. Perhaps we are going about this backwards, searching randomly throughout the various areas. Seeing that large map in the temple got me thinking. Old Bandar Zar had close ties with our founder, Valentýn Vladislov, closer ties than with any other baron. He chose to make his private stashes on Adapazan. People are creatures of habit. If I had to guess, old Bandar Zar probably lived or worked somewhere around this Republic State of Adapazan here on Voss. He probably stored those journals somewhere in this territory. Pacov is very likely to be there too."

"According to the map, the Republic State of Adapazan covers that section of the Russet Mountains from this eastward extension onto the desert south and westward for perhaps five hundred miles. The Republic of Rehor is the southernmost portion of the Russets, right below Adapazan. I think that we three groups should fan out and focus our searches in this roughly five hundred mile by five hundred mile zone of Adapazan."

Jarmila concurred. The connection did make sense from all she understood of Bandar from his copious writings. He was a creature of habit. Zoran then ordered,

"Okay, my group will head into the Russets from here at the temple, moving west and south. Yada, you take your group to the extreme southern border and work your way northward. Evsen, your group starts on the far western edge and work your way eastward. We'll meet somewhere in the central portion of this territory. Keep an eye out for the dragons. They are still watching us from afar. I don't trust them."

For the next few days, the groups entered caverns and searched through the ruins of numerous towns, yielding more treasure and a few more weapons, but little else. Well, there was one other thing. Yada's group came across a stone pyramid but it had no discernable entrances and appeared to be some kind of possible religious structure.

Then on the 20th of December, Karel, in his giant falcon form out circling around looking for potential ruins, spotted a very large one, too large for one group to search. All three parties joined up there and surveyed the scene. Here was perhaps the largest of all the cities they'd so far found. Nestled on the top of a minor Russet peak in the extreme southwestern corner of the Republic State of Adapazan's territory where the foothills began lay the walled city. It covered some twenty square miles, with stone homes and buildings flowing down the terraced slopes of the peak. A large keep sat on the very top surrounded by fortress walls reminiscent of those at Castle Dorumova. The parties scattered, searching the ruins for clues.

Honani wandered about on his own and made the discovery. His ambling brought him to the main entrance gates where the largest pave roadway, now completely overgrown with vegetation, stretched off to the west. He turned around to look back at what had once been an impressive sight and saw the ruins of an archway. He cast a few spells and cleaned the accumulated dirt, weeds, and thorn bushes off of the cracked stone and saw writing on along the arch. Pacov. He was heartily thanked for his discovery, with many hands slapping him on his back. Well done was echoed by many, none more so than Miroslav and Jarmila, who felt totally vindicated. There was a place called Pacov. Thus, the journals must be here somewhere!

Zoran then sent Evsen to fetch Jarka. No way was he going to delve deep underground looking for some secret stash without his expert trap finder present. Thus far, nothing they had searched had held any traps. Long ago, someone or something had mostly knocked them down. Certainly Bandar would have kept his precious journals protected with powerful spells.

She arrived most excited. "So it is real! There is a Pacov Fortress after all. I really didn't think you'd be able to find it. Way to go Honani. Now for this Sublevel 5. Must be underground."

She took an orienting look around and marched up to the ruined keep at the very center of the peak. "Has to be under here, Zoran. This would be the heart of the fortress. Somewhere, perhaps buried under all these collapsed stone walls must lie a stairs downward. Let's move all this debris off this central area. Spell time, gang."

Levitate spells flew right and left. Such a simple spell was known to everyone here. Rapidly, the countless stones which had once formed the walls of the keep were moved off of the central area of the peak. Before long, three stone stairwells appeared and they focused on clearing out each one, uncertain which one would lead them ultimately to their destination. It was certain that no one had been down these stairs in millennia.

Ever cautious, Jarka then had Zoran, Karel, and herself cast their Roving Eye spells, conjuring a remote giant eye that they then moved on down the stairs. Each one took a different set. The objective: to see what lay ahead without risking their lives. She based her extreme caution on all of the many protections that the barons currently had in place in their own fortresses. Nearly all had their Circles of Ascensions located in the depths of their keeps, surrounded by all manner of protections, some physical, some magical. Just walking down into the depths beneath a keep could well spell a surprise, sudden, and violent death for the unwary. She anticipated no less here.

"Trap on step twenty!" Jarka called out. A bit later, Karel and Zoran, having been alerted by Jarka, also discovered a trap in their stairs, but on different steps. These were merely physical traps, activated by the weight of a person on the step. A stone block would be dropped on the unwary. Jarka herself disarmed each of the three. All three stairs led to a different section of a series of connected rooms. Satisfied, they divided up into their three teams and each group headed down separate stairs. "Remember to search for traps every inch of the way once you get to the rooms down there," she cautioned everyone. Karel grumbled. Of course he'd check for traps.

The rooms had once been the granaries for the keep and now contained only the dust remnants along with several sets of human remains, ghastly eyeball-less skulls staring up at the intruders. It was a little chilling. Zoran assumed that they had been trapped here when the walls of the keep came crashing down, blocking all the stairs. At least they didn't starve to death, he presumed. Two more stairs led further downward.

Once more, they cast their Roving Eye spells and slowly moved them down the stairs, casting additional Light spells as needed. Meantime, the others set about casting Permanent Light spells around this first level. This time, Zoran and Jarka each found a Symbol Trap, marked by a faint magical rune on the wall beside the steps. If the unwary had walked past it without speaking the disarm word, the spell would detonate today, just as it would have a millennia ago. Magic does not fade with time, Jarka pointed out to the others. Karel growled. Of course it didn't.

This second level contained smaller rooms and most chambers were laboratories of one kind or another. Jarka recognized a potion making lab, for example, though all of its contents were now completely worthless. She would have liked to examine a potion maker's book, but the instant she touched it, the book disintegrated into a pile of dust — she being the first in a millennia to disturb it in any way.

Two stairs led on down. While the others joined them and cast Permanent Lights around the area, Zoran and Jarka worked on the downward stairs as before. This time, they both discovered Protection Wards cast about every ten feet down the stairwell. They cast their Dispel spells four times, safely removing each one. Zoran noted that one of these wards, if triggered, would have caused the person to go insane and run away. Another would have frozen the person to the spot, unable to move his or her legs. Someone definitely did not want the uninvited to gain access to these lower levels.

This third level held the treasury and armory, both heavily protected with numerous spells and traps. The trio of Karel, Jarka, and Zoran spent an entire hour detecting and canceling them. Because of the sheer number of them, all three checked over each other's work to make sure no one missed a single trap. At last, the others joined them and they began opening up the rooms. "Jackpot!" declared Karel upon opening the main treasury room. He'd already opened the minor treasury only to find piles of silver coins. Valuable, yes, but not very. This room, however, was quite different. Gold, gems, and some fine jewelry sparkled in the Permanent Light that Karel placed just inside the door. Of course, the tables on which the things had rested had long ago turned to dust, dropping the coins, gems, and jewelry onto the stone floor in a confused mass of dust and valuables.

"Hum, small jackpot, Karel," Evsen commented as he took a look inside. "I'd say that whoever owned this cleared out most all of it before they left here. Still I am not complaining." Karel grinned. Neither was he.

The armory contained a number of rusted, now worthless swords, and one enchanted dagger, still shiny after all these years. "Looks like they took their weapons with them," Zoran theorized.

Leaving the others to collect what treasure was still here, Zoran and Jarka worked their magic on the next pair of stairs that led further down beneath the mountain. Again, they defused more traps. This fourth level was far smaller than those above them, and they were at least a hundred feet below the surface, maybe more. Here the rooms appeared to have once been plush bedrooms, probably the secret hiding place for the fortress rulers, he guessed.

Among the decomposed bedding, the others discovered a number of minor magical items, a woman's hair brush, a man's razor, a pitcher that always seemed full of cold, clear water, for example. Once more while the others searched the dusty rooms, gathering up what seemed valuable, the two worked together on the single stairs that led even further down. Miroslav and Jarmila were right behind them for this would be the mysterious Sublevel 5 where the journals must be hidden!

Discovering no traps here at all, Jarka and Zoran rechecked every step downward twice over. "I can't believe this!" Jarka exclaimed, having finished her third complete search of the narrow stairs. The four headed down to a small, single room. "Sublevel 5," Jarka pronounced. "Light!"

Looking over each other's shoulders, except Jarka who was in the lead, they saw a small room with a single bed, desk, and chair. All had turned to dust and collapsed. However, a magical writing quill lay on the floor where it had fallen. Jarka picked it up and stowed it safely in her pouch. Quickly the four cast their Permanent Light spells, making the room appear as if it were lit by bright sunlight. For russet colored walls stared back at them.

"So where are the journals?" asked Jarmila.

"Don't rush me," Jarka said, as she cast her Detect Traps spells and slowly examined every inch of the room. Satisfied there were none, she cast her other detection spells. Finding nothing, she took out her dagger and began tapping lightly on the stone walls, looking for hollow sounds which would indicate a secret compartment or room off of this one. She found none.

"You mean they aren't here anymore?" Jarmila nearly cried. "Well, I guess he took them with him and we just don't know where he put them on our worlds."

"Oh don't give up *yet*," Jarka exclaimed. "That's why you have *me* here. I really did not expect to find them this easily." She continued her work. An hour later, still stumped, she sat down in the middle of the floor to think. Presently, she jumped up, "Ah ha! I have it! Unlock Doors!" She cast her spell. Normally, the spell would unlock all normal doors which were locked in a fifty foot radius around her body. However, just as she suspected, right in the center of the room in mid-air, a shimmering two-foot square door appeared. "Extra-dimensional door," she announced for the other's benefit, adding, "similar to the one we made to store all Bandar's stuff by Zoran's Circle of Ascension. Now what was that code on the paper?"

Hastily, Jarmila retrieved her copy of it and called out, "A52C96. Why? What do we do with. . ." she didn't finish her thought or sentence. The instant she finished uttering the last syllable of the code, the door opened wide. Everyone looked inside. Twenty perfectly preserved journals lay perfectly positioned. Each had a large letter on its binding, going from A to T. Each volume was about a foot square and two inches thick. All four cheered and relayed the news to the others who were standing on the stairs outside this small room.

Zoran handed the precious journals one by one to Miroslav and Jarmila, who packed them very carefully into the bags that they brought with them, five volumes per bag, four bags worth. There was nothing else inside the extra-dimensional closet and when Jarka shut the door, the whole thing vanished once more.

Everyone headed up the stairs to the more spacious Sublevel 4. "Okay, mission accomplished. Time to head for home," Zoran announced. "Well done all of you."

"Say, we have been finding a number of magical swords in some of these ruins. How about letting Strike Force One stick around and search for more?" asked Viktor. "We've already found enough to arm a second Strike Force. If we end up having to fight the dragons, these will be extremely valuable." He didn't mention all of the other treasure that they had been finding, however.

"Agreed. Honani, you and your group can stay too, if you like. As far as the treasure goes, why don't you divide it in half? You divide one half of it into sixteenths, one for each planet, including Asami. You divide the other half amongst yourselves as your reward for jobs more than well done."

"Thank you Baron Zoran, that is most generous of you," Viktor replied, very diplomatically. Kaya grinned.

"Just keep your guard up at all times. There are still reds and blacks around, mostly up north. Evsen, give me a report at the end of each day. Hang on to the rods you have in case the dragons decide to attack you," Zoran added. He received a big round of thanks.

A few minutes later, Jarka, Miroslav, Jarmila, Karel, and Zoran arrived back at his fortress, carrying their precious journals with them. Mission accomplished!

That was not the same comment that Werner, the black, said, at nearly the same time, however. Late November, Werner and Dario received some most shocking news. Zoran and a large party were on Voss. He immediately stepped up the security around the Breeding Caverns, as they now called their new site. "How the Hell did he find us this time?" Werner screeched.

Angry, he and Dario headed to Voss at once to see what the situation actually was. The next day, circling high above the tiny figures down in the desert of Anwyn, Werner spotted Zoran. Now he kept them under constant surveillance. Quickly he concluded, "We are in luck, Dario. Zoran must only know that the women are here on Voss, but he does not know where they are being held. He doesn't know the location of the Breeding Caverns. That is apparent."

A few days later, Werner became worried again. "There can be no question of it; they are searching every cavern they can find. They have to know the women are being held on Voss and are looking into every cavern. Well so far they are looking far from us up here in the north. Still, in time they will likely find the Breeding Cavern. We must take drastic steps, Dario, drastic steps.

"We should send out Invisible spies," Dario concluded. Werner agreed. For weeks, their spies reported back on the various explorations of the three groups. Then, one day they reported that all three groups merged and were searching one set of ruins down south.

"Wait a minute. This doesn't make sense, Dario. Why would they be removing all the debris from a collapsed building? Obviously, we are not keeping their women in such a place. Come on; we need to see this ourselves." The two cast Invisibility and headed down to the ruins. No one was above ground when they arrived, but three stairwells led deep underground.

"What are they doing?" asked Dario.

"For once, old friend, I have no idea, but at least they do not seem to be looking for their women. Perhaps we are catching a well-deserved break," Werner replied. They waited patiently.

Sometime later, the humans appeared climbing up the steps to the peak. They noticed that Zoran and three others were carrying four bulky bags. Further, Dario pointed out that the humans seemed extremely pleased about something.

"We have been duped, Dario! Zoran must have found some kind of new super-weapon that lay hidden here on Voss. He was searching for that all this time. Now he has found it. Look how happy they all are, as if they know that now they will easily be able to kill all us dragons!" Werner concluded.

"We are doomed by this secret weapon! No, no, no! There must be something that we can do, Werner, but what?" Dario pleaded mournfully.

"Wait, look, the others are not leaving. It looks like they are continuing their searches. Hum, we need to keep a close watch on them. Are they looking for the Breeding Cavern after all or are they after more super-weapons? We must know, Dario. Come on. We must follow them.

A few days later, they had answers, sort of. "One thing is obvious, Dario. They are raiding all these places looking for magical weapons to use against us. They are trying to arm an army so they can attack us."

"True, Werner, but that doesn't rule out the possibility that they are also looking for the Breeding Cavern as well," Dario pointed out. Werner conceded that point.

"We must not let them stop us," Dario continued. "This time, we *are* being successful. We have each added another fifteen new dragons to our folds. I just got word, another fifteen have been born and are now being taken their new mothers. That makes forty-five so far, with another fifteen are due in just a few more days, at which point we'll each have added another thirty to our folds. That, dear Werner, is most impressive."

"Of course, of course, but now we have to address the cramped cavern problem that we are facing. We unfortunately underestimated the space requirements. At this point, we have sixty breeding dragons and our cavern complex is honestly overcrowded, though we are making do. Before we can take another batch in here in December, we will have to setup another Breeding Cavern. With these humans possibly searching for our Breeding Caverns, it might be wise to make several more and split our current sixty up a bit. We don't want all our dragons in one spot." Both dragons chuckled at Werner's jest.

"Okay, I will take care of things here on Voss," Dario declared.

"And I will see what I can do to stop them from using their new super-weapon against dragon-kind," Werner stated and then left Voss.

Chapter 33 Up and Down

Yuletide week was nearly there, four more days and the week-long yearly celebrations would begin, starting with the big dance at the Stodgy Inn. Zoran had slept in this morning, while the rumors flew. The secret mission on Voss had been successful, but what was it?

At eleven, Zoran was finally ready to face the world. Per his orders, he had everyone assembled on the fortress parade grounds. He stepped out on a balcony to address them all, magic students and fortress staff alike. Barons Tomas and Jan had brought their key staff here as well, anticipating some exciting news.

"Thank you all for coming. As many of you know, for many weeks some of us have been on a secret mission. Now we are back and the rumors are flying. At this point, I want to set the record straight. We kept our mission a secret from many of you because there are dragon spies in Brn. If word of our mission spread to them, our lives might have been in danger. Now that we are back, I am going to fill all of you in, because in a way, you are all involved in what we found."

"Brother Miroslav and High Priestess Jarmila found a key map to the location of old Bandar Zar's missing journals. These journals were written before and document the events prior to the founding of our Federation of the Sixteen Planets. It is our belief that they contain vital, crucial information on dragons and their relationship to us humans. The map led us to Voss!"

Gasps echoed among the crowd, many knew that name — the planet from which the dragons came. "Yes, Voss. We have found those missing journals, but we have found things that are perhaps just as important. Our founding fathers, in our case old Baron Valentýn Vladislov, actually was born on Voss and came here to Adapazan from Voss. We found a preserved mural in an Anwyn Holy Temple which showed all of the sixteen republics that formed their political organization. There were sixteen and all had the same names as our sixteen planets! Yes, there was the Republic State of Adapazan, the Republic State of Gladno — yes, a republic for each one of us."

After the buzz died down he went on, "Unfortunately, it is a dead world now, long devoid of human habitation, probably for at least two millennia. A few dragons inhabit the far north and normal wildlife is now abundant once more. Yes, even antelope have rebounded and are commonplace there. We had several encounters with black and brown bears, as we accidentally strayed into their domains. Still, we found the ruins of towns and cities, proving that our ancestors lived there."

"Yes, we found isolated stashes of long forgotten treasure, gold, gems, jewelry, which we've brought back. More importantly, our fighters have also found many enchanted weapons which are still in excellent shape. We have literally doubled the number of magical blades in existence and I don't need to tell you just how important that is. Strike Force One and Honani's Star Dancers are still on Voss, searching for more of these valuable weapons. We've taken another small step towards being able to protect our people from the dragons."

After the cheering and clapping died down, he finished up, "In the coming days, these valuable ancient journals will be thoroughly studied. You may expect that we will be sharing the key information that we learn about our ancestors with all of you in due time. I know, some of you think this is most interesting. Others are saying so what? How does this help us now? Well, it is our hope that the journals will give us some clues about how to defeat the dragons, should they continue harassing us humans. In the meantime, Yuletide is nearly here so relax and enjoy the coming holidays."

He moved back inside listening to the applause. Not long after, his crew joined him for a briefing. Tomas spoke first, "Dad, I've been tracking the abductions while you were gone. Here's the picture. The nighttime random abduction of young women has definitely slowed down. As of now, only four women have been taken from Adapazan. Equal numbers have been taken from all of the other planets, except Asami, who continue to report that none are missing there. Who knows if Goro even knows, but for now, I am accepting that at face value. Leo and Stefan were able to trace and follow the most recent abductions on Valtr and located the rendezvous location. Unfortunately, they were not strong enough to stop the mass of dragons from stepping into the Shadows with the latest batch of fifteen women. Still they verified the pattern. Dragons, red and black, snatch a single victim from each of the fifteen worlds and bring them to the rendezvous point, where they cast more spells on the women just before taking them off-world through the Shadows. At least, dad, we've only lost four women. That's better than before."

Baron Jan reported on the fall harvest and the current levels of food storage in the subterranean cities, planet-wide. He was good at figures and kept accurate records. Zoran always made good use of what a person could do. Jan was not a fighter. After more reports, Zdenka gave her report on the many students.

"Well, dear, you are going to have to sit in with my advanced students this week, starting now. The Seventeen are just about to make their breakthroughs, you too, Karel. They are so close that they can taste it — Danika's words. Perhaps even more important for the other women, they are about to tackle the Morph spells. I don't have to tell you how critical that is for the handicapped women. We simply must see that they make it over that hurdle by Yuletide. That would really give them something to celebrate."

"Whoa! Are you saying that all Seventeen are about to make Archmage?" Zoran asked in disbelief.

"Yes, dear, they are. True, each one has all sorts of gaps in the spells that they know how to cast, just as we all do. However, they are now preparing to deal with the top power spells. That's why I need Karel and your help immediately. I've pulled Verushka, Marek, and Nadia out of their classrooms to help as well. Lida, Reyna, and Jarka are now running the classes until further notice. I am very hopeful that we can nudge all Seventeen through these tough spells."

"Wow. Okay, you have my undivided attention. The history can wait!" Zoran was truly excited. Seventeen more powerful Archmages was unheard of — the sheer power that these women represented was enormous. Lead on, oh master mage," he teased.

While Jarmila and Miroslav headed to their extra-dimensional study room around the Circle of Ascension, Zoran and Karel followed Zdenka into the top floor of her tower, where the Seventeen were already back at their studies, eager to tackle these most challenging spells. True, for the last few months, each woman had to face disappointments. One by one, each discovered that no matter how hard they tried or how badly they desired to know how to cast some of these more powerful spells, some spells were simply beyond their ability to learn and master. Danika, for example, had her heart set on knowing how to cast Self-project, a spell which created a duplicate of her body at some distance from herself, while her real self was then invisible. Attackers, namely dragons, would be attacking this image and not her own body. Yet any spells that she subsequently cast would appear to be originating from this image of herself. Eventually, she laughed it off, "I guess I am not meant to be able to hide behind an image of myself." Others chuckled, but they too wanted this skill. Most were unable to learn how to cast it.

So it had gone through the two additional levels of spells beyond this one. Each woman found herself able to learn fewer and fewer of these power spells. Now they all had reached the ultimate power spells. Each one knew that out of some eighteen known spells, they only had to be able to cast one, just one, and they would become Archmages. Their power, fame, and renown would be second only to the barons and baronesses across the sixteen planets of the Federation. They threw themselves into their studies harder than ever before, perhaps too hard, as Zdenka continually reminded them. Effort didn't count; knowledge, intelligence, and patience did.

Danika was determined to somehow master the Premonition spell first. She was married and she and Rafael were planning to start a family once she finished her studies. Having lost her husband and two babies to the dragons two years ago, she swore that she'd never again let that happen, that she'd never again be taken so totally by surprise. Hence, she had to know this spell!

Zdenka decided to work with her on this one, since this was Zdenka's power spell that she so often used. Once again, Zdenka's incredible knack of spotting the precise thing that one of her students was doing incorrectly paid off. After struggling with the spell for hours, Zdenka pointed out, "Danika, something is interfering with your casting. You are putting a barrier between yourself and the spell's activation. You have the words down, your intention is fine, but can you see a barrier between you and the spell's powerful energies?"

"Oh! Oh, I didn't think of that. You don't suppose that . . ." She canceled her morph spell, returning to her real form, that of an armless woman.

"Now try it," Zdenka suggested. Once more, Danika went through the complex chant. This time, when she made the final connection, the spell detonated.

"Oh! It worked! It worked," exclaimed Danika, very elated and excited as the significance of her achievement flooded into her mind. So did the premonition. She whispered it to Zdenka, who smiled and congratulated her.

"Let's keep this to ourselves for now. Okay, which one do you want to tackle next?"

"Okay, I wonder if I should refrain from doing these while morphed?"

"I can't say, Danika. That was what was interfering with this spell, but I don't know if it will interfere with the others. Now you can tell for yourself."

She decided to not re-morph and to deal with the awkwardness of using her feet for everything as she scanned down the list of spells, trying to decide which one to attempt next.

Meanwhile, in spite of the cold and snow, Archmage Karel took Eliska up to the roof where he kept his falcons. Why? She was trying to learn Karel's power spell, Change Shape and wanted to duplicate his favorite form, a giant falcon. Eliska always dreamed of soaring like the falcons and hawks that she'd watched for hours on end as a child. Now if she could just master this one spell, she would be able to change her shape and become for a time any living creature, swamping the Morph spells completely. In fact, she could become a real dragon complete with its breath weapon and then change into another form in barely a second's time! Under Karel's guidance, after she canceled her usual Morph spell and returned to her real armless self, her childhood wish came true. A giant falcon suddenly stood beside Karel. At once Karel disappeared, a second giant falcon appeared and the two took to the skies, soaring for over an hour before returning to the roof top.

Kate was envious of Zoran's powers to completely nullify all magic in an area for a time. She saw this as a most effective way to defuse tense situations before they erupted into conflicts. Kate was big on trying to get others to compromise and not fight. Zoran, therefore, worked with her personally. Although she was having lots of troubles with the spell, he kept at it. He got his breakthrough as a teacher when he cleverly spotted what Zdenka had just done with Danika. He made the same suggestion to Kate, who obeyed and canceled her Morph Self spell. "Oh, this is so awkward, baron," she protested slightly, as she tried to reposition the book with her feet so she could continue to read it.

"I know. Now forget that and let's give it another shot. Full intention. You really want this to occur. It is solely your intention that maters, Kate."

Again, she went through the relatively brief chant. Suddenly her spell detonated, much to the chagrin of the other students in the room. All spells in the room were suddenly canceled without warning. Several women dropped their books as their arms vanished. Lilia cursed, "Damn it! Who did that?" Others called out similar annoyances and then in a flash, they all realized what had happened, as Kate sat back with a satisfied grin on her face. She'd just Canceled Magic! She was now on par with Zoran. Kate radiated immense satisfaction and pride, well-deserved though.

Katerina, on the other hand, still held intense hatred against the dragons who so destroyed her life and family. She wanted to be able to strike back hard if they should ever again threaten her and her new fiancé. Thus, Verushka had her up on the roof of Nadia's tower as she tried hard to create a fiery storm of meteors, which would rain down hard, smashing and perhaps killing a dragon. Zdenka decided not to ask Emil to come and work with Katerina because the woman wanted to use this spell to slay dragons. Thus, Verushka did her best to help Katerina work out the glitches in the spell's casting. After long hours in the cold, the two were rewarded with a blaze of fiery meteors raining down harmlessly on the distant mountains behind the fortress and tower. Katerina had a self-satisfied look on her face when she and Verushka later rejoined the others.

To become an Archmage, one only needed to be able to cast one of these top power spells. Karel knew only the one. Zdenka and Zoran both could cast three. By Yuletide, each of the Seventeen had mastered three and a few had four of these spells down pat. Unfortunately, the remaining spells they were not able to grasp. Still, the Seventeen and all of Brn had something to celebrate on the 25th, when Zdenka publically announced her new seventeen Archmages. Indeed, the citizens of Brn went wild in their Yuletide celebrations this year. Having one Archmage in their town meant security and power, but with over twenty now in residence, they felt totally secure. No dragon could ever touch them or they supposed.

This news dwarfed all of the other many accomplishments of the remaining women. For thirteen other women, their accomplishment was all that mattered to them. Glass eyed Andrea spoke for her five dear friends, "Now we are no longer doomed to eternal blackness and dependency on mages for our lives. We can see again when we ourselves choose to — never again can anyone ever take that away from us!"

Similarly, Marcella's comments were echoed by her six other constant companions, being taught by Zdenka. They all were armless. "Ladies, at last we have our lives back. No longer are we helpless and dependent on others. Not ever again!" Archmage Verushka's sixteen similar women from Jing and Terra expressed similar opinions. All had mastered the Morph Self spell and could at will change their form, usually to their own selves prior to the dragon abduction. They could have arms whenever they desired, which was usually all the time.

On the morning of Yuletide, Zoran summoned the Seventeen new Archmages to his private study. "Congratulations one and all! This is one of the finest moments in my life — to stand here and talk to you women. You are shining examples of how resilient we humans are. I am so proud of you that I can hardly sit still! You have triumphed over immense personal tragedy, pain, and suffering. Yet, you never gave up. Here you are today, seventeen of the most powerful people in the Federation of the Sixteen planets!"

"I don't have to tell you this, but I will anyway. With great power comes great responsibility. We Archmages are looked upon to be the guardians of our people, to protect and help them. I know that each of you will live up to those expectations. To that end, I want to offer each of you a position here on Adapazan, helping me oversee our great world. If you accept, I will see that each one of you has an Archmage tower built for you as soon as possible and a guaranteed income for as long as you work for me, a very tidy sum, I might add." He then discussed the details of his offer, made possible by the treasure that was already recovered on Voss.

Always the spokeswoman for the Seventeen, Danika replied, "Baron, when I was abducted, at first, I just wanted to die, to join my husband and babies. I was helpless and could not even imagine how I could possibly live any longer. Then, I realized that I really did not want to die. I saw all these other women in the same position that I was in and I sort of snapped. Somehow I wanted to live and to be able to help them. True, when I first came here, for a brief time I wanted to follow in the footsteps of that poor woman who jumped off the roof, but I was so helpless I couldn't even open the doors in the way to get there. Then, I remembered your words to me just as you came to rescue me. 'Okay, Danika. Everything will be all right. I am coming to rescue you. Be patient. Help is coming.' You cannot know how hard I clung to those words, Baron Zoran. Be patient. Help is coming. You were true to your word. Now I am finally in a position to pass such help along to others in need. I speak for us all; you can count on us. We will not let you down!"

"Thank you, Danika, thank you one and all. Now I've wasted enough of your time. Go get dolled up for the Yuletide dance!" They didn't need to be told a second time. Giggling and chatting about his incredible offer, they left through a Mystical Door.

"Dear, where are you going to put seventeen more towers around here?" Zdenka teased him. Zoran laughed.

That evening when Rafael came to pick up Danika and Neda to take them to the Yuletide dance, he was a bit surprised. "My love, no arms tonight?"

She smiled, "Dear, I've decided to be myself as much as possible instead of using the Morph Self spell. Look, I am two years older now. If I always go around morphed to when I had arms so that I can look like myself and have them, then I am going to look only twenty-one forever while you turn old and grey. That's not fair to you. I'll morph when I need to, so don't worry. Don't worry, dear. We've all reached the same decision. If we are always morphed, we will never seem to age. Besides, dear, we have other spells we can use to help us with things."

He gave her a loving kiss. "Now we can start our family. Maybe Neda will have a little brother or sister next year."

"I want a sister, dad," Neda giggled, imagining what that would be like. "I'm twelve now. I think Dragon wants to marry me when I get older. Mom, can I get married when I am fourteen or do I have to wait longer?"

Both Rafael and Danika spoke in unison, "Wait longer." Both chuckled that they had the same thought at the same time. She added, "Eighteen is soon enough, dear. Get to really know Dragon, his good points and his bad ones. After all, if you marry him, you will have to live with the bad points too."

"But dad doesn't have any bad points," Neda protested.

"Yes he does. He never cleans up his messes." Both adults laughed.

As they approached the doors to the Stodgy Inn, Dana and Adrianna joined them. Adrianna said, "Danika, you look gorgeous tonight. Congratulations, by the way." She smiled; the world was now perfect once again.

On another world, Wenzel, the ancient black, commented, "Well, it was just a case of dumb luck, Werner. Who could possibly have known at the precise time that you attacked the browns, their Strike Force One would be right there with all the barons, eh? Just dumb luck. No matter. The Breeding Program is working flawlessly now. However, we both know that Zoran is lying to his people when he says they only wanted to retrieve lost journals. How stupid does he think everyone else is, eh? I agree, he has found some super-weapon to use against us dragons."

"We will use that and also the fact that he openly is telling the world that he's recovered many, many enchanted weapons from Voss. Who is he going to use them against? Dragons, naturally. That coupled with the fact that he now has added seventeen new Archmages to his arsenal can be used as proof of what we have been saying all along. Give them time and there will be hundreds of Archmages there."

"The browns and blues have their spies in Brn and surely now know that they really are all becoming Archmages. Combine that with the weapons and the super-weapon and I think that you can easily convince the browns this time. You'll have your majority and we can get on with exterminating these puny humans once and for all," Wenzel declared.

Later that day on yet another world, Werner, the black, Lothar, the black, Alistair, the green, Frank, the green, Dario, the red, and Dante, the red, met with an extremely worried Donatello, the brown, and Pietro, the brown. Also, Cezar and Jenryk, the whites were present along with Bolivar and Ernesto, the blues, and Aeton and Barnabus, the greys.

Donatello, the brown, spoke nervously. "We have heard from our spy in Brn. Indeed, the first batch of women has completed their magic studies. It is as Werner warned us months ago. All seventeen have become Archmages. Even if we wanted to attack Brn and Zoran, now it would be suicide for us to even try! It is no leap of faith to presume that in another year or two he will have hundreds of Archmages there in Brn!"

This disturbed the blues and greys considerably. Werner allowed them to stew a bit longer before he spoke up. "I am afraid that Dario and I have further bad news. As you know, we've been keeping our breeding dragons on Voss for safe keeping. We do not want these human killing any more of our newborns or our young dragons. While we were there, we discovered even more alarming news." All six neutral dragons perked up, listening intently to what Werner was saying.

"Zoran and his men spent months on Voss!" He exaggerated slightly. "Why? Well, at first, we thought that he was trying to find our caverns to kill our babies and children." All six gasped. "However, we soon saw that was not at all what he was doing. Instead, he and his men were robbing all of the human graves on Voss, stealing hundreds of magically enchanted swords! He's brought them all back to Brn. Now why would he need hundreds of enchanted swords?"

"To kill dragons!" Cezar, the white, spoke up angrily.

"Who else? But there is more to it. In fact, Zoran was looking for some lost super-weapon that the humans on Voss once wielded millennia ago, and he has found it. We know that he brought it back to his fortress in Brn, Adapazan! He has been telling others an outright lie — that it was merely some lost books that he retrieved. Ha. No one will fall for that outright lie. We are not that stupid, are we?"

"No!" Cezar called out. Werner was playing Cezar like a shawm, the white tooting at just the right points.

"What do we do?" asked Donatello, the brown, at last. "Is there no other choice but war with the humans?"

"Oh sure, Donatello. You can wait until the humans decide to wipe out all you browns or enslave you and put you to work in their mines," Werner, the black, replied sarcastically, knowing that at long last he would prevail.

"I move that dragons go to war with the humans and end this before they can make the Archmages who will enslave or kill us all," Donatello, the brown, said with a heavy heart. He did not want war, but now could see no other viable option.

"I second it and call for a vote," Cezar, the white, added immediately, very much afraid of the future if nothing was done this time.

Aeton, the grey, said, "The golds are not here, but I don't think their vote will matter." The vote was unanimous. If Aldrick was present, the vote would have been seven to one and he would have been outvoted anyway.

"How can we possibly attack so many Archmages?" asked a still worried Donatello, the brown.

"Simple. We attack and wipe out outlying towns and villages. That will force them to spread out their Archmages here and there to help defend the other towns. Split up the huge force of Archmages and defeat them one at a time," Werner, the black, replied. All of the neutrals breathed a sigh of relief. This might work after all.

"We make our first attack on their Yuletide night. They will all be off celebrating and will be easy targets, wholly unprepared. We need to coordinate our attacks and hit several towns on every planet that night. We have much to plan and little time in which to do it," Werner, the black, added.

Zoran announced the new Archmages formally at the start of the Yuletide dance. The applause that the women received was quite loud. Many openly whistled and yelled their cheers. Then the dance began. A while later, Zoran once more began his open dance with any woman who desired to dance a few steps with their baron, his long standing tradition. Right in the middle of the dancing, several Archmages shrieked, including Zdenka. The musicians stopped playing, startled by the screams. All eyes turned to the six who screamed. Zdenka, shaking visibly, called out to a hushed room, "Dragons have just attacked several towns on Adapazan!" Others backed her up, their Premonition spells had also activated.

"Party is over!" Zoran's Magnified voice echoed in the large pub's room. "Everyone, head home. Begin packing what you need. After we find out what is going on, I may issue the order for everyone to enter our subterranean safe house. At least get yourselves prepared. Gang, everyone back to the fortress. We have to get to those towns as fast as possible!"

As Zdenka opened her Mystical Door for herself and Zoran, she whispered, "The dragon war is beginning, isn't it?" Zoran's face looked grimmer than she'd ever seen it before and she had her answer.

Chapter 34 In the Beginning

Wenzel, the ancient black dragon, sat in the back of the huge cavern high in the unreachable mountains of Rehor, unreachable by humans that is. His huge face sported a satisfied grin, his long envisioned annihilation of the humans on Rehor was about to begin. Wenzel's hatred of humans spanned all of twenty-two years, ever since the humans had opened up these new worlds to dragon-kind. If asked why he hated humans, he would have answered, "They have divided dragon-kind and thus have kept we blacks from attaining our rightful place among dragon-kind." No one asked him, though.

He hated the golds even more than humans. His open hostilities towards the Gold Dragons dated back some four hundred-fifty years to when he was a young black, just getting started on Voss. There, the golds ruled over all dragon-kind, forcing all others to their will, as far as Wenzel was concerned. Only the golds had two breath weapons and they also frequently knew more magical spells as well, a sore point with the blacks.

However, Wenzel knew that blacks were the most powerful of all the species of dragons. The close allies of the blacks, the reds were certainly lesser. Why? If you asked Wenzel why he thought that, of all the dragon species, that blacks were the most powerful, he would have given you a dissertation on the topic. The golds and reds shot out scorching hot flames from their mouths. Yet, those very flames dissipated almost at once. True, normal humans would be incinerated in such a blast, but the searing hot flames were transitory — their effects: gone in seconds. Same with the whites. Their cones of intense cold and frost, while it could turn an ordinary human into a frozen, dead statue, that freezing blast was also transitory, lasting mere seconds. Still, the reds and whites could dole out much death and destruction to many humans caught within their expanding cones of death. Yet, the whites were inherently the weakest of the dragon species, the easiest for humans to kill. Besides, they were the smallest in size as well.

The browns were strong, but totally ineffective as dragons, according to Wenzel. They shot out an electrical charge from their mouths which affected only a single target at a time. Pathetic. Only one human dead per attack, pathetic in Wenzel's eyes. However, considering the past two year's losses of blacks and reds, coupled with those of the greens and the significantly fewer numbers of the remaining species of dragons, Wenzel had moved the browns to the top of their allies.

The greys, according to Wenzel, were hardly worth considering as dragons. Their breath was merely a suffocating smoke cloud. Only if a human were foolish enough to stay inside the cloud would he choke to death — yet another pathetic excuse for a dragon. Thankfully, there were few of the greys.

The blues, Wenzel could tolerate, since their neurotoxin breath permanently paralyzed the humans who were caught in its spray. Permanently immobilized — that was the key that impressed Wenzel. While not dead, the humans might as well be. Too bad the blues seldom left the oceans.

Wenzel was ambivalent about the greens, however. He respected their rotting slime immensely! Such a powerful weapon! Its effects were long lasting and most difficult to neutralize fast enough to prevent the rotting slime from eating through human flesh in short order. Amazingly good weapon. However, the totally chaotic nature of the greens forced Wenzel to drastically lower his opinion of them. He often joked, "Give a green a direct order and he will swear that he will follow it, only to do something completely different." That kind of behavior knocked the greens to the bottom of the heap of dragons. You simply could not count on them for anything. Too bad though, they had such a great weapon. Now however, their numbers had been so drastically reduced that their impact on the war would be minimal. The greens might become extinct during the war. Perhaps, Wenzel thought, that might not be a bad thing.

No, the blacks were the most powerful and most worthy of all dragons because their breath weapon, a cone of caustic acid, was not only deadly and covering a wide area impacting all who were in the cone, but also because its effects were long lasting. Their acid could even eat through stone in time! It was terribly hard to neutralize because of its high acid concentration.

Thus, Wenzel knew that blacks should be the masters of dragon-kind, not the egocentric golds. Golds favored the humans, so humans had to go. Then, he could concentrate on eliminating the golds as well, a more formidable task. Thus far, his protegee, Werner, the black, was doing an excellent job of carrying out his plans for total domination of all worlds and dragon-kind. He listened in to the War Council of Werner, the black, smiling to himself.

Werner, the black, shuffled his papers into order. "Okay, then let me summarize what you Battle Leaders have said. I want to make sure that we have accuracy here. We blacks have ninety-five adults ready to fight. Another five are on Voss protecting our thirty mothers, children, and infants." He did not mention the additional thirty newly hatched infants from the recent breeding program nor did he mention the same number of new red infants. He and Dario, the red, kept these a secret from the other dragons at this time.

"The reds have ninety adult fighters, with an additional five protecting their nursery on Voss, where they too have thirty mothers, children, and infants. The greens have only thirty adult fighters now, with five mothers and children who will have to be protected. The whites are fielding one hundred adults and are keeping thirty mothers, children, and infants safe. The noble browns," he tossed a bit of honor toward Donatello, "are fielding the largest group of adult fighters, one hundred twenty, keeping thirty mothers, children, and infants aside and safe. The blues are fielding seventy fighters, keeping ten mothers and children safe. The greys are sending twenty-four into the fight, with seven mothers and children remaining behind. Do I have the correct figures from each of you?" Many heads nodded or said yes.

Alistair, the green, spoke up, "We should hit Jing first. We greens nearly had all resistance on Jing eliminated. Even now, they barely have enough force to man their three fortresses. We could easily wipe them out and take control of Jing." This was what he most desired: to retake what he had somehow lost because of Zoran's interference.

"Ahem. Alistair, some of these worlds have very few humans on them, that is true. To win this war, we must destroy the barons, the Archmages, and their mages. Once those are gone, any remaining humans pose us virtually no threat whatsoever," Werner, the black, countered. "Thus, we must all remain focused on the real threat to dragon-kind. As everyone here knows, it is Baron Archmage Zoran Vladislov and his imperial army of Archmages on Adapazan that poses the most serious threat to all of us."

"But he is too strong for us and many of us will die if we attack Zoran," Cezar, the white, protested.

"Ah, Cezar, you are so right!" Werner, the black, played his fellow dragons perfectly. "It would be suicide for us to go after Zoran's fortress now, even with our combined forces. You are absolutely right. No, we have to go after him on another avenue. We must get him to spread his Archmage army out over many other areas. We can easily take down a single Archmage. Once his army of Archmages is eliminated, then we can assault him directly."

"But what about Aldrick, the gold," Cezar, the white, continued to raise significant worries. "He is friends with Zoran. Everyone knows that."

"Quite true, Cezar. The golds have two choices. They can side with us or they can side with their human friends. If they side with the humans, then we will destroy every last gold. I'm sure that if you whites team up on a gold, you can freeze one to death. They are not impervious to your frost breath, good Cezar. No, let Aldrick choose."

"Do you think that the golds will really side against their own kind and fight with the humans?" asked Aeton, the grey. He knew that his smoke weapon would be useless against a gold, while the gold's fiery breath or electrical charge could well wipe him out.

"I do not know, but if the golds do side with humans, then they are not worthy of our species and deserve to be extinct. Now then, how do we get Zoran to fan out his Archmages so that we can pick them off one by one? Simple," Werner continued. "We attack all of the worlds, focusing on those that are his allies. He will be forced to come to their aid and thus weaken his position."

"Our first objective is to strike a killing blow while they are all celebrating their Yuletide holiday. Our strike must convince all of the barons that we dragons are all at war with them. I assure you that they will all then be begging Zoran for help. Thus, he will start to send out an Archmage here and there. That's when we begin to pick them off, one by one."

"Now then, to the specifics. There are five hundred thirty-four of us. That means we can send thirty-three of us to each of the sixteen planets for this First Strike. We need to let Zoran and the barons know that they are fighting all of us dragons, that we dragons stand united! Each Strike Force of thirty-three will have at least one grey, two blues, seven browns, one green, six whites, five reds, and six blacks with them," Werner, the black, explained.

He went on, "Dario has suggested that one of the local dragons on each planet help choose the towns to attack and lead the Strike Force. That makes sense to me, I know next to nothing about Asami, Bolivar, whereas you know your planet well. I'll lead the assault on Adapazan. Dario will lead it on Rehor. Alistair, you take your

Jing. Donatello, you take Chana. Pietro, you take Anwyn. Aeton, you take Isi. Pietro, you take Alta. Cezar, you take Gerde. Jenryk, you take Dietmar. Frank, you take Maeve. Bolivar, you have Asami. Lothar, you have Valtr. Dante, Gladno. We will pick others to deal with Gonda, Terra, and Cosma. Make your first attack at ten on Yuletide night. Once the target is eliminated, move onto the two other ones. Be sure to leave a few survivors to tell their barons all about our devastating assaults! Victory shall be our, for we dragons are the most powerful beings in the universe!" The dragon leaders cheered and dispersed to begin their organization of the sixteen strike forces.

The Night of Terror began simultaneously on sixteen worlds. On Jing, Alistair, the green, led his force of thirty-three to two larger towns some twenty miles from the main fortress, palace, and Circle complex at Nanchan. The combined power of so many dragons was beyond anything that Alistair ever imagined possible. Within minutes the towns of some ten thousand each were laid to waste. As the dragon horde left each one, massive fires roared. Dead littered the streets as well as inside many stone buildings, while other bodies were consumed inside the burning homes. Of all the sixteen leaders, only Alistair failed to follow Werner's orders, though Werner, the black, fully expected this. The awesome power of his strike force went to Alistair's head and he decided to attack Nanchan as the third target, over the protests of several blacks and reds. They went along with Alistair's orders, because Werner had made it clear that Alistair was in command while they were on Jing.

Baroness Wen and her new husband, Baron Wenceslas, were hosting a Yuletide party in her fortress at Nanchan. Archmage Ivana was there along with her thirty students, many of which were in the middle of learning their grade two spells. Over a thousand people jammed the Meeting Hall, where the High Council met when on Jing. Security was tight. All the thousand soldiers were on active duty until midnight, though they were promised the day off in the morning. A group of twenty musicians were playing as the closing hour drew close.

Over the dance music, someone yelled, "Dragons! Dragons are attacking!" The music stopped instantly and the soldier repeated his warning over and over. Panic set in at once. Deafening sounds of thunder drowned out the cries of the thousand party goers. The browns were blasting away at the very walls of the keep within the outer walls of the fortress. While people pushed and shoved to get to the exits, part of the outer walls gave way. Across the room, Wen saw two reds moving in to take the place of the browns that had smashed the stone walls. Two blacks were already hovering just outside the gaping hole. Wen watched in horror as two ever expanding cones of searing flames streaked out into the Meeting Hall, followed by a pair of caustic acid cones, slopping onto bodies right and left. Death screams, horror screams, screams of intense pain filled the room, along with a hideous, foul smelling odor. If that was not enough, a huge pile of rotting slime splashed in through the hole next, ensuring death to any who managed to survive the fire and acid. Complete panic ensued.

Archmage Ivana had insisted that Wen carry her Rod of Dragon Slaying on her person at all times. Over the din and chaos of people, Ivana screamed at Wen to use her rod. Unable to make herself heard, she Messaged Wen, who stood beside her husband in shocked disbelief. Ivana relaxed a little as Wen's hand mechanically obeyed, bringing the rod up before her. Now the Archmage looked to her screaming students, trying to rapidly figure out how she could save them, all thirty women. Ivana opened a Mystical Door into her tower, and began Messaging each woman, ordering the terrified student to race through the door. One by one those who were close to her obeyed, but some were too far distant. A few had not survived the fire, acid, and slime, having had the misfortune to have been on that side of the room when the attack came.

Finally, Wen recovered and began to act. She shot a Bolt of Lightning out of the hole in the wall, striking a black. As always, she found herself on the familiar grey plain, staring into the cold black eyes of the dragon. Unnerved, the dragon won and her spell did nothing. Her husband, Wenceskas acted as well. Using a Magnify spell, he ordered everyone to head to the basement. "Orderly evacuation! Stop pushing and shoving those in front of you!" His admonition had little effect, however. Stark terror reigned. Ivana saw that she could not rescue any more of her students and used another spell to step beside Wen and the safety of her rod.

Once there, Ivana began to cast Disintegrate spells at the dragons as fast as she could, ignoring the additional cones of fire and acid being shot in again through the hole in the wall. Alistair's green head suddenly had a two inch hole bored straight through it. The seventy-foot long snake-like massive body dropped down out of sight, smashing onto the stone floor of the courtyard within the fortress walls. Then a black met the same fate. A red dodged out of the way. Finally no other dragons attempted to peer into the jagged gap in the wall.

Ivana hoped this would spell the end of the attack. They waited patiently, staring across the smoke filled room at the opening into the nighttime sky. No more dragons took a chance on looking in. Instead, the browns began firing more of their massive electrical bolts at the edges of the hole, being careful to stay out of the way of the deadly spells. More and more of the stone wall crumbled.

"My god! The wall is giving way!" Wenceslas screamed! "We have to abandon our position now!" He grabbed a hold of Wen and Shadow Walked her into her private study, deep within the adjoining palace complex. Finding herself alone, Ivana teleported into the safety of her tower, where fifteen of her rescued students were standing looking out of the first floor window, stark white and shaking with fear. Ivana continued to act, casting her protective spells on the Archmage tower, including Force Walls over the windows. At last, she too stopped to view the attacking dragons and watched as the entire wall of the keep crumbled, bringing down much of the roof and three floors with it. Many more people who were still fleeing the keep were crushed by the tons of falling stone. At last, the dragons circled overhead and then disappeared from the sky. Ivana knew that the attack had ended, but she saw the brilliant flickering glows of many fires set throughout Nanchan by the reds.

"My god! It's really happening," she finally muttered to herself.

"What — what — what do we do?" asked one terrified student.

"Okay, we can help put out the fires. Students, with me. Use your Make Rain spells. Let's work together and pull down some heavy rains on the burning buildings. Come on; we have to help." She latched onto all the women in one long line and teleported them out into the main streets of Nanchan. At once, the women began their chants, forcing the clouds to open up and deluge various small areas where homes and buildings were blazing. Once they had one block of fires out, they moved on to another street, repeating their actions. Around two in the morning, they finally returned to their tower, exhausted, but they'd put out all of the fires.

Wen and Wenceslas had recovered from their shock and began using the remaining soldiers to begin to search for survivors. When Ivana returned with her students, she had them cast numerous temporary Light spells to assist the men searching the rubble. Around three, word reached Wen of the near destruction of two other towns and she sent two of her new mages to check on the damage there. They returned shortly, grim faced and Wen knew that her worst fears were true. The reports she'd received had been accurate; two towns were virtually destroyed. She sent a dozen soldiers back with the two mages to search for survivors.

At last, she sat down and Mind Linked to Baron Zoran, reporting what had happened here in Nanchan and on Jing. Several days later the final totals were complete. Between the three attacks, around twenty thousand people had died and another thousand suffered injuries, many of those were trampled in the panicked exodus.

On Asami, Bolivar weighed his targets carefully. This world had two hundred thousand six hundred and five islands scattered around the blue ocean waters. Most were very small and held only a few inhabitants, hardly worth attacking. The largest island was a hundred miles long and fifty miles across, rising a whopping fifty feet above the sea level. Here was their largest city and fortress and primary Circle of Ascension, Paru, where Baron Goro lived. Following Werner's orders, he could not attack the fortress there. However, there was a huge harbor nearby where many of the yachts were docked. Since these humans depended upon their large fleet of yachts, Bolivar attacked them, having the reds set them all on fire. He destroyed half of the Asami fleet that night. The attack shocked Baron Goro and sent panic waves across the island.

Their second largest island Shima Yubi housed another fortress and Circle at Tesaki, located on the eastern end of the island. Again, he dare not attack the fortress. However, at the western end of the narrow width island was Ma-meido, a secret and heavily guarded pearl collection site. This he attacked, destroying the entire above ground facility there, sending a hundred mermaids fleeing underwater to escape the destruction.

He then attacked and destroyed their main fish factory on the third largest island. This totally crippled Asami's second largest export business, fish. All told, a little over three thousand died on the water world that night. Unfortunately, Baron Goro was unable to keep the secret of his mermaids any longer. Besides having to frantically rescue them, would be rescuers who rushed to Ma-meido discovered them, floating helplessly in the shallow waters. Their shallow beach home was completely destroyed and they had no place to come ashore, let alone eat and sleep. Those who always provided them their meals were now dead.

Some of these mermaids had recently been relocated from their home island of Orochi, which he ceded to Bolivar, the blue. All told, on Asami, Baron Goro had some three hundred-fifty mermaids. With Ma-meido gone, he had very serious problems to handle, to say nothing of the furor that arose over the discovery of the secret mermaids.

On Maeve, Baron Ailfrid and Baroness Breana were at Cullen, a nearby town from their fortress, performing the age old Maeve tradition of welcoming in the new year. Ever since the founding of Maeve a millennia ago, the ruling baron was required to officiate at this celebration of life and subsequent dance. Dense forests covered the habited portions of Maeve, and they were famous for their finely crafted hardwood furniture. Most of the buildings on Maeve were, naturally, wooden structures, which only aided the dragons in their attack of devastation. As always, Ailfrid carried his precious Rod of Dragon Slaying with him at all times now. He was petrified of the beasts.

At ten that night, Baron Ailfrid was thoroughly enjoying the pomp and ceremony being heaped on himself and his wife as the official rulers. Official — in that he had inherited the original Circle of Ascension from his father, the late Bran Ahren. His brothers were also barons and controlled the two recently built new Circles of Ascension. The festivities ended as half of the outside wall of the large wooden building came crashing down, compliments of four dragons joining forces. As utter panic swept over the thousand plus who were dressed in their finest for the celebration, Baron Ailfrid grabbed his wife's hand and Shadow Walked them out of the stampede of human bodies trying to get out of the way of the falling walls and out of the building. They stepped into the snow covered street.

Unfortunately, three dragons were standing there; two reds were in the process of belching forth cones of their deadly fire into the panic stricken masses. The coward froze, staring up into the cold black eyes of a Black Dragon. Instinctively, Ailfrid raised his Rod of Dragon Slaying high before himself, while still holding onto his wife. He knew that the dragon's acid would not be harming him, the rod was his protection.

Unfortunately for Ailfird, the black also knew about the rod. Instead of belching up his acid, he simply leaned over and bit the man's head off. Baroness Breana shrieked in shock and terror. The black burped and exhaled a small amount of acid over the woman, whose skin began to dissolve. Her terror screams turned into those of extreme pain, but she died seconds later.

Standing in the shadows was Conchobar Ahren, a bastard son of the late Baron Bran Ahren. Conchobar hated his father, but the baron had at least given Conchobar his rightful Ceremony of Ascension when he turned fourteen. Beyond that, the baron had abandoned Conchobar to his own fate, for which his bastard son never forgave him. Left to his own devices, he'd practiced sword fighting with anyone who would teach him. His style was a conglomeration of more than a dozen fighter types. Later when his father finally died and Bran's three legitimate sons took the thrones, Conchobar had acted on his own behalf.

Seeing that Bran had left him nothing when he died, Conchobar decided to help himself to an inheritance. His father had a prized enchanted bastard sword. While everyone was attending the funeral pyre and ceremony, Conchobar slipped into the fortress and stole the sword. No one ever found out how the sword had disappeared. Years of street life had taught Conchobar well.

This evening, he had come to Cullen to watch his half-brother make a pompous fool of himself. Security was tight and he'd not yet found a way into the building when the dragons swooped down on Cullen. He stepped back into the shadows of a nearby building to watch, his hand on his sword. Before long, he saw his foolish brother appear and hold the rod up before the huge black dragon. Conchobar knew all about the rod. It was now common knowledge that Ailfrid possessed one of Baron Zoran's magical rods which would protect the wielder. Of course, only a few actually knew of the rod's true powers.

Conchobar saw the utter foolishness of Ailfrid and watched the young baron and baroness get killed by the black. Even though he had no love for Ailfird, Conchobar acted. He saw his chance. He raced from the shadows, dove for the rod now lying on the snow covered ground, grabbed it, and rolled back onto his feet. Now he was facing the three dragons. The three beasts were taken by surprise, giving Conchobar time to draw his blade, thus negating any chance that the black could attempt to bite him as it had his half-brother. A red belched fire onto Conchobar, and to the young man's surprise, the rod activated and the searing flames swept past him, leaving him untouched. Conchobar acted.

His sword struck the red, piercing its hide. The startled beast let out a cry of pain and surprise. The other red backed away, recognizing the man was wielding an enchanted blade which could well slay him. Conchobar moved forward and successfully landed a strike on the black, wounding it as well. Now all three backed off and took flight, the reds then belching fire onto nearby buildings. Conchobar raced after them, but was unable to physically injure any other dragons. Once the dragons left Cullen in flames and ruin, Conchobar was hailed as a hero for driving the beasts away. Many had seen him dashing about trying to attack the dragons. After that, he found his horse and rode to the fortress, where he relayed what had happened and laid his claim to the throne. None dare defy him, since he had Bran's famous sword and the Rod of Dragon Slaying. Later on, his other two half-brothers arrived to survey the destruction, and they too had little choice but to acknowledge Conchobar as the new baron, though both began scheming to find ways to get that rod from him. It was Conchobar who later Mind Linked to Baron Zoran, introducing himself, proclaiming he was the new baron, and told Zoran what had happened on Maeve. All told, three towns were burned to the ground and around ten thousand on Maeve perished during the three separate attacks that night.

By the time that Zoran received the final reports from the Night of Terror as it was thereafter known, each of the sixteen planets had lost around ten thousand people, on the average, some more, some less.

Yuletide evening around ten there in the Stodgy Inn, Brn, one of the musicians called out, "Okay ladies. It's that time again. Here's your chance to dance a few steps with your baron!" This was a long standing tradition that Zoran always insisted upon doing — allowing anyone who desired to dance a bit with their baron. "It does wonders for everyone," he once explained to Tomas, who had asked why he did it. After all, it was a security risk. One of the women could be an assassin from Rehor. Nevertheless, Zoran always went ahead with it. As the women giggled and stepped forward to get their turn, suddenly Zdenka screamed loudly, along with five other women. All eyes turned to the six who screamed. Zdenka, shaking visibly, called out to a hushed room, "Dragons have just attacked several towns on Adapazan!" Their Premonition spells had detonated, taking the six Archmages by complete surprise.

"Party is over!" Zoran's Magnified voice echoed in the large pub's room. "Everyone, head home. Begin packing what you need. After we find out what is going on, I may issue the order for everyone to enter our subterranean safe house. At least get yourselves prepared for that. Gang, everyone back to the fortress! We have to get to those towns as fast as possible!"

As Zdenka opened her Mystical Door for herself and Zoran, she whispered, "The dragon war is beginning, isn't it?" Zoran's face looked grimmer than she'd ever seen it before and she had her answer.

Within minutes, Baron Tomas arrived with his forces, followed within minutes with a terrified Baron Jan and his forces. Zoran ordered, "Chika, Akira, you stay here, up on the roof please. Message us if you detect any sign that dragons are heading to Brn. Jan, you take a third to Zavis near Dorum. Tomas, take a third to Velin, Sholov Province. I'll take the rest to Zelen, Zovou Province. Stay alert!"

Zoran noted that the three towns that were attacked were scattered across the continent. From Zavis in the far east, to Zelen in the far west, and Velin in the middle, the dragons had spread their attacks out widely. He suspected this was on purpose, drawing his forces to extreme distances from Brn. He anticipated further attacks, though none came this night.

"Light spells — someone cast them from high above so we can see what we are doing!" Jarka called out as soon as they landed outside the small town of Zelen, an iron mining town. Here most of the houses were made of stone boulders with a limestone mortar holding them together. Roofs were often thatched and most were in flames when the group arrived. "Careful! Watch where you are stepping! Slime rot here and acid there!" she quickly advised the others. Karel grumbled again, these were plainly obvious to him.

Heavy snow added to their difficulties and at last, several Archmages began using their spells to lift large sections of the snow up, dropping them on the fires in an attempt to rapidly extinguish them. They met with some success. Meanwhile, Jarka, Zoran, Zdenka, Karel, and Danika began searching for survivors. Danika found the first of the seven survivors, a brother and sister, hugging each other. They were outside in the cold snow with only their long underwear on. She quickly took them inside the remains of their home but regretted that move. Their parent's bodies lay on the front room floor. Nevertheless, she got the two numb children to their rooms, now smoke filled, and got them dressed warmly. A few spells removed the smoke. At least their ceiling had been spared. The melting snow had put out the fire on their roof, though it had collapsed onto the attic floor.

An hour later, they returned to Brn with the seven survivors. There was not much else they could do until daylight came. Tomas reported finding ten survivors at Velin, while a terribly shaken Jan reported six at Zavis. This town was barely fifteen miles from Dorum and his own Castle Dorumova! That scared him.

Zoran contacted the Warlord of Zovou Province, the fifty year old Warlord Petr. After telling him about the total destruction of his outlying town, he asked him to take care of the funeral arrangements and that he would join him there in the morning. Petr was extremely upset. "Is this the start of the dragon wars?" he asked.

"Likely, I'm getting reports from similar attacks on the other fifteen planets. I'll keep you fully apprised of the situation," Zoran advised.

"We should be extremely careful when we are there tomorrow," Jarka cautioned. "It could well be a trap set for us. The dragons will be expecting everyone to be at the ruins gathering up the dead. Prime time to attack us and wipe us out!"

"Yes, we'd be out in the open and could easily be taken by surprise," Zoran admitted. "We'll use extreme caution. Keep several Archmages Invisible and on guard watching the skies." She felt a bit better about it now. Zoran didn't think the dragons would attempt to attack them though. With seven Archmages in each group, they would be able to extract a very heavy toll on the dragons.

The survivors, cleaned, fed, and in some cases clothed, were then questioned. They learned two key facts from the twenty-three survivors. One, every colored dragon was represented, save golds. Two, the attack group numbered thirty-three. During the long night, Zoran received similar word from the other barons. Each world had had three towns destroyed by a large group of dragons of all colors, save gold. The exact number in each swarm varied, but usually around thirty-three.

A sleepy-eyed Jarka commented over breakfast, "Well, we know one thing for sure. We are facing an army of five hundred twenty-six dragons. Archmage Ivana got two last night. We know the enemy's strength."

"Hey, we know one other peculiar thing, dad," Tomas pointed out. He had stayed here with Zoran during the night to help coordinate and stay abreast of the incoming messages. "One of Velin survivors said that they saw a black carrying one Milena Dezda away with him. I did some checking last night, dad. It seems that she has had some magic training. She's classified as an Adept, but has mastered a number of grade one and two spells before she reached her maximum ability to learn magic. She's twenty and was Velin's magic assistant, carrying out little useful things for the townsfolk. She was known for Levitating heavy stone blocks, helping the construction of new homes and additions in Velin. I wonder if she is part of the abduction of women-to-be-bred project of theirs? Or are they planning to torture her for information? If that's the case, I can't imagine what she could possibly know that the dragons desire to know."

"Right after breakfast, I'll speak with Kachina and see if she can locate her. I wonder if others were taken as well? How about re-questioning all the survivors, Tomas?"

"You got it, dad!"

A while later, Zoran met with the Isi native. He explained the abduction of the Adept Milena Dezda. "I am truly sorry, Zoran. Please don't ask this of me right now. The whole Shadowland around us all is completely saturated with the heavy emotions of fear, terror, panic, pain, and suffering. I would be overwhelmed if I even made the slightest contact with it right now."

"Okay, I understand. No problem. Thanks for being honest with me." Zoran left and headed to his private study. Already other barons were demanding a conference with him. What should they do? What ought they do? What could they do? His head was swimming and he felt the onset of a pounding headache. He sent for Jarka once more.

"Yes, boss?" she said as she stepped out of her Mystical Door, teasing him a little.

"Have a seat. I want to bounce something off of you." She did so. "Pretend for a moment that you are the dragon leader and have just launched this unprecedented attack on all sixteen worlds at the same time. Given that, would you be launching more of these attacks today, tonight, or would you be waiting for a reaction from us humans and barons?" He knew that he soon had to address all of the barons and that they would all be looking to him for advice on what to do next.

"It's to their advantage to attack at night, er, I mean mine, if I am the dragons. Humans don't see well at night, especially to coordinate defenses and such. So I would not attack during the daytime, only at night. After delivering such a blow, I think that I would wait and see how the barons react. With the exception of Wen, none of the barons was attacked directly, and none of the fortresses were attacked. That tells me that they are either afraid or very leery of them and the rods, naturally. As long as the barons and Archmages stay concentrated in a few locations, they will be tough targets to take without heavy dragon losses. I'd guess that they will wait and see before launching more attacks. However, they will undoubtedly raise more towns," Jarka suggested.

"That is a good point, Jarka. If we stay concentrated, we have a chance. Thanks. I have to deal with fifteen or more barons. I will relay that advice. Don't spread out. I think that it may be time to move as much of our populations into the subterranean cities as we can, just to be safe," Zoran concluded. She left and Zoran took a deep breath and then began constructing a large Mind Link to one baron on each of the other fifteen planets.

Okay. Don't all talk at once. We have all suffered at least three dragon attacks on towns on our worlds. We have a new baron for Maeve with us, Conchobar Ahren. Now then, my advice — which you don't have to follow necessarily. I believe that the dragons will take a wait and see what we do next approach and will not attack us later today. Jarka and I think that they will continue to make nighttime attacks, because we are far less defensible then. She and I think that the dragons want us to send out our forces to other towns and cities so that they can pick us off more easily. So here on Adapazan, I am keeping our forces in our three key fortresses for the time being, lending aid of course for brief times when needed. Thus, I am recommending that we begin to get as many of our people into our subterranean safe houses as we can.

Thanks to Archmage Ivana, the dragons lost two during their attacks. Jarka and I now put their number of attack dragons at around five hundred twenty-six more for us to kill. For now, let's focus on getting as many of our people into safe quarters as we can and worry about going after the dragons a bit later. I know that we are not going to have enough underground room for everyone, but let's do our best and then see where we are at. If your fortresses are attacked directly, message me, and I'll see if I can get to you in time to help repel the dragons. Let's all Mind Link each day say around this time to coordinate our efforts.

Remember, that is one thing that we have that the dragons do not — our ability to Mind Link and thus coordinate our actions. We must make use of this as much as we can. Okay, questions?

Baron Leo here. What are we going to do to protect those whom we simply cannot get below ground?

I don't know yet. Perhaps we can bring them into the fortresses, at least until our fortresses fall, Zoran suggested. *Hey, I have to go. Aldrick the Gold Dragon is here. Maybe I can find out from him what the devil is going on. I'll get back to you in a bit.* He broke the link.

"Welcome old friend. Sad, sad day," Zoran rose and shook Aldrick's hand. He'd morphed into his human form to visit the baron. Bernard had brought him in, passing by the security forces. Aldrick looked old, Zoran thought. This crisis was taking a toll on him as well.

The gold sighed. "Yes, it is the saddest day ever. We golds have been out-voted, seven to one. The others have gone to war against all you humans. Alas, at this time, there is nothing that I can do to stop them."

"That's what I figured, Aldrick. You and I, we've done our best, but it just wasn't enough in the end. Still, I am keeping the barons from making retaliatory strikes at the moment. I don't want to kill off your species either. Have a seat."

After sitting down, Aldrick sighed and said, "We golds are in a terrible position, Zoran. We have two choices really. One, we can side with the others and help wipe out the human race. Two, we can join you and help wipe out our own race."

"Three choices, Aldrick. You can sit back and not participate on either side. That way, you will not be party to either genocide. Plus, you and I may yet find a way to end this war on peaceful terms that does not involve genocide of either of our races. I'd prefer this choice, old friend," Zoran replied, hoping that the gold would seize this alternative.

"I don't like doing nothing, but if we can find a way to stop this, then I wouldn't be doing nothing, would I?" Aldrick mulled over his suggestion, finding a part of it that he could accept. "Is there really anything more that we can do?"

Zoran shrugged his shoulders. "At this instant, I don't even know why all of a sudden they decided to go to war."

"Three things finally pushed them over the edge. First, your Seventeen all became Archmages. Is this true? They all did?" Zoran nodded. "Interesting. Perhaps they need to worry! If the other hundred plus also become Archmages, then they have signed their own death warrants. Anyway, they saw that your people have been gathering up enchanted blades from grave sites on Voss."

"Correction. We found them in various homes and keeps. We've never dug up any graves that I know of, Aldrick. Yes, we need them to help protect ourselves, obviously. What's the third?" Zoran had anticipated these two, he did not the third.

"The blacks are claiming that you uncovered a super-weapon of the ancients on Voss and brought it to Brn to use against dragon-kind. That, I find hard to believe."

Zoran threw his hands up in disgust. "Aldrick, we went to Voss in search of twenty ancient journals of one of our founders, Bandar Zar. We hope that it will illuminate our ancient history. Did you know that all of the original sixteen founders came from Voss?"

"What? Voss? No way!"

"Yes, we found a mural in a temple that said Voss was originally the Democracy of the Sixteen. The map showed sixteen areas of the planet with names like: Republic State of Anwyn and the Republic State of Adapazan. Every one of our worlds' names was there as Republic State of such and such. All of them. Our ancestors came from Voss millennia ago, Aldrick. Incredible. Anyway, we humans thought that was interesting and that Voss may contain some clues, since all of you dragons also came from Voss, albeit a millennia later on."

"That is most interesting, Zoran. Yes, I always knew that there were ancient ruins scattered all over Voss. There has never been a human there that I know of, not in my long lifetime nor that of my father. I'm sure that he would have mentioned it if there were. So no super-weapon?"

"No, right now, I kind of wish there was one, if you take my meaning. Three towns destroyed on each of the sixteen worlds, nasty business. I can show you the volumes if you like."

"No, I am not interested in human history. I am more worried about the other golds, though. Emil wants to stay on the sidelines. Renata wants to go to war on your side. A few want to join the other dragons if only to end the war quickly. I will take your suggestion to heart and see if I can convince the other golds to do nothing at this point and yet be ready to help out if we can actually figure out some way to handle this mess. I have no doubts now, old friend, that this will get much worse for both our races before it gets better."

"I wish with all my heart that I could disagree with you, but you are probably right. Many more will die on both our sides before we can end it. Somehow, someway, we must get the war stopped before either race is wiped out," Zoran replied.

The two shook hands and Bernard escorted Aldrick out of the Brn fortress. Just then Evsen made contact with him from Voss. *Hi boss. Say, the others in Strike Force One have been getting messages from their home worlds. Their barons are asking that they return and help fight the dragons. Neither I nor they want to disband the Strike Force. Suggestions? What do you want us to do? We've found another dozen weapons.*

Right now, the dragons are attacking in masses of thirty-three, far, far more than your Strike Force could possible handle at one time. Coming back right now will serve no real useful purpose. Having more enchanted weapons is. So my suggestion is to continue your searches for the next few days. Let's see what the dragons do next. Honestly, if thirty-three attack us here, it will take all of our Archmages to defeat them. Swords are really only effective one on one, not against an aerial assault of this magnitude. Long range spells are our only real hope, unless you want to jump onto a dragon and fight like Chan and Wen do.

Okay boss. I'll relay your ideas to the group. I think they will see it your way, especially if you send for us if an attack comes. We all want to fight the dragons, that's why they all volunteered for the force.

I will message you if an attack comes where we can actually fight back. So far they have randomly struck small towns and then only late at night. No chance for us to fight back. Evsen broke the link and Zoran sat back thinking. More blades would be useful. Perhaps he ought to ask the barons to supply fighters to man up a second strike force that would be able to respond to an attack on a moment's notice, coming to their aid. Of course if he did that, who could he send as the Adapazan representative? He was running out of Duska fighters.

As if in answer, though later he figured Evsen was behind it, Dusan Dragon came to see him. He was Archmage Nadia's husband and Evsen's older brother, Jarka and Bernard's eldest boy. "Say, if you are planning to man up a second strike force, how about letting me be Adapazan's representative? I'm doing very little at the moment. I know that Dana is tied up training everyone he can. How about it?"

"Well, I was just considering it. We have accumulated enough weapons for another one. However, I don't want them going out hunting for dragons. Rather, I would like them to be ready to respond instantly to any ongoing dragon attack on any world. They could come to the rescue as soon as they were notified that dragons were attacking somewhere."

"Hey, I like that even better. Bet Evsen would too."

"Okay, I have to make you do the same as Evsen. You have to get your folk's permission before I'll consent," Zoran replied.

An hour later, though Jarka and Bernard had misgivings about both their boys being on the front lines of the war, so to speak, they agreed. Zoran promised to see that Dusan also had one of Karel's rods with him as well. Then, he contacted the other barons. As expected, they were delighted with the prospect of having two Strike Forces that would be ready to come to the aid of anyone of them who was being attacked.

Next, he went to check on how the populating of his subterranean city was going. The Seventeen Archmages were handling this operation. Why? They wanted to guarantee that no dragon spy attempted to sneak in along with the worried citizens of Brn. Thus, far, none had.

"So far so good, Zoran," Archmage Danika reported. "Most are all right with this move. It is winter and so little commerce happens. Most are worried about their homes or businesses getting damaged, but when I tell them that you've promised to replace them if that happens, they stop fretting. I hope that they don't get cabin fever down there. We've got a whole lot of Permanent Light spells set up, so it ought to be nice and bright. Of course, we also provided leather bags to put over them when they want to sleep."

"Excellent, Archmage Danika. Excellent. I have a feeling that we will soon be taking on many others from other worlds too. I don't think it is possible to house everyone on all our worlds in underground safe houses. We've not had time enough to make that much space. I best go check on how Baron Jan is faring."

"Tell Eliska hi for me. She's with him making sure no dragons enter his complex as well," she replied. As he headed over to Castle Dorumova, he began to worry about just that. So many people lived in small hamlets and villages. How could these be protected? They had no underground safe houses available, only the larger towns did. He just did not have enough mages around to handle the constructions via magic spells. Using miners to dig them would be impossibly slow.

Chapter 35 The Ordeal of Milena Dezda

Milena Dezda turned twenty-one in November and now had a thriving business going — Dezda Operations. Overly tall at six-five, or so she considered, only recently had her thin frame begun to fill out in all the right places. She attributed the sudden interest of men in her to just that. As a young girl living in Orlovia Province, she always had been taller than all the boys that she knew. Her parents had fled the invasion of Sholov Province some twenty-four years ago, living in exile until ten years ago when Baron Zoran began the rebuilding of the Province and his son took charge of the new Circle of Ascension there.

Among the exiles from Sholov was an old mage, Kamil. He'd taken an interest in this tall, skinny girl and began teaching her to use magic. Milena had quickly learned all of the many useful spells and had been officially given the Adept badge. From there, Kamil continued to work with her, though they only did so of an evening. Still, Milena continued to learn. "One day if you study hard and practice lots, Milena, you may become a mage like me," he'd often tell her. Well, that all ended five years ago when the old man had died of natural causes.

Shortly after that, her own parents moved into new quarters in Velin, Sholov Province, some twenty miles from Baron Tomas Vladislov's new Fortress and Circle. Here, she began to put her spells to work, quickly finding work for an Adept. Soon, she discovered that her "real spells" could make her even more money, and she'd set up her small business, Dezda Operations. Stone masons now frequently hired her to levitate heavy stones up to their places on the buildings that they were constructing. It saved them scaffolding time, which saved them money as well. One thing was certain, under Baron Tomas, new constructions were sprouting up nearly everywhere in Sholov Province. Milena was doing quite nicely for herself as Yuletide approached and the stone masons ceased work until the spring thaws came.

Yuletide night, nearly everyone was packed into the Moose Lodge for the annual party. In Velin, like most all towns, Yuletide was the party event of the year. Besides marking the end of one year, it ushered in the new year full of hopes which under Baron Tomas' leadership stood a good chance of being fulfilled. For the first time in her life, Milena found herself being the center of romantic attention from young men, instead of ridicule. She was so tired of "how's the weather up there" comments that she'd heard all her life. True, she had a thick skin by now, but she was having a harder time with the men's sudden change of viewpoint and all because the rest of her body finally caught up to her height. She had not considered that her bit of magic spell use and that she now had a small profitable business going had anything to do with all the young men asking her for a dance. In spite of her confusion over the why, she enjoyed the attention that she was getting tonight.

Everything came to a sudden, violent end when the dragons swooped down on Velin. Two browns came smashing through the roof, ending the festivities in a blink. Surprise shouts turned to screams of terror, as all eyes in the packed room gazed upwards at the swarming mass of multicolored dragons circling overhead. As the dragons began sending down death and destruction, Milena, unwilling to go down without a fight, cast her single Magical Missile at the nearest brown dragon. She found herself even more confused. Now she was no longer in the room of panicking people, many of whom were dying from the searing flames and streams of acid covering their bodies. No, she was on a featureless grey plain. Worse, there was the dragon that she tried to attack, glaring back at her.

This is so strange, she thought. Oh well, fire another one. She tried to get off another of her Magical Missiles, but immediately found herself back into the chaos with the Moose Lodge. Screams of pain and terror swamped her hearing. Heat, foul smoke and the odor of caustic acid deadened her olfactory senses and threatened to choke her. Dense smoke from the fires and acid fumes blocked her vision as much as the swarming mass of people, pushing to get out of the giant room.

Strength! She cast the spell on herself to avoid being pushed hard into the wall by the throng forcing its way towards the exit. Milena pushed back and slipped over the wooden bar, falling to the floor behind it. Just as she felt free of the mob, another blast of flames reddened the already smoke filled room. The mass, which had been pushing her, now shoved the bar over on top of her. How long she was stunned, she didn't know, but at last the heavy weight on her chest brought her back to the present. She pushed upwards, but only moved the heavy bar a little. "Levitate!" Now the bar slowly moved up off of her. The smoke was clearing. She felt the cold from outside coming into the room from where the roof had been. Charred bodies littered the floor like embers of some giant's fireplace's half-burnt logs. She got to her feet and stepped over the fallen and piles of caustic acid to get outside the huge hall.

She stepped out into the cold and snowy ground only to come face to face with a black dragon, who was counting a few terror stricken survivors! The dragon made a noise that sounded like "Hum." Then she recognized the spell that it was casting, Sleep.

No, I don't want to go to sleep! Fight it, Milena, fight it! She thought to herself. Movement, yes, she was moving through the air. She opened her eyes and found herself hanging from the claws of an enormous beast, flying through the air. *Is that Velin far below me? What's happening to me?* "Let me go!" her weak sounding voice broke the stillness of the night, barely audible above the flapping of the huge wings as the dragon sought to gain altitude.

She had to get away. Strength! She again cast her spell and struggled to break free from the powerful claws of the dragon. If she could, she had just the spell ready to break her long fall to the ground far below. If she could just break free. No luck, even with her enhance strength, she could not force the powerful claws open. Mentally, she went through all the spells that she knew, trying one here and there. Shock, Scare, Spook, Burn. Nothing worked on this powerful beast. At last, she stopped trying. Something strange was happening to her. A grey-blackness swept over her. She was disoriented, falling and yet not falling, the claws still held her in a vice grip. Milena felt nauseous and would have vomited only she couldn't figure which way was down.

Suddenly the world appeared once more, the nausea vanished as suddenly as it had come. World? What world was this? Desert sands? There were no deserts on Adapazan, none that she had ever heard of — where am I? Screams. She heard several other screaming women. Twisting around in the claws, she saw five other women clamped between enormous claws of other dragons, all circling in the moonlight. Warmth! Wherever here was, she thought, it was nice and warm.

Another dragon swooped in close to her. It chanted. Suddenly, everything went black, a total, complete, and utter darkness. She screamed as she recognized the spell. It was one that she flatly had wanted nothing to do with. Blind! The dragon had permanently blinded her. Memories of her old mage teacher came back. He had tried to teach her that spell, but she recalled her reply, "Absolutely not! What a horrible thing to do to someone. No way do I want to permanently blind someone. Never." Now she wished that perhaps she had not been so headstrong. If I'd have learned it, she thought, then maybe there was a way that I could undo it. "Please, I can't see. Undo this, please." The dragons didn't answer her. Another spell hit her. This time she didn't feel any different, though she certainly didn't know what the spell was. Now she felt the dragon moving once more, but she relaxed; there was nothing that she could do about it now. "If you are going to kill me, just do it!" she called out feebly.

Time passed and Milena struggled with the idea of time. How am I ever going to tell time now? I can't see anything anymore. How will I know when it is morning? How will I know when I am supposed to go to bed? Milena became more and more confused as she tried to focus on how she could survive like this. Then, the claws let go of her and she fought hard in the utter darkness to keep her balance and not fall down! That was scary, she thought. "Where am I? Why are you doing this to me?"

She heard more chanting but recognized the spell. Someone was trying to Charm her! Well, that won't work on me, she thought. Oops. Maybe I better play along with them. If they think I am charmed, maybe I can figure a way to get away from them. How? I can't see where I am even at? Which way is home? More confusion overcame her thinking processes.

Another spell detonated and she felt her shoulders being touched. Immobilize! Milena knew this spell but it was too late for her to counteract it. If she had been able to see and had been concentrating, she knew that she ought to have been able to avoid the spell's effects. Her body went rigid and she could not move a muscle, no matter how hard she tried. She felt her body being lifted and being laid on a flat surface. A bed perhaps? What's happening? Oh my god! No! Milena didn't need eyes to know what the somebody was doing to her now. She was being raped! She threw all her energy into trying to throw the man off of her, but her body didn't move even the tiniest fraction of an inch. She was Immobilized. I'll kill him! She swore to herself. I'll kill him, I swear I will if it's the last thing I ever do!

Well at least that was quick, she thought. Maybe now they will let me go. They've had their fun and jollies. Wait! Men are in cahoots with the dragons! Oh no! Who is that man? Why is he using dragons? What's going on? Her mind now raced down other avenues. She heard more chanting. This time, she did not recognize the spell, but held a little hope that whomever was chanting was going to release her now and let her go back home. Home? They were all dead now, aren't they? The horrors within Moose Lodge came back to her and she shuddered, though her body didn't move.

No, something was definitely happening to her body! She felt herself becoming positively huge. No, make that enormous. A voice spoke, "Ah, there, that is much better now. Milena, we have rescued you from the humans. We have been able to get you out of the human form that the humans forced you into. You have your dragon body back once more. What have those vile, wicked humans done to you, dear Milena?"

"Huh? What are you saying? Oh, I can move again. I feel so strange! I can't see. What's going on? Why do I feel so weird?" Milena asked, growing more and more confused. If only she could see. "I can't see. Help me."

"We are so sorry that we could not rescue you any sooner from those awful humans, dear Milena. We have managed to get your beautiful Black Dragon body back. They had been forcing you to always stay in your human form, the beasts. Your black body is very beautiful, Milena. But we are so sorry about your eyes. The humans have torn them from your sockets. Foul beasts! We promise you that we will extract revenge ten-fold for what the humans have done to you, a beautiful black dragon."

"I am not a Black Dragon, am I?" she asked growing more confused by the minute. None of this made the slightest sense.

"Don't you remember Milena? My god, what have those humans done to you? You are a beautiful Black Dragon! The humans captured you a month ago. They have blinded you and forced you to remain in your human form against your will. It took us a whole month to find where they were holding you captive. We swooped down and killed many of the wicked humans who held you captive and rescued you. Don't you remember any of that? Perhaps, they have also cast powerful spells that altered your memory. Feel your huge wings, your massive tail, and your powerful claws. We are so terribly sorry that they tore your eyes out. Now you can no longer soar high in the sky with us. But don't worry, we will take good care of you. You are safe in your cavern, but they probably erased those memories of yours too. Since you cannot see any longer, you must be careful. If you walk too far from here, you could step off of the cliff and fall a thousand feet to your death. How can you ever fly again? We don't know. You would not be able to see where you were flying and could easily fly right into a tree or cliff wall. Werner says that it is too perilous for you to attempt to fly anymore. So we will take good care of you, most beautiful Milena."

She felt her body as best she could. There was a tail, a long one at that. She felt her claws. They seemed awfully real to her. She felt her neck, so incredibly long! Her face, it was huge and her teeth — her claws told her they were enormous. At last, Milena no longer doubted that her body was that of a huge dragon. But how? "I am a human, not a dragon," she finally replied.

"Yes, the wicked men who captured you cast all sorts of awful spells on you, poor Milena. We hope that we killed all of them who did this awful thing to you. Are you hungry?"

"Well yes! I am ravishingly hungry!" She recognized an intense hunger in her belly. She smelled the carcass of a freshly killed animal being pushed across the stone floor towards her nostrils. Before she knew what she was doing, her massive body was devouring the antelope.

Later on, the kind voice began talking once more, "We have examined your beautiful black body, Milena and you are so very, very lucky. The humans have not harmed your baby that is growing inside of you! You will still be able to have your baby, perhaps in some sixty days. That is a miracle, Milena. At least they cannot take away your motherhood from you. Now that is something to be thankful for, isn't it?"

"Huh? Pregnant? I am? This is all so confusing. I am not a dragon, am I?" she replied, her confusion only growing.

"Of course you are a perfect Black Dragon, Milena, only the vile humans have tortured you and done awful things to you. Still, take comfort, you are not alone. The humans captured several other dragons too, torturing them much as you. We've been rescuing them right and left. Some of them are sleeping next to you. Oh, we've put a chain on your ankle. When it goes taught, do not try to go beyond that distance. The chain marks where it is safe for you to walk. We all fear that if you go farther, you will fall off the cliff to your death and not even be able to see it. Promise me that you won't go beyond the chain's limit, dear Milena."

"Well okay, I don't want to fall. I can't see," she agreed, becoming terrified of even the idea of falling into the unknown space.

"That is good. Why don't you take a nap now? I expect that you are exhausted from all the torture that the humans put you through."

She yawned. "Yes, I am tired, very tired. Wake me in the morning. I can't tell if it is morning or night anymore."

"Yes, of course we will. Rest now." She curled up, her long neck curved around her massive body, resting it on her side. Milena fell into a deep sleep.

Deep sleep gave way to some awful nightmares. Dragons were burning her friends alive. She awoke with a start, raising her head up high. Bang! Her head hit solid stone some twenty feet above the floor. "Ouch!" she exclaimed, pulling her head down. It banged into something soft to her right. It moved.

"Oh, you bumped into me. I am Vesna. Who are you? I don't recognize your smell."

"Milena. What's going on? I can't see. I am blind. Sorry. I must have hit my head on the ceiling."

"Yes, I have done that too, Milena. We are all blind. We have all been captured and tortured by the humans. They tore out my eyes. None of us can see anymore. That's an awful thing to do to a dragon. I am so sad. I'll never be able to fly again. I do so love to fly. At least the fellows are taking good care of us and the humans didn't find my baby. I'm going to have a fine, strong baby one day soon. How badly were you tortured, Milena? Did they try to do awful things to your mind too?"

"But I am a human or I was," Milena protested.

A voice to her left spoke up, "That's all right, Milena. We understand. I am Rada. The humans tore my eyes out too. They messed with my mind, but I won. I still know that I am a Black Dragon! They couldn't convince me otherwise. I am so very glad that they didn't harm my baby. I'm pregnant too, due in a few more weeks, I think. I don't know how I could have continued to live if they had killed my unborn baby! Those awful humans. I hope Werner wipes them all out!"

"Same here," another voice called out from further to Milena's right. "I hope they kill them all! I'm Marjeta, by the way. They didn't get my baby either! She's right. I don't know how I could have had the strength to carry on if they had ripped my baby from me! There are a dozen of us here now. None of us can see, but they are looking after us very well, Milena. Just be careful not to go beyond the reach of the chain. We can't see anymore and there is a steep cliff just beyond the cavern's entrance. I know that I can fly if I fell, but if I can't see, I will end up flying into something and get badly hurt or worse. Just be careful of that. I wish I could see you, Milena. He did say that you were one of the prettiest blacks ever."

"But I am a human, I think," Milena tried to explain the unexplainable.

"We know, Milena. The humans cast vicious spells to alter your mind. I do hope that you didn't reveal any of us dragon's secrets to them. I don't think that I did," Marjeta said soothingly.

Another voice from even further to her left called out, "It's all right, Milena. Give yourself time. Many of us were brainwashed by the humans. Even I thought that I might be a human when I first got here. I am Katerina, by the way. Give it time, Milena. Slowly your real memories will come back to you. At least that is what our caretakers are suggesting and hoping."

Poor Milena only became more and more confused. *I have memories of mom and dad. See, I was a little girl, well a big one. The kids all teased me about being taller than they were. Oh, was that because I was really a dragon? Is that why I was so tall? No, that can't be. I got taught magic by the old mage. I have to be human. No, I heard that dragons too can cast spells. But I am a young woman, I know it. I feel so strange. My body feels so different, so huge, and so weird. I can't be a dragon, not really, or can I? I don't understand this at all. What's happened to me?* She began to cry.

She felt two head on long necks moving their necks along hers. "There, there, Milena. It will be all right. Just give yourself time to remember who you are. The nasty humans have so wiped out our memories, but they come back in time I think." She recognized the voice of Vesna.

Katerina spoke up, "Say, Milena, can you remember how to cast any of your spells? The humans have wiped my mind totally clear. I cannot remember how to cast the simplest of spells any more. They've really robbed me of my own magic spells!"

"Me too," Vesna added. "They wiped my mind out too. I can't recall how to cast even one spell anymore. It is just awful, a dragon who can't cast anything! Vile humans!"

"I can remember my spells," Milena said more to herself. "But I can't see. I know. Levitate!" She felt her body rising up slightly.

"Oh! Everyone! Milena is doing it! She remembers her spells!" Vesna called out. She and Rada had their necks and heads wrapped around Milena's comforting her. Both felt Milena's body rising. Many other women complimented and praised Milena.

"Well, at least the humans didn't wipe her mind as badly as they did ours! That is something. Melina, you are one lucky Black Dragon!" Vesna pointed out. "The rest of us were not so lucky."

"It, it must be awful to have lost your ability to cast your spells," Milena admitted and sympathized with the dragon women. Are they even women or is that a human term? I am starting to think like them! Oh god. No, I am a woman. I am not a dragon, but then I do seem to be a dragon. This is all so confusing!

After that, Milena found that the other dozen female dragons around her all looked up to her. Rada pointed out that the only thing more humiliating than a blinded dragon was one who had lost their ability to cast magical spells. Milena felt a little better about everything now, since at least she could cast her spells, though most were entirely useless if she could not see anything.

Her days, if days they even were, consisted of chatting with the other females, whose talk mostly centered on the babies growing inside their wombs. At seemingly random times, food would appear and a water barrel always seemed to be full. All slept quite a lot, though. During the quiet times, Milena continued to examine all her memories. After all, Vesna said that her memories would slowly return to her. What had the humans done to me? Did they give me a whole bunch of false memories? What kind of spell would do that? Where are my dragon memories anyway? I keep on seeing only my human ones. Confusion continued to cloud Milena's mind.

Evsen and his Strike Force One continued to scour Voss for more likely sites to explore. Their goal: find all the enchanted weapons they could find and all the treasure as well. Naturally, they found more of the latter, though they now had ten more enchanted swords that were still functional. The news of the Night of Terror struck these fourteen fighters hard. At first, they wanted to head home and launch a strike of their own against the dragons. Evsen had been able to point out the folly of that. With Zoran's request that they stay and search for more weapons that could be used to kill dragons, they calmed down and agreed. With the news that a second force was being equipped using the blades that they had found previously, the fourteen took a renewed interest in finding even more. They were doing something positive about it. Viktor suggested that soon they might be able to equip a third strike force! Their morale was high.

On the other hand, Honani and his Star Dancers were becoming bored with the perpetual rummaging through long abandoned ruins. For days, they had kept their eyes turned to the north where the reds and blacks were often seen circling in the sky or sweeping down. Sometimes, Honani spotted one returning north carrying an antelope in its claws. Just what were the dragons doing there began to prick all five's curiosity. No other dragons were on Voss, only these reds and blacks. They were only at that one location in the far north of the Russet Mountains. They never ventured far from that area. Were they hiding something? Honani had that thought more than once, so did his companions.

The fourth day after the nighttime attack of the dragons, Honani took his group northward, telling Evsen, "Today, we are going to look for sites further north." Evsen didn't suspect anything and agreed. After Shadow Walking part way there, the five spent an hour looking for dragon dung. After finding one pile at last, the five smeared some of it on themselves.

"Invisible and here we go. Let's see what those dragons are up to, shall we?" Honani suggested.

"It can't be good," his wife, Awinita added. The five Shadow Walked to the northern mountains and began watching and searching for likely caverns. A few hours of methodical searching yielded five different cavern complexes that the dragons were using. Reds and blacks each had two that appeared to be for the sole use of their respective colors, but with the fifth, dragons of both were spotted entering and leaving.

Stay Invisible and stay in the Shadows as much as possible. Let's explore that one first," Honani suggested, pointing to one the reds were using exclusively. The five slipped deeper into the Shadows and moved towards its entrance, dodging a red that came swooping in, carrying an antelope. By being mostly in the Shadows, the many traps failed to detonate. Inside, they were quite surprised to find a dozen red dragons chained to a wall in one side chamber. They moved on deeper inside. They found three more chambers, each with an adult female caring for ten baby dragons. One of the females received the antelope and was now in the process of ripping it into smaller pieces for the young.

An hour later, they discovered the second reds-only complex was laid out much the same. Another three females were raising another thirty baby reds and another dozen were chained to a wall. Two hours after that, they finished searching the blacks-only caverns, discovering nearly the same thing. Three females were caring for thirty baby blacks with a dozen more blacks chained to a wall.

Finally, they scouted out the remaining cavern complex. This one was definitely much larger but many of the chambers were now empty, though they counted some sixty empty chains attached to the walls. There were, however, another dozen blacks and reds chained up in one side chamber and one dragon appeared to be caring for them. Since the unchained dragon was not with the dozen at the moment, Honani decided to have a closer look at the chained ones. Why would dragons chain up their own kind? Had they stumbled across a combination prison and nursery? As he semi-materialized, although still invisible, he used extreme caution. At any moment these dragons could spot him and their combined breath strikes could well wipe him out several times over. *How strange! Look at their eyes!* He sent.

All five fully materialized along the wall opposite the dozen chained dragons. Unlike the cold black eyes of the dragons that they had seen, these dragons' eyes were a cloudy grey. *They've been Blinded!* Awinita sent. They heard noise coming their way and hastily stepped back into the Shadows. The caretaker dragon entered and paused, sniffing the stone on which the five had just been standing. Evidently the caretaker found the smell to her liking and went about her duties, collecting up several piles of dragon dung.

Honani took his group far from the dragon lairs and materialized. "Well, I don't know what is going on there, but it sure is strange," he began, casting Clean spells to remove the dragon dung from himself. His companions did the same.

"I counted sixty blinded dragons. What does that mean?" asked Askook, baffled. Awinita shrugged her shoulders.

"That's the strangest sight I've seen. However, there are sixty baby dragons in there. If we could make a surgical strike, we could extract revenge for the four dozen villages that the dragons destroyed four days ago," Honani suggested. All five chuckled and agreed with his idea.

"They have an extraordinary number of traps on their entryways," Cheveyo noted. "Surely they consider these caverns of immense importance. Mothers guarding babies — well, I suppose that could account for it, though we have killed a number of baby dragons to get the blood for Milan and Archmage Karel. Still, I think that they are overreacting to our few kills."

"We should take them out, but will Evsen go for it? Killing their young, I mean," Donoma asked.

"He might not, but I know someone who would," Honani answered with a wry smile. "I will be back shortly." He Shadow Walked back to Brn and Messaged Archmage Karel. A minute later, Karel appeared out in front of the fortress in the nearly deserted street where Honani stood waiting.

"Well met again, Archmage. I have something interesting to tell you." He outlined what they had discovered and what he wanted to do. "I don't think the Evsen or even Zoran would go for it, but you and I, we know that these dragons need to be taught a lesson. Sixty babies have got to get their attention and let them know that they cannot wipe out four dozen of our towns without paying the price."

Karel grinned, "I like it! You were right to come to me with this. Zoran isn't really taking any revenge for the massive slaughter of our people. I don't have a squeamish stomach. This must be done. We cannot allow another sixty dragons to mature and enter the fight against humans! Come on; let's do it now. Let me get a few things that we're going to need."

Ten minutes later, Karel and Honani rejoined the four other Star Dancers. Karel handed each one of his Rods of Dragon Slaying. "Now here's how we go about it," Karel began outlining his plan for revenge. "We leave the blind dragons alone; we can easily come back later and finish them off." Everyone agreed with his method of attack which would minimize the risk to themselves. After Karel cast numerous protective spells on all six, Honani Shadow Walked them to the first cavern complex.

Peering out of the Shadows, Karel saw that Honani's description was accurate. He gave the signal. Several Silence spells activated and the six materialized on either side of the female dragon that was caring for the ten babies. While the five began hacking the red, Karel fired a Disintegrate beam into the dragon's head. She died several times over. Two minutes later, the ten babies were history and the six were again safe in the Shadows, moving to the next chamber. Fifteen minutes later, they moved on to the next red's nursery. Forty-five minutes later, the deed was done and Karel had sealed the entrances with Force Walls, preventing the other dragons, that were out either scouting or hunting for antelope to feed them all, from entering the caves.

Next, he proceeded to deactivate the many traps at the entrance of the shared cavern. Leaving Donoma to stand guard, the five headed to see about dispatching the dozen blind dragons.

"Is someone there?" Milena called out. She thought she had heard footsteps, which only added to her confusions. Dragons didn't have footsteps, humans did. But she was supposed to be a dragon. "What's going on?"

"You are right, Blind spell. All of them. What the devil is going on here? Why would they blind their own dragons?" asked Karel himself. He certainly didn't expect Honani to know.

"Humans! Help, humans. Stand back. I'll blast you with my breath!" yelled Vesna. Karel held his rod steady.

"Want me to start hacking them?" Honani asked.

"All right, take that you vile, wicked humans!" Vesna cried out and opened her mouth. Honani held onto his rod tightly, expecting the worst. Karel seemed amused, however, though he kept his rod at the ready. Nothing at all happened.

Karel couldn't resist taunting the dragon. "My, you are slipping. Not even a tiny drop of acid. Surely you can do better than that before we slay you!"

Vesna tried and tried, but nothing happened. She began crying. "The humans have cut out my acid glands too. It's not bad enough that they blinded me and wiped all memories of my spells from my mind, they had to go and cut out my glands too!" She sobbed and wailed. Karel noted that the others also tried to breathe fire and acid onto them as well, but not one of them could manage the slightest breath effect. Nada.

Karel rubbed his head. "What the devil is going on here? We cannot cut out their internals. Hell, we don't even know what their internals are. What is she talking about — wiping out their knowledge of magic spells? Well, there is such a spell, but we've been killing dragons, not wiping their minds. It would take an Archmage to do that in all likelihood. I'd rather have a dead dragon than an alive one any day. This is devilishly strange, Honani."

"Hey, five are returning with antelopes," Donoma called out.

"Hum. Honani, I am casting an illusion spell here and then you stick around in the Shadows and see what happens when they discover the slaughter. Cheveyo, take me quickly to each of the other caverns, fast. I have spells to cast in a big hurry!"

Cheveyo took Karel from cavern to cavern as rapidly as he could. While Karel cast a powerful illusion spell over the captive, blind dragons, Cheveyo canceled the Force Walls. He stepped the two into the Shadows just as a red entered the cavern, carrying an antelope. The male's reaction was the most hideous howl that the two men had ever heard, dampened considerably because they were mostly in the Shadows!

Before long, five more adult males arrived and added their howls to the din. "Even the breeders! They killed them all! My god! Dario has to be informed. Come on. Let's get out of here fast." The six reds left. Before long and after similar reactions, some twenty males, both red and black, took flight and then vanished from the sky, stepping into the Shadows themselves.

"Quick, we might not have much time before this place is overrun with dragons," Karel pointed out. He returned to the first cavern and stood before the chained dozen.

Honani said, "They sure fell for the illusion that these dozen were as dead as the others. Now what? Kill them quickly? They sure are a strange lot. Something is really off with them."

Milena spoke up. "Well you would be off too if humans tortured you and blinded you and did awful things to you. But I can't see myself. I am a dragon, aren't I? It feels like it anyway."

That did it. Karel cast his Dispel Magic and watched shocked, as a tall, naked woman appeared where the black dragon had stood. The chain around her leg dropped to the floor.

"My god, a Morph Other spell!" Honani declared.

"I am sorry, I don't know that spell. But I'm going to Sleep all of you right now!" Milena cast her Sleep spell, but could not see if anything had happened. Then she exclaimed, "I have hands again! What is happening to me? I am not a dragon after all? This is so confusing."

"What have they done to you, Milena?" Vesna called out, waving her head wildly about trying to feel for Milena who was now drastically smaller than she had been.

Honani cast his Dispel Magic and suddenly Milena's eyes returned to normal. "Oh! I can see again. Oh, I am human. Vesna! You are a big Black Dragon after all! Oh! Now you are a human, Vesna, this is *so* confusing!" Karel had just cast his Dispel Magic on Vesna and she returned to her human form. Cheveyo followed up, returning the woman's sight to her. Quickly, the others joined in. Askook and Awinita handled the next, while Donoma and Cheveyo worked on the next. Karel and Honani headed down the line, canceling all of the Morph Other spells, allowing the others to remove the women's Blind spell.

To their dismay, Rada screamed, "Foul humans! Give me back my dragon body!" She started pounding her fists on Askook. Meanwhile two others, yelling the same thing bolted out of the cavern.

Honani heard them yelling back to the others, "We are free. Quick, run and jump off the cliff and that will bring our dragon forms back so we can fly and warn the others!" Before they could do anything to stop them, three women dashed out and disappeared. Later, Honani saw their bodies smashed on the rocks far below the cavern's mouth.

Karel acted as soon as the two dashed off, followed by the third woman. He cast Sleep on the remaining nine women, but Milena didn't obey the spell. "I know that spell. You can't Sleep me. Where did they go? Did they really change back into dragons and fly away? I'd like to fly. The old mage told me that perhaps one day I could fly. Why are they sleeping now? What's going on? Why am I so big down there? Oh! I was raped, I remember now." Milena chatted on.

"Milena, I have a job for you. Your companions are getting a much needed sleep. Can you stand guard over them a little while? We need to get to some other women too," Honani asked her.

"Oh sure. I can shoot a Magical Missile if anyone comes. Oh, I have a memory of shooting one at the dragon who was looking in the hole in the roof of Moose Lodge, but maybe that isn't my memory. I'm not sure of much of anything anymore," she rattled on.

Honani took the initiative. "If all these chained dragons are Morphed women, we can't get them all out of here quickly. I'm going to Message Evsen to lend a hand." Karel grunted and reluctantly agreed. Within a minute Evsen and the rest of Strike Force One arrived, homing in on Honani.

"Archmage Karel? What's going on?" asked a very surprised Evsen.

"We need your help getting these abducted women back to Zoran's infirmary. They were morphed into dragons and are so disoriented that the best thing for them is to Sleep them and transport them that way. Three dived off the cliff thinking they were dragons and could morph back into dragon form and fly away. Be quick about it, I don't know how soon other dragons will return," Karel answered.

Honani added, "We will undo the spells and bring the women here. This is Milena and she knows some spells and can guard them for you."

"Yes I can Magic Missile them if they return," Milena spoke up. "I don't think that I am really a dragon anymore, but maybe I am. It is all so confusing."

Thirty minutes later, Honani Shadow Walked Karel and Milena back to the infirmary in Zoran's fortress. They were the last to leave Voss. All told, they brought back forty-five women. Except for Milena, most of the women were causing all manner of troubles for the Archmages, however. Being in various degrees of pregnancy wasn't the problem.

Once roused from the Sleep spells, many of the rescued women shrieked, cursed, and tried to pummel their care givers. Some tried and tried to somehow change back into their dragon bodies. Some even tried to escape the infirmary. Hence, Zoran had to place guards near the doors to prevent them from slipping out.

At last, Archmage Nadia found a workable approach. "Dragons, please, we need to get your human forms all cleaned up and cared for. Once that is done and you get fed, why then we will get you back into your proper dragon forms. You don't want to be dirty or filthy in your dragon forms now do you?" While they grumbled and griped, forty-four women went along with the suggestions.

Jarka cleverly mixed a little sleeping potion into their food. Thus, once cleaned, clothed, and fed, the women fell asleep, all except Milena who continued to chat away, adding her confusion into the mix. Since she was at least being semi-rational and not trying to harm anyone, Nadia allowed her to stand guard over the sleeping women.

"Oh yes, I can do that. Now that I can see, it really isn't bedtime, is it? They must be very tired. I will cast my Magical Missile if anyone tries to harm them while they sleep," she rattled on.

An exhausted Nadia met with Zoran and Tomas moments later. "What has happened to them?" Zoran asked, though he already knew the answer. He was looking for confirmation.

Archmage Nadia explained, "It is the damnable Morph Others spell. You know as well as I do that if someone is Morphed without their consent, there is a good chance that they will thereafter believe that they are the morphed creature, even when the spell is undone. In this case, it was far worse, they were morphed into dragons. The coupe de gras was having them blinded before the morph occurred. Unable to see what they were turned into, they only have disembodied voices telling them. These women have been literally brainwashed into believing that they are dragons who have been tortured and harmed and raped by humans, then later rescued from we humans by dragons. Since the dragons were taking total care of them, they bonded heavily with their dragon care givers. In short, we have forty-four insane women."

She went on, "You should have seen them eat. Not one used any silverware, rather they bent over and ate like dogs. Presumably that is the way that the dragons eat in the wild, though I've not seen such."

"Well, they are rescued. I guess now the question is will they recover their sanity?" he asked.

Nadia answered, "Some of them have already born a baby dragon. They claim that their dragon care givers helped them regain human form only to be raped again and returned to their dragon form. Why? I've given this some thought while I was working with them. I believe that the dragons have discovered that if the women are morphed into dragons, then they can have their babies safely and then be re-impregnated. In short, they become reusable baby factories for the dragons! Hideous and with no end in sight!"

"Well, that explains why there were so few women abducted this time," Zoran put it all together. We've only lost four women from Adapazan, when I was expecting to lose dozens. Damn, reusable baby factories! What will the infernal reds and blacks think of next?"

"Let's hope that it all ends here," his daughter replied and left to get herself something to eat. Zoran headed off to discuss the findings with Honani and Karel.

He found them discussing everything with Evsen, Dusan, and the members of Strike Force One. "Well done all of you, and especially you Honani, Karel, Askook, Cheveyo, Awinita, Donoma. We've worked out what happened to the women." Zoran then gave a complete explanation to the group, though Karel already had surmised most of it, except the reusable baby factory concept. He growled even more when he realized Zoran was absolutely right about that detail.

"Evsen, for the time being, it may be way too dangerous for you to go back to Voss. The dragons will certainly be hunting for all of you now. Instead, I'd like Strike Force One to train up Strike Force Two — get them up to speed on the tactics that you have found successful. I suspect that we will need your services soon," Zoran suggested. Evsen agreed, but he felt a little uncomfortable teaching his older brother.

Later, Archmage Danika dropped by to report. "The last of the Brn folks are now underground and getting settled in their new quarters. That leaves only your fortress guards, staff, and the three Archmage towers still occupied. I'm a little worried about nighttime security. If the dragons continue to attack in the middle of the night, we will all be in bed. The many magic students will be as well, including our new arrivals."

"Yes, I have been considering just that. Way too risky. If I rely on guards, they can be easily handled by simple spells, leaving us at risk. Further, I can't have an Archmage on duty all night either. Here's what I'm thinking. At night, we move everyone below ground. In the mornings, we come back up topside. Of course, Jarka will claim that we must anticipate that the dragons could be lying concealed in any room waiting for us to surface."

"Precisely my thinking. I've worked out a spell modification today and bounced it off my fellow Archmages." Danika explained her idea, "We can put up a Modified Force Wall over every entrance point of the towers and fortress. I've tied an In Case Of spell to the walls. If the wall is breached or the new spell is dispelled, a loud Alarm spell detonates, alerting us to the breech. That way we could feel pretty confident that the rooms are safe."

Zoran replied, "Let's get that widely implemented, Danika. Well done indeed. There is also the possibility that the dragons could Shadow Walk and arrive inside as well, bypassing normal security. I will have to work on that one a bit, but I think I can find a way to be alerted if that should happen. Let's get everyone drilled on your spell modification and get everyone settled in below. I am leery of staying above ground much longer at night."

Danika added, "One other thing, Baron Jan is really going to need Archmage help enlarging his underground living quarters. There are far more people in the capital city and immediate surroundings than here in Brn. May I take a number of Archmages over there tomorrow and lend him some help?"

"Absolutely. Then, we have all of the outlying towns and villages. I really am worried about how many more innocent lives are going to be lost before we get this dragon mess under control," Zoran admitted.

Danika smiled, "You really do care about the average person, don't you? I admire that. Zdenka is lucky to have found you." She smiled and left.

Since the rescued women were sleeping, they decided not to take them underground this evening. Instead, Archmage Verushka assigned all the Archmages two hour night watch shifts. Always, they would be pairs and always one had a Rod of Dragon Slaying with them. Fortunately, nothing happened during the night.

The next day, the women's pregnancies had to be handled. This was made all the more difficult because they still considered that they were dragons who were now prisoners of the humans. Worse, their future babies were being murdered and they reacted as one might have anticipated. Finally, the Archmages and Jarka had no choice but to cast Immobility on the women before they terminated the dragon fetuses in them.

Milena Dezda began to recover from her induced confusion, especially after she experienced the Roman Candle Effect when the dragon that she was carrying was aborted. "Dragons don't do that do they? I must not really be a dragon, right?" she said timidly.

"Of course not, Milena. Say, how would you like to continue your magic education here with us?"

"Really? Me? Learn more magic? Well sure that would be great! I do know quite a few spells that the old mage taught me. I'd really like to be able to fly. Is that possible?" she began chatting about magic and soon forgot all about the nightmare confusion she'd endured.

What to do about the other forty-five women was the real problem. Bluntly, they were insane, believing utterly that they were dragons, not humans. "Wish there was a Cure Insanity spell," Zdenka exclaimed exasperated and commented more than once that day.

She did have use of a Forget spell, but that only impacted what had happened within the last hour or so. Some of these women had been in dragon form for nearly a half of a year. They again had the women sleep in the infirmary a second night. Since the women were still basically mad, they dare not risk bringing them into the underground safe house. Once they were sleeping again, thanks to several Sleep spells, the Archmages conferred.

"I don't see any improvement happening anytime soon," Nadia said sadly. "They've really been brainwashed by their terrible treatment."

"I agree. I just don't see that we have any alternative but to use the Mind Wipe on them to wipe their minds of all memories from the last six months or so," Zdenka said with a heavy heart. She hated to do this to anyone, permanently destroying their memories. For the women, somehow half a year would have suddenly gone by and they'd have no recollections of any of it. Well, if the horrors that they suffered were gone, that might be a benefit, she thought. Still, wiping someone's mind was a very last resort.

Even so, Zdenka waited another day, hoping for some improvement in the women's insanity. Unfortunately, there was none and she begrudgingly gave the orders for the many Mind Wipes. All the Archmages partook in the process, most handling three of the women. Of course, the women were once more confused about how they got into Baron Zoran's infirmary at Brn. That they had somehow lost all recollections of the last six months of their lives only added to the confusion. However, Zdenka explained to them that they had been kidnaped by the dragons and rescued. "You have not been harmed and the barons of your respective planets will be coming soon to take you back to your families." Why?

The Archmages made a startling discovery. The Mind Wipe had also neutralized all of the magical energies that had built up in their bodies. Not one would be a viable candidate to learn magic, not like the other rescued women had been. True, a couple Zdenka thought could possibly become Adepts if they wished. Milena, on the other hand, was now stable and studying away with her other students in her tower. Within the next two days, all forty-five women were returned to their home worlds, ending this latest dragon breeding scheme.

Chapter 36 Repercussions

Werner, the black, and Dario, the red, were livid with anger. "All sixty of our new born babies had their throats slashed? Someone will pay for this and pay dearly!" Werner swore, his tail knocking a chunk of the roof of his cavern down. Several more bits of rock dropped unnoticed to the stone floor. "No more mercy killings! These humans deserved to be tortured, made to scream in pain, made to beg us to put them out of their misery!"

"Torture the vile, evil beasts!" Dario spat on the floor, resisting the urge to blast everything around him with his fiery breath. That would of course harm many of the blacks who were with him and that alone kept him from doing so. "Who could have done this heinous deed? It has to be Zoran's gang. They were the only ones on Voss. Death is entirely too good for them! Torture them for days! Make them pay and pay and pay!" he shrieked loudly.

A half hour of ranting passed before they calmed down into mere seething pots of hostilities. "Okay, Dario, we have to be cool about this. We cannot get all of the dragons together and attack Zoran directly because of this. They will be asking too many questions which neither you nor I wish to answer right now. After all, we were not supposed to be continuing our breeding program."

"Let's get the breeding program going once we eliminate all of the humans who threaten us. We'll make the humans our personal slaves and breeding women," Dario suggested.

"Yes, I like that. Put the men to work in all the mines and breed the women until our numbers are in the thousands! Good thinking, Dario, good thinking," Werner replied with wry smile. "So any more reports of the barons sending out their Archmages and mages and Duska to protect all the smaller towns and villages?"

"Er, not yet. The browns haven't yet reported in on their observations. Rehor and Adapazan apparently have not done that yet. Perhaps they need more convincing?" Dario said snidely.

A wicked grin formed on Werner's huge muzzle. "Yes, we should give them some more encouragement. Send out the word: tonight let us repeat our initial attack. Take out three more of the smaller towns on the sixteen worlds."

"Torture some? Can we? Can we?" Dario asked and then begged.

"Yes, let's have our blacks and reds each snatch one and bring them to our nursery on Voss. We'll torture them there, right where our own babies were executed. Once we finish our torture sessions, we'll dump what's left of them on Brn as a personal message to Zoran," Werner declared emphatically.

"Excellent. Pull their arms and legs off and drop all the appendages onto Brn too. A rain of human body parts! That ought to shock them and throw fear into their minds!" Dario declared with passion in his deep voice.

"Say, Dario, you have a good point. Drop their body parts onto Brn, arms, legs, heads, whatever. That should shock them to their very cores! Great idea, but we must make the captives suffer horribly first, before we let them die. It is the least that we can do for our sixty babies who did not have the slightest chance against the blades of the humans!" Werner agreed.

"Hey, even better idea: let's leave some alive to tell old Zoran just how bad it was," Dario laughed wickedly.

Werner roared, "Sometimes, old friend, I think you are meaner than I am." He meant it as a compliment!

"Oh my god! Zoran, come quick!" Archmage Nadia had just begun her daily survey of the tower, fortress, and Brn. Until this morning, all was quiet and a bit eerie, Brn lay completely deserted; its inhabitants safely below ground. On the snow packed main street of Brn that led to the main gates of the fortress was a ghastly sight, more than one stomach wrenched that morning.

Seldom had Zoran flinched, but he did when his eyes gazed out onto the street from atop the fortress walls for the first time that morning. His eyes caught limbs, human arms and legs, scattered about, hundreds of them. Then, he saw what remained of the victims, mutilated torsos, many headless, many with their chest cavities sliced open. There was almost no blood to be seen, which told him that these poor souls had not been killed here. "Body drop!" the vitriolic voice of Archmage Karel came from behind him. He turned to see the Archmage standing there, fists clenched, anger seethed through the man.

"Right. Lack of blood. Killed elsewhere and left here as a message for me," Zoran concluded. "Look, there's a sort of blanket covered mound. I dread seeing what else might be there."

Jarka led the way, cursing repeatedly to herself as she gingerly stepped around the remains, some no larger than the fingers of the victims. "Some are from the desert worlds. Check skin colors." she spoke a little louder, making her slow way to the blanket mound. As always, her first thoughts were to search for survivors, though she didn't expect to find any among this horrific scene.

As Zoran caught up to her, he said, "Dragons were careful and didn't get within my Alarm activation spells. Damn them! They've stooped to a new low!"

Jarka carefully lifted a corner of the blanket expecting more gore. "Oh dear god!" she gushed, her free hand coming up to her mouth and covering it. Zoran looked over her shoulder and flinched.

"Over here! Survivors," he called out. Mystical Doors appeared beside him. This was faster than trying to step over all the body parts littering the snow-covered street. He saw what remained of ten men, women, and children. Six were comatose, in deep shock, four had already died and what was left of their bodies were now frozen. Zoran picked up the two little girls and Shadow Walked them into the infirmary. Jarka followed, carrying what was left of a young woman. He didn't see who brought the three men, however, he was too busy covering them up and casting Warm spells to counter the girls' hypothermia.

His two physicians came rushing in. Jarka had summoned them from the subterranean city below. "Oh damn! What happened to them?" one asked as he pushed Zoran aside and began examining the first girl who was barely ten.

"Dragons got them. Looks like they are into torturing them now," Zoran said extremely softly. He too was going into shock over these sights. He sat down and put his head between his knees for a minute.

Jarka and the two physicians poured several healing potions down the six victims, hoping to stabilize them at least. One man came to and screamed before he realized that he was safe inside a warm room and there were no dragons present. His arms and legs had been torn from his body, but the dragons who had done it had crudely healed him with their healing droughts, just enough to keep him alive.

His name was Tomas and accompanied by continuous sobbing, he told them what had happened to his village. The dragons had taken him and others away to some cave filled with dead baby dragons. There, he was made to watch the hideous, inhuman torture of over fifty men, women, and children. At last, they tortured him until he begged them to end his misery. Instead, they crudely healed him and told him to tell what he'd seen to Zoran. "Please," Tomas sobbed, "I can't live like this. Please put me out of my misery. If you have any feelings left, please, please kill me, please, I beg you."

"Me too, please," the voice of another man who had only one arm and no legs joined Tomas. He'd awakened and begged as well. He did say that his name was Miklos. The other man had only one leg left and no arms. Josef also wanted to die, but did as the dragons had ordered. He told Zoran what he'd witnessed.

"Let us see what we can do for you men first. If we cannot help you recover from this, then I give you my word that I will do as you ask," Zoran finally gave his consent. After all, these men could not live as mutilated as they were.

The screams of the eighteen year old woman now demanded their attention. She had awakened from her nightmare only to find herself still in it. Her eyes had been torn out after she'd passed out witnessing the brutality of the dragons on the other victims. Both her legs were missing below her knees as well. After casting Calm spells on her four times, she finally relaxed and told them her name, Rickena. She described what she'd seen before they sliced off her legs and then forced her to drink something that kept her alive. Then, they'd removed her eyes. She required three more Calm spells while she was describing what had happened to her.

"We're going to get you four a bath and cleaned up first. Then, we'll tend to your wounds if they still need attention. Once that's done, let's get some hot food inside you," Zoran rather ordered more than suggested. While they were being bathed, the two children roused at last, finally coming out of their hypothermia. Both had been very near death themselves. Another hour and they would not have made it.

The ten year old girl was Dona Lida, and the dragons had removed her legs at her knees and arms at her elbows, leaving her four stumps. The eleven year old girl was Viera. The dragons had literally pulled her arms from their sockets and then poured her full of their ill tasting droughts, which, according to Viera, somehow stopped the massive bleeding but not the pain. "Those dragons are really mean, aren't they?" she said when she finished telling them what had happened.

"Yes, Viera, they surely are," Zdenka agreed. "Come on. Let's get you pretty girls all cleaned up, shall we?"

"But I can't do anything anymore," Dona Lida protested.

"Me either," Viera added.

"Oh, we will just have to see what we can do for you ladies," Zdenka countered.

Two hours later, the six were cleaned, fed, and given a sleeping potion. The Archmages met together to discuss what could be done for the six survivors. Archmage Karel said, "One thing is for sure, I aim to make those dragons pay for what they've done!"

"Yes, but what can we do for these six?" Zdenka tried to get him back on the real issue facing them.

"Well, only Viera has any chance at all of living some kind of life. At least she has her legs," Danika pointed out. "The others, poor Dona Lida — well I don't see how she can, or the others either. Perhaps, we should allow them to die."

"Life is precious. We have to save them if possible. I have been thinking about it while you all were cleaning them up. What if we use Morph Others on them? You know, Morph them into what they looked like before the attack?"

"Clever, dear," Zdenka spoke up. "There are only two problems with that — well maybe not problems exactly. Obviously, the spells could be dispelled. We could promise them that if that ever happened, to let us know and we'd recast the spell for them. However, their morphed forms will never seem to age. They could really be fifty years old and yet still look as they were before the dragons tortured them."

"That will be really a problem for the children," Zoran pointed out.

"We should give them that choice, dad," Tomas pointed out. He'd come to help clean up the hideous mess and was sitting in on the discussion, hoping and praying that he never had to deal with this up in Sholov Province. "They might prefer to just die."

After some discussion, they decided to follow this route. "Make your decision after we cast the spell on you, Miklos, Tomas, and Josef. At least see how it could be for you," Archmage Zdenka suggested. She'd just explained to the six the only thing that they could honestly do for the survivors. The morose men grumbled but allowed the Archmages to cast their Morph Others spells on them. All three men now appeared whole again, just as they had looked a week ago.

However, Tomas spoke for them. "This is all well and good, but we've lost our wives, our children, and our homes, and Josef here, his business. We have nothing more to live for now. Nothing. We are not fighters. We just want to join our lost loved ones, please."

Still, Zoran didn't want to kill them. "Why don't you men take a few days to get used to everything? I can offer you employment with my staff here in Brn. You are all fit and can start life anew here in Brn." He ought to have seen it in their eyes, but perhaps it was because he didn't want to see it. Grumbling, the three agreed, and Zoran took them on a tour of the fortress grounds. He left them in the huge dining hall to eat their breakfast and returned to see how the women were fairing.

Rickena was eighteen and cheered when her eyesight returned. She had been a good quilt maker prior to the attack and was extremely pleased with the "cure." She didn't have to be asked twice to stay here in Brn and make her quilts, especially when Zdenka offered to give her a fully supplied shop. "After this dragon war is over, I'll see that you get a fine shop. In the meantime, we've got temporary quarters below ground where you will be safe and can make quilts there. Many people will need them since it's rather chilly down there." She was pleased with the offer, safety was now extremely important to her.

Meanwhile, Archmage Danika and Eliska had a long show and tell talk with the two girls. "See, these are our true forms, exactly like you, Viera. I know, Dona Lida, you haven't got all your legs now, but you do have more arms than we do — that's something."

"You think that we could really learn magic spells and change ourselves like you two do?" asked Dona Lida, eagerly.

"Really?" added Viera.

"If you study really hard and practice a whole lot, I think you both just might," Archmage Danika replied. The girls giggled and promised to do so. When Zoran returned, he found that Danika had taken on Viera as her first magic student, while Eliska had just accepted Dona Lida as her first student. Both Archmages whisked their new students off to Zdenka's tower to get them started.

Zdenka could not help herself. She eavesdropped in on the two as they began the girls' training. "Now one thing that our teacher, Archmage Zdenka taught us is that the Morph spell can easily be undone by other magic. So she made us learn to do many things by ourselves. We will Morph you both back to your old bodies after your lessons are over each day. However, we insist that you try to do your studies as you are now, using your feet, Viera, and your short arms, Dona Lida. We'll help you with the harder things, but if some evil mage undoes your morph spell and your real body returns to the way that they are, you have to be able to still function and recast your spells."

"I get it. We have to be independent. Okay, I'll try," Dona Lida replied. "This is going to be so much fun, Viera. We are going to become real mages!" Her childish enthusiasm had returned. Zdenka smiled and went about her own teaching duties.

Later that day, some of the men who were picking up the mess in the street for burial found the bodies of the three men. Instead of eating breakfast, they'd made their way to the walls and jumped to their deaths. Zoran sighed when he was informed, the men had lost just too much for them to recover he realized at last.

Archmage Karel visited Honani. "I want to go dragon hunting. Can you help me find some of their lairs, where at most one or two live? I am going to butcher them as they are butchering our people. You just find me their dens and get me there, I will do the rest. You don't need to risk your life." Honani smiled and agreed.

Late that night, Karel limped back into his laboratory and guzzled another two healing potions. He was a wiser man now. Honani had returned after supper with the location of a red's lair. He'd located this one months before but had verified that the dragon was there resting. Karel was pleased and within minutes, he stepped Karel out into the dragon's lair. "I had a false sense of security," Karel muttered to the walls of his lab. True, he had slain the beast and did what he'd set out to do — slaughter the beast, leaving parts of its body scattered around its lair in a bloody mess. However, the dragon was clever. Seeing the rod in the Archmage's hands, it chose to attack him with its claws and vicious bite instead. While Karel was protected for a time, he had the fight of his life and very nearly lost it. Bruised and wounded, he'd guzzled his two healing potions on the spot and then proceeded to cut body parts off of the slain red. He also confiscated the dragon's valuables, sharing a portion with Honani.

"There has to be a better way of slaying these foul beasts!" he growled to the walls. He pulled down all of his many spell books and began researching various ways to cause a painful death. His wife, Chika, found him in the morning asleep over his books.

"What happened to you? Your clothes are a mess and is that dried blood on them? Are you all right? I was worried last night. You didn't come down to bed," Chika asked, growing concerned. Her annoyance had vanished, replaced by fear.

"I had a dragon to slay, dear. I've realized that we need more than my rods if we are going to win this war. Can you bring me some breakfast? I have much research to do. I am getting an idea."

"Okay, just do be careful. Let me know when you are going off like that!" she chided him a little and left.

"I will. Say, find Rafael the blacksmith, you know, Danika's husband. Tell him I need to see him at once," he asked, returning to his books. He growled at himself for having fallen asleep. How much time had he lost?

Later, Rafael knocked and entered. "Son, I need another golden rod made as soon as possible. Take what gold you need from that pile. Same dimensions as the other ones you've made, but this one is going to be quite different. The war is escalating and we need better weapons. Go on, don't just stand there."

"I am not allowed to be at my shop without someone watching over me as look out. Dragons could attack us at any time. I think that was the baron's orders," Rafael pointed out.

"Okay, okay, I'll watch over you. Now let's get going. I need that new rod today!"

While he had the rod finished in two days' time, the enchantment became problematical. In short, he was trying to tie two very powerful spells together in tandem. This consumed enormous magical energies, and this new rod would only hold enough for one casting before recharging. Hence, he had to work on modifications. He added a large diamond to the gold core, wrapping it securely to the rod. This worked better. The enchantment charges were split between the gemstone and the gold core, enabling the user to cast this tandem spell twice before recharging. Well, this was better than nothing, but would it work? If so, then he could perhaps work on a much large scale model, one that would hold numerous charges.

Finally, on the last day of January, he paid Honani to take him to another dragon lair for testing. This time, he let Chika know that he was off to test his new rod. She didn't realize and he didn't specify that he was going after another dragon! Honani brought him to a black's lair high in the mountains of Rehor this time. As before, after stepping Archmage Karel out of the Shadows onto the stone floor, Honani slipped back out of harm's way and watched him.

"Well, well, well, who do I have marching into my lair?" the black dragon raised its head to glare at Archmage Karel who held both his old rod and the new experimental rod in his hands.

"I've come to test my new Rod of Dragon Bursting on you. I hope you don't mind. This will take only a second of your time. Of course, if it works, that will be your last second of life — an excruciatingly painful one though, much like the pain and suffering that you dragons did to our people. Nice touch depositing their many bits on our main street, but it made lots of us angry, though."

"After I rip your puny arms and legs off of you, I think that I will pour my drought down your throat and keep you alive for a while longer," the black retorted.

"I hardly think that's going to happen. Well, test time. Dragon Burst." Karel spoke the simple command word of the rod. Of course, he'd have to change that to avoid accidental discharge of the rod. A huge flash of magical energies momentarily illuminated the cavern. The energies streaked into the dragon's belly, roughly in the center of its huge body. Then the tandem spell detonated. The black dragon let out a hideous cry of intense, unimaginable pain. The air rushing out of its mouth suddenly changed to tiny particles of dust! Horror blazed from its eyes, then they glazed over, death had come to this black. As Karel watched, the dragon completely dried out, almost mummified! He'd turned all of the water in the dragon's body into dust particles, though it took several seconds to get to the water near its hide and face.

Karel was covered in dust, but he brushed himself off as a startled Honani reappeared. "Good god! What have you done to that dragon? That was incredible! What a weapon you have invented, Archmage Karel Ambrose!"

"Well, yes, worked well. Only get two shots though — takes way too much magical energies per detonation. Have to work on that some. Come — let's confiscate its loot, shall we?" Karel said nonchalantly.

Back in Brn, Honani began telling everyone about this new super weapon and within minutes of their arrival, Karel found himself once again at the center of everyone's full attention. Honani Mind Linked everyone to himself and replayed his memories of what he'd just witnessed. Needless to say, everyone began talking about this new invention at the same time, pleasing the Archmage. The other Archmages demanded to know the spells.

"Well, I've put two spells in tandem. First, the Rod of Dragon Bursting executes a Teleport spell, placing the piggyback spell in roughly the center of the dragon. That is all the wielder must do, focus on the center of the dragon. Then the tandem spell detonates, rapidly turning all the water in the dragon's body into fine particles of dust. Although this process is swift, it is incredibly painful to the beast. Of course, it takes an Archmage to wield this new rod, because we have to smash down their resistance to magic, as always. Very effective. Of course, it uses up huge amounts of magical energy with each use and right now, I can only get two charges at most in the rod. I will work on that. We need lots more than two charges if this is going to become highly effective in the field." Karel enjoyed all this attention and went on about its design.

Inwardly, Zoran was ambivalent. He desperately wanted to find a way to end the hostility between the races without genocide on either side. Yet, with the viciousness of the recent dragon attacks, he needed more effective ways to protect his people. A bit reluctantly, he gave Karel approval to improve its design.

Werner, the black, again waited several days to see what the reaction to their latest attack would be. He hoped that this would be enough to force the barons to send out their mages and Archmages and perhaps even Duskas to the outlying towns and villages, where the dragons could pick them off one by one. After a number of days, he saw that this still was not happening. Worse, word came to him that a red had been slaughtered, its body butchered into many pieces. He fumed, but Dario was even angrier. While they planned their next operation, one of his blacks failed to report for duty. He sent a messenger to fetch the black and received word back of the black's hideous death. Werner and Dario both visited the lair.

"My god, Werner! You were right! Zoran has indeed got a new super-weapon to use against us! Look what happened here! There's nothing left of him but dust and hide! How can this be?" Dario exclaimed, becoming frightened. The black looked like some monstrous hollow mummy that had been dead for millennia!

Even Werner was shaken by the sight, but he did summon all of the other dragon leaders to examine the deceased black, murdered hideously in its own lair. This put a great fear into all of the other leaders, who now felt absolutely certain that Werner was right. Zoran had indeed brought some monstrous new super-weapon back from Voss. The question now was what would they do about it?

"Okay, enough of this toying around with the humans. Tonight, we go after some of their larger towns. Pick ones with at least ten to twenty thousand inhabitants. As always, leave a survivor or two to spread fear in their leader's minds," Werner ordered.

Because of the vastly larger sizes of the targets, Werner had the groups of thirty-three dragons join together into one large band. Nearly a hundred dragons of all colors were to sweep down on the sleeping large town and wipe the humans out. Good plan.

Unfortunately, Werner soon began receiving most troublesome reports. While the dragons were being successful at torching many homes and using their brute strength to smash stone buildings, they could find no humans there. "The town has no humans in it," the relay dragon for the Adapazan dragon horde reported to Werner.

"What? Where did they go? This cannot be. What new devilry is this? I shall see for myself!" Werner Shadow Walked to Adapazan and surveyed the burning large town, not fifty miles from Castle Dorumova, the heart of Adapazan. "Search the homes. They must all be hiding," he ordered and watched the hundred dragons do just that. The dragons had to settle for merely burning down the town of Cerven. Now Werner had even more to ponder. What had happened to all the humans? Where were they?

He sent out spies to check on many towns and villages. Most of the larger cities and towns were nearly devoid of people, while all of the smaller ones still were quite populated. At first, Werner, the black, suspected that the barons had evacuated the larger cities, moving the populations either into outlying villages or perhaps within their fortresses and strongholds. To him, this seemed a reasonable explanation. However, still the barons refused to send out their forces to protect their smaller villages from the dragons. He knew that stronger measures were needed and soon.

Chapter 37 Ancient History

During January, Brother Miroslav and High Priestess Jarmila Zar spent every waking hour pouring over the twenty newly discovered journals of Bandar Zar. They were safe inside the extra-dimensional room in Zoran's Circle of Ascension chamber. Here they stored all of their precious volumes, some of which detailed the construction of these Circles. The room held tables, desks, and chairs, in addition to the bookshelves. The room was well lit and very conducive to their studies.

Both soon became fascinated with the writings, taking notes as they followed the sometimes meandering journal entries of old Bandar Zar. Magic seemed in wide spread use on Voss, much as it was here in the Federation of the Sixteen Planets. However, Bandar was something of a rogue. He apparently was a skilled Mage, but was kicked out of several magic schools and never made the official Archmage status.

> The idiot Archmages didn't take kindly to my constant hounding them about how a certain spell worked or why it should behave the way it did. I raised a big stink when I demanded of Archmage Jakob where precisely the useful spell Clean actually **put** the dirt. Doesn't a single magic user want to know where his debris has gone? Idiots, all of them. There is far more to magic than these supposed Archmages even know. Ah well. I'm conducting some experiments to find out where it does go. Perhaps somewhere there is now an enormous pile of dirt. Imagine some folks on another world complaining, "Oh no! Here comes another one of those dirt rains again! I do wish it would stop raining dirt down on us."

A bit later, they learned a bit about how the Democracy of the Sixteen worked. Evidently, Bandar thought even less of the political rulers, they concluded.

> Got into a long discussion with Valentýn last night over our illustrious Democracy. Perhaps, he is right, when it was founded some three hundred years ago, the concept worked. Each person has one vote; all votes are equal. Rule by majority votes. Valentýn claims it would work if the voters were informed. I pointed out how easy it is for the politicians to lie to the populace, but I ceded the point to him. Perhaps it had once been a workable form of government. Not so today. Far from it. If you want to know the hotbed of graft and corruption, look no further than your local politician or senator — con artists, all of them. It is a well-known fact that money in the hands of the right senator or politician will get you what you desire.
>
> Granted, there are exceptions. Senator Valentýn is one. There is not a corrupt bone in his body. I ought to know. Still, the senators have passed so darn many laws during the last several hundred years that an entire school of magic is needed to sort out what is and what is not legal in any situation! Honestly, we average folk have no idea whether anything that we do is legal or illegal! I point out the recent case of Archmage Milos and his request to

build a tower on his own property. It took the Legal Mages nearly five months to determine that he could build it if it were located five feet further west than he intended and only had four floors. Honestly, what has our Democracy come to? A seething, indecipherable mass of conflicting laws, added to each term by our illustrious senators.

Valentýn ceded the President point to me. Our latest illustrious President Hamil from Anwyn has won with a landslide of popular support. Not in centuries has there been such a speaker who could say all the perfect words that his audience most wanted to hear. I claim he is using a simple spell, but as yet, I can't prove it. He won the last election by promising each special interest group just what they most desired. Of course less taxes for the poor, yearly handouts to the poor under the banner of Welfare for the People, and "tax the rich" won him millions of votes. Who wouldn't want less taxes and more handouts? But what has he done since he's been in office? Nada. Yet, each week he addresses the populace with yet another of his charming, perfect speeches. Worse, the fools continue to buy into it! Fools. He is bringing doom down onto them all!

"I don't think he liked the way that Voss was being run," Jarmila concluded. Miroslav agreed. A lot of the first journal contained similar entries, some even more scathing than these. Finally, they came to something far more important.

The dragon scene is coming unraveled. For years now, the President and senators have been slowly giving in to the demands of the dragons. Valentýn has shown me their latest demands. "The Democracy is to hand over one half of its yearly revenue to the dragons as rightful and just payment for their many services to the Democracy." Valentýn and I debated long into the night and went through three pitchers of ale as well. Perhaps that explains why we both have hangovers today. However, Valentýn did ask me a key question — one that I had not considered before and one that ought to be answered. Just where did the dragons come from and how did they get here to Voss? He rightly pointed out that until fifty years ago, there were no dragons on Voss. Yet, today, everyone accepts the fact that they are here. Curious that no one has asked that question. I promised him that I would find out.

"Now we are getting somewhere," Miroslav pointed out. "I hope he found out and wrote it in his journals somewhere. That might be useful to know."

A little later, Jarmila chuckled. "Hey listen to this entry, dear."

Got into a big argument today with Archmage Nadezda. I asked her just where do we go when we Teleport. I had to explain though. "Look, we are at Point A and we cast our Teleport spell. We arrive at Point B. Where are we while we are en route to Point B?" She brushed me off and told me not to bother her with such inane questions. Well, we have to at least travel through space of some kind or other. I should look into this myself, since no one seems to either know or care.

A few days later, Jarmila found another interesting passage. "Listen to this, dear. I think that we are getting closer."

> Eavesdropping can sometimes prove fruitful. While in the Mages Guild, I overheard a conversation. Apparently, the late Archmage Kazimir Kornel was the man responsible for bringing the first dragons to Voss! His diaries were recently sold at auction and purchased by Archmage Nadezda. She refuses to see me or let me read the diaries, however. Must speak to Valentýn about it tonight. He has connections.

"So what happened after that?" Miroslav asked.

"Don't know yet. Hang on. There is another entry."

> Got the copy today. Spells are duplicating it now. Must return it before dawn.

"I hope he tells us what it said. It sounds like he got the diaries," she added. "Then, he is off on another discussion of the troubling times they were in. I wish he'd stay on topic."

Miroslav chuckled, "Dear, these are merely his field notes, more like a daily diary." Both laughed. It was not until Volume B that Bandar wrote more about the Archmage Kazimir and his diaries. Miroslav found the key entries and read them for his wife.

> Archmage Kazimir was an experimenter and created his laboratory in the shape of a huge pyramid. He claimed that it focused the Energy of the Universe into whoever was inside. I doubt that. Nevertheless, he did invent a device that allowed him to scan the universe of Shadows for other inhabited planets. He named this the Shadows. His diaries say that he found eight such worlds. Later, his viewer allowed him to become the first person to ever see a dragon — his claim, not mine. So what did he do next? How did the dragons get here? Too drunk to continue tonight.

"See dear, too much ale is not good for you," Jarmila teased him. Both grinned. "What's he say next?"

"Unfortunately, it is about the continued deteriorating relations with the dragons. Apparently, their President is giving away more and more concessions to the dragons and the people are protesting. However, the President's perfect speeches continue to win back their support, even though he continues to do the opposite of what he is saying he'll do. Bandar's calling them fools once again and idiots too," he replied.

Later on, he exclaimed, "Hey, listen to this."

> Deciphered Kazimir's cryptic notes. His magical invention at the pyramid allowed him to search across the vast space of the universe in search of habitable planets. He cleverly devised a star-sun blocker and a giant planet blocker — not sure what he means by that last bit yet. He found eight other worlds. He did what I would have done — invent a way to take a closer look at them. Ah, so it was Kazimir who made the first contact with the dragons. He stated that each of these new worlds that he found contained a different color of dragon. Question: how did he manage to communicate with them and how did he manage to bring them to Voss? Will have to wait. Too tired

this early morning.

"Wow, he did bring the dragons to Voss and then Zoran brought them to our worlds. How ironic," Jarmila noted. "What's he say next?"

"More of the political stuff. Another argument-discussion with Valentýn. Have to read more, dear." An hour later, he came across more relevant notes. "Say, here's a bit more."

> Kazimir named them after the color of the dragons there. The Gold Planet, the Black Planet. Well, I would have picked better names. How did he communicate with them? Come on, Kazimir, out with it.

"That's all that's in this entry," Miroslav said disappointedly.

Shortly, Jarmila found the continuation of that thread of discussion. "Here we go, dear."

> So old Kazimir wasn't so smart after all. A Gold Dragon named Tereza sensed him watching her via his magical device. It was her curiosity that got it all started. Kazimir says that she magically came to him. I wonder how she did that? Ah, Kazimir states that Tereza knew many magical spells and Morphed into a human form so that she could speak with him. Interesting, but how did she travel from her world to Voss? He ought to have logged that piece of critical data. Wish he had also noted what she said to him. Maybe it's later in his notes. That's something that I would have logged — first contact and all that. Probably he felt badly that it was she who came to him and not the other way around. Got to remember to tell Valentýn about this tonight.

"Next part is washed out. I think Bandar spilled ale on his journal page. Here, he continues the next night," she continued, fascinated with the writing.

> Kazimir's notes indicate that she taught him the magic on how to move through space. According to him, she called it Shadow Walking. Fascinating. Come on, Kazimir, how is this Shadow Walking done? Well, I'll be, Tereza seduced the old mage! Ha. So that's how she got him to agree to allow some of her friends to come to Voss originally! Interesting. Wait til Valentýn hears about this twist!

The next page continued the same thread, but was a night later.

> Got drunk with Valentýn. He pointed out many salient facts that we need answered. Promised him I'd continue with this, as if he had to ask. Today's translations yielded a bit more information. The golds came and Morphed into human shapes per Kazimir's request. He didn't want to shock people. Duh. Well, that was smart, considering how huge a dragon is! No brainer, Kazimir. The old lecher traded magic spells for her affections! Sex will do it every time! Ten more pages of drivel, come on, old man, out with the key data. Have to wait. Too tired to translate more of his love-sick notes tonight.

Unfortunately, Bandar's subsequent pages dealt with several nasty events on Voss. Dragons and humans were definitely having serious problems getting along with each other. It wasn't until the next day that the two finally found more on this thread.

> Kazimir documented the fact that other colored dragons began appearing on

Voss about a month after Tereza arrived. According to the old mage, it was Tereza who encouraged interspecies breeding, but only with those highly knowledgeable in magic. Ah ha! The dragons were just using you, old fool!

The next entry continued on from this point.

Finally, Kazimir! He reports that eventually Tereza taught him to Shadow Walk. Come on, where are your notes on how it is done? If you didn't write that down, Kazimir, I swear I will dig up your bones and resurrect you and force you to divulge that!

"Gee, Bandar really wanted to know how Shadow Walking is done, didn't he?" Jarmila noted. "I wonder if it was Bandar who taught everyone else how to do it? These journals are priceless!"

"Eureka. Here it is, dear. Bandar is describing how Shadow Walking is done. Say, it is just like we do it. Someone who can do it has to take you into the Shadows and show you around. Kazimir says that he got ill at first, nausea, just like we do. After that first trip, he could then do it himself. Interesting. Whoa, listen to this!" Miroslav exclaimed.

So it is *not* something that one can *read* about its casting and then learn to do it. One has to be *taught it* by another who can Shadow Walk. Damn! I **have** to learn how to do it. I wonder how I can coerce a dragon into teaching me? Where there is desire, there is always a way, heh, heh. I have an idea just how I can do it. Kazimir is long dead, but dragons live ten times longer that we do. I've got to find this Tereza dragon.

"Did he find her?" Jarmila asked.

"Don't know yet. Several more entries about his fruitless searches for her. Let's see. Ah, here we go."

Found Tereza today. I can see why Kazimir fell for her. Her human shape is most appealing. Going to meet with her tomorrow.

The next entry is a bit smudged.

Met Tereza officially. I have gotten what I wanted. Note: dragons love magic and spells. I agreed to teach her several mid-level spells in return for a Shadow Walk session. She claims that I will only need one such session. We'll see.

"He continues the next day."

Beyond my wildest dreams! I am changed now, **physically**. I can tell, something is very different within me. This is the coolest thing ever! Going to teach Valentýn to do it tonight. My reactions are significantly increased. Not sure what else is altered. More later. Got to meet Valentýn at the pub.

"There is a substantial gap in terms of days before the next entry, dear," Miroslav explained.

Valentýn and I have been Shadow Walking to the eight dragon planets. Coolest thing ever! Tereza suggested that we should learn how to do it before we reach adulthood or full growth. He and I barely qualified, since we are now twenty-one. Valentýn has been codifying the physical changes that we've undergone. Our reaction time is half of what it was before. He's also discovered that we are alerted to trouble coming our way before we are even aware of it. Could be a very useful aspect.

Valentýn has a good friend in the Republic State of Valtr. We're going to see her tomorrow and induct her into Shadow Walking too. She's his betrothed, Zelenka Pavel. She's medically trained, so I am hoping that she can shed more light about our physical changes. Will they be permanent or just a temporary thing?

"His next entry is four days later. I guess that he had to do some traveling or he was too occupied to keep his journal up," Miroslav suggested.

Zelenka took to Shadow Walking rather well. She's been dissecting old Kazimir's body looking for any changes. She's found a gland in the base of his brain that is many times larger than normal. While one case doesn't prove anything, our going theory is that this gland is somehow enlarged when we learned to Shadow Walk. I found it kind of gory and a bit unnerving digging up his grave. Tomorrow, I am going to introduce my fiancé to Shadow Walking too.

Ari loved it! I asked her to marry me. Yahoo! She agreed as long as she is called Ari Zar and not Rayna Ryba Zar. She hates her given name. Still haven't been able to get her to tell me why, but I think that kids must have teased her about being a fish when she was a little girl.

"Rats, the next entries are political again," he complained. "He and Valentýn believe their Democracy is going to collapse and that there will be a conflict between humans and dragons soon. Ah, they are trying to figure out what they can do to avoid it. Listen to this."

Valentýn and I believe that we are witnessing the fall of the Democracy of the Sixteen. We both want to abandon the sinking ship. He suggested that we see if we can find other planets that would support human life. If we can find some, he would like to Shadow Walk there and leave Voss before we get caught up in the great battle that he foresees coming. He's leaving the discovery of the planet up to me. Ha. And just how am I to do that? Well, I am going to see if I can find old Kazimir's pyramid. If so, can I activate it and search the universe as he once did? Worth trying. Besides, I am dying to see that magic invention of his.

"His next entry continues this thread. Listen to this!"

Found Kazimir's pyramid. Was under an Invisibility spell and an Antipathy spell that keeps everyone from getting too close to it. I found it by noticing that I kept avoiding going to the area in which it was located, even though I saw nothing there at first. He had a lot of second-rate traps set. Defused. Inside, found a mess, but the machine still works. Following Kazimir's directions, I located the eight dragon worlds. All are nasty, except the Gold Planet. Red Planet is fiery hot. I'd never survive there. White planet is snow covered and presumably way too cold for humans. Tomorrow I will begin our search.

"What did he find?" asked Jarmila. "Let me read a while." She took the volume from her husband, who grinned. This was fascinating reading for the two.

My patience was rewarded. Four days. Found a great looking planet. Valentýn likes it and has declared it will be New Adapazan. We're going there tomorrow to check it out more closely.

"The next entry expressed Bandar's thrill of discovery. Listen to this."

How do I put down in words what I felt as I set foot on a new world on which no human has ever set foot? It is indescribable! Exhilaration. Elation. Extreme pride and self-satisfaction. Forget it. I can't. The new world is very similar to our Republic State, only it is a whole world and not a small part of a larger world as it is here on Voss. Valentýn says that we now have the opportunity of a lifetime — to begin a whole new way of life. He thinks that we should colonize the planet. Valentýn always does think big.

The political climate here on Voss is deteriorating at a rapid rate, though I swear the average person is completely blind to what's going on and where it is leading.

Perhaps we had way too much to drink tonight — I dread my hangover in the morning, but we agreed to actually go through with the notion of colonizing the new world. Leave the planning to me, he says. You find more worlds. I've got other friends who might well be interested in bailing out of Voss before it sinks. I like that idea better. So tomorrow or perhaps the next day, I will see if I can find more worlds. My head is likely to be mush tomorrow.

"The next entry was extremely short."

It is mush! But the ale sure was good.

"Ah, politics again," Jarmila announced.

Well, our Democracy has sunk to a new low. Some dragons — eye witness accounts vary slightly — attacked a village in the Republic State of Rehor. Death toll is estimated to be two thousand dead. Our illustrious President has called for the dragon's representatives to explain their attack. The senators voted on a declaration of war against the dragons in retaliation, but they ended up in a tie vote. Nothing whatsoever is actually going to be done, save perhaps the imposition of some unenforceable sanctions against the dragons. Pathetic.

Valentýn and I had a lengthy conversation about this today. We've agreed that we need to abandon Voss and start over on some new worlds. He claims that we ought to find sixteen planets, each similar to the conditions within each of the Republics. He must have a whole lot of friends. Well, I agreed to see if I can find them.

Did find a water world tonight. Am hopeful I can find more, though it is mostly a blind search and it takes a lot of time. Thought about calling these new worlds New Adapazan and New Asami, but opted for just Adapazan and Asami. At least we can tell the planets apart this way.

"Looks like he scribbled some notes but continued writing a week later," Jarmila noted.

Tonight, met with Valentýn and fifteen other men. Apparently, each is from a different Republic State. All are fed up with the Democracy and are keenly interested in backing our search and colonization of these new worlds. Damn, these men have money! I am hopeful this will be a most successful venture.

We discussed how we would govern these new worlds. I suggested they were jumping the gun and we should settle them first. I was outvoted sixteen to one. The consensus was to abandon democracy altogether. Valentýn's suggestion of a benevolent monarch won the support of the others. I laughed. These sixteen men planned on becoming the benevolent monarchs of the sixteen new worlds, assuming I can find that many. Now they are planning how many others to bring along to settle and colonize these worlds. Money. The sums that they are throwing around make my head spin.

I then asked them if they were all going to learn to Shadow Walk. Valentýn pointed out that perhaps we should restrict such knowledge to the chosen rulers and their most trusted friends. I suggested that we should call those who can Shadow Walk Duskas, meaning exactly that — Shadow Walkers. For once, they agreed with me. Pavel suggested that they call themselves barons and their wives baronesses. Matous suggested that each baron rule his own planet, but Pavel added that the barons ought to meet at least twice a year to work together as a group and deal with issues concerning all of them. Weatherby suggested these be called High Council meetings with each baron getting one vote. I asked what happens if the votes are tied. I was promptly told to shut up and find the planets.

Valentýn suggested that I be put in charge of teaching others to Shadow Walk. Pavel suggested that some sort of official ceremony be used to help make this appear official and said that the ceremony was up to me to work out. Matous wanted some kind of bond between our ruling locations, but they decided to leave that up to me, since I was in charge of Shadow Walking, et cetera. I think that I am being dumped upon. I think that I need lots more ale at this point.

"Wow," exclaimed Miroslav, "you can see the formation of our Federation! These original sixteen men plus Bandar set the whole thing up! Incredible. Here's a bit more on it.

Ari and I decided that I will find the planets and find a way to hook them all together via the Shadows and such. She will become our High Priestess and deal with the initiation of others into becoming the Duskas. Ari is really getting into this whole idea. She says, "The worms are going to destroy us all, so we best get ourselves out of here." My gut tells me she and Valentýn may well be right about the worms. Heard about another village being attacked last night. It's getting a bit grim.

The two read more pages and finished the current volume and tore into the next one. For quite some time, the entries denoted more incidents with the dragons, the discovery of more suitable worlds, and Ari's invention of appropriate "ceremonies" to go along with the "Shadow Walking" skills. Ari decided to call the most important one the Ceremony of Ascension, because the person was ascending to new, undreamed of skills and abilities. After that, many pages were filled with Bandar's notes about the advance planning sessions, preparing the way for the mass exodus to the new worlds. During these same days, according to Bandar's journal entries, the worms' raids on small villages across the Republic States grew more and more frequent.

The later journals contained even more of the newly designated barons' plans for colonizing the new worlds. All of it was done in secrecy so that the dragons would not find out about the exodus of a large number of humans from Voss. Further, the new barons had High Priestess Ari Zar perform her Ceremony of Ascension on their wives and trusted kin. It would be these who Shadow Walked the many others who wanted to join them, along with the vast amount of supplies that the barons planned to bring with them.

Each baron was limited to bringing along a total of one thousand people to help colonize their new planet. However, Bandar was quick to point out some immediate problems facing several of the barons. Asami was mostly a water world and those living there would need to be importing much of their food supplies from other barons. Likewise, the two desert planets would need to import agricultural products as well.

"Interesting, Jarmila, right from the day that the worlds were first settled, there was the acute separation into the 'have planets' and the 'have-nots.' That struggle has been with them ever since," Miroslav pointed out.

"Yes, dear, but remember, the original barons made their own choice to settle on a 'have-not' world. Today, the people living there don't have that choice, unless they are Duska and can travel off-world," she countered.

As the days passed, the volumes outlined more and more of the plans for the mass exodus of Voss. Already the future barons had worked out advanced trading arrangements, much to the relief of those whose new worlds were going to be problematical for long term survival of humans, such as Asami and the desert worlds. While the two found this interesting reading, it didn't offer any real help for Zoran and the Dragon War currently being fought above ground. Still, they could not help noticing the parallels between ancient Voss and their worlds now. Back then, the reds and blacks appeared to be the driving force behind the war, just as it was now. Only in the present war, somehow all of the dragons were involved, except the golds. However, by Volume P, the other colors of dragons had been pulled into the war on Voss, again excepting the Gold Dragons. It was at this point that the Exodus to the New Federation began with the barons leading the way.

Bandar and Ari did not leave with the first wave. The barons insisted that they wait until temporary dwellings had been constructed.

"The safety of our two saviors is of paramount importance." Well, now Ari and I are saviors. Still, she thinks this is a wise move on their part.

The two continued their study of the journals, though only four more volumes remained. In Volume S, they came across some fascinating entries, wholly unexpected. The two read over each other's shoulders.

Had a most surprising visit today. We have been staying at Kazimir's Pyramid. It is defensible and isolated from habitation centers which have so far been the targets of dragon attacks. The Gold Dragon Tereza came to visit us today, canceling my defenses neatly and causing us a bit of a scare. She brought along her son, Kazimir. I learned that he is their son, as incredible as this sounds. Tereza named him after her human husband and great mage.

She confided some very interesting secrets to me. Dragons dearly love magic. Apparently, on their native worlds, magic is at a premium. On Voss, we humans command vastly more magical powers than the dragons. Initially, that provided the impetus for the original crossbreeding of the two species. Some of the dragons hoped that a merger of the two blood lines would create dragons that have a much higher ability to learn powerful magic. According to Tereza, this has come to pass rather significantly. Her son knows more spells than she does.

"That humans also make vastly superior teachers of magic is now proven," Tereza told me, adding, "that jealousy is the driving motivation behind the reds and blacks attacks on the humans of Voss. While they too have benefitted from interspecies breeding, they cannot stand the simple fact that you humans command more magical powers than they do." We had a long chat about this.

At last, she brought up the reason for her surprise visit. She wants me to try to teach Kazimir three spells: Magically Enchant an Item, See True, and the ever useful In Case Of Emergency spell. It seems that his previous teacher was killed by the blacks three days ago. Tereza said, "If you will do this for my son, I will tell you the great secret behind Mage Kazimir's machine here in the Pyramid — how it was able to bring dragons to Voss in the first place. I encouraged him not to document that feature in his writings."

Okay, I bought it. My curiosity was roused. Was there more to this machine than searching the Shadows for worlds? Tereza certainly knows how to play me. I spent several days with Kazimir and found him a most willing student. What surprised me was both Tereza and Kazimir respect me and even Ari too, quite unlike the other dragons who are ravaging Voss. He picked up two of the three spells. He just could not get the hang of the In Case of Emergency spell. At last Tereza accepted her son's limitations with this spell. Both seemed extremely pleased that he was able to Magically Enchant items around the interior of the Pyramid. Of course, none of his enchantments were permanent. No, that would require a far more powerful spell, Make Permanent.

As they were leaving, I overheard them talking and finally figured out why she had taken this unprecedented step to have her son learn these spells. She could cast Make Permanent but had failed repeatedly to learn how to enchant items. Now between the two of them, they could create magical items. Note to self: I wonder what new troubles I have inadvertently unleashed upon the worlds?

What did I get out of this? A most intriguing fact: Kazimir's machine had a secret feature. Once it was focused upon one of the dragon home worlds, by using a special hidden lever, he could activate his Power Attraction spell. Tereza explained that he used it to pull the unsuspecting dragons from their worlds to Voss, dragging them through the Shadows, whether they desired it or not. At first, they did not desire to be abducted, but once here, Tereza explained, they then accepted it. Personally, I cannot wonder if this was also partially why the dragons were now attacking us humans on Voss for having brought them here against their wills? However, I am not going to ask a black or red this question, obviously.

I respect old Kazimir even more now. However, I also sense that his own ego got in the way of his logic. A wise man would have studied the dragons before bringing them here to Voss. I, too, would have brought the golds, but certainly not the reds, greens, or blacks. Isn't hindsight just perfect? Ari is chuckling as I log this entry.

As the end of January came, Miroslav and Jarmila finished Volume T. Both hated to read the last entry, for their connection to their ancient lineage was ending. There were no more "volumes," no more revelations of Bandar Zar.

Valentýn has told us that it is time for us to depart Voss forever. He and his men have suitable accommodations for us awaiting our arrival on Adapazan. This is for the best, as Ari is expecting our first child in four months. We cannot bring up our son or daughter here on Voss; we cannot hide from the ravaging dragons forever.

Ari has convinced me to leave these journals here on Voss in my private room and to start afresh on our new world. I hate to part with these, but I can see her reasoning. We are leaving Voss behind forever and starting a new life on New Adapazan. Besides, I can always return to Voss and retrieve them if I ever need them. Still, it is hard to part with these twenty volumes. In a way, they are sort of like my own child. Okay. Ari can be most persuasive — new life so new journals. Besides, ahead of me lies my greatest magical challenge yet: how to magically tie the sixteen worlds together and to keep the Duska training to those who can best use it for the benefit of the common man.

"Well, that does it," Jarmila sighed. "The last one. So much makes so much more sense now."

"Yes, it does. I wish that we had known all of this all along. Perhaps we would have made far wiser choices," Miroslav suggested, referring to the many barons who made ill-advised bargains with the other races of dragons, particularly the reds, blacks, and greens. "We best go relate our last findings to Zoran. I hope this helps him in some way."

Chapter 38 Weather Plays a Role

December's foot of snow had been hard packed on the streets of Brn. With the population now underground deep beneath Zoran's fortress, the mild January weather had not been noticed much, as all attention had been on the dragon war. A howling blizzard marked February's arrival, not only in Brn, but across most of the main continent of Adapazan.

"How can we fight in weather like this?" Baron Tomas asked his father. The two braved the whiteout conditions to survey Brn from Zoran's fortress rooftop. Archmage Karel had long ago moved his falcons inside to his laboratory. Both men wore heavy parkas, thick boots and mittens. Scarves wrapped their faces leaving only their eyes exposed to the howling winds and biting snow.

"We can't, son. I can't even see out outer walls. If the dragons hit us now, we might as well just head for the safety below ground. Let's get inside while we still can just barely see the door," Zoran suggested. Bent low against the fifty mile an hour wind, the two snow encrusted men moved slowly to the door and safety. Once inside, they shut the door but it took their combined strength to do so, pushing the foot of snow which had blown in against the door in just the few minutes that they had been outside.

"Warm! Clean!" Both men cast spells rapidly, removing the layer of snow that covered their parkas, pants, heads, and boots. "Worst start of a February in a long time, son. I doubt that even the dragons can fly much in this weather. We've got a breather. Let's put our heads together and see if we can get some bright ideas." They briefly checked on the Archmage towers and watched the many students filing in from breakfast, ready to learn new spells. Zdenka and Verushka paused to give their husbands a quick kiss before following after their students. At least the hundred plus students would not have to worry about being interrupted by dragon attacks today, Zoran thought.

The two men walked the nearly deserted halls to his private study. It seemed so strange without the many staff present, going about their daily duties. All non-essential personnel were now safely below ground. All across Adapazan, the dead of winter was mostly a quiet time. Families were forced to stay indoors. Little commerce took place and then only the essentials such as another load of coal or firewood. While not ideal, the accommodations in the subterranean towns were working out for the twenty thousand plus Brn residents. Rest and relaxation gave way to boredom broken by games of cards and darts.

From the distant fighter training room, the clanks of steel upon steel filtered into the study. Strike Force One members were training up Strike Force Two members on the tactics that they had found more workable. Dana was also training up more men to join the fortress guards in the event that the dragons attempted an assault of the fortress. Zoran whipped up a pot of hot tea and the two men stared at the huge map of Adapazan, sipping their tea.

"I like your little flags, dad. Looks like we have all of the towns and cities over ten thousand covered with some kind of subterranean habitations," Tomas pointed out. "Trouble is, not everyone chose to evacuate. Hope that they don't pay a steep price because of that."

"True, but son, over half of our people do not reside in these larger towns. How the devil can we possibly protect a hamlet of a hundred? A lone farmstead? A small mine or smelter? They dot the provinces."

"What are the other barons doing on their worlds?" Tomas asked. Although he suspected that he already knew the answer, he hoped his dad would have some new news.

"Worse than we, I'm afraid. Most have either larger populations or fewer mages to deal with the underground constructions. What about sending out our mages to some of our smaller towns and having them build some underground safe houses? Is that too risky? Jarka seems to think so."

"I agree with her, dad. I have a feeling that the dragons are just waiting for us to spread our Archmages out. As long as we stay grouped together, any dragon attack will meet with very heavy losses on their side. At the moment, that is our best defense."

Zoran sighed. What could he do to protect his people? Outside, the weather was doing what he couldn't.

The dragon strike group of thirty-three swooped over Adapazan, fighting the howling winds. While the whites loved the weather, all of the other dragons despised it. "We can't see a thing, not even the roads! This is utter folly!" a red complained bitterly. Reluctantly, the black leader agreed and the group returned to their respective worlds and caverns.

Three days later, the sun finally appeared. Brn was hardly recognizable buried beneath drifts some ten feet deep. Bundled up against the bitter cold, Zoran and Tomas Shadow Walked around the continent checking on the situation. Everywhere, enormous snow drifts sculpted the landscape into something one might see in a desert. Instead of sand, here it was snow. Whole villages were nearly buried. Both men had a most difficult time locating any of the more remote villages. Gone were all their familiar landmarks, replaced with snow dunes. All traces of the winding roads were gone.

"Well, dad, if we can't find the villages, then certainly the dragons cannot either. It looks like our weather is protecting our people," Tomas pointed out the obvious. Zoran smiled and they gave up their reconnoitering mission. It was hopeless.

Two days later, the weather turned bad again, dumping another two feet of snow in and around Brn. The weather patterns continued all throughout February — two or three days of very heavy snow followed by a couple of days of sunshine and bitter cold. In the far north, the warlord reported at least twenty foot snow pack with villagers making tunnels to get around between buildings. In the milder Dorum area, the snow pack was nearly record breaking at ten feet. As expected, Adapazan had no dragon attacks during February.

Werner, the black, and Dario, the red, huddled in the warmth of Dario's lair. "Damnable weather is defeating us, Dario. It is almost as if these Archmages are now controlling the weather!"

"They very well could be doing just that!" growled Dario, the red. "We can still attack on Asami, but what's the point? The desert worlds, Anwyn and Chana, are ripe for the pickings as is the swamp world of Jing. Adapazan, Rehor, and Gerde are buried under huge snow packs. Even the forest, hills, and plains worlds are deep in snow this winter. I guess our war will have to be postponed until the spring comes to the many worlds."

"Hum, maybe not. So far, Zoran has refused to disperse his Archmages out so we can get at them and with this dismal weather we cannot even find their villages to attack. Maybe a different strategy is needed just now. Perhaps it is time that we pool our resources and begin taking out the barons in their fortresses. Say we attack Anwyn. If Zoran come to their aid, we have a chance to take out some of his Archmages."

"You are assuming that these barons will come to the aid of their fellow barons," Dario, the red, sneered.

"I expect that they will at least send along a token Archmage or two for us to kill. Let's send for Donatello and get his input on which fortress would be the best target for us to strike," Werner suggested.

These sixteen new worlds that Bandar discovered and to which the beleaguered folks on Voss fled were not wholly devoid of sentient life forms. Adapazan had its Yellers, banshees, megalowolves, slithers, and paleowasps. The desert planet of Anwyn had its own unique dwellers, the sand sprites. Solitary creatures except during mating season, these highly magical beings dwelled within the endlessly shifting sands. They did not appreciate the sudden arrival of the thousand from Voss.

When Tudyr Anwyn, Duska-trained and a brother of the first baron Padrig Anwyn, attempted to build a stone fortress around the oasis of Fair Wyn, the sand sprites reacted with deadly force. Unknown to the new arrivals, Fair Wyn was the Holy Site of the sand sprites. Three quarters of the small force under Tudyr perished during the two day battle. Tudyr himself was captured and brought far beneath the surface of the sands to face the wrath and justice of their Monarch Betrys, the Fair.

An agreement was reached or so the legends say. Tudyr sent a messenger to his brother telling him that the region around Fair Wyn was off limits and belonged to the sand sprites. In return, Tudyr's life was spared, but he was forced to spend the rest of his days there in the underground lair of Monarch Betrys, the Fair. No one ever explained why Tudyr didn't just Shadow Walk away from captivity. Legends say that he and Betrys became lovers and had seven children.

Indeed, today the oasis of Fair Wyn has a several dozen adobe homes around it and the hundred plus inhabitants trace their lineage back to Tudyr and Betrys, a merging of the human and sand sprite lines. The barons of Anwyn ignore the oasis and still know virtually nothing about the original inhabitants of Anwyn, these sand sprites. However, the villagers at Fair Wyn do provide water and shelter for human traders and passersby. Still, direct contact with the human population of Anwyn is kept to a minimum. and the barons continue to avoid this region of their vast desert continent. Most humans simply believe that this area is haunted by evil demons.

Another native life form was the sand worm. These enormous worm-like creatures loved to swim in the desert sands as if it was water. Further, they often burrowed into the bedrock far below the sands, carving out intricate mazes of tunnels and chambers. When the sand worms left, the sand sprites subsequently turned these chambers into their homes. Sand worms ignored humans and sand sprites completely. However, the brown dragons soon discovered that these worms were a delicacy delight and began hunting them for food. Of course, the sand sprites greatly disliked this and thus during the last twenty years, a great animosity had arisen between the two species, though the browns had yet to realize the existence of the sand sprites.

Early February, Donatello, the brown, now firmly behind the war against the humans, sent his browns out on regular attacking patrols. Unlike the other dragon's breath weapons, the brown's electrical bolt only impacted a single target. Thus, the browns needed to make more frequent raids and/or resort to physical attacks with their mighty claws and teeth. He sent out patrols of a dozen browns and their orders were to sweep the desert clean of the smaller human establishments. Anwyn had thousands of oases, each one supporting a small number of human settlers, usually between one and two hundred.

February 4th was an ordinary day in Fair Wyn. Dozens of barefooted children ran around the warm, packed sands of the main street that encircled the five hundred foot, clear blue waters of the life-giving oasis. They were engrossed in a game of tag while several women sat with their backs against the crude adobe walls of their homes weaving baskets or mats from the yucca leaves they had gathered the day before. While technically wintertime, the warm sun was welcome on their pale, white faces, driving the previous night's cold from their bodies.

Megan and Rhys Seren of Fair Wyn traced their lineage back to Tudyr and Betrys, though on separate lines. In their thirties, they had four children who were out playing tag. Their eldest was nine and their youngest was four. Megan's physical appearance was more closely aligned to the sand sprites. Her complexion was quite fair, pale white some would say. Long yellow tresses of her thick, curly hair fell to her knees, though she often kept it tied back in a ponytail. Her eyes were green. She stood six-five, a little on the short side for her people. Compared to the more robust humans of Anwyn, most would say that Megan was extremely tall and quite thin, possibly frail. In contrast, Rhys took after the Tudyr side. His hair was long, thick, and black as were his eyes. His skin, while pale, held a slight tinge of yellow in it. He stood six-eight, but was also thin, owing to the sand sprite lineage. None of the men had any facial hair, again due to the sand sprite line.

Both Megan and Rhys could Shadow Walk, but seldom, if ever, left their beloved Anwyn. Both were very able users of magical spells. Unlike the Federation, these people had no formal magical training levels or titles. They simply loved magic and it was apart of their very beingness. Here in Fair Wyn, Megan and Rhys were the undisputed most powerful casters and the pair were always experimenting and learning new ways of casting and variations of spells. Unlike the Federation, they had no formalized or ritualized methods of teaching magic. Instead, those who knew a spell simply taught it to those who did not know it. If one was unable to learn a certain spell from a given teacher, he or she tried it again with another teacher. Evenings were often spent in small groups, with one person teaching the others a particular spell or variation or perhaps handing down their verbal history to the younger children.

Brown Dragons were occasionally seen flying high in the skies around Fair Wyn. None had ever ventured close though. That did not mean that the inhabitants had no opinion of the dragons. Because the dragons often dined on the sand worms that made the underground burrows in which the sand sprites lived, the hundreds of Fair Wyn were rightly upset with them. Once Rhys had ventured to find and speak with the leader of the browns, Donatello. He had asked them to stop eating the sand worms and had explained what the worms were doing for the ecology of Anwyn. The browns didn't stop and now often used some of these underground tunnels and chambers for their own lairs. Before this day, there was some long standing animosity towards the Brown Dragons. All that was about to change.

A dozen browns came swooping in low over Fair Wyn, just above the date and palm trees that lined the oasis. The dozen children stopped their game of tag and looked up at the approaching dragons, pointing excitedly to the huge flying beasts. Their wide-eyed enthusiasm was replaced by fear. The leading dragons let lose their breath electrical bolts directly upon the gazing children. Their small bodies jerked and smoldered from the massive currents flowing through their bodies, killing them nearly instantly. The children's screams brought the many adults racing out of their adobe homes only to encounter the wrath of the dragons.

More electrical charges detonated, but many of the adults cast their defensive spells which in essence shorted the current into the ground beneath their feet. Seeing this, the browns landed and went into melee with the remaining adults. One reared up on his hind legs and batted the humans near him with his powerful front claws. Another tried to bite others with his huge, sharp teeth.

The adults countered with spells, from Magical Missiles of many variations and varieties to Lightning Bolts of their own. None dared use Balls of Fire because of the close proximity of everyone else. A few shot Disintegrate spells as well. Some spells were effective, others not.

When a human was struck by one of the swinging claws, his or her body went flying off as if it were a billiard ball. Broken ribs, arms, and legs were common results, along with great torn gashes in their torsos and/or appendages. Many who did not rise up again were later trampled to death by the dragons that continued unabated in their carnage of Fair Wyn.

"The children, Rhys!" Megan exclaimed wildly, dodging a giant claw aimed at her head. Ducking and rolling across the sands, she scrambled to her feet and continued making her way to the children. Rhys was delayed by a dragon and he wisely chose to back up and open a Mystical Door. He stepped into it, avoiding the dragon's attack and stepped out beside the body of his oldest boy. Rhys knelt down and felt for a pulse, but didn't expect to feel one from the charred body. Anger seethed and grew within him.

Megan raced to her eldest daughter but likewise found she too had been killed. Ten feet away, she spotted her other daughter and moved to her side. Cradling the wounded five year old in her arms, Megan watched the life force depart from the little body. Grief swelled in her bosom as she rocked back and forth, crying, "No! No! No!"

Rhys glance her way, saw that she held their daughter and frantically looked to find their young four year old son. "Oh no!" He spotted the small body, which had been squashed by some dragon as it had attacked and killed another child before moving to attack the adults. Rhys snapped. Anger filled his mind. Another dragon moved towards him now, intent upon killing him. Rhys cast his spell, Sand Spike. He became part of the sand beneath his body, which seemed to vanish utterly in the eyes of the approaching dragon. As the dragon neared the location where Rhys had been, suddenly an enormous spike of fused sand came thrusting upwards from the sand, as if the hand of some giant was thrusting up an enormous stalactite of granite or basalt, rock hard. This was Rhys in his sand body form spell. The spike thrust into the belly of the brown exiting through its back, severing its backbone in the process. One second after the attack of Rhys, the spike protruded ten feet above the back of the brown, who moaned a painful death howl. As suddenly as the spike had come, the sand comprising it returned to the sand that formed it and trickled to the ground like some enormous sand timer whose glass cylinder had just been shattered.

Megan, seeing the attack form used by Rhys, nodded and cast her Sand Spike spell. Her body too disappeared, blending into the sands beneath here she had knelt. A small wave moved across the sands to the nearest dragon that was attacking other adults. Megan moved beneath the dragon and executed her attack. Again, a giant stone spike flew up from the ground, puncturing the dragon's hide, slicing through its belly, and thrusting up eight feet from the top of its back, killing it slowly and painfully. An instant later, sand grains fell back down to the ground and Megan's wave moved onwards. A second wave, Rhys, was right beside hers.

Three other adults spotted the effectiveness of the Seren's attack spells and followed suit. Before long, six more browns were skewered by Sand Spikes. The browns, never having seen such devastating attacks against themselves and expecting little to no resistance whatsoever, lifted off, fleeing for their lives, leaving eight of their original twelve browns dead there at Fair Wyn.

While Rhys and several others used their spells to move the eight dead dragons far out into the desert sands, others tended to the many wounded and lined up their dead. Half of the adults were wounded, some severely. Nearly all of the village's children had perished, only two survived. When Rhys returned, joining Megan, he tried to comprehend the devastation but was numb.

At last, he took charge. "Okay, let's get everyone to the safety of the Below." One by one, he and Megan began teleporting the wounded far beneath the surface into their private chambers that the village often used, abandoned Sand Worm tunnels. Here they stored their precious food supplies, safe from the desert thieves, such as hyenas and scavenger birds. After the fifty wounded were safely brought Below and made comfortable in their quarters, the remaining fifteen adults returned for their dead.

Each of their fallen was brought to another Below Cavern, the Cavern of the Dead. Carefully, Rhys and Megan prepared their four children, brushing out the girls' hair and straightening their clothes. At last, they placed their yucca sleeping mats over their children and conducted their own private farewell ceremony. Nearby, others were doing the same thing. Here in the Cavern of the Dead, the deceased would quickly dehydrate forming mummified bodies that slowly turned into dust, joining with the sands of Anwyn.

Finally, the two grief stricken parents returned to their own chambers Below. Both broke down, sobbing and holding each other tightly. Their home, once filled with four children, now seemed utterly deserted, devoid of the sparking life it once had had. As their tears subsided, one or the other would look around their vacant chambers and notice one of their children's things and their crying began anew. Finally, their intense grief subsided.

"Why, Rhys? Why did the dragons attack us? We've never done anything to them?" wailed Megan.

"I don't know. I surely do not know. This was wholly unprovoked. I simply will not allow this to continue. I am going to Message their leader, this Donatello fellow and ask him!" Rhys had now risen to anger. He sat down on his yucca mat and focused, casting his Message spell.

Donatello. Rhys Seren of Fair Wyn here. A dozen of your Brown Dragons just attacked our humble village and murdered our four children and killed many others. I am giving you this sole opportunity to explain why this happened.

We are at war with you humans. You have killed many of our children and many of us dragons. It has to stop. Donatello replied via his Message spell. He had not yet heard from the other four returning dragons on their successes at wiping out small human establishments in the vastness of the desert. Thus, he did not know of the staggering losses that band had suffered.

I agree, this has to stop and it will! This cannot go unpunished, Donatello. I will give you Brown Dragons twenty-four hours to leave Anwyn and never return. If any are still on this planet after that, they shall suffer the rage of my retribution. I give you my solemn word: all remaining dragons on Anwyn will be killed. I will show them no mercy, just as your dragons did to our helpless children! He broke the connection.

"I gave them one day to vacate Anwyn. After that, I will begin systematically killing every last dragon on Anwyn!" Rhys proclaimed.

"I am with you, Rhys. I will show them no mercy!" Megan supported him. "Come, let us prepare our things. Anwyn is big. We will need supplies. I shall not stop until the last dragon on Anwyn is dead or gone from here forever!"

"Excuse me, Rhys, how come our spells didn't work so well on them?" a fellow villager asked.

"I don't know. They are dragons. However, our Sand Spike spells have proven most effective. We shall use them to kill all the remaining dragons on Anwyn. I give you my solemn word on that, Agrona," Rhys declared vehemently.

"Do you want some help?" she asked.

"No, you are in charge of the village for now. Keep everyone Below where they are safe from the wonton ravages of these out of control dragons, while Megan and I get rid of them forever," Rhys ordered. She bowed and returned to her own chambers; she'd also lost a child this day.

"How can that be? Eight dead? A tiny village oasis? No Archmages?" Donatello fumed and paced his cavern worriedly. Shocking, distressing, impossible — unless this was Baron Zoran's secret super-weapon. He glared at the four surviving browns. "Are you sure that Zoran was not there?"

"Er, we don't know him, but I swear we saw no one holding rods or anything. A few cast paltry spells at us and a couple got lucky with their Magical Missiles. I sensed none of the Archmages — excepting, well, we did get a sniff of magical energies from the village as a whole. I thought it rather unusual. None of the other villages have had such an aura about them," one brown replied.

"I swear, boss, it was powerful magic that we've never seen before! The sand, the desert sand just formed into these giant spikes and ripped up through their bodies. It was awful," another replied. He added, "And we didn't see anyone doing it, no person holding a rod causing it, no one standing still concentrating — just nothing. The terrified villagers were in complete chaos, just as they always are when we attack."

Ignoring the warning of Rhys, Donatello was completely past the twenty-four hour mark. He was not about to be bullied by some unknown human. Well, that was not entirely true. He had seen this fellow once before quite a long time ago. As with most humans, Donatello paid him no mind at all and didn't recall the incident at all. It was as important to him as a five-year-old grocery shopping list might be to your mother. "Okay, gather our whole force here on Anwyn. Let us go retrieve our dead and see what we can learn from the battlefield," he ordered.

Thirty-two browns soon took flight and Shadow Walked to the oasis of Fair Wyn. Circling high above the oasis, Donatello saw the crystal blue waters and the green tops of the trees standing in sharp contrast from the orange-brown desert sands that stretched off in all directions. His shape eyes zeroed in on a brownish mass and he gracefully glided down towards that patch, growing more and more angry the lower he descended. Carrion birds and hyenas were gorging themselves on the carcasses of the eight slain browns. A dozen birds and sixteen scavengers dashed off in all directions as the enormous black shadows of the winged dragons swept over the sands near their feast.

Seeing no villagers, Donatello landed beside the remains and sent a dozen into the village to look for survivors. "Bring anyone alive to me. Count their dead," he ordered and began his own inspection of the fallen browns. Each of the dead had an enormous puncture wound right through the middle of their bodies as if they had been skewered by some gigantic spike! "My god! What did this? It must be Zoran's super-weapon! Okay, I am going to bring Werner to see this. Round up all the remaining villagers. We will want to interrogate them thoroughly when I get back with him." Donatello lifted off of the desert sands and stepped into the Shadows.

"Dearest, you were right! The dragons have returned to the scene of their crimes. Do you suppose that they want to bury their dead, much as we do?" Megan asked. She and Rhys were invisible and sitting on the ruins of the roof of their adobe home. Rhys had insisted that they be patient and wait. Now they were rewarded, though Megan was a bit daunted by the sheer number of browns circling around them. They watched as the group landed.

"That's the leader, Donatello, over there looking at the dead dragons. I'll give him time to bury his dead and then decide to leave Anwyn. I know my warning of twenty-four hours has just elapsed, but he is here now and is seeing for himself that we mean what we say. Look, the dragons are entering the village once more. Be ready to Sand Merge if they get too close to us," Rhys cautioned his wife.

"They are going through each home. They aren't taking anything. What are they doing? Looking for us?" she asked. She overheard the dragons talking and had her answer. They were looking for survivors. Rhys had once again been right in having the survivors go Below to safety.

As the dragons approached the remains of their adobe home, both cast their spell and merged into the desert sands around their home. Two small waves of sand, like a silent sailboat's wake, slipped out of the village a short distance and then stopped. None noticed two tiny spikes of sand protruding inches above the surrounding sandy desert floor. Both continued to watch and listen. Rhys hoped and prayed that Donatello would heed his warning and leave Anwyn. Both were surprised when a short while later, Donatello returned with a number of blacks and reds with him.

"It is a good thing that you have spotted this new weapon of Zoran's," Werner, the black, said as they landed. "Let's see what it has done to your poor fellows. We were just about to launch and all-out attack here. Oh my! What could possibly have done this? I've never seen anything like this before," Werner exclaimed, shocked at the huge puncture holes in the eight carcasses. He examined the dead browns a bit before suggesting, "Donatello, we should leave and discuss this matter. You are sure that the messenger who ordered you to leave was not Baron Zoran?"

"Absolutely, unless he has totally changed his entire appearance. Let us go then." Donatello lifted off followed by a large number of dragons. A few remained behind, rapidly burying the eight dead and giving them a brief ceremony.

"That sounded hopeful," Megan said. She and Rhys canceled their spells and returned to the surface and their bodies. "He did say we should leave. Do you suppose that he meant to leave Anwyn like you asked?"

"I couldn't tell for sure. We should give them the benefit of our doubts, after all, that's what we want — for the dragons to abandon Anwyn. We'll wait a little longer, dearest," Rhys replied.

"Look, there were no signs of Zoran at that oasis, Donatello. Besides, how could Zoran possibly know that your forces were going to attack that tiny site? You yourself told me that your browns merely swept across the sands looking for likely targets. They chose to attack Fair Wyn on the spur of the moment. I cannot fathom how Zoran could possibly have known about it or even had time to interfere," Werner, the black, countered Donatello's insistence that the destruction of his eight browns was the work of this new super-weapon that Zoran's people had brought back from Voss.

"Rather let us consolidate our striking forces tomorrow. The weather is atrocious on many of the worlds at the moment. We cannot even find the towns on Adapazan — so much snow. We will attack the baron's fortresses here on Anwyn and see if we can lure Zoran and his army of Archmages here and eliminate them," Werner, the black, explained his newest plan.

Chapter 39 The Battle for Anwyn

The second week in February brought no relief from the snows. As Zoran looked out at Brn from his snow covered roof, half of the city was buried in drifts nearly ten feet tall. In normal times, the townsfolk would have been steadily shoveling out after each storm. With all of the people now living far beneath his fortress, the snow continued to pile up with each passing storm.

Baron! We're under attack! Dragons! Hundreds of them! Help us! My brothers have just reported that their fortresses and Circles are also under attack by hundreds of dragons! We cannot possibly withstand this massive assault! Help us or Anwyn is lost! Baron Cadfeel fairly screamed across the Shadows as he frantically Mind Linked to Zoran, the only person that he thought could possibly save him. If asked, he would have had no idea how this massive assault could possibly be withstood.

Zoran began systematically Messaging his extended groups. Evsen and Dusan took their Strike Forces to the Beawenn Castle and Ceri Castle respectively. Archmage Karel accompanied Evsen's Strike Force One. These two groups had been on alert and had practiced for just such an emergency call. Hence, within two minutes of the Message from Zoran, their groups raced off into the Shadows to come to the aid of the two younger barons. Meanwhile, Zoran gathered up his group and issued the crucial Rods of Dragon Slaying to many of the Archmages.

"I don't like this, Zoran. We are going to the rescue of one of your archenemies?" Jarka complained and asked.

"They are humans first," he replied. "If Baron Cadfeel is correct, there are hundreds of dragons attacking his fortress at Alun Castle. If the force is too great for us to handle, we get out. No heroics. Stay close to your Duska. Everyone: cast all of your protection spells, and we'll Shadow Walk to Anwyn and see if we can stop the battle." Several minutes later, the large group slipped into the Shadows, adrenaline pumping in the early morning frost.

As Zoran brought his group partially out of the Shadows above Alun Castle, everyone saw instantly that the baron was not exaggerating the magnitude of the assault on his stronghold. His fortress had a twenty-foot outer wall entirely surrounding the castle proper, the tall Archmage tower, and the many internal buildings. A large number of soldiers were manning the walls, vainly trying to shoot arrows into the circling dragons. The castle itself was two stories tall and made from imported granite stone. The tower was four stories tall but Archmage Byrnn Arwel was standing beside Baron Cadfeel on top of the castle, utilizing the protection of the rod that the baron held aloft. Two other mages were beside him as well as two other Duska relatives.

Acrid smoke clouds rose around them, the blacks had soaked the area with their caustic acid and it was now eating into the stone roof. Zoran had most of his group alight on top of the Archmage's tower. No sense landing in the acid and having your boots eaten away. A dozen black dragons were circling around the castle, along with a dozen reds, blues, and whites. With forty-eight in so close a formation, they were having trouble navigating and attacking. Circling further out and not yet in the fray were several dozen blacks along with another thirty dragons of various colors. Several dragon bodies lay crumpled on the ground, victims of Archmage Byrnn and the baron. Many dozen of the soldiers were also dead, their smoldering corpses littering the ground just inside the walls.

The instant that they appeared out of the Shadows, the Archmages and Duskas fired off their first round of devastating spells, bringing down some twenty of the dragons. Surprise took its toll that first minute. Jarka and Bernard focused on conjuring water to wash the acid off of the castle roof while Zoran, Zdenka, and the others fired their deadly spells.

"My rod is dead! We can't take another dragon's breath here, Zoran! What do we do?" yelled a terrified Baron Cadfeel.

"Move in close to us!" he yelled back.

The dragons quickly altered their sweeping attacks, now focusing heavily on the large group of Archmages on the roof of the taller tower. Within a minute, ten dragons had shot fire, acid, and freezing frost at the group, nullifying their rods completely. The next wave hit them with all manner of magical spells, and many of their protection spells were dispelled. Much to the annoyance of the Seventeen, half of them found their Morph spells canceled and were once more armless facing the onslaught of dragons. In spite of the chaos, another six dragons fell from the sky, victims of the Archmages' deadly attacks.

Archmage Danika suddenly found herself armless once more, but she managed a smile. Zdenka had been right. In a battle, you never know when the Morph spell might be dispelled. She dodged a blast of fire and managed to keep her balance in the process. With so many on the roof top, they had very little room to maneuver without interfering with their companions. Using a Magnify spell, Zoran ordered, "Make for the grounds inside the walls, spread out!" Mystical Doors flashed like firecrackers. Everyone stepped out onto the stone courtyard, spreading out in the process. Still, Zoran knew that if the dragons made another massive sweep with their breath weapons, many were going to get killed. He reached a decision. "Move inside the castle. Baron, get your men inside too before they are all slaughtered."

Dodging cones of searing flames, freezing cold, and acid streams, the group raced for the main doors. The baron's soldiers didn't need a second order to abandon their walls. They dashed across the bodies of their fallen comrades and tried to dodge the onslaught, making for the doors as well. Hundreds did not make it; their dying screams only adding to the surreal scene in the desert morning.

"Throw up Force Walls over the doors and windows!" Zoran yelled and the many mages complied.

"My god, you really are armless, Archmage!" Baron Cadfeel exclaimed as Danika moved to cast one over the window nearest her.

"Morph got dispelled," she replied hastily, glancing around for more windows to protect.

"Well, that will keep us safe for a minute. Everyone: recast your protection spells. Let's see what they do next," Zoran ordered. "Anyone hurt?"

That was a rather dumb question. Many had already been injured by the flames, acid, and frost. Jarka and Bernard raced around from person to person doling out her precious healing potions until she ran out. "That's it on the healing droughts, so don't anyone get injured anymore," she yelled with her Magnify spell.

"I have a bad feeling about this," Jarka whispered to Zoran. "We are like rats in a cage in here. What are they doing out there?"

"Circling and bringing in a host of browns," he called out. He wondered why the browns? Then he got his answer. The browns fired off volley after volley of their powerful electrical bolts at the stone walls and doors. The doors splintered on the first round, but the five Force Walls held and would have to be dispelled for the dragons to gain access.

"Guess the strength of my castle walls is going to be sorely tested," Baron Cadfeel muttered. "What can we do? Join the others below ground?"

Just then, a section of the wall stone shattered. A large chunk flew out hitting Archmage Eliska, knocking her to the ground, smashing her left arm, and then settling down on her shattered arm. Screaming in pain, she panicked for a moment. Zdenka hastily cast a Force Wall, re-enforcing what remained of that wall and quickly four others added more walls as well. As Jarka raced to help Eliska, the Archmage began laughing. She canceled her Morph spell and awkwardly regained her feet.

"How silly of me. Cancel my Morph and no more pain. Duh! I'm fine, Jarka. Thanks for the hand up. See, there is a benefit in being armless for real," she jested.

Her brief levity was quickly lost amid the sounds of dozens more electrical blasts against the stone. The browns were very effective at shattering stone, Zoran discovered, making a mental note of this tactic. Both he and Zdenka looked at each other and smiled. Simultaneously, they had the same thought. When their fortress was being constructed, they had painstakingly inserted Force Walls in between the layers of their fortress walls and the sides of their fortress proper. This tactic the dragons were employing now would be mostly nullified if they attack their Brn fortress in a similar manner.

Bernard grumbled, "Well, against so many dragons, we have managed to last a whole three minutes without getting killed, just wounded. Now here we are stopped in our tracks and trapped like rats in a cage. Fine how-to-do."

"Dear, we wouldn't have lasted even this long if the dragons had not chosen to split their forces among three targets. I wonder how the others are faring?" Jarka replied, growing more and more nervous. Their two sons were leading the two strike forces, helping defend the two newer castles of Anwyn. She didn't dare Message them for fear of distracting them.

"What are we going to do now? We can't surrender. The dragons will just kill us," asked Baron Cadfeel. He was growing more and more nervous with each electrical blast against the crumbling stone wall.

"I had no time to contact the other barons to have them send help. Besides, there just isn't enough room for all of us to effectively battle these beasts," Zoran sighed. "If the walls come down, perhaps we should head to your underground city and make a stand there. If they knock enough walls down, it may well block the entrance to your subterranean city and actually protect everyone down there from the dragons." He tried to make a positive statement for the baron's sake.

"Dad! The north wall is crumbling! More Force Walls everyone!" Baron

Tomas yelled, calling everyone's immediate attention to the gaping hole which had just formed. A gap some twenty feet wide gave everyone a clear view of the huge number of dragons poised just outside the castle wall. Dozens of Force Walls went up, ensuing that the dragons would need to cast many Disintegrate spells to bring them down. Mere Dispel Magic spells would not cancel them. However, time would. This temporary barrier would only last a few minutes. Hence, several Archmages cast their Make Permanent spells on a number of these, ensuring that they would have to be brought down by Disintegrate spells.

Baron Cadfeel's eyes drifted away from the present. His two brothers were contacting him, relaying the disasters at Castle Beanwenn and Castle Ceri. "My god, the two new castles are in ruins, Zoran! Many lost their lives there including five from the two Strike Forces. They are all holding up in the subterranean city areas. They say that they are now safe. The entrances are buried beneath tons of fallen stone and the dragons seem to have left."

Jarka and Bernard frantically Messaged their sons, Evsen and Dusan. Upon hearing Cadfeel's mention of the five dead, Zdenka glanced at the two. Worry lined her face. Momentarily, the big smiles on their faces told all. "They are alive!" Jarka exclaimed, tremendously relieved. "Evsen said that they didn't have much of a chance to counterattack. There were just too many dragons. They did get five and six between the two strike groups, though, before they had to run for cover."

Just as Zoran was about to suggest that they all evacuate to a safer location as well, Danika called out, "Look outside! What is happening?" Howling winds whipped up the orange-brown desert sands. Visibility shrank to a mere few feet. Grains seeped into the castle sliding between the small cracks in the many Force Walls.

"Sand Storm!" Baron Cadfeel yelled above the howling winds. "I've never seen one this fierce and come up this fast!"

Megan spotted a flock of twenty browns flying in a formation and called it to Rhys' attention. "I bet they are heading off to attack some other human village. Looks like they are ignoring your warning."

"True, they are not leaving like I asked. Well, let's follow them and see if we can find a way to get to those browns. I can see that Donatello needs more convincing to leave. Come on, after them," Rhys stated dryly.

Before long, they came upon one of the human fortresses. Castle Alun with its huge oasis rose above the horizon. "My god! Look at all those dragons!" Megan exclaimed. "So many different colors too! Now what do we do?"

"Megan, we can't deal with that many. We wait and bide our time. Look, there are a few humans battling them," Rhys pointed out the obvious.

"Are the humans fighting our battle too?" Megan asked, slightly confused by this unexpected turn of events. Seldom had she been here where the humans made their stronghold.

"Looks like it. Perhaps the dragons are attacking every life form on Anwyn," Rhys theorized. "Say, a whole bunch more defenders appeared. Wow! They just killed a mass of the dragons. Incredible."

"My god, Rhys! Look! Dozens of flames, frost, and acid are spewing all over the newcomers! They will be dead for sure!" Megan exclaimed.

"No, wait. They have moved their position. Come on. Stay invisible, and let's get a closer look," he suggested. "Our enemies, the browns, are not doing much at all." They moved to a different vantage point, balancing precariously on one of the many merlons of the protection parapet around the now vacated Archmage tower's roof that was soaked in acid and scorched from the many searing flames from the reds.

"Look, they are being forced to retreat inside. My god, look at all the dead soldiers!" Megan exclaimed. "Why are the browns not attacking?"

"Dunno. Look, now the reds, blacks, and whites are moving off. Maybe the battle is done," Rhys suggested.

"No, the browns are moving in. What are they going to do?" Megan replied. As they watched, the browns began systematically unleashing their massive electrical bolts into the stone wall of the castle proper. Soon, both watchers realized what the browns were doing — destroying the very protective stone of the castle, exposing the helpless humans inside.

"Darn, Megan, there is no sand in there, only the stone floor within the walls. If there was only sand, we could get ourselves some browns," Rhys pointed out.

"We have a golden opportunity, Rhys, to get us a bunch of browns. Let's bring on a sand storm and pile sand in there!" Megan suggested, growing excited about the possibility of finding a way to directly attack the evil browns that had killed their four children.

Both stood up, raised their arms towards the clear deep blue sky and began chanting in unison. After a couple of minutes, they ceased and waited. A huge whirlwind formed around the entire area, whipping up the desert sands. "Now, down into the sands we go, Megan." The two opened a Mystical door and stepped out onto the sands beyond the fortress proper. There they cast their Sand Spike spells. Two small waves seemed to float on across the sands and into the fortress grounds, where already a foot of sand had been deposited.

Overhead, the non-brown dragons decided to abandon the attack. This freakish dust storm made flying nearly impossible. One by one, the dragons flew off into the Shadows, leaving the browns still on the ground, trying to smash their way inside the castle proper. As Zoran and the others watched, a brown attempted to push his way in through the Force Walls. It took all of them working together to counter the massive force of the dragon's push. Just as they were beginning to weaken, an enormous spike of sand shot up from the ground, puncturing the brown's belly and shooting four feet above its back. Over the howling of the storm, the final bellow of intense pain shook the very foundations of the castle.

Another bellow followed shortly after that and then another. While they could not see the second one, they did glimpse the sand spike suddenly slaying the third one. Upon hearing these hideous cries from their fellow dragons, several reds and blacks, who were preparing to Shadow Walk to safety, stopped and fired off several cones of searing flames and acid in the general direction of the cries. While they could not see anything there in the sand storm, they hoped to perhaps hit whoever was harming their brown companions.

As the group watched, they saw the sand spikes being hit with the flames and acid. Part of the tip of one sand spike fused together, while acrid smoke came from the second spike as the acid seeped into the sand. Almost as suddenly as the sand spikes appeared, they vanished, leaving sand grains falling and whipped away by the winds. Then, another two hideous moans suggested the sand spikes had reappeared a little further away, but Zoran and crowd could not see them through the swirling sand. The browns promptly left as fast as they could.

As suddenly as the howling winds had arisen, the winds stopped. Silence was total and most pronounced to those inside. As they looked out, visibility suddenly returned. They saw the bodies of five dead brown dragons scattered before the breech in the castle walls. Just beyond that point, they saw two strange humans suddenly appearing, rising up out of the sands.

"Come on, outside everyone," Zoran called out. "They seem to be injured." Dozens of Mystical Doors opened and the large group stepped out on the massive mounds of sand that the sudden storm had deposited within the fortress and particularly up against the breech in the wall.

"Rhys! I'm hurt! My arms are burned! I can hardly bend them!" Megan cried, her voice a mixture of pain and fear.

"Me too, my chest is burning from that acid stuff! Oh no, the humans are coming out. I don't think I can focus enough to cast any spells," Rhys replied, fighting back tears of pain from his still smoldering chest.

"Hello. Are you injured? Perhaps we can help you," Baron Zoran spoke first.

"Darn, I wish I hadn't used all our healing potions," Jarka exclaimed, rather annoyed that she didn't have any left. It would have been nice if she could have come to their aid.

Bernard chuckled. He pulled two vials from his chest pockets. "Here you go. I sort of saved two back just in case you got hurt. I wanted to make darn sure that I didn't lose you, my lovely mage."

Jarka hugged him. "Brilliant dear! Thanks." She took the potions and walked closer to the two very strange looking humans, if human they were. "I have a healing potion for each of you. It should help get the healing process going and take the pain away at least." She handed each of the two a vial, noticing how tall they were. Both towered over her. Megan was six-five. Jarka guessed that this strange woman was perhaps ten years younger than she, but her complexion was quite fair, pale white, though her arms were blistering from second degree burns. Her ponytail of long yellow tresses of her thick, curly hair fell to the backs of her knees. Even though in great pain, Jarka saw her green eyes were full of life. Still, the woman was quite thin and frail.

"I can't move my arms," Megan grimaced as Jarka offered her the potion.

"Here, I'll help you drink it," she replied, carefully pouring it into the tall woman's mouth, before handing the second one to the even taller man. Rhys was even taller, at six-eight with long, thick black hair and eyes. His skin was also pale, but held a slight tinge of yellow in it. His physique was also quite thin, exacerbated by his extreme height. He readily accepted her potion but watched Megan carefully.

"Oh, it is working already! I can move my arms at last. Look, Rhys, the blisters are going down a little," Megan exclaimed, rather surprised at the efficiency of her potion.

Rhys then spoke, "Thank you for the healing potions, mage. We are nearly immune to the brown's electrical discharge when we are merged with the sands, but the searing flames and acid very nearly killed us. We've never encountered red and black dragons before, only the wicked browns who murdered our four children a few days ago. I am Rhys Seren of Fair Wyn and my wife, Megan."

"I'm Mage Jarka Dragan. My husband Mage Bernard. Baron Archmage Zoran Vladislov and Baroness Archmage Zdenka. I'll let him do the talking." She deftly passed the ball of introductions to him.

"Well met. Were you two responsible for the timely sand storm and the deaths of these five browns?" Zoran asked.

"Well, yes, we needed sand in order to cast our Sand Spike spells. We discovered that regular spells sometimes do not work on the dragons, but our spike thrusts are totally effective. We've killed over a dozen so far. I gave Donatello, the brown leader, one day to leave Anwyn forever. He obviously didn't and now we are going to kill every last brown on Anwyn until they do leave us in peace. We owe that much to our four children," Rhys explained.

"I am Baron Cadfeel Alun, ruler of Anwyn. We have never met your people before. This Fair Wyn oasis — we have always avoided it. Strange spirits dwell there. However, I too wish to thank you for your timely aid."

"We are descendants of Tudyr and Betrys and the sand sprites. Until now, we have shunned interaction with you humans, but we saw another chance to slay some more browns and took it."

"We fight the same foe, Rhys, Megan," Baron Cadfeel seized the initiative. "Let us work together to rid our world of these dragon worms. They have already murdered thousands of my people and now apparently many of your people."

"Indeed, we fight the same foe. Yes, we have lost some of our people, but now all are safe beyond the reach of any dragon. Anwyn provides, as always," Megan agreed with him. "We had best be on our way. We need to heal and recover."

"If you need anything, please let me know," Baron Cadfeel suggested, hoping to gain two powerful new allies. They nodded and stepped into the Shadows, a clear sign that they were Duska born and trained outside of the Circle of Ascension and its Ceremony of Ascension. How this could be eluded Baron Cadfeel, but Zoran now had a very good idea, thanks to the journals of Bandar Zar. Here was a whole sub-culture that had been unknown until now. He intended to explore it later on.

The group began to inspect the battlefield now, looking for survivors, though that prospect was grim. That's when Zoran finally noticed that Baron Jan was missing. Quickly, several headed to the top of the Archmage tower, where he was last seen. What was left of his body lay in a pool of the caustic acid. His Rod of Dragon Slaying lay beside him, its charges gone. He had been too slow in reacting to that initial onslaught of dragon retaliation.

"Damn!" Zoran swore. Although Jan was his half-brother, he still had a strong bond with him. While Jarka and Bernard began casting acid neutralization spells, what remained of the two Strike Forces arrived. Dusan was limping noticeably and Jarka made for him as soon as she could. His left leg was badly burned.

"Not Jan?" he said as Bernard levitated the remains to the ground.

"Afraid so, Dusan," Zoran replied, as Archmage Nadia rushed to Dusan's side, rather worried by his limp.

"Damn! Bad day all around. Lost five of our fighters and the rest of us are pretty banged up. Got any more healing potions, mom? I'm okay, love," he added to his wife.

"Back home. We should get you and the others who are hurt back there soon," Jarka hovered over her son almost as much as Nadia was.

"I'll take Jan back and Dusan too," Nadia offered.

"Thanks, Nadia. Okay, I hereby appoint you, Nadia as the new Baroness of Castle Dorumova. Dusan, you are now its baron. I am certain that Reina will want to take their kids back to Gladno for now," Zoran announced. "She doesn't like our long, cold winters. Besides, she will want the comfort of her own sisters and brothers right about now."

"Baron, what about merging the two strike forces into one? Let us go dragon hunting now, once we resupply," Evsen asked. "Karel wants to come with us as well. This way, we ought to have enough power to take some of the dragons out in their lairs. If we let them mass like they did today, we don't stand a chance."

Zoran agreed and the strike force members also departed to get more healing potions and gather their needed supplies. Before long, only Zoran, Danika, and Eliska remained, helping Baron Cadfeel deal with the aftermath. Around noon, at least one baron from each of the other worlds arrived, bringing mages and a few Duska with them. All wanted to see firsthand the destruction and to lend a helping hand. Near dusk, Zoran, Danika, and Eliska finally headed home.

"For once, all the barons are working together," Danika observed. "Still, I don't see how we are going to be able to fare much better if hundreds of dragons attack us in Brn. I'm sorry about your brother, Jan."

"Thanks. He was ill suited to being a fighter. I probably should not have asked him to come along. Yet he upheld the honor of being a leader of our people. I will remember him for that," Zoran sighed, thinking of the young boy he had rescued twenty-two years ago. Images of how Jan had loved living in a castle swept over him. Yes, those would be the images that he would remember, the childhood innocence and awe.

"It is really all my responsibility. I brought the golds to our world in the first place. The other barons felt pressured to bring other dragons to their worlds to counterbalance my golds."

Danika nodded, adding, "Yet, had you not done so, as I understand our history, Adapazan would still be a slave state to your despot father's ruthless whims. Focus on all the good your decision has brought not only to we of Adapazan but to many other worlds."

"True, Danika, but now it has also brought death and maiming to tens of thousands as well. I must find a solution and stop this war before it consumes us all."

Danika reached a decision. "Count me in on helping find that solution, Zoran. Let's put our heads together. There must be something that we can do other than this continued killing. I know Archmage Karel is now on a killing-dragons rampage. I think he took the death of Baron Jan personally somehow. We must be overlooking some tiny fact that might be the kingpin to ending this war."

"Help accepted. Let's get back and clean up. Meet in my study in say an hour," Zoran proposed.

An hour later, Jarmila and Danika, now bathed and wearing a fresh dress, joined him in the study. They found him staring at his huge maps of the Federation of the Sixteen Planets. He'd cleaned up as well and had brought a fresh pot of tea and biscuits for the women. "Evening. Nadia is conducting a funeral for Jan tomorrow morning. Help yourselves," he said solemnly.

"Want me to pour your cup?" Jarmila asked Danika. The Archmage had canceled her Morph spell and was in her true form.

"Please, I tend to spill too much using my feet to pour a cup when the pot is full. Thanks," Danika replied, scooting a chair out with her foot and sitting down.

"How come no arms?" Jarmila asked.

"This is the way my body really is. Besides, my Morphed form never ages. I'm comfortable with myself now, Jarmila. I only use my magic when it is really needed."

Jarmila flashed her a smile as she poured two cups, positioning Danika's where her foot could best reach it. "Use magic when it is really needed — that is admirable, Archmage. After all, I think far too many of us depend utterly on magic in our lives. Perhaps there can be too much of a good thing."

"What's that? Use magic when it is really needed?" Zoran broke in on their chat. That phrase echoed in his mind, sounding a chord within him.

"Oh, I was just telling Jarmila that I only really use my magic when it is really needed. I have learned to do many things with my feet now, so why depend upon magic when my feet can suffice?" Danika replied.

"Jarmila! What was Bandar Zar's notes about using some magic of his machine when needed? I remember you telling something about it. A secret feature or something?" Zoran asked rapid fire.

His daughter thought for a second and then remembered. "Oh, he said that Kazimir's machine had a secret feature. Once it was focused upon one of the dragon home worlds, by using a special hidden lever, he could activate his Power Attraction spell to pull the unsuspecting dragons from their worlds to Voss, dragging them through the Shadows, whether they desired it or not. Is that what you meant?"

"Ah ha, he used magic to drag the dragons from their original worlds to Voss. Danika, you might have just given us a way out of this mess!"

Chapter 40 Death and Destruction

The next day amid a furious snowstorm, Zoran had High Priestess Jarmila Zar conduct the funeral services for his half-brother, Baron Jan Vavrin. Walking the halls of Castle Dorumova brought back memories of his mother's funeral and her Ceremony of Passing, so similar to Jan's. A solitary chime sounded. Then a choir of two dozen voices singing a religious chant was heard as they solemnly entered from the main doors, headed by the High Priestess Jarmila.

His daughter spoke clearly and solemnly, "We are gathered here today to honor Baron Jan Vavrin, baron, husband, and father. Our wishes, dear Jan, are to see you safely off on your voyage to the hereafter." She spoke about the highlights of his life, the joy that he brought to his children, and so on. Then, she began the official last rites, little of which Zoran could understand, even though this was the second time that he heard them. At last, the choir began another song and pushed the floating coffin slowly out of the Great Hall. Magical fires and lights seemed to issue forth from his coffin as it moved, symbolic of Jan's passing from one realm into another. After several minutes, the sounds finally died down as the choir moved on down the long halls, taking his body to its final resting place outside the castle.

After the brief ceremonies, a weeping Baroness Reina Matous Vavrin bade them all farewell. She took their two children, Lilia and Vilem, back to Gladno, where she could stay with her brothers and sisters there.

"Okay, Dusan, Nadia, I proclaim you are now Baron Dusan Dragon and Baroness Archmage Nadia Vladislov Dragon. Will you both accept the duties and responsibilities that come with running Castle Dorumova and our original Circle of Ascension here beneath the fortress?" Both agreed and the task was done, except for the fact that Dusan was leading Strike Force Two and Nadia was teaching magic to numerous women here at Brn.

"Since everyone is here, let me tell you what Archmage Danika and I are about to do," Zoran explained. "We are going back to Voss and to see if we can get the machine of Mage Kazimir to work. If so, we may have a way to remove all of the dragons from our worlds. She and I will be gone for some time. In my absence, Baron Tomas will run Adapazan in my place. If there are further massive dragon attacks, send all that we have and try to eliminate as many dragons as possible, but above all, avoid getting yourselves killed. I don't want to come back to another funeral."

"Hey, dad, I'm coming too," Jarmila broke in. "I'll be bringing Bandar's notes, which may give you some more clues. Besides, Tomas, Nadia, and mom insist. I'll do the cooking too," she added with a wry grin. She knew that the mention of cooking would seal the deal. Zoran was all thumbs in the kitchen. The three headed off to say goodbye to their families and to pack.

Dusan and Nadia quickly headed over to their new huge castle and fortress. "What an ill time for Jan to die. I should be out fighting dragons and you're swamped with your students. How are we going to be able to be in two places at once?" Dusan exclaimed, running his hands through his hair.

Just then Tomas stepped out of the Shadows. "Hi sis, I came to help get you both hatted up on your new duties. Plus, now that dad's going to be gone for a time, I've got a few ideas of my own that I want to try out — a possible way to reduce the dragons numbers without any danger to us. First, we must see to the Circle and Castle security. Come on; let's be swift about this. Ah, here comes Kate now." Archmage Marek and Duska Akira's eighteen year old daughter stepped out of the Shadows. She was engaged to Milan, Archmage Karel and Duska Chika's son.

Tomas explained, "I've asked Kate here to take over the Circle and castle duties for you so you are free to deal with the dragons and the women students. I hope this is all right with you sis and you, Dusan."

"Perfect! Yes, very much so. Thank you Kate!" Dusan replied, quite relieved. "Let's get the security protocols altered quickly." The four set about the lengthy task of re-establishing the security guards and wards on the primary Circle of Ascension of Adapazan and the huge castle. That took until suppertime.

Over dinner, Tomas explained his latest idea. "I remembered something that dad told us. When the dragons are moving through the Shadows, they can't see us if we are there too. Remember, dad told us that he cut a dragon with his sword as it moved through the Shadows as it came to Adapazan. What if we take a whole lot of Duskas and we position ourselves around the planets. When we spot the dragon swarm coming to raid another village, we inflict as much damage as we can while they are still in the Shadows. We'd be perfectly safe from any counterattack. Plus, it might spook them, making them afraid of moving through the Shadows."

The next day, the two strike forces met as a group, along with Honani and his group and Archmage Karel. Tomas outlined his plan. Dusan then took over, "Look, they are not likely to bother Adapazan now, because the snow depth is at record levels. I think that we can rule out Rehor, Dietmar, and Gerde as well. Both of those are mountainous or snowy planets and are in the middle of their winters."

Evsen added, "We can rule out Asami too, nothing there but oceans. The dragons decimated Anwyn, which is a desert world. I don't think that they will be launching another major strike there. Similarly for Jing, since there's not much to be gained there either. That leaves nine planets that could well be facing the dragons' next assault. We should focus on them."

Honani volunteered, "You know, on Isi, there are quite a lot of us who can Shadow Walk. If they could be armed with magical weapons, they could help protect their world. Plus, why not get all of the other barons to round up some of their Duskas, arm them with magical blades, and have them do the same thing. If Zoran is right about this, they will all be safe as long as they remain in the Shadows."

"Good idea. Even if the Duska numbers are small, as long as one of them spots where the dragons enter that world, they could Message the others and make a good strike when the dragons exit. I'll bet anything that they leave by the same route that they enter a world," Dusan suggested. "Gang, this way we would finally be able to kill dragons in quantity."

"As long as we are in the right place at the right time," cautioned Evsen. "Let's make this happen!" Their teams cheered.

Archmage Karel grumbled. This plan would leave him high and dry. "You don't need me then," he muttered and left, teleporting back to his lab. He began making preparations of his own.

"So how did your meeting go?" his wife, Akira, asked him. She had sensed him arriving home and came to see him.

"They've got their own plans that leave me out. So I'm going to go to Anwyn and help out those deadly spell casters that we discovered. Between the three of us, I think that we can wipe out all of the Brown dragons on Anwyn. Dear, I'm going to need you to take me there, once I make all my preparations. If I am lucky, I might learn their fancy Sand Spike spell."

"Dear, that's terribly dangerous," she replied, her voice trembling a little.

"I know, but we all have to do our part. See if you can round me up several dozen of Jarka's healing potions to take with me." He continued to pack a bag with what he thought that he was going to need for his extended stay on that desert world. Two hours later, Akira kissed him goodbye and left him on Anwyn.

Baron Cadfeel personally teleported him to the oasis of Fair Wyn, where he met up with Rhys and Megan. Both were still slowly healing from their burns from the last battle and Archmage Karel endeared himself right away by giving them several more healing potions.

Soon, they made an effective team. He used his power spell, changing into a giant falcon. Flying high in the sky, he systematically located dragon dens. Once found, the three joined forces and eliminated them. The brown's powerful electrical bolts didn't harm Rhys or Megan and Karel managed to protect himself with his rod. Still, it was slow going. They were lucky to find a dragon a day.

The Shadow attacks began to work almost at once. Within a month, all the dragons left Isi. With something like a hundred Duskas taking turns hovering just above their world in the Shadows, every time any dragon attempted to arrive or depart, they were attacked and wounded by these unseen men and women.

Unfortunately, the damage inflicted upon the smaller towns of the other worlds was growing. In that month, twenty were raised. Approximately forty thousand men, women, and children perished. Still, the barons were reluctant to spread their Archmages out over their worlds. One alone could not stand against a raiding party of thirty dragons.

The 1st of April, the dragon leaders met in secret, high in the mountains of Gerde. This was their Spring War Council. Donatello, the brown, spoke first, "Well, that's that. All of us browns are now relocated to the deserts of Chana. There are no dragons left on Anwyn, thanks to those three illusive dragon killers!" He was referring to the deadly strikes of Rhys, Megan, and Archmage Karel. "At least their three fortresses are mostly destroyed. That's something anyway."

"Yes, but now we know for sure that we were not facing Baron Zoran's Ultimate Weapon there on Anwyn, just powerful Archmages," Werner, the black, pointed out. "Plus, we have now figured out how to avoid the Shadow Assassins who struck our forces as they made their raids on the planets. Again, we were all fooled into believing we were facing that Ultimate Weapon of his. Instead, a simple Invisibility spell has nullified those treacherous attacks."

"Yes, but," interjected Dario, the red, "we still have not gotten them to spread their Archmages out so that we can pick them off one by one. The humans are sacrificing all of their smaller villages. Plus, where have all the humans in the larger towns gone? We don't know that either."

Wenzel, the black, spoke up, "They've have gone underground. That's the only answer that remains. Look, we have seen in town after town the absence of humans. They have to have gone somewhere and the only possibility that remains is underground."

"Ah, if so, then we can starve them out," Werner, the black, picked up on his master's conclusion. "They have to eat. Once they've eaten up all of their supplies, then they will have to surface and we can get them then."

"The real problem is all of those Archmages," Wenzel, the black, pointed out. "These barons are intelligent. They have resisted our attempts to draw them out to protect the smaller villages. Rightly so. Had they spread them out, we'd have won the war already. We must not underestimate their resourcefulness. We need to change tactics here."

"What do you recommend, Wenzel?" asked Werner, the black.

He replied, "Since they are keeping their powerful forces all bunched up, we need to force them to do battle with us. We should join all of our forces into one huge group and one by one assault each of their main fortresses and circles. We will lay bare their fortresses and towers. If they come out to fight us, our numbers will annihilate them once and for all. On the other hand, if they remain cowards in their holes, then their precious fortresses and towers will be reduced to rubble. Either way, we inflict enormous damage on them all. Who knows, in the process of destroying their fortresses, we may accidentally totally block their underground entrances, trapping them all forever beneath the ground where they can die of starvation. The main thing is to have enough of us present to kill them all should they decide to surface and protect their fortresses and towers."

He added, "I will predict that in two months' time, total victory shall be ours. All of these sixteen worlds will be under our total control. We can then put the surviving humans to work for us. Our victory is assured now, my fellow dragons." The group cheered and began making preparations for their first huge assault.

Chapter 41 Ancient Technology

Jarmila, Danika, and Zoran arrived on Voss on the 16th of February. He gave them a guided tour of the planet from the edge of the Shadows, pointing out the old sixteen Republics. There were still a very few reds and blacks around the far northern mountains where they had kept their captured women prisoners. Hence, Zoran decided to make sure that there were no more "breeding" dragons being kept there, that is captured women from the sixteen worlds of the Federation. All three breathed a sigh of relief. They found none.

Zoran led them next to the pyramid that they had found during their reconnoitering mission some time ago. It was located in the south-central portion of the rectangular continent at the extreme southern edge of the tall mountains which bisected the continent. Just west of this location a few hundred miles lay a dense forest. Another forest began some two hundred miles to the southeast. The desert of Anwyn began almost at the pyramid's eastern edge. Rugged hills lay to its south down to the ocean some three hundred miles further south. Tall grasslands waved in the breeze as the three materialized just west of the pyramid.

"Well, it is a pyramid, just like Bandar describes," Jarmila commented upon getting her feet securely on the ground. "We should check for traps and such," she added, imagining herself as Mage Jarka. Zoran grinned, picking up her thought. All three activated their spell and proceeded to walk slowly around the base of the huge structure. The pyramid was a perfect one, geometrically speaking. Each side was a hundred feet long, making the top vertex about seventy-one feet tall. All three spells revealed a hidden entrance on the south face, but no traps as yet. Bandar had long ago removed the original spells which hid the pyramid from sight and kept people from discovering it.

The entrance door did have a highly powerful Guards and Wards spell on it. It took both Archmages to dispel that one. Further, the door itself did not appear to have any door knobs or locks on it. The three spent an hour working out how the door actually opened. Jarmila finally resorted to her notes from the journals. "He is merely teasing us, dad. He says that to gain entry, knock, knock. What does that mean?"

Of course, all three tried saying "knock, knock" as well as physically knocking on the door. "Can't be that simple," Zoran teased his daughter.

"Maybe he means the Knock spell," Danika volunteered.

"Okay, in case this is a trap, you both stand way back while I try it," Zoran ordered. Once the two women were well back, he cast his simple Knock spell. Instantly, he vanished from sight, startling the two.

"Dad? Dad! Where are you?" Jarmila shouted, startled and suddenly quite worried.

I am just inside the door. One second. Okay, I have a Light spell. I see, the door is not really a door like we know them. It is a permanent Mystical Door. The Knock spell is its trigger. Okay, you two try it. I'm out of the way, Zoran Messaged the two worried women. A moment later, they appeared just inside the door, three feet from Zoran, who had a Light spell on his sword so they could see.

The three were in a small hallway. Pegs on the walls held cloaks at one time. All that remained of one was a pile of dust on the floor below a peg. Three doors led to their left, right, and straight ahead. The hall was barely ten feet square. Danika spotted a globe and pulled the old bag off of it. The bag disintegrated in her fingers, but a Permanent Light now illuminated the hallway. "That's better. I bet that we will find these globes all over this place. I suggest that we leave them all on so we can see well."

"Ah, no one has been here for ages. Look at the dust on the floor," Zoran pointed out. All three felt relieved at this observation.

"Dad, do you realize that we are probably the first people to set foot in here since Bandar?" Jarmila whispered in awe.

"Looks that way. Okay, most likely the center door heads into the main facility. We should check out these side passages first and see if we can set up some way to sleep, cook, and eat. We're going to be here for some time," he suggested. "Again, everyone check for traps everywhere. I don't trust this place in the slightest."

The right door led to a kitchen and pantry arrangement, following along the outer wall. The left door led to a bedroom, which at one time had been extremely elegant. Now, however, even the bed had turned to dust. The three cast numerous Clean spells that day, preparing the site for living. They did find a golden pitcher that was enchanted to provide endless water. It still worked, much to their pleasure. In the kitchen, they found an enchanted stove that provided heat for cooking. The numerous pots and pans were still serviceable. By the end of the long day, Jarmila was able to prepare them a hot supper. Zoran's first worry that they would have a tough time with living arrangements vanished.

The next day, they set to work, entering the center door which led to the machine and numerous workshops. The device itself commanded their full attention and awe. Located in the central portion of the pyramid, a giant tube pointed upwards. A movable seat was at one end of the tube, along with dozens of controls, buttons and levers. Essentially, this was a device that looked through the Shadows. Hence, unlike a telescope, it needed no opening to the sky, which is why it had survived all these millennia.

Wisely, the three decided to study absolutely everything here, correlating them with Bandar's crude notes before they attempted to operate the device. Their study was long and arduous. Two weeks passed before Zoran and Danika felt comfortable sitting in the chair and operating the device. Already, they'd pasted labels onto the various buttons and levers, outlining the purpose of each.

Now their task was to find each of the dragon home worlds from which they'd been pulled to Voss. That took them another two weeks of sixteen hour days, but at long last they had identified the various home worlds.

"Okay, now we can work out how we are going to pull the dragons off of our worlds and send them back to their own," Zoran explained at long last.

"Yes, but we are going to have to Mind Wipe them or else they will just Shadow Walk right back here," Danika countered. "But we can't Mind Wipe them of their knowledge of our worlds. What's to keep them from coming right back?"

"Don't know, Danika," Zoran admitted. "That's the flaw in my plan. I think that we can pull them all off our worlds and put them back on their own worlds. However, you are right, Mind Wipe can't be used. Still, we ought to test it first on the few dragons that are here on Voss. Of course, they can come right back if they want to. I am open to ideas."

"Let's see if it even works first," Danika answered pragmatically. "If it doesn't work, then the Mind Wipe is moot. If it does work, we can then work that detail out."

He agreed with her practicality and together, the two set the controls. First, they would force all of the blacks here on Voss back to their original world. Then, they'd do the reds. After making all the adjustments, Zoran pressed the Activate Program button. "How do we know if it is even working?" asked Jarmila.

"Ah, look there, on that screen. I am seeing a couple dozen dots. They are moving," Danika pointed out. The three watched fascinated. When the process was finished, she asked, "Ought we take a look up north and see if the blacks are gone?"

Zoran smiled. Holding their hands, he stepped them into the Shadows and headed up north several thousand miles. While they saw a few reds flying about, they saw no blacks. He took them into one of the massive caverns that the blacks had been using. It was empty. Satisfied, he returned to the machine room. "Okay, Danika, you get to do the reds."

She grinned. "With the utmost pleasure!" A few hours later, the reds too had vanished from Voss. As the hour was late, Jarmila headed off to fix them supper, while the two began discussing just how they could prevent the dragons from returning.

The next day passed and still neither had an answer. Hence, Zoran decided to discuss this with his friends, Aldrick, Emil, and Renata. Leaving Danika and Jamila in charge of the machine, he headed back to Adapazan.

An hour later, he sat on the cold stone floor of Aldrick's cavern. At least, Aldrick, Sophie, Emil, and Renata had changed to their human forms and were sitting across from him. "Well, I've asked you here because I have now got a way to send each of the dragons back to their original home worlds." He went into a lengthy explanation of the ancient history of Voss as well.

"So I can now send them back. Yet, I am at a loss about how to prevent them from just Shadow Walking right back here. Besides, I owe it to you to discuss this with you four. I consider you good friends. Really, I don't want to send you back against your wills."

"Hum, this is fascinating, Zoran," Archmage Emil finally replied. "Indeed, we four have finally decided that if the dragons attempt to attack Adapazan in force, then we will come to your aid. Already, there has been too many deaths on both sides. It has to stop."

"Thanks, I agree, it has to stop. I don't want to be a part of genocide either," Zoran replied.

Aldrick spoke up, "You know, there might be a way. The blacks believe that you originally went to Voss to obtain some kind of Ultimate Weapon. Perhaps this can be used to convince them not to return. Obviously, as they are being pulled from where they are currently at and into the Shadows and deposited on their home worlds, from their point of view, that would seem to be an Ultimate Weapon. Perhaps as you are transporting them, you could tell them that if they return, then the next time you will deposit them in the center of a sun. Give them a scare."

"Say, I like that. But would they believe that?" Zoran asked.

"I don't know, but it is worth an attempt. I know that many of the golds here would like nothing more than for this whole fiasco to end. If they were also returned to their original home worlds, I think that they would actually find that highly interesting. As far as we four are concerned, we'd like to come back one day. Sophie is pregnant. Down the road, we'd like to bring our son or daughter here to be trained, if we can," Aldrick replied.

"Absolutely, just let us know when. We'll see that your child gets the best magic training we have. Congratulations, by the way," Zoran grinned. Sophie seemed very pleased with his offer.

"Also, Zoran, I would encourage you to get this process going as soon as possible. Some of my spies out among the blacks are reporting that they are going to change tactics. All available dragons are going to assault one of the main fortresses and tower. Their objective is to render it to rubble or to get the Archmages to do battle with them so they can be eliminated. Even with your magical rods, no one can withstand a hundred dragon breaths at one time. In a month, all of the baron's fortresses and towers will likely be reduced to rubble," Aldrick explained. "That's why we've finally decided enough is enough. Please hurry with your plans, if possible."

Zoran was stunned by the news, but inwardly, it was not unexpected. Long he knew that if the dragons combined all their forces into one group, they'd be unstoppable. "Okay, I best get going then. I will let you know if it works and I will do the golds last." He shook their hands and stepped back into the Shadows, heading for Voss.

Back at the pyramid, Zoran outlined what he'd learned. "Oh know, we have to get this going fast! We can't let those dragons totally destroy all of the fortresses and towers!" Danika gushed.

"Right, but we need a way to put my threat into each dragon's mind as they get pulled back to their home world," Zoran countered.

The three began reviewing all that they knew about the operation of the machine. Finally, Jarmila pointed out, "Say, dad, how about the Thought Transfer option. Bandar says it is there, but he never tried it out."

"Brilliant!" Zoran praised her. Quickly, the three set to work on learning how to use that option. A day later, they were ready to test it out on several of the blacks who had returned to Voss already. He worked out his message carefully, bouncing it off of Danika and Jarmila several times, until they all agreed on the proper wording. Then they fed it into the machine:

Baron Zoran here. I am using my Ultimate Weapon from Voss to send you back to your original Home World. If you ever return to Voss or to any of the sixteen worlds of the Federation, I will again send you back, only this time, your arrival point will be in the middle of your planet's sun. Do not ever attempt to return here. This is the only warning that you will ever get.

The next morning, Zoran received a panic stricken message from Baron Leo. *Zoran! Hundreds of dragons have just appeared over my fortress! They are going to destroy us entirely! Help!*

The machine was still setup for the black's home world. Zoran didn't reply, but he and Danika hastily went down the checklist, double checking all settings. Then he pressed the Activate Program button. "Keep your fingers crossed!"

"But I don't really have any fingers anymore," Danika teased him. Jarmila grinned.

Two hundred plus dragons stepped out of the Shadows over Gladno. Wenzel and Werner led this massive assault, knowing full well the close ties that Baron Leo had with Baron Zoran. Their plan was to draw out Zoran and his many Archmages and once and for all eliminate them. Baron Leo took his entire staff down into the underground tunnels where most of the city's population was staying. No way was he going to attempt to defend the fortress and tower, not against such a force as this. He resolved himself to the total destruction of his fortress.

Just as the blacks were about to make their first sweep, one by one they simply vanished from the air. Wenzel and Werner found themselves flying through the Shadows. Try as they might, they could not break loose. They also heard Baron Zoran's words in their minds. It gave them quite a shock, before they materialized above a strange world, filled with other flying black dragons. One by one, over a hundred blacks appeared behind them.

Dario, the red, suddenly saw all of the black dragons vanishing. He called out, "Hey, everyone, hold off a minute. Where have all our blacks gone? Werner?" He sent a Message to Werner, but the spell didn't activate. Werner was gone! Suddenly, he thought of Zoran's Ultimate Weapon. "My god! It exists! Abort! Abort! Abort the attack. Flee, flee for your lives! Zoran has just killed all of the blacks!"

One by one, the huge dragon horde stepped back into the Shadows, vanishing without a trace. Baron Leo listened for the sounds of the destruction of his fortress, but heard nothing at all. Finally, curiosity got the better of him and he teleported to his manor house's roof top. He was invisible, of course. To his utter astonishment, all of the dragons were gone. No damage had been done.

It took an hour to get all of the blacks handled. They had to keep resetting the origin point from one planet to the next to be sure that they got all of the dragons. Blacks handled, the three worked as rapidly as they could to reset the controls for the reds. Danika did the honors for the reds. She activated the machine, sending the reds back to their home world. An hour later, they reset the controls for the greens and repeated the process. Five hours later, they finally finished sending the white, blue, brown, and grey dragons back to their home worlds. That left only the golds.

Zoran then sent a Message through the Shadows to Aldrick, who replied, *We are ready. I've told the other golds what is about to happen. They are prepared. All have their bags packed and ready. Thank you for finding a way to avoid genocide, my friend.*

You are most welcome. Please come back whenever you wish. Just be a bit clever when you do. No sense attracting undue attention to yourselves, Zoran replied. Aldrick chuckled, recalling how he'd first met Zoran so many years ago. Then, Zoran activated the machine for the last time, sending all of the golds back to their home world.

"We had best reset it for the blacks," Danika suggested. "Of all the dragons, I trust them the least. I wouldn't be surprised to see some of them sneaking back here."

"True, we had best stay here at the controls for some days just in case," Zoran admitted. "I will arrange a meeting with the other barons and let them know what we've done. You two keep an eye on things."

Two hours later, the many barons assembled in Zoran's Great Hall, along with Zdenka and the many other Archmages, Mages, and Duskas. All had heard Baron Leo's frantic call for help, but wisely had declined, realizing that against so many dragons, it would be suicide to go to Gladno.

"I'll keep this very brief. The dragon war is over," Zoran began. "Danika, Jarmila, and I have been successful on Voss. We've pulled all of the dragons from our worlds and those on Voss, sending them back to their original home worlds. Each had a message from me saying that if they returned here, I would pull them back again, only materializing them into their own suns. I hope they don't force me to do that, though. What I need from all of you right now is to keep a very thorough look out for any dragons trying to return to your worlds. Message me off-world if you spot any. I just need its color. I will explain everything more fully when we next meet in a few weeks for the Spring Council."

"You saved my fortress, Zoran! I will never forget it," Baron Leo spoke up.

"But what about your golds?" Baron Clav growled.

"Gone too. All dragons on all of our worlds are gone for now, baron. However, don't go getting any ideas of invading Adapazan. I can just as easily bring them back again," Zoran threatened his enemies.

"I'll keep watch, but I expect to hear how this miracle was done when you come to the council," Baron Clav replied antagonistically. Old hatreds still had not melted.

"Good, that's all. I need to get back in case some of them try to return. Keep me posted," Zoran explained and then departed.

"That has to be the shortest meeting in history," Baron Leo commented. Everyone laughed.

"Most significant too," Baron Stefan added. "I can't believe this dragon war is over! Incredible. How could he and Danika and Jarmila have managed this? Guess we will have to wait a few weeks."

Chapter 42 Adjustments

Back at the pyramid on Voss, Zoran now faced an ethical dilemma. Just how much of all their ancient history should he reveal to all the barons? Ought he bring all of them to the pyramid and show them how to use it? If so, then others could take turns watching for the return of the dragons and dispose of them. On the other hand, his enemies could well bring them back and have them attack Adapazan or other allied planets.

"Look, this whole pyramid and its operation was almost lost to us forever, dad," Jarmila spoke her mind. "It's really a miracle that we even discovered it. Who knows, maybe fifty years from now, the blacks will return. By then, you will be dead and buried, but the dragons live for hundreds of years. Our children have got to know about the pyramid and how to use it. We've got to keep this site and this machine protected and ready. Besides, everyone ought to know our history, even if it is ancient."

"Even our enemies?"

"Who knows who our enemies will be fifty years from now, dad. Look, two years ago, Jing was our enemy and now they are our allies. Likely Anwyn is now with us too," she countered. "I think that we ought to teach each baron and baroness how to use this thing."

"What about telling them that anyone can become a Duska if they are given the ceremony while they are young enough? Baron Clav might just get the idea to make hundreds of them and send them to attack us," Zoran countered. "That's in the journals as well."

Danika spoke up. "If you censor part of the journals, then that alone will raise the suspicions of our enemies, Zoran. They won't trust you. I agree with Jarmila. Make each world a complete copy of the journals. Still, we should put strong defenses around the pyramid and retain control of it. Perhaps some of the "have-not" barons would like to relocate to Voss. There is a whole world here where they can pick and choose where they want to live. Certainly treasure hunters will want to scour Voss. I love our endless water pitcher and that fine stove in the kitchen here. Quite a lot of other magical items are likely to be found here on Voss as well. I think that the "have-not" barons will have far too much to do now than try to bring back the dragons or to attack us. But I do think that you should quickly get all of our Archmages brought here and grooved in on how to operate the machine. That way, we don't have to be stuck here for weeks doing nothing."

Zoran agreed and began bringing all his Duska and Archmages here to the pyramid, where Danika showed them how to operate the machine. Meanwhile, Jarmila and Miroslav worked on making sixteen copies of Bandar Zar's journals A through T. Zoran decided against duplicating Bandar's journals written in the new worlds just yet. They were not particularly relevant to the current situation and he didn't want to reveal that anyone could become a Duska, if they were not yet twenty-one years old.

The 15th of May, Zoran summoned all of the barons and baronesses with their advisors to his fortress at Brn, filling up his plain Great Hall. While High Priestess Jarmila and the Archmages began handing out the large stacks of copied journals of Bandar Zar, Zoran addressed the anxious assemblage.

"I've taken the liberty of inviting all of you here for this vital meeting. As of now the Dragon War is over. So far, they have heeded my warning not to return to our worlds or to Voss. I have a whole lot of explaining to do. Much of what I will be telling you can be found in the copied journals of Bandar Zar which our priestess Jamila has copied for you, one for each world. I will summarize the salient facts."

"Originally, our ancestors lived on Voss. There is a wall fresco which denotes where each of our groups came from on Voss, where their lands were located." He began relating the key turn of events that happened millennia ago. Then, he discussed in detail the pyramid and its unique powers.

"Danika, Jarmila, and I found a way to reverse the pull and we forced each type of dragon off of our worlds and sent them back to their original world. As they were in transit, we told each dragon that if they should return to our worlds or Voss, then I would send them into a sun. So far, they have not attempted to Shadow Walk back here. However, as you know, a dragon's lifetime is more than five of ours. Hence, I feel that it is crucial that we pass on our hard-learned knowledge of the machine's operations to all here and to our descendants, in case the dragons try to return in say a hundred years. Soon, I will be taking each of you to Voss and showing you how the machine works. The idea being that between our worlds, there will be someone who can run the machine if the dragons again make their appearance on our worlds in the far future."

"On a different note, Voss is totally habitable. I have laid claim to the mountainous lands that were the Republic of Adapazan and in which the pyramid lies. So yes, I want to keep control of the pyramid constructed there so that I can keep the dragons at bay. However, this is a golden opportunity for those of you who consider your world a 'have-not' planet. I would like you barons from Rehor, Jing, Dietmar, Anwyn, and Asami to have the first choice of lands on Voss. Once they have picked, then let's allow the other neutrals to make their picks. The 'have' planets will then choose from what's left. This way, perhaps we can end this eternal conflict between the 'have' and 'have-not' planets."

His wholly unexpected announcement took the enemy barons by surprise. Zoran allowed the murmurs to run their course. "So I'll take you first to the pyramid and show you the machine that has saved us all from the dragons. After that, I'll take you to the wall plaque that shows the lands that your ancestors held. From there, you are welcome to scour Voss and begin making your picks of new lands. I sincerely hope that we are now embarking on a new era of peace and prosperity for all of us. Oh yes, Zdenka wants me to tell you that we will continue training all of the women until they have gone as far as they can in their magic training."

When he finished, he received an enthusiastic round of applause, even from his archenemies. Zoran took this as a positive sign. Then, he and his Duska companions began Shadow Walking over two hundred men and women to Voss and the pyramid, where Danika gave them a guided tour and explained briefly its operation.

Later, Baron Leo and Baron Stefan took him aside. Baron Stefan asked, "Do you think that the dragons will come back? Will they stay away?"

"I don't know, barons, but that is why I want all of us to know how to run the machine. That way, if they do come back and kill me, the knowledge of the machine will not perish with me."

They grinned. Baron Leo added, "I like the way that you are keeping physical control of the pyramid. I sure would not trust it in the hands of Baron Clav. He might just try to make another deal with the blacks and reds, bringing them back." All three men chuckled.

The End.

Other Books by Vic Broquard

Without Warning (fantasy)

The Trident Series: (fantasy)
      Volume 1 The Trident and the Book
      Volume 3 The Trident and the Scepter
      Volume3 The Trident and the Resurrection

The Adventures of Elizabeth Stanton Series: (science fiction)
      Volume 1 The Evolution of the Path
      Volume 2 The Great Messiah
      Volume 3 Of Kings and Queens and Troubadours
      Volume 4 Chaos in the Aftermath
      Volume 5 Power Plays
      Volume 6 Age of Exploration
      Volume 7 Abducted
      Volume 8 The Emperor and Empress
      Volume 9 A Job Worth Doing
      Volume 10 Degradation
      Volume 11 The Second Crusade
      Volume 12 When Worlds Collide
      Volume 13 Dark Ages

The Lindsey Barron Series: (fantasy)
      Volume 1 The Rod of the Apocalypse
      Volume 2 The Board of Governors
      Volume 3 The Crown of Moses
      Volume 4 Dominus for President
      Volume 5 The National Health Care Program
      Volume 6 States Justice
      Volume 7 Cross and Double-cross

Zoran Chronicles Series: (fantasy)
      Volume 1 A Dragon in Our Town
      Volume 2 Dragons, Power, Courts, and War

Planet of the Orange-red Sun Series: (science fiction)
      Volume 1 When Kingdoms Fall
      Volume 2 Dark Ages
      Volume 3 Age of the Towers
      Volume 4 Difficillis Exitus
      Volume 5 Age of the Lords
      Volume 6 The Renegade Tower
      Volume 7 Rebellions
      Volume 8 The Aliens Return
      Volume 9 Power Struggles
      Volume 10 Guilds, Genetics, and Gods
      Volume 11 Magi, Witches, Swords, and Superstitions
      Volume 12 The Voyage of the Eagle's Seed
      Volume 13 Justifications
      Volume 14 Responsibilities

The Return of the Wizards: Twelve Companions – The Making of Wizards (fantasy)